Hennessey was pale, ███████████ the gringo norm. His eyes were glued to the television screen that showed the imminent collapse of all his hopes, the destruction of his life. On the screen people were jumping from the flaming towers to smash their bodies below. It was better than burning.

Hennessey's own cell phone rang. Jimenez picked it up, answered, then—not without some reluctance—passed it over. "It's Linda," he announced in a breaking voice.

Like a drowning man grasping desperately for a life preserver, Hennessey took the phone.

"Honey, where are you and the kids?" he asked, desperately.

He heard screams and cries in the background as Linda answered, "I'm here at Uncle Bob's office . . . the children are with me. I am so sorry, Patricio."

Hennessey felt his heart sink. "Is there any way out?"

Her answering voice held infinite sadness and regret. "No . . . I don't think so. The only way off would be helicopters, now. And I do not hear or see any. It's getting very warm in here, husband. We'll have to go soon. Why don't you talk to the kids? Do not worry; I will wait as long as possible but I will not let our babies burn if I can help it. Goodbye, Patricio. You know I love you."

"I love you, too, Linda. I always have," he wept.

"Dad?" Hennessey heard young Julio say, voice quavering, then firming up. "I am being brave, Dad . . ."

BAEN BOOKS BY TOM KRATMAN

A State of Disobedience

Watch on the Rhine, with John Ringo
Yellow Eyes, with John Ringo
The Tuloriad, with John Ringo (forthcoming)

A Desert Called Peace
Carnifex
The Lotus Eaters (forthcoming)

Caliphate

A DESERT CALLED PEACE

TOM KRATMAN

BAEN

A DESERT CALLED PEACE

Copyright © 2007 by Tom Kratman.

A Baen Books Original

Baen Publishing Enterprises
P.O. Box 1403
Riverdale, NY 10471
www.baen.com

ISBN 10: 1-4165-5592-7
ISBN 13: 978-1-4165-5592-6

Cover art by Kurt Miller
Maps by Randy Asplund

First Baen paperback printing, January 2009
Second Baen paperback printing, April 2009

Library of Congress Control Number: 2007023559

Distributed by Simon & Schuster
1230 Avenue of the Americas
New York, NY 10020

Pages by Joy Freeman (www.pagesbyjoy.com)
Printed in the United States of America

A DESERT CALLED PEACE

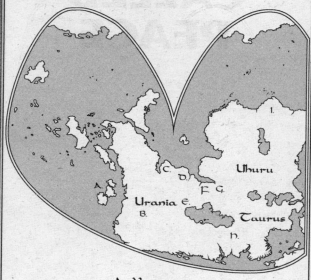

A. Yamato

B. Zhong Guo

C. Sind

D. Kashmir

E. Pashtia

F. Farsia

G. Sumer

H. Volgan Republic

Nova

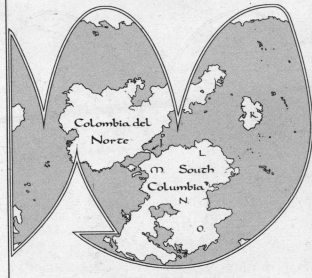

I.   Republic of Northern Uhuru

J.   Republic of Balboa

K.   Atlantis (UEPF Lodgment)

L.   Atzlan

M.   Colombia Central

N.   Federated States of Columbia

O.   Secordia

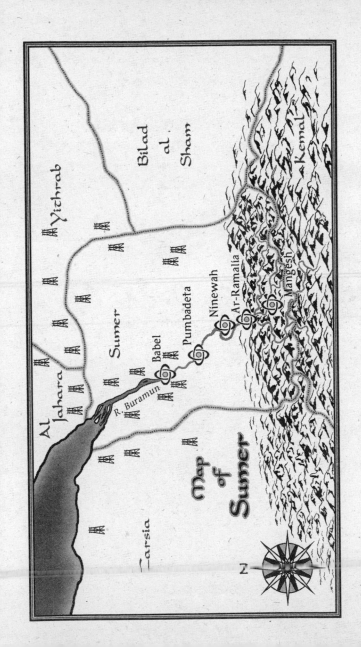

Solitudinem faciunt; pacem appellant
(They made a desert and called it peace)
—Tacitus

Acknowledgments

Special thanks to the many people who helped with this, from concept to copy editing: Yoli (who puts up with me), Matt Pethybridge, Sam Swindell, Bill Crenshaw, Mr. Dunnell, Mo Kirby, Sue Kerr, my brother John, Scott Connors, Genie Nickolson, *Obras Zorilleras* on Baen's Bar, Toni Weisskopf, Modean Moon, and, of course, Jim Baen.

If I've forgotten anyone, chalk it up to premature senility.

Dedication

For Oriana Fallaci, who had more sheer balls—and infinitely more wisdom—than nearly any man on the planet.

And for my comrades, CSM Joshua McIntosh and 1SGs Epolito Martinez and Chris Coffin. Miss you guys. Save me a spot, huh?

Dear Reader:

You can take this book as a commentary on the somewhat cyclic nature of history, if you want. ("History doesn't repeat itself, but it does rhyme.") You can take it as a commentary on the endless war between the Christian or secular West and Islam, if you want. You can take it as a critique of the phenomenon of monocultural planets that dominate science fiction, if you want.

If it pleases you, you can look at it as a cautionary tale on choosing one's enemies well . . . because you are going to become much like them or because they're going to become much like you. If you're of a legalistic mindset, you can think of it as a lengthy commentary on the law of war. If you loath transnational progressivism, surely there is something here for you.

The one thing you must never do, though, is to think of it as a commentary on the current war or the leadership thereof.

Unless, that is, you *want* to.

Tom Kratman

PROLOGUE

They called him "the Blue Jinn." He took a small and perverse pride in the title. Blue jinni were evil jinni. That his enemies thought him evil was . . . pleasant. Even more pleasant was the sight of his enemies, beaten and bleeding, captive and bound.

The Jinn looked over those enemies in the late afternoon sun. Sinking in the west, the sun's light was carved by the mountains to cast long, sharp shadows across the ground. Much of that ground was covered with the head-bowed, broken prisoners.

One of those captives, Abdul Aziz ibn Kalb, held his bleeding head upright. Abdul Aziz glared hate at his captors. These were a mix of Pashtun mercenaries—tall and light eyed; light skinned they would have been, too, had the sun not burned them red-brown—and shorter, darker men. All were heavily armed. All sneered back the hate Abdul Aziz felt, mixing with that hate a full measure of disgust and contempt.

Aziz's hate mixed with and fed on fear. Along with several hundred other male prisoners, and nearly a thousand women and children, Aziz waited to hear his fate. The male prisoners' hands and legs were

1

taped together. Not far away, the women and children waited unbound. The two groups were close enough together that Abdul Aziz could see the noncombatants as well as a small group of his enemies ascending a low hill to his front.

Leading that group, Abdul Aziz saw, was a uniformed man, medium in height, and with his face and head wrapped with a keffiyah. Another looked oriental. Three more were dressed much as any mullahs would be. A sixth wore the white dress of the emirate of Doha. The last was another man in uniform, bearing the rank badges of a *subadar*. Trimly bearded, tall and slender, with bright gray eyes, the *subadar* looked Pashtun to Abdul Aziz.

That man in the lead partially unwrapped the keffiyah from around his head. Aziz had never seen him before, but had heard enough descriptions to recognize the "Blue Jinn." The Jinn paused and lit a cigarette. He puffed it contemplatively for a few moments. Then he sat back easily in a chair, almost a throne, that had been prepared for him by his followers out of hastily felled and trimmed trees. Even at this distance Abdul Aziz saw the eyes that gave the Jinn his name. Though it was just a trick of the sun, the eyes seemed to glow from the inside like malevolent coals.

A dark-clad, bearded mullah walked to the microphone of a portable public address set standing in front of the chair and began to speak.

"I have consulted," he announced, "with the man you probably know as the Blue Jinn, and whom you see to my right, concerning your fate. He, in accordance with the Sharia, has turned the general resolution of your cases over to myself and my fellow mullahs. We have pronounced sentence of death upon you, in accordance with the will of Allah, for complicity in murder."

It was widely speculated that the mullah only consulted the quarter gold Boerrand the Jinn allegedly paid him for each desired "legal" death sentence he passed on. The Jinn never admitted this. Neither did he deny it.

"Your young children shall be taken back to your enemy's country," the mullah continued. "Your women, and the girls over twelve, are awarded to his Pashtun Scouts as prizes. Mr. Yamaguchi," and the mullah's head nodded to indicate the oriental man who had accompanied the party, "and Mr. al Ajami," another head nod, "represent certain interests in Yamato and Doha that might wish to buy some of these women and girls from the Scouts. Having consulted with the Jinn I have informed him that there is no religious prohibition to this, that you are all apostates and your women may properly be enslaved. For his part, he says he could care less what happens to them so long as it is within the law."

A wild and heartrending moan emerged from the cluster of women as the grinning, leering Pashtun began to prod them away to the processing area. Aziz felt a sudden relief that his wife had been spared the ignominy of rape followed by sale into prostitution.

"As for the rest of you, as I said, you shall die. But the Jinn tells me to inform you that he is solicitous of your souls."

The mullah stopped speaking and backed away from the microphone. The Blue Jinn stood and took the mullah's place. He spoke in decent Arabic, Aziz was surprised to discover, though his accent was somewhat heavy.

"Some years ago the actions of your leader and your movement robbed me of my wife and children," the Jinn announced. He turned to the chief mullah. "What does Sura Eighty-one say, O man of God?" he asked.

The mullah recited aloud, loud enough for the microphone to pick up so that the prisoners could hear, "When the infant girl, buried alive, is asked for what crime she was slain . . ."

"What does it mean?"

"It means, *sayidi*, when Allah asks who murdered her, for no infant girl can be guilty of a crime."

"Does Allah approve of burying infant girls alive, then?"

"He does not. Sura Eighty-one, the Cessations, is concerned with the end of time, Judgment Day, and the punishment of the wicked. God will punish the murderers of infant girls."

The Jinn's face twitched in the smallest of smiles. "Ah, I see. What does the Holy Koran say about those who bring disorder to the world?

"It says, O Jinn, in Surah Five, the Table, that those who fight against God or his Apostle, bringing disorder to the world, should be killed, or have the hands and feet cut off on opposite sides, or be exiled, or be crucified."

"I see," said the uniformed man. "Do those who kill infant girls fight against God? Have these men brought disorder to the world?"

"They have. They do," answered the mullah, "for this is expressly forbidden under Islam."

The Jinn turned back to his captives. "I loved my family, even as—one supposes—you love your own. I swore, when they were murdered, to avenge myself on all who had contributed, even passively, to my loss. Thus you shall die. I am, though, as Mullah Hassim told you, very solicitous of your fate in the hereafter. So before you die, you will be thoroughly Christianized."

Then the Jinn smiled, nastily, and turned to his *subadar*.

"Crucify them."

PART I

CHAPTER
ONE

To reap the harvest of perpetual peace . . .
—William Shakespeare, *King Richard III*

UEPF *Spirit of Peace*,
Earth Date 25 November, 2510

Klaxons sounded piercingly throughout the ship as black-uniformed crewmen and women hurried through the cramped metal corridors to this or that necessary duty. Despite the soft, gripping soles of the crew's footwear, needed in the reduced gravity aboard ship, their feet made a rumbling sound that passed through the air and hull. Not a few of the crew's pale faces looked mildly nauseated. Transition through the rift, jumping thousands of light-years in an instant, affected some people like that. Others it seemed not to bother. Nor was there any predicting in advance; the only way to find out was to endure the transition.

A voice followed the klaxons, emanating from someone on the ship's bridge. "All hands, all hands, secure from transition. Rotating ship in five minutes. Sail crew, stand by to deploy the sail for braking. Captain to the admiral's quarters."

High Admiral Martin Robinson, United Earth Peace Fleet, was one of those affected badly by the passage. He'd hoped it would not prove so and had his hopes dashed moments after the bridge had announced, "Transition in . . ."

Robinson's looks belied his age. Despite being two centuries old, his face remained unlined, his back unstooped, his blue-gray eyes clear and bright. His heart and lungs and all the other organs worked as if they inhabited a twenty-one-year-old body and were no older than that themselves. Even his hair was blond, without a trace of silver or gray, and his hairline unreceded.

Anti-Decay Accelerating Factor, or ADAF, drugs had been available, at least to Earth's elite, for centuries. As a Class One, the highest of Earth's six castes, the high admiral was very elite indeed.

Yet neither the apparent age nor the real age had helped one whit to spare Robinson the misery of transition. One moment he had been fine, if a bit nervous. The next had seen his mind temporarily erased as his body disassembled and reassembled in an imperceptible instant. With the next he was on all fours on the deck of his cabin, projectile vomiting, moaning, and cursing.

It was in this position, vile smelling puke forming a puddle beneath him, washing over his hands in a flood and spreading to stain the knees of the black uniform trousers, that the captain of the *Spirit of Peace* found her admiral and the incoming system and fleet commander.

The captain of the ship, Marguerite Wallenstein, accompanied by two of the voiceless proles that handled janitorial services for the largely middle to upper-caste crew, hurried to kneel at the admiral's side and help him regain his chair. The proles set immediately on hands and knees to cleaning up the vomit while Wallenstein went to a nearby cabinet and took from it an amber bottle and two glasses. She poured herself and the admiral a drink.

Color was just returning to Robinson's drained face as he gratefully accepted the glass from Wallenstein.

"I was warned what to expect but nothing—," the admiral began.

"Nothing prepares you for it," Wallenstein finished. "I know. It gets better—a bit, anyway—after you've done it a few times."

"How many times have you . . . ?"

"This is my fifth transition," Wallenstein said, "and hopefully my next to last."

Younger than the admiral by some fifty years, Wallenstein looked to be the same age. A leggy, slender and svelte Scandinavian, she was a Class Two, ranking just below the admiral in the hereditary order of United Earth. Like him, she received full benefit of all the ADAF therapy and might, with luck, live to see five hundred. Not precisely beautiful—nose a bit too large and eyes a bit too small, she still exuded much of the earthy sexuality the application of which had seen her through difficult times in her rise within the hierarchy of the UEPF. What low shipboard gravity did for her breasts didn't hurt, either.

A competent officer, Wallenstein had ambitions.

Chief among these was to be raised to class one, followed by promotion to admiral, even high admiral, and then to take what she considered her rightful place among the ruling caste. It would be a rare honor and achievement. She also knew that without a powerful sponsor it would never come to pass.

The proles finished their odiferous task and, bowing deeply and respectfully to the captain and the admiral, made a quiet exit from the suite. Neither of the upper-caste officers bothered to return the bows, even symbolically. They forgot about the proles as soon as they, and the smell of vomit, had left. Who knew or cared what proles thought, after all?

"You should have waited in freeze, Martin," Wallenstein said reproachfully, once they were alone.

The admiral shrugged, already half recovered. "It seems to pass quickly. And I *did* want to experience the transition, *once* anyway. Speaking of freeze, though, what of our passengers?"

"No malfunctions, if that's what you mean," Wallenstein answered. "They'll stay in freeze until a few days before we assume orbit. We haven't the stores to feed and water them without recourse to Atlantis Base, anyway."

Robinson nodded his understanding and agreement. Moreover, it would be months before the ship would be able to take orbit around the target world. He had great respect for the position—or at least for the *power*—of the clergy of Earth, but really didn't want them for company for all that time. The representative of the caliph of Rome, in particular, grew tiresome very quickly, despite the body she would share gleefully and for the asking.

And on that not entirely happy thought, Robinson considered inviting the captain, once again, to his bed.

It would be a long braking maneuver before the ship assumed orbit and, while he could, by right and tradition, bed any female of the crew he wished, he had found the captain's technique most agreeable, especially in low gravity. Wallenstein would make *Peace*'s long descent to the planet something other than a trial.

Peace was one of thirty-three ships now in system. Four of these were of the same, *Spirit,* class. Another twenty-three were of one of the older but similar classes. The Spirits were slightly larger than the rest, but only slightly. They were ovoid, at just under two hundred meters across and three hundred long. Their silvery skin shone when the sun was just right. Only on closer inspection could one see that the apparently smooth surfaces were pocked with the marks of hundreds, or in some cases thousands, of strikes by astral debris.

Still, at a distance the ships—all twenty-seven that could be seen from below by the locals if the locals used powerful telescopes, as some did—seemed pristine, powerful and invulnerable.

Only one of the petty states that infested the surface of the planet below had made any effort to match the power of the majestic and apparently invulnerable fleet. Just how successful that attempt had been was a matter of considerable conjecture, both above and below.

All of the ships, newer and older, were said to be armed to the teeth. Those arms, specifically *Peace*'s arms, had been used exactly twice since the once invulnerable fleet had been established. It was too risky to do so now, though. Having seen two of its cities destroyed by nuclear fire from the fleet, the state so victimized had moved Heaven and Earth to eliminate the fleet's invulnerability.

That state, the locals called it the "Federated States of Columbia," had made the effort in a spirit of revenge as much as survival. "Once burned; twice shy" was the common saying. Having seen two of its cities burned off the map toward the close of the great war that had convulsed the planet decades before, their equivalent saying had become, "Twice burned; a third time and we nuke you until you glow." The Fed bastards had actually had the effrontery to demonstrate that the threat was not idle, tracking, intercepting and destroying a robotic courier ship to prove their point. An armed and decidedly hostile standoff had ensued with more than a thousand (the exact number was deep-classified) of FSC nuclear-tipped and hypervelocity missiles pointed into space, and a like number of Peace Fleet warheads aimed expressly at the FSC. Moreover, it was widely believed that the FSC maintained, in addition to its nuclear missiles, some hundreds of mobile railguns and charged particle beam weapons capable of reaching into space either to defend against incoming UEPF warheads or, if those weapons were as good as they might be, even reaching out to touch the ships of the fleet.

The Peace Fleet might have destroyed the FSC, damn the retaliation, then, except that at the same time the FSC had demonstrated the ability to deluge Atlantis Island, the Peace Fleet base on planet, with too much nuclear fire to intercept. Since the families of the crews were on that base . . .

Besides the twenty-seven ships locked in geosynchronous orbit, six more were held farther back, one behind each of the planet's three moons—in order of size: Hecate, Eris and Bellona—and three more guarding the rift point. These six were of varying types but, while having some defense capability, were designed generally for the support of the "tooth" elements of the fleet. This was longstanding practice, not a reaction to the FSC's threat. Indeed, insofar as Earth itself was concerned, there had been *no* reaction to the threats. Earth no longer understood threats, it had been so long.

In Orbit Above Terra Nova, 19 April, 2511

The blue-green planet turned slowly and majestically below, its day-side pastels interrupted only by concentrations of white clouds. The right quarter of the planet was plunged in night. Cities came into view as bright sparks and thick lines, especially along the planet's southern hemisphere.

Watching the scene on the wall-mounted view screen that hung in his sleeping cabin, High Admiral Robinson shook his head in something between dismay and disgust. *So many people, twelve times or more what we have on Old Earth. And so uncivilized. Before I left home I was briefed that they were a potential threat, but only when you see the size of their cities, so much brighter than our own now, do you realize just how many of the barbarians there are, just how much potential for violence they have.*

The picture on the sleeping cabin view screen was better than the one in his main cabin. For all that, it was still flawed. Multicolored lines flickered across it from right to left. Sometimes they were wide, sometimes quite narrow. They were always an annoyance and they never went completely away.

It had been a long braking before *Spirit of Peace* assumed orbit over the new world. *Give Wallenstein her due, she's as competent a skipper as she is a bedmate. She's brought her command in flawlessly. Now if she would only stop hinting that she wants me to back her for a rise in caste.*

The Spirits—*Spirit of Peace, Spirit of Unity, Spirit of Harmony* and *Spirit of Brotherhood*—were the newest ships in the fleet, the most recent having been launched just over one hundred and twenty Earth years ago. The others were much older. One of the others, the UEPF *Kofi Annan*, was nearly four centuries old. Earth could not build another. Even the ancient *Annan* was beyond her ability to recreate.

And that was the problem. The new world, Terra Nova, could not build them or their like either, yet. *Yet* was the operative word. The day was soon coming when the natives *could* build starships. The day was coming when the natives *could* come up looking. Worse, the day was probably coming when they *would*.

And Earth couldn't resist them now, thought the still youthful high admiral of the fleet, watching the screen and lying in his extra wide bunk next to the peacefully snoring Wallenstein, *not if they manage to get off-planet and out of the system. Barbarians.*

Robinson looked over at the captain and considered giving it another go. Why not? Despite his centuries of age, the ADAF therapy had given him the vigor of a young man, along with the skill and grace of a much older one. Anti-agathics were one of the truly remarkable breakthroughs of Earth's medical science. It was no mean achievement and had contributed much to the peace, order and stability of Old Earth that its critically important leadership actually had the time now to truly run things. Indeed, no one given the full treatments had yet died of any natural cause. Perhaps, if Robinson lived to see his third or fourth century, further breakthroughs might extend his life indefinitely. On the other hand, it *had* been a century since the last DAF gene advance. At least, he could not think of another since. He wasn't actually sure that anyone was even trying. Very few of even the very few progeny of the elites seemed much interested in science anymore. They were fewer even that chose to serve in the United Earth Peace Fleet and those were few enough.

Hands clasped behind his head, High Admiral Robinson turned his attention to the dull gray ceiling, thinking back on the Earth he had left so regret- fully almost a dozen months before. Earth was such a paradise compared to the hellhole below, teeming with about twelve times more people than a world that size could indefinitely support. And most of those were poor, sometimes starving, and afflicted with more disease than one could find at home outside of a laboratory.

Earth was peaceful, as well, and had been for more than three centuries. The structure ensured peace, with the half million or so Class Ones supervising perhaps three million Class Twos, who in turn supervised twenty or so million Class Threes, the entirety lording it over the half billion proles of Classes Four through Six. The proles didn't really matter, of course. They were nonpolitical now, living in peace, growing the food and obtaining what raw materials could not be gotten from recycling. They did the limited manufacturing still permitted and possible. They knew their place.

Barring a few malcontents like Wallenstein, everyone on Earth knew his or her place now. *We're not so foolish anymore as to leave decisions to the ignorant or the ambitious. Especially do we keep the proles out of things. What would they have to offer, anyway?*

Indeed, there was hardly any such thing as ambition anymore. One was born into a caste and stayed there. Only within the Peace Force was social mobility still seen as desirable, and even there it was highly constrained. The highly pneumatic Captain Wallenstein was unlikely ever to see Class One, for all the time she had spent in a long life servicing her betters.

Whatever the drawbacks of the system, and Robinson knew them better than most, at least it was generally peaceful.

The same could not be said for Terra Nova, which had become one huge slugfest, periods of peace intermittent, at best, between bouts of war, reprisal, massacre and genocide. Robinson shook his head with disgust.

There was a knock on the door. "Come in," Robinson commanded, rising and throwing on a robe, walking to the main cabin, and ordering the door to his sleeping chamber to close.

"Maintenance crew, Your Excellency," said the Class Three technician. "Got the replacement screen for your cabin. New stuff, Your Excellency, just brought up from Atlantis Base by shuttle. Be only a few minutes to install it."

"Be at it, then," Robinson ordered. Then, since the installation was likely to prove noisy and bothersome, he retired back to his sleeping cabin and the captain. On the way he happened to notice the box the view screen came packaged in. *Kurosawa Vision Solutions, 101 Imperial Way, Kamakura, Yamato, Terra Nova. Fragile: take special care when moving,* the carton said.

Kurosawa always took extra special care of the products it sold to the fleet.

Special care or not, too much of the fleet is going that way now. Earth sends so little, and the ~~rat~~ are growing so old.

Indeed, of the twenty-seven ships in geosynchronous orbit around the planet, two of them were little more than husks with rotating skeleton crews aboard. The meat of the things had been cannibalized to keep up the rest of the fleet.

And how many more will I have to order cannibalized to keep the fleet going? Robinson wondered, as he lay back down on his bunk. *And how much can we continue to buy from below without arousing suspicions about our real status? Wouldn't those bastards in the FSC like to know they could nuke half my fleet now with impunity?*

Buying from the Terra Novans had its problems. For one thing, the fleet had little to offer in exchange. Food was impractical to export over interstellar distances

despite the rift, which made personal travel in cryogenic suspension reasonable. Besides, the Novans who
could pay for food didn't need to. Indeed, the fleet
purchased all its food locally, along with the petro-
chemical fuel for the shuttles. This was explained to
the Novans as simple economics; cheaper to buy locally
than to import. This wouldn't have hurt Robinson so
deeply if it had been the only reason. The fact was
that Earth could not send food or petrochemicals even
if the Consensus wanted to.

There were only four worthwhile and practical
things to trade to the Novans to keep the fleet running. Technology was on, but it was under ban by
the Council and had been for centuries. Besides, what
Earth had were all the far ahead of what the Novans
capable of making for themselves now. Gold?
Half the gold of Earth was already on Terra Nova;
same for the silver, platinum, palladium and rhodium.
There were plenty of proles to trade as slaves, but
the Novans, most of them, had little use for slaves.
And the Moslems, and especially the Salafis, who did
have use for slaves, only wanted pretty young girls and
boys. Since there was a strong market for those on
Earth as well, saleable slaves were a tight commodity.
Moreover, you never really could tell what the proles
knew. If they were questioned, and the Novans realized what Earth had become, it could be a disaster
for the fleet as well as the Earth.

Art, Robinson sighed. *I am reduced to selling Earth's
artistic patrimony to keep in being the fleet that keeps
Earth from being overrun in a hundred years or less
and looted of, among other things, its art.*

Ah well, I should be grateful I was able to talk the

*caliph into turning over to me so much of the contents
of the Vatican's cellars. Fortunate, too, that he valued
them so little. Then again, with even the followers of
Islam so few, and most of those barbarians in the
reverted areas back home who could care less about
the caliph, I suppose he needed the credit as well.*

Robinson closed his eyes and dozed fitfully. He
was awakened, sometime later, by the same technician
who had come to install the new view screen. "We're
done, Your Excellency. Also, your aide, Baron Fiske,
said to tell you the shuttle is ready to take you to
Atlantis Base whenever you're ready."

The shuttle itself was the same silvery color as the
Peace Fleet ships. As the shuttle door split, it also split
the blue and white symbol of United Earth. This was
a map of the Earth, from the northern hemisphere
with the southern hemisphere distorted out of scale,
on which had been superimposed marks for longitude
and latitude, the whole being almost surrounded by
a laurel wreath. There was symbolism in that, with
the poor south exaggerated in apparent importance
but the white and European north still in the commanding center.

The doors closed behind Robinson with a *whoosh*.
He walked the few carpeted steps to his chair and
buckled himself in. Even more than the ships, the
shuttles needed replacing. Roughly a third were unfit
for flight for lack of parts. Moreover, though the skins
were the best product of Earth at the height of its
technological achievements, the composite of which
they were constructed was no longer produced. Terra
Nova, specifically the FSC, produced something similar

(in fact, the nose cones of the missiles it had aimed at the Peace Fleet were made of it), but that was unacceptable for any number of reasons.

It was becoming a logistic burden as well. The shuttles that were still working had to be used overtime. This cut into their maintenance and led to even more failures. Moreover, though logistic effort had been saved with the skeletonization of the crews of the two cannibalized ships, and more by reducing the crews of others by a variable percentage, this put in danger the entire fleet.

And I haven't a clue as to what to do about it, Robinson fumed. *One problem's solution just creates another problem. If I'd known then what I know now, I doubt I'd ever have accepted this assignment.*

Instead of worrying about it, uselessly, the High Admiral stretched out in his chair and slept. He dreamt of the skiing, which he missed, north of the town of Atlanta, by the huge and growing Dahlonega Glacier.

It was going to be one of *those* cocktail receptions, Robinson decided.

"The FSC has become a rogue state," insisted the slender, well coiffed blonde. This was the intense—and, so Robinson thought, even more intensely vapid—commissioner for culture from the Tauran Union, one of the new supra-nationals coming to prominence on the planet. The commissioner was on Atlantis with special permission to bid for *objets d'art* for a consortium of TU museums. "Unni Wiglan," she had introduced herself as.

Robinson considered her for what she was likely to be worth. As high admiral he could have his pick of the Novan women at the reception, of course. On the other hand, although he had a taste for blonde women (that hair color having become rather rare on Earth), she really seemed so earnestly dull that he wasn't quite sure that the no-doubt enjoyable use of her body could quite make up for the torment of having to listen to her talk afterwards. With mixed feelings, he decided, *No, it really* wouldn't *be worth it.*

Robinson simply asked, "And what do you think we can do about it?"

Which question ended that discussion, as well as short-circuited any discussions in the immediate future that might have been of a more pleasant nature.

It was *a good question, actually,* the high admiral later reflected in his ashore quarters. *What* can *I do about it? Options? Hmmm.*

A. I nuke the planet. It'll cost me the fleet and Atlantis Base—no big deal since I don't have a family here, and I could make sure I was safe and away before we struck—but at least I can still nuke them. Set them back . . . oh . . . maybe four or five hundred years. Then they come looking for Earth.

B. Get the Novans to nuke each other. Not hard but they'll probably nuke my fleet, too, on general principle. The FSC would, for a certainty; bastards can hold a grudge. So they nuke each other and us. Sets them back also four or five hundred years. Then they build a fleet and come looking for Earth.

C. Leave things alone. Within one hundred years my fleet is a worn-out ruin. Within one hundred years the Novans are more than capable of launching their own ships. Then they come looking for Earth.

D. Change Earth. Not going to happen. Half the reason they sent me here, instead of leaving me home, was that I was even capable of thinking about changing Earth. History ended there and the Consensus doesn't want it to start up again. Besides, what would we do with half a billion educated, industrialized, militarized proles? Ugly thought, that is. And if the wretches started to actually think?

E. Change Terra Nova. But how . . .

The auction went well, a beneficiary of Terra Nova's cosmopolitan upper class's newfound fetish for the luxuries of Old Earth. With what the serfs on Atlantis could grow, Robinson had enough to feed his fleet for another few decades, and even to buy—under the table—most or even all of the parts and fuel he needed. It put him into rather a good mood, actually, an especially good mood when he considered the portion, twenty percent of the auction's proceeds, that was his by right as the high admiral of the fleet.

So good was Robinson's mood that he was even willing to listen to Unni Wiglan, the commissioner for culture from the Tauran Union.

"I was thinking about your question, High Admiral," the leggy blonde said between sips of champagne. "I admit, I was a little shocked at it. I am, all we cosmopolitan progressives are, so used to thinking of Earth—its advanced social development, technology and culture—as being so superior to what we have that it sometimes comes as a surprise that you are not omnipotent."

Robinson shrugged. "Earth is very far down the road," he said, without mention of whether that road was the right one or not. From his point of view things were pretty good; worth upholding and defending, in any case. Would he have felt the same if he'd been born a prole, forced to eke out a living from the soil or burrow in its depths for ore or freeze on the fishing boats that dotted Earth's oceans? Would he still think so if, instead of his own potential five hundred or more year lifespan, he knew he would have been extraordinarily lucky to reach even an eighth of that? Would he think so if, instead of being able to bed lissome blondes like this one, he had to share his bed with some toothless prole crone? Somehow he doubted it.

"Yes," Unni agreed. "That's precisely it. Earth is far down the road that Terra Nova should be on, but isn't. The reason we aren't is the damned Federated States. By looting the world, by taking a totally unfair share of its resources, by exploiting the poor, the Federated States are able to make a more proper system, one like Earth has, seem inefficient. So, other nations here—doesn't that word make you ill, High Admiral? 'Nations?' As if there could be any nation but the nation of Humanity—follow the FSC's lead. And we can't make any progress here on Terra Nova at all while the FSC stands in the way."

"I am not sure what I can do about it though, my dear Unni." *Sure. Why not make the slight effort to remember the bimbo's name? Costs nothing and might pay, as long as she doesn't* insist *on talking afterwards.*

"I can do something about it," interrupted a dark man who had slid up unnoticed.

Robinson looked over at the newcomer. Then he looked up . . . and up.

The man was tall, nearly two meters in height. In front was a long, untrimmed beard, half gone to gray, that hung to his waist. His head was covered with a checked cloth, held in place by a retaining band made of cylindrical beads interspersed with spherical ones of gold. Robinson thought the cylindrical beads might be of some precious stone, though he could not immediately identify it.

"I can do something about it," the dark man repeated. "I am Mustafa ibn Mohamed ibn Salah, min Sa'ana, emir of the *Ikhwan*."

"Oh, Mustafa, piss off, won't you?" said Unni. "You've tried that trick with the FSC so many times and nothing has come of it."

"Silence, infidel houri," Mustafa commanded. "I lacked the means. The high admiral can give me those means."

Wiglan stiffened under the insult. Robinson made a moue. He asked, "What "means?" And what is this *Ikhwan* of which you are . . . the leader?"

"The *Ikhwan* is the Brotherhood, the Brotherhood of true believers," Mustafa answered. "What we need are nuclear weapons. Give me a dozen such and I will break the FSC."

"That, I am afraid," Robinson answered, "will never happen. Our weapons are identifiable as ours. And, while we could—and did—use them on the FSC in past days, those days are *long* past."

"Then help me in other ways."

INTERLUDE

21 January, 2037,
51.716 AUs Out From Sol

The trickiest part had been the sail. It had to resist tearing, or be self-repairing, or be otherwise repairable, while also avoiding becoming overly charged, electrically. It had also to be very lightweight and highly reflective; the amount of propulsion provided by photons from the Sun and other sources striking the sail being very low except in the aggregate.

In the end, and after frightful expenditures, it was decided that self-repairing was too hard. The nanites that did effect repairs on the sail were not, strictly speaking, a part of it. They worked though, even in the vacuum of space and even while under bombardment by the sun's unfiltered rays. The sail was quite porous, the diameter of the pores being less than the wavelength of the light that forced the sails forward.

The mechanism for setting the sail was simplicity itself. Instead of a complex mechanical operation to raise and lower it, a series of gastight tubes were sewn around the exterior and connected to the main ship by much thinner tubes. Gas was pumped into the tubes to set the sail, pumped out while thin filaments were retracted to furl it. Heating elements within the tubes kept the gas from freezing and collapsing in the cold of deep space.

Other problems, microminiaturized electronics and an extremely lightweight spacecraft body, had been easier. Indeed, they had been almost natural outflows of ongoing, purely terrestrially oriented, research. It was a short step from nanotube body armor for soldiers to a nanotube spacecraft body, for example. The programming had been even easier if not precisely simpler.

Not to say that the ship was cheap. It had eaten up almost all of the United States' National Aeronautics and Space Administration's somewhat constrained budget for the better part of two decades. The less said about the scandals, the overruns, the bribes from various foreign subcontractors, however, the better.

The ship, if one could call a robot a ship, was named the *Cristobal Colon*. Many had held out for a different, generally more culturally sensitive and less eurocentric, name. These ranged from Saint Brendan and Leif Eriksson (obvious nonstarters) to Sinbad to Cheng Ho. Since the Americans were footing the bill, however, they got to choose. Moreover, they were, at the time, going through one of their periodic bouts of extreme nationalism. "Cristobal Colon" seemed good to them and the rest of the world could lump it.

The robot, or ship, was just under two meters in diameter and approximately nine long. Various projections—a radio telescope here, an antenna there—were attached to the outside. The computer that controlled it was deep inside, or as deep inside as one can get with a cylinder two meters across. The sail dwarfed the robot ship, though the sail massed very little and the ship several tons.

The ship was very fast, as men reckoned such things. Boosted by lasers fixed to the moon and floating in space, by the time the ship reached the point it was at it was going a very appreciable fraction of c. Everything was operating normally, though there was a bit of trouble in the Number Thirty-three vent. There were nearly a hundred such, however, which allowed Mission Control or the robot to steer the thing a bit. Even with one such operating at suboptimal efficiency, there was no danger.

Imagine the consternation at Mission Control, then, when the robot and sail seemed to wink out of existence completely. . . .

CHAPTER TWO

I loved you
And so I took the tides of men into my hands
And wrote my will across the sky in stars . . .

—T. E. Lawrence

Cochea, *Provincia del Valle de las Lunas*,
Republica de Balboa, Terra Nova,
10/7/459 AC

Art, precious metals and the occasional young slave were not the only in-demand product of Earth. Music, too, was popular, in particular the wild and violent sounds of the twentieth century. Earth literature also had its place on the new world. Both had been brought by the original immigrants in the form of computer discs. Much had been lost, of course, but much had survived the days from when the old computers wore out. Indeed, developing new machines capable of reading the old discs had given Terra Nova a leg up in artificial intelligence, generally.

As with many immigrant tongues on Old Earth—American English, Quebecois French and South African Dutch, for example—many of the languages of Terra Nova retained many features that had been lost to their mother tongues. Indeed, a man or woman of the twentieth century would likely have found the English of the Federated States more comprehensible than that commonly used by the Anglic-speaking proles of Old Earth. In any case, this made much of the older music of Old Earth quite in tune with Terra Novan listeners.

Of course, Latin hadn't changed in millennia. It was Latin—Satanic flavored Latin at that—which flowed from the speakers in the book-stuffed library:

> *O Fortuna*
> *Velut Luna . . .*

High on one wall of the library hung an ornate, embossed certificate, in Spanish, signifying a high decoration for valor from the Republic of San Vicente. The gilt name emblazoned on the award was Patricio Hennessey de Carrera. Posted beneath the certificate, framed with obvious pride, hung a letter of reprimand—in English—from a general officer of the Army of the Federated States of Columbia. It was addressed merely to "CPT Patrick Hennessey." Both certificates—dated fifteen years prior, long before Hennessey's promotion to his terminal rank—described the same series of events, though in rather different terms.

The library was large, with bookcases covering three of the substantial room's four walls. Against the fourth, under the certificate and the letter of reprimand, stood a desk and chair, each made in the main of dark-finished Lempiran mahogany, hand crafted and richly carved. A man approaching middle age, just beginning to go gray at the temples and with a face weathered beyond its years with the wear of sun and rain, sat at the desk, eyes fixed on a book.

The book was one of many. Reaching floor to ceiling, the volume-packed shelves of the library held the essence of a lifetime's interest and study, more than seven thousand volumes in all. Even over the broad, deep desk more bookshelf space was stacked and—like the other shelves—filled to overflowing. Still more reference material resided on computer micro-discs inside cases stuffed to the brim.

Despite appearances, there was an order and a theme to the volumes. The library was, in the main, about war. If there was a book on the plastic arts—and there were several—the owner had studied them because he knew that art had propaganda value in war. If there was a book on music—and there were dozens—that was because music, too, was both a weapon of war and a remarkably subtle yet powerful tool for training for war. If there were books on the Marxism that had made its reappearance under the Volgan tsar during the Great Global War—and there were some few—it was because the reader believed in knowing one's enemy.

There was even a copy of the Koran.

However, most of the library was more obviously military. The collection covered, as nearly and completely as possible on Terra Nova, every human age and culture as it pertained to armed conflict. An English translation of Vegetius rested next to another copy in the original Latin. Apparently not as confident

in his Greek as in his Latin, the reader kept most
of Xenophon in bilingual texts—Greek and English
alternating pages. Plato, Rousseau, Machiavelli, Aristotle, Hitler, Lenin, Mao, Annan, Nussbaum, Harris,
Steyn, Fallacci, Yen, Peng and Rostov . . . war was
about philosophy and politics, too, and so the reader
studied those as well.

Eyes fixing upon the Nussbaum work, a gift from
his parents many years prior, the reader thought,
*Amazing that that line of thought should have suc-
ceeded in contaminating not one but two worlds. What
utter nonsense!*

A stranger, given time to realize the single-minded
purposefulness of the library, might eventually have
concluded that the reader considered war his art;
perhaps all he cared about.

The stranger would have been wrong. War was not
all the reader cared about, nor even what he cared
most about. It had been a job and was still a hobby;
it was not a life.

The reader, one Patrick Hennessey, late of the
Army of the Federated States of Columbia, put down
the book he had been studying and closed his eyes,
deep in thought.

*Decision Cycle Theory, the Observation-Orientation-
Decision-Action loop, plainly was working against
Nagumo at Midway on Old Earth. How and why
is combat on the ground different? Friction? Scale
and scope? The vulnerability of large single targets
like aircraft and aircraft carriers compared with the
endurance and ability to soak up punishment of ground
forces composed of many small units and separate
individuals? Nagumo's pure frigging bad luck?*

Hennessey's aquiline face frowned in concentration. Pale blue eyes, normally slightly too large for the size of that face, narrowed. A viewer would not have been able to see the darker circles around the irises that typically gave those eyes their frighteningly penetrating quality. "The eyes of a madman," said some, not always jokingly.

Have to think on this one. Hennessey resumed his reading.

The satanic sounding Latin piece ended, to be replaced by:

> "*I see a red door and I want it painted*
> *black*
> *No colors anymore I want them to turn*
> *black . . .*"

To Hennessey the music was a drug, a way of purging the unwelcome feelings and emotions, most of them dark, that otherwise might have taken possession of him. Between that, his calming scotch, cigars and cigarettes, and—most especially—his wife, he kept the surge of feelings under control or, at least, at bay.

A cigarette burned in the ashtray on the maple inlaid into the mahogany desk, smoke curling up about twelve inches before being sucked outside by a ventilation fan. The fan dispersed it to a courtyard surrounded on all sides by the house Hennessey and his wife, Linda, had had built following his departure from the FS Army.

The cigarette was interesting, or, rather, the tobacco in it was. Despite many disapproving clucks from progressives back on Old Earth, a number of the early colonists had made sure to bring tobacco seeds. Once planted on Terra Nova, the tobacco had come under attack from a virus unknown on Old Earth. Whether this virus was native to Terra Nova, or a mutation from the earlier transplanting by the Noahs, or something unmodified and native to Old Earth that had either died out or never been identified; no one knew. The subject was hotly debated.

The effect of the virus, though, was to remove nearly all of the carcinogens from the tobacco. It remained addictive and was still rather unhealthy. It remained highly profitable to sell, the more so as it was considerably safer than Old Earth tobacco.

Of course, the sale and use of tobacco had come under even more virulent attack as Terra Nova developed its own brand of "progressive." Couching their arguments in terms of health, what these truly objected to was the profitability of the commodity. Progressives hated profit.

They hate profit, Hennessey thought, *unless it's their own.*

Hennessey knew about progressives. Especially did he know about cosmopolitan progressives, or Kosmos. He should have; he'd been raised to be one. The lessons had never quite taken.

Hennessey's library was in the very back of the house and reached from inner courtyard to rear windows. By turning his chair towards the rear Hennessey could see the one hundred and twenty-five foot waterfall that had made his wife, Linda, fall in love with this particular piece of land. The waterfall had its memories,

memories that brought a smile to his face. *There by the swimming hole, under the screened* bohio . . . *when the kids were all asleep . . . Oh, my . . .*

The smile disappeared when Hennessey looked at his hand as it picked up the cigarette. He took a satisfyingly deep drag and pulled the cigarette away. *Dainty disgusting thing,* he thought, holding his hand out. *Sickening for a soldier to have such small, miserable, soft hands. Oh well, the rest isn't so bad. And it isn't like I'm a soldier anymore, anyway.*

"Not so bad," was it. He was never going to win any beauty contests but . . .

Hennessey was somewhat slight of build and regular featured, with extraordinarily intense blue eyes. A reasonably well formed chest topped slim hips, themselves atop legs unusually massive, the result of many, many miles of heavy-pack forced marching in his younger years. They were infantry legs, plain and simple. Even several years of relative idleness had not robbed them of their strength. He *was* developing a slight paunch, something he made some effort to combat.

Turning his attention away from his utterly unsatisfactory hands and fingers, Hennessey's eyes wandered over the bookcases containing his library. He put the cigarette down, replacing it in that hand with the iced whiskey. The cubes made a tinkling sound as he sipped while continuing to peruse the library's shelves.

Hennessey's eyes came to rest on a simple metal-framed picture of Linda, his wife, now visiting his—mostly estranged—relatives in the Federated States.

He looked at the picture and glowed with love, thinking, *I am one lucky son of a bitch.*

Twelve years now they had been husband and

wife; twelve years and three children. And *still* she looked like the eighteen-year-old girl he had married. If anything, so her husband thought, she was more lovely now than when he had married her.

Next to the one portrait was another, that of Linda with their son and two daughters. *We do damned good work, don't we, hon? Miss you.*

Hennessey looked up from his family portraits. He thought about waterfalls, then left the library to take the short walk down to the one behind the house. There was a small *bohio*, or shed, there, along with some garden furniture. He sat down in one of the padded chairs, losing himself in the sight and sound of the splashing water.

God, I love this place, he thought. He didn't mean merely the waterfall, nor even the entire property. He meant Balboa, possibly the only country in which he had ever felt truly at home.

Odd thing, that. But what's not to love ... outside of, maybe, the government here? The people are bright, hardworking and friendly. The men are brave; the women loyal and lovely. The land is ... well, "beautiful" hardly does it justice. He watched Linda's multicolored pet "trixie," *Jinfeng,* sail across the waterfall. It came to rest on the branch of a large mango tree and began to eat the fruit it found there.

Just beautiful.

Balboa, being largely jungle and also somewhat sparsely settled, retained more than the usual amount of pre-settlement flora and fauna. *Jinfeng* was one example. But mixed in with the green of the jungle around the waterfall were some other species, bluegums and tranzitrees, the latter so named because their bright green-skinned fruit was intensely appetizing to look upon, and the mouthwatering red pulp inside intensely poisonous for man to eat.

Lower animals could eat tranzitree fruit without ill effect. It was conjectured in some circles that tranzitrees had been developed and placed on Terra Nova by the Noahs—the beings who had seeded the planet with life untold eons ago—expressly to prevent the rise of intelligence. Certainly the tranzitrees had been artificially created, as had bolshiberry bushes and progressivines. The latter two were, likewise, poisonous to intelligent life but harmless to lower forms. Their complex toxins did build up in some food animals, were they allowed to eat of them, rendering those animals equally toxic. This, too, would have tended to limit the development of civilization, even had early intelligent life managed to survive the tranzitrees, bolshiberries, and progressivines, by limiting the food supply.

The tranzitrees had no real use but aesthetics. The bluegums, on the other hand, were cultivated locally for their edible nuts, high grade lumber for cabinetry and furniture, and the refinable resin—a rubberlike compound—which gave them their name. All were blue, as were the trees' leaves. The leaves were used to make a rather good dye.

Of course, there's no law in this place. It's all who you are related to, who you know, who are your friends, what bribes can you pay, and how much clout do you have. A well-connected man can get away with murder—some of my in-laws have—manslaughter, anyway.

Want to set up a new business? "Well, my brother-in-law is at the planning commission. I am sure he could help you if you made it worth his while." *Need to buy a chunk of land?* "My cousin, the procurator, could probably help but he doesn't come cheap." *That's all fine for me; I'm connected through Linda's clan. But what about the average Joses? They're screwed, unless, that is, they know somebody.*

Add a little law, a little integrity, to the government and this place could be perfection.

The maid, Lucinda, found him under the *bohio*, lost in thought.

"*Señor?*"

"Yes, Lucinda?" he asked.

The woman was older, from a poor family, and never terribly pretty. Nonetheless, her family had been in service to Linda's for generations. This explained why she had taken a job even at the wretched salary earned by a domestic in the undeveloped and unindustrialized parts of Terra Nova. Hennessey tried to treat her kindly and, had she been asked, the maid likely would have voiced no ground of complaint.

"*Señor*, there are two men here to see you. One is from the *Fuerza Civil*; a Major Jimenez. The other is General Parilla. You know, sir, the old dictator?"

"Xavier? Here? Great! And Parilla? Wonderful, Lucinda." Hennessey rousted himself from his chair and walked briskly to greet his old friends and former enemy.

He reentered by the back office door, then walked briskly across the cobblestoned way that led through the courtyard. In the open courtyard Hennessey stopped briefly to study the clouds gathering overhead. To himself he muttered, "Storm again, from the west, it seems. Oh, well, I've always liked the rain."

The door leading from the courtyard to the foyer was open, befittingly so in country so warm. Hennessey passed through it without pause and saw two men, rising politely from the overstuffed chairs in the iridescent bluegum-paneled foyer.

Rank *had* its privileges. He thrust out a welcoming hand first to retired (*forcibly* retired) General Raul Parilla; short, dark, gone a little fat now with his years of service behind him. Most of the general's still abundant hair had gone to gray.

The general returned the clasp warmly. "Patricio, it is good to see you again after all these years."

"Sir . . . you too, sir." Hennessey meant it. Cut off, as he was, from his old army, he valued the contact even with a foreign one. Though it would be pushing things, really, to call Balboa's Civil Force an army.

Smile broadening at his other guest, Hennessey greeted a friend of much longer standing and even deeper feeling. Indeed, so close were he and Xavier Jimenez that neither of them much minded that they had once fought each other nearly to the death . . . and *had* fought to the deaths of many of their followers.

Where Parilla had grown a bit rotund with the years, Jimenez remained whippet thin, a lean, black hunter and racer.

No words passed between Jimenez and Hennessey. With friends so close, none were needed.

"Lucinda," Hennessey called. "Please bring a bucket with ice, a bottle of rum, some coke and some scotch to my library. And three glasses, as well, please. Gentlemen?"

With that, Hennessey led the way back across the courtyard. Parilla and Jimenez stopped to admire a statue of Linda Hennessey that stood at one end.

"She hates that thing," Hennessey said, "but it helps me when she's gone."

"It's a beautiful piece of work, though," Parilla commented.

"So's Linda," said Jimenez.

First Landing, Hudson, Federated States of Columbia, 10/7/459 AC

There was a screeching of tires followed by curses and the tinkling of broken glass as Linda began to walk across the street to the restaurant where she was to meet with her husband's cousin, Annie. She scrunched her neck down, looking somehow guilty, and proceeded to cross.

For some women the word "breathtaking" was only bare justice. Linda Hennessey was one of them. Though she would never have claimed to be so, she was beautiful; simply beautiful, the kind of woman who can stop traffic on a busy downtown street just by *being there*. Hennessey had *seen* her do just that, more than once. It didn't usually cause a traffic accident, though. Still . . . that happened, too, sometimes.

On the other side there was a man leaving the restaurant in company with a woman. He walked into a lamppost. Linda tried not to notice.

She had to repeat herself three times to the maitre d' before he actually heard a word she said, and *he* was plainly gay. That wasn't caused by her accent. A wave of awed silence washed across the restaurant floor as she was led to the table where Annie awaited. Conversation didn't resume until she was seated and, for the most part, out of sight.

Dark complected, she had a high cheekboned, heart-shaped face set off by large, liquid brown eyes. She also had a classic 90-60-90 centimeter figure and though for modesty's sake she wore a bra, she didn't need one. Her breasts stood out and up on their own, as if she'd won the war with gravity and dictated her own terms. She had perfect teeth, even, straight and white like newly polished ivory. Her midnight black, wavy hair gathered light and cast it about her face like an angel's halo.

Unusually enough, her looks meant little to her. They were a gift to share with her husband, yes, as well as a gift to pass on to her children. But she hadn't earned any of that perfection; she'd been born with it. She didn't even have to work at it. Even though she valued those looks less than someone who did have to work at it might have, she knew they usually had an effect on people, and generally a very *positive* effect.

Thus, she didn't understand, she could never understand, just why her husband's family loathed her so. She was *sweet* to them, as she was sweet to everybody. She dressed well. She carried herself with a bearing that was aristocratic, true, but never arrogant. She never condescended. She spoke well, both in the Spanish they seemed to refuse to admit was a civilized language and in rather cultured, if accented, English, as well.

It was surprising, then, that neither her looks nor her character did any good at all with her husband's family.

Linda sighed. *Patricio's family has never liked or accepted me. I suppose they never will. No, that's not quite fair,* she amended. *With the exception of this one cousin, they despise me. But Annie is always friendly. These trips would be a lot more difficult than they are but for her.* Linda smiled at her husband's cousin, seated opposite her in the crowded First Landing restaurant.

Annie Hennessey was taller than Linda by almost half a foot. Where Linda was dark with midnight hair, Annie was pale white and dark blond. Not as pretty—well, *few* were—she was still quite an attractive, and exceptionally well built, woman in her own right. She felt none of the common jealousy at Linda's uncommon looks.

Linda sighed again. "Why don't they like me?" she asked.

"Like you?" Annie asked. "Honey, *everyone* likes you . . . oh, you mean the family. Well . . . they're just assholes." Leaning forward across the table to be heard over the hubbub of the crowd, Annie said, "The thing is, Linda, dear, that you make them feel inferior. After all, what is my family but a bunch of broken down farmers who grafted themselves onto some down and out families of WASPs? Well, and a few well-to-do Jews, too, of course.

"But *you* on the other hand? When the first major colonization ship to this part of the world made its final approach orbit you had ancestors to wave to it from below. When they put up their first building, you had ancestors that said, 'There goes the neighborhood.' You even come from old money. Oh, not so much as we have, I know—not nearly—but it's *older*. And that counts, my dear.

"You make Uncle Bob's skin crawl, because everything

he has clawed his way to, everything his father and his grandfather and his great-grandfather clawed their way up from, you came by naturally."

Annie stopped speaking and sawed and speared a bit of steak from her plate for emphasis.

"Is that why he insists on seeing me and the children at his office? Surrounded by his tokens and triumphs?" Linda asked.

"That . . . yes," Annie responded, slowly. "Other things too. You see, our family has been in decline for more than forty years. Not in money, but in people. We lost about half when the UEPF bombed Botulph. After that, few of the women wanted children. Of those few, some couldn't have any. Bob's wife never had any, for example. And when you subtract the couple of gay boys and the occasional girl who will never have children . . . nope, we are in decline."

Annie paused and leaned back in her chair, looking back across the veil of years. "I remember when I was a little girl everyone setting so much store by Pat. It used to kill me the way he was doted on. Yes, even us girl cousins . . . we *all* spoiled him rotten. He seemed to have something the rest of us had lost; a certain, oh, spark, I guess. Uncle Bob in particular expected him to grow up to take over the business."

Linda snorted. "Patricio? Business? He despises business."

"Oh, I know," Annie agreed. "He always did. Me, too. So I don't do it; I just live off the trust fund."

Annie sipped at her drink, sipped again . . . again. "I always understood him better than the others did. If I had been a man, I'd have joined the army too, to make my own escape."

She continued, "So, anyway, when he ran off to join the army at age eighteen, it just infuriated Bob. And *enlisting* rather than going to one of the military academies? Well, we haven't had an enlisted man in our family since Great-great-great-uncle Bill with the 12th Wichita Infantry in the Formation War. Then, when Pat insisted on *staying* in the army . . . well . . . it took the heart right out of Uncle Bob at first. That was when he cut Pat off, you know. It wasn't anything to do with you."

"Well, here I have one son and two daughters," Linda said. "They carry the name, they've even got your family's color rather than mine. And the women of *my* family insist on having children . . . lots of them. Speaking of which . . ."

"Yes?" Annie asked, expectantly.

Linda just smiled and held up three fingers, then slowly raised her little finger to make a fourth.

Cochea, 10/7/459 AC

As Linda and Annie dined in First Landing, in the Federated States, Hennessey, Parilla and Jimenez pored over maps from the Federated States invasion of Balboa, in 447, called "Operation Green Fork." Hennessey was working on a history of that invasion—something neutral and objective to balance the often propaganda-distorted works already in print. He had to work on *something* to keep busy and to feel useful, not having a job to call his own anymore. Indeed, he had several projects going at any given time. One of them was a translation into Balboan

Spanish of a novel by an Old Earth writer he knew only as R.A.H.

Jimenez pointed a long, thin finger at the map. "Right there, Patricio. Right on that damned corner was where the war started."

Hennessey straightened up from the maps. "Tell me about it, Xavier."

As Jimenez spoke, Hennessey went to his computer and began to type, fingers blurring over the keyboard.

Zabol, Pashtia, 10/7/459 AC

Some miles from the center of the city of Zabol a bearded man hunched over a keyboard. Very slender and tall, as were most of his people, the man had to hunch deeply, uncomfortably, to perform his task. In the dim light the glow of the computer monitor illuminated his face to the semblance of a demon, though in daylight his face was quite decent and even handsome. Distantly, an electrical generator groaned, the sound traveling down damp, narrow hallways. The generator brought light and heat, and powered the fans that brought fresh air to this elaborate complex of caves and tunnels painstakingly carved and blasted from the living rock. The complex was one of several, not all of them in Pashtia.

Abdul Aziz Ibn Kalb brought up a free e-mail service, Firestarter, and then typed a sign-in name— "islandsrfrdude"—and a password. The screen changed to reveal an account with nothing but spam in the inbox, and no messages sent. He began to compose a meaningless message.

Composition completed, Aziz attached a photo as a jpeg file. The photo, properly processed, contained a message, simply, "CA39, Desperation Bay, Execute, 11/7."

Aziz saved the message to his draft folder, which was actually physically located on a server far, far away. He then closed the account. When it was opened later in the day, in Yithrab, it would be copied to a different account and saved into yet another draft folder and server. From there it would be opened in Lancaster in Anglia and copied yet again to a different account. Finally, when opened in the rebuilt city of Botulph, in the Federated States, it would never actually have been sent. There would be no easy trace to Zabol or to Abdul Aziz.

That task completed, Aziz typed into the computer, "Wahoo.sig."

Botulph, Federated States, 10/7/459 AC

"The orders are received. We go tomorrow."

"*Allahu akbar. Allahu akbar,*" the swarthy men congratulated each other, shaking hands and slapping backs in unconstrained joy. *God is great; God is great.* Now, finally, they were chosen to strike a great blow against their greatest enemy. Now, at last, they would bring home to the Great Demon the meaning of war. Could there be any doubt of their coming success, their cause being just and the Most High being on their side?

"Shall we rehearse again?" asked the youngest member of the team.

The leader smiled indulgently and answered, "No need, Samadi. We have rehearsed so many times any one of us could cut a throat in our sleep. Go out. Have a good time. Just be asleep before midnight and remember that tomorrow night you will be feasting among the houris of Paradise."

Samadi simply shook his head in the negative and went to his room to study his flight manuals.

Yusef, the convert, likewise didn't go out. Instead he pulled out the guitar that he loved and began to play and sing something of his own composition:

"I've been dreamin' fait'fly
Dreamin' about the jihad to come . . ."

INTERLUDE

21 January, 2037 to 14 March, 2040

...to emerge, unknown to Mission Control, somewhere . . . else.

The robot didn't know where it was; the star and
constellations matched nothing in the catalogue. It
didn't know how it got there. Most disconcertingly,
it had lost touch with Mission Control. It blared out
a distress signal. It blared in vain.

This was where good programming came in. While
this precise turn of events had definitely not been
foreseen—no one on Earth remotely suspected the
existence of such a flaw in space—other emergencies
had, which would have required a certain amount of
independent judgment on the part of the ship.

The robot did know it was still functioning. It did
know there was a star ahead. It could sense that planets orbited that star. It knew that it had a mission.
And it had a star map of the stars as it emerged in
the now system, which map was updated over. With
this, and what could be gleaned of the solar system
in which it found itself, the robot got to work.

Having a star ahead was important, for without photons to brake its flight the robot-ship had little choice but to continue on to wherever the solar winds or inertia might take it. Its own maneuvering capability was quite limited.

Accordingly, the ship began furling the sail, pumping out the gas that held it erect and reeling in the filaments that connected it to the ship. When this was done, the entire assembly was rotated using some of the small amount of conventional fuel carried, to where the robot decided the sail was best suited to braking. It was then unfurled. The light from the sun was not sufficient to fully brake, however, if the ship followed a purely straight path. The robot began calculating an orbital path that would allow it to come very close to the light and heat of the foreign sun, thereby chopping its velocity to something it could work with.

This took several months, months well spent in analyzing the system. It found, for example, that the fourth world was in the right range to support life. It found further that the other five planets spinning about the local sun were not, being either far too hot or far too cold. There was no asteroid belt.

The fourth world, further, showed an oxygen nitrogen atmosphere, had an albedo indicating that it was about seventy percent covered in water and thirty percent in land, and had polar icecaps and some seasonal variation, though less than Earth's. It had small moons, three of them, which were certain to produce tides, though of lesser intensity than did Earth's sole companion, Luna. Spectral analysis showed plant life in profusion and limited volcanic activity. The closer the robot-ship came to the world its programming had settled on, the more it saw weather, as well.

The robot-ship was never designed to land upon any world, whether of its origin, its intended target, or this new and unknown place. It was equipped to explore, nonetheless, if a found world had an atmosphere. In the last half of its cylinder, carefully cradled, rested two parachute landers and two high altitude gliders. It released one of each over the fourth world as it passed close by.

The glider was never intended to come to a rest and did not. Released from the ship at low velocity relative to its target and with wings folded, it simply went ballistic until reaching the first thin traces of gas in the fourth planet's troposphere. At that point it deployed its wings. Solar powered itself, with a small propeller for propulsion and control surfaces for minor adjustments, it fought for control against the wind that threatened to rip it apart and the gravity that sought it in a deadly embrace. It was touch and go for a while but—to give NASA's executives their due; when they take a bribe to buy a Japanese-built gliding drone for interstellar exploration work, they at least make sure the drone can do the work before cashing the check—the glider skipped along, its microminiaturized camera and radar mapping the surface.

The gliding drone lasted quite some time. Not so the first parachute lander. It actually had a much easier time of it, initially, surviving entry into the planet's atmosphere and coming to rest lightly under its deployed parachute. It even managed to release its parachute precisely as it touched down, the wind carrying the 'chute off and allowing the lander to use its cameras and other sensors unobstructed. Sadly, however, as it was sending a continuous stream of video information to the *Cristobal Colon*, said stream showing a number of very large and tusked herbivores, one of the herbivores stepped on it, crushing it completely. The ship had to wait several months before it was in position to deploy another, and that came down on a different part of the planet.

The other glider-drone, too, was eventually deployed, thus cutting the mapping time down considerably. After all, there was a limited amount of time left to complete the mission and the *Cristobal Colon*, while it was never bright enough to actually understand what had happened to it, was certainly intelligent enough to follow its programming and retrace its steps.

CHAPTER THREE

My sons were faithful . . . and they fought.
                                    —Padraic Pearse, *The Mother*

Cochea, 10/7/459 AC

Hennessey leaned back from his keyboard, blanking his mind of distractions as he tried to match what he remembered from the invasion of a dozen years before with the sequence of events as related by Jimenez. That was, in fact, the entire purpose of the exercise, to construct an objective history of the 447 invasion by testing it against *both* sides.

And besides, Hennessey thought, *my side had all the histories written by ourselves. What will happen to the memory of good men who fought and died on the other side if Jimenez and I don't write down their story?*

For himself, he remembered his mechanized infantry company standing by on radio listening silence from just after sundown until the order came to roll.

53

The armored personnel carriers—or "tracks," boxy M-224s—he had pulled into hide positions off the main road that led from Fort Muddville to *Ciudad Balboa*, paralleling the Transitway. The engines he'd ordered to be left idling—an armored vehicle once stopped could not be guaranteed to start again—while he and his subordinates went over the plans and contingencies for the umpteenth time.

Hennessey remembered, too, the mix of excitement and eagerness, on the one hand, and regret that his company's target for the attack was also the responsibility of his best friend, on the other, to defend. Although it hadn't been his first action (it *had* been his first *official* action . . . but there was that letter of reprimand over his taking "leave" in San Vincente, after all), he remembered being nervous.

When he'd first been told, he had asked to be given a different mission, *any* different mission. The battalion commander, however, had very reasonably pointed out that the Federated States wished to keep even enemy casualties low.

"And, *Captain* Hennessey," the colonel had emphasized, "since Captain Jimenez of the overstuffed and underarmed brigade we call the Balboa Defense Corps *is* your friend, since you command the most powerful ground striking force in the country and since the fall of Jimenez's charge, the *Estado Mayor*, can reasonably be expected to cause the rest of the BDC to fold, there is a) some chance that you might be able to induce him to surrender and b) no chance that anyone else could."

"No, sir, not a chance, sir," had been Hennessey's answer. "Zip, zilch, zero, none, *nada*. You don't know

him like I do. Jimenez is first rate all the way. His
mother could ask and he'd tell her to fuck off, the
same as he will me."

"Do it anyway," the colonel insisted.

Hennessey's reminiscences were suddenly interrupted
as the rain promised by the afternoon's darkened
skies came down in a deluge. Its heavy pounding on
the tiles of the roof and the stones of the courtyard
returned him to the present.

Even as it did so, Jimenez remembered, *It rained
that night, too. . . .*

*The rain had come quickly, taking in its wake the
trash and the smell, and even covering briefly the
sounds of the city under its soft hammering. People
scrambled for shelter or ignored the downpour as
the mood took them; for this was Balboa City, on
the closing end of its long wet season, and the only
possible weather forecasts were "it is going to rain"
or "it may stop raining soon."*

*The deluge passed as quickly as it had come. From
his sheltered vantage on an upper floor of one of the
many buildings of Balboa's Estado Mayor, or general
staff, complex, Xavier Jimenez, Captain, Balboa Defense
Corps, sighed as he watched the streets nearby fill
again with people.*

*Jimenez missed the rain as soon as it passed, missed
the feeling of solitude, of peace, of being subsumed
in nature. Balboa was the rain; the rain was Balboa.
Jimenez loved both very dearly.*

*Casting a wary glance skyward, Jimenez was pleased
to see the clouds still blocking the stars above. He
said softly, and only to himself, "Not tonight. They*

won't hit us tonight. Not with the clouds so low and thick."

He did not say it aloud, but whispered the words, "But they will hit us. I wonder if it will be Patricio who comes for us here. We're important; he's the best. I think it must be. I'm so screwed." Another sigh escaped him, this time for things that could not be helped, things as inevitable as the rain.

Dozens of automobiles passed by the Estado Mayor every minute. Had any looked up, they would have seen Jimenez smiling, white teeth sparkling in an angular, coffee-dark face. They would not have seen his hands as they clenched and unclenched to no perceivable rhythm.

Pushing the sight and sound of the automobiles from his mind, twisting his head to look directly at the corridor leading to the office of his country's "Supreme Leader," General Antonio Piña, Jimenez's smile grew even broader. "Son of a bitch," he muttered under his breath. He could have spoken aloud, since that same dictator was either passed out drunk, or, if he retained some semblance of consciousness, certainly engaged in fornication with one or another of his bevy of mistresses.

The smile closed, a sneer taking its place. Some things were just too disgusting to maintain a smile over, even for him. Jimenez turned his gaze back to the street below, watching the passing cars as one might watch fish in an aquarium, relaxing, vicarious, mindless existence . . . like watching the rain.

Below, a corporal of the guard stopped a car. This was an unusual enough break from the pattern to catch Jimenez's attention. He watched closely, intently.

He watched as the car leapt forward, missing the corporal by mere inches. He watched as the corporal grabbed a nearby rifle, charged it, and raised it to his shoulder. He saw the rifle give off three spurts of flame that lit up the area as if by a strobe, each shot driving the corporal's shoulder and body backwards a few inches.

Under the glow of an overhead streetlamp, the rear window of the automobile shattered under the fire. Jimenez saw countless tiny flakes of glass burst into the air then fall, sparkling, to the dull pavement below.

"They shot up the car, killed your man," Jimenez explained. "That was understandable, if unwise. But then they grabbed that naval officer and his wife . . . threatened them, beat him and assaulted her. I tried to stop it but . . ."

Hands clenching convulsively, Jimenez turned from his station and began walking briskly to the nearest staircase. His booted feet tap-tap-tapped on the hard stone floor.

Reaching the staircase, one hand grasped the banister as a pivot for a forceful turn. His feet beat rhythmically on the stairs as he descended. Soldiers and flunkies, each and every one perplexed at the unexpected shots, took one look at the fixed, fierce and even painful smile on Jimenez's face and looked quickly for something else to do, someplace else to be.

Jimenez burst through the door, then trotted for the complex gate. Armed guards were all around. Some stood idly. Others, those nearer the gate, were plainly at a heightened sense of alert. Jimenez trotted through them all without a sideward glance.

Reaching the gate, Jimenez slowed his trot back to a brisk walk. As if in compensation, his hands' clenching became almost frenzied and his smile grew broader still. He headed straight for the guard shack from which the shots had been fired.

Reaching the shack, Jimenez found it to be empty. He looked around until, under the city lights, his eyes caught on the former occupants. They were surrounding two civilian-clad people—one man, one woman; both, Jimenez was certain, from the FSC. Gringos—the name had been carried across the stars. They were too well dressed, too light skinned, too blond—especially the woman—to be anything else.

Jimenez stopped for a moment, watching intently. In his gaze the crew surrounding the gringos began to beat the man mercilessly. A knee intersected his groin.

The woman's head bent down as if she were crying. One of the Balboans grabbed her hair and pulled her head erect again. Jimenez thought she must have been threatened then, as she began shaking her head back and forth in obvious terror.

More words were spoken, none loud enough for Jimenez to make out clearly. He saw one of the troops smash the gringo's head back against the wall. Another made a half-ways grab at the woman's breasts, then reached down instead and patted her thigh meaningfully.

Jimenez's smile grew brilliant. Hands forming fists, he strode forward.

From clouds overhead and to the south the first hints of another warm sprinkling began to descend.

✧　　✧　　✧

Hennessey stopped typing. He looked up at Jimenez and asked, "What happened next, Xavier?"

"I heard the corporal say, 'Kick the fucking spy again.' Then some private did, kneeing this navy type's groin. That navy officer—he was a tough man . . . very . . . well, he hardly made a sound. But his wife was crying, streams of tears running down her face, begging for her husband. She looked terrified. Who could blame her? Not I."

"Raul," Hennessey turned his head to address Parilla. "You were the commander of the old *Guardia*. They weren't like that before. What changed? What do you think caused them to act like that? With a woman, I mean?"

"Piña," answered the short, brown and somewhat rotund Parilla in a single word. "Our drunken idiot 'Supreme Leader.'"

"Him? How?" asked Hennessey, raising a single eyebrow. In principle, he agreed, of course, but wanted Parilla's thoughts.

"Oh . . . I doubt I have to explain this to you, Patricio." When the eyebrow remained raised anyway, he continued, "Look, we had a little tiny force in Balboa before I was ousted. Maybe two thousand men. Maybe a few more. But they were select. Good men. Piña brought in . . . oh, Christ, Patricio, some of the people he brought into the force weren't much more than criminals themselves."

To Parilla's side, Jimenez just nodded in silent agreement.

"And then he had to get rid of, get out of the way anyway, a lot of good people. It was only my nagging that kept our friend here in service. Somebody, after all, had to set an example." Parilla leaned over and ruffled Jimenez's hair just as if the younger were still the old man's aide de camp.

Hennessey laughed, more at the gesture than at the words. He turned back to Jimenez. "What happened then, Xavier?"

Jimenez sighed and shook his head with a mixture of regret and disgust. "I saw the corporal lift the woman's head by her hair. I heard him say . . ."

"What? You afraid he won't be able to perform in bed, bitch? How about I have a half dozen of my men give you the last decent fuck of your life?" The wife's mouth just formed a silent "O" of pure terror. She began to plead for herself then, as well as her battered husband.

The corporal released her hair and turned back to the husband. He asked, "You want that, boy? Shall we gang-bang your wife? No? Then tell me what the fuck you were doing here. Just out for a stroll, you say. No doubt."

A private put his hand under the husband's chin and pushed up hard. The naval officer's head slammed into the wall behind. It struck the exposed brick wall hard enough to split the thin skin over his skull.

Even now Jimenez smiled at the memory, the same smile he had been using since boyhood whenever something *really* annoyed him.

He went on, "So the private's still holding this poor guy's chin and was cocking his arm to hit him in the face when I reached them and grabbed his arm."

"He said, and I remember this clearly, 'What the

fuck . . . ?' Then the private looked at me over his shoulder. Oh, Patricio, it was good to see. His eyes got big—like saucers—when he realized who I was."

"I smiled at him. Patricio, I confess . . . I was not always as even tempered as I am now. The private knew what that smile meant. He looked . . . well . . . a lot more frightened than that poor woman did."

The corporal's eyes bugged out. He stuttered out, "Ca-Ca-Captain Jimenez. Sir. They're spies. We were . . ."

Jimenez cut off the explanations and excuses. "I know what the hell you idiots were doing. I can see what you were doing. But I don't think you know what you were doing. Let the gringos go . . . with apologies. And pray it's enough."

The corporal insisted they were spies. That's when Jimenez lost his temper. He grabbed the corporal's uniform shirt and slammed him against the wall, following up with two quick punches to the solar plexus.

"That navy officer *was* spying, you know? Probably without authorization but still spying," commented Hennessey. "Then again, maybe he *had* authorization, too. I had awfully detailed and up-to-date information when my company rolled out."

Jimenez sighed. "Yes, I know. I knew that even then. But I still didn't want a war we could not even hope to drag out very long, let alone win."

Hennessey was a bit odd about impending combat. He'd fret nervously, go to see everything, to check on everything, to look into the face of every one of his soldiers. And then, as it got closer, he'd simply begin to calm down. It was almost as if he was detaching a part of himself. Perhaps it was the part that was human. Certainly it was the part that seemed most human. In any case, when the time came, with something like an internal mental click, he would drop off fear, drop off trivial personal concerns, and become something very like a machine.

"Up there! The windows!"

A few vehicles ahead of Hennessey, a young soldier twisted his body to realign the heavy machine gun mounted atop the armored personnel carrier. "Target!" The flash from the muzzle lit the buildings to either side as fifty-caliber bullets, long bursts in steady streams, streaked out to punch through the thin walls of a third story room. The pounding of the heavy machine gun was a palpable blow over the entire upper half of the gunner's body.

The gunner, ears covered by his track commander's helmet and hearing under assault by the fifty's steady booms, could not tell that the shrieks coming from inside did not somehow sound military. Even Piña hadn't thought to conscript five-year-old girls.

From the other side of the street a single, mostly hidden, muzzle flash sparked. A bullet forced its way between the aramid fibers of the gunner's armored vest. He gasped and slumped down to the footstand. Blood began to drip, then gush. It flowed across the raised dots of the metal floor plates, gathering in the lower flat parts.

Confusion on his face, the dying soldier called out once, "Mama?" Then his body went limp, dead.

The soldier's platoon sergeant roughly pulled the

body off of the stand. With one hand he dumped it to the floor even as the other hand scrambled for purchase on the inside of the hatch well. The platoon sergeant pulled himself up into the hatch, drew his remaining arm through, then grasped both spade handles of the fifty cal.

Again, there was the faintest flash from the side of the street opposite where the gun pointed. The platoon sergeant felt something strike his armored vest, then ripple through his left shoulder. He felt more than heard the crunch of splintering bone.

Not too bad. Doesn't even hurt much. *He reported to his company commander.*

"Sergeant Piroute, you don't sound right," *Hennessey said coldly and calmly into the radio. He ignored normal radio procedure; Balboa had no real electronic warfare capability.*

"I'm fine, sir. Just fine. A little hit. Not bad."

"Can you carry on?" *Hennessey asked, still ice cold.*

"Yes, sir. No sweat, sir," *the platoon sergeant answered as his well drilled right arm jerked the fifty's charging handle, twice; ka-chink, ka-chink. Steadily, the gun turned towards the dimly perceived flash. The sergeant's thumbs pressed down on the gun's smooth butterfly trigger. Again, long, steady bursts lit the night. Fountains of powdered cement, wood and stucco emerged from a wall where the fifty's bullets struck. On the other side of the wall a sniper—young and brave but not too well trained suddenly found himself minus the legs that had held him up. His dying thoughts were of his mother.*

Heated by a lodged fragment of a tracer, a piece

of wood began to smolder. Soon enough it would blaze.

The platoon sergeant, still ignoring his own wound, spoke orders into a microphone. The tracks rolled forward, toward Balboa's Estado Mayor.

"You managed to drag it out a lot longer than anyone could have expected," Hennessey said, by way of condolence.

"You pushed faster than anyone should have expected," Jimenez retorted.

Behind him was nothing but fire and smoke and dead bodies, some of them carbonized. The nauseating stench of burnt flesh overlaid that of burnt wood and diesel exhaust. Ahead of him was more smoke, more fire . . . and much of the fire was of the directed variety, the bronze-jacketed lead variety.

Hennessey ducked his head barely in time to avoid a random burst in his direction. The bullets made sharp cracks overhead. They were too close together to make out individual rounds. He spoke into a radio and, on command, a helicopter gunship came in low to rake a threatening section of the compound with cannon fire and rockets. Another command and a team of his infantrymen rushed the wall to emplace a demolition charge.

"Fire in the hole! Fire in the hole!" the men shouted, racing back to the cover of their armored personnel carrier. Again Hennessey ducked as a dark, angry cloud blossomed from the wall.

His men resumed their fire as the last of the demolition-spawned fragments pattered on the ground.

Hennessey lifted a hand, then swung it forward. One platoon, still covered by the armor of their carriers, raced for the breach. Hennessey's own track followed.

He didn't think it funny, at the time, that he was not afraid. It was just one of those things that was. Some people were calm before the storm and mere wrecks in it. Hennessey was always at his calmest and coldest under stress.

If the defenders were afraid, none of the attacking force could see it. Outnumbered, outgunned, to a degree also outfought, but not surpassed in courage, they continued to hurl their defiance at their assailants.

With a clang of metal on metal Hennessey emerged from the rear door of his carrier. He spared a quick glance at one of his platoon leaders. Phil will be fine, he thought, seeing one of the medics apply a bandage to a wounded leg. Another wider glance encompassed the men. They seemed ready.

Hennessey smiled confidently, nodded once and shouted, "All right, motherfuckers . . . Let's gooo!"

With a roar the men followed.

They followed as if into a vacuum. Bodies lay sprawled everywhere, in every manner of undignified death. Here lay a headless torso, there a torso-less head.

Hennessey shook his head with regret. He thought again of his old classmate, Xavier Jimenez, probably even now lying dead somewhere in compound. Jimenez would never run, this Hennessey knew.

Around him, to either side, his platoons and squads fanned out across the compound. Occasionally, shots rang out wherever an FSA trooper simply felt he *could not take the chance. This was the price of a fierce resistance; a price the Balboans had understood when they had decided that honor demanded that resistance.*

Hennessey heard a scream rising above the sounds of battle, the scream coming from a burning building. Poor bastard, he thought. Horrible way to die. Why the hell didn't they surrender when they saw it was hopeless?

Of course, he knew the answer. I wouldn't have. Jimenez wouldn't have either. And the men will follow their leaders . . . if they're good men . . . and have good leaders. And Xavier is a good one.

A fire team leader, a corporal, led his three men to the sound of the scream without being told to. Dodging from cover to cover, they reached the building just as it collapsed. The screaming grew for a few seconds, then petered out into sobs amidst the smoke and falling sparks. Then the sobbing stopped, small mercy.

From off to one side, at another building, one of Hennessey's troopers called out, "I've got five of 'em, here."

A sergeant ordered, "Bring 'em out."

The answering voice was composed half of shock and half of wonder. "I don't think so, Sarge. They're all fucked up."

Hennessey jogged over to investigate. He passed the trooper standing flush against the wall by the door, entering a room taken straight from hell. Bodies, parts of bodies . . . above all, gallons of blood that lent the air an iron stench, even above the smoke. He looked for signs of life. He looked for his friend.

Hennessey knelt beside one body that still showed

signs of life. With grief shaking his voice he asked, "Oh, Xavier, you big, dumb, brave fuck. Why the hell didn't you surrender when you had the chance?"

To his surprise the body answered, "Because I had my duty, Patricio."

"We sure as hell tried to get you to surrender, you know."

"I know that too, Patricio. But we had taken our oaths. We had our duty as we saw it." This time it was Parilla's turn to nod in silent agreement.

"It was too late, though?" Hennessey enquired.

"Patricio, it was always too late. It was too late when Herrera was killed in the plane crash that—I am morally certain—Piña arranged. It was too late when General Parilla here let himself be tricked out of office by Piña." Here, Jimenez referred to one of the cleverest coups in human history, where one would-be dictator, Antonio Piña, convinced a rather reluctant dictator, Raul Parilla, to resign his military post in order to run for the civil office of president . . . then ensured there would be no civil elections.

Parilla muttered, "Son of a bitch cocksucker," under his breath, then added, with a rueful smile, "I've got to admit it was clever, though."

"It was too late," Jimenez continued, "when the thieving son of a bitch lined his pockets with the money we might have used to build and train a force big enough and powerful enough to make your president think twice about invading until we could solve our own problems. It was too late when some of us launched the coup in October, 447, and failed. It was always too late."

"Speaking of which," Hennessey interjected, seeing that his guests had begun to look weary, "it's late, in general. I've had Lucinda make up guest rooms for both of you. If you'll tell her what you would like for breakfast, I am sure it can be arranged. In any case, we need to turn in."

The three stood then, leaving the study and walking across the courtyard to the bedroom side of the house. The rain had stopped; the skies cleared. Hennessey looked skyward at the familiar constellations—the Smilodon, the Leaping Maiden, the Pentagram—and wondered which of the bright points of light overhead were the ships of the UE Peace Fleet.

INTERLUDE

4 August, 2040, Mission Control, Houston, Texas, USA, Earth

The budget had been busted with not a damned thing to show for it. Then had come the scandals, the resignations, the heavily publicized trials . . . the obligatory appearances for public flagellation in front of a posturing Congress. Then had come very damned little money, let me tell you, brother. NASA was reduced to minor projects, as flashy as possible, to try to overcome the bad press and re-fire the public's imagination for the potential of space travel.

One such flashy mission—it amounted to little more than another photo op of the rings of Saturn—was underway now.

About the only thing positive to come out of the loss of the *Cristobal Colon* was that any number of astronomers and physicists had turned their attention to the area in which the probe had disappeared. There was a theory on the subject.

Based on the presence near the area of microwave variance that the physicists described as "lumpy," it seemed that the area concerned was very similar to conditions believed to have existed when the universe was virtually brand new. The theory was that the speed of light was not the same in that area as it was more generally.

This theory, by the way, was not exactly correct.

An assistant flight director, bored and contemplating a night with a couple of cold beers, a hot shower and a hotter woman suddenly saw something on his screen that ought not—no way in hell—be there. He fiddled. He even faddled. But there it remained.

When in doubt, delegate. When delegation is impossible, buck it up to higher.

"What the . . . ? Skipper? Skipper, you've got to come see this!"

Impatiently, the 'Skipper'—a retired naval officer entitled mission director for the Saturn mission—made his way to the terminal. His face was old, weather-lined, and leathery, but he walked erect. A careful observer might have noticed a certain swaggering gait that told of a life at sea now confined to the land.

"Yes, what is it?" the skipper asked.

"The *Cristobal Colon* just sent us a distress signal, sir."

"That's not possible. The thing disappeared three and a half years ago and never a peep."

"Look for yourself," the assistant flight director insisted, indicating his monitor screen with a pointed finger.

The skipper fumbled in his shirtfront pocket for glasses—bifocals, dammit!—and, placing them low on his nose, craned his head to look at the screen.

"I'll be dipped in shit," the skipper muttered,

then continued, a growing excitement in his voice, "Don't just sit there with your teeth in your mouth. Answer it!"

A little shamefaced, the assistant flight director began typing on his keyboard. A series of protocols appeared on the screen. He scrolled through them at practiced speed. *But which is . . . ah, there.* Selecting one, and hitting return, the assistant flight director sent a signal down the line. The signal reached a largish antenna somewhere in the Rockies and was promptly beamed into space. Then came the roughly one hundred and four thousand second wait—about thirty-one hours—while the signal went out to the *Cristobal Colon,* was received and returned.

From that point until the ship was recovered the *Colon* sent an almost continuous stream of the most absolutely, most amazingly impossible data Mission Control, Earth for that matter, had ever received.

There were those who came to wish that the ship, the data, and the program had or would disappear. They had their reasons, and some of those reasons were very good ones.

CHAPTER FOUR

Blessed are they that mourn, for they shall be comforted.

—Matthew 5:4

Cochea, 11/7/459 AC

She glided through his dream like a goddess on a cloud; glowing with her own inner light. The halo of her hair shone with semi-divine vitality. Her perfume was the lightest fresh mist in his nostrils. Perfect rounded breasts danced—thinly veiled—before his eyes, enflamed aureoles outlined in the fabric that covered them. As ever, his eyes were dazzled.

She came to her husband, pressing herself against him and inclining her head to be kissed. Her lips opened slightly, dreamily, in invitation.

As they kissed, Pat ran his hands over her back, skin so smooth that but for the seam of the pajamas he couldn't tell where silk left off and equally silky skin began. No matter that she had borne him three children, no mark showed anywhere on her body.

Hennessey buried his face in the junction of her neck and shoulder, reveling in the richness of long flowing hair the color of midnight; savoring her warmth, her wondrous scent.

She backed up, pulling and leading him towards the bed. At the bedside, goddess-fingers deftly removed his shirt, undid his belt. As she began to kneel, most un-goddess-like, she whispered, "I love you, Patricio. Only you. Ever . . . forever." Her husband groaned, fingers flexing involuntarily in her hair, as sweet soft lips and roving tongue found and teased.

Sensing the right moment, one of Linda's feet replaced a knee. She arose gracefully, kissing her way upward.

How they moved onto the bed he did not know. Where their clothes went he did not know. One moment they were standing, she in pajamas and he half in working clothes. The next, he lay atop her, the two naked together, her back arched, face flushed with desire. A greedy, grasping hand guided him into her. A small gasp escaped her lips as he began to fill her body as he filled her heart.

For his part it was as if he had entered heated honey. He reveled in the wet heat. His hands roved and stroked, caressed, squeezed, fondled with more than fondness.

Together, they began the age old dance; long slow strokes together. Her moans were more than music to his ears. They inflamed him, drove him on and on, faster and faster. With her moans turning to cries of ecstasy, he groaned, shuddered, spent himself inside her.

Patrick Hennessey smiled in his sleep.

Columbian Airlines LTA Flight 39, Federated States of Columbia

One of the distinguishing features of Terra Nova, with only its three small moons rather than Old Earth's single large one, and its lesser axial tilt, was that the weather tended less to extremes than had the world of Man's birth. This had made certain technologies that had proven suboptimal and unreliable—even dangerous—on Old Earth rather more competitive on the new. One of these differences was that lighter than air aircraft, blimps and dirigibles, were somewhat more practical and safe.

LTA aircraft still had a number of limitations. They were slow, and so—since the development of large, fast and efficient propeller and jet powered passenger aircraft—not generally used anymore for intercontinental passenger service. Materials for building them both light and strong were either expensive or lacking and so they were not generally used for heavy freight. (Though several companies, notably in the Kingdom of Haarlem, the Republic of Northern Uhuru, and Anglia, were working on this.) For war purposes, though the LTAs had been used extensively early on in the Great Global war, they had been found to be simply too big, too slow, too easily spotted and, because of this, altogether too vulnerable. As helium was relatively expensive, and since the weather was so much less of a threat, Terra Novan airships had stuck with using hydrogen for lift. This, too, made them less suitable for military use.

Instead, LTAs kept a niche in local light freight drayage, regional and infracontinental passenger service, and—naturally—sightseeing. There was nothing quite so good as a mid-size LTA for touring the ice fields of southern Secordia, the Great Ravine that roughly bisected the Federated States of Columbia, the Balboa Transitway, or the First Landing skyline.

The five men sat up in First Class, Yusef playing on his guitar and singing in Arabic . . . much to the annoyance of the other passengers and the flight crew. He played his new song, happily unconcerned that the song referenced airplanes and they were actually on an air*ship*. That was the sort of trivial detail only the infidels worried about.

> *"I've been dreamin' fait'f'ly*
> *Dreamin' about the jihad to come*
> *I know deep inside me*
> *The holy war has begun"*

The other four men of the team unbuckled themselves and stood in the aisle, clapping their hands, dancing, and singing along:

> *"War plane getting nearer;*
> *RIDE on the war plane!"*

One of the other, business class, passengers rang for a stewardess. "Miss, can't you get those bearded heathens to please shut up and sit down?"

"I'll try, sir," she answered, smiling. She walked up to one of the dancers and asked, politely, "Sir, could you please—"

And then the ceramic knives came out.

Cochea

Hennessey sliced off a bite of ham as he, Parilla and Jimenez took their breakfast in the courtyard, not far from the statue of Linda.

The sun was up, a pleasant breeze blowing. The head of the waterfall was just visible from the spot where they sat. The air was fresh and clean, washed by the previous night's rain. The mosquitoes were vanquished by day. Nor was anything allowed to gather anywhere near the house that might draw or breed flies. There was only the smell of the flowers, Linda's carefully nurtured garden in the courtyard, and of the repast: bacon, ham, eggs, corn tortillas, some cheese Lucinda made herself from the few score cows the Hennesseys owned, mostly for the sake of Linda's family tradition. Above all was the smell of strong Balboan coffee, grown by one of Hennessey's in-laws in a high, cool mountain valley halfway to the southern coast.

The courtyard was doubly screened in, overhead. The finer mesh was intended to keep out mosquitoes and flies. The coarser, steel wire mesh was prevention against entry of the unsavory *antaniae*, nocturnal flying lizards with batlike wings and highly septic mouths. Like tranzitrees, bolshiberry bushes, and progressivines, *antaniae* were neither terrestrial in origin nor Terra Novan, but showed evidence at the cellular level of being artificial creations.

A portion of the screen, a panel of perhaps four feet by six, had receded when light sensors told it the sun had risen enough to drive off the bugs and the winged lizards. Just as Hennessey took the bite of ham an emerald, blue, red and gold reptilian bird—or flying reptile; it was somewhere between the two, though most called them birds—appeared at the opening, circled almost incredibly slowly twice, then descended to land in front of Linda's statue. There it squawked several times before twisting its head to cast an accusing glare at Hennessy.

"She's still not back, *Jinfeng,*" Hennessey called to the bird. "Come over for your breakfast."

Hennessey picked up a still warm corn tortilla and held it down between the level of the table and the level of the courtyard's ground. The bird looked at the tortilla, then looked with vast suspicion at Parilla and Jimenez in turn. Hennessey wriggled the flat fried corn cake to distract the bird.

"My friends won't harm you, *Jinfeng.* Come get your chow."

The bird opened its beak wide, wide enough to show that it was lined with teeth. A warning? Possibly. *Jinfeng* and her kind had not survived—so far—on Terra Nova by failing in the paranoia department. Then she waddled over, her long boney tail scrapping along the stone walkway that ran the length, also the breadth, of the courtyard while the claws on her partially reversed big toes went *click-click-click.*

She stopped beside Hennessey's chair and reached out with a three-fingered claw sprouting from her wing for the tortilla. Before eating it she gave another screech, this one sounding almost polite. Then she raised the tortilla to her beak and began ripping off pieces with her teeth.

"You don't see many of those around anymore,"

Parilla commented. "There were a lot more when I was a boy."

"They're smart, you know," Hennessey said. "At least as bright as a grey parrot."

"If they're so smart," Jimenez asked, "why are they nearly extinct?"

"It's the feathers," Parilla answered. "I daresay if you were that good looking, my ebony friend, people would be hunting you, too. Besides, coming near extinction, in the presence of man, is no shame . . . except to man."

"And they still do hang on," Hennessey added, flipping the bird a slice of fried ham that it caught and likewise bolted down. "Linda's been looking for a mate for this one."

"Speaking of hanging on, why did so many of you stay and hang on in the *Estado Mayor*?" Hennessey asked again, as breakfast neared its end. "Don't get me wrong. I think you did the right thing. I admire you dumb bastards, I did even then. But it *was* hopeless."

Jimenez sighed and shrugged. "We knew that. But what's a principle worth? What's honor worth, Patricio?

"Not everybody did stay in the *Comandancia*, you know. Truthfully, I do not know how many took off as the screen between the Transitway Zone and the *Estado Mayor* collapsed. For a certainty, very few of the real thugs Piña brought in stayed."

"We found well over a hundred bodies inside," Hennessey reminded. "And only the five of you that were too badly wounded to fight were taken prisoner."

Jimenez winced. "Oh, I know, Patricio."

"Damn shame. You had some good kids with you that day."

Jimenez smiled. "Yes. They were the best, the ones who wouldn't give up."

Parilla interjected while spreading butter on a piece of toast, "You will note, young Patricio, that those were men Herrera and *I* trained, for the most part—the old guard. I wish to hell we had their like again in the uniform of the country."

"We do, General," Jimenez objected. "The Civil Force boys are as good as what I commanded in 447." He grinned ruefully. "One of the good side effects of having been abandoned by most of their officers is that a lot of good men survived who would have been killed had they been properly led."

Parilla scowled as he buttered a bit of toast. "But they aren't an army, Xavier. A country *needs* an army."

Jimenez looked down at his own plate and, nodding, frowned. "Yes . . . well we're not going to get an army again; so we have to make do."

"We *could* have an army again, if . . ." Parilla didn't finish the sentence.

Hennessey thought for a bit, then said, agreeably, "You have good people. They make good troops. If you ever get an army again and need a little help . . ."

"Yeah, well," Jimenez said, "no one believes that here. We lost, after all."

"So did the Sachsens in the Great Global War," Hennessey objected. "Xavier, General . . . you know I was in the Petro War, too?"

Jimenez nodded as did Parilla.

"Well, let me tell you this. Six companies and fewer than a dozen independent platoons of Balboan light infantry—outnumbered, outgunned, hit without warning in the middle of the night—gave the FS Army more

trouble than fifty divisions of heavily armed Sumeris.
That's the truth; from someone who fought both. Your
boys had *nothing* to be ashamed of."

Parilla smiled with pleasure. In truth, the Armed
Forces of Balboa—be they called "Civil Force," "Defense
Corps," or "*Guardia Nacional*" had been and remained
his one greatest love. To hear good words of an organization and tradition for which few in the country had
much use anymore did him a great measure of good.

Just as Parilla was touched by the admission, so too
was Jimenez. Normally a block of black ice to the world,
still his voice choked a bit as he tried to formulate fum-
bling words of thanks. Before he could get those words
out he was interrupted by Lucinda, gone suddenly pale,
bursting in on them.

"*Señor, señores* . . . come quick. Something terrible
in the Federated States. On the *Televisor*. Come
quickly!"

Exchanging worried glances, the three arose and
hurried to the television room.

Columbian Airlines Flight 39, 0827 hours, 11/7/459 AC

Legs splayed, the stewardess lay face up with her
open eyes staring blankly at the ceiling of the first
class cabin. Her throat was raggedly slashed and a
great pool of her blood stained the carpet around
her. The blood likewise stained the back of a now
abandoned guitar.

Forward of the stew's corpse, halfway up the flight
of steps that led to the bridge of the airship, was

another, smaller, pool of blood. It dripped from the
steps down onto its donor, the airship's purser. His
throat had been cut at leisure, after he'd been beaten
senseless. It was a much neater slash.

At the head of the stairs, there was a bolted door
that now sealed off the bridge from the rest of the
ship. Inside were eight men, three of them dead and
on the deck. Of the five living, all were covered in the
blood sprayed from the throats of the crew as they
were sliced open. Two of those living sat the pilot's
and copilot's seats. Another two guarded the bolted
door against some desperate bid on the part of the
passengers to regain control.

Yusef, the final member and commander of the
team, stood behind the two flight-trained hijackers.
He had a mobile phone pressed to one ear on which
he received reports from the other teams. With each
report the smile in his blood-dripping beard grew
wider, more jubilant.

"The Merciful, the Compassionate One smiles upon
us in all his glory," Yusef exulted. "The other two
airships are also in our hands."

Samadi, at the pilot's controls, pointed and exclaimed,
"Brothers, look! There beats the heart of the beast."

Looking out the bridge's forward window, Yusef
nodded with anticipatory satisfaction at the immense
skyscraper that was their ultimate target.

"If you hanker after Paradise, Brother, then fly us
into the base."

Samadi smiled nervously and nodded. He was not
nervous over his impending death; that was nothing.
But he was only the best pilot among them, not
necessarily a good one. Pushing forward on the yoke

with one hand, the other pushed the throttle all the way forward. The speed of the ship began to climb up to maximum.

Behind them, in the passenger compartments, the rest of the airship's passengers began to scream at the changing attitude, altitude and speed. The hijackers ignored those screams completely.

Headquarters, Terra Nova Trade Organization, First Landing, Hudson, Federated States of Columbia, 0829 hours, 11/7/459 AC

As with all poisons, Linda thought, *toxicity is in the dose.*

The ground floor of the TNTO was also the floor of the Terra Novan Trade Appeals Board, the planet's sole *effective* international court. Thus, that floor simply swarmed with lawyers. The density made Linda's skin crawl.

One child in her arms, another held by the hand and the third trailing along, Linda stepped onto an elevator heading up to the office's of Patricio's family firm.

"Your destination, please," the elevator's speaker asked.

"Chatham, Hennessey, and Schmied," Linda answered clearly, though with a slight but utterly charming Hispanic accent. The machine running the elevator understood it well enough, in any case.

With a smooth sound the elevator began to shoot upwards until it reached the 104th floor. There it came to an equally smooth stop. The doors opened to either side with a *whoosh.*

Heart pounding, as it always did whenever she had

to meet some of her husband's family—Annie alone excepted—Linda Hennessey and her children stepped off of the elevator. A sign high on a wall announced, "Chatham, Hennessey, and Schmied," the name of the family business.

"Why do I put myself through this?" she asked of no one in particular. She asked and she answered, "Because family is important and I do not want my husband to have lost his . . . especially if I can help it."

"Come on, kids," she ordered, then led two of them forward. Linda carried Milagro, the baby.

Imperious, impervious, unsmiling and unfriendly, Pat's Uncle Robert Hennessey watched without any expression at all as Linda led and carried the children into his office. *If my own wife . . . useless mouth . . . . had managed to have children perhaps I would not resent this woman having taken my only—practical—son. I should not blame her . . . but I just can't help it.*

In her own way equally impervious, Linda smiled with a warmth to rival the sun of her homeland. She glanced about Bob's office, mentally comparing his trophies and mementos—golf, business, and such—with her husband's, much to the favor of the latter. *I am proud to be the mother of my husband's children.*

Truth to tell she found the entire office to be borderline tacky, unrestrained and unrefined. It wouldn't do to mention that, though.

"Linda," Bob greeted, without noticeable enthusiasm.

She didn't answer directly. Being old money, she was probably better at playing status games than Uncle Bob when she cared to play them. Instead, she placed Milagro down on the floor and said, "Go see your grand-uncle, *niños*."

The two little ones scurried around Bob's imposing desk. The eldest, the boy, strode like a young prince, before putting out his hand to shake, formally. By that time Milagro had already climbed aboard.

Still sitting in his chair, his throne, Bob looked down into a lovely little girl's enormous brown eyes, saw the image of the nephew that was more like a son, and felt his heart melting.

He looked up to say something to Linda. She was looking out of his office window, wide eyed, speechless, an expression of shock written on every curve of her unlined face. Bob's eyes followed and saw. Mouth gaping wide, he exclaimed, "Oh, my God!"

Columbian Airlines Flight 39, 0849 hrs

The airship hit near the base of the skyscraper. Its structure, even while coming apart, was just strong enough to force its nose through the thin walls and into the main lobby with its toxic dose of international lawyers. As the ship lost speed to the collision, its engines in the rear broke loose and drove forward, smearing passengers and crew alike, before tearing out of the remains of the front and smashing into the shocked barristers. With the engines came a great invisible cloud of hydrogen gas, pouring into the open lobby before igniting from a spark created by the one of the engines tearing through a steel support.

The hydrogen began burning in front, incinerating several score shrieking attorneys. Then the flames raced through the rich oxygen-hydrogen mix present in the tunnels carved through the ship by the flying engines.

Flame then burst out of the rear, tearing open the hydrogen cells there. The contents of these, once mixed with oxygen, effectively exploded, driving the remains of the ship, and much of its hydrogen, farther into the lobby of the TNTO. There it burned hot enough to incinerate several thousand more international jurists, as well as to set aflame anything therein remotely flammable.

Yusef and company, however, didn't get to see any of that. They were dead and on their way to wherever and whatever might prove to be their final reward, moments after the ship's nose touched concrete.

Terra Nova Trade Organization, 0849 hours, 11/7/459 AC

Arms clutched protectively around the now crying Milagro, Bob rushed to the side of the fallen mother. Julio followed.

"What happened?" she asked, groggily.

"I don't know, I don't know," answered a shocked Bob as he helped her to her feet. "The LTAs never come *that* close. Jesus, it hit us!" He thought about that for a moment, then amended, "No, it *crashed* into us. On purpose. Christ!"

As Bob spoke, the fire sprinklers came on overhead, sprayed for a few seconds, and then died as pressure from below fell to nothing. The pipes had been cut. Unchecked by the sprinklers, smoke and the hint of flame began rising past the exterior windows.

Milagro began coughing as faint smoke filtered into the office complex. Minutes passed as Linda soothed the child, Julio calming the next oldest beside her.

Just as the last tears were wiped and the last sniffles snuffed, Julio looked up and pointed out the window and across the city to where another airship closed on a building only *just* less grand than the TNTO. That was the headquarters for the Global News Network, based in First Landing.

Julio said, "Mom, there's another one . . ."

Cochea, 0903 hours, 11/7/459 AC

Hennessey and his two friends missed the first impact. However, like the rest of the world, they saw it replayed over and over in the next several minutes.

"Dear, God!" Hennessey exclaimed, once he made the visual connection. Stomach sinking and heart pounding he added, "That's my uncle Bob's building." He raced for the phone, frantically dialing his cousin Annie's number in First Landing.

1050 5th Avenue, First Landing

"Dammit, *dammit*, DAMMIT, STOP that ringing!" Bad as the ringing was, the sound of her own shout seemed enough to tear the top off of Annie's head. She shuddered and pulled a pillow over in an attempt to shut out the nagging phone. No such luck. It continued to ring.

"Shit," she muttered. "May as well see who it is."

Slowly, reluctantly, not a little angrily, Annie stumbled to the phone.

"Who is it?" Annie asked, her voice still distorted

by alcohol. After Linda had left her at the restaurant, she had consumed more than her share of Black Russians before going home alone.

"Annie, it's Pat. Where's Uncle Bob right now?"

Anger drained from Annie's voice. "Oh, hi, Pat. I imagine he's at the office. Why?"

Hennessey's voice in the telephone receiver was frantic. "Turn on the TV, Annie. Something's happened at the TNTO."

"Sure . . . okay . . ." Annie walked unsteadily to pick up the television's remote. The set came to instant life just in time for the woman to catch the second airship slamming into GNN Headquarters. For several seconds she stood dumbfounded, then blurted into the phone, voice breaking with tears, "Pat . . . Linda and the kids are in there!"

On Annie's screen, another plane struck low at the World League Headquarters. There were three buildings burning now on the First Landing skyline, with smoke and flames beginning to billow up and out.

TNTO, 0915 hours

It was pandemonium. Office workers ran to and fro frantically, looking for some escape. Cute little secretaries in short skirts wept. Some people, those a bit calmer or braver, punched numbers into their cell phones for a last goodbye to their loved ones.

The smoke inside was worse now, though it was still not clearly visible to the naked eye. Outside, however, it was an angry black cloud rising past the windows like a swarm of vicious wasps. Tongues of flame licked up occasionally, though the greatest flames were just visible through the smoke, dancing around the GNN building.

Milagro—clutched in Linda's arms now—coughed from the smoke and cried. Her elder sister, nicknamed "Lambie," tried to be brave though a quivering lip and dampened eyes betrayed her. The boy, Julio, put an arm around Lambie's shoulder and hugged her close and tightly.

Uncle Bob had left them for a few moments to check on the possibilities of escape via elevator or stairwell. He returned, looked at Linda, then shook his head slightly. *No way out.*

At his nod, she steeled her face and pushed her emotions away before they themselves ran away with her. For the nonce, she also pushed away the decision: burned or crushed or fallen? *Oh, my babies, why? What did you ever do to harm anyone?*

A hand gently brushed the baby's hair and cheek, brushed away a tear and a bead of sweat. The floor was growing noticeably warmer. "Don't cry, Milli, we'll be fine," she lied.

Taking his cue from his mother, ten-year-old Julio said much the same to Lambie. Even as he spoke those few words of comfort, he looked at his mother meaningfully. *We're going to die, aren't we, Mom?*

Linda answered, indirectly, "I wish your father could see you now. He would be *so* proud of his son."

The boy smiled, as best he could manage, and nodded. He wished his father could see him, too, see him grow up to be a man. He had wanted to be a soldier like his dad. Well, he would act like one now.

Bob stood there for a moment, watching the silent

interplay with admiration. *I was so wrong. What a woman my nephew found. What children she brought to our family. I,* he concluded, *have been an utter ass and a fool.*

He walked the few steps to Linda and handed her his cell phone. "Here, call your husband if you can get through. Give him my regards . . . and my regrets." He patted her shoulder, not ungently, nor even lacking a certain late-blooming admiration and affection.

Linda took the device and smiled up, gratefully.

"I have something else I have to do," Bob announced.

The uncle, the old tyrant, walked to his desk, fiddled with a computer that had no wires coming from it, then began to speak.

"John," he said aloud to a face that appeared on his screen, "there's not much time. Can I do a codicil to my will over this line? I can? Good. Prepare to copy this then. 'I, Robert Hennessey, being of sound mind and body . . . '"

Cochea, 0924 hours

Hennessey was pale, Parilla saw; paler even than the gringo norm. His eyes were glued to the television screen that showed the imminent collapse of all his hopes, the destruction of his life. On the screen people were jumping from the flaming towers to smash their bodies below. It was better than burning.

Hennessey's own cell phone rang. Jimenez picked it up, answered, then—not without some reluctance—passed it over. "It's Linda," he announced in a breaking voice.

Like a drowning man grasping desperately for a life preserver, Hennessey took the phone.

"Honey, where are you and the kids?" he asked desperately.

He heard screams and cries in the background as Linda answered, "I'm here at Uncle Bob's office . . . the children are with me. I am so sorry, Patricio."

Hennessey felt his heart sink. "Is there any way out?"

Her answering voice held infinite sadness and regret. "No . . . I don't think so. The only way off would be helicopters, now. And I don't hear or see any. It's getting very warm in here, husband. We'll have to go soon. Why don't you talk to the kids? Do not worry; I will wait as long as possible but I will not let our babies burn if I can help it. Goodbye, Patricio. You know I love you."

"I love you, too, Linda," he wept. "I always have."

"Dad?" Hennessey heard young Julio say, voice quavering, then firming up. "I am being brave, Dad . . ."

TNTO, 1003 hours

The air was very bad now. The windows people had knocked out in order to jump had let in as much smoke as fresh air. Ashes floated on the fire-fanned breeze.

Uncle Bob, Linda and the kids crouched low, breathing what oxygen there was in the hot, stifling, and murky office.

"Not much more time . . . Linda," Bob said. As if to punctuate, a chorus of heartrending screams came from down the hallway. The fire had eaten through the floor, consuming a half dozen office workers who had been steeling themselves for the jump. The screams seemed to go on and on.

Linda stifled a sob as she hugged Milagro and Lambie to her breast. With tears rolling freely down her face, she said, "It's just so *wrong*. What did my babies ever do to harm anyone? What did *I* do? What did Patricio do that he should be left all alone?"

Bob just shook his head. He had no answer that would help. He looked out the window towards the GNN building, even as a cloud of dust and smoke began to billow out from it.

"It's collapsing," Bob gasped through the smoke laden air. He gestured toward the open main area of the office suite "The fire is getting worse. We have to go now."

Linda nodded, sniffed, suppressed a cough. "One last thing first." She took her arms from around the girls briefly, put her hands on her stomach and said, "I baptize you in the name of the Father . . ."

It was almost time to go. The heat rising from the floor, telltale of the flames below, was already too much to bear for long. Nor could anyone on the floor stand for all the thick, toxic smoke that hung above.

On the other side of the suite, a man laughed. "Infidels," he cried in a foreign accent, "see the judgment of Allah. See the wages of your iniquities. You will all die here and burn in Hellfire forevermore for your crimes against the will of the Almighty."

Uncle Bob recognized the voice and answered back, with more force than reason, "God will send you and all your kind to Hell, Samir, you miserable, treacherous bastard."

Julio looked calmly at his mother. Ten years old

or not, he was her son, and his father's. "Mom, will Daddy make them pay, the men who did this?"

"That will be as it will, my baby," Linda answered. "But . . . knowing your father, I can't imagine that he will not. He is . . . he can be . . . a very harsh man."

Linda looked at the flames rising behind her. "Almost time, children. Pray, now." She began to recite, "Our Father, who art in Heaven, hallowed be Thy name. Thy kingdom come . . ."

Others joined in the final prayer, and one began to sing a half-remembered hymn, in English. Yet Linda recognized the song by its Spanish version. She, then the children, then another dark and lovely young girl in a short red shirt joined in, in Spanish.

Perhaps because she was an island of relative calm in a sea of insanity, people clustered around Linda. Most stopped praying, a few going silent but more joining in the hymn. In English it was known as "Abide with Me."

As the song neared its end, Linda and Bob stood. It was easier to stand near the smashed-out window than it had been in the smoke-filled interior. Bob took Julio in one arm and wrapped the other around Linda's slender waist. Linda, with one arm around Lambie and the other holding Milagro stopped singing for just a moment to say, "Close your eyes, babies," and to kiss each of the little girls atop their heads.

She resumed singing and began to walk forward, others following. At the very edge she hesitated, but only for the tiniest fraction of a second. She and Bob took the last step forward, the hymn echoing in their ears: "Help of the helpless, O abide with me . . ."

It was a long way down. Linda felt her speed build.

Her stomach seemed to want to come out of her mouth. She heard the babies she clutched so tightly scream as if from a great distance. She reached terminal velocity and the falling sensation in her stomach disappeared.

There was a brief sense of shock and then . . . nothing.

Cochea, 1028 hours

"Don't look, Patricio," implored Jimenez, voice strained with despair for his friend.

"No . . . don't," whispered Parilla, shaking his head slowly.

Hennessey ignored them, his eyes fixed on the television image. Down went the Center Tower, slowly, majestically. With it went his wife, his three children, possibly a fourth, too. Linda had hinted before she left for the Federated States that she might be expecting. He gave off a soft, wordless cry.

In the background Lucinda bit her hand to stifle wracking sobs. "The babies, the babies, the babies . . . my Linda . . . I changed her diapers as a baby . . . my little ones . . ."

Overwhelmed with grief, Hennessey just let his head hang, tears running down his face to gather and drip from the end of his nose and chin. He made no sound, yet his shoulders shuddered spasmodically.

Not knowing what else to do, Jimenez walked to the liquor cabinet, extracted two glasses and a bottle, then poured a light drink for himself and a much larger one for Hennessey.

"Here, Patricio, drink this. For a while, it will help."

Eyes of the Prophet,
Zion-occupied Filistia, Terra Nova,
11/7/459 AC

As Hennessey wept, even as thousands and millions in the Federated States and some few other places wept their grief and shrieked their anger, a series of rather differently spirited and impromptu—but, one cannot doubt, wholehearted and completely sincere—demonstrations erupted around the globe. From one end of the Salafi and Moslem quarter to the other cheering people took to the streets, automobile horns blasting, people dancing, women warbling the Arabic call to battle and victory.

Hennessey, thousands of miles from Shechem watched one such woman, her face transformed with radiant joy.

Parilla whispered, "Bastards. Fucking bastards! They should be destroyed."

Jimenez watched the image carefully, engraving every line of the harridan's face onto his mind. "'What though the field be lost?'" he quoted, whispering. "'All is not lost; Unconquerable will and study of revenge, immortal hate and courage never to submit or yield.'"

University of Ninewa, Sumer, Terra Nova

In contrast to the smoke and flames of tall buildings crashing down, the university was white and placid. Students and professors, some of them white coated, gathered in small groups to converse worriedly and even frantically.

From a third-story window overlooking the central green square of the campus, a Sumeri brigadier general watched out. His name was Sada and he, and the brigade he commanded, were here to guard. What they guarded only Sada knew and he wasn't telling.

Turning away from the campus scene Sada looked back at the television screen that showed, over and over, the destruction in First Landing. He sat, heavily, and put his head in his hands. *They're going to crush us for this,* he thought.

INTERLUDE

One of the questions the data from the *Cristobal Colon* could not answer was, "Why?" Another was, "How?" The last was "Who?"

None of these questions was ever to be entirely satisfactorily answered, though theories abounded. Answering the last by calling the "Who" of the matter the "Noahs" was hardly a satisfactory explanation. Some other questions could be answered, though. Most of these were about Earth.

It was learned, for example, from a video recording made and transmitted by Parachute Lander Number Two, that *Smilodon*, the saber-toothed tiger, was an ambush hunter and did use its long canine teeth to rip open the bellies of its prey, wherever that was possible.

Because this is what the *Cristobal Colon* had found: an Earthlike world, teeming with life from well before the last ice age but after the age of dinosaurs. The trees were there, the flowers and plants, the mammals, the reptiles. Everything was there except for man, though there were small groups of pithecines scurrying about. These, apparently, had been seeded before the mutation or mutations that led to *homo sapiens*.

Moreover, several low passes by the glider drones had indicated the presence of huge numbers of whales, of shoals of fish, and of birds. Number One Drone had almost come to an early end as a result of failing to note, until it was almost too late, an enormous flock—though flock hardly did the thing justice—of passenger pigeons over the southern part of one of the lesser continents.

There were dodos and there were great auks, though that news awaited further exploration as neither drone nor lander had seen any. There were cave bear, giant ground sloth and great Irish deer, though the rediscovery of these, too, took time. Phororhacos, the eight-foot-tall carnivorous bird of South America was there, as was the giant moa.

There were no dinosaurs, though there were a number of fairly large reptilian species. There were also no horses, though eohippus was found in some numbers.

There was no trace of who had done this, no archeological remains, no cities, no settlements, no landing sites. Yet it was clear that at some time between the end of the dinosaurs and the arrival, or at least flourishing, of man, some people or some things had made an effort to preserve life as it was found on Earth at that time. Close estimates, based on the flora and fauna to be found in the new world, suggested a timeline of between three million and five million years, BC. Yet not all the animals and plants found fell into that range. Some seemed newer, still others older. Some were completely alien to both New Earth and Old

It was then suggested that evolution on the planet itself had continued, creating new species through the same mechanism as on Earth. This, however, failed to solve the riddle of the older animals, thought extinct on Earth well before the presumptive date of the transplanting. Some believed that the fossil record on Earth was by no means complete; scientists and explorers could have missed or misdated any number of species. Moreover, since coelacanth had hung on for some fifty million years longer than scientists had thought before it was rediscovered, why should not have archaeopteryx?

The fossil record of the new world was quite limited. There were no missing links and most of the animals found seem to have suddenly appeared.

It was not—and is not—known if the Noahs who had seeded the planet had also created the rift that allowed instantaneous transport between Earth's solar system and the other or if they had merely used something that was already there. As to whether man could make use of the rift, reliably, that awaited events.

In the event, man being man, extinct species on the old world tended to become extinct species, extinct out of zoos anyway, on the new.

CHAPTER FIVE

In peace, children inter their parents; war violates the order of nature and causes parents to inter their children.

—Herodotus

Cochea, 12/7/459 AC

Hennessey had first laid eyes upon his future wife at a national festival. She had been seventeen then, one of the dancers garbed in the national costume the Balboans had brought with them from Earth, the pollera. Linda's hair had been done up in an intricate array of gold and silver. There was no word adequate to describe her. Perhaps "stunning" came close.

As he had first laid eyes on her, so had she— without at the time knowing—laid hands upon his heart. In a phrase, he had fallen, abjectly and completely. And he didn't even know her name.

In his dream, Hennessey again watched the dance,

again pushed his way through the crowd, again steeled himself for a very informal self-introduction.

The dream Linda, as she had so many years before, smiled warmly . . . friendly . . . confident as only beautiful young women are confident. The brash gringo had a certain something. She admitted as much to herself.

They walked as in a dream and the walk was a dream. "I am going to marry you someday," Hennessey said. "You and only you."

Linda had scoffed. "You just met me. We haven't even been properly introduced."

"No matter," he answered. "You and only you."

"You are so sure? What makes you think I would marry you? Besides, I am only seventeen."

"No matter. The girl is mother to the woman. I will wait." He seemed very certain.

She laughed, white teeth flashing in the sun. "How long will you wait, brash gringo?"

"Forever . . . if I must," he answered seriously.

"Forever is a very long time," she countered.

"For you, and only you, I would wait 'forever.'"

Young Linda inclined her head to one side. Her eyes narrowed, judging, studying. "Hmm . . . perhaps you would at that."

A face rapt with amusement turned suddenly serious. "Do you smell something?"

Hennessey's nose wrinkled. He sniffed. "Smoke. From where?"

He and Linda looked downward at the same time. "Oh," she said in surprise.

The hem of Linda's green-embroidered pollera was on fire, the fire racing up and out. Hennessey knelt to try to beat the flames out with his hands. The fire

*raced on, ignoring his efforts. She began to scream
as the flames reached her skin. "Please help me," she
cried. "Please."*

*For all Hennessey's thrashing hands, the personal
inferno spread. His hands turned red, then began to blis-
ter. The blisters broke. His hands began to char. All the
time he never stopped trying to put out the flames.*

*Linda screamed with agony, her cries cutting through
Hennessey's heart like a knife.*

*Hennessey looked up. The girl was a mass of flame.
Fire leapt from her hands to her head. Hair crackled.
Gold and silver ran like water. The flames began to
consume her face.*

*Ignoring the fire and the pain, Hennessey wrapped
his arms around the girl, hands still beating frantically
to put out the fire that was eating her alive. The fire
must have eaten its way inside her as well, for her
eyes—once brown and warm—turned red, hot and
then burst like overripe grapes.*

Still screaming, Hennessey sat bolt upright in his
bed. He wept for a little while, as quietly as he was
able. Then, to the sound of *antaniae* outside the house
calling "*mnnbt . . . mnnbt . . . mnnbt,*" he walked to the
liquor cabinet and grabbed a bottle. He didn't bother
taking a glass.

Ciudad Balboa, 13/7/459 AC

Linda's family had volunteered en masse to drive him
to the airport outside Ciudad Balboa so that he could
catch the first plane—airships made the run, as well,
but were just too slow—to First Landing and, perhaps,

push the authorities to find the bodies. Though he'd appreciated the offers, he'd declined. The sympathy of both parents, all twenty-two aunts and uncles—not including those by marriage—and one hundred and four legitimate first cousins had quickly gone from warming to oppressive. They'd meant well, he knew, but seeing every face around him in perpetual tears had come to make things worse, if that were possible.

It had been good to drive, to have to concentrate on something besides his murdered family. Even the mind-diverting task of ducking the larger potholes was welcome. Through the little towns along the highway that led from the San Jose frontier in the east to the Yaviza Gap to the northwest, he drove slowly and carefully. At the larger towns he would stop sometimes, gas here, lunch there. Once he stopped to take in a view of the *Mar Furioso* that he and Linda had once enjoyed together. That had been painful. Finally he came to the great bridge that led over the bay to the city. He almost smiled at a particular memory of the bridge. Almost, not quite.

The city had changed since he had first seen it. It was still clean, remarkably so for a large metropolis in Colombia Central. But the buildings had grown to the sky over the last fifteen years. He looked up at them briefly, then turned his eyes back to the road as unwelcome thoughts invaded his mind.

Though much had changed, much was the same. Driving through *Ciudad* Balboa's streets he was cut off, tailgated, honked at and cursed with friendly abandon. Pretty girls walked the sidewalks and the parks. Young men looked, watched, pursued. Food and flowers wafted on the breeze, competing with the sea.

Emerging along the coastal road, *Avenida del Norte*, Hennessey almost managed to enjoy the fresh sea breeze off the high tide-covered beach and mud flats. To his left he passed the *Restaurante Bella Mar*, where Linda had taught him to appreciate sea food for the first time in his life. To his right he smelled the flowers of Parque Prado. He came at length to the Hotel Julio Caesare, arguably the best hotel of any real size in Ciudad Balboa, almost certainly the most ornate.

After a bellhop had unloaded the bags, a red uniformed valet took his car and parked it in the patrolled garage. Hennessey took a receipt in return and, followed the bellhop through marble and gilt and gracefully hanging palm fronds to the front desk to register.

He planned to spend a few days at the hotel, using it as a base while he waited for flights to the Federated States to recommence. Nothing was allowed to fly anywhere near the FSC at the moment and none could say when air traffic would resume. It was possible that airship service would begin before fixed wing did, though most thought this unlikely under the circumstances.

As it turned out, it would be several days.

He spent his evenings, and evening came early this close to the equator, drinking in the bar *cum* disco on the ground floor of the hotel. A wretched dancer—Hennessey described himself as the worst dancer in the entire history of human motion—he still enjoyed looking at pretty girls on the dance floor. He enjoyed it, that is, so long as none of them reminded him too much of his wife. This wasn't a problem, generally, since most of the women in the disco were light skinned. Though of a quite prosperous family,

Linda had been very mixed-race and rather dark. Since the Julio Caesare was expensive enough to be only for either the well to do (or less moneyed cosmopolitan progressives, or Kosmos, who slurped lavishly at the public and donative troughs), there were few women of plainly *mestiza* backgrounds. None of these had been quite pretty enough to bring forth painful memories.

His first night at the hotel a few women, either too insensitive to pick up on Hennessey's pain or kind hearted and sympathetic enough to wish to relieve the pain if possible, approached him. It wasn't difficult for Hennessey to tell the difference. The former he sent packing with few words. The latter he spoke to as much as they might care to speak, or as much as he could stand to.

The second night in the city a pair of women, a tall and light one and a slightly shorter dark one, sat down not quite beside him. It was the darker one who broke the ice. She said her name was Edielise. Hennessey didn't catch the last name and didn't really much care to. He answered her questions, asking only enough of his own for politeness' sake. He covered his reticence by taking another drink whenever the girl seemed about to say something that might call for a thoughtful response.

The other girl, who remained silent throughout the conversation, thought, *What a typically arrogant gringo. Here Edi is trying her best to be polite and all he can do is nod and grunt. He's hardly even responding at all.* Hennessey and the darker girl had been speaking English the whole time. Pushing her own drink away, the lighter of the two said, in Spanish, although she too spoke excellent English, "Come on Edi, this gringo is too dull and stupid to waste time on."

Hennessey, who also spoke quite good Spanish, answered quickly, "Maybe you're right. I might be dull and I'm probably stupid too. Mostly, though, I'm just tired, drunk, and sad."

A little angry at her comment, and a little drunk as well, Hennessey told her why he was as he was. "You see, my wife and three little children were killed two days ago, in First Landing in the Federated States."

He delivered the words with the kind of apologetic tone that sounds like "it's all my fault" but makes the hearer feel that it is entirely their fault. Then, while the two girls sat dumbfounded, Hennessey excused himself and left for his room. He didn't feel any better. It had been cruel, pointlessly so, and worse, he knew it.

When Hennessey reached his room he was already cursing himself for being a boor. *It wasn't their fault,* he thought. *They were just trying to be civil. Tomorrow maybe I'll go to Cristobal. I'm not fit for civilized company right now.*

After Hennessey left, the taller, lighter girl—her name was Lourdes Nuñez-Cordoba—stayed in the disco for a long time feeling very small, very dark, and very ashamed.

Lourdes was only twenty-four, slender and pretty enough, too. She looked even younger; she had lived a somewhat sheltered life. She'd never known anyone who had so much real hurt in his voice as that gringo had. *What a bitch I am, what a pure bitch. That poor man's lost everything and I had to insult him. I didn't even have a chance to apologize. Damn.* Turning to her friend she asked what the gringo's name was.

"I don't know his last name. It was a funny one. His first name was Pat, he said."

Gesturing at the door with her head, Lourdes said to her friend, "Let's go home. I'll come back myself tomorrow, early, and see if I can catch him before he leaves. I hope he'll accept an apology. I feel so terrible."

When Hennessey awoke the next morning, hungover and needing a shave, he cursed to see the time. "Dammit, almost eleven. I wanted to get out of here no later than nine."

He went to the shower to scrape off the previous day's accumulations. Normally he liked to sing in the shower, old ballads of war, revenge, and rebellion that he had learned at his grandfather's knee. This morning, the idea of singing was enough to make him want to puke. Instead, as he soaped off, Hennessey's mind wandered to the events of the night before. He felt genuinely guilty at having lashed out at the poor girl who'd called him dull. He didn't blame her a bit; he *had* been pretty dull. Realistically, he did not blame himself too much, either. He resolved to try to be a little kinder in the future. Wrapped in a towel, he left the shower and picked out the clothes he would wear for the day; a short-sleeved green shirt, blue jeans and running shoes. The rest he began to stuff into suitcases in no particular order.

By noon Hennessey had finished packing. He rang for a bellhop, *"el butones,"* to come and carry his bags to the lobby of the hotel. At the front desk he tried, and generally succeeded, in being pleasant to the obligatorily polite receptionist. He was about to turn to leave when he heard a very sweet voice behind him hesitantly ask, "Pat?" He turned then to see who belonged to the voice he didn't recognize.

"Oh, it's the girl from last night." Hennessey forced a welcoming tone into his voice. He took one of her hands in both of his. "Look, I'm *really* sorry for having left the way I did. I really haven't been quite right for a few days now."

However, as soon as she had recognized him, Lourdes had immediately begun a lengthy and heartfelt apology of her own. Talking at cross purposes, and simultaneously, the two continued for half a minute before the realization that neither had heard a word the other had spoken stopped them both completely. Twice more they began to speak at the same time only to stop cold again. Finally Hennessey decided to be a gentleman and let Lourdes speak first.

Almost taken aback by being allowed to speak after three false starts, Lourdes said, in English, "I'm so sorry for saying those terrible things about you last night. I feel like such a horrible person. No wonder you didn't want to talk after losing your family like that. Will you please, please forgive me?" Her enormous brown eyes were eloquent with sincerity.

Hennessey shook his head as if he didn't understand why she should feel repentant. "There's nothing to forgive. Your friend was doing her best to cheer me up. I wasn't in the mood to be cheered, I guess. You were perfectly right to call me stupid. But I don't know any other way to be right now. I should be apologizing to you. An a matter of fact," he added with a sad but ironic grin, "I *was* apologizing to you."

A sudden rumbling in his stomach told Hennessey that it had been almost a full day since he'd taken any

sustenance beyond a heavy dose of alcohol. He asked
the girl at the front desk if he could leave his bags there
over lunch. Of course an establishment as thoroughly
accommodating as the Julio Caesare would have no
problem guarding a few bags. On an impulse Hennessey
asked Lourdes if she would care to join him.

"Are you sure you want company?" she asked.

"Please. I promise to be civil. And I've never cared
to eat alone."

Nodding assent, Lourdes joined Hennessey on the
way to one of the Hotel's four restaurants. Before leaving the lobby Hennessey tipped the bellhop who had
moved his bags. Despite the receptionist's assurances
that they would be safe it couldn't hurt to keep the
help on his side.

The young woman was fine company, perhaps because
she was trying her best to cheer the sad man accompanying her. Over a meal of prawns on rice, her conversation
kept up a light mood. Hennessey was surprised to find
himself sometimes honestly smiling.

Objectively—and without lust, it was far too soon
for that—Hennessey found himself appraising the girl.
*Looks twenty-one, maybe twenty-two. Nice hair, light
brown shading to blond. Good facial structure, high
cheekbones. Nose a little prominent but overall a good
shape. Slender and tall, her breasts would look better
on a shorter woman. Nice posterior. Very beautiful
eyes, large and liquid brown. Also a good heart or she
wouldn't be here with a broken down, miserable old
fart like me.*

As the meal neared its close, Lourdes asked the question she had wanted to ask since Hennessey had left the
disco the night before. "How did your wife die?"

Hennessey paused before answering. It wasn't easy for him to think about. He returned his fork to the plate and sat back against the chair. "Lourdes, that's some of my problem. I don't know, not exactly anyway. All I do know is that she and the kids were caught in my uncle's office building when the airship hit. That, and that they were not killed right away." Hennessey paused to rub away the beginnings of a tear.

Lourdes likewise didn't respond immediately. After a brief pause of her own she simply said, "Poor man."

The mood chilled, the meal was finished mainly in silence. Assuming that the loss of his family was too painful for him to talk about any more, Lourdes went along. Soon the lunch was ended. Before the two left the restaurant, Lourdes—feeling quite forward and even daring—wrote her home and business phone numbers on a napkin, and pressed it on him. "Pat, when you come back to Balboa, and if I can help you in any way, please call me."

Hennessey nodded as he paid the bill. Then he escorted the woman to his car and drove her to her work. When he returned to his hotel he was informed that he would be able to fly to the Federated States the following morning.

First Landing, 17/7/459 AC

"I won't stand for it. I just won't stand for it. That money's mine. I'll sue, I swear I will. I've made promises. There are 'causes' . . ."

Annie, seated in a typical lawyer's client's leather chair turned to her cousin, Eugene Montgomery

Schmied, and said, "Oh, shut up, you mincing little fairy."

I hate squabbling families, thought the attorney and executor, John Walter Tweed. Steepling his fingers in front of his receding chin, he cast his eyes on Eugene and said, "That would be a very grave mistake, Mr. Schmied. Your uncle arranged his will quite carefully. Should you—or anyone—in person or by proxy attempt to contest his will or its codicil you will be utterly cut off from everything. This state will honor such an 'in terrorem' clause, I assure you. And First Landing is *so* chilly this time of year." The lawyer smiled nastily.

The reading of Uncle Bob's will and its last minute video codicil had started with a rash of crocodile tears, all but for Annie—whose tears were sincere, and Patrick—who felt nothing. Indeed, so still and detached was he that he might as well have been the chair he sat upon, that, or a corpse himself.

Tweed cleared and throat and asked, "Now if I may continue without further interruptions? Good. Colonel Hennessey . . ."

Deadpan, he said, "I'm not a colonel anymore."

"Nonetheless, your uncle referred to you as such in his codicil. His so referring also indicated a true change of heart as concerned his feelings toward you. So, unless you object strenuously, I will continue to so address you."

Hennessey shrugged his indifference.

"Very good then. To continue, you are, in the main, your uncle's primary beneficiary. What this means, as a practical matter, is fourfold. You have inherited the chair of Chatham, Hennessey and Schmied. You have also the control of your grandfather's trust, the William Hennessey Fund. You are the inheritor of his personal and real property upon the demise of your aunt, Denise—Robert's wife—who retains a life estate. . . ."

1050 5th Avenue, First Landing, 17/7/459 AC

Annie shivered slightly as her cousin tossed a switchblade knife onto the kitchen counter before removing his suit jacket. "Where did you get that thing?" she asked.

Hennessey pointed to a place over a cabinet. "Right there, where I stashed it the last time I visited."

"You really haven't changed since you were little have you? Everything is violence. Why?"

He quoted, "'Force rules the world still, has ruled it, shall rule it. Meekness is weakness and strength is triumphant.'"

"You can say that? After everything that's happened?"

"After everything that's happened, Cuz, how could I say anything else?"

Annie didn't like knives. She didn't like guns. She, quite reasonably, didn't like violence. But cousin Pat would not be found dead without a weapon; he'd always been that way. She changed the subject.

"What are you going to do now, Pat?"

He shrugged. "Go home . . . back to Balboa, I mean, not Botulph. Bury what I have of my family . . . first haircuts and things . . . then . . . hurt a lot. Drink a lot. Eventually die."

Annie grasped at straws. She did not want her cousin to die, nor even to hurt. She did not want to mention, or even let his mind dwell on, what the fireman had told them near the wreck of the TNTO earlier in the day, namely that it was unlikely that much in the way of remains would ever be recovered. She asked, instead, "What about the company? The trust?"

Again, he shrugged. "What do I care? The only good thing about Bob changing the will is that Eugene won't have the money to send to 'Save The Whales,' 'Meat is Murder,' 'Fur is Forbidden,' or the World League. For the rest? Eh? Who cares?"

"Actually," Annie said, "he seems to have acquired a taste for swarthy men, of late. I'd expect a lot of the money to go the People's Front for the Liberation of Filistia. And, Pat? It's a lot of money."

He just looked at her, so much as to say "can't buy me love."

Herrera International Airport, *Ciudad* Balboa, 18/7/459 AC

David Carrera, Linda's brother, was waiting at the *Aduana*, the airport customs office. Although a lieutenant in Balboa's "Civil Force," the successor—such as it was—to the Balboa Defense Corps, itself a successor to the old "*Guardia Nacional*," still David wore civilian clothes.

Eyes scanning the thickening line at the *Aduana*, David finally caught sight of his brother-in-law. *Sallow skin and bags under his eyes; Jesus, Patricio looks like crap!*

Moving forward to the officer in charge of Customs, David flashed a badge, pointed and spoke a few sentences. Rank had its privileges. The customs man smiled assent, then gestured for Hennessey to come forward.

Waved through after a very cursory inspection, Hennessey passed Customs then stretched out a hand to David.

David smelled alcohol, a lot of alcohol, on Hennessey's breath. He decided to ignore it, asking only, "How was your flight, *Cuñado?*"

"It was all right." He shrugged. "Right up to where I nodded off to sleep and awoke screaming. The stewardesses were upset with me; bad for passenger morale I suppose, especially these days. On the plus side they fed me booze until I fell asleep again, that time without dreaming."

The two walked without further words to where Hennessey's car waited. At his mother's insistence David had taken a police flight down to the airport to drive Hennessey home. Before turning the keys over to David, Hennessey removed his jacket, opened the trunk, and put on a shoulder holster bearing a high end, compact forty-five caliber pistol in brushed stainless. Then he put his light jacket back on.

Trees, rivers, bridges, towns; all flashed by without comment or conversation. Only once on the long drive eastward did Hennessey make a sound. That was when he inadvertently drifted off to sleep and awakened, as usual, screaming. He did not say of what he dreamed. He didn't need to; David knew already, at least in broad terms.

At length the car passed into *Valle de las Lunas*, then up the highway toward *Ciudad* Cervantes, the provincial capital.

Just before reaching the city, Linda's brother flicked the turn signal to head down the gravel road that led ultimately to Cochea, the Carrera family ranch, and the house Hennessey had shared with Linda.

"No," said Hennessey. "Take me into town please. I need to go to the liquor store."

David sighed, nodded, flicked off the turn signal and continued straight ahead into the city.

Hennessey heard it as a warbling cry, coming from hundreds of throats. He recognized it immediately; he had heard it in the very recent past.

As little emotion as he had shown, now his face became a cold stone mask. "Drive towards that sound, please, David," he requested.

Again with a sigh, David turned the wheel of the car to bring it in the direction of *Parque Cervantes*, the practical center of the city. The park was square, with a bandstand in the center, surrounded by broad, paved streets. Stores fronted the streets, facing the bandstand.

Traffic slowed as they neared the park. Reaching the southeast corner, David merged into the traffic and did one complete loop around the square.

While David watched traffic, Hennessey watched people. There, in the middle of the park, around the bandstand, stood a fair mob, certainly several hundred, perhaps even a thousand. Though as swarthy as Balboans, they were not Balboans. Hennessey would have known this from their signs—"Death to the Federated States," "Allah smiles upon the *Ikhwan*," "Long live the Salafi Jihad," and such—the women's tongues flicking back and forth in a Yithrabi victory cry; and the happy faces of people celebrating as though it had been themselves who had struck against a great and infinitely evil enemy.

"There are a lot of damned wogs here now," David commented. "They call themselves Salafis and are nothing but trouble."

"Salafi means those who follow Islam's oldest ways . . . or think they do," Hennessey explained.

"What's the difference?" David asked.

"Well . . . for one thing, I think Mohammad probably had a pretty fair sense of humor. The Salafis don't." To himself he whispered, "Then again, neither do I now . . . and I follow the old ways, too."

His finger pointed, "Pull over and park, please, David . . . in behind the car with the green bumper sticker."

Tanned from years in the Balboan sun, with hair naturally dark where it wasn't tinged with gray, only Hennessey's gleaming blue eyes might have given him away for the gringo he was. No matter; he kept his eyes narrowly slitted as he emerged from the car, leaned against its side and watched the local Salafis at their victory celebration. No flicker of emotion betrayed what he was feeling over people celebrating the murder of his wife and children.

Even as the celebration began to break up he did not move from the car on which he leaned, arms folded nonchalantly.

He smiled broadly as a group of six men walked toward the car just ahead of his own; the one with the green bumper sticker that said, in Arabic, "There is no God but God."

The Salafis joked and played amiably among themselves as they came closer. Hennessey's smile broadened even more.

CLICK.

He said, loudly and in adequate, if badly accented, Arabic, "Your Prophet was a sodomite and a liar. Your mothers were whores. Your fathers were their pimps. Your wives specialize in fellating barnyard animals and all your sisters came from sex change operations. You are fools if you think your children are yours."

David looked questioningly at Hennessey; the Balboan had not a word of Arabic. He needed none, however, to understand the import of what was said. This was as plain as the wide-eyed rage and hate on the faces of the men who now ran toward them waving signs like clubs and shouting their fury. One young man, in particular, outdistanced the rest.

For a moment David knew fear. He need not have. Lightning-fast, Hennessey's left hand pulled back his light jacket even as his right sought to draw the pistol.

Hennessey's right on the pistol, his left swept up to block and deflect the sign that the nearest of the Salafis sought to brain him with. Whispering, "Bastard," at the same time, he drew the pistol and smashed its muzzle once, twice, three times into the area of his enemy's solar plexus. Every blow felt like the lifting of a burden. The Salafi's breath left his body in an agonized whoosh.

One down, five to go. Before gravity could pull the first one to the ground, Hennessey had brought his focus to the main body of his assailants.

The gang attacking Hennessey could see in his

eyes that this one was not going to run. They could also read that their intended victim intended to kill or maim as many as he could before he went down. They could see from the gun that he had the means to do so. Like any street gang, anywhere, these were no heroes. While they all would have advanced confidently on someone who showed the slightest fear, when faced with a target like Hennessey they stopped cold.

Had they run, some might have lived.

A quick but delicate squeeze of the trigger and the pistol recoiled in Hennessey's hands. His mind provided details his eyes could not possibly have seen; a burst of flame, the spinning half-ounce lump of bronze-jacketed lead, the bursting of shirt and flesh and blood and bone. The first target's back arched as he was impelled to the ground.

A chorus of screams arose from bystanders, Christian and Salafi both, as the crowd ran and sought cover.

The four still standing didn't have time to close on their victim before the next of them went down with a slug that ripped through his arm and one lung. Again, Hennessey smiled slightly at the satisfying recoil. His victim, now fallen to the street, wheezed faint screams, blood bumbling from his mouth and the hole in his chest.

The other three, torn between fight and flight, made the worst possible decision; they did nothing, frozen in fear. Quickly but carefully aligning the barrel, Hennessey shot one through a head that burst under the impact like an overripe melon dropped from a height. Recovering the pistol from its heavy recoil, his smile grew broad now as he squeezed the trigger yet again to ruin the left side of another assailant's chest.

Hennessey didn't need X-ray vision to know that he had exploded the man's heart.

The last Salafi standing was like a deer caught in the headlights of a semi-tractor, frozen, helpless . . . already dead.

He did not shoot that last one standing; not immediately. Instead he walked forward calmly, spit in the frozen man's face, and then kicked him in the crotch. The Salafi bent over and melted to the ground.

"Attack MY family will you? Celebrate their murder?" He took a short step forward, bent over at the waist, then calmly placed the hot muzzle against the man's head. Again, he shrieked, "Attack MY family will you?" The Salafi barely registered the pressure and the smell of crisping hair as his brain went scampering like a frightened rabbit. With such a helpless target, Hennessey had leisure to rise and walk around to a better firing position. He didn't want an innocent bystander to take a bullet that passed through his intended target.

Carefully gauging angles, he knelt down and pulled the thug's head up by the hair, jammed the pistol—*hard*, hard enough to break the skin and the bone beneath—into the man's face. Then he grinned even more widely, withdrew the pistol slightly, and fired. David, standing nearby, was spattered with blood and brain.

Hennessey stood again and turned his attention to the first man, the one who had tried to brain him with a sign. The Salafi began to beg for his life in mixed Spanish and Arabic. Hennessey said, "Fuck you," then shot him through the stomach, savoring the resulting scream.

Hmmm . . . one bullet left. He looked over the bodies. One, the one he had lung-shot, was still breathing. Hennessey shot him again, in the head. The slide locked back and Hennessey pushed a button to let it fall forward. Then, from habit, he flicked on the positive safety and turned the pistol in his grip, his index finger passing through the trigger guard. The pistol was now a hammer, not a firearm.

He walked forward, face lit by a glowing smile. Speaking with unnatural calm to the former celebrant, Hennessey explained that shooting was really too good for swine like him.

The pistol swung almost too quickly for the eye to follow. There was a crunch of bone, a spray of crimson, and another scream. Again and small chunks of hair attached to flesh joined the crimson spray. Again and teeth flew.

Again . . . again . . . again . . . again . . .

"Patricio? Patricio, stop. He's dead. Please stop."

Hennessey became conscious of a hand gripping his shoulder. "What?"

"He's dead, Patricio. You don't need to hit him anymore." David shook his brother-in-law's shoulder to pull him back to the present.

Dully, Hennessey asked, "Dead?" He looked down. "Yes, dead. Good."

"We need to get away from here, *Cuñado*. You know, before the police come. Christ! I *am* the police. Shit!"

"No," Hennessey answered, "Better to take care of it now."

He calmly wiped the blood- and brain-stained pistol on the shirt of his victim. Then he laid the pistol on the ground, stood, and turned to lean again against his automobile. In the distance a siren shrieked.

Suddenly, unexpectedly, Hennessey realized that he actually felt *good* for the first time in just over a week. He pulled out and lit a cigarette, enjoying the first puff as he had not enjoyed anything since his family was murdered.

"So you see," Lieutenant David Carrera explained to the investigating police corporal, "my brother-in-law here was minding his own business, watching the demonstration, when these foreigners simply attacked him with their signs. I don't know why, though. They were speaking their foreign gibberish. Perhaps they thought to kill another harmless and innocent gringo to add to the tally of those they murdered in First Landing."

The corporal looked skeptical. Hennessey, seeing the skepticism, suggested, "Why don't you call Major Jimenez, *Cabo*? I'm sure he can set this all straight."

The call was unnecessary, as it turned out. As soon as Jimenez, the local Civil Force commander, had heard the words on the radio, "gringo . . . shooting . . . Salafis" he had put two and two together, come up with the name "Hennessey," and set out for the scene.

Jimenez didn't ask Hennessey anything. *He is just too likely to tell me the truth. And I think I don't want the truth.* Instead, he asked David, who repeated the story he had told the corporal.

Jimenez looked at the six dead Salafis and the spreading pools of blood. He looked at Hennessey's blood-spattered and bone- and brain-flecked pistol.

He looked at the corpse nearest the car and noted that his head was more a misshapen lump of mangled flesh and crushed bone than a human being's. Then he pronounced his learned judgment.

"An obvious case of self-defense, Corporal. Let the gringo go."

Cochea, 25/7/459 AC

Hennessey looked better than he had, thought Linda's mother. He had even told her that the nightmares had, if not quite stopped, at least lessened since he had shot those demonstrators. *May they go away and never come back. Poor man.*

Around a small hillock overlooking the Carrera family ranch and the stream Linda had swum in as a girl, Hennessey, the remaining members of Linda's immediate family, a dozen and a half aunts and uncles, her last surviving grandparent, and about seventy of her one hundred and four legitimate first cousins (and a half dozen or so illegitimate but recognized ones) stood in the rain for a funeral service. A five-foot tall marble obelisk rose above a shorter plinth placed on the hill. It was blank for now but would soon bear a bronze plaque inscribed with the names of Linda and her three children, plus a gender neutral name for the unborn. As the priest went through the funeral service, Hennessey wept.

I will never see her again. Never hold her in my arms again. All my dreams for the two of us, all my—our—dreams for the children are gone; dead. What's left? Nothing.

Oh, Linda, you were . . . are . . . my life and my love. I wish I were with you, wherever you are. I wish I were wherever I could bask in your approval. I wish I were wherever I could be warmed by your glow. I wish . . . I wish . . . I wish.

At least you are there with the children. Someday, maybe soon, I will join you. There is nothing for me here anymore. Nothing.

Linda's mother had arranged for the funeral. Hennessey himself had the monument cut, polished, and set in place. He hadn't been able to think of anything else positive to do.

Hennessey's mind wandered back to the thought of being with Linda. However, the one place he would not permit the thought of was the precise place, wherever it might be, where Linda's and the children's bodies rested. He could not bear the idea of the unknown, unmarked grave. He could not bear the thought of them rotting unprotected, of being eaten by worms and insects. *No!* screamed his mind, whenever his thoughts ventured anywhere near that subject. *Too far, too awful. Do not trespass.*

When the priest was finished, and the relatives had said their condolences and left, Hennessey continued standing alone in the rain while Linda's four brothers and her father filled in the grave containing a sample of her hair, a few personal belongings, jewelry and such, hair clippings from the children, a toy for each of them, plus another for the probable unborn.

Never very religious, nonetheless Hennessey prayed to God to take care of the souls of his wife and children. As he prayed, his tears mixed with the rain and fell to the ground at his feet. After a long while, he left.

INTERLUDE

There was a planet teeming with life and able to support more life. There was another planet; old, worn out, depleted and allegedly groaning with overpopulation. What could be more sensible than to colonize, to relieve Earth's burden by transferring man to the new world?

Not that it was simple, by any means. No large numbers could be sent off world without some means of either reducing the trip's duration to a few months or putting passengers in suspended animation. For that matter, even with a much faster ship, the number of people that could be carried went up geometrically if they didn't need to be fed and used no oxygen during the trip.

Still . . . great oaks from little acorns and all. Cryogenic suspended animation seemed possible, but needed work. In the interim, a ship could be built to take at least a token number of colonists off world. This would be expensive, to be sure, but perhaps not so expensive as not sending people off world.

Design took years. Development of materials to meet the design took more years. Actually building the thing—as important, building the shipyard in space that would build the thing—and its external laser auxiliary propulsion and putting those stations in place took decades.

She was to be called the *Cheng Ho*, after the great Chinese eunuch explorer. In design, externally, she was similar to the *Cristobal Colon*, but much larger with a diameter of just at one hundred and seventy meters.

Gravity was a problem, there being serious adverse medical ramifications to extended periods in null g. This was especially bad for a ship intended to carry people to a planet, where they were expected to live, that had gravity almost indistinguishable from that of Earth. No one had yet come up with a true artificial gravity and perhaps no one ever would. Continuous acceleration was deemed impractical. Magnetism was right out. All that was available, known and practical was that an acceptable artificial gravity could be produced through spinning the ship.

Internally, *Cheng Ho*'s decks were to be cylinders within cylinders, with the exterior living deck providing just under .4 g's when in full spin. The machinery needed to run the ship was set within the innermost of the cylinders. Storage took up the intervening spaces, together with a modest investment in agriculture, this last being partially a supplement to food storage but equally a means of recycling air.

The *Cheng Ho* was never expected or intended to land anywhere. It would be built in space, travel in space, and live out its useful life in space, shuttling its cargo up and down. Surface planetary gravity would have crumpled the ship in an instant.

Yet it had to be built somewhere and by something. That something was a toroidal station, put together just inside of the asteroid belt. The station itself spun and that would provide the initial spin to the *Cheng Ho*. Gravity on the exterior ring of the shipyard was on the order of .76, a very comfortable load.

Within the toroidal ring of the shipyard the *Cheng Ho* was built from the inside out, the central cylinder serving in place of the keel of a sea-bound vessel. A series of mining and refining outposts on the moon and in the asteroid belts provided the limited metal needed. Sections that would have been far too heavy if metallic were made of composites, both in space and on Earth, and lifted to the construction site.

Construction of this first true interstellar colonization ship took decades.

Passengers were selected six years prior to launch and subjected to a three-year training program before being allowed to board.

CHAPTER SIX

From evening isles fantastical rings faint the Spanish gun . . .

—Chesterton, "Lepanto"

Cochea, 26/7/459 AC

It was warmth; it was peace.

With the song of birds in the air, Linda and Patricio sat on a blanket spread on the side of a small hillock. To the northeast gurgled the creek in which she had swum as a girl. Between the hill and the creek, on grass weeded and kept smooth by family retainers, Julio, Lambie and Milagro played a game of ball, Milagro, in particular, giggling madly as her two older siblings tossed the ball to and fro over her head.

It was contentment; it was happiness. His love was with him and the results of that love were with them.

Hennessey heard Linda say, "It's hot, Patricio. Here, why don't you have a beer?"

While keeping one eye on the children, he held out

126

a hand for the bottle she offered. As he took it, his nose was assailed by the stench of rotting flesh. He closed his eyes and whispered, "Oh, no."

When he could bring himself to open them again, he looked at his wife. She knelt motionless by his side, flesh turned black with decomposition and bones beginning to show through as the flesh fell away in long rotten strips and irregular pieces. She made no sound.

Pained, frightful cries came from the children. "Daddy! Help us!"

Almost too frightened to look, still Hennessey turned his gaze toward the creek. The children's game had stopped; the ball sat still on the smooth grass. They stretched blackening arms out toward him, pleading, imploring. Even as he watched, little Milagro exploded in a cloud of bone and rancid meat. Lambie and Julio shook and shivered, screamed and begged, as their bodies fell to ruin.

Hennessey looked back to Linda. She was no longer there. In her place lay a neat pile of disconnected bone. The children's screaming stopped. He looked back for them.

In their places, too, were little piles of joints and ribs.

"Martina? This is Patricio. Would it be all right if I stayed with you and *Suegro* for a little while?"

Finca Carrera, Cochea, 29/7/459 AC

Poor Patricio, thought Linda's mother, Martina. She looked out to where her son-in-law sat unmoving on her front porch, the picture of human misery. Some food she had brought to him lay untouched, except by the flies, on the porch railing.

It's like he's died inside.

He had told them he had no remaining relatives—barring one cousin—that he wished to see in the Federated States. And even with Annie he found it difficult to talk.

When he had called a few nights back, his voice choking with misery and horror, and asked if he might stay for a while, the family had naturally taken him in. *Though it seems to have done little good. Still, it can't have been good for him to stay in that house.*

Nothing worked. Hennessey took no interest in anything. He just sat there on the porch, day after day. What passed through his mind no one knew. The only interruptions to his vigil came when he took the short walk to Linda's and the children's "grave." Sometimes, too, he slept in the bedroom the family had provided. Just as often, however, he would fall asleep in the chair on the porch. He hardly spoke to anyone. He drank far, far too much.

Arranging some flowers on a table beneath the window, Martina thought, *Poor broken man; he's got nothing left. I don't think I've ever seen a sadder sight than the way he just sits there, day after day, no hope or purpose.*

She resolved to demand that her husband find something to interest Hennessey, something to give him even a little interest in life. *Maybe cousin Raul can think of something to help. He's mentioned that he thought very well of Patricio.*

✧   ✧   ✧

Linda's father shook Hennessey's shoulder. "Patricio, there is someone who wishes to see you."

At the insistence of his wife, the father had invited distant cousin and old family friend, Raul Parilla, to come to talk with Hennessey. He'd been there when it *happened*. And Patricio had always spoken of Raul with respect. Perhaps it might do some little good for his son-in-law to talk with the retired general.

Parilla remained one of a very few influential Balboans interested in giving the country an army again. Linda's father was not one of them, though the more politically minded Martina *was*. The fact that there was such a group was an open secret. As Parilla had told *Señor* Carrera, they did little more than debate about it. The group had accomplished precisely nothing yet . . . and it had been years.

Hennessey didn't even look up. Twirling the ice filled glass in one hand, he said, "I don't want to see anyone, *Suegro*. Please ask whoever it is to go away."

"You will want to see this one, Patricio. It's General Parilla. He wants to ask you for some advice. Talk to him, won't you? For me, if nothing else."

Shrugging, Hennessey agreed. Parilla had been with him that day, that counted, as did their long standing friendship. "Okay, *Suegro*. I'll see him."

Linda's father led Parilla out onto the porch. Hennessey stood up; though he knew the general well, and though neither was any longer in service, old habits die hard. The two shook hands and sat down. Linda's father left them there.

Parilla lit a cigarette before beginning. At his first exhalation, he said, "How have you been, Patricio . . . you know . . . since . . . ?"

"I don't know how to answer that, Raul. Not well? Yes, that. I have not been well."

Giving a quick fraternal squeeze on the shoulder, Parilla said, "Well, man, I can understand *that*. I wish . . . but there weren't any words that day. And I have none now. Except I am so sorry."

"Yes. Me, too, Raul. But sorrow doesn't help. Nothing helps. Only that one time have I felt any better, and shooting strangers on the street is not something I can make a hobby of."

Parilla nodded understanding. Jimenez had told him the story. In the same shoes, he could not imagine feeling or acting any differently.

"I came here to ask advice, Patricio."

"Yes, so said my father-in-law. I don't know what help I could be, but if I *can* help . . ." He let the words trail off.

Parilla's mind groped back over fifteen years, to the day he had first met a much younger Hennessey, then a lieutenant leading a joint Federated States-Balboan small unit exercise at the Jungle Warfare School at Fort Tecumseh, on the southern side of Balboa. Despite having his recon party compromised, Hennessey had managed to win through in the problem, a company raid. Since Parilla had only a very basic idea of how to conduct a raid at all, he had been impressed.

"I think you can. But tell me . . . you never have, you know . . . why aren't you still with the Federated States Army? And . . . too . . . why don't you go back now? I remember; you were *good*."

Hennessey nodded quietly, then paused to think about his answer.

"Well," he began, "I can't go back. They don't want me."

"Why not? It makes no sense to me, your leaving. It never has."

Hennessey sighed with pain, an old remembered ache to go along with the fresh agony. "There's nothing I can tell you that won't sound like sniveling, Raul."

"I know you are not a crybaby, Patricio."

Muscles rarely used stretched Hennessey's mouth into something like a grimace. "No. No, I'm not. You really want to know?"

Seeing that Parilla did, he continued. "Raul . . . you know that in the army, nearly any organization I suppose, you will often be forgiven for being wrong. What they never tell anyone is that you are very unlikely to be forgiven for being right."

Parilla looked honestly perplexed and said so.

Another deep sigh from Hennessey. "It had to do with training; my approach to it. I'm not the only one it ever happened to. You remember General Abogado? He got bounced for much the same thing, though he had some other issues, as well. In any case, let me ask a question of you, Raul. In the old *Guardia,* who trained the privates on a day to day basis?"

"Their sergeants and corporals mostly. Is there a better way?"

"No. None. At least given good sergeants and corporals. But that isn't the way it worked most places in the FS Army. There, oh, since time immemorial, most of the day to day training has been closely supervised by officers. Mostly, it doesn't work very well, either."

"No. I can't see how it could," Parilla agreed.

"Well . . . I did something a little different. I had been watching and experimenting with the training of individual soldiers very closely for nearly two decades. In all that time, every time someone mentioned 'individual training,' the stock solution was: "'tighten up the training schedule,' 'waste not a minute' . . . you know, all that rot."

"I decided to try something a little different. I made my subordinates loosen the training schedule, to leave a lot of gaps and holes for the sergeants to use. Then I made them put on the schedule certain things that had to be done by Thursday night . . . or else. Told them I would test for it, too."

"Well, they didn't believe I was serious. It was too different a concept. The first week I tested—had my sergeant major test, actually—the whole damned battalion failed and so I held them over the next night until nearly midnight retesting. Next week it was about five-sixths of the battalion to just after eleven PM. Then about three-fourths until ten or so. By the time six weeks rolled around I had privates going to their squad leaders and saying, 'Forsooth, Sergeant, I am in desperate need of getting laid. The only time to do that is Friday night. The only way to have Friday night off is to pass the *muthafuckin* colonel's test. So *teach* me this shit, please.'"

"About that time *my* boss got wind of it; tubby little fart of a dumb-assed tanker. 'Tuffy' was his nickname." Hennessey sneered with contempt. "Don't ask me how he got or why he deserved the nickname 'Tuffy;' the evidence was pretty thin on the ground. He was so fat he couldn't squeeze through the hatch of an armored personnel carrier without greasing his ponderous gut.

Anyway, he was a clueless, stupid shit. I explained what I was doing and he told me to stop. I answered, 'No, sir. Relieve me if you want but this is starting to work pretty damned well.' Well, he wouldn't do that. But he hated it. He hated me, too, for defying him."

Parilla likewise didn't understand why Hennessey had done this, and said so.

"The trick," Hennessey answered, "was that the sergeants had for decades been conditioned to being told what to do and had had driven out of them any native initiative they might have had. They were . . . over-supervised, if you will. Worse, they'd grown to *like* not having to think or use initiative."

"But weren't *you* over-supervising doing it your way?"

"At first, yes," Hennessey admitted. "Clearly. But the difference between legitimate and illegitimate oversupervision is in the end game. Once I had them in the habit of finding and using time, I let them run with it. It worked . . . oh, quite well. We had an individual training test a few months later. They call it the MIB—Master Infantry Badge—test. The rest of the brigade shut down for three weeks to prepare for it. My battalion rolled to the field, doing any number of things that had nothing to do with the test.

"We came in the day before we had to take it. I told the boys to get a good night's sleep. We'd take the test in the morning and clean equipment the day after.

"When the smoke cleared I had something over seventy percent of my battalion max the test. This had never been done before. Normally it's just a couple of percent of any given unit that maxes. Pissed off my boss to no end."

"I do not understand," Parilla interjected. "You

do something that well . . . surely it makes your boss look good."

Listening through an open window Martina heard Patricio laugh and felt a sudden relief that her son in law was still at least *capable* of mirth.

Hennessey answered, "Uh . . . no. Surely it does not. The rest of the brigade failed miserably by comparison. Made him look bad, in fact."

Parilla's eyes widened. "Ohhh . . ."

"'Ohhh,' indeed. A commander can stand having nothing but mediocre units under his command. What he can't stand is having mostly mediocrity and one very superior unit. Makes him look bad, by comparison, you see.

"But that wasn't the worst of it. A couple of months later the brigade had an organization day. Lots of athletic competitions and trophies, things like that. Well, my boss volunteered my battalion at the last minute to be the duty battalion—picking up trash and such—for the division, for that day. So I went out with about one-sixth as many men as the other battalions, a fair number of mine being people who had been hurt in training."

"Jesus, he really *did* hate you, didn't he?"

"That was *my* guess," Hennessey muttered. Then he added, "We beat the rest like we owned them too, cripples and all. Why, for one competition I didn't even have enough people to field a complete team and we won anyway. My brigade commander was so pissed about it he stormed off the parade field just before awards presentation."

Parilla snickered. "Surely he couldn't relieve you over that?"

"No. That came later. And, in a sense, tubby little turd or not, he was right.

"You've got to remember, this was in the most intensely leftist and pacifist years of the Gage Administration in the FSC. Peacekeeping and Operations Other Than War were the big thing. Everybody had to play along. Not that I think Gage ever really believed in any of it . . . or even cared. But he was beholden to his base and they *did* believe in it.

"Raul, I couldn't. I just couldn't do it. I looked at my boys, thought about the way the world *really* was . . . and I could not, not, *not* train them to pass out multiculturally sensitive, vegetarian rations to starving refugees in the hinterlands in a multiculturally sensitive manner. I kept training them to fight, orders to the contrary or not.

"That was the last straw. The brigade commander fired me. I resigned my commission. And so, here I am. And so, my wife and kids were in First Landing on 11/7." Hennessey's voice broke at that last and it was a long moment before he could look up.

"What a damned waste," Parilla said. "I've known you had real talent for this sort of thing since I first met you. What a waste you can't do it anymore."

Parilla leaned forward with an almost conspiratorial air. Speaking softly, he said, "Patricio, you know I am part of a group—we probably don't deserve the name 'conspiracy,' more like a debating club for now—that would like to see Balboa fully sovereign again, which means rearmed. But we haven't the faintest idea of how to go about such a thing, you see. I thought, since you're about the only man in the country outside of the FS Marines who guard the embassy, who has ever even been in a real army, that you might be able to tell us."

Recovered, Hennessey answered, "Go ahead and ask. I may be able to help a little."

The direct approach? Parilla wondered. *Yes.* "How could we rearm ourselves?"

Hennessey thought about it for just a few seconds. Looking from the same window through which she had seen him before, Linda's mother saw the first sign of any interest in anything since he had returned to Balboa.

Hennessey gripped the lower half of his face in his right hand, thinking hard. "Much would depend on the attitude of the Federated States. If they were hostile, then you're likely screwed . . . although there are a number of techniques you can use to hide an armed force if the legal government will help. For one thing, you can use front organizations: boys' and girls' youth groups, civilian labor groups . . . unions, fraternal organizations, police and fire departments. I'm assuming here that the Morales government wants nothing to do with that."

A sneer crossed Parilla's face. "That is unfortunately correct. The *traitors* actually had the gall to legislate away our ability to defend ourselves; like San Jose did." Parilla spat with contempt.

Parilla paused, then admitted, "Well, that's not entirely true. The new Civil Force is in most respects a blurry mirror of the old Balboa Defense Corps. But it is a singularly ball-less version of the BDC."

Hennessey nodded. "Then it will be almost impossible unless you can either change the government or change its mind . . . or fool it."

"I see. Well, what can be done without a change of government?"

Hennessey leaned into his left hand and rubbed his temple. After a moment he answered, "Staff work. You can prepare Tables of Organization and Equipment. If you have money, you can buy some equipment and hide it, possibly at sea. You can send people to work with other countries that have armies. You can prepare programs of instruction and plan to set up training facilities even if you can't actually set them up. Perhaps a military high school—another one, I mean—might help."

"How would *you* prepare for something like that?"

"Me, Raul? I couldn't. Not any more."

Parilla cut him off. "Oh, horseshit, Patricio. You live here. Your roots—new ones to be sure, not as deep as they might be—are still here. Here is where your blood rests. And we *need* you. We've got 'Progressivist' Santandern guerillas from FARS and the SEL pressing our western border. We'll have the homegrown variety soon enough, too, if we don't do something. We are the trade route for the world. And the same people who killed your family will eventually figure that out and come for us, too. That is, they will if they aren't already here and waiting. I suspect they're just waiting."

Hennessey's eyes were pained. There had been a time when . . . ah, but it was too late now. "I still can't. Look . . . Raul. I'm just . . . broken. I'm not good for anything anymore. I just don't have it. And even if I did, without Linda I am . . . not to be trusted. I don't really trust myself."

Parilla muttered, "Bullshit," then stood as if to leave. He turned, paused, and then turned back. "You know, Patricio, we need you. I told you; no one in Balboa has ever even *been* in a real army. The nearest to one we ever had your country crushed and *you* helped them do it. We could offer you much no one else can: a new home, a life worth living, useful work to do. We would not be ungrateful for the help; you know that."

"I still can't. I'm not the man I was." *Without Linda to control me I am afraid of what I am capable of.*

"Well . . . think it over some, at least."

Hennessey shrugged. After Parilla left, Hennessey went back to twirling the ice in his drink, occasionally glancing toward Linda's grave.

His blank look was suddenly replaced by a deep and lasting frown. *Could it be possible? There is a framework here, the Civil Force. There are some good people, men like Xavier, in it.*

He debated within himself. *But, no. Twelve years have gone by since they thought of themselves as infantry. Riddled with corruption, Xavier has told me. No recent training in heavier weapons. No experience in combined arms or higher staff work.*

But . . . couldn't I give them some of that? Surely I could. And I have friends still, good soldiers, who could help.

Money? It always comes down to money. And even if Uncle Bob's estate does end up in my hands, it's a pittance compared to what's actually needed. I am no Crassus and I'm not going to be, either.

Not enough to maintain an army. Enough for a staff? Yes . . . at least enough for a staff. And then . . . maybe someone else could pay to maintain an army if one were raised.

Ah, no. Forget it. It was true what I told Parilla. My heart and soul are gone from me. They died with Linda and the kids. I just can't.

Can't? Why not? I was a good soldier before I met Linda.

Good? Yes. But she made me a human one. Before I met her? I was near to being a monster.

So be a monster. This is the time for monsters again; monsters have already arisen.

Hennessey's frown cleared. He remembered how very damned good it had felt to shoot men who'd cheered the murder of his family. He wondered, *How good might it feel to kill the men* actually *behind killing my family? Might the nightmares stop then?*

His heart began thumping and stomach churning with the excitement of the possibilities. With his left hand he reached over and poured his drink onto the ground outside the porch. Then he walked into the house, hugged his mother-in-law, shook his father-in-law's hand and left.

"I need to do something at the house," he announced as he walked out the door.

Hennessey Residence, Cochea, 2/8/459 AC

The sound of *Jinfeng* squawking miserably at Linda's statue came through the window. Hennessey heard it only dimly.

Instead, there was music, Old Earth music, playing in the background.

"I see a red door and I want it painted black . . ."

At the *casa's* front door, Hennessey met Parilla

and shook his hand warmly before leading him to his library. Parilla had an electronic slate tucked under one arm.

Hennessey began, "It was good of you, sir . . ."

"Please, Patricio; 'Raul.'"

"Raul. I thought since this was a formal mission . . . oh, never mind. 'Raul.' It was good of you to return to see me. I think, maybe, I can help you now." *Yes, I can help you . . . and I can help me . . . now.*

Parilla positively beamed. "Ah! Wonderful. How?"

Hennessey had already thought about it enough. He had spent days thinking about it. "I will collect a small staff, house them somewhere out of the way, and put them to work on some of the things I mentioned before. While I am doing that, you need to be setting up the government to knuckle under for rearmament. You can do this?"

Parilla thought about it for a moment. "I can do *some* of it."

"Well . . . that's a start. Perhaps some propaganda can do the rest. In any case, soon the Federated States will need an ally; an ally that doesn't blanch when the body bags start coming home. If a way can be found to hasten that day, so much the better."

Parilla pointed a finger at Hennessey. "Could you do that kind of preparation for rebuilding a Balboa Defense Corps that really mattered outside of Balboa? Really?"

Hennessey didn't hesitate at all. "Yes. Really. Only . . . let's not call it the BDC. Too politically correct for my tastes. Also too much of an image marred by defeat. As a matter of fact, I think we should partially detach the force from Balboa. Your government is very sensitive to world opinion and very fond of the Tauran Union, the World League, and the UEPF."

"*La Armada*," Parilla suggested.

"Maybe that. But maybe not, either. The people who legislated away the name while leaving a shadow of the reality are plainly people more interested in image than facts. Call it an army openly and they'll be more likely to resist."

Parilla pushed Hennessey's objections aside for the time being. "Patricio tell me, what would you do specifically? Wait. Let me fire up my slate to write with."

"No," Hennessey said. "If it's electronic it can be tapped. At this point let's stick to old fashioned."

Terra Nova's levels of technology were approximately those of very early twenty-first century Earth. Like that place and that time, too, the levels were very unevenly distributed across the planet. Uhuru, outside of the Republic of Northern Uhuru, for example, was little advanced in some places above the neolithic level.

Even in those areas—the Federated States and Secordia, Yamato, the Tauran Union—which enjoyed the highest levels of technology available, there were some differences from the world of Man's birth in its twenty-first century after the birth of Christ.

Terra Nova had no truly and completely peaceful use of space. The Global Locating System put up by the Federated States had some peaceful *uses*, true, and it had been permitted by the UEPF because of those presumptive peaceful uses. But it was there, the Feds had paid for it, for its use in war. As much could be said for the communications satellites that circled the planet.

The major use of space, however, was manifest in the extensive system of systems set up by the Federated States of Columbia to engage and destroy the UEPF if the latter ever again had the temerity to try to dictate terms to the former. And that sat unused but threatening.

Medical technology was somewhat less, in particular with regards to epidemiology and infectious diseases, generally. They had their diseases there, of course, but most of those Man had brought with him to the new world he already had considerable resistance to. The planet itself had none of importance.

Given its sad history of war and massacre, however, the planet's medicos were quite capable of dealing with trauma.

Militarily, the planet was on a rough par with twenty-first century Old Earth, as well, much to the delight of medical interns who wanted the practice.

In electronics Terra Nova was perhaps a bit further behind, being at the level of Old Earth just before the close of its twentieth century. For example, small personal computers were common, but somewhat slower, larger and heavier than might have been expected based on the level of military technology. Personal computers and mobile communication devices—cell phones—small enough to surgically insert were still the stuff of dreams and fantasies there.

One area where Terra Nova was far ahead of where one might have expected was in hacking. This, perhaps driven by the endemic warfare, was very advanced. Indeed, it was so advanced that no one was safe, ever. It was so advanced that the Globalnet, the equivalent of Old Earth's Internet, was far less well developed.

Hacking on Terra Nova could be said to have retarded every other aspect of information technology.

It was suspected, in some circles, that the UEPF was responsible for much of the hacking.

Hennessey swiveled in his office chair and took from the top of his cluttered desk a pen and notebook, which he handed to Parilla. The older man considered this, considered the subject matter, considered the effects of what they were about to discuss on those who might object, and decided that using his electronic slate might be a bad idea after all. He took the pen and notebook.

Moments later, notebook in hand, a beaming Parilla prepared to take down Hennessey's thoughts.

Hennessey pulled a pack of cigarettes from a breast pocket. He took one paper tube out and stroked a match to light it. With smoke curling about his head in an infernal halo, he began, "I have friends who were once good soldiers in the Federated States Army . . . some other armies, too, but who despite being good soldiers—very good, actually—never made any great success of things. In some cases this was *precisely* because they were superior soldiers. They have left the service early or have retired. I would hire some of them to come here to do the staff work."

Half turning his head away, Parilla focused one eye on Hennessey. "Could you trust them to be discreet?"

"They are my friends. Yes, I would trust them." *The ones I will pick? Oh, yes.*

Parilla asked, "How much would this cost?"

Hennessey didn't need quick calculations. *Those* were long since made. "For the first year a fair figure might be about one point eight million FSD"—Federated States Drachma, also legal tender in Balboa and much of the rest of the planet—"not more than two point two million; plus perhaps a lump sum of about four million to start up. The annual figure could go as high as three million or even four but I really don't think it will cost that much, not before we start to recruit and expand."

Parilla took a deep breath before telling Hennessey, "Patricio, I would like you to take charge of this project, to make all possible preparations for Balboa to have its own armed force again, in truth as well as in name. Will you do it?"

"I'm sure I can't afford the whole thing on my own. My uncle's estate is tied up for now. I have an income, and it's comfortable, but it wouldn't pay for anything like this, not even with the insurance from my family." *But what I have, this project has.*

Parilla answered, "You won't have to. I never thought you should." He shrugged his shoulders and looked heavenward in mock shame. "We do have certain sources of funds . . . not always aboveboard but also not often traceable." Parilla's hands spread in helplessness at the wickedness of mankind. "Piña wasn't, sad to say, the only ruler of the country ever to have a foreign bank account. I can have a reasonable down payment on the start up amount—say, FSD 450,000—tomorrow. The rest will take a couple of weeks. As for greater amounts for actually recreating a force? Well, Piña took two hundred and seventy-five million a year in unofficial taxes from the Cristobal Free Trade Zone. Most went to line his pockets; his and his cronies. But we could raise probably four hundred million per year now without hurting trade overmuch. And we are not *that* poor a country. Our gross domestic product runs nearly twelve billion. A couple of hundred million more could be squeezed out of government revenues. That's not small change. That all assumes, of course, that the government can be made to see reason."

Even while thinking, *I don't want the government to pay for it. I want to pay for it, to maintain control of it, and to use it to destroy my enemies,* Hennessey nodded agreement. "Then I will go back to the Federated States in two days to begin."

Saulterstown, Shelby, FSC, 5/8/459 AC

Military installations bred military towns. Saulterstown, right outside of and dominated by Fort William Bowen, was typical, from "Sarge's Used Auto" to "Post Pawn Shop." Typically also, the military town was full of ex-soldiers. Hennessey had come here to find and recruit one in particular.

He knew couldn't make his plan work alone, that he would need help. So he had drawn up several lists of people that had worked with or for him over the years who might be available. Most of these he eliminated as unsuitable. Forty-nine remained. He stood now outside a firearms store owned by one of them. It looked depressed. A few posters of guns decorated the walls. Through the windows he could see rifles and pistols in glass cases. Still, this was much the most bedraggled looking gun store he had ever seen. He walked in.

"Is Terry Johnson here?" he asked the sole clerk on duty.

The crop-haired, wiry man behind the sales desk put down the rifle he was inspecting and instead looked at Hennessey. Something about the civilian clad man in front of him suggested, *rank . . . serious rank; dunno why he's in mufti but it shines through in civvies or not.*

He answered, "Nah, sir, Terry's not here. He's supposed to be in later, sir."

"Do you know where I can find him, Sergeant?" The sergeant—that was as obvious to Hennessey as his own, former, status had been to the other—serving as a salesman didn't know that either. He returned his attention to the rifle.

"Well, if you don't mind, I'll just wait." Hennessey amused himself by walking around the store, examining some of the guns on display, reading the few posters on the walls. As he walked and looked, he tapped impatient fingers on the glass cases.

One of the items on wall display caught Hennessey's eye. It was apparently a plaque from Terry's former Direct Action team in the 5th Special Service Group. The plaque showed a picture of Terry's team members behind a burning red smoke grenade. It was inscribed: "To Captain Terrence—'Terry the Torch'—Johnson From his Team Mates of Det 3, Co B, 3rd Bn, 5th SSG." Hennessey looked at the men in the picture and realized that the sales clerk was one of them.

"Did you leave Group, too?" he asked, pointing to the picture.

Again the clerk, laying the rifle aside, returned his attention to Hennessey. "No, sir, I'm still with Group.

We all—all the old team, that is—pitch in from time to time to help Terry make a go of this. Doesn't seem to be working though."

Won't do to have an active member listening in when I talk to Terry. We'll go elsewhere. Even if the kid would keep quiet, no sense putting him in a conflict of interest. Sure, the FS is likely to approve what I'm planning in the long run, but in the short they might be . . . difficult about it. Especially might those assholes at State be difficult about it.

He continued to pace about the shop. Asking to examine a Zhong Guo-made copy of a Samsonov assault rifle with a folding triangular bayonet, Hennessey filled the time with small talk about weapons. The sergeant-clerk was a particular fan, Hennessey learned, of some unusual calibers—.410 Kiowa, .34 Suomi, and 6.5mm Jotun.

Terry Johnson muttered a curse as he yanked the wheel of his decrepit pickup truck to avoid a newly loosened piece of the road fronting his shop. He turned into what passed for a parking lot, all gravel and mud, turned again and rolled to a stop beside the blank brick that made the place's southern wall.

He noticed first a high-end rental car parked outside. This suggested a well-heeled customer inside, a rare enough event. *Hell, it's a unique event.* Even so, Johnson went first to check the mailbox that stood by the juncture of the highway and the concrete walkway leading to the front door.

"Bills," he muttered with disgust. He flipped through the little stack quickly. *Overdue, past due, past due, overdue, overdue, cancellation . . . shut off notice . . . Fuck! FEB*—the Firearms and Explosive Bureau—*wants to inspect me? Fuck.*

Life used to be a lot better than this. It used to even be worth living.

Shaking his head, Johnson walked to the door, opened it, and stepped in. The customer inside turned around. He was wearing a smile and what looked like an expensive suit.

Johnson stopped and looked at Hennessey. It had been years since last they had met and Hennessey had aged a great deal since. For a few moments he puzzled over the familiarity.

Recognition dawned. Johnson wrapped Hennessey in a bear hug, planting a sloppy kiss on his forehead. "Pat! How the hell are you?"

"Lemme go, you nasty fuck!"

Disentangling himself, Hennessey calmed immediately and answered, not quite truthfully, "It could be worse, Terry. Yourself?"

Johnson lifted and dropped one shoulder. "A long story. It could be better. What the hell are you doing here in Saulterstown?"

"I came to see *you*, Terry. Let's go have a little chat."

The two left Johnson's gun store in his beat-up old truck and drove to a nearby restaurant. They spoke of old times in Balboa and traded information on every mutual acquaintance they could think of. This continued throughout lunch and on into the drinks that followed. Then Hennessey began to probe Johnson for his own history since he had left Balboa in 447.

"Well, I got married. That was a really big mistake.

We did *not* get along. We got divorced about eighteen months ago." Johnson raised his beer in a unilateral toast. "Free at last; free at last; praise God Almighty . . ."

Hennessey was unsurprised. Johnson had never had any real sense when it came to women. That Johnson had been married, Hennessey knew through the grapevine. That he was now divorced was a plus.

Hennessey asked, "Is that how you ended up out of the army?"

"No. I know what you're thinking. 'Bad woman drives good man to drink' or something like that. Actually the divorce didn't bother me all that much." Johnson paused. A painful memory caused him to scratch at the tabletop. "Pat, do you remember how you told me to stay away from SSG?"

Hennessey nodded and shrugged. He couldn't see any sense in bringing up *that* whole thing again.

Johnson continued. "I should have taken your advice. It was everything you warned me about, only worse. 'Good people in a shit matrix'; wasn't that what you said? In short, my battalion commander lied to me, then screwed me for following the order he gave me himself."

This sounds interesting, Hennessey thought. He made a hand motion—*come on*—for Johnson to continue.

Johnson raised a quizzical eyebrow. "You really want to hear this? Okay. My team and I were on a deployment to the Yithrab Peninsula, one of those trivial but rich little oil kingdoms. Exactly where doesn't matter; it's secret anyway. I got orders from my motherfucking, son-of-a-bitch battalion commander to do a blank fire attack on a police fort. It was a training mission so I didn't think anything of it at the time. When I went to the police fort to recon it, however, it did not, repeat *not*, look like a good place for a blank fire raid."

Johnson put up his right hand and raised one finger for each reason he had thought the raid a bad idea. "These guys had serious security out; machine gun bunkers, even a few anti-tank weapons, all live ammunition so far as I could see. They did not look to me like they were planning to take part in any blank exercises. They *did* look like they were expecting the Army of Zion to roll over the ridge at any moment.

"Anyway, I got on the SATCOM and told my battalion commander that I didn't think this exercise was a good idea and why I thought so. He went ballistic on me over the radio. Insisted that it was all laid on and coordinated, etc., etc., et-fucking-cetera. That, and that he wouldn't come in my mouth. I said I still didn't want to do it. He ordered me to." Again Johnson clenched a fist at a memory that still rankled.

"So we did the raid. I couldn't use live ammo on the cops and I didn't want them to have a chance to use live ball on my guys. So I improvised. We attacked with more pyrotechnics than you have probably ever seen used in one place. We had hundreds and hundreds of grenade and artillery simulators. Smokepots, signals. The works. The attack went just fine. *God*, it was pretty." Johnson sighed with pleasure, then frowned. "Only thing was . . . the police fort sort of . . . uh . . . burned down. To the ground. Must have been more wood in the place than I'd thought."

Hennessey laughed. He *could* just see it. "You and Kennison and fire. It just doesn't mix."

"Anyway, it turned into a big international stink. I claimed I was following orders, which is not a bad defense if you haven't committed a war crime. My battalion CO denied ever giving me any orders, the cocksucker. My word against his, and he was an SSG 'good old boy.' I had a choice of resignation or court-martial. I resigned. I should have listened to you," Johnson summed up.

"So, Terry, since you don't owe much to the army anymore what are you going to do with yourself for the rest of your life?"

Johnson shrugged. "I don't really have any plans. I get about ten thousand a year from a family trust fund. I'm a part-time sheriff for this burgeoning metropolis. I load a bread truck three days a week. I had really hoped to make something of the gun store but it's costing me more than it's bringing in. That's even with free help from my old team. There are a surprising number of obstacles the government throws in your way if you want to run a gun store. I really don't know what I'm going to do, Pat."

Hennessey nodded with understanding. *Toss the bait . . . plunk.* "Would you like to get back into uniform again, Terry?"

Johnson shook his head vigorously. "With the army? No thanks. Sure, I miss the army . . . or I miss the old days in the army, anyway. I thought about joining the Territorial Militia but they're as fucked up as can be. I don't think I could stand it. In any case, no, I don't think there's a place for me there anymore."

And good bait must wriggle, must never stop being

bait. "Answer the *precise* question, Terry. Would you like to get back into uniform?"

In the open question there was an implied one; Hennessey's tone said as much. Just what was being implied . . .

Johnson thought about the implications for a moment before answering, "Okay. You win. Like I said, I miss the service something awful. Yes, I'd like to soldier again."

"Can you follow orders; my orders?"

"You've always been senior to me, Pat. You taught me more about training and fighting than all the military courses I've ever had . . . in less time, too, come to think of it. Why do you ask?"

Set the hook. "Remember, Terry, how we used to bullshit from time to time about having our own army; what we would do to make it a great one? Well, there is a chance we can do just that over the next few years. I have come into a large amount of money recently." Which was true; even if his cousin Eugene prevailed in court, Hennessey still owned a huge chunk of the family business—"It's enough to get the ball rolling and keep it going for a while. It could be parlayed into an army with time and a little luck." *Reel him in.*

Johnson didn't hesitate. "I want in."

"We'll be going back to Balboa."

"*Balboa? Girls? Booze? Never being fucking cold? Be still my heart.* I want in even more than I did before. It will be great to see Linda and your kids again. By the way, how many do you two have now?"

"*We* don't have any, Terry . . . Linda and the kids are dead. I'd rather not talk about it, if you don't

mind. Terra Nova Trade Organization . . . that's all."
Hennessey forced the pain from his voice as he forced
it from his conscious mind.

*That's a lot worse than a divorce. Poor Linda . . .
poor kids . . . poor Pat.* Johnson turned his eyes toward
the table. "Okay, Pat. There're no words I can say
except . . . I'm sorry."

"Thanks. Me, too. But getting back to business; I
will be in charge. I *am* a dick, remember."

"Yeah . . . but you're at least a competent dick. And
you've always been in charge; you know that. Now
please quit tormenting me and tell me the plan."

Hennessey looked up for a moment, unconsciously
rubbed his hands together, then answered. "For now
the plan is to recruit a small staff. Half of that will be
your job, the recruiting I mean. Carl Kennison—you
remember him?—is going to do some of it too. I'm going
to go look us up an old friend to be our sergeant major.
His name's McNamara. You don't know him. Good man,
though; you'll be impressed, trust me. I'll also be going
to First Landing, Anglia and Sachsen for a few other
people I've worked with over the years.

"Mac and I will go on ahead to Balboa to set up a
headquarters. You and Carl will recruit and round up
the rest of our group. Most of them you don't know
either. I'll give you a list of names, addresses, and
personal histories when we get back to the car. The
list also has the pay scale I'm willing to offer."

Johnson interrupted. "Speaking of that, what is
the pay?"

"In your case it's forty-eight hundred a month, tax
free, plus room and board. Is that acceptable?"

"Very. Please continue."

Hennessey pulled out a checkbook. "I'll be turning forty thousand over to you. With that, you'll need to get around to where these people are, swear them to secrecy, sign them up, and get them, and yourself, flown to Balboa. I'll expect an accounting except for five thousand, which is your personal flat rate for expenses. You want to live like shit and save some of it, go ahead and live like shit.

"I don't expect you to make any sales pitches. I'll be giving you a personal letter for each man you're to recruit. The letter will explain the deal generally. I've noted on the list the duty positions I'm offering, with the priority of assignment for each one. By the way, you are to keep control of the letters. Let them read them, then get them back.

"There are twenty-two people on your list and as many for Carl. I don't need or want that many. They are prioritized, also. As soon as you have filled all the duty positions I've assigned you to fill, stop looking."

Hennessey paused again. "Do you have a decent car, Terry?"

"No, not really. I had one but I had to get rid of it when I left the army. I just have the beat-up old pickup we drove here in."

Hennessey tapped a finger against his nose a few times, thinking. "That's just as well. You won't have a lot of time to drive from place to place. I'll tell you what; I'll add eight thousand to that forty thousand. I want you to fly to each city or the nearest city you can get to with an airport or airship field. Use rental cars to get around once you get in the right general location."

"Might be cheaper to buy a beater"—a beat up, used

automobile—"and have it flown or carried along with me by airship, barge or train," Johnson observed.

"Mmm . . . no, Terry. I don't think you'll have time. Just fly and rent if that's at all possible."

"Your drachma."

Desperation Bay, Lansing, FSC, 7/8/459 AC

The city had partially taken its name from a disaster that had overtaken an early group of settlers to this part of Terra Nova. The broad freshwater bay that provided the other part could be seen from the airport control tower. The monument placed at the spot where most of the settlers had, ultimately, died could not be seen for the city that had grown up along the forty miles of shore.

In an uncomfortable chair overlooking the airship arrival gate, Dan Kuralski waited impatiently for the stranger who had spoken to him over the telephone two days prior. The stranger had identified himself as Terry Johnson. Johnson had said that he would be arriving today and was carrying with him an employment proposal from a mutual friend, Pat Hennessey. At first, Kuralski had been only mildly interested in the proposal. He was doing well enough financially as a computer programmer. He didn't really need the work. But then the stranger had said that the work would be soldierly. Kuralski was reminded of Kipling's words; the lines that went, "The sound of the men what drill. An' I says to me fluttering heartstrings, I says to 'em Peace! Be still."

Okay, OKAY. I make decent money as a programmer; let's not pretend that I like it, though.

That was why Kuralski was at the airport today to meet a total stranger. He had heard the sound and it had made his heartstrings flutter. Kuralski flat *hated* being a civilian.

From the window of the waiting area, off in the distance, Kuralski caught sight of a huge cigar shape turning nose first to the terminal. From the dirigible fell, almost as if thrown, six heavy cables. These swung freely below until each was caught by one of six special trucks, each with a grasping crane mounted above it. Even as the six trucks took command of the cables, the motors—forward, after and center—rotated as if to push the ship broadside into the wind. Their combined pushing was enough, apparently, to hold the ship fairly steady while the trucks carted the cables off to mules—super heavy locomotives—that sat on twin tracks leading to the terminal. The dual tracks ran in a wide figure eight so that the mules could be positioned wherever the dirigible might find minimal cross wind.

At the mules the cables were transferred, with each mule taking one. These were then tightened. Kuralski couldn't see it but knew from experience that the airship did the tightening, not the mules. Slowly, the dirigible inched down until it hung not more than twenty meters above the concrete of the field. At that point the mules, centrally controlled by a computer, began to roll the ship slowly forward in a long curving arc. After some forward travel, a switchback guided the mules off the figure eight and onto a twin track that descended and then ended at a concrete cigar shape hollowed out into the ground, just in front of the terminal.

At the terminal the ship winched itself down the rest of the way, easing its belly into the artificial depression. As the ship descended, from each side of the depression emerged a dozen or fourteen steel pillars, erecting themselves in a closing curve and dragging behind them what amounted to windbreaks—though their official term was "sail"—that, coupled with the reduction in cross area and change in aspect, enabled the airship to sit quite safely on the ground.

Shortly after the ship was safely moored, Kuralski saw in the crowd of debarking passengers someone matching the description Terry Johnson had given of himself. He went up to meet the man.

Johnson was the first to speak. "Dan Kuralski?" he asked, putting out a hand.

Kuralski nodded. "And you would be Terry?"

"Yes, Terry Johnson. Pleased to meet you."

The two men shook their introductions. Kuralski gestured toward the door and the parking lot beyond. "Come on. We can use my car."

Both men were graduates of the Federated States Military Academy at River Watch, though of different classes. They didn't know each other. They did tend to know a number of the same people, though. During the drive they traded information on mutual friends and acquaintances just as Hennessey and Johnson had done a few days before. The fact that their classes were three years apart and they had never served in the same location limited their conversation. They drove in silence a while before Kuralski asked, "Where do you know Pat from?"

"He was my Company XO when I was a platoon leader in Balboa. And you?"

Kuralski smiled at a half-forgotten memory. "We've never actually served in the same unit. The way the school schedule worked out we always seemed to end up going to school together. The Basic Course at Fort Henry was where we first met." Dan laughed aloud.

At Terry's quizzical look he elaborated, "My first acquaintance with our friend Pat was when he chewed me out for not keeping my foot in the same fixed position and my mouth shut while standing at ease. You would have thought that in four years at the academy someone would have taught me the proper position for standing at ease. *I* thought they *had*. We argued about it, which amused everyone but Pat and myself. Finally he just told me to shut up and do what I was told. It was kind of funny, one shavetail chewing out another. I was more shocked than anything, shocked enough to shut up anyway. You know: rank among lieutenants, virtue among whores? After he fell the formation out I went up to complain. He told me to go look it up. I did. Unfortunately for my self-esteem, he was right. That, and a few other occasions where other people doubted him, convinced me that when he insists something is right; it's right . . . or he wouldn't have insisted."

Johnson chuckled. "That sounds like him; he's an anal bastard, all right. Where else did you go to school together?"

"Ranger School. The Advanced Course at Fort Henry again. Then the Combined Arms Center for the short course."

Johnson said, "You know, Pat taught me a lot about being a combat leader. When he was XO he used to just *dog* all the platoon leaders out trying to teach us everything from the proper employment of barbed wire obstacles to how to conduct a raid to understanding, and, more importantly, ignoring when required, the principles of war."

Kuralski agreed, "Oh, he's good. At least as near as you can tell from peacetime operations."

"Wartime, too," Johnson answered. Seeing the look on Kuralski's face he half-explained, "Oh, you didn't know about him taking leave from Balboa to go to San Vicente with a Vicentinian pal of his to fight the Arenistas? Big stink, that one. And then, because he knew the country, his mech infantry company from Fort Leonidas was tapped to deploy to Balboa for the invasion. I understand they did quite well."

"I didn't know about those," Kuralski answered.

"He can be pretty closemouthed about such things," Johnson agreed.

Abruptly turning off the road they were on, Kuralski pulled into his driveway. Johnson followed him into the split-level house that stood next to that driveway. Once inside Terry noticed a number of pictures of a woman. *Crap. A married man might not go.*

Kuralski motioned for Johnson to take a seat in the living room. Johnson placed a briefcase on the couch beside him and took out an envelope. He handed the envelope to Kuralski.

Kuralski opened the envelope, took out the letter inside, and began to read:

2/8/150

Dear Dan:

The bearer of this letter, Terrence Johnson, is representing me. He is well known to me, trustworthy and loyal. You may speak with him as if you were speaking to me.

I am writing to offer you a job, working for me, as a military planner and consultant. The job will be performed in another country. You do not need to know at this time which country. Suffice to say that it is a pleasant, hot and wet but otherwise comfortable place, with a large city and an active nightlife. Do not expect, if you accept this offer, to have overmuch time to enjoy the nightlife.

Your particular job will be as chief of a small staff I am assembling. You will be second in rank after myself. The pay is initially 4,800 FSD per month, plus room and board. All of that amount is tax free. Life and medical insurance will be provided. Terry will arrange transportation.

You may assume that nothing I will ask of you is illegal, likely to be of interest to the Federated States in the near term, or harmful to the Federated States in any way in any term.

If you decide to join up, let Terry know immediately. I would give you time to decide if I could. I can't. I must ask you not to repeat any of this. Terry will collect this letter, and your decision, now.

I hope you will join me. It's not like I couldn't find someone else to do the job, but I really want it to be you.

Sincerely,

Patrick Hennessey

Kuralski felt a small flush of warmth at that last sentence. He looked up from the letter, toward Johnson. "He doesn't allow much time to decide, does he?"

Johnson answered, "If you think about it, if someone needs a long time to decide something like this, then he probably doesn't need to go. Have you decided?"

Kuralski looked around at the interior of his house. Fading memories, painful ones as often as not. There was nothing there to hold him. "I'll go. Can I have a few days to get my house on the market?"

"You can take fourteen days from today. I'll send you tickets as soon as I finish making arrangements. You'll have to take care of your own passport, if you don't have one." Johnson offered his hand a second time. "For Pat, let me say 'Welcome Aboard.' Ah, what about your wife?" he asked, pointing at a picture.

"Dead. Cancer. It's why I'm not in the army anymore. I had to take care of her and so I missed my chance to command a company. No command; no chance."

"Oh. Sorry. Pat didn't know."

"Thanks. No reason he or you should have. Anyway, it would be worth the trip just to see Linda."

"She's dead, too. Pat said it was on seven-one-one in the TNTO."

Kuralski bowed his head and began to fight back tears.

"You loved her too, didn't you?" Johnson asked.

Kuralski just nodded and said, "Yeah . . . yeah, I did. But, then, who didn't? What a woman."

Johnson smiled grimly. "I know. And pity the poor bastards who murdered the family of Pat Hennessey."

INTERLUDE

31 December, 2049, Brussels, Belgium, European Union

Margot Tebaf's chauffeured limousine passed row upon row of empty, boarded-up shops and unmaintained apartment buildings. *It seems like only yesterday,* she thought, *when those shops were open and vibrant, when there were flower boxes at the windows of the apartments, when the streets were clear. Has it been thirty years?*

The driver cursed as one of the front tires slipped into a pothole. Nobody was maintaining the cobblestones anymore. He muttered something unintelligible but ugly sounding as he maneuvered around a pile of uncollected trash, then cut the wheel hard to avoid the charred and rusted ruins of a burned and ancient automobile, parked—if that was the word—so as to jut out into the street and make passage for those still able to afford private transportation more difficult.

Perhaps it was an ambush point; the city's crime rate was so high now that the police hardly bothered taking reports. Outside of the neighborhoods dominated by the European Union's bureaucracy, they didn't bother with enforcing the law even when it was violated before their eyes.

Margot's gaze avoided the street—too ugly—and looked instead at the little towers above, each ringed with green neon lights.

To a viewer of even twenty years before, the streets would have appeared remarkably clear of motor traffic. Instead young, unemployed men wandered aimlessly, followed often enough by black-clad women trailing masses of children. The men glared at the passing limo. Margot might have feared attack except that her auto was armored. It was also preceded and trailed by armed police escort vehicles.

The one-way glass of the limousine's windows allowed Margot to see out without anyone seeing in. Thus, no one saw her shiver when she considered what things might be like if Europe were a democracy in anything but name and merest appearances.

Thank the god that doesn't exist that my ancestors were wise enough to destroy democracy before we had a barbarian majority in our midst, she thought.

That was only one of the many depressing thoughts impinging on Margot's consciousness. Looming even greater than the barbarization of Europe was the continuing, annoying, *infuriating* prosperity of the United States.

Americans; I hate those bastards. And there are nearly five hundred million of the swine now. While my poor Europe is dying out. And the reason there are so many of the damned Yankees? Not only do their women bear children, just like the Moslems, in unsustainable numbers, but most of the young Euro women willing to have kids went there . . . or to Ontario, or the Republic of Western Canada, or Australia. Others fled east to Poland and Russia.

All our most talented young people left for other climes, leaving what remained to pay for the pensions for the old, the welfare for the immigrants, or the absolutely necessary government that runs things and keeps the peace, that ensures the people are cared for, cradle to grave.

Except that we can't care for them anymore, even with over ninety percent of conscripted youngsters devoted to social issues instead of the military. We have hardly anything to export now, except retired "workers" and Moslem children. And no one wants to buy, or even accept, those.

The limo turned to the right and began to slow. Ahead, the leading police escort pulled off to one side of a guarded steel gate. A guard emerged and questioned the driver of the police escort. Apparently satisfied, the guard turned and signaled to someone inside the small armored shack in front of the gate and to one side. Magically—Margot wondered how long it would be before such things were explained away as the work of magic or of the *Jinn*—the gate slid out of the way. She wondered, too, how long before the gate, *all* the security systems, *all* the technology of Europe broke down, never to be replaced.

She pushed such thoughts aside as the limousine began to move forward through the gate and toward the imposing glass and steel building surrounded by still meticulously maintained grounds that was the Headquarters for the European Union.

CHAPTER
SEVEN

Give me a place to stand and I will move the Earth.

—Archimedes

I'll make my own goddamned lever.

—Patricio Carrera

Air Balboa Flight 717, 9/8/459 AC

Hennessey was a smoky wraith hidden in a wreath of smoke. He did not recognize anything around him. Somehow, though, it felt very high in the air. There was a floor beneath him above which he floated. Though floating, he felt the heat emanating from the floor.

He was drawn forward by laughter. The smoke parted as his shade moved on and through its swirling screen.

The laughter came from a swarthy man. "Infidels," cried the man, "see the judgment of Allah."

A voice he recognized shouted back, "Allah will send you to hell, you miserable wog bastard!"

He was drawn forward by the voice and away from

the hyenalike laughter. "Uncle Bob?" he asked. There was no answer. The shade could not see the wraith, though the wraith could see the shade as it shook its fist. "Uncle Bob?" the wraith repeated.

The shade turned and knelt by a small group. Hennessey recognized his wife, his children. Others were there too, none of whom he recognized.

"Daddy will make them pay, Mom, the men who did this!" Hennessey saw his son, Julio, looking at his mother with certainty in his eyes.

"He will, my son," Linda answered, "and terribly."

"Terribly," echoed Julio.

"I will. I swear it. I will!" whispered the unheard wraith. "Their great-great-great-grandchildren will have nightmares."

Linda looked at the rising flames behind her. "It is time to go, children. Pray now." Linda began to pray, the children joining. Even Hennessey's uncle joined in, as did many others.

The prayer over, Linda began to sing. Hennessey recognized the song, "Abide with Me." Linda had always loved that one, the wraith remembered. He was not surprised that she had chosen it for the last canto. The singing grew in volume as more people crawled over and joined in.

The wraith saw Linda and Uncle Bob stand, along with the others. They held the children in their arms as they began to walk forward, still singing. Linda's hair billowed in the wind from the smashed out window.

"God, even now she is so beautiful," whispered her husband's shadow.

Then Linda squeezed her children tightly to her, waited to feel their answering hugs . . . and took a single

step. As Linda, Bob and the children fell forward, oth-
ers shuffling up to take their places, Hennessey heard,
"Help of the helpless, O 'Abide with me . . . "

High above the ground, in a first class seat toward
the front of the airplane, his sergeant major seated
beside him, Patrick Hennessey awakened, pulled a
medium weight blue blanket over his head, and—as
silently as possible—wept.

Herrera Airport, *Ciudad* Balboa, 9/8/459 AC

"Ahhh. Smell t'e flowers! T'ere's no place like Balboa!"
Hennessey smiled indulgently at the tall, razor-thin,
gray-haired black man walking at his left side. They
moved quickly through Balboan immigration and into
the baggage area. At the *Aduana* a senior customs agent
recognized Hennessey from his previous trip and waved
him, the other two whites, and the sole black man forward to the front of the line. With a conspiratorial smile,
the *Aduana* agent fell over himself to make the group's
transit through the terminal as trouble free as possible.
Within mere minutes Hennessey and his companions,
John McNamara, Command Sergeant Major (retired),
Matthias Esterhazy, late of the Sachsen Reichswehr's
Fallschirmstuermpioniere, or Airborne Assault Engineers, and Her Anglic Majesty's former Royal Sapper,
Gary Clean, were standing at the counter to pick up
their rental car.

"Where are we goin' first, sir?" asked McNamara
in a melodious Maiden Islands accent. Esterhazy and
Clean kept silent, looking around with curiosity.

Hennessey answered, loudly enough for all three of his companions to hear, "First, Sergeant Major, we're going to check in at the Julio Caesare. We've got reservations already. An acquaintance of mine—nice girl, 'Lourdes'—has reserved rooms for us. Then we'll need food, I think. This afternoon, after lunch, we'll go look at buying a headquarters. I want you there for that. It may take us a couple of days to find something appropriate."

The CSM nodded. "I've given t'e set up some t'ought. Once we find t'e right place, just leave it to me."

"As always, Sergeant Major."

As the rental car pulled up, Hennessey thought to ask: "You were never stationed on the *Ciudad* side, were you?"

"No, sir. I've been here, of course, but only to pass t'rough."

"Okay, I'd better drive. I know the way. I'm also more used to the . . . shall we say . . . *élan* with which they drive here."

The drive from the airport to the Julio Caesare was uneventful. Check-in, too, at the hotel went smoothly, as expected. The rooms proved more than adequate. As Hennessey was unpacking, the room telephone rang. "A young lady to see you, sir. 'Lourdes,' she says her name is."

"Yes, fine. Please have her escorted to my room."

"I am here to see one of your guests," Lourdes told the man at the registry counter. "Patrick Hennessey."

The man looked her over briefly and came to a rapid conclusion—*Hooker. A high-end model, I suspect.*

Lourdes' already huge brown eyes widened further

still. *He can't really think . . . oh, no . . . I don't look . . .
I don't dress . . . I hardly even wear any make up . . .
he can't really. Dammit I'm a good girl!*

She said nothing except to sigh as the man picked
up the telephone and announced her, then signaled
for a bellhop. The bellhop came up to stand beside
her, a wide smirk on his face. *He thinks so, too?*

Lourdes followed the bellhop to the elevator,
embarrassment—and not a little anger—growing inside
her with each step. She stewed in simmering juices
while waiting for the elevator doors to open. She
thought, *I should have just asked for the room number and told them I could find it myself. But then . . .
no . . . if I knew my way around the hotel they would
probably be certain instead of just guessing.*

Lourdes and the bellhop rode up past several floors
before the bell chimed, the elevator stopped and the
doors opened. She let herself be led to Hennessey's
room quietly, like a sheep to slaughter.

Hennessey opened his door, a few minutes later,
in answer to the bellhop's knock. Tipping the man
a tetradrachma and dismissing him, he gestured for
Lourdes Nuñez-Cordoba to enter. She hesitated,
automatically. Helping find a house for someone you
barely knew was one thing; being alone in a hotel
room with a near stranger was something a Balboan
girl of good upbringing just didn't do. The thought
of what the hotel staff had assumed about her made
her skin crawl.

Overcoming her rearing, Lourdes walked in. "It's
very nice to see you again, Patricio."

"And you, too. Have you been well?"

"I'm all right, but my work has closed because of the world's economy since the First Landing attacks. I know after all you've suffered that's small beans, but I'm out of a job. My family has been supporting me. With business so depressed, and so many people out of work, I doubt I will find another job soon."

"You already have one, working for me, if you want to and are willing to put up with some conditions."

Lourdes immediately raised a suspicious eyebrow. "What conditions?" she asked. *I am a good girl dammit! You may be good looking, but you are not THAT good looking.*

Understanding, in part at least, Hennessey chuckled slightly. "Probably *not* what you're thinking. First, your job will be general clerical, with some supervisory responsibilities, work gangs and such, and some teaching. Second, the pay is twelve hundred per month plus room and board. You'll earn your pay, believe me. I am not easy to work for." Twelve hundred per month was good pay, very good, by the standards of the Republica de Balboa.

"I don't believe that."

"Believe it, Lourdes. I'm not a nice man."

"I don't believe that, either." The woman thought for a while. *This is the best offer I've had lately.* Reaching a decision, she answered, "I'll take it."

"Good. I'd hoped you would. You're on the payroll as of the beginning of the eighth month. I'll have your first monthly paycheck for you tomorrow. Oh, yes, there is one other thing before you commit yourself. I expect absolute loyalty, discretion, and obedience from those who work for me. You must also never tell anyone, not your boyfriend, your parents, or your priest—no one—what you do for me or what I do. Can you do that?"

"I don't have a boyfriend right now. I'm a Baptist, so I don't have a priest. I can keep quiet." She hesitated. "Are you planning something illegal? I don't want anything to do with drugs . . . or guns."

"No drugs. And we won't be *running* guns, if that's what you're worried about."

"All right then. What's my first job?"

"For now, you're going to lunch with me and a few close friends. Then we'll meet the real estate agent you found for me."

Chorrera Province, Republic of Balboa, 13/8/459 AC

"*Señor*, I am certain this will fit your needs," announced the fat, greasy-looking real estate agent. He may have been fat and greasy looking, but Lourdes had checked and he had an enviable reputation for fair dealing.

It had taken four days, and fourteen houses and ranches, before the agent had finally brought them to something appropriate. Lourdes had not understood what was wrong with the others they had seen. Hennessey hadn't bothered to explain. The one in front of which Hennessey, McNamara, the realtor, the two engineers and Lourdes stood seemed close to fitting the bill. It was some eighteen or twenty miles east of Balboa City, on a promontory overlooking the ocean, a mansion of sorts, old and built of stone, with a high stone retaining wall fronting the highway to the south and east. It had the "haunted house" look that said it hadn't been occupied or properly cared for for some years.

"What do you think, Sergeant Major?"

McNamara's head leaned a bit to the side, contemplating. "Security potential is good, very good. We've got cliffs on t'ree sides. Hard for someone to get in directly. A little wire would make it even harder. T'en t'ere's t'e wall around it. T'at can be improved a bit, too; wire . . . broken glass . . . watchposts or security cameras . . . t'at sort of t'ing. I figure an easy one hundred and fifty meter clear zone inside t'e wall, twice t'at on t'e side facin' t'e road. It's t'e best we've seen so far. And, you know, sir, it's actually a perfect place to control t'e highway from t'e city to t'e interior, if we ever needed to. I'd like to see it from t'e air before you buy it t'ough."

"Good thought." Hennessey considered for a moment, then said, "Lourdes, please take the car and the sergeant major back to the city. Go to La Punta Airport. Rent an airplane or a helicopter, if you can, with a pilot. Then, Sergeant Major, I want you to check this place out from above. The agent can drive the rest of us back after we look over the inside. We'll meet you back at the hotel."

Restraining the impulse to salute—barely— McNamara contented himself with a nod and left. Lourdes turned and followed McNamara quietly as Hennessey and his engineers, Esterhazy and Clean, walked forward to inspect the mansion.

"Where do you know Patricio from, Sergeant Major?" Lourdes kept her eyes on the road as she and the CSM chatted.

"T'e old man? We go back a few years. Have kind of a mutual admiration society. He t'inks I'm about t'e best sergeant major he ever met." McNamara chuckled and flashed a smile brilliant in his homely black face. "And I *am*. I know he's about t'e best commander I ever met . . . at any rank."

"What makes him so special?" *Besides that he's cute . . . and I don't think you care about that.*

"If you were a soldier it would be easier to explain. I don't know how to explain it to a civvie."

"Try."

"He's a warrior; t'e real article, no fake. He's afraid of absolutely not'ing. A lot of people aren't afraid of deat', and neit'er is he. But it's rare not to fear even disgrace . . . and he don't. Why, when our brigade commander once told him to stop training to fight or get relieved . . . but never mind t'at. Long story. Sad one, too." McNamara sighed despondently.

"He wasn't always well liked in t'e army. As a matter of fact he was sometimes hated. Smart as hell; *too* smart for some. Too . . . aggressive. Also he's t'e best trainer of infantry, any soldiers really, t'at I've ever seen. I've never met anyone who even came close, and I've worked for t'e big boys. He can take a group of nice clean-cut kids and make t'em into fanatics in about six mont's. And he loves soldiers. We tend to reciprocate when we get a boss like t'at. After a few months' acquaintance troops'll die for him."

"I find it hard to believe that," Lourdes commented.

McNamara gave her a look that was half pitying.

Seeing the look, Lourdes said, "He told me that he wasn't a very nice man."

The sergeant major laughed aloud. "T'at's a crock. If you're one of his t'ere's no battle he won't fight for you; not'in' he won't do. Take me, for example. I was slowly dyin' from sheer lack of purpose. T'en he came about two t'ousand miles to find me and give me a reason to go on living, to make my last years good ones. No, he is a *very* nice man. Besides, you should see him some time, when t'e bullets are flying and the mortar rounds going *crump*. Eyes glowing from *inside*, I swear to it."

"And what are the two of you going to do?"

"I don't know all of t'e details yet. What I do know is t'at we're goin' to work to make an army for Balboa to help in t'is war . . . and to make it a good one. He's bringin' in anot'er eighteen or twenty people, specialists sort of, to help wit' t'e work."

Lourdes thought about that as she drove. *A "good" army? My country has never had a "good" army. Whatever army we have had has typically been just an instrument of oppression, corruption, or—more usually—both. But those problems are out of my ability to influence in any case. Who knows, maybe here I might be able to do some good.*

Hotel Julio Caesare, *Ciudad* Balboa

"Another drink, Top?"

McNamara thought it over briefly. "No, sir, enough for me already." He refrained from saying, "enough for you, too." Not his place, so the sergeant major felt. *Besides, Patrick Hennessey drunk is still a better commander than ninety-nine out of one hundred are stone sober. Even so, Hennessey sober is better than Hennessey drunk.* Mac's tone betrayed his thoughts.

Hennessey understood the tone. He even agreed. Sometimes he worried that the alcohol was becoming too much of a crutch. He signaled the waitress for one more, not a double this time. Contented, McNamara let it pass.

Over drinks in the hotel's bar, the sergeant major, Hennessey, and the engineers discussed the potential, and potential liabilities, of the latest house they had inspected. The agent had said FSD 1,435,000 was the asking price. Hennessey had shamelessly whittled him down to $1,185,000, even so, but still without firmly committing to buying the place. He wasn't entirely sure. The house was a little run down, despite its setting and architecture.

"The place needs work, Sergeant Major: painting and floor refinishing inside, some new windows, some plumbing and electrical work . . . phones, computer links."

Esterhazy interrupted, "More zan zat. Ve'll have to pour concrete to make a basement floor and finish ze valls if ve're going to get any use out of ze basement. Zat's important, *nicht wahr*?"

Hennessey and the engineers had discussed probable interior setups on their inspection. The house, though huge, would be hard pressed to hold everyone and all the needed offices and other spaces. Once the wives arrived with the children . . . ?

"But it *can* be done," insisted Clean, in a properly middle-class Anglian accent. "Take some bloody time, though."

"T'at's not a problem, sir," Mac added. "When t'e

troops get here, I'll put 'em to work so you wouldn't recognize t'e place."

Hennessey shook his head. "No. I appreciate the money saved, Sergeant Major, but I wanted the place to be ready for them when they arrive. First impressions and all. Then, too, some of the troops aren't going to be staying in the headquarters indefinitely. When the married men's wives arrive, those men will be moving out. It wouldn't be like they were doing the work for themselves."

"Sir, don't be dumb about t'is. You're payin' t'em yourself. T'at makes it all right to have t'em do work for you. Besides, what t'ey make t'emselves? T'at t'ey'll appreciate."

"Okay. Conceded. But I need some of the rooms ready as soon as possible anyway. Okay," he said, making a final decision, "we'll take the place; finish off the individual areas later. The common areas, my quarters and yours, Lourdes' and Gary's, and the basement floor I need done now. Gary, it's your project, yours and Lourdes'. We'll also need a domestic staff, one or two cooks, a housekeeper. I've got one of my in-laws looking for some suitable women. Those, and a groundskeeper."

The CSM started to say that the troops incoming could take care of that too when Hennessey cut him off. "Sergeant Major, when they get here I've got too much for them to do for them to be polishing brass. And you'll have too much to do yourself to spend a great deal of time supervising them polishing brass. Besides, you know you hate that shit."

McNamara shrugged.

Hennessey and McNamara discussed a few details

about setting up the headquarters. Then Hennessey turned over to Clean a large bundle of cash, FSD 40,000 in fifties, to fund the initial work he wanted done. "There's more available when you need it," he said to the sapper. "I'll want receipts."

Giving the CSM the keys to their rental car, he said, "Sergeant Major, in the morning I'll be heading up to *Valle de las Lunas* for a few days to see some people. I'll rent another car at the hotel desk. Check us out of the hotel when the house is minimally fit to move into." He reached into his pocket, pulled out his checkbook, opened it and began to write. "Here's a check for the full price plus closing costs for the headquarters. I'm turning in. Oh. And Gary? Put up a sign on the front. We'll call the place 'Casa Linda.'"

Ciudad Cervantes, 14/8/459 AC

After a seven-hour drive to Linda's family's city residence, Hennessey was ready for the cold beer her brother, David, handed him at the door. The beer was *Nacional*. It was not *good* beer. Hennessey recalled that Linda had done a television commercial for that company in the mid forties, the family owning some stock in the enterprise.

Hennessey asked, "Do you have the list?"

David nodded, "Yes, Patricio. Seven hundred and thirty-eight names and addresses of the parents, wives and children of the soldiers who were killed in the invasion twelve years ago, and those reserve troops of the Sovereignty Battalions who fought and were killed, too. I also have the list of the two hundred and fifteen soldiers and SB troops who were permanently disabled. It has taken me almost all this time to finish compiling it. Why did you need it?"

Hennessey didn't answer directly. "Has the government started paying support to any of them yet?"

"No. Did you expect they would? Crippled and unsupported, those men and their families are walking advertisements for antimilitarism. Much more likely they'd throw the disabled troops in jail than give them money."

"I suppose I didn't expect them to help, not really. Never mind, we'll take care of them for a while, thanks to my Uncle Bob. I want you to find a lawyer here in Cervantes. Your family keeps one on retainer, don't they?" Seeing David nod, Hennessey continued, "Good. Set up a trust fund. I'll give you a check to start it off. Then I want every wife and set of parents on that list to get two hundred drachma per month. Send an additional hundred for each kid. If there is a particularly needy case let me know. We'll try to cover that too."

"There *is* one case I'm aware of, over in *Las Mesas* Province. One of our mid-rank NCOs who was killed, a Sergeant Cordoba, had a very young daughter named Marqueli. His parents are dead. His wife just died." David saw that Hennessey flinched.

"The mother was working to send the girl to school. I'm afraid a hundred drachma won't cover that. Two-fifty might, if she's very careful and can work, too."

"Fine. Put her down for two hundred and fifty a month. Any others?"

"I'll have to check. It would have been easier if you had told me why you needed to know."

"I know. Sorry. I wasn't sure myself until about a

week ago. Let's just say that I'm buying good public relations. Do you have my domestic staff?"

"I have the two cooks you wanted, plus a grounds-keeper. And Lucinda has agreed to take the new job. My mother will send one of her girls over to keep up your old place. All three women are noted for keeping quiet. The groundskeeper is one of our workers. They also don't have any great grudge against gringos. That's important, isn't it?"

"Very. Now, tell me, have you arranged to move yourself to Balboa City?"

"Yes. I start the beginning of next month."

"Good. I'll want you to make as many connections as you can. Will you be stationed right in the city?"

"Yes, with DEBI, the Balboa Department of Investigations. I'll be working for a Major Fernandez. Which thought doesn't thrill me . . . Fernandez has a reputation for extreme measures."

Hennessey shrugged. "Too bad. It's still a useful posting."

"I don't see what difference it makes, Patricio. The government is not going to let us rebuild an army."

"Well . . . I need to talk to Parilla about that in a couple of days."

Ciudad Balboa City, 16/8/459 AC

They met at Parilla's house, a well-furnished and sprawling two-story colonial mansion in the city's Old Cuirass district. They spent no time inside, but retired upstairs to converse in the privacy of a patio overlooking the tranquil waters of the Bahia de Balboa.

"Not a chance, Patricio," Parilla said, with finality. He'd really thought he could do better. It was a sickening and frustrating defeat that he hadn't been able to. "I can raise maybe eighty-five percent of the votes we need in the legislature. The rest? They're shitting in their pants at the thought of resurrecting the Defense Corps."

"Bribes?" Hennessey asked.

"Still not enough. And we can't just bribe those who are opposed to us. In fairness, we'd have to bribe the entire crew that would vote our way or they'd vote against us out of spite. That's more money than my little fund has in it. Millions more. Many millions."

Hennessey sighed. "And I've had worse news. I'm afraid my pussy cousin in First Landing is going to tie up my uncle's estate for some years, too, so I don't have all that much to help with; just my personal bequest. Less now, really, what with the market down. I've sent one of my people, Matthias Esterhazy, to First Landing to see what he can do."

"But I thought you said that your Uncle's will would cut—what was his name? Eugene?—cut him out of the will if he contested it."

"Yes, so my uncle's lawyer told me. But apparently, from Eugene's point of view it's a good bet. He gets a lifetime income, a comfortable one, if he keeps quiet, true. But he's filthy fucking rich if he sues and wins. And, apparently, an 'in terrorem' clause, with a videotaped codicil to a will, under unusually stressful circumstances, is just weak enough that he might win. So says the lawyer now, anyway. He's advising that I settle."

"Are you willing to settle?" Parilla asked.

"Willing? Up to a point. If I could keep enough to fund our little enterprise, I would settle. Problem is, Eugene hates my guts. Can't say I blame him, either. We've loathed each other since we were kids. He would never settle on any terms that were acceptable to me, anyway. Besides, even though the Salafis would chop Eugene's head off in a heartbeat, he still supports them. I don't want to see that much money going into the other side's coffers. Even if he gave it to charity, that only frees up a different pile of money for war and terrorism."

"So. I see," answered Parilla. "Well, in any case, I just can't deliver the votes, Patricio. Not enough; not at a price we can afford."

Hennessey scowled. "Hmmm. More than one way to skin a cat. Raul, do you know any good propagandists?"

Drama Department, University of Balboa, 18/8/459 AC

The campus really should have been moved. Sitting, really sprawling, as it did between the financial district, the high-end shopping district, and the hotel and casino district, the land on which the university sat was not only too valuable for its current use, it wasn't even convenient any longer to the bulk of its students.

Leaving Soult to guard the Phaeton, Hennessey walked to the drama department. Rather, he searched for it on foot. It was only with difficulty that he finally managed to find it. When he did find it, a secretary showed him to the office of Professor Ruiz, with whom he had an appointment. Hennessey had gotten Ruiz's name from Parilla along with an introduction. The professor had a reputation of being a nationalist to a degree even greater than the university norm. When Hennessey had made the appointment, he had given his name as Patricio Carrera. Under Balboan law, he'd become Hennessey de Carrera at the same time Linda had become Carrera de Hennessey.

Ruiz's office was shabby and rundown, as was much of the university. Books, papers, and binders littered it in the universal academic decor. The professor was not run down but his glasses were dirty and his tie-less shirt wrinkled.

Ruiz made a place for Hennessey to sit by moving some books from a chair to the floor. Once Hennessey had sat down, Ruiz asked, "And so how may I help you, Señor Carrera?"

"Professor, I want to fund a series of projects, one of them a movie. Your name was given to me by General Parilla as someone who might be inclined to make the kind of movie and oversee the kind of projects I want."

"And what kind of movie would that be?" Ruiz asked.

"Frankly, I want a propaganda movie. I want—"

Hennessey stopped speaking when Ruiz's secretary brought in two cups of coffee. Ruiz passed over the sugar and waited for Hennessey to continue.

"As I was saying, I want to make a propaganda movie . . . about the 447 invasion. I am told you might be able to make such a movie, given funding."

Ruiz brightened immediately. He began to wax about

the terrible atrocities—largely fictional—committed by the Federated States, the suffering of the people, the destruction of the economy. Ruiz paused. "But aren't you a gringo, yourself?" he asked, doubtfully.

"I am. And I am not remotely interested in an anti-FSC movie. Oh, don't misunderstand; the Federated States is going to have to be the enemy. But I need them to be an honorable enemy. As for atrocities; that's not the message I wish this movie to send. Perhaps later we'll do another . . . on a different kind of atrocity." Hennessey smiled before continuing, "The kind of film you are thinking of tells about the evil of the Federated States. What good would that do, even if true? We have bigger enemies. Worse ones, too, now. Enemies of our entire civilization. So, really, Professor, what good?"

"It would help rally the people against this puppet government. That is quite a bit, don't you think?"

Hennessey shrugged. "Up to a point. But I don't want to demoralize the people. I have a different idea. Let's not spend our effort showing the Federated States as bad. Anyone here in Balboa who believes that already doesn't need further convincing. Instead, let's work on showing Balboa and Balboans as good. With, and I cannot emphasize this enough, the glaring exception of General Piña, of course."

Ruiz looked confused and uncertain. "But everyone in the country would agree even more on that. What's the point?"

Hennessey thought that Ruiz was perhaps over-optimistic. Few in Colombia Latina, Spanish- and Portuguese-speaking Columbia had any real faith in their own governments and societies.

He answered, "That depends on how we go about it. I want a film about Balboan soldiers doing their duty unto death. I want you to write a script, or have one written, about the last stand of the BDC in the *Estado Mayor*. I want the film to give three main messages. First, I want the movie to show that the BDC troops in the *Estado Mayor* fought as well as any troops ever have, as well as the gringos did . . . or better. Since I was there at the time, I can assure you that this is the truth. This will tell the people that they are not inferior, not helpless. Second, and without going to the level of the ridiculous, I want the movie to show that the only reason the BDC lost was because they were outnumbered and outgunned, not outfought. Third, and this will probably require the greatest artistry on your part, I want the message sent that while the battle was physically lost, morally it must be seen as a victory."

"There were so few survivors—at the *Estado Mayor*, I mean—that it will be difficult to be accurate."

Hennessey smiled grimly. "So much the better. Without witnesses there will be few to criticize what the story shows if we're broadly and generally realistic. Get copies of some of the movies made by all sides during the Great Global War, *The Fighting O'Rourkes*, maybe. Maybe *Kohlstadt*, too. You'll see what I mean."

Ruiz hesitated. "I would like to do the script myself, but I don't know anything about soldiers or fighting."

"Don't worry about that, Professor. I have several first-class technical experts coming who can assist you. In addition," Hennessey handed over the draft of the history he had been working on with Jimenez, "here's an accurate version of the truth as seen by both sides."

Ruiz flipped through the draft quickly. His English was acceptable for the purpose. "How quickly do you need this done, Mr. Carrera?"

"In the GGW films like this were turned out in as little as three months. I'll give a little more time than that; five months, say. At the end of that time I want to see a rough cut. Can you do the job on five hundred thousand?"

"If I start today, and can keep costs low, which is a very big *if*, then yes."

"Then start today, Professor Ruiz. I'll be in touch."

"You mentioned other projects."

Hennessey nodded. "Ah. Yes. Several, assuming the movie makes a reasonable profit. I need radio and TV propaganda. I need newspaper propaganda. I will want a series of soap operas; '*Novellas*,' you call them. I am thinking of six."

"Concerning?"

"Well, for the first use as a working title *El Rasul*—the Prophet. I want it to be on the oppression and betrayal of Christians under Mohammed when Islam first reared its head on Old Earth. Historical accuracy is unimportant. I want to plant the thought in Balboa that Islam is evil and false in its very roots. For the second, *Los Esclabos*, a romance of Christian lovers torn apart by Moslem slavers. He goes to a galley, she to a harem, to rape, and then to a brothel. For the third, *El Martillo*, I want the turning back of the Moslem tide of conquest at Tours, on Old Earth. Also a romance . . ."

"Why so many romances?" asked the professor.

"Because I want the *women* of Balboa enraged at the very thought of sharing a planet with Salafis. For the fourth, *Lepanto* . . ."

Casa Linda, 22/8/459 AC

With a substantial expenditure of cash, Lourdes, Clean and McNamara had worked a miracle or ten in getting as much of the house ready as they had. All of the floors had been redone, the walls of the common areas on the first floor painted or papered, barring only those that were already paneled. The paneling was old mahogany, individual planks of fine wood, and far too nice to cover. Lourdes was given the task of furnishing the place.

"Use your own judgment," Hennessey told her. "You dress well. I trust your taste. Besides, the people I have coming are used to *army* furniture: often poor quality, almost always tasteless. They'll be impressed if the stuff isn't outright *ugly*. Hmmm . . . try to stay within budget, Okay?"

Lourdes was warmed slightly. *He likes the way I dress. He thinks I have good taste. He . . . he* trusts *me.* She flashed him a brilliant smile, which quickly turned to a frown when he failed even to notice.

Hennessey's own quarters, and some of the common areas, had been filled with some of his own, or rather his and Linda's, furnishings. David had taken some leave from his job and overseen the move. Hennessey now sat on one of those chairs, sipping a scotch on ice. Among other things the CSM had done to prepare the place was to furnish a bar. Hennessey swirled the ice and sniffed, savoring the peaty aroma.

The CSM and Lourdes were currently at the airport picking up the troops. Hennessey thought they might even be on their way back by now; David would see the troops through the *Aduana*. He was filled with a curious sense of—almost—happiness such as he hadn't known in some time. Whether this was because he was soon to see many old friends, because it heralded the start of real work again, or because he was an imperceptible measure closer to his goals, he couldn't have said.

Johnson and Kennison had wired ahead with the names of those they had recruited, the names encoded by prearranged numbers. The list had pleased Hennessey immensely; twenty-four good men—including himself, McNamara, Esterhazy and Clean—were all anyone needed for the early stage of a job like the one he planned. He had them . . . plus Lourdes. *Lourdes? Pretty girl. Nice girl. In another time . . . another life . . . oh, well.* He pushed her from his mind.

Hennessey had wanted to go to the airport but McNamara had talked him out of it. In retrospect, he had realized, the sergeant major was right. It was better for McNamara himself to get the troops, billet them, put out the rules of the house, and then have Hennessey make the grand entrance. The troops had signed on for a military enterprise; the more like a military enterprise this looked, the happier they would be. *Stage management? Not my forte. So I will, for once, listen to someone like Mac who understands it.*

There had been some discussion, too, as to whether or not the troops should come in separately. Ultimately, McNamara had nixed that.

"Too much bot'er. Besides, if t'ey come in openly an toget'er, lookin' like t'ey're supposed to, soldiers, t'e customs and immigration people will be too afraid to say anyt'ing about it . . . for now. But if t'ey come in separately, t'ey would look like a bunch of criminals— damned suspicious, anyway—to anyone who can add t'eir names, origins, and destinations up and come up wit' *us!*"

Hennessey had, eventually, agreed.

From the upper back porch of Hennessey's quarters he could see for some dozens of miles out over the *Mar Furioso*. The smell of Balboan cooking wafted up from the kitchen below and on the other side of the house. It reminded him of Linda, painfully so. He continued to gaze out over the ocean, mulling his plans over in his mind.

Hennessey sat there, just staring at the distant waves and thinking, for perhaps an hour. Then came from below the sound of moving vehicles, two vans and a step van hired for the occasion, grinding up the gravel of the front drive. This pulled him from his reveries. The sergeant major's melodic Maiden Islands voice, loud but not shouting, and the opening and closing of automobile doors, told Hennessey that his new command had arrived.

Inside the first floor foyer, the sergeant major had the troops pile their bags against the wall by the stairs. He then brought them into the living room opposite what even Lourdes was beginning to call "the mess."

Mac said, "Welcome, gentlemen, to your new home. Later, I'll be showin' you to your quarters. For now I want to give you t'e rules of the house and t'e organization. First off, t'e house rules. You are expected to keep your own quarters clean; t'at goes for both officers and noncoms. It ain't because t'e boss can't afford more maids. It's because we want as few outside ears listening in as possible. T'is might change, later.

"Meal times are 0800 to 0900, 1130 to 1230, and 1800 to 1900. T'e kitchen is t'e province of t'e chief cook. She's a tough old bitch, so no snackin'. If you miss a meal, other t'an in t'e line of duty, tough shit. If it's in line o' duty, she can maybe be persuaded.

"Second is t'e schedule. Physical training will be conducted from 0600 to 0715, Monday t'rough Saturday. I will lead it, initially. Starting next week we will begin to rotate leadership of t'e PT sessions. T'e CO has ordered weights. T'ey should be here in a couple of weeks . . . or maybe a bit less. T'ere's a room down in t'e basement we've set aside as a weight room.

"Blendin' in. For t'ose who don't speak Spanish, Miss Lourdes here will be giving lessons from 1930 to 2100 nightly, Mondays t'rough T'ursdays, until you do. T'e rest of t'e time you work on t'e CO's project.

"Saturday afternoons and Sundays are off unless you have duty. Two men, one officer and one NCO, will be on duty during t'e weekend days. One NCO will pull duty from 1800 to 0600 on weekdays. T'e CO and I will not be pulling t'e watch. T'ose who pull t'e weekend duty will have the followin' Monday off. Check t'e schedule on t'e bulletin board, which, as you can see," McNamara jerked his thumb to the rear, "is right behind me. If you are not on duty or workin' you are off and can do what you want. Now, how many of you are married?"

McNamara raised an eyebrow. "Still married, Daugher? Your wife is a saint." Seeing five other hands raised the CSM said, "T'at will be fine. T'e CO is going to have t'e outbuilding, I suppose it used to be servants' quarters, converted as soon as possible to make married quarters. He's also going to put up a few houses for t'e spillover and, eventually, some bachelor quarters. He's going to hire an English speakin' teacher from t'e locals for your kids. T'e school will be in t'e old stables down the hill, once it's ready. Your families are invited to t'e eat in t'e mess when t'ey arrive. Your wives will be expected to help out wit' social occasions at need."

No one objected to that. The few who were married had wives who were used to the unremunerated obligations the military laid upon them.

"T'ere is no rule against drinkin' when not on duty. If you want to have a bottle in your room t'at's no problem. I've set up a bar. Drink prices are posted behind it. If you want to use t'e bar just check off what you took and it will be deducted from your pay. Beer wit' lunch and dinner are free."

That raised a cheer, and not a small one.

One of the men, Siegel, interjected, "Oh, crap. If Hennessey's giving out free beer you *know* this is just gonna *suck*."

"Quite correct, Sig," McNamara agreed. "T'ere ain't no such t'ing as a free lunch . . . or free beer."

"We will not be wearin' uniforms for t'e next several months," the sergeant major continued. "Frankly, we're not even sure yet what t'ose uniforms would look like, t'ough I am pushing t'e CO to go for Tan Tropical Worsted. You are required to look presentable. Haircuts are not optional. If you can stand t'em in t'is heat, mustaches and neatly trimmed beards are encouraged.

"T'e maid will take care of your laundry on days I'll post on t'e board. You are expected to bring it to t'e laundry room yourself.

"Some time next week we'll have t'ree cars and a light truck you can sign out. T'e Phaeton sedan is t'e CO's; leave it alone. If you take a car on personal business you will sign it out from t'e duty NCO and return it wit' a full tank.

"We have no medical personnel. T'e sick will go to Balboa City for treatment. T'ere's a small, first class hospital t'ere used to dealing with FSC types. English speakin' an' everyt'ing."

One man, Daugher, raised a hand. "Weapons, Sergeant Major?"

"Our weapons are limited to two pistols, mine and t'e CO's, and a couple of Samsonov rifles. We'll be gettin' more in a few days. Among other t'ings, we will all be goin' to town tomorrow to apply for permits to carry a weapon concealed. T'e CO is payin'. His brot'er in law will . . . facilitate. T'e CO will also be payin' for your personal sidearms. T'ey will all be forty-fives."

That elicited smiles from everyone. There wasn't a man present who didn't believe that most any pistol was good enough . . . as long as its caliber began with a "four."

"Lastly, t'is. You are to avoid any contact wit' anyone here in Balboa except in line of duty. You may not discuss any aspect of what we do wit' anyone. You will report any attempt to get information about our activities to me. Any questions before I send for t'e CO?"

Seeing there were none, the CSM asked, "Miss Lourdes, would you go get t'e boss, please?"

After Lourdes left, the sergeant major added, "One ot'er t'ing. I don't know if t'e CO has any interest in t'at one. Keep your fuckin' hands off, anyway. T'at means, among ot'ers, you, Daugher."

"Oh, Sergeant Major . . ." Daugher began, plaintively.

"Hands off, boyo."

Lourdes shivered as she left the foyer. *Those men. They look so dangerous there in a group, not at all like Patricio and the sergeant major; they're civilized men even if a bit rough. And the way that tall blond one kept looking at me? I don't think I like him.*

Reaching the door to the porch just off of Hennessey's private quarters, she knocked politely. "Patricio? The sergeant major says he's ready for you now."

Hennessey looked up and gave a friendly smile, friendly and no more than that. "Thank you, Lourdes. I'll take it from here but I would appreciate your checking on dinner, if you would."

"Certainly. Will you need me for anything before dinner?"

"No. No, thank you. Everything should be fine." Hennessey considered that for a moment. "Hmmm. Attend anyway."

A mildly uncomfortable few minutes were spent between Lourdes' departure and the moment McNamara saw Hennessey about to enter the conference room. He announced, "Gentlemen, t'e commander."

Everyone rose to attention as Hennessey walked to the center of the room in front of them. *Yes,* he thought, *this will be a good crew. The most talent I've ever had working for me at any one time, I think.* Before beginning to speak he looked over the assembled men recently arrived. He ordered, "At ease. As you were." Those who had risen resumed their seats.

By the door stood Johnson and Daugher. Tall, blond, strong as an ox, and disgustingly *Aryan* looking, Daugher had personally killed—with his bare hands alone—almost as many people as were in the room and always in "self defense." Johnson was at least as strong, but more restrained.

Framing those two were Soult and Mitchell, more like younger brothers to Hennessey than subordinates. Years before they had been Hennessey's drivers at different times in different units. They looked nothing alike, Soult being rail thin, sharp featured and clean shaven while Mitchell was something of a mustached human fireplug.

Beside Mitchell, short, balding, and wearing glasses, Dan Kuralski's looks were deceiving. However much he might have looked like an aging professor at some small university, his heart and mind were those of a soldier.

Must see about getting Dan remarried while he's here, Hennessey thought. *I wonder if Lourdes can be any help there.*

Next was Carl Kennison. *Irwin Rommel, Robert E. Lee, Heinz Guderian and Ulysses S. Grant could probably not have passed a body fat test. Huang? Zhukov? Tamashita? No way. Welcome to you, too, my chubby little genius.*

However pudgy he looked, Carl could bench press almost three times his body weight. He had also run Hennessey into the dirt on more than a few occasions. Carl had not been picked for either his appearance or his physical strength. Hennessey remembered that in Carl's unusually long time as a second lieutenant he had had the distinction of having received a letter of reprimand once a week for a three-month period from a full colonel or higher—without even once repeating reprimanders. Little things: kicking his company commander in the groin (he had argued "accident" but no one believed it had been anything other than perfectly deliberate), burning down a Federated States Militia brigade headquarters ("Hey, who thought that tent would be so flammable?"), loading forty-six men on a single (stolen) quarter-ton vehicle with trailer and taking them for a drive (*two* letters from that one).

I like a man who can break the rules.

On a chair behind the table sat Aaron Brown, a diminutive tanker—and one of only three blacks in the group. Brown's tank company had been the normal attachment for Hennessey's infantry battalion some years before. Seeing Hennessey's eyes on him, Brown said aloud, *"Es braust unser panzer,* sir."

"Im stuermwind, dahin," Hennessey finished. *Our tanks roar through the stormwind.*

Next to Brown was Michael Morse, a former squad leader for Hennessey. *Okay, so Morse isn't the brightest soldier who ever lived. I'll take an honest man with a good heart who tries really hard before I'll take some glib shithead looking out for Number One.* Hennessey was well pleased that Morse had joined his group.

There was no smile for the next man, just a nod of respect. Hennessey had wanted Michael Bowman in the crew despite the fact that he was a borderline psychotic.

Have to keep that one busy; not give him time to start contemplating his navel. Bowman was as capable as Morse, considerably smarter, but not quite so reliable. *A dangerous man. Well, so are we all.*

Esterhazy—here for only a few days before he had

to return to First Landing where he was watching out for Hennessey's interests—and Clean stood in the back of the room along with several others. Hennessey nodded in turn to "Dutch" Rudel, a chemical officer but also an FS Army Ranger; Greg Harrington, the only other tanker in the group, besides Brown, but much more valuable for his logistics skill than his ability to order a charge; Lawrence Triste, a first rate intelligence officer; and Tom Christian, infantry, but with long experience in personnel administration.

Hennessey was especially pleased to see the men in the last group: "Sig" Siegal, looking like a koala bear in mufti; Fletcher, serious as always; Prince who knew Hennessey's training methods and could be counted on to see them through, and Clinton, whose happy smile belied a fine mind and a meticulous sense of order.

Siegal's brains, linguistic ability—he spoke Spanish, French, German, Italian, Arabic, Turkish and Tagalog—and knowledge of weapons, organizations, and the undeveloped world in general would be indispensable. "Fletch" was a communications man. Prince was an 'expeditor.' Warren Clinton was as conniving a supply man as ever doctored a property book.

Fletcher, Clinton and Siegal were the only new arrivals to have stayed in the army long enough to have retired.

Hennessey looked each one in the eyes before beginning to speak.

"Gentlemen, you smell bad and you're ugly. Jesus, it's good to see you."

That earned a small laugh.

"You've all heard my introductory speech at one time or another. I don't see the need to give it again.

I won't ask you why you decided to come. Your reasons are your own so long as you follow the rules and do your jobs.

"You probably won't get rich here working for me. I think I can promise you that we're going to have a lot of fun over the next several years. Military fun, the only kind worth having for people like us.

"Ranks? Don't worry about mine. Officers retain the ranks and seniority they had in the FS Army. The sergeant major is *the* Sergeant Major. *Don't* fuck with him. Fletch, you were a first sergeant, I believe. You will hold WO4. Former sergeants first class are three's. Former sergeants and staffs are WO1's and 2's respectively. When the time comes to wear insignia that is what you will wear . . . assuming we finally decide on a set of insignia. For now it doesn't matter.

"The mission: We are going to recreate a real army for Balboa, to plan the foundation of something that can be of use to the Federated States at need. The first part of that will be pretty dull. Later, it should get a lot more exciting . . . when we actually can start building and training; better still, when we can deploy and fight. Still, don't expect too much right off. Don't worry about who's paying the bills.

"Organization. We are a staff. I intend for us to set up under something close to the old Sachsen model, not the one the Federated States inherited, if you dig deep enough, from the Frogs of Old Earth. That means that personnel administration, instead of being the 'One,' is the 'Two,' Roman numeral two. The Roman numeral 'One' shop is the Operations, Logistics, and Intelligence office—Ia, Ib, and Ic, respectively.

"Assignments are as follows. Dan, you are the Chief

of Staff. Carl, you are the 'One.' Larry and Sig, you have the Ic, Intel. Harrington has the Ib, Logistics. Mr. Clinton will assist you, Greg. You're also in charge of the household."

Hennessey turned his gaze to Johnson. "Terrence, you are Ia, Operations and Training. Morse, Bowman, Fletcher, Daugher, Prince, and Brown are all in your shop. Likewise you have—and let me introduce—Gary Clean, late of Her Anglic Majesty's engineers and 'Dutch' Rudel, late of the 39th Parachute Division.

"Tom Christian has the II, personnel. Mitchell assists you, Tom. Matthias Esterhazy has some considerable experience in banking. He's our comptroller. The sergeant major is, as stated, *the* Sergeant Major. Sergeant Major, Soult will assist when he's not working for me directly. Lourdes, although normally you would work for Captain Johnson as our Spanish teacher, for now you work for the sergeant major and myself.

"That is all for now. This evening, after chow, I'll give you your immediate work priorities. If you have questions, hold them until then. The sergeant major will show you to your rooms and offices. They're a mess but at least they're furnished. You can thank Lourdes for that. You'll also be doubling up until I can have quarters prepared for the married folks. When you figure out what you need to fix your rooms up, drop a request with Mr. Clinton."

It was a festive time. After all, how often do a group of men get together with a real prospect of renewing their wonderfully misspent youth?

Lourdes and the domestic staff had done a fine job. The dining room—*Why did Patricio insist on calling it the mess?* she had wondered. *It's not a mess at all.*—was bedecked with flowers and wreaths. Candles burned unnecessarily in sconces.

Table space had been a problem. Hennessey's old dining room table, his and Linda's, had been large enough for twelve with chairs to match. Lourdes had brought in a card table suitable for four, and moved in another one from the kitchen that could handle eight or even ten in a pinch. Crystal, silver and china had had to be a mix of three different sets each.

Still, as Hennessey admitted to himself, *the girl has done wonders. Note, though, we need to knock out a wall, expand the mess, and get regular seating for thirty-six to forty-eight.*

Daugher took one look at the tables and announced what they all thought. "This is some good shit."

The table was garlanded with tranzitree flowers the women had picked from a patch growing halfway from the house to the sea to the north. The flowers were harmless. Bluegum wax candles burned in sconces in three spots along the walls, centered and at both ends. Many people liked the smell of bluegum candles. The aroma they gave off was something like, although milder than, myrrh.

This being an occasion of some celebration, dinner centered on a frightfully large turkey, roasted and stuffed, an equally large prime rib from the *Finca* Carrera, and an impressive ham from the same source. To the usual trimmings for these were added some typical Balboan dishes: empanadas, a sort of meat turnover, fried yuca, a fibrous tuber, poisonous if not properly prepared but superior in taste to potato, and *maiz rojo*, which was *not* corn though it *was* red.

From the market the cook had obtained half a dozen steaks from a freshly caught baby *carcharodon megalodon*. These she'd soaked in milk and then broiled with butter and garlic. Next to the meg steaks sat a tureen of *sancocho*, or stew. The meat in the stew was a mix of normal beef with several kinds of reptile not to be found on Old Earth and becoming rare on Terra Nova.

The bread was made from a seed taken from a plant that resembled an orange-colored sunflower, except that unlike the sunflower it never grew above two feet in height. The plant, like the *maiz rojo*, the tranzitree and the bluegum, was one of those that were either native to Terra Nova or had also been transplanted by the Noahs from somewhere besides Old Earth. Before being ground the seed resembled nothing so much as very tiny corn kernels. Once ground they made quite a good bread though, because of the flour's high gluten content, nothing that resembled cornbread. The bread tended to a buttery yellow color. The plant and its flour were called "Chorley."

As it *was* a sort of Thanksgiving for people who had never again expected to be able to do the work they felt they were born to, wine was served, along with the beer. When dessert was finished, and plates cleared away, the sergeant major lit a candle, the "smoking lamp." The cook brought in a tray of single malt scotch with glasses just as the smoke began to curl to the ceiling.

Standing, Hennessey began to speak.

"Everybody moved in, all right?" he asked. Seeing the general assent, he continued. "Notebooks ready?" He paused to allow the men to get out writing materials.

For the few who pulled out electronic ones, he said, "No E-Slates. Security. Take a notebook and pen."

He waited until they had and began, "Good. We have two initial tasks, one minor, and one major. The minor one is ourselves. You've all had a chance to see what your quarters and offices need. You'll fix them yourselves on your own 'copious free time.'"

That was a joke that spanned solar systems and centuries. It received the laugh it deserved.

"A little more complex is the question of arms, equipment, and uniforms. Uniforms will have to wait. We couldn't wear them for a while yet, anyway. Sorry. For arms, we need enough to defend ourselves against minor threats and possibly to take out a minor target ourselves. Let me make clear here that, no, I have no one and nothing in particular in mind. It just pays to be prepared."

Hennessey focused his attention on Bowman and Daugher. "So, no, you two, it is *extremely* unlikely I will be asking you to kill anyone any time soon. Calm down."

Hennessey turned his gaze to Harrington. "Greg, I'm going to put you in touch with my brother-in-law, the guy who eased your way through customs. He's in the Civil Force. Good kid. Have him put you in touch with a black market supplier. I believe he knows at *least* one. I want two antiarmor weapons and a fair supply of ammunition. Get us two light machine guns, it doesn't matter which, and a dozen and a half rifles, Samsonovs would do but don't feel bound. Make sure that the rifles match the LMGs, whatever you buy. Get starlight scopes for each. Also get four or so pair of night vision goggles. Don't buy Volgan for those. I also want two

sniper rifles, Dracos, M-12s, or even bolt-action hunting rifles. Oh, yes, get us a machine gun the caliber of
which matches the sniper rifles. Don't buy a Federated
States MG-6, no matter how cheap it is; the odds of
it being just plain worn out are too good to risk. Get
a forty-five and shoulder holster for each man. If the
dealer has silencers for the pistols, get one for each and
have the pistols threaded.

"Also, the day after tomorrow I'll give you a check to
go to town and get a pickup and three passenger cars.
You'll also need to pick up the Phaeton I ordered a few
days ago. Task the One shop as needed for drivers.

"When you're downtown it should be possible to buy
twenty-four sets of body armor . . . hmmm . . . make it
twenty-five; get a slender one for Lourdes, too. Don't
scrimp on those. Get the best available. Gentlemen,
Lourdes, give Captain Harrington your sizes before
going to sleep tonight.

"Greg, I also want you to look into the possibility of
buying a boat, forty or so feet and fast. Don't commit
to it yet, though. Look around a bit. As a matter of
fact, we are probably—no, certainly—going to need
merchant ships as well. Look into it.

"The maid could probably use another washer and
dryer. See about getting a big freezer for the kitchen.
It's got to be cheaper than paying someone to do a
daily grocery run the way you fuckers are bound to
overeat."

Harrington looked mildly distracted as he scratched
notes on a pad. "Can I borrow Miss Lourdes for a
translator?"

"Sure."

Hennessey turned to Johnson.

"Terrence, you are tasked to help with the making of a propaganda *cum* recruiting film. We'll discuss that in more detail later.

"So much for ourselves, for now."

Hennessey began to pace around the room as he spoke to the group as a whole. "The *major* task, however, is to design an army for Balboa for the future. That is what will consume most of our efforts for the next few months. Dan, as chief of staff I want you to direct that. Start with the assumption Balboa could, were the funding available, raise and sustain a force of about thirty thousand regulars, maybe ninety thousand reservists and perhaps three times that in militia. Assume that between Balboa and the rest of Colombia del Norte we can find as many as thirty thousand volunteers a year. The reservists and militia are critical because you just can't politically trust professional Latin soldiers. Eventually, given the fantastic degree of governmental corruption, they *will* overthrow their governments. The reservists and militia are to counter that.

"That size force is the illogical and unreasonable extreme," Hennessey continued. "Start there anyway. Once you have done that, shrink it to what is possible; a single corps of about fifty or sixty thousand that is capable of deploying one division of eleven to fourteen thousand in support of the Federated States in the war now ongoing. Match the huge force to the smaller corps so that if it ever *did* become necessary the corps could be expanded with minimal confusion, battalions expanding to regiments, regiments becoming divisions, and so on. Again, that's just in case the illogical and unreasonable come to pass."

Everyone present, with the exception of McNamara, Esterhazy and Clean who had heard Hennessey thinking out loud for some time, was a little shocked. Not a few wondered if their boss had flipped. He had, of course, but not in the way they were thinking.

"The corps is the important thing," Hennessey said. "Note carefully, however, that I can't pay for it now and neither can Balboa."

Okay, so he hasn't quite flipped completely . . . in the way they had been thinking.

"What I want you to do, Dan and the I-Shop, with a big assist from the II, is design it carefully and completely. Then further shrink that. I don't know what I *can* pay for, not yet anyway. So shrink it in four forms: to a division of about eleven to fourteen thousand, to a large brigade of about eight thousand, to a regular sized brigade of about four or five thousand, and to a combat team of around two thousand. Which we decide to go with will depend on funding."

Okay, that's reasonable . . . but a frightful amount of work.

"I would have told you to optimize this first force for Pashtia. But I think that is going to kick off within a couple of weeks—"

Triste interrupted. "My sources say three, Pat."

"Fine, three then. It will in any case be too soon for us to have anything to offer to the FS. So the question is, 'Who's next?' Larry?"

Triste didn't have to think. He already knew. "Sumer," he announced with absolute certainty in his voice. "Sumer . . . but not soon. I am thinking maybe early in 461. In theory it could be summer of 460 but the heat . . ." Triste's voice trailed off.

"I concur," Hennessey said. "Sumer in early 461. It will take at least that long for the Federated States to build up the logistics in al Jahara for a—what do you think, Larry?—a four division invasion."

"About that," Triste agreed. "Or maybe only three plus maybe two Anglian brigades or possibly even a full division of the Royal Army along with some odds and ends from other contributors. All will, I am sure, be most welcome to help out and there is hardly a country on industrialized Terra Nova that hasn't lost some people to the TNTO attacks. For poorer allies the Federated States will gladly foot the bill, I am sure."

"Mmm . . . yeah," Hennessey half agreed. "The FS will be happy to pay the operational costs for anyone joining in the fight. I don't want them to pay for us, or not yet anyway. I think our bargaining position, for later on, will be much better if we—if I—can pay the initial costs."

Esterhazy interjected, "You are right about zat, Pat. But have you considered just vhat a fair price would be for the FS to pay for a . . . oh, say . . . a full division of Balboan troops?"

Hennessey pulled out a cigarette and lit it. McNamara, and not for the first time, thought that his chief would kill himself young if he didn't cut down.

"I've thought about it and made a few inquiries, Matthias, yes. For the FS to maintain one full division overseas in action, even low intensity action, requires them to keep three divisions on the books. So one division deployed costs three divisions worth of normal pay and operating expenses. That's about fourteen billion drachma a year. The cost of one division at war at low intensity is maybe—frankly no one I spoke to was quite sure—sixteen or seventeen billion a year more. Annuitized retirements, long-term medical care, disability payments to the badly wounded, etcetera, would probably add another four billion to that. I *think* the total cost is about thirty-five billion per committed division, per year. And that says nothing about the political costs of combat casualties or the benefit, propaganda-wise, that comes from having a strong ally in the fight."

"We won't have to charge them anything like their own cost," Hennessey said as he flicked an ash onto his plate. "We can pay the Balboans maybe forty percent of what a soldier from the FS gets and they would still consider it princely. Lourdes?"

"I don't know," she answered. "What is the pay for a soldier in the FS?"

"A new private receives about twelve hundred drachma a month," Hennessey answered. "Plus room and board."

The girl did some quick calculations in her agile mind then said, "We have unemployment here that fluctuates between fifteen and twenty percent, and most of that is concentrated among young men. *Their* unemployment rate is over fifty percent. Four hundred and eighty drachma a month would be considered, along with room and board, very good, yes. And those boys are not unemployed because they are lazy or untalented. In fact, our literacy rate is almost one hundred percent, considerably higher than in the FS," she added, not without some pride. "People here are unemployed because they lack connections, not because they lack ability."

"I know. So, gentlemen, we can pay a lot less and still be considered generous. Food is cheap here, too," Hennessey added, pointing to the remains of the bird. "That turkey you just massacred cost about a third of what it would have in the FS. Moreover, our troops will not have the expectation of the best, most cutting edge, equipment. In all, I think we can pay for a corps of fifty or sixty thousand, with a division deployed and fighting, for about four to four and a half billion a year."

"If that's true, Pat," observed Esterhazy, "then you could charge the FS nothing more than the cost of one of their divisions deployed, say sixty percent of their total cost, and still make a fortune."

"Even at half," Hennessey corrected, "we can make a fortune."

"Where's all that money going to go, Boss?" Daugher asked.

"Mostly we'll plow it back into Balboa," he answered. "This war will last a very long time. Ideally, I would like, before I die, to set things up so that the force we build can continue that war indefinitely and independently, without having to ask for help from anyone.

"Anyway, enough about fuzzy finances. Back to the concrete. Dan, do the whole Table of Organization: numbers, equipment, ranks, individual gear, training base, et cetera. Maximize ground combat forces. Design, to the extent that is possible, for things the FS Army is either not good at or lacks the capability for. For example, they are always short infantry, so design for primarily infantry missions: counterinsurgency, city fighting, reduction of complex fortifications. Plan for a very austere logistic and admin tail. I have a preference for Volgan equipment, where it will do. With them having gone about half belly up I think there will be a lot of useful military equipment for sale in the near future for cheaps. Nonetheless, consider a mix of Volgan, FS and Tauran Union equipment. Zion may have some useful stuff, too."

Kuralski looked up from note taking and asked: "What kind of fire support? What kind of control system? ATADS?" This, the Advanced Tactical Artillery Data System, was a digitalized system for controlling and massing artillery fire. *No one* entirely trusted it.

"No, Dan," Hennessey answered. "How's the quote go: 'Real soldiers don't trust ATADS'? Number of guns and throw weight are the semi-developed world's solution to the artillery battle. Now that you mention it, though, put the forward observers in the combat support/ weapons company of the maneuver battalions. I've never liked the idea of people who have to fight together being strangers to one another."

Hennessey continued. "Assume that we will never be able to afford a high tech battlefield communications system. No microwaves, few or no frequency hopping radios. Regular radios and wire are what they need."

Kuralski observed, "I'll need a computer to keep track of all of this. It will save months of work."

"Fine. Have the log shop get you one, the best available. And don't scrimp on computer security. On second thought, Greg, better make it about six. This isn't our only concern."

Hennessey turned to Rudel. "Dutch, don't worry about NBC"—nuclear, biological and chemical— "warfare beyond defense, individual protective masks and suits, recon, and some decontamination capability. This isn't that kind of country. Worry about defensive training.

"Nauseating as the thought is, I half expect to have to call whatever force we build 'Military Police.' Don't let the name fool you. It's to be a combat organization, having within it all arms and services. And it has to be ready to deploy and to fight by early 461."

Everybody looked doubtful about that. A mere year and a half to go from a standing start to something resembling an army in battle? Ridiculous! Absurd! Impossible!

Except they'd seen Hennessey do impossible things before.

Hennessey paused briefly, then added, "In the back of your minds, I want you to keep the concept of a 'nation in arms' . . . just in case.

"A last word before we adjourn for the evening. For various reasons I have found it useful to go by my wife's maiden name, 'Carrera.' It's a name of some local importance. It also became one of mine—here, at least—the day I married her. Mostly it may help to allay suspicions about our obviously gringo origin. Force yourselves to think of me that way from now on: *Carrera.*"

Hennessey tossed off the dregs of his drink, then grinned evilly. "The fucking wogs are going to remember it, I promise you."

Casa Linda, 5/9/459 AC

"Sir, there are four Civil Force officers and an NCO here to see you."

Jamey Soult stood at a respectful attention, a habit Carrera had never succeeded in breaking him of. "Shall I have the rest of the boys stand to?"

"Quietly, Jamey. Have Sergeant Major collect up five or six of them. Silenced pistols. You stay with them. Have them keep out of sight and earshot. I'll call if I need you."

Soult left quickly to summon aid. *Those people go after the boss and there'll be hell to pay; I promise.*

Carrera walked down the stairs to meet the men who were very likely there to arrest him. *Why the hell didn't David let me know this was coming? He should be in a position to know.*

When Carrera entered the living room where the Balboans waited, he relaxed immediately. They all had the look of men with no intention of arresting anyone. They stood up when he entered the room.

Taking the Balboans in with a single glance, Carrera saw that they were a major, about as high a rank as existed in the Civil Force that had replaced the BDC, two captains, a lieutenant and a sergeant major. He knew none of them by sight, however their uniforms all bore name tags that identified them.

The major's name was Fernandez. He was small, slight and mildly stoop shouldered. Withal, he looked like nothing so much as a pharmacist. Certainly, his appearance gave no hint of the frightful reputation of which David Carrera had warned.

After shaking hands, Fernandez asked, "*Señor*, are you the same Carrera that has been supporting the families of those killed in the 447 Invasion?"

"I am."

"May we ask why you are providing for them out of your own pocket? And why now, rather than before?"

"Now," Carrera answered, "because I only recently

acquired the wherewithal to help them. As to why, for no reason than that I thought it wrong for the parents, wives, sons, and daughters of brave men to go in want if I could do something about it."

Besides, it may be that I am to blame for their loss. In part, anyway.

"I see," said the major. "An unusual generosity. You are from the FSC, are you not?"

"I am, though I make my home here."

Fernandez began a staccato interrogation, pausing to bite on his lower lip between questions. "Why should you do that? Why should you come here now? What do you intend here? We know that you have a small army here on the premises with you. We also know that you were once a military officer, that you were part of the invasion force, and that you lost your family in the Terra Nova Trade Organization attack. I have investigated. And no, I have not *yet* informed the government."

Hennessey—no, "Carrera" now—said simply, "Revenge."

Major Fernandez smiled. "That is a worthy goal. It was also worthy to plant your brother-in-law in my department. However, though your brother-in-law is a nice kid, he has no business in intelligence . . . so please get him moved."

"I don't know where else to send him."

"Major Valdez, from 5th Company of the Civil Force, will take him. He said to me, just a few days ago, 'I'm down one platoon leader, anyway, as soon as I fire the stupid son of a *rabiblanco* bitch who's wrecking my *chingada* third platoon now.'"

The other officers with Fernandez tried to control

smiles. They failed. Everyone in the Civil Force knew about Valdez, his general loathing of pure whites (though he loathed pure indians, too), and his foul mouth.

Patricio Carrera agreed, "Okay. Fine. David should be glad of the change. I hadn't intended to offend anyone. I just wanted to keep tabs on things."

"You didn't offend me. It is impossible to offend me. Unless you're a Piña or someone riding on his coattails or some gringo trying to run our country. *That* would offend me."

"You do not care for your former 'Supreme Leader'?"

Fernandez gave an evil, angry laugh. "No. Not me. Not my men. Not anyone in my department. Piña? When the going got tough that cowardly son of a bitch got going."

"Oh. I see your point. Major Fernandez . . . I will *not* run out on you. But I will tell you that in the course of avenging myself on the stinking wogs I am going to help make Balboa free, really free, for the first time in centuries. That . . . and I know what I'm doing."

Carrera paused, then made a decision. "Follow me, please. Just you. Say nothing."

With a shrug, Fernandez motioned for his men to remain while he followed Carrera downstairs to the staff area. It was empty at the time, as McNamara and the other on duty were currently upstairs checking pistols and ammunition.

Carrera flicked on a light. Fernandez saw three entire walls each covered with an intricate diagram of lines, circles, boxes and numbers. There were many gaps in the diagram.

"*This* is why I'm here. I don't want to 'run your country.' I just want to help it build an army; like any other country has. This is part of that, though it's a long way from complete. Tell me, Major Fernandez, have you ever even been in a *real* army? No, I thought not. Not your fault. But you do not, cannot, know what goes into creating one. Do you know what schools you need? What equipment? How many spare parts of what type? Ammunition? How many trucks to operate at a given distance from a port? How many drivers and mechanics? How much does it all cost? How long will it take to do X? Is Y what you should really be doing?

"I *do* know. And I'm here to show you . . . you and the rest of the old Defense Corps."

Fernandez moved closer and looked over one of the diagrams. He noted that there were many blank spaces. *This Carrera doesn't have all the answers then. But I didn't even know the questions.* He considered this. At length he nodded his head slowly. "Perhaps you do know. Perhaps you do, indeed. How can I help?"

"In many ways, Major. Notably by keeping the government off my ass and out of my business. And by giving me whatever you can to make them support this effort."

"My department can help with this."

"Then *viva* Balboa, Major. Will you and your men join me for a drink?"

"Thank you, sir, no. My men are still on duty and I need to get home to my daughter. I am a widower, you see, and I'm all she has."

INTERLUDE

1 January, 2050, Brussels, Belgium, European Union

Margot Tebaf awakened in a strange bed. There was nothing particularly unusual in this; she and her husband had an understanding.

She risked a glance at the other form in the bed. It was hidden by the covers. *Hmmm. Large, so probably male. But who was it?*

Margot wracked her brain frantically. There had been a lot of champagne, stronger drink as well. Well, it *was* New Years, after all. She'd been talking to someone . . . some expert in demographics and migration patterns. What had he said?

Oh, yes. It's coming back now. He said that this new planet may be the answer to all our problems. And not just the EU's problems, but the UN's, the progressive movement's. Everything.

We are losing talented and fertile young people to the United States, Canada, Australia, New Zealand and South Africa. They produce there, in the cutthroat, dog-eat-dog competition of the capitalist system. That makes our system look bad by comparison—never mind that it is much the fairest and most gentle system in the history of the world—and pulls even more young people away.

But if the new planet can be used to attract those tired of Europe and, better still, if it can also be used to attract a number of those stinking Americans out of their own stolen homeland, the drain on us will lessen and they will begin to lose some of their power and their arrogance.

Margot muttered aloud, "Oh, how I *hate* those bastards."

The body next to her stirred. "What's that?"

"I was thinking about what you said last night . . ." She found, to her consternation, that she couldn't produce a name to go with the body she had spent the night with.

"Dominique, Margot. It's Dominique," the body answered, apparently unperturbed.

"Ah, yes. Dominique. Explain to me again, please—I had *so* much to drink last night—how we can use the new planet to hurt the United States and save ourselves and the Earth?"

"Well, it would take a lot," Dominique admitted. "We would need . . . oh . . . call it one hundred ships, more or less, each capable of carrying fifty or so thousand colonists."

"Ships, yes, but how big?"

"I've asked someone in the navy about that. He told me to think of the size of the United States' supercarriers or the very large ships that carry crude oil. Built in space because otherwise we would never get them off the Earth."

"We couldn't afford that," Margot said, suddenly looking very glum.

"No, no, of course not," Dominique admitted. "Certainly we could not ourselves. But we, China, Japan and the United States could, collectively."

"Why should they participate in a project that ultimately hurts them?" Margot asked.

"Because in the short term it helps them," the other answered, reasonably. "Have you ever known an elected politician who really thinks long term? No. Long-term thinking requires what we have here in Europe, an elite that cannot be turned out of office over the latest blip in the economic forecast.

"It's more than that though, too, Margot. If we can get some substantial numbers of the more extreme Moslems to leave Earth—though I confess I have no good idea yet how to do that—the more moderate ones will make life uncomfortable for the extremists who remain. Then they'll leave, too."

"Wouldn't *that* be wonderful," she mused aloud.

"Indeed," Dominique agreed.

Margot admired such clear thinking. She pulled the covers down and bent her head over to show how much she admired it.

CHAPTER EIGHT

If you prick us do we not bleed? If you tickle us do we not laugh? If you poison us do we not die? And if you wrong us shall we not revenge?
—William Shakespeare, *The Merchant of Venice*

Zabol, Pashtia, Terra Nova, 7/9/459 AC

Even through fifty meters of rock and soil the men below could *still* feel the bombs going off overhead. They shook the ground, making the lights flicker and raising dust to fill the narrow cramped corridors and rooms. No matter, the cave was deep and safe. Even at its entrance, where the FS Air Force could toss bombs with frightening precision, strong baffles prevented any harm from reaching those lower. Besides, there were dozens of false entrances for each real one, though they were tolerably hard to see. Even the FS had *some* limits on their ability to bomb.

Feeling quite safe from the bombing, Abdul Aziz ibn Kalb still withered under the glare of his chief.

Not that the glare was directed at him personally; no, not at all. The glare was directed at a report just received from the organization's cell in, of all places, Balboa. Interference on the part of the *Ikhwan*'s great adversary had delayed receipt for some time.

"How dare they? How *dare* they? By the nine and ninety beautiful names of Allah how damned dare they shoot down five believers and beat a sixth to death? How dare they even think of joining this new 'crusade' against us? Little pissants!"

Aziz forced himself to stand tall and corrected, "*They* didn't. Just one man killed six Salafis in an outlying town. "Self defense," the local police said. Maybe it was, too."

"No matter; the lives of any number of infidels are as nothing compared to the life of even one of the true believers. And then there's this other swine trying to raise political support for aiding the Columbians. Well, we'll just have to put a stop to that."

The chief rubbed worry beads between thumb and forefinger. "What cells do we have in Balboa?" he asked.

Aziz had an answer ready, of course. He'd expected the question. "We have one 'expeditor' cell, one informational cell, three direct action cells and one command cell. Twenty-three people total."

"The direct action cells? What are their missions?"

Again, Aziz had the answers ready to hand. "One of them is trained for ship seizure and pilotage. They were intended to be able to grab a ship and ram the locks of the Balboa Transitway. But it has to be a special ship, one carrying explosives or LNG, or perhaps fertilizer, to really do damage."

"Any such ship coming through the Transitway soon?" the chief asked.

"No, Sheik, we really weren't thinking about attacking Balboa for a few years. The other cells are directed at, in the one case, the trans-Isthmian pipeline that sends oil from the State of McKinley to the Shimmering Sea for shipment to the Federated States' west coast. Heating oil mostly. In the others, they are bombers. Their status report says they are capable of detonating two to four truck bombs."

The chief mulled a bit. "Pipelines and truck bombs. Hmmm . . ."

Casa Linda, 21/9/459 AC

"Don't sweat it, Dan. You and the boys have worked miracles."

Despite the words, Carrera could not keep the disappointment out of his voice. It was true; the staff *had* worked miracles. They knew the required personnel and equipment strength down to the last item. By dint of sixteen hour days—eighteen hours, some days—they had designed tables of organization and equipment for every required formation. They had devised detailed programs of instruction for officers, senior noncoms, and enlisted men. They had charted out training areas, ranges, and had at least a tentative plan for barracks. They had the sketch of an adequate recruiting organization. Working with Jimenez, Parilla and Fernandez, they had most of the core cadre sketched out as well: mostly good people with only a few politically necessary hacks.

What they could not do was take that cadre of officers and senior noncoms, having only the most limited of combat arms experience, with no background in armored warfare, artillery, combat engineering, chemical warfare, mountain operations, counter-guerilla warfare, complex staff planning, a *host* of esoteric military skills and attributes, and make them competent overnight.

Apologetically, Kuralski answered, "Three years, Pat . . . or maybe four at the outside. *That* we could do ourselves. But not in fifteen months. Not in time for the spring, 461 campaign." Kuralski hesitated, then said, "Pat, outside of a couple of us we don't even speak enough Spanish yet to train them."

"I understand. Not your fault." Carrera sighed. "Go hit the rack, Dan. Maybe something will turn up."

Carrera closed his eyes and put his head in his hands, elbows resting on the kitchen table.

Before leaving, Kuralski turned and said, "Pat, Daugher had a death in his family in Dragonback Pass. He's asked if he can take a couple of weeks' leave. Bowman wanted to go with him, said he'd never been to Dragonback. Any problem?"

Carrera, despondent, said, "Sure. Let them go. No problem."

Satisfied, Kuralski left Carrera alone with his troubles.

Lourdes found him there like that, unmoving, head still in his hands. She padded in on bare feet, silently. At least, if Carrera had heard he gave no sign. She thought, *How very sad and tired he looks. Poor man.*

She reached a hand to pat him lightly on the back. The hand never touched; when it was a bare inch from him she drew it back. He had never invited her to touch him in any way. She didn't feel right doing so now.

Instead, Lourdes backed off, walked around the wooden table and took a chair opposite her boss.

That, Carrera heard. Though his eyes remained closed he recognized her familiar sounds. He said, "Hello, Lourdes. What's keeping you awake so late?"

"Nothing, really," the girl answered. "I came down for a glass of milk and found you here. What's wrong, Patricio?"

Eyes still shut, chin resting on steepled fingers, he answered, "Everything."

"Do you want to talk about it?"

"Want? No. Need? Maybe so. I am trying to build a force to avenge my family. You know this. We have made some pretty good strides in that regard, too. But I have three problems . . . and they appear insurmountable."

Lourdes made an inquisitive sound. Carrera continued.

"First off, no matter what we have planned, the staff informs me—and I believe them—that there is no way for us to put a useful force into the war in a timely fashion. 'Three years,' they tell me, 'maybe four.' Then there's Parilla. He thought he could swing the government around to supporting us. He can't. He's pulled every string, called in every favor, and we're still short the votes we need. Lastly, my damned cousin. I could afford to bribe enough politicians if I had control of my Uncle Bob's estate. I do not. Cuz found a lawyer who would . . . at least I guess he would . . . support him for an estate fight. So it looks like everything we have done so far is wasted."

Eyes still shut tight Carrera moved his right hand to massage both sides of his nose with index finger and thumb.

"It looks pretty hopeless."

Lourdes chewed on her lower lip, thinking. "I can't think of anything to do about the will or the government, Patricio, but . . . oh what's that word in English?"

"Try Spanish," Carrera suggested.

"No, no," Lourdes insisted. "I don't think we have a similar word. I'll remember it. I'll . . . *outsourcing*?"

Carrera's eyes flew wide. The irises swiveled like twin turrets to focus on the girl. "Say that again."

"Outsourcing. You know, where you hire outside . . ."

"I know what it means." A trace of excitement crept into his voice, along with some self-contempt. "I have many flaws, Lourdes. One of these is pride. One of the effects of that pride is a tendency not to look outside myself or whatever group I control for help when I need it. Lourdes, go wake Dan, would you? Then call the airport and get me a flight for ummm . . . where the hell did I read Abogado had settled down to? Ah, I recall. I need a flight for Phoenix Rising, in the Federated States. Hmmm. For the day after tomorrow, I think. Lastly, make me an appointment for tomorrow afternoon with a corporate law firm in Ciudad Balboa."

Lourdes nodded and got up to go.

Carrera held up a hand to stop her. "And Lourdes? Neither I nor all my damned geniuses could come up with that trick. But you did. Thank you."

Unsure as to quite why, Lourdes felt a bounce in her step and happiness in her heart as she left the kitchen.

City Recycling Plant, Phoenix Rising, Oglethorpe, FSC, 23/9/459 AC

Some things in human civilization are eternal. Among these is the tedious, tiresome and, above all, odiferous task of waste disposal. Carrera could smell the plant from five miles away. Worse, the speed of the auto was greater than olfactory fatigue could deal with. The stink only grew worse.

Nor had it ended by the time he was invited into the office of Major General (Retired) Kenneth Abogado.

"It was good of you to see me, General, on such short notice," Carrera said, "and especially right after Thanksgiving."

General Abogado merely smiled. (Though perhaps "shit-eating grin" described the smile better.) He smiled first because it pleased him to be remembered as a soldier and as a general officer; not everyone with whom he came in contact had the good manners to do so. He smiled second that an offer had been made to him— better said, suggested to him—that might, just might, help him escape from the constant smell of human shit being recycled. Life had been hard for Abogado since leaving the army—hard, disappointing and degrading.

"My name is Pat Hennessey, though I go by Carrera now. I doubt you remember me, but we've met."

Abogado frowned in concentration. He stared for a moment at Carrera's eyes.

"I remember now," he said. "You're the one who lectured me when you were a lieutenant on the problems with subcaliber ranges; how the other full scale things that visibly ruined the training effect.

"And you had the beautiful wife," he announced, remembering a single dance at a single officers' event with the single most beautiful woman he had ever seen.

"Yes. The general has a good memory. As for my wife . . . 'had' is the word," Carrera said bitterly. "In a way that's why I am here."

Abogado started to open a desk drawer where he kept a pistol. Then he remembered he had never even considered trying to sleep with this man's wife. He closed the drawer and relaxed.

Carrera explained to Abogado, coldly—no tears now, no emotion showing through his armor—what had happened to his family.

"Son, that's a tough break," was all Abogado could say.

"Very tough," Carrera agreed, nodding. "Nor am I going to just take it. But I seem to have hit a wall." In a few sentences he explained what he had done to date in Balboa and what he was trying to do.

"I have several problems, but only one of those can you help me with."

"Help? How?"

"You are familiar with Professional Military Personnel Resources and what they do?"

"I know about them," Abogado spat out bitterly. "They shut me out. Just shut me out. And me the best trainer of infantry in the goddamned army, too."

"I'm not a huge fan of PMPR, either, General. And yes, you were very good," Carrera agreed. "Would you like the chance to train soldiers again?"

Ordinarily Abogado would have played a little hard to get, to sweeten the deal, whatever it was. However, at about that time the wind outside shifted and an overpowering whiff of recycled and recycling human feces assaulted his nose. "Where do I sign?"

"Not so simple," Carrera cautioned. "You haven't even heard what I need."

"Seems obvious. You need someone to train and lead an expeditionary force."

Carrera sighed. He hated to disappoint the old man. A bastard Abogado may have been, but he'd been very kind and patient with up-and-coming lieutenants. Yet . . . Abogado *was* old. He might have been quite something in his younger days. Indeed, he had been quite something. But he could never stand that kind of pace again.

Carrera sighed and shook his head again. "No, sir. We have a commander already. And a deputy. And a staff. What I need is a school. You have done that, and done it very well. That's why I am here; to offer to let you do so again."

Abogado kept the disappointment off of his face and out of his voice. Yet, *I am not too old,* a part of his mind insisted. *I am not!*

"Details?" he asked resignedly.

"In the big picture," Carrera said, "I am having a lawyer down there form a corporation. It will be called FMTGRB: 'Foreign Military Training Group, Republic of Balboa.' Inc., of course. Or, rather 'S.A.' Means the same thing.

"If you accept my offer, the day-to-day running of this corporation will be yours, within certain guidelines my people in Balboa are working on."

"And this corporation is to do precisely what?"

"Well, I am willing to listen to reason on this but basically I need a group to train officers, warrants and senior noncoms. I need one shortened Command and

General Staff College course for about one hundred officers. Then I need that CGSC to morph itself into a general purpose, all-arms advanced course for about another hundred. Then I need it to morph again into a combined Officer Candidate School and Officer Basic Course. After that, this group is to change back into a small CGSC, a small Advanced Course, and a continuing OCS."

"Clear enough. I would need maybe twenty . . . oh, possibly twenty-four good men for that. I could find them, I'm sure."

Carrera nodded. This was close enough to his own estimate. "Second, I need a Noncommissioned Officers Academy. We will need to take Senior NCOs and bring them into the real military world, take middle and junior NCOs and prep them to be platoon leaders and platoon sergeants—"

Abogado interrupted, "You mean send them to OCS?"

Carrera shook his head in an emphatic *no*. "They'll need much of the same training, yes, but I intend to follow the Sachsen model in this and keep a very small officer corps, about three percent of strength. Most platoons will be led by NCOs. Anyway, call this Group Two of FMTG; the officer group being Group One.

"Then I need something like FS Army Ranger School—call it, 'Cazador School'—to take the best of new privates and select from them those who have that . . . oh . . . certain something that makes for a really good officer or senior NCO.

"The last groups are a little fuzzy right now. My staff is still working on requirements. Basically, though, we'll need a center for training and testing of large battalions or small regiments, a service support training

group that will also train specialists and warrant officers, a small naval school, a flight school for both
helicopters and fixed wing aircraft, and you will need
a small headquarters yourself."

Abogado whistled. "Tall order."

"Yes. Very. Can you do it?" Carrera asked.

The old general raised one quizzical eyebrow. "Can
you fund it?"

"Not yet," Carrera conceded. "Rather, I can fund
part of it now, but not all, not just yet. That must
await developments."

"You mean, 'Don't quit my day job,' right?" Abogado's voice was heavy with disappointment.

Carrera pondered for a moment. "No. Quit your
day job. Get away from the smell of shit and come
back to the land of flowers. You, at least, I can support for a term of years."

"Let me make a few calls, first. Is that all right?"

"Surely, General. But, to be fair, I ought to tell
you I have appointments over the next two days with
Generals Schneider at the Catlett Foundation and
Friesland on the other side of Phoenix Rising."

Abogado scowled. "Cancel 'em. I'll take the job.
By the way, what does it pay?"

Carrera smiled broadly despite the smell of sew-
age. "Enough."

First Landing, Hudson, FSC, 23/9/459 AC

"I have had about enough of this place," announced
Bowman. Daugher muttered agreement under his
breath.

The two *had* flown to Dragonback. There they'd met some of Daugher's old motorcycle gang and borrowed a car. Then they'd driven to First Landing in an all-nighter.

Daugher and Bowman hated the city, hated the stink, hated the noise. They hated the silly disguises they felt called upon to wear—yuppie glasses and false mustaches, a slight amount of stage makeup, and practiced walks. Likewise they hated Hennessey's nasty little cousin for putting in jeopardy their own best hopes for the life they wanted to lead.

(For they still could not think of him as Carrera. For too many years had he been "that motherfucker, Hennessey" for them to change easily.)

They were following Eugene now. He hadn't been hard to find and he was not hard to follow as he walked from his upscale apartment to some unknown destination. Though the streets were dark, there was just about enough light to make out Eugene's dainty mince.

They almost lost Eugene when he turned a street corner. Racing to catch up they saw no sign of him when they had made the same corner. Music blasted from somewhere. The two raced to the next corner. Nothing, no sign.

"Shit!" said Bowman. "Lost the little bastard."

The two turned back, frustration seething within them. After a few minutes' walk, Daugher tapped Bowman on the shoulder before pointing upward to the opposite side of the street.

"The Peeled Banana?" Bowman could hardly believe it. "You think?"

"I think it's worth *looking*," said Daugher.

Bowman shrugged, "Maybe so. After you."

With a similar shrug Daugher led the way. The interior was not so bad. Oh yes, it was full of more homosexuals than Daugher had seen since being let out of prison on an overturned conviction for murder. But they seemed not the terribly aggressive type. He began to relax . . . slightly. Then he saw two men, neither of them Eugene, kissing in a corner and a flood of unpleasant memories returned.

"I hate queers," he whispered, too softly to be heard.

Daugher and Bowman went to an open spot at the bar, one where they could see the—no pun intended—comings and goings of the clientele. There they sat, nursing their drinks and avoiding mixing, for nigh upon two hours.

"Not a sign," observed Daugher. "Might as well hit the road; try again tomorrow."

Bowman nodded agreement, then said he had to visit the men's room. Daugher thought about counseling against that, then decided the joke was too good to spoil.

Thus it was a very surprised Bowman who entered the men's room and saw a kneeling Eugene, servicing what was almost certainly a very new acquaintance. Ignoring his intended victim, Bowman did his business and left. Before he left, however, he had cause to note a window, about head-high, that ventilated the men's room.

"Bastard's in there," he told Daugher when he returned, "blowing somebody. One window, big enough to stuff a body out of. You'll have to be quick."

"Then he's been in there since we arrived," whispered Daugher. "Must be 'ladies night out.' Anyone else inside?"

"Just the blowee."

Daugher did a few quick mental calculations. "Okay, you can't go in there again. That might draw suspicion. I'll . . ." he stopped speaking as the bartender passed within earshot . . . "I'll wait until the guy with him comes out, do the job, stuff him out the window and come back. Then we can leave."

Eugene, apparently, either had great talent for the enterprise in which he was engaged or lacked any at all. It was quite some time before the man Bowman had seen with him emerged. By that time another had gone in and stayed. Then another. It was past ten PM before they knew Eugene was alone.

"And . . . we're off," Daugher whispered, tapping his fingers on the bar.

"Oh, aren't you a big one," Eugene observed as Daugher undid himself to urinate in the trough. "Want me to take care of that for you?"

"Sure, brother," Daugher agreed as he turned around.

The last thing Eugene ever felt was the blow from above that rendered him unconscious. He never felt the hands that gripped shoulder and chin and twisted his neck in a way human necks were not intended to go. He never heard the crack of his own neck breaking. When his wallet was removed from a back pocket—*Well,* thought Daugher, *there needs to be some better motive for the killing*—Eugene's body was already beginning to cool. He was thus spared the embarrassment of shit filling his trousers. Likewise he never knew that his bladder had let go. He felt neither the scraping as he was lifted up and pushed out of the small ventilation window nor the noisy impact on the trash cans below that window.

Daugher did up his trousers and left an empty men's room behind him.

"Done?" Bowman asked.

"Very done."

"You realize, right, that if they connect us to the murder the boss is screwed?"

Daugher thought on that. "Yeah . . . but's what to connect us? By the time I did it, the bartender had changed, so he can't connect the time the queer was in there with the time I went in there." He showed Eugene's wallet. "Motive: money. What connects us to a need for money? Nothing. Did the boss have a reason to want the fucker dead? Yes. Would we have killed him if the boss had asked? Clearly. But we weren't here; as my old motorcycle gang will swear on a stack of bibles, we were in Dragonback Pass. So they've got nothing, even if they suspect the boss."

Bowman considered that as the two walked. After a few contemplative moments he agreed.

First Landing, Hudson, FSC, 27/9/459 AC

Lourdes had passed on the news when Carrera had called in to the *Casa* Linda from his hotel in Phoenix Rising. He was shocked, at first. Then, secretly, he was pleased. That made him feel terribly guilty. Still, try as he might, he had not been able to shake the pleasure of Eugene's most timely demise. His shame grew with that failure, warring with his joy.

I am a low-down, no good, bastard. I should be

ashamed, he thought, *and I am. But even so, I am glad the piece of shit is out of the way.*

Having flown up for the funeral, Pat had listened patiently to the Jewish branch of the family's rabbi droning on and on about Eugene's many virtues; his love of animals, his support for equal rights, his staunch activism. *All true enough, I suppose, provided you add in "eager support to terrorist organizations."*

Now, standing in bright winter sunshine at the graveside, with Eugene's heart-broken mother weeping into her third husband's arms . . . *Aunt Sarah was always good to me. Always. Too bad she has to suffer. She deserves better.*

Cousin Annie, smelling more than a little of strong drink, leaned against Pat Hennessey for support. His arm helped her stand as she shook with great shuddering sobs. She whispered, over and over, "Poor Eugene. Oh, the terrible things I've said to him."

As the funeral began to break up, Pat half carried Annie to Aunt Sarah's side. The two women fell upon each other with weeping. Pat and Sarah's current husband held back.

Finally, Annie backed off and Pat took Sarah in his arms, cradling her aged head with one hand. "I am sorry," he whispered to her. "For you, I am sorry. I know what it's like."

EXCURSUS

From: *Legio del Cid: to Build an Army*
(reprinted here with permission of the Army
War College, Army of the Federated States
of Columbia, Slaughter Ravine, Plains, FSC)

If there were any attribute that perhaps could be
applied to all Moslems, and especially the more radical
Salafis, everywhere, it would have to be their exquisite
sense of timing.

True, of course, self-deception was nearly universal—
witness their continuing, and apparently groundless,
belief that they could somehow defeat the Zion Defense
Force and drive the Jews into the sea. Witness, too,
the steady frequency with which the Jews drove the
Moslems farther into the desert instead. Yet many
Moslems knew better. Indeed, it was precisely those
who did know better who made some of the most
fertile ground for terrorist recruiting and joined the
Salafi *Ikhwan*.

Bombast, too, was something of a cultural characteristic, one closely related to self-deception. And even
among the terrorist crew, those who had given up on

232

victory through real strength, bombast was quite unre-markable. Yet, even here, there were exceptions.

But the sense of timing, that inner light that tells one the precisely *wrong* time to take an action—if not all Moslems enjoyed it, then certainly the culture was pervaded with it, they all received the dubious benefits of it . . . and in a sense, all had come to expect it.

Has a young Federated States just ended a war with a great maritime power? Obviously this was the best of all possible times to begin piratical attacks on FSC shipping. Was an older and much more powerful Federated States about to show a little more even-handedness in Zionic-Moslem relations? That was the surest sign possible that a planeload of handicapped orphans on their way to a once-in-a-lifetime trip to Fantasy World was about to be blown from the sky. Has Zion's prime minister announced he is willing to trade a modicum of security for some chance at peace? Pay that man's life insurance premium because as certain as daylight he'll be dead at Salafi hands before the month is over. Is the Federated States about to engage in a great military enterprise to free one Moslem state from another oppressing it? Be certain that both the Moslem adversary and its friends will do everything possible to insure that the timing of their predictable defeat is perfect . . . for the Federated States. It was as if an entire culture was locked onto one of those decision-making diagrams, one where every block is labeled, "make serious mistake here," and that culture must always, always, *always* choose the "yes" arrow . . . and at the worst possible time.

So it happened that in the Republic of Balboa in the fall of 459 . . .

✧   ✧   ✧

The first sign of the attack came at a pumping station in *El* Toro, Balboa. An oil tanker was being refilled with crude from the McKinley oil fields when, suddenly, the station ceased pumping oil and began to spurt air. The puzzled pumping crew immediately called the sending point at the small oil port, *Puerto Armados*, on the northern side and was informed that pressure was down all along the system.

No one was injured directly by the explosion of the pipeline. Several hours later a small family of share-croppers downhill by several miles drowned—husband, wife, and two small children—in a flood of silently moving McKinley crude.

The next attack, coming only minutes later, was much more noticeable. A parade celebrating the adoption of Balboa's first constitution passed by a step van loaded with several tons of ammonium nitrate based fertilizer, soaked with fuel, and containing also a number of propane tanks. The thin, sheet-metal walls of the van had been reinforced with thick glass originally intended for one of *Ciudad* Balboa's newest high rises. As it happened the nearest object to the van was a float carrying a bevy of young high school girls. When the bomb detonated, the glass shattered into shards and flew outward. Without warning the little flock of dark-eyed Balboan beauties was turned into a red paste obscenity in the blink of an eye. Hundreds of bystanders were killed or injured.

Within seconds, another explosion rocked the city, this one in the busy shopping district of *Via Hispanica*. Windows to small shops and exclusive boutiques were driven inward to tear and rend shoppers and store clerks alike. Several dozen people, those in the immediate vicinity of the blast, simply ceased to exist, blown to atoms. Among these were some numbers of children as well.

Unlike the first two, the third and fourth attacks in the city were suicide bombs. The third detonated at the very peak of the stately Bridge of the Columbias. Twenty-one cars were blown completely off of the bridge on both sides. Some dozens more were destroyed or damaged depending on both distance from the blast and luck. The pavement was blasted entirely through at the spot where the bomb detonated. The enormous steel arches holding up the bridge, however, withstood the blast fairly well.

The last bomb was crashed into the presidential palace, a lightly guarded mansion. It being a national holiday, the president was at home.

Her body was never found.

PART II

CHAPTER NINE

Cui Bono (who benefits)?

—Cicero

UEPF *Spirit of Peace*, 27 April, 2511

The trip back from Atlantis Base had not been uneventful. One hundred and sixty-seven kilometers out from the docking bay a short had developed. Robinson had been the first to notice the distinctive stink in the recycled air. He'd wondered, later, if that had been because the flight crew had simply grown used to such smells.

In any case, it had been he who had first noticed and sounded the alarm. It was a damned good thing he had, too. A short in the lights was one thing, and likely survivable. A short in life support that turned into a fire was something else again.

The pilot, copilot and high admiral managed to scramble into EV suits in time. Sadly, the steward, while even quicker, had a faulty suit and suffocated

239

before Robinson's eyes as the cabin filled with smoke and the pilot broke seal to cut off the fire.

It was that, the image of a man dying slowly and miserably in front of him, far more than the fanatical glare in Mustafa's eyes, that decided Robinson to think further on the wild Salafi's scheme.

To start a war, the high admiral mused back in his cabin aboard the *Spirit of Peace.* He laughed slightly at the thought. *That wasn't exactly in my portfolio, now was it?*

On the other hand, he reasoned, *there wasn't anything in my orders about* not *starting a war. And there was that section about securing the blessings of peace for the Earth. I can hardly do that with my fleet crumbling around me, now can I?*

Robinson turned his bolted-down swivel chair towards his desk, laying his two elbows down and leaning forward to rest his nose lightly on his two middle fingers.

Difficult, difficult. I'll have to keep it almost all to myself, do it almost all myself. Some of the things Mustafa had in mind? My crews would balk, most of them, and I can hardly afford a mutiny in the fleet.

But the benefits? *If we can break the FSC, who on Terra Nova could resist a rising progressive tide? The TU? They're the model for progressivism on that planet. The other, continental, supranationals? They aspire to become like the TU. Bharat? Nationalist in some ways, yes, but such a hodgepodge of ethnicities they could be broken up with little more than a nudge to some of the separatist groups. Zhong Guo? Almost as badly mixed as Bharat. They could be handled.*

Then, too, this could be exciting and I'm bloody bored.

"Computer?" Robinson demanded of the Earth-tech model sitting atop his desk.

"Yes, High Admiral."

"Create a file. Label it . . . mmm . . . 'Pax 2511.' Restrict it to my voice only, both additions and access."

"Done, High Admiral."

Robinson paused, organizing his thoughts.

"Computer, add to the file all that is known to us about the Terra Novan World League and the Tauran Union. In particular I want profiles of all the major players. Then I want you to find whatever is known about the Salafi *Ikhwan*. Get me everything available on the subjects of guerilla warfare and terrorism. Lastly, for now, I want an economic analysis of the Federated States of Columbia, Terra Nova. Emphasis is on vulnerabilities. After you are done, erase all traces of your search, except for what remains in the file, Pax 2511. Work."

"Working, High Admiral."

UEPF *Spirit of Peace*, 28 May, 2511

"Mustafa hasn't the slightest idea of what he's about," said Robinson aloud in the privacy of his quarters. His eyes had grown a bit tired from reading the material he had had collected and which was on display on the Novan built view screen mounted on the wall. He looked away, resting them on a painting he had kept for himself out of the recently auctioned Vatican collection.

"He really thinks this god of his—which does not

and cannot exist—will do all the heavy thinking and lifting. He really believes that if he and his followers will only sacrifice and fight, then everything else will work out by divine will. Do I *really* want to entrust the future of my fleet, my planet and my class to a lunatic like that? I think not," the high admiral scoffed.

For over a month Robinson had been studying the problem. In that month he had come no nearer to a solution than he had been when he had last visited Atlantis Base. The FSC, with its three hundred million people, its industry and economy that dominated the planet, its matchless armed forces, was simply too tough to break under the limited attacks Mustafa had in mind. Add in that it was quite capable, albeit at a terrible cost, of swatting the Peace Fleet from space and . . .

"Not a chance," Robinson said to himself. "And not a chance I will give him the nukes to make his attacks more effective. Simple analysis would tell the Feds where they had come from; they've already got plenty of material to compare them to from the remains of the two cities we leveled in their Great Global War. And they *would* retaliate; there's no question about that. They couldn't then, with no way to loft a warhead into space, but now they could and they would.

"Tough problem."

He stood and began to pace.

"Should I have the bio people transfer some form of disease to Mustafa? No . . . no, I don't think so. There are some things that even *I* can't contemplate doing. Bio war is one of them."

Robinson turned his eyes back to his view screen and continued reading.

UEPF *Spirit of Peace*, 29 May, 2511

The conference room had been paneled in rare, iridescent Terra Novan silverwood by one of Robinson's predecessors. It lent the room a warmth that was sadly lacking in most of the ship's areas. The table was likewise from below, as were the chairs that now held some nine members of Robinson's staff.

There'd been nothing for it but to bring some of his staff in for some small parts. Not that Robinson had told them anything important or ever intended to; far from it. But there were questions he didn't have time to answer and which the computer was simply unable to bring the required creativity of thought to bear upon. He needed human help.

"First question," Robinson began. "What can we consider to be progressive forces and organizations on Terra Nova?"

"Assuming by 'progressive' you mean the kind of forces which brought peace to Earth and prominence to our ancestors," answered his sociology officer, Lieutenant Commander Khan, a very white and blonde atheist who happened to have one prominent and progressive ancestor from old Pakistan, "then the answer is fairly simple. Progressive forces include the supranationals like the World League and the Tauran Union, the entertainment industry, the news industry, the humanitarian industry, the legal industry—especially that part of it devoted to international law—and those elements of the economy, like Oak Tree Computing, that are detached from any given nation state and benefit from the global economy the Terra Novans have developed in the last ten or twelve years."

"Humanitarian *industry*?" queried Robinson.

"It's an industry like any other," answered Khan evenly. "What they manufacture is guilt and good feelings. The good feelings they sell at a high premium to those who need to feel good about themselves. They're no different from a company that makes cold remedies, except they are dealing with the relief of guilty emotions rather than sniffles. That, and that those who manufacture cold remedies are not also in the business of making colds."

"I'd always thought of those as existing to do good," the high admiral objected.

Khan, the realist, smiled. "They manage to do pretty *well* by doing good, Admiral. And it is highly questionable whether they do any real good, at least of the kinds they claim and probably even think they do. Do they feed the hungry? Surely. And they will keep feeding the hungry, as long as the hungry look pitiable enough to collect money for doing so. But the net result of feeding the hungry tends to be the destruction of local agriculture, which ensures a continuing supply of the hungry, a continuing supply of poster children, and a continuing supply of donations to assuage guilt.

"Then, too," Khan continued, "they can afford to pay for the best local housing wherever they go, and that drives the price of local housing beyond the reach of all but a very few locals. Do they educate people? Indeed they do, and thereby ensure that the most capable people get enough education to leave the place of their birth and go where the money and living are better. Alternatively, they will tend to hire highly educated people in these undeveloped hellholes they inflict themselves upon and use them for highly skilled work . . . like driving around and translating for the humanitarian aid workers. Oh, yeah, *that's* value added."

The fleet's Druidic chaplain interjected, "I remind you, Ms. Khan, that it was precisely those kind of groups that helped our ancestors bring Earth to peace and stability at last."

"The admiral asked me for analysis, Your Wisdom," answered Khan respectfully. Atheist or not one had to respect the power of Earth's official clergy of which the Druids were a part. "I make no moral judgments. What I have told him *is* the effective operating method of the local international humanitarian aid community, as it was for our own planet's. They are a plague to whatever place they visit, but they are equally a boon to the cause of international progressivism."

"What Sosh has said is true, Admiral," added the staff communications officer. "But it could not be true unless the news media and entertainment industries of which she spoke were willing to accentuate the positive and cover up the negative."

Khan nodded her head in agreement.

Robinson tapped his fingers against his face, thinking. "How long," he asked, "before the Novans can achieve interstellar travel?"

Estimates ranged wildly from "Fifty years" to "Centuries."

Engineering disagreed. "Twenty years, Admiral. Possibly as few as fifteen."

That was a shock.

"Explain that estimate," the high admiral ordered.

"The state of their technology right now is about where Earth was in the early twenty-first century. But that's only in general. They're already ahead of where we were in some areas—the Federated States of Columbia is, in any case—because a), they know a lot more of what is possible than our ancestors did and b) the FSC has been fanatical about space research ever since your predecessor nuked two of their cities."

"That doesn't mean they *will* though," Ms. Khan objected. It really was a frightening thought, the barbarians of Terra Nova loose in space.

"No," Engineering agreed. "But they could and *that* is what the High Admiral asked."

"Could we prevent them from doing so short of war?" Robinson asked.

"No." Everyone agreed. "No."

Khan added, "Though the kind of war might make a difference."

Atlantis Base, Earth Year 14 June, 2511

They met in Robinson's ashore quarters, a spacious house set apart from all other buildings by a high wall and broad, green lawn. Lit naturally by tall, narrow windows, the apartment was furnished in the best of Earth and Novan styles, kept spotless by a crew of dimwitted proles. The tables were gleaming wood; the couches and chairs supple leather. Thick rugs covered the porcelain tiles of the floors and rare art hung on the walls.

"We cannot be directly involved, Mustafa. Understand that much from the beginning. We can guide you, help you, partially fund you and give you a certain amount of intelligence. But we *will* not get directly involved under any circumstances."

Barely, Mustafa restrained the urge to pronounce UE's high admiral a "coward." Then again, the Salafi doubted that the word would have meant much to the high admiral. Mustafa was certain that the idea of cowardice had left the UE lexicon every bit as completely as had the concept of courage. Besides, coward or not, the man was an infidel, an atheist, and that was, in Mustafa's opinion, infinitely worse.

"Money?" Mustafa sneered. "I have money. Intelligence? Allah will provide victory to us or not, as he wills, without your "*intelligence*." I am wasting my time here."

"Not so fast, son of the desert." Robinson was really thinking *son of a bitch* but that would have been impolitic to say. "Our aid means more to you than you imagine."

In one of those little quirks of fate that sometimes happen, the Fleet chaplain, Druid though he was, had proven of more value than all the rest of Robinson's other counselors. The Druid, at least, understood Islam, though it could hardly be said he approved of it.

"Allah will provide," Robinson echoed. "Allah will provide your weapons, then? Or will you have to find them yourself? Allah will make the Federated States complacent, or will you have to be clever on your own behalf and in His cause? How do you know, Mustafa, that Allah did not provide *me*? Or do you question that all things, to include me, come to pass only through his favor? I am shocked, *shocked,* that you think to spurn the gift He has provided."

Robinson keyed the intercom on the table at which he and Mustafa spoke. "Bring my car around for my guest. My business here is concluded."

"Wait," the Salafi said, holding up a hand. "Perhaps I was hasty. We may yet be able to do business together."

Atlantis Base, Earth Date 19 June, 2511

Unni Wiglan was thrilled, *thrilled,* that the high admiral had invited her, personally, to return to Atlantis Base for consultations. The prestige alone was invaluable. And the comfort of being in the one place on Terra Nova which gave proof that her values were true? Priceless.

She'd shown the high admiral her gratitude, too, in a number of ways.

Better, the high admiral had shown himself to be a man of both caring and culture. He'd been nothing but questions and concern about the very things Unni herself cared about: improving the low regard in which the World League was held, limiting the anarchic and archaic "sovereign" rights of Terra Nova's two hundred and twelve nation-states, the plight of the people of Filistia, groaning under the heel of Zion, among other worthy causes. She'd been especially pleased when the high admiral had dismissed Zion's claims with the words, "Bloody Jews."

United Earth *had* no more Jews; they'd all been either killed or sent off world to the colony the Arab

League had given them to entice them away.

And then there was the great concern the high admiral had shown for the Terra Novan natural environment. He'd himself noted that in the last two hundred years Terra Nova's mean temperature had increased a staggering .3 degrees Celsius. "It just can't go on, my dear Unni. Why, in a thousand years the planet will become uninhabitable. And did you know, my people say you may already have reached the tipping point; that, or you soon will. There's no time to waste."

Here, *finally*, was a representative from Earth who understood, who cared. For the first time in her life, Unni Wiglan thought there might be some hope for peace for her planet.

UEPF *Spirit of Peace*, Earth Date 28 June, 2513

"Computer, view screen on," Robinson ordered. Immediately the computer turned on the wall-mounted Kurosawa. "Find me the news, Federated States. Make it the Global News Network."

". . . and it's a bright and sunny day here in First Landing, Hudson," the announcer said. "Not a cloud in the sky and . . . What the fu—? Oh, dear God . . . there's been a terrible accident at the Terra Nova Trade Organization."

Robinson winced as the view switched from the studio to a tall tower, standing alone but with other, similar ones in the background. The tower had a gaping hole near the base from which smoke poured out. He winced again when another airship slammed into a second building and then again when a third skyscraper was hit. Both of those shots were seen distantly, as the second and third towers were across the city.

He didn't really feel it, though, until the camera on site focused on people beginning to jump from the upper stories to avoid burning to death. Shivering, he remembered back to the smoke-filled cabin of the shuttle, to the face of the crew chief suffocating in the faulty EV suit.

"Poor people," he whispered. "But what am I to do? Wait until you're strong enough that it becomes *my* people jumping from burning buildings? I'm sorry for you; truly I am. But it was necessary.

"I hope, I really do, that no more, or not much more, will be necessary."

INTERLUDE

31 January, 2050, Turtle Bay, New York,
New York, United States of America, Earth

The speech was televised. Moreover, it was watched
with keen interest in certain quarters.

Margot Tebaf had prepared long and hard for the
occasion. The best speechwriters available to her had
taken her thoughts—hers and Dominique's, who had
quickly become rather more than a casual fling—and
turned them into shining prose, a beacon to light the
dark night and turn it to day.

Margot's speech was, from the progressive point
of view, exactly on point. Perhaps many, even most,
viewers thought it full of pious platitudes, inanities
and wishful thinking. She and they simply didn't share
the same concepts, even the same vocabulary. In that
sense it was a failure, but a predictable one. Moreover,
those people really didn't matter. In the more important sense, for people who did share the same world
view and did matter—the news media, the European
Parliament, the various humanitarian aid and human
rights activist organizations around the world (of which

there were hundreds of thousands, large and small), and the increasingly hereditary bureaucrats at the United Nations—the speech was a resounding success.

They could read the code phrases put into the speech by Margot's speechwriters. *They* knew that "increased political stability" was a nicer way of saying "deportation of troublemakers." *They* knew that "fair distribution of human talent" meant "keep the highly talented from emigrating out of their own hellholes to the United States."

Moreover, the insightful among the viewers saw something that Margot grasped, if at all, only in embryonic form. If they could cut off the flow of immigrants to the United States, and make this new world the only permissible outlet for people who simply didn't care for transnational governance, that would be good. But what would be infinitely better would be the effect of moving those same people *out* of their home countries in even greater numbers than the United States had ever been willing to accept. For each one that left, say, Europe weakened the resistance to supranational and transglobal governance while each weakening of resistance led to more supranational and transglobal governance. This, in turn, led to more people wanting to leave which, if allowed, would still *further* weaken resistance to transglobal governance.

It was, the viewers saw, a perfect solution, an *elegant* solution. Moreover, it did not have the distressing side effect of increasing resistance, and providing an unfortunate counterexample, within the United States. To one another they said, "What's not to like?"

And so the consensus grew—for it was a consensus, not a conspiracy—*this new world is the solution to our problems here on Earth.*

CHAPTER TEN

Among other evils which being unarmed brings you, it causes you to be despised.

—Machiavelli, *The Prince*

Casa Linda, 29/9/459 AC

If one picture was worth one thousand words, how many words were saved by half a dozen, in living color? The pictures fronted a newspaper that lay unopened upon the desk. There was no need to open it. That front page said everything necessary with its display of dismembered arms and legs, broken bleeding children, and people burned and blasted almost beyond recognition.

They have given me what I asked for, thought an inexpressibly saddened Patricio Carrera. *But I will not thank them for it. I wish they had not.*

His eyes wandered down again, down to a picture of a little girl. This one, at least was alive. Bloody, she was; covered in blood from head to foot. In the picture her skin showed through only at the twin tear tracks on her cheeks. The little girl was standing perfectly well. She was quite unhurt.

The baby's mother, however, was a ghastly, exsanguinated ruin—torn and bloody meat—lying on the street before her.

Though Carrera was saddened, an element of celebration charged the air of *Casa* Linda. Men passing in the hallways of the house spontaneously lifted their hands to "high five" as they passed. *The Boss can do it now! We're going to war!* Daugher and Bowman butted heads, literally and for the sheer violent joy of the thing, every time they passed in a hall.

Carrera, himself, was rather more restrained. He had a plan. He had all the diagrams. He had tables of manning and equipment, pay scales, grade requirements, training schedules . . .

And I have guilt. *Is it my fault, my doing, that these people were attacked? Or would it have happened eventually, anyway? I suppose I'll never know.*

Lourdes interrupted his thoughts with a cup of coffee. She pretended not to notice as he quickly wiped a forming tear from his own eye. "What happens now, Patricio?"

"I don't know, not for sure. I don't yet have the authority. I don't have the money; I don't have the equipment, I don't have the men. I don't have the land to train on. I don't have the uniforms, the ammunition, the barracks . . . even tents we lack. All I have is a plan and control of *some* money, with more on the way . . . that, and a few connections."

Lourdes glanced down at the newspaper, then back to her boss. "But you and General Parilla have an appointment with the acting president in just three days, Patricio. Isn't that about getting all those things?"

"Yes. But Parilla and I both have our doubts about how easy it will be. Even after this," he said as his hand gestured towards the paper.

"I have faith in you, Patricio. You will get what you need."

He sighed. Maybe the girl was right. "Lourdes . . . you're a reasonable girl, as reasonable as anyone in the country. Do you believe we . . . Balboa should go to war over this?"

Lourdes' eyes flashed pure Castilian fire, glowing hot with rage and hate. This fire would have been commonplace during the *Reconquista*, the centuries-long drive to rid Spain of the hated Moslem. On Cortez's march to Tenochtitlan to conquer the Mexica a similar flame had lit the eyes of his conquistadors. Aboard the ships of the Holy League the night before the bloody naval battle at Lepanto, Don John's sailors' and marines' eyes had shone so. It was the very fire that had once made Spain "the nation with the bloody footprint."

"Oh, very much, yes. Yes, yes, *yes*." Her foot stamped. "You must make them *pay* for this!"

Carrera nodded, satisfied. A hand reached out for a cigarette. "Lourdes, would you get Professor Ruiz on the phone for me? Then call Parilla's secretary and see when he will be available."

Saint Nicholasberg, Volga, 30/9/459 AC

Smoke curled up from half a dozen vile Volgan cigarettes to gather and congeal along the ceiling and
walls of the room. A small buffet—and that was *not*
vile at all—sat pillaged on a table near the room's
only door. Inside, men no longer young argued over
their state's future.

"Stefan Ilyanovich, I tell you for the last time
there is no more foreign exchange to be had." The
speaker, Pavel Timoshenko, a sub-minister of finance
for economically moribund Volga, spoke, on behalf of
his chief, to an assistant to an industrial minister.

A note of something like hysteria crept into Ilyanovich's voice. "Our factories are crumbling. We are losing
even the ability to extract our own oil. We are in desperate need of the technology that only the East, the FSC
and the TU, or Yamato can supply us. And you tell me
we cannot even buy it." Ilyanovich looked despondent,
almost crushed. He hung his head in despair.

Timoshenko, not wanting to appear unsympathetic,
said, "My friend, it is not that we would not buy it if
we could. It is not even that the East will not sell to
us. Since the Reds"—for the tsar who had instituted
Tsarist-Marxism in Volga had, like his philosophical
predecessors, chosen that color to symbolize his social
revolution—"have been gone, the East, most of them
at least, are quite willing to sell. But they will *not*
give it away. Welcome to the free marketplace." He
reached over to squeeze Ilyanovich's shoulder.

Ilyanovich looked up. "Then sell something, before
we have nothing left to sell."

Timoshenko shook his head sadly. "That's just the point. We have nothing but the very raw materials to sell. And no one wants to buy. The world is glutted. Even the price of gold is down, what with all the precious metal the UEPF has dumped, or we would sell that."

"Weapons?" Ilyanovich held out his hands in plea.

Timoshenko shook his head, shrugged. "Ordinarily we could sell our weapons. But all of our former clients deserted us as fast as we deserted them. It doesn't matter; they have no money. And those who can buy don't want what we have. They want newer, more modern, Columbian or Tauran arms."

The men present looked to the representative of the ministry of defense. After finishing off the caviar-laden cracker in his fingers, and wiping the corners of his mouth with a napkin, Vladimir Rostov answered the unspoken question.

"We make good weapons," he said. "Yes, they're different from the East's but, in the main, about as good—in some cases better, used properly—and always much, *much* cheaper. How could they not be when we pay the workers who produce them about ten percent of what their western equivalents earn? But after decades of selling "chimp models"—they look the same as the best equipment but have all of the really good features taken out—no one wants to buy who can afford better. Forty years of our arms, in Moslem hands, being bested by Zion and the FSC hasn't helped matters. We have managed to sell some heavy rocket launchers to al Jahara, true, but that is all. When they wanted tanks they went for FS models. When they wanted infantry vehicles they bought Anglian. They could have good, top of the line,

T-38s—hell, I would sell them T-48s!—for what they can afford to pay. But they aren't even asking."

This was a bad sign indeed. For forty years the old empire had bartered its weapons for hard currency, needed raw materials, and political influence. Now its successor, the Republic of Volga, couldn't sell them even without the political strings. And weapons were about all it had to offer. Millions upon millions of tons of finished arms and munitions sat rusting, unused and unwanted, in military storage yards all over the country. The times were bleak.

Rostov tapped the table top in anger. "It is worse, even, than the picture I have painted. The FSC are already beating the Salafi fanatics in Pashtia like they own them. As soon as that is done they'll be going after the next state on their list; quite possibly Sumer again. Then they'll go after another. Then another. In a few years, not more than six the General Staff thinks, most of our former ex-clients are going to get the living shit kicked out of them by the Federated States-Kingdom of Anglia Alliance. The Sumeris still have almost exclusively Volgan heavy equipment. Even what we didn't build ourselves is mostly based on our systems; closely enough that few can tell the difference from the outside. They're almost all "chimp models," but who will care about that? When the FSC and the Anglians are through, our reputation for making arms will be destroyed for a century. Two centuries!"

Rostov rubbed a chin perplexedly. "Hmmm. I wonder if . . . no, I suppose not."

Ilyanovich reached for a glass of hot, overly sweet Volgan tea. "Is there no way to save that reputation? We have the arms, thirty thousand tanks in storage or more, enough possibly to see us through some of the hard times ahead if we could sell them for even a fraction of their value, at something better than scrap metal value anyway."

Timoshenko held up his hand to silence the others. He had studied and traveled in the East, even during Imperial days. During that time he had picked up a few decidedly un-Volgan ideas. One such was coming to him now.

"Comrades, it occurs to me that there is one chance. If we can somehow show that our arms are second to none—okay, *okay* . . . at least good *enough*—we can sell them in the future. The money we get from that will give us the ability to buy some high technology, enough to continue getting our oil and other minerals out of the ground. That will bring more hard currency and a favorable, or at least less unfavorable, trade balance. We must have positive advertising. Can we not get our forces to Pashtia?"

It was the representative of the Foreign Ministry's turn. "Forget it, Pavel. We are definitely not invited in any major way. Border and convoy guard maybe. Probably not even that."

"Not even that." The one soldier in the group added, "It wouldn't make much difference even if we sent in the Guards. Since we left Pashtia and since the breakdown of the government, our army is a wreck, good soldiers—some of them anyway—in a broken organization. Besides, the point Pavel wants us to make is, I think, that our weapons are good in rich undeveloped world hands. This point cannot be made if they are in Volgan hands."

Timoshenko ended the discussion by suggesting,

"Comrades, let us await developments a bit, shall we? Perhaps the horse will learn to sing after all."

Las Mesas, Republic of Balboa, 30/9/459 AC

Young Ricardo Cruz looked into and past the television screen. It cannot be said he really even saw the images. He had no need to. He had seen them before, or others much like them, over and over, perhaps one hundred times in two days.

Cruz's girlfriend, Caridad, sat next to him. He had his arm around her. Unlike more usual occasions, now she had to make no effort to keep his pawing teenaged hands away. She really liked Ricardo so she didn't always fight very hard. But even token gestures were important and she was a little disturbed that she needn't make any.

He was a good looking boy, was Ricardo, his appearance marred only by somewhat unevenly prominent ears. Olive of skin and brown of eye; at five feet, seven inches, Cruz was a bit taller than the national norm. He towered over Cara's five, one.

"Ricardo," Cara insisted, "stop fretting so. You are only seventeen. There's nothing you can do to help. Only the gringos can avenge us."

Cruz said nothing, but his mind seethed and stomach churned at the harm done his country and his people. The idea of some other country doing the job that he felt deep inside was his own didn't sit well either. He'd always been a boy to take personal responsibility for things.

❖   ❖   ❖

A fourteen year old Ricardo heard the girl crying. He heard, too, the predatory laughter of what had to be at least three or four boys. Neither the laughter, nor the jeers, nor the numbers much affected him. The crying, however, did.

He began to walk briskly to the door of the three-bedroom adobe house he shared with his parents and three siblings. On the way he paused to consider taking with him the machete he used to help with the harvest in season. It was a good tool, strong, flexible, very sharp and not too heavy. But was it the right tool?

Better to have it and not need it, *he thought,* than to need it and not have it.

He took the machete.

On the front porch of the house he saw them standing in the road. There were four, plus the girl. They were well-dressed, rabiblanco-*dressed.*

Money, *he thought.* Money come to have a little fun with the farm girls.

He didn't recognize any of the four boys but he'd seen the girl before in a class a grade behind him. He thought her name was Cara and that she lived a couple of miles down the road farther away from town. There were books lying in the dirt of the road, a cheap orange backpack, as well. He thought they must be hers since none of the boys looked the type to care much for schoolbooks.

One of the boys held the girl—yes, Cara's her name—from behind while another unbuttoned her white, schoolgirl's blouse and felt inside. The last two stood to either side until one of them bent down to grab her legs and pick them up. She struggled and cried for help as they began to carry her off to the woods abutting the road.

"*I don't think so,* maricones."

The three carrying Cara stopped and looked. The fourth member of their party lay face down on the road, blood pouring from his scalp to mix with the reddish dirt of the road. Some lunatic stood over that one, with a bared machete one hand, the scabbard in the other, and a remarkably serene look on his face. The punk with the machete was considerably younger, they thought, and considerably smaller, they could see. This didn't seem to bother him any more than did the fact that they were still three to his one.

"Keep hold of the meat," said the leader of the boys to the one holding Cara's arms. "Come on, Manuel, let's show this campesino piece of shit who he can and can't fuck with."

"Si, Eduardo," answered Manuel.

Little Cruz might have been. But his young arms had been strengthened by many seasons' hard labor with the machete. What work had the rabiblancos ever done much harder than lifting a poor maid's skirt? Young Cruz stood his ground as Eduardo and Manuel advanced on him.

And stopped dead when he didn't run. In that moment's hesitation Cruz sprang forward like a panther. Eduardo was the nearer. Cruz feinted high, then swung the machete around Eduardo's upflung arms and cut inward, below the ribs. The rabiblanco gasped and looked down at where his blood welled out from his deeply sliced side, pouring over the silver metal blade. Eduardo screamed and promptly fainted.

Cursing, Cruz tugged at the machete. Crap, it's caught on the ribs. Shoulda cut even lower. While he was worrying at the machete, Manuel's fist—he

*was perhaps made of tougher stuff than his chief,
Eduardo—struck Cruz beside the head, knocking him
to the dirt and causing him to see stars.*

*With Cruz apparently out of commission, Manuel
bent low to see to Eduardo's wound. This was found
to be rather a bad mistake as Cruz, stars or not,
launched himself directly from the road to crash into
Manuel's side. The two went tumbling over in a flurry
of punches and kicks, a mix of Manuel's punches to
the farm boy's face and Cruz-delivered knees to the
groin. Two or three such were one or two more than
Manuel's gonads could take. Cruz left him puking
in the dirt and walked—staggered, really—to where
Eduardo and the machete lay joined.*

*Using two hands, Cruz roughly pulled the machete
from the now moaning Eduardo's side, bringing forth
another scream and a renewed flood of bright red
blood. Bloody machete in hand, still staggering, Cruz
began to close on the last member of the rape party,
the one holding the girl. This one lacked Manuel's sense
of determination. Having seen three of his friends—all
older, bigger and stronger than the little demon who'd
attacked them—the last of the would-be rapists simply
took to his heels, leaving Cara alone.*

*She ran to Cruz. "Thankyouthankyouthankyou for
saving me!"*

*"You're welcome," he answered. "But now could
you lead me home? My eyes have swollen so badly
I really can't see."*

Cara shuddered, remembering the way she and
Ricardo had met. *He's the bravest boy I've ever met,*
she thought. *If he goes to war, he'll surely be killed.*

Cara took a very personal view of things. She liked Ricardo . . . a great—oh, a *very* great—deal. She didn't want him killed. She couldn't even stand the thought of him being hurt. And the Federated States could be counted on to fix the problem without Cruz's help. So why should he leave her and risk his life, even if it were possible?

Finca Mendoza, *Las Mesas*, Balboa, 1/10/459 AC

A mere dozen miles from where Cruz had sat with Cara, another Balboan boy, Jorge Mendoza, sat alone in front of a television. In his hand he held a memento, a set of collar insignia, from his brother, Arturo, fallen a dozen years ago in battle against the gringos.

To say that Jorge did not like Federated States was an understatement. His brother had been a hero to him, a great smiling, kindly presence. Ever since Arturo's death beside his commander, Captain Jimenez, Mendoza had hated the Federated States, its people, and everything the two stood for.

Not by any means alone among the population of the underdeveloped parts of Terra Nova, Mendoza had been neither shocked nor even particularly disapproving of the attack on the Federated States a couple of months previously. To him, the people killed had had no faces. They were merely the great, opposed, *other* which had done his beloved big brother to death.

Other people did have faces though, faces as clear as Arturo's. Those faces smiled out at him from the television; faces of men and boys, young and old; faces of mothers and daughters; faces that could have been his own family's.

Mendoza's hatred for gringos ebbed a bit. Only so much hate could a heart hold and his had to make room for the Salafi *Ikhwan*.

Vice-Presidential Palace, *Ciudad* Balboa, 2/10/459 AC

"That bastard!" fumed Balboa's new president, Guillermo Rocaberti, pounding the tabletop. Rocaberti had taken the oath of office as president, but had not yet had time to move into the presidential palace. The palace needed considerable repair anyway, so he was in no hurry.

Surprised at the unexpected bang, the president's aide looked up from the screen. He asked, "Which bastard, *Señor Presidente*?"

"I'm not *sure* which one. Whoever put that goddamned 'public service message' on the television."

Rocaberti pointed at a silent television showing row on row of small portrait pictures of the victims of the Constitution Day attacks. Had the TV not been deliberately silenced, a voice would have been heard calling for rearmament and vengeance.

"That is not entirely clear, sir. Ex-General Parilla is reported to have a hand in it, but there is also supposedly some gringo involved."

"Gringo?"

"Yes, sir. There is a small group of them, a couple of dozen or so, we think. They've kept a low profile since they came here a few months back. We don't know much about them except that they have ties to Parilla."

"Soldiers?"

"Maybe ex-soldiers . . . mercenaries, perhaps."

"Why wasn't I told? Are they planning a coup?"

"Told what, sir? They haven't done anything. And Major Fernandez has reported them to be harmless, on extended vacation, actually."

"Wonderful! Fernandez! Do you think for a moment that Fernandez is anything but an outright enemy of this government? Never mind answering."

What's that bastard Parilla's plan? A new Balboan Defense Corps? A new Guardia Nacional? He half won the plebiscite seven years ago, so we were never able totally to get rid of the armed forces. On the other hand . . . hmmm. Maybe this might be a way to get them out of the way for a while. But they'll be back. Eventually, they'll be back. They always are. So, no, unless I can figure out a way to make sure they never come back, I've got to fight this.

"Get me Ford Williams on the phone. Now!" The aide quickly dialed the number of the country's second vice-president.

The National Assembly, Ciudad Balboa, 3/10/459 AC

It had cost Parilla no money but much political capital to arrange this meeting with Guillermo Rocaberti and his Cabinet. This was to the good as, with the cost of the extensive advertising for which he and Carrera had personally paid, immediate funds were beginning to run low. He had no choice but to get the government to agree to send a military formation to the war.

Pending funding from Carrera's uncle's estate, neither he nor those who supported him could afford to do this again if the propaganda campaign didn't work. In the president's conference room, richly paneled and decorated, Parilla was being grilled by a very suspicious group of politicians.

"General Parilla, what difference does it make if the Federated States wins this coming war with us or without us?"

Parilla turned his attention to the Minister of Police. "*Señor*, it could make all the difference in the world. If we help with the upcoming war, to the extent of our abilities, we will have a claim on the Federated States. We can expect further aid, possibly money to improve the Transitway, jobs . . . a greater prosperity.

"Leaving all that aside, however, the major reason to help them is that *we have been fucking attacked*. Our people have been murdered. The blood of our innocents has run in our streets."

Parilla pointed to Carrera while addressing the group. "My friend here believes that the FSC is likely to be generous under the circumstances."

The minister of police looked dismally at Carrera. "No blood would have spilled, most likely, had this man not killed six Salafis."

No more than had Jimenez did Parilla want Carrera to say a word about that. He just might tell the truth; that he had been angry and half mad with grief and so had baited the Salafis into attacking him. Not that Carrera had ever admitted it. Indeed, everyone close to him avoided asking precisely because they were sure he *would* admit it. That particular truth must not get out.

Parilla merely answered, "That was self-defense . . . so said the investigating officer. So said that officer's commander, Xavier Jimenez."

The policeman lifted a scornful and skeptical eyebrow.

Greasy looking, though said to be an honest man, Balboa's minister of justice, Ruben Arias, turned to Carrera. "You are from the FS, so no doubt you have a claim to understanding them greater than ours. But tell me this; we have a long and unfortunate history of military rule. If we let you and General Parilla bring about this force you have spoken of, what is to keep them from restoring military rule once again?"

Carrera stroked his own face lightly while formulating his answer. "You ask a good question, *Señor* Arias. I have thought upon it much before coming here today. I think, in the first place, that the lesson of the invasion twelve years ago—that the FSC will not tolerate military rule in this continent—will not soon be forgotten by the soldiers.

"Nor are we speaking of keeping a large standing force. This will be a one time only event. When the war is over you could disband the force or reduce it down to a manageable size, fold it back into the Civil Force or even turn it into a reserve formation." Carrera brought his hands together to illustrate. *Of course, since the war is going to last at least a century, reduction in force is a most unlikely possibility. Besides, You'll get rid of my army over my dead body.*

Arias continued on that point. "That is very easy to say, *señor*. But what if they won't lay down their arms afterward?" He folded his arms, looking triumphant.

Parilla took up the challenge. "Who controls the

spending in the country? Surely, *Señor* Arias, you do not think that the men who volunteer for this expeditionary force are going to want to continue in arms if they are not paid?"

Arias saw an opening. "And that is another thing. How are we to pay for this? We are financially . . . well, if not prostrate, then by no means in good shape."

Without elaborating on Carrera's part in the planning, Parilla answered, "My people have estimated the cost of this operation at just over four hundred million drachma a year over and above the aid we can expect from the FSC. That is, it should be about that if we scrimp a little. Before the invasion Piña was taking almost three hundred million per year in illegal taxes from the Cristobal Free Trade Zone alone. You gentlemen can make that illegal tax a legal one . . . and a larger one, too. That alone would pay for the operation. But it is still very unlikely that we will have to pay for the whole thing ourselves. The Federated States can be expected to provide support if we ask."

Back and forth the argument went. For each objection raised by the Cabinet, Parilla and Carrera had an explanation of a benefit to be derived. As the opportunity arose Parilla dropped narrow hints of the personal gains that might accrue to the men present if they were to approve. "Just think of the benefits to our economy, gentlemen. We'll take several thousand young, aggressive and unemployed—hence dangerous—men out of circulation for a while. They will earn money that they will spend freely, being young men. Soldiers eat a *lot*! This can only help our many farmers." Parilla knew that many in the room had significant agricultural interests. "Farmers—and they make up much of the country, you recall—will buy more. New shops will be opened and old ones thrive. And gentlemen, one way or another foreigners will pay for it all. Even if we get not one centavo in aid, these are solid gold to us. My own financial interests will advance as will those of everyone here."

Parilla thought, *And if I didn't act as if I were in this for my own financial benefit you would all be certain I was planning a coup, wouldn't you? Then you would fight us even harder. Well, believe the worst of me; it's no more than I know is true of you. To most of you bastards there's no good reason to do anything except for a personal or family profit. So if you want to think Patricio and I are in it for the money so much the better. You probably don't know that Patricio himself is on the verge of enough wealth that any petty graft available in Balboa shrinks to insignificance by comparison.*

Still, despite best efforts, Parilla and Carrera could see the politicians weren't buying. Parilla turned to Carrera and said in a whisper, "I told you they wouldn't be reasonable. Fortunately we've planned for such a contingency."

Before going in to confront the president and Cabinet, Parilla had insisted on preparing another means of persuasion. As he had told Carrera, "Patricio, you know how to raise, train, and use military forces for military objectives. Trust me when I say that I know how to use them for other objectives. I've had practice. And I've understudied some of the best."

Parilla gave a signal to Jimenez, who had accompanied them to the meeting. Jimenez slipped out quietly to make a brief telephone call. Within twenty minutes the men in the meeting room could hear the sound of singing, the measured tread of booted feet. Marching men approached.

Outside of the National Assembly Building two thousand former members of the Balboan Defense Corps, most of them also current members of the Civil Force that had replaced the BDC, marched in formation to positions surrounding the building. They were all uniformed and armed.

At Parilla's orders, Jimenez and Fernandez between them had done all the necessary coordination to bring every conveniently located unit—police and paramilitary, both—into position to threaten the government ministers. To any within sight of the demonstration it looked exactly like an impending coup d'etat.

Parilla had not been content merely to show a greater force at his disposal than the government could muster. A very substantial bribe had insured that the president of the Republic's own guard—constitutionally distinct from the Civil Force—would ostentatiously leave the assembly building and join the rest of the demonstrators. Perhaps if Rocaberti had had longer in office to cement his ties with the Presidential Guard they would not have defected. As it was, he did not have those ties cemented.

Loudspeakers carried by the leaders of the units began to state the demands of the defenders to be sent to the war to crush those who had attacked their country.

Looking from the window of the meeting room the assembled cabinet ministers saw their only supporting military force leave to join the demonstrators. Arias was the first to realize that the men meeting with Parilla and Carrera were now defenseless.

"I suppose you planned this?" he accused Parilla, banging his fist on the conference table.

Parilla shook his head and answered, quite untruthfully, "No, *señor*, I did not plan, though I knew it might happen." None present believed him. He hadn't expected them to. The lie was for politeness' sake only.

"This won't get you anywhere, you know. Even if you force us to approve your plan, we are not the Assembly. They must vote on it."

Parilla didn't answer but looked out the window to where a series of automobiles were disgorging a carefully selected quorum of the National Legislative Council, the seventy-two member body that had the power to approve the essential elements of Carrera's plan. It had taken a fair amount of the time he'd had available to determine who would support the move to send an expeditionary force to the war. Two were members, somewhat distant members, of Carrera's late wife's family. Her father, at her mother's insistence, had persuaded them to vote in favor. Others had been bribed or promised bribes for their votes. A fairly large number hadn't needed much persuading. In all, Parilla had assembled enough legislators to both constitute a quorum, just, and to insure that he would win the vote.

After watching the legislators being disgorged from the cars that had brought them, Parilla turned away from the window to address the Cabinet. Sounding sincere, he said, "In a few minutes we will be able to legally enact the legislation the country will need to shoulder its burden of responsibility to the world community and avenge our own dead. I think that the men outside will not permit much debate on the matter. Mr. President, I suggest that you use all of your political skills to push this vote through as quickly and painlessly as possible."

Arias stood straight. "I, for one, have no intention of permitting this to happen. I will not stand by and make some gringo the commander of the forces of the Republic. You can *kill* me if you wish," he sneered. "But I will not go along."

Soothingly, Carrera said, "*Señor* Arias, you wrong me. I have no intention of either harming you or being the commander. For one thing, I *was* a gringo; for all that I live here in Balboa now. The troops have no great reason to trust me. They don't even know me. Moreover, having a gringo commander will make the whole thing smack of an FSC ploy to keep effective rule over Balboa.

"No, sir, I will not be the commander. I wouldn't accept it, at this time, if it were offered. General Parilla, however, is fully suited to command this force. He has my loyalty. He plainly has the loyalty of those men outside. He is the only former military ruler in Balboa's history ever to voluntarily step down from office to return real rule to an elected civilian government. *Señor* Arias, you may relax. General Raul Dario Parilla will be the commander of this force." *I will merely be his executive officer . . . very executive.*

Arias did not, repeat *not*, trust this gringo son of a bitch in the slightest. He had one last strong card to play to stop him and he used it.

"Gentlemen, there is one little problem," Arias said. "Get the entire legislative assembly to vote for your little project and it still wouldn't matter. It would require a plebiscite to recreate a true armed force for Balboa. That would take months to set up and tally the votes on."

"That is true, *señor*, as far as it goes," Carrera conceded with a shrug. *Thank God for good lawyering.* "But it is certainly within the power of the Legislative Assembly to sponsor a nongovernmental organization within the Republic. Much as the Gauls have sponsored Justice Without Borders or Helvetia has sponsored our planet's version of the Red Cross. The . . . oh, for now let's call it *El Legio del Cid* . . . could even pay to the Republic what the World League pays to contributing states for peacekeepers, one thousand Federated States drachma a month each for troops actually deployed. That is, of course, assuming the FSC supports us as I expect they will. Seriously, General Parilla and I can promise the Republic one thousand drachma per man actually deployed, per month, after operational costs are paid but before any other expenditures are made. Gentlemen, that is, potentially, sixty to one hundred and fifty-six million drachma a year. Where else; *how* else, could the government increase its revenues by over fourteen percent so easily?" *Where else could you find that much extra money to steal?*

President Rocaberti scowled darkly. This bastard gringo had been talking to some lawyers, and apparently rather good ones. And the plebiscite had been his next to last card and last really good one. He'd played it and lost. There was only one thing left and he doubted it would work, not if they had serious financing as he had considered evidence—witness the desertion of his personal guard—that they did.

Looking into Carrera's eyes, the president felt a chill. *He's polite enough here, now. But he's got the look of madness about him. One last effort then.*

"We cannot tax the Cristobal Free Zone to support what is, in essence, a private activity. The merchants would be up in arms," Rocaberti insisted. "It would be unconstitutional."

Inwardly, both Parilla and Carrera smiled. They'd expected this. Indeed, they'd wanted it. By refusal to fund, the government also gave up any semblance of control. All that blather about controlling the force by withholding funding? Gone now, with the refusal to fund. Moreover, they had a full list of demands to be made. The haggling then began.

By a reasonably large majority the Legislative Council ordered the creation of a nongovernmental organization, or NGO, final name to be determined, of not more than thirteen thousand, five hundred expeditionary troops plus required support back home (and the legislators had no clue as to how much support back home might be required), to secure the Republic from foreign enemies. It further required Raul Dario Parilla to negotiate a memorandum of understanding with the Federated States for the use and support of that force. The NGO so created was to quell the scourge of terrorism wherever it might be found. The legislators passed as well the enabling legislation to facilitate and govern such a force.

Casa Linda, 4/10/459 AC

Down in the cool and damp basement of Carrera's headquarters, the sergeant major stubbed out another cigarette as he labored to sort personnel files into a semblance of order. The files had been provided by an assistant to Major Jimenez. Except for meals, hasty ones, and brief periods for sleep, no one on Carrera's staff had taken any time off from their duties since Balboa had been attacked. Carrera was working himself no less than he and McNamara were working the men.

Beginning on the night of the 28th the house had been the scene of constant meetings and coordination sessions between Carrera and members of the Civil Force. At some of these the sergeant major had been present. Other members of Carrera's staff attended others.

It wasn't really McNamara's job to be selecting personnel. The Staff's II—the personnel management office, under Tom Christian—should have been doing it. They, however, were tied up in other things, notably coordination between Balboa and Abogado's nascent FMTGRB. So it was left to Mac to fill in the chain of command for the force that Carrera intended to lead into the war. To this end he was currently matching files to positions. The commanders and primary staff had long since been filled. The sergeant major was working on secondary staff now.

Siegel came in burdened by another stack of personnel files. "An action passed on is an action completed,' Top," he announced, dumping the files in front of McNamara. "These ones have been cleared by Fernandez."

McNamara looked at the top of the stack Siegel had brought. There, in plain English, was a summary of each file in the stack. "Sig, what t'e hell are you doing here? You're way too smart for t'is."

"Doing here? You mean with the old man?"

Seeing that this was exactly what McNamara meant, Siegel continued, "Oh . . . I just follow him out of idle curiosity."

The sergeant major tapped his fingers impatiently.

"I'm only half joking, Sergeant Major. Most people are predictable. The boss is not. Just watching him operate is a laugh a minute; always has been. Oh, I don't mean *him,* so much as watching the people around him. You and me, for example."

"Get out, Sig. And go tell t'e cook to put on more coffee."

"Sure, Top. But don't *you* ever wonder about why we're here? You know, you can tell a lot about somebody by what he reads; what he thinks is worth reading. I was up at the boss's desk two nights ago and he had a book out, face down. Know what I saw when I picked it up?"

"No and I don't care, eit'er."

"Yes, you do." Siegel closed his eyes, dredging up the memory. "I read:"

> *"I loved you, and so I took these tides of men
> Into my hands and wrote my will
> Upon the sky in stars . . ."*

"Lawrence of Arabia, Top. And the CO had it specially marked."

"T'e cook, Siegel. Coffee."

McNamara watched Siegel make his exit, then made a notation on one file and shoved it aside. He reached for another.

Opening it, the sergeant major saw that this file was for a former BDC officer who had been in command of a company during the '47 invasion. For whatever reason, Fernandez had marked it "Politically Necessary." The officer, a Major Manuel Rocaberti, was a graduate of the Federated States Military Academy at River Watch, Class of 438. The file had not been signed off on by Jimenez. This was odd.

River Watch? This, with Fernandez's notation, was enough for the sergeant major. He had dozens more files to check out tonight. The Balboan officer, Manuel Rocaberti, was assigned to an important billet in the Ia, the operations office.

Office of the President of the Republic of Balboa, 4/10/459 AC

President Rocaberti made a few last minute notes on the speech he would give the people of Balboa telling them that their country had decided to pledge itself—sort of, in an only semi-official, nongovernmental way—to the war against the terrorists. Ultimately, what had decided him to cease resistance and to cooperate was not Parilla's or Carrera's persuasion, nor even the gutless capitulation of the Cabinet and Legislative Council. Instead, Rocaberti had been persuaded by the very attractive prospect of getting the old guard of the BDC out of the country for a while. Given a bit of time, and relief from pressure by the radicals of Piña's old political party and their BDC minions, Rocaberti thought he would have a much better chance of bringing a lasting democracy—which he defined as an oligarchy of the upper classes—to Balboa. It was the silver lining in this very dark cloud.

The president looked up from his note making. It was time to address the nation.

At the signal from the television man the president began.

"People of Balboa, eleven days ago our country was attacked. We were attacked brutally, suddenly, without warning and with no provocation on our part. We did *nothing* to provoke this attack in which hundreds of our people were murdered. The targets of that attack were not our country's defenders of the Civil Force, but inoffensive civilians going about their daily lives, innocent children, and our women.

"Even now a great army of vengeance and justice is being assembled from all over the world to resist and reverse this aggression, to free the peaceful people of the world from the threat of terror. Free peoples from every corner of the globe have pledged themselves to this worthy and noble task.

"In this desperate hour, the Republic of Balboa cannot shirk its responsibility to the rest of the world. Last night, in a late night session which was attended by myself, my Cabinet, the National Legislative Council, and those men of the Civil Force whose job it will be to carry the fight to come, the government of the Republic of Balboa, by an overwhelming majority, voted to facilitate the sending of an expeditionary force to assist the other democracies to end this plague.

"The patriotic and brave soldiers of the Civil Force will be the vanguard and center of our part of this *armada*. However, because they are few and the enemy many, because we need to secure our homeland as well as carry the fight to the enemies of civilization, the Legislative Council has authorized only that one thousand and fifty men of the Military Police companies of the Civil Force, exactly one quarter their strength, may transfer to the new. Any men recently retired may also volunteer without cost to their pensions.

"Still, the new organization will need several thousand volunteers to bring its units to the size needed for this operation. I call upon the young men of the Republic to give of themselves by volunteering for this enterprise."

Like hundreds of thousands across Balboa, Ricardo Cruz, aged seventeen, sat among family and friend in front of the snowy screen of the family television. (For while satellite television was in theory available, the premium tacked on by the Rocaberti family that controlled it made it prohibitively expensive for simple farmers.) Cruz contemplated his immediate plans. *Tomorrow I will go down to the police station and sign up.*

He thought of Cara and her feelings on the subject. *She is so sweet . . . so pretty too. But she'll never understand that I have to go.*

Manuel Rocaberti, too, watched his uncle's speech. His feelings on the subject were far different from Cruz's, however. Only that morning he had spoken to his Uncle, the president.

"Shut up, Manuel. You owe this to the family," the president had commanded.

Manuel pleaded, "But, *Tio Guillermo*, I'm no good. I've tried and I just don't have it. I've no business being a soldier."

"You're not going there to be a soldier, boy. You're going there to be a spy, my spy. I don't trust Parilla and I trust his pet gringo with the electric eyes even less. Those bastards forced this fucking under-the-table rearmament down my throat. I don't like it."

"So what can *I* do about it? *Jesu Cristo, Tio*, I'm not going as anything or anyone important."

"Watch, report, impede if possible. It isn't likely that they'll really be able to raise this force, not from scratch. Parilla's never been in command of a real army. And this gringo of his was—what?—a lieutenant colonel? All of that? Even *you* were a major," the president sneered. "But I want you there to make it as unlikely as possible, even so."

INTERLUDE

29 July, 2067,
United Nations Starship *Kofi Annan*

The ship on-screen bore a name in English letters, though that name was Chinese.

The *Cheng Ho* drifted slowly in high orbit around the planet people back home were already calling Terra Nova, or something similar in their own languages. In Arabic, for example, it was "*al Donya al Jedida,*" in Chinese, "*Xing She Jie,*" though the Chinese were as likely to say, "*Xing Zhong Guo*" which meant "New Middle Kingdom." Then again, for the Chinese, very little could be even of conceptual importance that was not China and Chinese.

The *Cheng Ho* hadn't sent word to Earth in six years, despite having carried several dozen messenger-bots capable of, and intended to, carry news from the ship homeward.

Like the earlier robotic probe, the *Cristobal Colon*, the *Cheng Ho* had taken off, in 2060, propelled by Sol's rays and laser stations positioned on planets, planetoids and in space. The laser stations had, by that year, grown much more numerous and powerful, cutting the time of flight to the rift nearly in half.

There had been much celebration on Earth when the ship had begun its long journey to the stars. Every country, every ethnicity, and nearly every interest group had a reason to be proud. Indeed, each had a stake in the voyage, on an emotional level at least, as the passengers had been carefully handpicked to be the best and the brightest representatives of their respective ascriptive, ethnic, cultural or national groups. As a matter of fact, not only were they the best and the brightest, much care had been taken to ensure they were also the most forward thinking, the least intolerant, persons available from those groups.

The crew members were not quite as diverse, being largely American, English, Chinese, Japanese, Indian and Brazilian with only token members from other nations. But the passengers?

There were three hundred and sixty-four Moslems, one hundred and eighty-one non-Moslem Europeans, a like number of Americans, roughly three hundred each Indians and Chinese, and about eight hundred passengers from other groups and nations. The average IQ was over one hundred and forty and the average adult educational level the Ph.D.

Thus, it had come as something of a shock when, a year after launch, the captain of the ship reported a murder. Moreover, the shock to Earth when he mentioned "rioting youths" was enough to cause an initial news blackout against any further reports from the *Cheng Ho* as tens of thousand more "youths" rioted in sympathy across the globe The blackout itself was followed by considerable censorship on what news was later allowed, yet clearly the problem of "rioting youths" had remained.

"Well, nobody's rioting aboard her now," observed the captain of the follow-on ship, the UNSS *Kofi Annan*, an exploration frigate, the first of its class, fitted out to search for and bring back news from the *Cheng Ho*.

"No, ma'am," answered an ensign manning the remote sensing station as the *Annan* reached the outer limits of its sensing range. "With radiation levels that high there's nobody alive on board. Only one shuttle missing, too. And its bay doesn't look like it saw many dockings or take offs. Only light burning, you see, Captain."

The captain grimaced and nodded, grimly. Hitting a button on her command chair to activate the on-board intercom, she said, "Marines? This is the captain speaking. I want a recon team ready in thirty minutes, full hardened suits upshielded for heavy radiation. Major Ridilla, meet me in my cabin for instructions. Flight deck? Prepare to bring them to the *Cheng Ho*. I want you to dock and wait to retrieve them. Captain, out."

CHAPTER
ELEVEN

Gold cannot always find good soldiers, but good soldiers can always find gold.

—Machiavelli, *The Prince*

Casa Linda, 5/10/459 AC

For a change the *Casa* Linda was quiet. Differently from the past month, this day there were no shouting matches, no screaming in the halls. Even the keyboards and printers of the computers bought to design the force were silent. Above stairs, the only sounds were the hum of the window-mounted air conditioners, the sound of the kitchen staff going about its business, and the steady drumming of the incessant rain.

None of those sounds penetrated below to the basement which held, among other things, a plain but well equipped conference room. In this the entire staff, minus Lourdes but with Abogado added, had collected themselves for the final decision brief.

It was informal, that brief, as Carrera (once known

as Hennessey) was, himself, informal. He sat at one end of the table that ran lengthwise down the room. The primary staff, some of the important secondaries, and Abogado filled the rest of the spaces. The remainder sat behind Carrera on upholstered chairs in three rows of five. Soult sat at a keyboard, in front and all the way to the right.

There was nothing on the walls but for three projection screens opposite Carrera and thirteen carved poles with bronze placards and topped by gilded or silvered, carved eagles.

This is going to be an insufferable data dump, Carrera fumed. *God, I hate meetings. Nothing to be done for it, though.*

"Let's get to it," he began. "Matthias, what do we have to work with?"

The Sachsen cleared his throat and answered, "Not as much as I'd like. Ze most—und, Patricio, I mean ze *most*—I vas able to come up viz vas seven hundred fifty million. Vorse, you can't use all uff it. I leveraged you zo hard zat you simply must keep a reserve to cover any downturn in your family's fortunes . . . zay, eight perzent. You may be able to use zat, even to dip a little deeper later on, if ze economy improves, generally."

Carrera had hoped for more but . . .

"Fair enough, Matthias. Let's see the Table of Organization and Equipment you've come up with, Dan."

All three projection screens lit up. The two on the flanks showed spreadsheets. The right one was budget, broken down by major element of expense: Pay, Subsistence, Operations, Major End Items, and the like. Some of those were further subdivided as, for example, Major End Items which showed separate entries for Small and Crew-served Arms, Aviation, Armor, Artillery, Transportation, Command and Control, Intelligence, Medical, Foreign Military Training Group, and so forth.

The left screen was a detailed breakdown by rank and military occupational specialty, or MOS, for the entire force to include the rump that would be left behind to send support forward and train replacements.

The center screen was a diagram marked "Brigade Table of Organization." Carrera knew it already, in general terms. After all, he'd been in everyone's shit for the last five weeks as they struggled through. The chart showed one unit, marked as a rectangle with a large X feeding to each corner and a smaller one above to show the size; namely, a brigade. The larger X indicated the type, infantry. Above that box and to the right was a number, "4997." This was the strength, not subdivided by rank, they'd agreed on.

One line ran down from that box to touch another line that ran almost from one side of the screen to the other. Twelve short lines descended from that longer one to a series of boxes. These twelve boxes had other symbols inside. Four showed large X's for infantry, one marked with the X and oval symbol for mechanized infantry, and one with crossed arrows for special operations troops or "Cazadors."—the word meant basically the same thing as "Jaegers," "Chasseurs," or "Rangers." Still others were marked for Artillery (a single large dot representing a cannon ball), Combat Support ("CS"), Aviation (a propeller), Service Support (SSP),

Headquarters (HQ), and Naval (an anchor). Numbers showing above these boxes ranged from "372" for the smallest unit, the Cazadors, to "578" for the largest, the Service Support people.

Above each of that series of boxes were drawn two vertical lines, indicating that the units were "battalions."

"Let's just call a fucking spade a spade, shall we?" Carrera said. "We're forming with the intention of hiring ourselves to the Federated States. That makes us mercenaries even though we may call ourselves 'auxiliaries.' Traditionally, mercenaries form 'legions.' Moreover, we're going to be about the same size as a traditional, Old Earth Roman legion. Additionally, if you subtract the aviation and naval groups, we have ten sub-units just as did the legions of ancient Rome. And while we're at it," he added, "note that the sizes of our battalions are a bit small to really be battalions. Call *us* a legion and them fucking cohorts. Or celibate cohorts, for that matter, I don't give a shit."

A really good subordinate must sometimes read his leader's mind, even in fairly trivial matters. Carrera had hand picked some pretty good ones. He was unsurprised, therefore, when all traces of the word "Brigade" were instantly replaced with "Legion" and all references to "Battalion" became "Cohort."

"It occurred to several of us, too, Pat," Kuralski explained.

"No comment, General Abogado?" Carrera asked.

"Your command and control is going to be stretched with twelve subunits reporting directly to headquarters," Abogado answered. "On the other hand, when I was commanding the old 391st Separate Brigade here I had one mech battalion, plus two infantry, one special forces, one combat support, one military police, an aviation, a service support, a jungle operations school, an attached infantry battalion attending the jungle school, an international school and a headquarters battalion all reporting to me, plus two full brigades of the Territorial Militia that would have deployed here in the event of war. So I think it's in the realm of the *plausible*, at least. Moreover, I didn't command the air force and naval commands here. Instead I had to coordinate. Command is easier."

"Yeah, I'm not worried about that. Okay, if we can't afford it, it's a pipe dream. Let's talk money, Dan," Carrera said.

Kuralski nodded. "The biggest element of expense is troop related: pay, subsistence, allowances, operations, training—which includes maintenance—and training *ammunition*, for the brigade, err, legion. It's based on paying forty percent of FSA scales, housing them in tents, feeding them at local costs for food . . ."

Clinton, the supply man, piped in, "Sir, myself and the log officer checked local wholesale prices on that and matched them against FS Army ration schedules. No more than one hundred drachma per man, per month to feed the troops *well*."

"Yes," Kuralski agreed, "but we don't know if that would be feeding them what they like. I suspect feeding a good local diet will be a little cheaper."

"Enough cheaper to make a difference?" Carrera asked.

"Not really. Might save a hundred D per man for the year. Not even half a million drachma, overall."

"Okay, continue."

"Ammunition and personal and crew-served arms are so tightly interwoven that we really need to talk about them together," Kuralski said. "And we never could come to an agreement among us as to which to go with. It makes a pretty whopping difference in cost, at one end, and battle performance on the other, with proficiency in the middle. The short version is that if you buy Volgan, you can afford a war gun, a training gun, and ammunition to the tune of fifty or sixty *thousand* rounds of training ammunition per man. If you buy Tauran or FS, you can afford one rifle and maybe four thousand rounds per man. Of course, the Volgan arms are simple, reliable, and none too accurate. The best compromise we could come up with was to buy Volgan and add three Draco sniper rifles to each section."

"What's that save us over buying FS or Tauran with, say, fifteen thousand rounds per man?"

"About nine million," Kuralski answered. "That's an estimate, we haven't worked out any deals yet."

"Works. Do it: Volgan, if we can get them. Besides, they're more accurate than they get credit for if they're properly zeroed."

"We can get them, surely. There are also a lot of Volgan equipment clones out there," Kuralski reminded, "so it's probably fairly *safe* to plan that way. And Sachsen is allegedly sitting on hundreds of thousands of unusually high quality Samsonov rifles and machine guns, too."

He went on, "The next largest element of expense is aviation equipment. That isn't counting training on that equipment."

"Dan and I have worked on that one together, mostly by e-mail and phone," Abogado interjected.

"I don't know all that much about training for pilots and such, though I can deal with maintenance training well enough. Most of what he's talking about using is Volgan or really, *really* simple Tauran and FS birds. I think that, rather than set up an aviation subdivision of the FMTG, we ought to send pilots and maintenance personnel overseas. I've looked into the prices and, in the short term anyway, that would be cheaper . . . a little. Maybe later, once we've got enough local pilots trained and a larger scale organization, it might be worth it to bring the aviation training base home."

Carrera looked over the screen showing cost factors. Aviation stood out above everything but personnel and training costs. The figure, "FSD 115,000,000," was a little shocking.

"How do we save some money there?" he asked.

"I don't think we can cut numbers, Pat," Dan answered. "What we have listed—eight converted crop dusters for attack birds, twelve medium and four heavy lift helicopters, eight cargo, six recon and twelve remote-piloted vehicles—is about the minimum to do the job. The basis was to be able to lift the critical elements of an infantry cohort and the Cazador cohort in two lifts, assuming an eighty-five percent serviceable rate for the transport helos. Almost everything else was based on that. Oh . . . and we'll need two more helicopters for medical evacuation. We can save something if you're willing to go with used, rebuilt helicopters and to substitute short takeoff recon birds for choppers for the medevac."

"And save how much?"

"About eighteen million. Note, here, that this is a bad bargain, unless you find more money at some point to buy newer aircraft. Older and cheaper also means sooner to wear out."

"All right. Buy used. You have a line on used?"

"For a lot of it, we do. For some we're still looking. IM-71 medium lift helicopters, for example, can be had for about one point six million FSD, each, used. IM-62 heavy lifters run about two point six. New they run over twice that, by the way. We've found nine IM-71s for sale. We're still looking for three. IM-62s are available."

"Okay, let's talk armor."

Kuralski laughed slightly. "If you think we fought over small arms, that was nothing compared to the fight over armor. If we thought you could afford it, we'd mutiny before letting you buy anything but Zion-built *Chariots*. Too damned expensive, even used. Sixty of those would cost two hundred and twenty to two hundred and forty million. It would break the bank, in other words.

"Instead, what you've got there under that sum of 'FSD 84,000,000' is our best *guess* of what it will cost for a mix of Volgan T-38s and PBM-23s. Until I can go over there—"

"You?" Carrera asked.

"I'm the only one who speaks Russian. Until I can go over there, that amount remains an educated guess. We do have fairly hard numbers and figures for some much less capable equipment, T-27s and the like. But that stuff is truly shit, well designed but what's available is so badly made it would be almost as criminal to use it as to not have anything."

Carrera looked like he had a very sour taste in his mouth. He mulled the prospect of losing his chief of

staff for anywhere from weeks to months and clearly
didn't like it. After perhaps a minute of looking sour,
he went along. "All right. You go to Saint Nicholasberg
as soon as possible to hunt arms. Moving right along,
who do we have among the Civil Force competent to
command the mechanized troops?"

Kuralski shook his head. "Xavier says there's no
one."

Carrera thought about that for a minute. *Harrington
or Brown and I need Harrington as a loggie.* He then
said, "Brown?"

"Sir."

"I dub thee, 'Sancho Panzer.' You'll command the
mech and tanks. You're going to go spend about a
month and a half somewhere where *nobody* speaks a
word of English to immerse you in Spanish."

"Sir!" The single word meant: *I won't let you down,
Boss. Promise.*

The brief moved along, covering artillery and ground
transportation.

"Twenty-four 105mm guns and six multiple rocket
launchers will cost WHAT?"

"We have an alternate plan to substitute twelve
122mm guns and twelve 160mm mortars, plus six
Volgan . . . "

By the time they got to individual equipment beyond
small arms . . .

"Twenty-two hundred FSD per man for body armor,
Pat. Unless you want to go with something Terry
Johnson has come up with."

Johnson stood up. "I knew that figure would floor
you. It floored me. So, off duty, I started nosing around
the Globalnet. There are two developments I think

you ought to consider. By the way, Harrington let me dip into discretionary funds to get this stuff."

Johnson bent over and pulled what looked like a thick vest from under his chair. This he passed to Carrera.

"What the fuck is this?" Carrera asked. "It's *light*."

"It's silk, Pat, regular old silk. Well, not *regular*. It's specially woven and encased in polytetrafluoroethane cloth. That model is what this company in Rajamangala had available to send us. It's thirty-four layers of heavy duty silk and, yes, at about four and a half pounds, it's pretty light. It will stop anything up to .45 caliber but *not* .44. It will stop damned near all shrapnel. Though both .45 and heavy shrapnel will *hurt*. It will *definitely* not stop high powered rifle ammunition. Neither will the twenty-two hundred drachma vest the FSC makes which is also, by the way, a shitpot heavier."

"Cost?"

"One fifty to five hundred, depending. I say depending because there are some modifications we can make that would make it lighter *and* make it more effective. Some mods would lower the price but one modification also raises it substantially.

"That modification is this." Johnson again reached down and handed over a four inch by twelve inch metal plate, about a tenth of an inch thick. The plate was deformed in five spots.

"This is what is called 'glassy metal' or 'liquid metal.' It's an alloy of five metals—titanium, copper, nickel, zirconium and beryllium—that really don't like each other. It's cooled very quickly so that the metals can't form crystals. What they do form is an alloy about seven-eighths as dense as steel and two and a half times stronger. It's also precision castable. What that means to us is that we can make a plate a tenth of an inch thick out of this shit and have it be as strong as a quarter of an inch of good steel. We might also consider using it for some other things; bayonets come to mind, and maybe helmets.

"I figure that we can make it something like the old Roman lorica, a series of thin plates maybe four inches by twelve or so and running partway across the chest and back, and over the shoulders, to cover all the really vital organs and the hard-to-rebuild shit, like shoulders, for maybe eleven pounds. Add that to the silk which, because we'll be able to make the chest and back portions thinner will reduce in weight, and you're looking at a fourteen pound set of torso armor."

Carrera looked skeptical. "You tested the metal?"

"I shot at it, yes. Those deformations are what I got firing different calibers. Got to warn you, armor piercing .30 cal and higher will go through if it hits straight on."

"Fair enough. What's the total cost for a vest with the metal plates, again?"

Johnson put out his hand, spreading his fingers and wiggling them slightly. "A little under five hundred drachma . . . give or take."

"And that saves us," Carrera summed up, "about eight or nine million drachma. Which, even if this shit turns out not to be as good, is still eight or nine million I could spend on training, training which is at least as likely to save life, by killing the enemy, as a vest is. Okay. I'll think on this one though."

Casa Linda, 6/10/459 AC

Carrera and Abogado spoke privately on the balcony that led from his office to overlook the *Mar Furioso*. A steady drumbeat of electric crackles told of myriad mosquitoes being fried before they could come to feast.

Abogado handed Carrera a thick notebook with rings. "These are people I've talked to about coming here for the FMTG that have indicated a willingness to come. No, I have *not* made an offer to any of them. It's set up by rank—former generals in front, then former colonels and lieutenant colonels, then other officers, other warrants, and noncoms—and the position I think they could fill. It isn't alphabetical."

Carrera shrugged, took the book, and began flipping pages.

Flip, flip, flip. "No, you can't have 'Moon' Mullins," he said, tearing a page out and laying it on the coffee table between them. "He's a toad, an incredibly stupid toad, and a sycophant. He brings out the worst in you; I've seen it." Flip, flip. "Hmmm . . . maybe." Flip, flip, flip. "Good choice on Frazar." Flip. "Lambert? No. He's the 'Salute in the Field' type. Had his Special Services Group operatives shaving when their mission required them to blend in with locals, none of whom shaved. Altogether too stupid for me to let near my boys." Flip, flip, flip, flip. "Bolger? Are you out of your fucking mind? Disloyal and treacherous. Mulholland? Nice guy but almost as stupid as he looks. Well . . . that's not *quite* fair; nobody could be that stupid. Maybe Mulholland." Flip, flip. "Mace? You have got to me shitting me! He could be a good stage manager in some major theater, great at putting on a show, but there's never a drop of substance behind the show. Add in . . . oh, off the top of my head, smuggling exotic birds and falsifying physical fitness tests. If he sets foot in this country again I'll have him shot. I wouldn't let him near my troops except in a sealed glass case marked, 'Be nothing like this man.'"

Flip. "Taylor's very good."

Looking up, Carrera saw that Abogado face had become a mix of frustration and worry. "Look . . . you saw these guys from one end. I saw them as peers or superiors and I saw something very different. The Army of the Federated States does a very bad job, generally, of choosing general officers. For the most part, they're charming men without an ounce of good character. How the hell could it be any different? In an environment where every decision is a moral one, where you get rated by fifty or sixty people before you're looked at for stars, the ones who make general are, almost entirely, those who *never* pissed anyone off. How does one never piss off the boss? Almost the only way is to have no real character, or at least no good character. The exceptions to that rule are just that, exceptional."

"I had character," Abogado objected.

"You were fucking the secretarial pool at Building Four on Fort Henry," Carrera pointed out. "I'll overlook that because you have other virtues. But let's not pretend that you aren't a rotter, too."

Casa Linda, 7/10/459 AC

True to his pledge, Carrera had not assumed command of the expeditionary force. When Kuralski asked him about that, he answered, "Dan, I don't need to be in the top position to be in control. I don't even want to be. Besides, I'll own every piece of equipment the legion is going to use, *and* be making the payroll. How much more control do I need?

"Then, too, Parilla's an old soldier, but he doesn't know much of anything about war, less still about modern war. He understands discipline, leadership and politics. I need him for that. But I'm quite sure he'd let me do what I want to train and lead the force, even if I weren't paying for it."

Parilla, escorted by Kennison, Morse, and Bowman, pulled up to the entrance of *Casa* Linda in Carrera's Phaeton. Once, when he had been the effective ruler of the country, Parilla would have been driven in his own. Since then he had fallen on somewhat harder times, although he was hardly living in poverty. Carrera would have been more than prepared to give Parilla the Phaeton, or to buy him one of his own, to get his cooperation. He knew that wouldn't be necessary.

When the vehicle stopped, Morse got out to open the door. Carrera and Kuralski came to attention and saluted although no one was in uniform. After Parilla returned the salute, Carrera walked down the steps to greet him.

"General Parilla, it is good to see you again." The two smiled conspiratorially.

After shaking hands, Carrera escorted the party down to the briefing room. The rest of his staff was already there. Lourdes served drinks while Carrera introduced Parilla to the staff. Then Carrera began the briefing.

"General Parilla, I have asked you here today to get your approval for a plan for raising, equipping and training an expeditionary force, roughly brigade sized, to participate in the war against the terrorists. I thank you personally for coming out of your way to meet with me here at my home. The *Estado Mayor* would once have been a more appropriate spot for this but, since this house is air conditioned and the *Estado Mayor* has been demolished, I thought you might prefer to be brought up to date here."

"And besides that," Parilla added, "this place is secure. There probably isn't another quite so safe in the country."

"This first item of business is the shape of the organization we have planned." Carrera gestured for a slide to be shown on the screen in the front of the briefing room.

"As you can see, General, we've named it a legion. It should be obvious enough why."

Parilla looked confused but let it go. "I confess I don't know, but do you think, do your people think, that this is a good design, Patricio? It seems odd to me."

Carrera frowned, not at Parilla but at circumstance and fate. He shrugged. "Honestly, in some ways it's a crappy design. But it has some serious good points. It actually is not designed for use so much as for expansion. In the expanded form, with every cohort grown to the size of a small regiment of about one thousand to fourteen hundred men, and the legion grown to the size of a division, it *would be fairly* optimal for the kind of war we expect to fight. As is, it is as much as we can afford, as much as we have the personnel to lead, and as much as we have time to train those leaders for. Matthias, explain to the general, would you?"

Esterhazy nodded and went over the finances. He didn't need to remind Parilla who was paying for everything.

Carrera interjected, "Basically, Raul, the hit my family's fortunes took in the TNTO attack has not been made good. The value of our assets is down to about forty-seven percent of what it had been."

"*Ja*," Esterhazy agreed. "If he vere to cash out assets now ze loss vould be enormous. His family vould object and he might lose control in a shareholders' fight. As is, if Patrick can vait, zere is no reason for ze assets not to return to zere prior value . . . in a couple of years."

"Matt's used his contacts to arrange loans secured by my holdings, Raul," Carrera added. "We have a line of credit for seven hundred and fifty million FSD, a personal loan, really, secured by me, er, rather secured by what will be my personal share once the estate is finally probated. That's all we have to count on."

Carrera sighed, a bit wistfully. "I'd have gone for a full division, anyway, and just used shit for equipment until we could afford better but the personnel and training issues make that more than a little problematic. As is, not only are we going out smaller than I'd like, and not organized the way I'd like; we're not going to be able to afford the best equipment either.

"There is no telling exactly how the war will roll out. It could be that Sumer folds immediately and we go right into a counterinsurgency war."

Seeing Parilla's somewhat quizzical look, Carrera stated, "Oh, yes; no matter what, there *will* be an insurgency, though I have reason to suspect the FSC is not even considering the possibility.

"It could be that there will be a major conventional fight, something like the last Petro War, though on a lesser scale, because Sumer has not managed to make good its losses. What we really expect though, is a campaign—more or less conventional—of about three to seven weeks' duration, followed by an insurgency."

Triste, sitting in the left rear corner, added, "You got that right. Those idiots in the War Department, to say nothing of that king of idiots, Ron Campos—that's the FSC's secretary of war, General—are really being obtuse about this. I don't think I've ever even heard of anyone engaging in such wishful thinking since the FSC got itself into that dumb-assed war in Cochin, forty years back."

Carrera scowled a bit. This was Campos' second stint as SecWar. Carrera had not thought the first sufficiently impressive to justify a second.

He continued. "Anyway, the legion is based in large part around the needs of counterinsurgency. Thus there are four infantry cohorts, each with four infantry centuries, plus combat support and headquarters and support, because a square organization is more suitable for controlling an area and the people on it than a triangular one is. Note though, that triangular is clearly better for maneuver warfare. There are Cazador and mechanized cohorts because the one is critical, and the other useful, for counterinsurgency. The rest is fairly self explanatory *except* for the size and shape of the aviation *ala*."

"*Ala*?" Parilla asked.

"Latin for 'wing,' as in 'cavalry wing.' But all the real cavalry is in the air now, so . . ."

"Bring up the aviation slide, would you, Mitch?" Carrera asked.

When the slide was shown, Carrera frowned. "General, this one makes only limited sense *except* in terms of its being a training vehicle for a cadre for a much larger air organization. It's the largest group after the service support cohort. It has fifty aircraft including remotely piloted vehicles. That doesn't include medical evacuation aircraft. Of those fifty, it has sixteen helicopters, twelve medium and four heavy. We don't know yet which medium and heavy lift helicopter we will choose or what we can afford. I am inclined towards Volgan and there are a sufficient number for sale, usually used and rebuilt, at an acceptable price. We are probably going to use modified crop-dusters built in the FSC for the close air support role." Carrera saw Parilla's smile and hastily added, "No, sir, don't laugh. They have impressive capabilities—over two tons of ordnance, thirteen hardpoints and can turn on a dime—and have already been combat tested in the close support role in Santander."

"In any case, in designing the air *ala*, our twin goals were: every asset that would be in divisional level air support wing must be there, and it must be able to lift the combat elements of one infantry cohort plus the Cazador cohort in not more than two lifts with eighty-five percent of the helicopters operationally ready. This does that but the personnel inefficiency when dealing with numbers of aircraft this low is just *appalling*.

"Naval slide, Mitch."

Parilla looked that over and saw a few light warships plus a number of merchant ships. He shrugged.

Soldiers were soldiers and didn't care about ships. One thing did catch his eye, though.

"What's this intelligence collection ship?"

Omar Fernandez, sitting next to Triste in the left rear of the room piped in, "That one's for me, General."

"We need to have a long talk about that, Fernandez," Carrera said, his eyes narrowing to slits. "And soon. Like, say, after this meeting is over."

"Anyway, General, that's it. You have detailed diagrams of the tables of organization in your packet. Pending your questions . . ."

Carrera stopped to sip at a cup of coffee. Parilla sat digesting the rest of the chart of the Headquarters. Parilla asked about the unusual staff set up.

"A good question, General. There are basically four staff arrangements in use in the civilized world. The FSC's system of four equal sections, which is what you are used to, and which they inherited from the Gauls in the Great Global War, is designed to be something of a committee. I believe it has a number of defects, chief among them being that these staffs inject an equality into the planning and conduct of military operations that has no place in battle. The Anglian system is needlessly complex and badly over officered; we don't have enough trained officers to hope to emulate it anyway. The Volgans could be said not to really have much of a staff structure below division level.

"Instead, the model we have chosen is the same staff form that the Sachsen used with great success in the Great Global War and before. Historical experience says that this is much the best form for a highly mobile force. To some extent I expect this to make up, partially, for the fact that our organization is not really geared to highly mobile warfare. This staff form also does not suffer the defect of permitting the rear echelon to act as a dead weight upon the fighting line. Instead, everything goes to support the front. Lastly, this form for the staff does not permit the personnel managers to have much of a say in operations. It locates the clerks so that they cannot harass the line with constant demands for timely information that no personnel management system can do anything useful with in a timely manner."

Parilla chewed his lower lip for a few moments before saying, "I don't think I like that, Patricio. Armies are composed of people; hence personnel management is a critical component of the force. It's as important as, maybe more important than, logistics."

Carrera jerked his chin slightly sideways, then chewed his own lip for a bit. "I am put in mind of a story I read once," he said, "a true story, about a day in August, 1944, Old Earth Year, when the American Army in France had a total infantry replacement pool of one rifleman for perhaps twenty or so divisions. Imagine, if you will, General, a situation where thousands of personnel managers are in a position to manage one poor rifleman. How privileged that man must have felt! I have always thought that if those personnel managers had been mostly infantry themselves they wouldn't have been managed quite so thoroughly, but there would have been more than one man to replace the hundreds killed and wounded that August day. Computers, by the way, do not seem to help this problem much once the shooting starts."

Parilla thought about that for a minute and decided Carrera was probably right. His face said as much. He thumbed through his hand-out packet and said, "I note you have General Abogado in charge of our foreign trainers. How is old Ken doing?" He remembered Abogado rather fondly from his days as commander of FS Army troops in Balboa.

Carrera smiled. "He's fine and raring to go last I saw him, Raul, which was here, two days ago. He asked about you. In any case, he says he'll be ready within six weeks to begin the first course he is going to be running for our senior officers, a sort of truncated CGSC, a command and general staff course. He'll also be running a number of other courses to train and select lower leaders and technicians."

"Good, good," said Parilla. "I remember—with envy, too, I admit—the way he used to train the FSC troops here. A fine old soldier."

"He was that," Carrera agreed. *Pity about having feet of clay. Still, Abogado is superb at what he does provided you keep him away from women.*

"Where are we going to train the troops, by the way, Patricio? Most of the old FS facilities have been sold off. The Civil Force lacks facilities, generally."

"Mitch, bring up the Fort Cameron slide, please."

The previous slide disappeared to be replaced by a map of a small area well known to Parilla from his days as commander of the *Guardia Nacional.*

"Sometime, someday when we can afford it, Raul, I hope to buy the Isla Real outright and turn it into a base for us," Carrera explained. The *Isla Real*, or Royal Island, was about eighty kilometers north of *Ciudad* Balboa and was about two hundred and seventy square kilometers in area. "But that alone will cost twice our total budget now to buy and build up. It will have to wait. In the interim . . ."

He pointed at the slide. "This is a map of the old *Centro de Instruccion Militar* at *Fuerte* Cameron. As you can see, it is sufficient to our current purposes, with enough range space and well-drained, open, flat areas for tentage. Most of the buildings will go for housing cadre, offices, and school rooms."

Again, Parilla accepted that. He asked, "What about rank structure? I see lots of old Roman military titles, few modern. Is there a reason?"

Carrera nodded. "We'll be working mostly with the Army of the Federated States and the Anglians. They are extremely rank conscious. I simply do not want them, initially, to have the slightest clue as to the ranks of our people they are dealing with. Thus, signifers are roughly second lieutenants, but could be considered first lieutenants or captains. Tribunes I through III are, for our purposes, 1st lieutenants through majors, but could be considered majors through colonels. Legates 3rd through 1st are lieutenants colonel through brigadiers. On the other hand, in Latin 'legate' means lieutenant general, three stars, or ambassador, which is a four star equivalent. The sole *dux*, or *duce*, is yourself. The centurionate runs from optio, basically a platoon sergeant, through 1st centurion, the senior noncom of a cohort, and on to sergeant major, of which *this* expeditionary force needs only one at this time, Sergeant Major McNamara."

"Seems silly to me, Patricio."

"Give it time, Raul. Are you ready for dinner?"

Adjourning to the mess, Parilla asked about a set of thirteen carved and silvered or gilded eagles perched atop poles.

Carrera gestured toward the table and chairs,

mahogany and intricately hand carved. "There is a furniture factory in *Valle de las Lunas*, *Fabrica* Hertzog, that does fine wood carving and makes some really superb furniture. They made this table, the chairs, the sideboard and the china cabinet. Good work, very good. When you gave me this mission, I gave some thought to what the units' symbols should be. I had *Fabrica* Hertzog make these up.

"We'll present them to the legion, cohorts, *ala* and *classis* at a solemn, probably half-religious, ceremony sometime in the future."

Carrera moved to take one of the eagles from its rack against the wall. He presented it to Parilla. "As you can see, sir, the eagles themselves are of gilded or silvered wood. The plaques we just had made up. They give the name and number of the unit that will carry it. This one, for example, is for the 8th Artillery Cohort, *Terremoto*." Earthquake. He put down the Eighth's eagle and picked up another. Pointing to its plaque he read off, "Eleventh Air Ala . . . Jan Sobieski, who beat the Turk at Vienna with his *winged* hussars." Carrera went down the list, pointing to each in turn. "Legion: Ruy Diaz de Bivar, Legio del Cid for short . . . First Cohort: Principe Eugenio; Prinz Eugen who led the Austrians against the Turks . . . Second Cohort: Roberto Guiscard, the Crusader . . . Third Cohort: Ricardo, Corazon de Leon, the Crusader . . . Fourth Cohort: Barbarossa, Crusader . . . Fifth: Carlos Martillo who stopped the Moslem advance at Tours in old France . . . Sixth: Vlad Tepes who fought the Turk for Transylvania . . . Seventh Combat Support: the sword of El Cid, Tizona . . . Ninth Service Support: his horse, Babieca . . . Tenth: the Headquarters,

Santiago Matamoros, Saint James the Moor killer . . .
Twelfth *Classis*: Don John who crushed the Turk at
Lepanto."

"You see where I'm going with this, right?"

Parilla laughed, "Oh, yes, I see, my friend."

Dinner commenced and carried on more or less
silently. Parilla was on information overload and the
staff knew better than to talk plainly. After all, they
worked for Carrera, not Parilla. When it was done,
and the maids were clearing the table, Carrera asked
the general—no, *el Duce*—yet again, if he had any
further questions.

"No, none. You have done a fine job . . . by the
way, what is your rank in all this?"

"We have to talk about that, privately. At this
moment I probably have no official legal rank beyond
a mandate from the Legislative Council to be your
deputy and to help prepare the Legion. Shall we repair
to the living room for a nightcap to discuss just that?
We also need to talk about your own rank." Carrera
nodded to Kuralski to keep the rest of the staff away
while he and Parilla chatted.

"The day after tomorrow I am flying to Hamilton,
FD to speak with, umm, my family senator. She owes
my family a great deal. She also needs our support
for future campaigns. Frankly, I despise the bitch on
principle but she ought be a useful conduit to greater
FSC support."

An hour and a half later, while Bowman and Morse
drove the general home, Kuralski, Sergeant Major
McNamara, Fernandez and Carrera relaxed on the
back porch of *Casa* Linda, overlooking the sea. The

salty smell of ocean, overlaid with the smell of decayed organic matter from the coast, wafted up.

McNamara chided his boss. "Now, sir, if you had been t'at good at dog and pony shows back in the FS Army you would have gone far. Why I can just picture you as some four star's aide de camp."

Carrera made a gagging sound and then leaned back in his chair and clasped his hands behind his head, satisfied at a job well done. "They tried to grab me to be someone's aide de camp three times, Top. The idea made me ill; I *despise* general officers, for the most part. And, besides, don't confuse inability with unwillingness. I could always dog and pony with the best of them. I just wouldn't do it without a really good reason. Tonight I had a good reason.

"And, Mac, tell the boys to put on the uniforms starting tomorrow. With the ranks I gave them when they first got here, with the proviso that Kuralski and Kennison are Legates I and the ex-captains are Tribunes III. And they can skip the promotion party for my having made Legate III. It's just another tool. Besides, we are going to be much too busy for that nonsense over the next several months."

"As shall I be, Legate Carrera," smirked Fernandez. "So if we could have that talk now . . ."

For such a sensitive matter neither the front steps to the *casa* nor even the dining room would do. Instead, Fernandez and Carrera repaired to the basement conference room.

"What the hell do you need an 'Intelligence Gathering Ship' for, Fernandez? There is no way I can afford the equipment you would need to gather intelligence from a ship. You have no people trained for the equipment anyway. I cannot afford more people from Europe or the FSC, either, not with what I am paying for trainers."

Fernandez gave a tiny and wintery smile. "It is not to gather intelligence *from* the ship. It is to gather intelligence *in* the ship. I have in mind a prison *cum* interrogation vessel."

"But why on a ship? We can put up tents and string wire much, much more cheaply."

"Yes, you can, Patricio. And you can have Amnesty Interplanetary, Liberation International, Freedom of Conscience, the World League and every other cosmopolitan progressive organization breathing down your neck and harassing you twenty-four hours a day. A ship—a ship that never comes to port—prevents that."

"But what do I care if . . . oh, you are talking about them objecting to . . . what shall we say? 'Rigorous' interrogation methods?"

"Precisely," Fernandez agreed.

Carrera considered for a bit. *There was a time I would not have permitted anything like torture. Now? Do I still care now? Maybe not. It would have mattered to Linda and that would have once made me care. Then, too, the bar on torture was a bar to torturing real soldiers, honorable men and women. What consideration do I owe to those who kill innocent people deliberately? Maybe none.*

"What do you have in mind and why?" Carrera asked.

"To begin with, Patricio, pain, force and violence, either physical or mental, are *always* at least implicit in any interrogation, in war or in peace. It may have been the rack and the hot pincers in the Middle Ages, or it could be a longer sentence—or at least not a *shorter* sentence—to some hell hole of a prison now, for failure to cooperate. The person being interrogated has no—let me say that again, *no*—reason to cooperate without some threat or violence."

"Yet some do," Carrera objected.

"Oh, yes," Fernandez admitted, "whether in police work or intelligence work, you will sometimes get someone who sings like a bird from the moment you bring him in. In ninety-nine cases out of one hundred, Patricio, even then he is responding to the fear that he might be subject to force and violence. And the other one in a hundred? He's likely to just be a nut from whom you can't get anything of value."

"Witch trials?" Carrera objected again. "Forced, valueless confessions? What about all those people on Old Earth who confessed to being what they could not possibly have been, and to doing what they could not possibly have done?"

Fernandez's face acquired the indulgent smile professionals sometimes confer on tyros. "In the first place," he said, "the price of confessing to witchcraft was, for a first offense, generally nil. Some not too onerous penance, and being watched carefully for a time thereafter. On the other hand, the penalty for not confessing was often quite awful. If we were interested in obtaining confessions for witchcraft, your objection might be valid. We are not. I am interested only in intelligence which can be corroborated, a very different proposition."

Carrera shook his head, unconvinced. "People will still say anything to avoid torture. You can't count on it."

"*Anything*, Patricio? That is what you said, is it not: 'anything'? Is not the truth also 'anything'? Will people not speak the truth to avoid torture as well?"

Fernandez knew Carrera smoked. He took out a cigarette and lit it before adding, "The trick is that you have to have something to work with, some intelligence the person being interrogated does not know you have that you can use to trick him with. You catch him in a lie and then you apply enough duress that he is terrified ever to lie again. Sometimes it takes catching him in two or three lies before you break him, but break him you will provided that you are ruthless enough and have some means of corroboration. Sometimes, if the interrogator is skilled, he can sense when someone's lying if not about precisely what. Then he applies duress until the man contradicts what he had said previously. That's tricky, though, and not everyone can pull it off.

"And then, too, sometimes you can get instantaneous feedback even if you know nothing. If you catch two people who know the same information, you separate them before they can concoct all that complete a story. Apply duress—oh, all *right!*—torture, until their stories match. Or, too, if you have a true ticking time bomb scenario, your feedback is when the bomb is found. You torture until then."

"It's sickening," Carrera said. Apparently he had some of his old sensibilities left, after all. He was honestly surprised at himself. "Just sickening."

"So? If you are willing to let men be crippled and killed for you under your command, don't you think you owe them a little nausea on your part to give them the best possible chance to live and win?"

Carrera started to answer, and then stopped cold. *Perhaps I do.*

"All right, tell me exactly what you have in mind and how it will operate."

Hamilton, FD, Federated States of Columbia, 15/10/459 AC

Carrera wore a suit and tie—*God, I hate ties!*—and carried an old leather coat over one arm. Unaccompanied, he entered the senator's reception area and announced himself as, "Patrick Hennessey. I believe I have an appointment."

"Oh, yes, sir" the receptionist said. "The senator was very explicit that you were to be given every courtesy and shown right to her office . . . but . . ." The girl looked stricken.

"But?"

"She's tied up in a meeting and won't be quite on time. "Fifteen minutes late, she told me, 'no more.' I'm terribly sorry."

"That'll be fine."

"If you will follow me, sir."

Hennessey followed the receptionist to a tastefully decorated office. He noted the probable expense with disapproval, then chided himself for being a cheap prude. Apparently the senator, Harriett Rodman, felt nothing was too good for her comfort and prestige. In the unreal political world of Hamilton he conceded that she probably had a point.

When he had asked the attorney, Mr. Tweed, about Rodman, he had answered, succinctly, "Corrupt, venal, power hungry. She can be bought, however, and for only a modest interest payment will stay bought. There is, after all, Colonel Hennessey, sometimes honor among thieves."

Hennessey thought, by her description, that Rodman would be perfect. A little money—very little, actually, in comparison to the family trust at full value—and she could be a strong arm at his side, pushing, prodding, nagging and threatening to force the Federated States' military to give things they otherwise might have been most reluctant to give.

He heard a sound from the open doorway. "Colonel Hennessey!" exclaimed Senator Rodman, almost as if she were truly happy to see him for himself. "I am *so* pleased to meet you . . . and so *terribly* sorry about what happened to your family."

Dripping mutual insincerities for the next two hours, Hennessey and the senator worked out a deal favorable to both of them.

UEPF *Spirit of Peace*

Khan and her husband had asked for a special appointment with the high admiral. Given the offices they held, the appointment had been readily granted. Rather than meet in his office, however, Robinson had, on a whim, told them to meet him on the *Peace*'s observation deck.

This was a small area, relative to the size of the ship, with a thick, transparent viewing point. Normally, the port was protected by thick, retractable protective shields. Those shields were withdrawn to the sides now, allowing Robinson unimpeded view of the planet slowly spinning below.

Neither Khan nor her husband were privy to the full scope of their admiral's plans and intentions. Some things were better left unsaid, after all. Nonetheless, from the high admiral's questions and interests they'd surmised some important portions of what he wanted, not merely what he wanted to know about, but also what he wanted to happen.

Khan, the wife, began the informal briefing.

"High Admiral, do you recall my saying that the kind of war mattered?" she asked. Seeing that he did, she continued, "Well, there is a new development down below that might change the nature of the war. Note, please, sir, that I only say it could, not that it will or must."

Robinson, who had been watching as the continents of Uhuru and Taurus slowly spun by, lifted his eyes from the planet and looked directly at the speaker. She was informally dressed in a long, flower-printed skirt. Her bare breasts stood out magnificently in the low, shipboard gravity, the nipples pert from the cool air blowing across the observation deck.

A much more attractive view than the cesspool below, thought Robinson. "What development?"

"One we did not predict and are still investigating," Khan, the husband, answered. "There is a force building, down below, that was not in any of our initial calculations. Right now, all we can say definitively, is that it will be about the size of a brigade, that it will be technologically primitive in comparison to the most sophisticated armed groups on the planet, but that it is unlikely to be constrained by the web of treaties and accords your predecessors have thrown up around most of the planet's armed forces."

"You mean to act like the Federated States?"

"No, sir," answered the wife. "We expect it to be much worse than that."

INTERLUDE

29 July, 2067,
alongside Colonization Ship *Cheng Ho*

The UNSS *Kofi Annan* adopted almost the same high orbit as the ghost ship, only a touch farther out. This allowed the captain of the *Annan* to watch as the launch neared the derelict and docked.

"There's still a charge to the batteries, Captain," the Marine officer in charge of the away party announced. "The hatch is cycling and . . . we're in. Good Lord, the radiation is bad! Skipper, this ship is so hot we couldn't even hope to *scrap* it for a thousand years."

"Very good, Major Ridilla. Put us on visual please."

"Wilco." The *Cheng Ho* suddenly disappeared from the bridge's view screen, being replaced by the view from the Marine's helmet cam.

"Where to first, Skipper?" asked Ridilla.

"Check out the bridge to the *Cheng Ho*," ordered the captain. The image on the view screen wobbled as the Marine walked forward under the small gravity provided by the *Cheng Ho*'s spin, his magnetic boots gripping the deck lightly.

"Stop," the captain ordered. "What's that writing on the walls?"

"No clue, Captain," Ridilla answered. "I can't read Arabic."

"Hold on the image, Major." The captain looked around the bridge. "Who can read Arabic?" she asked.

"I can, Skipper," answered a lieutenant at life support. "It's from Sura Forty of the Koran. It says, 'Whose is the kingdom on that day? God's, the One, the Dominant!'"

"Thank you, Lieutenant. Stand by and give me translations if Major Ridilla finds more. Proceed, Major."

"Aye, aye, Skipper."

Time passed slowly on the bridge, with little on the view screen but a trembling image and nothing to hear but the hum of the *Annan* and Ridilla's labored breathing.

"I've got bodies, Skipper . . . twelve . . . no . . . fourteen. Mostly young but there's one old guy with a beard. The radiation must have killed any bacteria and the cold preserved them."

The captain ordered, "Show me." The image on the view screen twisted down to show the fourteen corpses identified by Ridilla. They were all but one young men, half of them bearded and half clean-shaven, apparently locked with each other in deathgrips at a point where two corridors of the *Cheng Ho* met. One young man, frozen eyes staring blind at the opposite bulkhead, had managed to sit up before he died. The arms were clutched around a stomach wound and bloody icicles trailed outward from the fingers.

Other bodies, singly and in pairs, dotted the way

to the ghost ship's bridge. Most had apparently been killed by cutting or stabbing implements. There were only two obvious gunshot wounds, both of those outside the sealed hatch to the *Cheng Ho*'s own bridge.

"The hatch is locked tight, Skipper," Major Ridilla announced. "We are cutting through."

"I want the log for the *Cheng Ho*, Major. I want to know what happened on that ship."

CHAPTER TWELVE

Hardship, poverty, and want are the best school for a soldier.

—Napoleon I (Bonaparte), Maxim LVIII

We become brave by doing brave acts,
—Aristotle, *Nicomachean Ethics*

I love the infantry because they are the underdogs. They are the mud-rain-frost-and-wind boys. They have no comforts, and they even learn to live without the necessities. And in the end they are the guys the war can't be won without.

—Ernie Pyle

Fort Cameron, *Centro de Instruccion Militar*, 20/3/460 AC, 3:30 AM

A shrill blast of a whistle matched with a sudden glaring light awoke Cruz from a rather pleasant dream of

Caridad. She was walking toward him, wearing nothing but an inviting smile . . .

"Get up! Get up, you shitty little maggots. Move your nasty, lazy, *chingada* asses out of my tent. Put on your sneakers and shorts and *move*! You, *chico*! Do you think you're being paid to sleep all day? Out! *Out!* OUT!"

The infantry corporal—his nametag read "del Valle"—strode quickly down the tent between two rows of cots. As he did so he overturned each one, spilling its occupant out onto the muddy tent floor. Cruz, who had been sleeping on his back, landed on his face, driving mud into his mouth and up his nostrils.

From somewhere off in the distance a loudspeaker was blaring out some sort of martial music at an indecent volume. Dimly heard by the tent's occupants, other new recruits in adjacent tents were being subjected to the same treatment. The corporal no sooner reached the last cot than he began herding, sometimes with punches and kicks, the stunned and bewildered recruits outside into the street that fronted the tent.

Disoriented, tired, confused . . . and sneezing; Ricardo Cruz followed the rest of his tent mates, sheeplike, into the night.

Cruz had arrived at Cameron only about five hours before. He and seventy-nine other volunteers had been bussed from the police station in *Las Mesas* starting at seven PM the previous evening. A long and deliberately slow drive to the *Centro de Instruccion Militar* had brought them through Fort Cameron's front gate just after nine. The bus dropped the new recruits off in front of a mess hall. Met there by a friendly-faced sergeant, they were fed a light snack, and then issued running shoes and shorts, ponchos and poncho liners—thin nylon quilts—and smallish, inadequate pillows. This had taken until just before midnight.

Then that deceptively friendly, warmly smiling sergeant had guided them—they didn't yet know how to march—to their tents. Cruz had gone to sleep shortly after midnight.

So it was that an extremely tired Ricardo Cruz was hustled out into the street at three-thirty in the morning to face the wrath of his new squad leader. On either side of Cruz's tent's group, more of the new volunteers were also spilling out into the street. None had on anything more than their shorts, T-shirt, socks and running shoes. A couple still seemed to be pulling on shorts. One of these went down face first into the mud, a corporal's kick to his fundament providing the motive power.

Cruz had a moment to look around before one of the omnipresent corporals shoved him into the formation that was building in the dirt street. Opposite from where Cruz stood was a line of grim-visaged soldiers wearing running shoes and shorts, black T-shirts and hostile glares. Behind the line of men there was a square podium. From the podium two men oversaw the scene. One of these was short and stocky. He looked to be a rather medium olive color, though in the dark Cruz couldn't be sure. Next to him stood a very tall and slender, graying but not balding black man. The black looked somewhat elderly in the face as well, his skin deeply seamed by what must have been years of exposure to the elements. Still, he carried himself like a young man, a very proud young man. Over the shouting of the corporals and the murmuring of his fellow volunteers, Cruz could not hear what the black man was saying.

Sergeant Major McNamara, standing to the right of First Centurion Epolito Martinez, gave a few last minute words of advice before moving on to look over the next company of new trainees. When speaking Spanish, the sergeant major sounded very like a native of Cristobal, in the Republic, with only rare conversion of the English "th" sound into "t." That was no surprise to those who knew him; his wife was a native of that place.

"There's no moment more critical than this one, Martinez," the sergeant major said. "Too forceful and you'll frighten them silly for months. Too little and they'll stop paying attention in a few days. What becomes of your company in the next several months all depends on what you do here in the next few minutes. You have shocked them. That's good. The shock will keep them in line until you have time to build some discipline in them, especially self-discipline. Remember, though, it is a tricky job, creating self-discipline. The more you impose discipline from the outside, the less they will build on the inside. Tricky."

Martinez, although a soldier for more than fifteen years, was unused to the task of training new troops. He listened attentively to what the big gringo sergeant major had to say. As McNamara stepped off the podium, Martinez stepped up to its edge and began to address the company.

"Welcome, volunteers, to Fort Cameron. I am First Centurion Martinez. You will address me as 'Centurion.'

Together with your centurions of centuries, section leaders, and team leaders, we will, I am sure, turn most of you into soldiers the country can be proud of." Martinez shook his head in seeming regret, his face looking sad, even mournful. "Unfortunately, we will probably have to kill some of you first."

In the ranks, the men around Cruz—Cruz, himself, for that matter—gulped. The way Martinez had said it, there could be no doubt but that some of the new boys *would* be killed in training.

"Today marks your first day as soldiers of the *Legio del Cid*. It will be a day you will never forget. It will not be the hardest day you will ever face. Each day here will be worse than the day that preceded it. We will make it so, I promise. I promise you also hunger and fatigue, thirst and forced marches, hardship and pain. I promise *misery*. In the end, your only release will be when you yourselves are too tough to notice anymore. That . . . or when you die. To me it makes no practical difference which happens first.

"Centurions, take charge of your centuries." Martinez returned the salutes of his subordinates.

It was just ten o'clock at night, as Cruz lay on his cot waiting for sleep to overtake him. Outside a bugle played a soft call.

Oh, God, I hurt. First Bastard Martinez was right. To lie on this cot and not be in pain is the best thing I've ever felt, even though everything still hurts.

The day, too, had been as miserable as the first centurion had promised. From about a quarter to four to six in the morning, the company had learned the basics of marching. Then, from six to seven thirty, had come physical training. Given the number of push-ups awarded during the close order drill instruction, PT was agony. Cruz had lain on his back with his body twisted and his legs to one side until he thought his abdomen would rip apart from the stress. God, it had *hurt*! Push-ups had been interspersed with other exercises until Cruz's arms would no longer support him.

Sure, his previous life had been hard, as was to be expected on a cattle ranch and farm that occasionally dabbled in pigs and kept a coop of trixies, megalapteryx fowl, for their olive-green eggs. Even so, it was nothing like as bad as his first day in the legion.

A year on the farm wouldn't be as bad as today was.

Arms quivering, Cruz had flopped onto the ground, head held high to keep his face from the muck. Pain lessened immediately, though the horrible burning in his arms did not abate at all. *I can't do this anymore*, he'd thought. *No fucking way. These guys are insane.*

He was sadly mistaken, of course, except about the insanity part. Two instructor corporals had come up on either side of Cruz and convinced him he was underestimating his own strength; seriously underestimating it. A sneakered foot slammed into Cruz's left side, by his stomach so as not to break any ribs. Even as he writhed, arms crossing to protect himself, another foot rather more than nudged his kidney. Cruz barely held in a scream. More kicks followed. "Get back to your position, you fucking maggot," said a corporal.

Cruz strained to do so, arms quivering like jelly as he tried to hold himself off the ground.

The corporals waited until he had both his trembling arms beneath him. A shared nod and the feet moved together to kick his arms out from underneath him.

Uncontrolled, Cruz flopped belly down to the mud. After his torso stopped descending, his face continued on. Mud filled his mouth and nose. More kicks followed. "Get up, shithead."

Strangely, from somewhere inside, Cruz found the strength to get his body back off the ground. *Assholes.*

After Physical Training, the corporals had turned hoses on the dripping volunteers. Since no other showers had been made available, Cruz guessed— correctly—that the hoses were all the showering he was going to get anytime soon.

Breakfast had been served, though "served" may not have been precisely the right word, immediately after the hosing. Cruz had taken a full plate before discovering that he was too exhausted to be hungry. Yet another corporal had disabused him of the notion that food could be taken and not eaten. That, too, had been a painful lesson.

Issue of initial equipment had gone very quickly. There hadn't been much to issue: a plastic foot locker with a lock and key, several pair each of underwear and socks, a black baseball cap, a two-quart canteen, another set of running shorts, a toilet kit with toothbrush and paste, soap, shampoo and a razor with blades. First Centurion Martinez had told the troops that, until they had proven they were worth the expense, there was no reason to waste money on uniforms for them. In fact, uniforms were for the time being unavailable, but there was no reason to tell the recruits that.

The rest of the day had consisted of lectures, meals, close order drill, all interspersed with pushups and more creative punishments. Cruz's section leader, del Valle, was very fond of what he called "the low crawl." After hours of dragging his poor tired, scraped and battered body across the gravel and sand, Cruz's elbows and knees were weeping sores. By day's end two cots in Cruz's tent had been folded up and taken away, their former occupants kicked out after an interrupted public beating by the corporals.

Halfway through the beating a relatively tall, relatively light-skinned officer appeared. Cruz couldn't see his name tag and didn't know enough to tell as yet the man's rank. It must have been very high though, so he thought, since the corporals stopped the beatings as soon as they spied him.

"And just what the fuck is going on here?" the white officer quietly demanded.

"Just a little discipline building, sir. We're making an example of these two to convince the others they can't quit."

Carrera held his temper in check, though he was truly pissed. He stood tense for several minutes as he gained control of himself. The corporals' nervousness increased in proportion to the time it took for Carrera to control his anger.

Finally he asked, genially enough, "Tell me, *Cabo,* just what do you think you can do to these men that the enemy won't be able to do more of and worse?" There was no answer. "At a loss for words, I see. Good. Let me tell you that there is *precisely nothing* you can do worse than the enemy. These beatings. Why bother? Who wants quitters? You? Would you trust your men in battle if the only reason they stayed was because they were afraid of a little beating?"

"Put that way, sir . . . I *guess* maybe not."

"Look, *Cabo*, I know this is all new to you, that you were probably a private just a few months ago. Maybe there might be a time and place for this kind of thing. But this is *not* the time and place. We are selecting the future of the legion. Even though we are a nongovernmental organization for now, we are building the future of Balboa, right here, right now. I want, I need, we *all* need, people who are not afraid of a little pain and people who will do what needs doing on their own."

"No physical discipline, sir?" The corporal sounded incredulous.

"Didn't say that," Carrera corrected. "There's nothing wrong with an occasional kick in the pants. And if someone mouths off to you, you deck him on the spot; hear me? There are some crimes that demand punishment public, graphic and as immediate as possible. But I do not want you frightening people into staying with us that really have no business in this business. Let them go. Encourage them, even. Make the training—*the training, I say!*—so fucking hard that only the best can make it. That will give you soldiers to count on. Now finish up these two—I don't want anyone thinking their corporals can do wrong—as soon as I leave. But don't do it again. And pass the fucking word."

Cruz had heard none of that. The white officer had left, the beatings had resumed but then ended shortly thereafter, and the miscreants were marched out of camp under guard. He fell asleep with dread in his heart about what tomorrow would bring.

Hotel Metropole, Saint Nicholasberg, 21/3/460 AC

In the hotel bar pretty, but altogether too young, Volgan prostitutes solicited the business that might keep them fed for another week or even another day. Easterners—journalists and businessmen, mostly—flirted, or negotiated, or simply bantered with the whores. Along the bar sat a balding, Russian-looking, man. The hookers paid him no mind. He didn't seem like he had the money they, or their pimps, required.

Being a bureaucrat, thought Dan Kuralski—seated at the bar, *ought to be a capital offense.* He sipped at his nearly frozen vodka. *And I was so happy to be coming here for this mission, Patrick, old friend. "One big shopping spree," isn't that what you said?*

In the days since arriving in "Saint Nick" in search of arms, Kuralski had been up one dead end after another. One bureaucrat in the Ministry of Defense told him that MoD didn't have authority to sell arms to other nations, let alone NGOs; that was for the Foreign Ministry. In the Foreign Ministry he had been told that, "Sorry, no, the actual sale of arms was being conducted by the military itself." Kuralski *had* managed to corner one Volgan general. This hadn't worked either; the general was too drunk at the time and reportedly too much of a worm when sober. Dan was about ready to go directly to a factory and make a private contract for what was needed. He would have, too, if it had been possible to go to a single factory and get each of ten thousand different items. There was no such factory or warehouse or, so far as he'd been able to determine, business. And precisely where the particular items required were being manufactured was still a closely guarded state secret. It was sometimes even a silly state secret. Who cared who made one-liter water bottles, anyway, for Christ's sake? But that was still Top Secret, Special Compartmentalized Information in Volga.

Preferably something slow and painful, Kuralski amended his earlier thought. He contemplated the very unhappy tone Carrera had used when last they'd spoken. He did *not* want to disappoint Carrera or to fail in his mission. The legion *needed* that equipment, dammit!

Kuralski sipped again at his vodka. Attention on the glass, he failed to notice at first the man who sat down beside him. When he did notice, and looked up to see, the Russian asked him, quite directly, if he was "the Balboan arms agent who was looking for heavy equipment for the upcoming war in Sumer?"

Arms agent? Me? I am just an errand boy.

"Not just heavy equipment," answered Kuralski. "We need virtually everything from rifles and machine guns on up. Why do you ask?"

In slow, heavy but correct English the newcomer said, "Ah. Permit me to introduce myself. I am Pavel Timoshenko. Word came to me of a Russian- and English-speaking Balboan looking for reasonably modern arms. Since I am in Economic Planning, I thought I might be of assistance. And you would be?"

"Forgive my rudeness. I'm Daniel Kuralski."

Timoshenko reached out a hand. "A Volgan?"

"Sorry, no. My grandparents were. They fled the Red Tsar, though. I was born in the FSC. I live in

Balboa now. It is perhaps a silly question, but what does Economic Planning have to do with arms sales?"

Timoshenko smiled. "In this country, Daniel, Economic Planning has to do with everything. Yes, even now, even after the fall of the empire. Not that the plans work, mind you." Timoshenko looked wistful, sighed resignedly. "When I was young it used to seem that they did, somewhat. In any event, nothing much works anymore." He shook his head dismally.

Timoshenko continued. "Right now, we are planning our upcoming economic collapse. It will happen, too; that plan we can be sure will work, unless we can get a major infusion of hard currency and technology. Which is why I am here to see you. What are you looking to buy?"

Kuralski answered, "Equipment for a large brigade, with technical experts to teach our men how to use it. However, whatever you might sell to me, I don't think we are in a position to regenerate the Volgan economy."

"My new friend, after three generations of Tsarist-Marxism, no one is in a position to regenerate the Volgan economy, at least, no one who would be willing to do so. We can still help each other, though."

Immediately suspicious, he didn't really believe in win-win situations, Kuralski asked what the Volgan was getting at.

Timoshenko looked up. For a moment he seemed lost to philosophy. When he spoke, he said, "What we need is good advertising. For decades we have been selling shitty equipment to everybody who couldn't afford better or was cut off from better for political reasons. Now that particular chicken is about to roost. The Volgan Republic is sitting on more than thirty thousand tanks; actually a lot more than that, if one counts everything. Some of them are crap, of course; the kind of *dreck* we used to barter for political influence to the undeveloped world. Still others are relics from the Great Global War. But we have first class equipment, too. Who will believe that, when the East's second best has been beating what we have been calling our best for so long that no one remembers that we—not the Sachsens, but *we*—built the best armored vehicles of the Great Global War?"

Blood will tell. Kuralski, too, felt a small pride in his ancestors and relations in thinking of both their tanks, and their courage, in fighting the Sachsen.

Timoshenko shifted gears a bit. "Tell me something; when you get over there, to the war zone, I mean, are your men going to fight?"

Kuralski thought about it for a minute. "My boss, though he is officially the deputy for the legion, is really in charge. He will fight. I don't think he would obey orders that kept him out of the fighting." Kuralski laughed, "He's pretty selective about obedience in general. So, yes, if there is fighting we will be in it."

Timoshenko turned his bar stool around to lean his back against the bar. "That's what we need. If we sell you some of our best equipment—maybe better than our usual best, and you take it to battle against the Sumeris, then the rest of the Yithrabis—especially the Oil Yithrabis—will see that we can still be their best buy for defense. It is only necessary that a couple of our tanks survive hits and kill the older tanks we sold Sumer for the point to be made. Besides the Federated States and the Sachsens, who would never help *us*, the Oil Yithrabis are the only ones with the money to make a difference to our economy."

Kuralski shook his head. "We couldn't afford to buy your best if it cost half, even a quarter of what the FS, Sachsen, or Anglia would demand for their equipment. We are not a rich country and the legion's—Carrera's—private resources are limited."

Timoshenko gave a deep belly laugh. "I see that you are unacquainted with the miracles of Socialist Accounting. Trust me on this. Things cost precisely what we *say* they cost. You can afford it."

Interu Inn, New Giza, Misrani Islamic Republic, 23/3/460 AC

On Old Earth it had once been possible to determine to a considerable degree of certainty the degree of oppression in any given country by the words used in its title. Generally speaking, the rule had been: "Republic equals republic. People's Republic equals dictatorship. Democratic Republic equals really oppressive dictatorship. People's Democratic Republic equals really oppressive and corrupt dictatorship, amounting to a family corporation, with genocidal tendencies."

This rule had held good, in general terms, on Terra Nova. Moreover, it had been taken and applied by Moslems, as well, for their own little experiments in statehood and linguistic sleight of hand. Thus, for example, the Misrani Islamic Republic was, in fact, a corrupt family-run dictatorship, with said family being among the most devout atheists to be found in the known universe. Much like "democratic" and "people's," "Islamic was a mere sop.

The suite Kuralski had taken at the Interu Inn of

the Misrani "Islamic" Republic was, at best, tacky, all gilt over cheap wood held together by glue. In this, it resembled the country as a whole.

While a hotel servant unpacked his bags in one room of the suite, Kuralski brought Carrera up to date over the salon's telephone line. The hotel's own phone he'd unplugged, substituting an encrypted one. Carrera spoke from Balboa on a similar device.

Kuralski felt flushed with success. Even so, he kept his voice low enough that the bellhop couldn't hear. "Yes, Pat, everything we wanted and more. And they're selling us good stuff, too. Some of it has never been on the general market before. White Eagle tanks, Pat, latest upgrade. Matter of fact, they're offering special upgrades for the thirty we need. Pat, the Volgans have *never* sold White Eagles to anybody; and it isn't because they're shit, either. They gave me a tour, including a ride and a firing exercise. Harrington would love them if he weren't too fat to fit inside. And we're getting PBM-100s for the light armor and mechanized infantry requirement. They've actually offered to let us have the PBMs at cost plus . . ."

"Yes, they've got some of their people working on the right allocation of spare parts. They also corrected a few mistakes in the publicly available information on some of their capabilities."

As Carrera's voice sounded in his ear, Kuralski turned to keep a watchful eye on the Misrani bellhop. *Yep, still out of the way.*

"Right. Their trainers are coming in three echelons, Pat. Expect the first at Herrera Airport on the sixth of the sixth month, and the next on the ninth. The last won't arrive until the end of the month . . . yes, they're sending enough to train our leaders. . . . Yes, we agreed that their folks get paid Balboan scales. It's princely to a place as depressed as Volga is now. Wait a sec, Pat . . ."

Waiting until the bellhop left the suite, Dan added, "Yes, from here I'll be moving on to Zion for some of the individual equipment. After that I'll go to Helvetia, then Sachsen followed by Castille. I have a very good line on five to twelve thousand Castilian-made, Sachsen-pattern helmets for cheaps, though the Helvetians are offering what might be a better helmet for about the same amount. . . . Yes, I'll check out both. Both governments are basically dumping them."

Kuralski was briefly silent, then answered, "Right; I'll keep you posted. I'm meeting with a Misrani about the tents tomorrow morning. When I get to Zion, how high are you willing to go on the Remotely Piloted Aircraft? Right . . .

"Okay, Pat. Of course I'm great. I'm lucky, too . . .

"Oh, I almost forgot; while I was in Volga I ran into a Volgan Airborne colonel with a serious problem. Things are bad over there, very bad. Even the army is not always getting enough to eat, and that is so even with the troops growing a lot of their own food. This colonel—Colonel Samsonov . . . yes, he's related, distantly, to the small arms designer—said they were going to close down his unit. I think I can put Samsonov and his regiment on retainer for very damn little. Do you think you might have a use for an airborne regiment, possibly reinforced to maybe two thousand men? Okay, I'll make a deal with this guy. It shouldn't cost more than about fifteen, maybe twenty thousand drachma a month to have them wait for the call. Those poor fucks will soldier for food. Pat, it was sad; Samsonov actually looked *hungry*."

Kirov, Volga, 23/3/460 AC

The factory was gray and greasy, and stank of ozone and motor oil. It was quiet, however, even more quiet than the lack of business would justify. The workers had ceased what passed for work and assembled on their shop floor to listen to their manager.

While Kuralski spoke on the phone to Carrera, another man, in the Kirov tank factory near Saint Nicholasberg, addressed those workers. Victor Khudenko had taken over the management of the factory almost eleven years before. In that time he had seen production standards slip from bad to worse to unbelievably awful; all in lockstep with the rest of the Volgan economy. Since the factory not only made the White Eagle—the few prototypes that were all anyone had been able to pay for, anyway—and the PBM-100, but also was located near a major port, it had been decided that this factory would fill that portion of the Balboan order.

Khudenko had not received the news with joy unstinted; however. He knew better than anyone what trash his factory had been turning out for the Volgan Army. He thought, sadly, about the superb designs that his workers ruined through their indifference. He also knew—and if he hadn't, Timoshenko had made it abundantly clear—that this would be the *last* order if these tanks were not the best ever made in Volga.

Desperate times; desperate measures, Khudenko thought. *If I just tell them we have an order and we must do better work than we have, it will be like every other exhortation they've heard, and ignored, over decades and centuries of Tsarist rule; in one ear and out the other. No . . . there must be more. There must be something to shake them up. Sad that I have to terrify them to make them see the truth. Sadder still if I don't and we all end up out on our asses.*

"Comrades," he lied, "I have very bad news. The State has decided to close our factory down in two weeks' time. We will all be given severance pay, another two weeks' worth, and, of course, we will have our unemployment coverage. I am told that we will all be given *some* kind of a priority for some other kind of work, as and when it might become available. What that means in today's circumstances . . ." Khudenko gave an eloquent shrug of the shoulders.

The factory workers stood in stunned silence. Their world had collapsed in four sentences and a fragment. Khudenko let them stew for a full minute. Then he let them have the other barrel.

"Of course, the State is taking back the factory housing complex. But I have managed to get an extension on the time we will be given before we have to get out. We will have thirty days from today. And we can use the plant trucks to move ourselves to our new homes as soon as we find them."

This time the workers were not silent. They were *outraged*. This was really too much. How could they explain it to their families? The factory floor erupted in angry shouts.

One worker stepped forward to shout at the manager. "They can't do this to us," he insisted. "We have rights. We have law."

Khudenko smiled. "Josef Raikin, you, of all people, have little ground to complain. How many times have you been heard to say that as long as the State pretended to pay a good wage, you would pretend to do good work? No, no, I am not singling you out, Josef. We are, all of us, equally guilty . . . of tolerating shoddy work even if we did good work ourselves. And now the time has come to pay the price."

Another worker stepped forward to stand next to Raikin. "It wasn't us that were guilty, it was the system itself. They made it so it doesn't matter whether we do good work or bad so long as the norms are filled. Why should we have to suffer?"

"Who else *can* suffer?" answered Khudenko, with seeming resignation. "Anyway, you can all take the rest of the day off to break the news to your families. Come back tomorrow at the regular time so we can start the process of shutting everything down." With that, Khudenko left the podium on which he had stood, leaving the workers to ponder dismal futures.

When the factory opened the next day, Khudenko was unsurprised to see a delegation of workers and foremen waiting by his office to see him. Nor was he surprised to find out that they had come to beg him to do something, anything, to save their jobs. Surprised? He'd *counted* on it.

Khudenko conceded that he had heard of an order for a foreign sale that had recently been received but it was probably going to go to the Mamayev Transport Machine Factory near Novy Kiev. It was only for thirty tanks and about twice that in infantry fighting vehicles, he told them.

The news infuriated the workers. Imagine, they

complained, Central Planning throwing good Volgans out into the street and giving the job to a bunch of stinking Kievens. Khudenko told them that, in these troubled times, the State was most likely seeking to avoid starting trouble in what had always been a troublesome region. The workers asked if there wasn't something Khudenko could do to steal the order from Novy Kiev.

Khudenko paused. His hand moved as if groping for an answer that was almost there. "Maybe if I could go to Central with some new plan, some new production technique, that would have us turning out the best tanks in the whole Volgan Republic, maybe then I could get Central to change their minds. Ah, but what's the use? I don't know what hasn't been tried before. Do any of *you* have any ideas?"

The workers pondered that question for a few minutes. Then one of them, Raikin, tentatively offered one possible answer. "I read once of a system they use in one of those Scandi places to make cars. They form a small team that's responsible for making the car from start to finish."

Another worker retorted, "That's fine for simple automobiles. We're talking *tanks* here. They're forty to fifty times heavier and a thousand times more complex. Besides, the factory is set up for assembly line operations. We couldn't set up the separate work spaces in time to make any difference."

A foreman piped in, "You're right, we can't do the whole thing the way the Scandis do. We could take part of it though. What if we assign a single worker, or maybe better, a small team to each tank? Automotive, firepower, electronics and . . . oh, yes, armor and welding. Four workers. They can walk it all the way through production, inspecting each step and having any mistakes fixed before the tank goes on to the next. We are only talking thirty tanks anyway so there will be extra people to do the walk through."

Khudenko raised an objection. "Yes, but who will guard the guards? And how will they control the line workers?"

The foreman pondered briefly. "Well, what if we give the control teams the authority to credit the work done? Do it badly and you won't get paid until it is done right. We have the norms to say how long a given job should take and how much it should be worth if done right. Then we'll have a special team check each tank from tooth to tail at the end . . . again, it's only for thirty tanks so we have the people. Any mistakes that the control team didn't catch gets taken from *their* pay."

"I like that," Khudenko answered. "But it's not enough. Give me something else I can go to Central with."

A young man with but one eye, the other being covered by a patch, and wearing a small gold cross at his neck, answered, "How about those new thermal sights? Not so good as the East's, maybe, but they would make these much more effective tanks. I remember that in Pashtia, fifteen years ago, there were times I prayed even to the God I didn't then believe in for a sight to see through smoke and dust."

Khudenko considered. "We can't make them here. And we've never been equipped for installing them."

"Well . . . maybe we can get the factory that does make them to send us thirty or so along with the workers and machinery to install them. I'm told they were designed to be the same dimensions as the passive sights we normally use so they could be retrofitted."

Hours later, with notebook full of some rather good, and a few silly, ideas, Victor Khudenko went in to his office and pretended to make a phone call. Through the windows the committee could see him gesturing frantically, wiping sweat from his brow, screaming, begging and pleading. They didn't know that acting had been a hobby of Khudenko's back in his college days.

At length, visibly weary, the manager emerged to tell the delegation that Central had agreed to give the factory one more chance. They had an order to produce ninety armored vehicles, thirty top quality White Eagles and sixty PBM-100s, by the first of June, 460. If that worked out they would be given another few months' probationary period. Khudenko then added something that none of the workers or foremen had suggested.

"If anyone drinks on the job; if anyone slacks off on the job; if anyone lets someone else drink or slack on the job; that man will be sacked. And no connections will save them. Spread the word men. Our *lives* depend on this. Our *families* depend on this."

Fort Cameron, 3/4/460 AC

From various parts of Terra Nova flowed uniforms, weapons, ammunition, and equipment. Though not yet enough for all needs, it was enough to keep the men training. Cruz now sported locally sewn jungle fatigues, in a digital, tiger-striped pattern. The material came from the FSC. In the absence of a single factory able to handle the order, seamstresses from all over Balboa had contracted to do piecework in their own homes to outfit their boys.

Besides the tiger suit, Cruz now wore jungle boots, and bore a rucksack, load carrying equipment, and a Helvetian helmet. He carried a North Sachsen-made Samsonov assault rifle that matched superior Volgan design with superb Sachsen workmanship. He actually wouldn't have minded going back to just the PT shorts, T-shirt, and sneakers he had been given initially. That uniform would certainly have made the current march a lot more bearable than it was.

The march had begun, as most days began here, well before sunrise. It was a forced march, a six or seven kilometer per hour *death march,* to a range on the other side of the post. Typically, breakfast would not be served until they reached the range. The century would spend the next week and a half sleeping out, learning about their new rifles and how to use them. Despite the pain in his feet, legs, and back, Cruz looked forward to the training. He passed a road sign that said the rifle range was only six kilometers away. Another hour, then, and they could take a break.

But then First Centurion Martinez, marching beside the century, turned over his right shoulder and gave the command, "Double tiiime . . ."

The company gave out a collective groan.

"March!"

The sound caused Carrera to stop his evening walk and just listen.

"Bagpipes? Here?" He turned and followed the

sound until he saw a lone man, much taller and lighter skinned than most, standing under a streetlamp with, yes, bagpipes held in his arms.

He walked over. The piper stopped playing until Carrera told him, "No . . . please keep going. At least until you finish the piece."

When he was done Carrera asked, "Where did you learn that?"

"Black Guard of Secordia, sir," the piper answered. He had an odd accent that took Carrera a moment's thought to identify as Gallic.

He asked, "Can you teach others? And what's a Secordian doing here?"

Herrera Airport, *Ciudad* Balboa, 6/4/460 AC

Generals Parilla and Carrera were on hand to see the first planeload of instructors and equipment rolling down the ramp of the Litvinov-68 heavy transport. The aircraft's Volgan crew supervised as some of the trainers carefully eased the first White Eagle tank ever to set tread in Colombia Central—or anywhere outside of the Volgan Republic and its satellites—out onto the airfield surface.

A Spanish-speaking Volgan colonel, about thirty-eight or thirty-nine years old, balding and graying but with spring in his step and a happy gleam in his eyes, ran over and reported to Parilla. Rendering a snappy hand salute, the Volgan said, "Colonel Aleksandr Sitnikov, Fifth Guards Motorized Rifle Regiment, reporting as ordered, sirs."

Parilla and Carrera returned the salute, introduced

themselves, and asked the Volgan what he had brought with him.

Sitnikov produced a manifest list showing that portion of the training package on the aircraft that had brought him to Balboa, as well as what was enroute from Volga over the next twenty-eight hours. The manifest had been thoughtfully provided in both Russian and extremely bad Spanish.

"I didn't prepare the list myself," the Volgan apologized.

Without asking, Sitnikov explained that most of what was coming to Balboa were "chimp models" but that a reasonable number of standard and above-standard systems were with him or enroute.

"For purposes of training these are very similar to, if not exactly the same as, what you will receive when the new systems are built. We will use these to train your leaders and maintenance personnel." Sitnikov made several checks on a form. "Where possible and where they are different we've brought subsystems that are the same as you will receive when you deploy to train with as well."

"For the rest, we have a larger number of the sort of "chimp models" the Volgan Empire usually sent to the underdeveloped world . . ." Sitnikov paused, then continued, ". . . well, they're better than chimp models, but not by all that much. These will do for teaching driving and basic gunnery. The artillery will be along later. Those pieces are all standard models." More checks were made.

Carrera asked about the trainers and maintenance specialists.

Sitnikov replied, "Each vehicle or artillery piece

has either its own *praporschik*"—warrant officer—"or
sergeant for maintenance and training. Most of them
speak some Spanish, mostly courtesy of a having spent
a tour in Hundred Fires when it was a Volgan satellite. The rest are generally good at the point-and-show
technique we use to teach our own non-Volgan speaking
recruits. In addition we are bringing a four-to-six man
team for each of your companies that will be using
our heavy equipment, plus another six to eight for
your mechanized and artillery battalions . . . oh, you
call them 'cohorts,' don't you? In any case, I am in
charge overall and of the headquarters support group
in particular. That consists of some combined arms
and logistic specialists. In all, I bring two hundred
and forty-seven men."

Carrera answered, "Very good, Colonel. The government has finally turned over the FS Army's old Imperial Range complex to conduct our training. We'll be
billeting your men there. It has enough barracks space,
screened and out of the rain, for your group; five large
buildings, some smaller ones for the officers, a mess
and a headquarters. If there is any spillover, we've
got tents. I'll want you to run your own local security.
We'll also have a bus service to bring your men to
where they can use our recreation facilities . . . as well
as the unofficial facilities—the brothels and bars—of
which there are many in *Ciudad* Balboa. I've got my
secretary lining up some Spanish teachers, but the
whores will probably do a better job of it."

As the first heavy equipment transporter pulled
up near the LI-68, Carrera motioned for Soult to
approach.

"Jamey," he said, "I would like you to stay here

with Colonel Sitnikov. When he has finished overseeing the unloading, and his men are on the buses to
go to Imperial Range, please drive him over to the
Officer's Club at Herrera Field."

Turning back to Sitnikov, he said, "Colonel, my
friend here will see to your needs. Please accept
our invitation to lunch as soon as you have seen to
your duties." It was, of course, not a request; nor did
Sitnikov take it as one.

Kirov, Volga, 7/4/460 AC

It sounded different, somehow, the factory. Raikin tried
to pin down precisely what was different about it, but
could not. Machinists ground at metal, as always. The
steam hammer pounded, as always. As always, the
actinic glare of the welders still strained the eyes. The
overhead cranes and tracks squeaked . . . annoyingly,
as always.

Raikin was surprised to find himself on one of the
quality control teams, the teams that had to walk each
tank through the production line. Odd, that; it wasn't
as if he had ever made himself the reputation as an
Udarnik—or shock worker—in the twenty-five years
he'd worked here.

On reflection, though, perhaps it was not so remarkable. On this team there was Raikin, senior and in
charge. He had served once, and cursed often, as a
young tank commander in a Guards tank regiment in
Northern Sachsen. All the teams—now that he thought
on it, all the quality control *teams*—were composed
of people who had served in tank or motorized rifle

formations and suffered firsthand from poor quality. Would it make a difference? Raikin didn't know. He admitted to himself that it just might.

Raikin fitted dark goggles over his eyes and bent low over a welder, himself crouching as he joined the tank glacis to the sides of the hull. Raikin was pleased to see the welder taking extra time and care to ensure a solid joinder. He thought about hurrying the welder along, but rejected the notion. He did not want *his* pay docked over the matter. Let the welder take his time, just so that the tank passed final inspection.

"Josef?"

Raikin stood erect and turned towards the speaker, Stefan Malayev, he of the black patch and single eye. "Yes?"

"The castings people are trying to palm off some second rate road wheels on me. You can see they're crude just by looking. I won't stand for it. I have a wife and two children and no slovenly son of a bitch is going to take food from their mouths."

Raikin nodded solemnly. "Let's go chat with the bastards, then, shall we? And if they won't listen . . . well . . . we'll go see Khudenko. That, or kick the fuckers' asses."

Imperial Range, 8/4/460 AC

Jorge Mendoza stood in ranks, eyes shining at the sight before them. *If we had had those . . .*

Atop a spotlessly gleaming T-38 tank, Colonel Sitnikov stood proudly, his hands on his hips. In a semicircle around Sitnikov, all around Mendoza, stood the nearly one hundred long-service BDC and Civil Force officers, noncoms, and enlisted men, none over five feet, six inches, plus another slightly larger group of new enlistees. These had been chosen to man the tanks and lighter armor of the *Legio del Cid*. Five Volgans stood between Sitnikov and the Balboans. Behind him, stretching for half a mile along either side of the access road that led to a number of the rifle and machine gun ranges at the complex, was a staggered double line of twenty-five more T-38s and PBMs. Twenty feet behind the Balboans stood Parilla and Carrera. Just behind them stood Siegel.

Sitnikov spent a few minutes, speaking in good Spanish with hardly a trace of accent, introducing himself and a few of his key personnel. He then explained, in fairly broad terms, the training schedule the tankers-to-be would follow for the next three months. Lastly he went into an enthusiastic description of the tanks themselves.

Sitnikov began, "My friends, what I am standing on is one of the best tanks in the world. "What is it about this tank that makes it so special?" you might well ask. Well, I shall tell you."

Sitnikov turned to his right, walked forward a few steps, and placed his hand atop the long barrel protruding from the turret. "This gun, the 125mm smoothbore, is the most powerful tank gun on Terra Nova today. Firing depleted uranium or tungsten-carbide penetrators, this gun will defeat the armor of any tank to be found on the modern battlefield, not excepting even the Cheetah II, the Federated States' Creighton, the Zion Chariot or the Anglian Contender, although not always in the frontal arc where the armor is thickest. Those tanks often can't even kill each other in the frontal arc. As far as the Sumeri tanks you will face, it would kill them at a range exceeding that at which those tanks can hit and penetrate the T-38's own armor."

Sitnikov moved back a step and placed his hand on a boxlike attachment sitting above the gun on a rail projecting from the turret. "Moreover," he said, "to destroy targets past the range at which the gun can hit or penetrate, the T-38 carries a number of rounds of the antiarmor missile, the AT-111 Mirror. This is a guided antitank missile, fired through the barrel. In all the world outside of the Volgan Republic, only the Federated States' Phillips light tank carries a similar weapon. But the Phillips' gun-missile system lacks the range of the Mirror. It also has the distressing habit of suffocating the crew with exhaust from the rocket motor. The Mirror has no such unfortunate defect."

Sitnikov removed his hand from the Mirror's guidance package, sat back onto the turret, and gave the turret a healthy slap. "*These* T-38s also boast steel-ceramic-plastic-depleted uranium composite armor similar to the type of armor found on the other most modern tanks. I must be honest, however, and tell you that the T-38's composite is not as strong as the armor used by the FS, the Anglians, and the Sachsens. That, however, makes little difference because the T-38 is much harder to *hit* than those tanks." At the key word 'tanks,' the five Volgans in front of Sitnikov simultaneously flipped over charts on which were drawn silhouettes of the other tanks he had mentioned, superimposed over the T-38's. Sitnikov continued. "As you can see from the charts in front of you, the T-38 is only about half as big a target as the others. Gentlemen, I assure you, in armored warfare *size does matter*. You can afford a little less armor when you are twice as hard to hit. Even so, your armor is not much less." His finger pointed at some layered, blocklike additions around the turret. "See these blocks? Your T-38s will boast the newest reactive armor, Engagement-5, giving an additional 120 millimeters worth of steel protection against solid shot and 500 millimeters against hollow charge, HEAT, ammunition. From the front, nothing the Sumeris have can penetrate. *Nada*, my friends."

Used to second rate, light armor—at best—the long-service veterans of the old BDC breathed a sigh of relief, even as the newer men grinned or, some of them, whistled.

For his part, Mendoza simply grew dreamy-eyed at the prospect of having one of these beautiful war machines under his control.

"Moreover, "Sitnikov continued, "the tanks you will receive once they are ready will have four significant advantages over even the usual T-38."

Sitnikov walked closer to the turret and pointed at a device mounted to the side of the turret, behind the gun. "This is called a "Blinder." When the tank or the infantry carriers are attacked by guided missiles, either automatically or when the tank commander flicks a switch inside, the Blinder will send out coded infrared signals that mimic those sent out by the guided missile. This confuses the missile's computerized guidance system so badly that the missile is usually sent into something like low orbit. That; or into the ground. Think of it as a nervous breakdown, computer style. The Blinder also warns and gives a directional indicator for laser beams "painting" the tank for a laser guided missile. In addition, it launches prismatic smoke grenades to screen you from the view of enemy gunners."

Pointing then at the oddly placed blocks around the turret, then at an ovoid device above them, Sitnikov announced, "Moreover, a number of the tanks you will receive in the desert will have mounted an active defense system, the "Sand Blaster." This is a system which automatically senses incoming projectiles, computes the best intercept point, then fires off the correct one to three of these other explosive blocks to deflect or damage the projectile. I have never personally used this system, but it is said to be amazing . . . effective against both missiles and kinetic energy weapons. Yes, even against tank-fired long rod penetrators. The Sand Blaster is new, absolutely new. Outside of a few prototypes, our own tanks do not have it yet. My government is giving it to you for combat testing.

"Then, my friends, look here at this box. This is a thermal imager much like those found in other world-class tanks. The tanks you will receive will have an improved version.

"Lastly, your tanks will come with the ammunition carousel and storage inverted to give you approximately three times as many antitank rounds, and fewer anti-personnel high explosive rounds. In the desert, facing tanks, this will be a good thing for you."

As Sitnikov moved back to stand over the tanks engine and wax lyrical over the power plant—in this case the 1250 horsepower turbine engine that replaced the less powerful 1000 horsepower diesel job found on most Volgan heavy armor, Parilla asked Carrera in a whisper, "Do you believe any of that?"

Carrera answered equally softly, "Oh, maybe every other word. That turbine is going to suck gas. Although I could be wrong; don't sell the Volgans short. Still, I doubt that Sitnikov believes it all, either. But it doesn't matter what you, or I, or even what Sitnikov believes." Sweeping his hand across the backs of the mostly young Balboans listening raptly to the Volgan, Carrera concluded, "All that matters is what *they* believe."

Though Carrera had spoken to Parilla softly, Siegel had heard. He leaned forward over their shoulders and added, "Actually, sirs, what the Sumeris believe is likely to be of some importance, too. You know, 'They can because they think they can' and all. Rather, 'They *can't* because they think they *can't*,'"

Carrera was puzzled at the reference. He asked, "Homer? The Trojan assault on the Greek camp?"

"Virgil, sir. The boat race."

"Ah, Virgil."

Parilla said, "You know, Patricio, there is something to be said for naming weapons rather than numbering them. Why don't we give these tanks and the other equipment names?"

"Not a bad idea. Any thoughts?"

"Yes, as a matter of fact. I was thinking that we could name the tanks for a predatory cat." Parilla held up his hands defensively. "Yes, I know, so did some rather unsavory characters both in our history and Old Earth's. Not all their ideas were wrong, merely for them having had them. So . . . yes, the most powerful predatory cat in this hemisphere."

"Smilodons?" Carrera asked. "I don't like that; having our tanks nicknamed 'smilies.' Or named for captive animals. Or named for a nearly extinct species."

Parilla grimaced. "I hadn't thought of smilodons. They were such a danger, and their fangs and pelts such a prize, that they're almost never found outside of a zoo anymore. How about we call the tanks . . . mmm . . . *'jaguars.'*"

Carrera shrugged. *The jaguars, beautiful as they are, are endangered, but nothing like old saber-tooth. They exist in zoos, of course, but they're mostly free. Maybe . . . oh, why the hell not?*

"What about the lighter armor, Raul, the PBM-100s?"

Parilla thought about that one before asking, "Those things swim, don't they?"

"Yes . . . yes, they swim pretty well, I understand. They've got waterjets underneath."

"Ocelots?" Parilla suggested. "They swim, after all."

Still atop the tank, Sitnikov was coming to the end of his presentation.

"Now, gentlemen, you may recall that I began by saying this is one of the best tanks in the world. Surely that is a matter of some worry to you, not being the best. Never fear, the only tank better than this is the White Eagle. That, with all the modifications I mentioned, is what you will actually receive for the fight. . . ."

Carrera and Parilla then left for a different part of Imperial Range. There the infantry, artillery, and other professional cadres were going through a training course in staggered groups, some pushing the new trainees while others learned to use the new equipment.

Knowledge was power, and Carrera wanted his subordinate leaders to have power over their troops by virtue of their superior knowledge. Therefore, they had to learn the new equipment before the trainees ever laid eyes upon it.

Kirov, Volga, 15/4/460 AC

"Damn your eyes, take it back!" an infuriated Raikin demanded.

"What do you mean 'take it back'? There's nothing wrong with that block. Nothing!"

Raikin reached out his right hand, grabbing a surly looking machinist by the ear. "You smelly little twat," he hissed. "I was boring cylinders when you were pissing on the floor and I *know* what is and what isn't a good block. Come with me."

Across the factory floor Raikin dragged the shrilly protesting machinist. A few people stopped to look briefly. Not many did, however. This had become normal. The tyranny of the quality control teams had replaced the dictatorship of the proletariat.

Reaching the block where it rested on a cart by his tank, Raikin pulled the machinist's head down. "Show her, Stefan."

With a grimace, the one-eyed man set a micrometer and showed the setting to the machinist. Then he plunged it into an open cylinder and rattled it around. The machinist could not hear the rattling, of course, not over the drone of the factory. But the micrometer moved where it should not have been able to move.

"Now come with me. I am going to show you, once and for all, how to bore a damned cylinder."

Hand Grenade Range, Fort Cameron, 21/4/460 AC

Private Cruz was feeling rather pleased with himself today. He had been among the first in the century to qualify to throw a live grenade. Earlier he'd raced through the grenade assault course, proving that he could handle one of the little bombs. Now he waited in line to move up to the pit from which he would throw five live fragmentation grenades. One of the instructor corporals motioned for Cruz to stand and move up to the pit.

At about that point it really sank in, *Holyfuckingshit! They want me to hold a live bomb in my hand?*

When Cruz reached the pit from which he was to throw his grenades he was met by First Centurion Martinez. Martinez looked the new private up and down and asked, "Feeling a little cocky today, are we, son?"

Cruz answered, "First Centurion, I haven't felt cocky since coming to this . . . establishment."

"That's good, *chico,* because today cocky can get you killed." Martinez returned to business. "Private Cruz, at this station you will engage targets under a variety of circumstances with live fragmentation grenades. Do you understand why these grenades are called 'defensive' grenades?"

"Yes, Centurion." He parroted, "They are called 'defensive' because if you throw them while advancing or even standing you will be within the burst radius when they go off. Therefore they are only to be used while behind cover."

"That is correct, Cruz. However, cover means different things. Let me ask another question. How long after you pull the pin and release the handle will these grenades explode?"

"About four to five seconds, Centurion."

"Also good. So you understand that if you throw immediately there is a good chance the enemy will throw the grenade back at you?"

Cruz answered, "Yesss . . . Centurion," rather more slowly and suspiciously. He wasn't sure he liked the direction in which Martinez was heading.

Martinez sighed and continued, a philosophical note creeping into his voice. Idly, he tossed a grenade up a few times, catching it on the descent. "You see, Cruz, any fool can throw a grenade as far as his arm will send it. Any fool can throw one as soon as he releases the spoon. You, however, are going to learn to be a very *special* kind of a fool." Martinez's tone changed. "Take the first grenade in hand, Private."

Cruz, paling, took a grenade from a table in the pit. Martinez ordered him to remove the safety clip, and pull the pin. Cruz obeyed. Then Martinez grabbed the wrist of Cruz's throwing arm and said, "At my command you will release the spoon and count to three with me. Then you will throw the grenade as far down range as you can. Release the spoon."

Cruz, eyes gaping wide, looked at Martinez like he had lost his mind. Martinez repeated himself, "Private Cruz, release the spoon."

Mouth suddenly open and gone dry, Cruz removed

his thumb from over the grenade safety handle and watched as the metal safety handle flew off. He followed Martinez in what seemed an impossibly slow count to three. It's possible that the count seemed especially slow because the private's heart was racing at several hundred beats per minute. Martinez then released the boy's wrist, allowing him to propel the grenade over the walls of the pit. Cruz leaned back against the wall, knees gone weak, at about the time the grenade went off.

Martinez gave the boy a few moments to let his heart stop racing. Then he said, "Very good, Cruz. Now you are going to do it again. This time, though, you will do it entirely on your own. After that, instead of throwing the grenade as far as you can, you will lob one so that it explodes just on the other side of the pit wall. Then we will go out into the impact area. There you will use one of your grenades to clear a section of trench. You will be inside the trench, but around the corner from where you throw the grenade. Then you will take out a bunker. You will not, repeat *not*, be inside the bunker. The amount of training we have lavished upon you is beginning to make you too expensive to just throw away. Private Cruz, take a grenade."

Later, while marching back to the company tents, Cruz reflected upon the day's events and what they meant to him. Certainly they showed that he could use a grenade. It was more than that, though. In Cruz's mind, the big lesson of the day was that he could overcome mind-numbing fear. His step acquired just a bit more spring to it.

Kirov, Volga, 22/4/460 AC

"Let her down easy. *Easy,* I say!"

Raikin turned from the crane lowering the fifteen-ton turret to its rest. "Stefan, are you sure, *sure* that the recoil system is solid?"

"I am sure, Josef. I made the bastards do it over twice. No leaks. No weak seals. I watched them from start to finish."

The one-eyed man hesitated. "Josef?"

"Yes?"

"It feels good, you know . . . seeing good work done and doing good work."

And Raikin suddenly understood why the factory sounded different. "Yes, it does, Stefan."

"Stefan . . . why don't you pick up the wife and kids and come by this evening after work. A little vodka. A little food. For you are right; it does feel good. I never knew it could."

Imperial Range, 24/4/460 AC

"Move out!" crackled in Mendoza's headset. He was already shifting gear to reverse. Smoothly he backed out of his tank's hull-down firing position. Another quick shift of the gears and twist of the steering yoke—*I am getting good at this*—and his Jaguar sprang forward and to the left. Mendoza's body was pressed back against the rough cushion of the driver's seat.

An alarm buzzed in Mendoza's ears. He swore as he brought the tank to a complete halt, brakes squealing as his foot slammed down. His hand felt for the gearshift, then threw the tank into idle. Mendoza popped the hatch and was immediately surrounded by a cloud of red smoke billowing from a canister. The acrid smoke irritated Mendoza's eyes and throat, forcing him to tear up and to cough violently.

Half out of the hatch, Mendoza twisted his body around to see his tank's Volgan trainer climbing aboard, face red with fury. With frantic gestures supplemented by curses in mixed Spanish, Russian and Azeri, *Praporschik* Suleymanov pounded on turret top, screaming. Reduced to their essence, his words amounted to, "Left! Right! Left! Right! Always you do the same. Don't you think your fucking enemy is going to pay attention? Shift! Vary! Alternate! Don't be so damned predictable!"

"Yes, sir," answered Mendoza's chief, Sergeant Perez, once he was made to understand the problem. To Mendoza, Perez said, "Don't take it to heart, Jorge. It's my job to tell you which way to go. So . . . my fault. We'll do better in the future."

"Right, Sergeant. Got a set of dice to randomize?" *Thank you, Sergeant Perez, for not blaming me. But I could do better and I will.*

Kirov, Volga, 3/5/460 AC

"Do you think we could have done any better, Josef?"

"Maybe," Raikin admitted. "But if so, I don't see where. I don't know about the others, but *this* tank has no flaws." He looked at the vehicle, admiring it from the fresh paint of its hull, to the gleaming treads to the spotless rubber around the road wheels. Soon a heavy transporter would come to take it to the port. He would miss it, miss the sense of purpose it had given his life.

"Did you test fire the commander's machine gun as I told you?" Raikin asked.

"Yes, even that. Two hundred and fifty rounds through the barrel, just as you insisted. Then I cleaned it. Do you think it is enough?"

"Maybe not. But we did do the best we could."

Stefan smiled. "We actually can do a little better."

Raikin twisted his head, looking quizzical.

"Well . . . I was thinking about that tank crew; the one that will get this tank. I have been out in the desert, alone and scarred shitless."

"So?"

Stefan pulled a liter bottle of vodka from his lunch pack. "Does anyone in the factory write Spanish? I'd like to leave them a note with this."

Fort Cameron Parade Field, 5/5/460 AC

For the first time since it had been formed, the entire brigade stood together in one place. Basic Combat Training was over. The various training centuries had been reorganized into the ten cohorts, one *ala* and one *classis*—the naval squadron—that would participate in the war. As part of these cohorts and centuries— basically very large platoons that could be expanded into companies, or maniples, as money and manpower became available—the men would now train on the more advanced tactics, skills, techniques, and weapons they would actually use when they went to war.

In front of the now-formed legion the president of the Republic, General Parilla, the defense attaché from the Federated States, Colonel Sitnikov, and various other dignitaries—including the Roman Catholic archbishop—stood on a reviewing stand. Off to one side of the stand, a band played a martial air as the cohorts marched onto the field under the command of Carrera. TV news cameras recorded the event.

Once formed on the field, the officers and the legionary, cohort and century eagle and guidon bearers marched to the center behind Carrera. At his command, they all marched forward to a position directly in front of the reviewing stand. After the archbishop of Balboa had invoked a blessing, the president and Parilla presented the legion, each cohort and each century with the eagle or guidon it would carry as its colors. They were the same eagles Parilla had seen in Carrera's mess. These were gold for the legion and silver for the cohorts, *ala* and *classis*. There were miniature bronze eagles for the centuries with guidons attached. Each eagle perched atop an enameled copy of the national shield of Balboa. The shields were attached to seven-foot mahogany poles carved in a spiral design. The eagles' wings stretched upward until they almost touched overhead. A bronze plaque under the shields proclaimed the unit number and motto of each.

After presentation the men swore their oath of allegiance to, "God and the legion," rather than to the Republic. This was not lost on the president of Balboa who made a long-winded prepared speech, even so. Parilla made a rather shorter one which also had the function of promoting all the corporals

in the legion to sergeant. The archbishop prayed for
God above to also bless and protect the men who
would follow the eagles. Then the officers and eagles
marched back to a position in front of their units.
With the brass band playing—it was borrowed from
the *Cuerpo de Bomberos,* the firefighters, as the pipes
weren't quite ready yet—the legion passed in review
by the stand. Then—no time for celebrations—they
went back to training.

INTERLUDE

29 July, 2067, UNS *Kofi Annan*, alongside
Colonization Ship *Cheng Ho*

The man on the view screen was plainly dying. His
face was pale, sweat running down it in sheets. His
voice was breaking with pain. Even so, he managed
to eke out, weakly:

"*Captain's log, UNCS* Cheng Ho. *Final entry.*"

"Turn up the volume, Coms," the captain of the
Annan ordered. "And see if you can get rid of some
of the static."

The image cleared; the volume raised. In the view
screen the master of the *Cheng Ho* grimaced with
obvious agony.

"*I haven't been able to stop the troubles. Maybe . . .
maybe if I'd had more Marines aboard. But rampaging youths . . .*"

Did the captain of the *Annan* detect a sneer in the
words, "rampaging youths?" She thought she did. She
almost missed the next few words:

"*. . . have sabotaged the reactor. We've managed . . .
just . . . to keep it from going critical. We have not*

*been able to . . . control the radiation. It overheated . . .
melted the shield. The ship's been flooded . . . with
hard rads."*

Annan's captain winced. A bad way to go.

*" . . . the Phalange flooded the reactor deck with
some poisonous gas they ginned up in the labs . . . too
late . . . we can't get at the reactor even to build a
temp shield . . . around it."*

"What the hell is a *phalange*?" the captain asked of
the bridge crew, generally. Her question was rewarded
with blank stares.

*" . . . to anyone who comes after me . . . I can't explain
what happened, how it all fell apart. I don't know
why we can't . . . all . . . just . . . get along . . ."*

The captain of *Cheng Ho* began to sob on the
screen. Unable to speak, he clutched as his midsection
for long minutes before crumpling and falling off of
his chair and off screen.

"Oh, my," whispered *Annan's* skipper. Then, setting
her face firmly, she ordered, "Major Ridilla, return
here with your men. I want the complete log for
the *Cheng Ho* brought with you. Take them to my
port cabin and give them directly to me and to no
one but me."

"Aye, Skipper."

CHAPTER THIRTEEN

And the plan of God was being accomplished.
—Homer, The Iliad, Book I

Ranges Eight and Ten, Imperial Range Complex, east slope of Hell Hill, Republic of Balboa, 10/5/460 AC

Shift gears. Back up. Shift again. Move forward to the left. Feel the restraining straps cut into your body as it's thrown forward when the brakes bite in. Stop at the next covered position. Shift gears. Back up. Shift again. Move *right* to the next covered position. Right, again. Left. Left. Right. Stop. *Incoming!* Back up *fast!* Pop smoke.

Perez's voice shouts in the microphone. "Two o'clock! Gunner! Sabot! Tank!" Buttons are pushed. The auto-loader selects a round of kinetic energy ammunition from the carousel, lifting it easily to the breech and feeding it in. The gunner and commander shy away from the autoloader; it has been known to feed in arms, shoulders and heads. From behind Jorge Mendoza's head comes the whine of a 15-ton turret moving smoothly on its bearings. Jorge braces himself.

"Target!"

"Fire!" The crash of the gun ripples Mendoza's internal organs.

"Hit! Hit!"

"Eleven o'clock. Gunner! Sabot! Tank!"

"Miss!"

"Repeat!" The loader recycles with a fresh round. Again the crash sends Jorge's stomach bouncing against his backbone.

"Hit!"

"Driver, move out!"

Shift gears. Back up. Shift again. Forward. Forward. "Ten o'clock! Gunner! Sabot! . . ." An alarm goes off in Mendoza's ears. "Shit!" As always after a failure, red smoke floods Jorge's compartment as soon as he opens his hatch. *Shit!*

Jungle-covered for the most part, *Cerro de Infierno* jutted up between the Gallardo Trench of the Transitway and the road that ran generally alongside it. The hill overlooked the relatively open maneuver areas of Imperial Ranges Eight and Ten. From his vantage point above the road, Carrera watched one of the legion's tank sections going through its paces. While the rest of the legion had been going through basic training, the tank and PBM-100 crews, largely composed of long service professionals with Basic far behind them, had been doing their individual and crew training on the Jaguars and Ocelots. They were now working up to section and century level operations.

Through his field glasses Carrera saw the four tanks move by bounds toward *Cerro Marieta* to the east-south-east. As one group of two moved forward, the other protected them, overwatched in military parlance, by searching for and engaging any targets that presented themselves. As he watched a pair bound forward, Carrera's attention focused on one tank in particular. He couldn't see what had hit it, but the expanding cloud of red smoke told him something had. Perhaps the crew didn't know either, though Carrera could see a red-faced Russian, he assumed it was a Russian, screeching a small four wheel drive vehicle to a stop and getting out. In his glasses Carrera saw the tank crew, already emerging, flinching from the anticipated lesson.

Carrera cursed himself for a fool. *I've made a mistake in this training plan. This range is simply too hard. Truth be told, this platoon has already been "killed" more than once over.*

The primary problem was that the jungle and the hills and ridges made the range available to let the tanks engage targets far too short. This meant that when targets appeared they were so close to the tanks that the Jaguars had little chance to traverse and engage before, realistically, they would have been hit.

Everything is a trade off in tank design. Engineers trade size against ammunition and fuel capacity, height against ability to depress the gun, armor against speed, and engine and speed against fuel consumption and—sometimes, in peacetime—safety.

Politicians trade off expense against numbers. Some-times, in the industrialized parts of Terra Nova, they traded safety and combat performance for environmentalist sentiment, too. Politicians on Old Earth had once made similar choices. If they'd never paid for those choices, their soldiers often had.

One of the trade offs the Volgans typically made was slow speed of an electrically powered turret traverse against the complexity of a hydraulic traversing system and the danger of its fluid catching fire if hit. The Jaguar, like all Volgan tanks, was notoriously slow in traversing its turret. There were actually ranges, close ones to be sure, where a fast man on foot could run in a circle around a standing Volgan tank faster than the turret could track him. This sounded like more of a design flaw than it really was. Volgans used tanks in mass and with supporting infantry always close by. Try to run circles around one Volgan tank in combat and the odds were good that a dozen others would perforate you before you had a chance to turn the first corner, *if* the infantry didn't get you first.

Carrera thought, *Once they get to the desert this won't really be a problem. Shots there will usually be so long-range that the typical engagement will require only a small angle of turret movement. On the other hand, if the boys start believing their tanks aren't up to it here, they're likely to carry that attitude over to the desert. This is definitely not good.*

Carrera reached a decision and it didn't take him long to do so. He told his driver to call on the radio for Brown, Sitnikov and Kennison.

Brown was the first to arrive, having been the nearest. "Sancho Panzer reports, sir."

When the other two showed up, a few minutes later, Carrera told them, point blank, "This range sucks. Not your fault; still your problem. The troops aren't getting the chance to engage targets at a realistic distance and they're getting their clocks cleaned by the targets because they can't traverse quickly enough to engage. Here's what I want done by tomorrow morning. Carl, you go get your hands on a dozen small boats with outboards and a dozen, no better make it two, without. Get five hundred feet of tow cable for each powerboat. Brown, find some ballsy fuckers from among your tankers to man the powerboats. Offer a bonus if you have to. Don't be overgenerous . . . say, no more than daily combat pay would be. Fit out the others with tank-sized plywood targets. We'll tow the targets behind the powerboats out in the ocean north of the FS Army's old drop zone at Vera Cruz. Sitnikov, move half the Jaguars you've dedicated to gunnery to Vera Cruz. We'll do long-range firing from there."

With a moment's reflection, Carrera added, "Carl, better get the word to the merchant freighters anchored out there to move. And find me a place to do a tank platoon attack where they can shoot at some distance."

Kennison thought briefly. "No place near the Transitway, Pat. *Rio Sombrero,* maybe? I'll look tomorrow after we get the Vera Cruz affair set up."

"Fair enough."

Santa Clara Schoolhouse, Balboa, 14/5/460 AC

The training schedule for Cruz's unit—now reorganized as Second Century, 1st Cohort—called for exercises in city fighting. That put them in this paint-chipped and abandoned, multistory and multilevel building. The building had once been a school. Of the two major sections one stood atop a hill, another at its base. A long, covered and enclosed walkway ran up the side of the hill, connecting the two.

No Volgans, except the five that were attached to the cohort for their equipment training, were present. City fighting was an area in which the BDC had been reasonably well trained prior to the 447 invasion. The cohort's own NCOs, therefore, trained their own troops in the tactics and techniques of defending and attacking buildings. Those NCOs had, themselves, spent the previous three evenings in refresher training run by Abogado's organization while their troops rested.

Cruz's section leader, del Valle, took his men from station to station within the building. He showed them how to clear a room, to watch for booby traps, to use a rope to climb up the side of a blank wall, and all the other usual techniques employed in combat in built-up areas.

The upper part of the school was used to practice offensive operations. In the lower part were set up a number of demonstration areas showing how to prepare to defend a building, from making fighting positions to blocking normal passages to making new passages to setting traps. Cruz's section leader explained each, pretty much as it had been explained to him by FMTG. By supper time the company was finished with the schoolhouse. Eating his supper, a heavy stew over rice, Cruz and his friends had to admit that today's training had been the most fun so far. And it hadn't really been very hard work.

After supper Cruz's squad leader rejoined the rest of the squad. He marched them over to one of the abandoned houses the Federated States military forces had kept for the families of its soldiers once stationed in Balboa. The house was on stilts. It was also in very poor shape, which explained why it was abandoned. Underneath the house were several piles of fortification material, barbed wire, lumber, sandbags, shovels, axes and picks. Just outside the area under the house was a huge pile of dirt.

Del Valle gave a half evil smile just before saying, "Fun's over. Tomorrow morning we will be attacked. We will work all night to prepare this house for defense. You can use those two shovels and that dirt for filling sandbags. Sanchez, you are the acting section leader. The rest of you stay here. Sanchez come with me."

Fort Cameron, 17/5/460 AC

Artillery was a mixed bag. The artillery cohort was organized into five firing centuries of six guns each, though in one case instead of guns the century had multiple rocket launchers. Of the other four, two had Volgan-built 122mm howitzers and two had 160mm Suomi-manufactured mortars. The Volgans, too, had manufactured mortars in the 160mm range but those had been one of the rare cases where Carrera had opted for something besides Volgan equipment. The Suomi guns were lighter, more maneuverable, easier to get into and out of action, had greater range and a more effective shell on target. Nor was the price terribly bad, though it was more than the Volgan guns cost. Still, mortars were so cheap, generally, that the price differential for a mere twelve systems was small change, even for a force trying to squeeze out the last bit of value from every drachma.

Carrera had ordered several hundred Volgan "Daredevil" laser guidance systems to be modified for the Suomi shells. These had actually cost more than the other mortars would have. The Volgans were happy enough with the deal.

While only *just* enough tanks and other armored vehicles to train on had been delivered, the guns and mortars were light enough to fit on just a portion of a single large cargo aircraft. The Balboans had the full complement of what they would take to war with them.

Under their Volgan and Zion artillery instructors (for Zion made the same mortar as Suomi and had a fair number of Spanish speakers to boot—for that matter, the Arabic instructors for the intelligence and Civil Affairs/Psychological Operations troops were Zioni), the drivers were learning to operate prime movers for the artillery cohort while the cannoneers drilled on deflection and elevation changes, fuse setting and charge setting. Under a large tent, with the sides raised to let in the breeze, two more Volgan instructors were working with those twenty-two Balboans who had been selected to be FDCs, fire direction computers. The subject for today was setting up an artillery plotting board.

Nearby, another Volgan, along with Carrera's man Mitchell, was showing ten more Balboans how to use a Global Locating System, or GLS. This was a hand-held device that took coordinates on the ground directly from satellites in geosynchronous orbit. The UE Peace Fleet took very careful notice of any Terra Novan ventures into space, but had allowed these satellites without too much fuss.

Gamboa River, Republica de Balboa, 18/5/460 AC

A large black- and red-painted freighter moved north-west on its way through the Transitway. About a half a mile west of the freighter was the site chosen for the legion's engineers to practice river crossing and some other combat engineer operations.

Like nearly everyone else in the legion, the engineers had only a partial set of equipment with which to work. This was unfortunate but, in an armed force expanding radically and rapidly, it was perhaps unavoidable.

Carrera took it philosophically; other armies in the past had expanded to a greater degree, faster, with less-qualified cadre personnel and less equipment. What the legion had would do.

Touring the place, he thought, with a certain grim satisfaction, *Fortunately the area is nearly perfect. The Gamboa River is enough like the one in Sumer at this point, broad and slow, to make a good simulation in case we end up having to force a river crossing.*

Even as he watched, some of the engineers, the bridge and ferry troops, practiced ferrying men and equipment across the river to the other side and back again. On the other side was a marginally maintained golf course. The shouts and curses of the engineers reached his ears but faintly. He smiled.

A simulated minefield had been laid out across the golf course itself. Naturally, the greens of the golf course had been chewed up by heavy vehicle treads. Some of the locals were less than pleased at losing their recreation facility. When they had complained, however, Carrera had told the civilians to "go piss up a rope."

From his vantage point Carrera watched as the pioneer century and the pioneer sections of the combat support centuries practiced clearing lanes through the simulated minefields. They showed no more concern for the civilians' feelings than Carrera had.

It will be a long time before the golf course even has a fairway again. Tsk. How very unfortunate.

Once, when the Federated States had maintained a large force in Balboa, the place had been dotted with military facilities. One such was the *Cerro Peligroso* ammunition dump, located very near the golf course. This consisted of some open areas, a ring road, a fence in absolutely terrible shape, and thirty-three ammunition bunkers made up of very thick concrete. The whole area was badly overgrown. The engineer troops were billeted in some of the bunkers, each of which was large enough to fit forty men comfortably. The bunkers, what with the thick concrete and the jungle vegetation overhead, were cool and pleasant, if a bit damp.

From a demolition range situated at the southeast corner of the long abandoned dump came an irregular concussive thumping. As unhappy as they were over their golf course, the civvies were even less happy about the constant explosions. Carrera had also spoken to them about that, briefly. *Go piss up a rope.*

Carrera walked by, just to see if the chain of command knew enough to keep the troops busy. Since the bunkers were abandoned but for a guard each, plus the cooks in the mess bunker, Carrera inferred that they did.

Near the bunkers, the ditch and entrenchment

excavators chewed lines in the ground wherever they could find an open area. *Must insure they know to fill those in. Mosquitoes.*

The water purification troops, engineers rather than logistics men, trained on the polluted waters of the Transitway itself. Quality control was easy for these men. The water they purified was all they were allowed to drink.

Amid the hubbub of roaring machinery, sputtering water ferry engines, and explosions, Carrera and the engineer century commander spoke.

"How's it going, Sam? Any major problems?" Carrera left unspoken the *and how can I help you?* It was possible that he couldn't help. No sense in offering what he couldn't deliver.

The engineer officer was another man from the Federated States. Originally, Sam Cheatham had come as part of Abogado's FMTG. He was tallish and a bit beefy, a graduate of the FS Military Academy at River Watch. Carrera had tapped him one day and asked if he'd be interested in joining the legion and commanding its engineer century. Promised that Carrera would make up the pay differential on the side, Cheatham had jumped at the chance.

Like the Ocelot sections that trained with the mechanized cohort but would eventually return to the infantry cohorts, the engineers of the cohorts' combat support centuries trained with the main engineer century for the nonce.

Everything's basically going well as far as our own jobs are concerned, sir," the engineer had answered. "One thing does worry me, though. We need to work with the combat cohorts we're going to support. That will happen on its own with the cohorts' own sapper sections. My century is a problem. If we could have even a few days each of working with the cohorts, I'd be a lot happier."

Carrera answered, "Yeah . . . me, too. After Advanced Individual Training is finished we'll have about eighteen days here in Balboa before we go over to major unit exercises under the legion. We can send your men down to work with the cohorts then."

And then we can pray it's enough. I think it will be enough.

Range 12, Imperial Range Complex, 21/5/460 AC

Cruz's hands still had not healed from all of the shoveling of dirt he had done at Cocoli the week before. His lungs also still hurt from all of the smoke he had sucked down when his squad was attacked. The defense had not gone well. Cruz's section leader, plainly displeased, had simply selected another building and the whole section had done it all over again the next day. The same had happened to all the other sections in the century. That defense had gone better. Best of all, six of the cohort's twelve sections had to do it all a third time. Not only did this give Cruz's comrades a satisfying opportunity to rub it in to those who still had to train to standard; while they were retraining the members of the sections who had passed were allowed to catch up on sleep. Since nobody had slept more than half an hour in two days, this was a most welcome break.

Now, at Range 12, the men prepared to do a dismounted live fire exercise, a fairly simple trench clearing operation. The section would use its rifles, its three Volgan light machine guns, and a medium machine gun in getting to and clearing the trench. Instead of hand grenades they had been given simulators. In the confined spaces of the trench system these were probably dangerous enough.

The men were set, but hidden by the jungle's foliage. At a signal from Cruz—he was acting as leader for this mission—the medium machine gun began to sweep fire across the top of the objective. Near the machine gun, but spread out to either side, were three men carrying "Draco" sniper rifles, which fired the same, high-powered, round. Between the two types of fire Cruz could reasonably expect the target to be judged "suppressed."

When he, personally, judged that anyone who might have been in the target trench would at this point likely have been on the bottom of it, shitting their pants, Cruz gave the signal—a simple whistle blast, for the machine gun to lift fires off the objective. It did, but only to the extent of firing high so that the sound of the bullets passing would at least continue to frighten anyone who might have been in the trench. The Dracos maintained their slow, aimed, deliberate fire. The assault party would just have to move through it, trusting to the marksmanship of the Draco men.

Most armies would have banned this as being far too unsafe.

Cruz then led the remaining men forward at the double, bayonets fixed, to a shallow linear depression in the earth. The men hastily threw themselves down into it. The machine gun resumed firing only a few feet over their heads.

Under his leaders' watchful eyes, Cruz and the rest threw simulators at the opposing trench. At this signal the machine gun lifted its fire off of the objective completely and began to pound a suspicious-looking position higher up the hill. Making ready to use simulators again, the men crawled forward to within a few feet of the trench. Two of them placed simulators directly into it. That was much less nerve wracking than using real grenades. After the twin explosions the rest rushed the last few feet up to the trench, firing downward from the hip as they ran.

The first two men jumped in, turned to the sides and fired at targets that suddenly appeared on either side of them. Meanwhile, Cruz and the rest crawled forward and entered the position themselves. Cruz ordered the rightmost man to stay put and guard the rear. Then the rest turned left and began bombing their way forward, throwing simulators to clear each section of trench before entering it to make a clean sweep with automatic rifle fire.

Fifty meters up the line the trench branched. Again leaving a man to guard that portion that ran parallel to the crest of the hill, Cruz and the others took the branch that went uphill. Bombing forward the entire way, Cruz reached the final objective, a small command bunker. He threw a green smoke canister to signal for the machine gun to come forward and sent one man to retrieve the two who had been left behind. Then he began placing the section in a hasty defense to repel any counterattack.

Behind Cruz, del Valle and First Centurion Martinez

exchanged glances. *Oooo, that was* nice. *Good kid;
very calm, very determined. He's done well. There's
potential here.*

Lying on his belly, waiting for someone to start
pulling up the targets that would signal the enemy
counterattack, Cruz thought, *damn, that was fun.* He
didn't notice that his hands had started bleeding again.

Fort Cameron, 24/5/460 AC

The window-mounted air conditioner hummed loudly,
causing the speaker to have to raise his voice to be
heard. It didn't really matter; Carrera listened with
only one ear, and absently, to the training status brief
being presented. He relied more on his eyes and ears
than statistical indicia, anyway.

The briefing officer, Tribune Rocaberti, was River
Watch trained, Carrera knew. The briefing reflected
that. It was also precisely why Carrera paid it little
attention. The briefing was thorough, painstaking, and,
inevitably, duller than watching paint dry.

Carrera had always found long meetings to be
physically and psychically agonizing. He interrupted
Rocaberti and told Johnson to stay and listen to the
rest. Then he left the conference tent.

"Take me to Imperial Range, Jamey," he told Soult.

"Sure thing, Boss."

Soult put the car in gear and pulled away on the
packed gravel road for the hour and a half long drive
to Imperial Range. Soult drove quietly for the first
half hour, before reaching the paved highway that
ran west to the Bridge of the Columbias and on to

Imperial Range complex. He did risk a couple of glances over at his chief, noting that Carrera's face seemed troubled.

"What's bothering you, Boss?"

Of the people Carrera had assembled for his staff, only three—Soult, Mitchell and the sergeant major—were actually the kind of friends he would trust with a personal problem. He thought about whether this was the kind that he could . . . or even should.

"I am beginning to feel like a disloyal rat, Jamey."

"Lourdes, right, Boss?"

"Yeah," Carrera admitted. *Who said enlisted men were stupid?* "I find myself thinking about her at odd times."

"Uhhh . . . Boss . . . we all find you *looking* at her at odd times, too."

"Everybody's noticed?" Pat asked.

"I think so. I mean . . . well, I'm sure you try not to look and all . . . but, yeah; sometimes you're pretty obvious."

Carrera sighed and turned his face to the right, watching the trees go by. After several minutes he turned back.

"The problem is, Jamey, that my wife and kids are dead less than a year. It just seems *wrong* for me to be looking at another woman now. It might be wrong *ever* to look at another woman with . . . any . . . oh . . . *significance.*"

"If you don't mind my saying so, Boss, that's bullshit. A man needs a woman. A soldier needs one more than most."

"Maybe," Carrera half conceded before turning his gaze back to the passing jungle.

✦   ✦   ✦

The staff car pulled to a stop near the large asphalt parking lot where Sitnikov had once given his introductory presentation on tanks. There was an infantry cohort—the schedule said it would be the 1st Cohort—sitting on the mown grass east of the asphalt, eating lunch from pouches.

"Hey, Cruz, look. It's the Gringo."

By now, everybody knew who *the* Gringo was. It was also known that he was a former Federated States military officer. It was rumored that he had lost his family during either the terrorist attacks on the Terra Nova Trade Organization in the FSC or during the attacks shortly thereafter in the Republic of Balboa. No one, no one at Cruz's level, at least, knew for sure which it was, though.

Cruz looked up to see Carrera watching another century as they practiced mounting and dismounting from the Ocelots. Each cohort had four, for general support, in the Combat Support Century. Any couple of sections might need to mount them in the coming fight so all had to be at least familiarized beforehand.

Cruz asked a question of common concern. "Why do you suppose he's here with us?"

Not quite understanding, his squad mate answered, "To make sure we're training all the time, not eating properly, and getting little rest. Why else?"

"Don't be more stupid than you absolutely must," Cruz said. "No, I mean what is he doing here in Balboa? It doesn't make sense to me."

"I heard a rumor that he is planning to overthrow the government and establish himself as dictator. I also heard, from an equally reliable source, that he is an agent of the Gringo imperialists to make sure we never rise again."

"Oh, *antania* shit. He spends way too much time training us to think he's against us. Nothing he's done suggests anything but that he's on our side. He spends all his time out in the field with us, trying to make sure we're ready to fight. That means he is not trying to keep Balboa down. I heard he refused the command of the legion, so it doesn't look like he wants to be dictator. No. He is here for some other reason. If he really did lose his family, like rumor control says, could it really be that he's here just for revenge?"

Sergeant del Valle, who *was* at a level to know why Carrera was there, interrupted the conversation to say, "Why he's here is none of your goddamned business, Privates. And since you two seem to have all this idle time on your hands to philosophize, you can wash out the Ocelot tonight after we're finished."

Casa Linda, 26/5/460 AC

While the maids puttered and dusted, Lourdes sang, softly but happily, as she busied herself with preparations. Carrera and his boys, most of them, were coming home from Fort Cameron for the first time in weeks.

"Over there, Maria," Lourdes said to a maid. "Put the whiskey out where they can find it first. After all that time in the jungle they'll want a drink. And I want Patricio . . ."

Lourdes stopped with sudden confusion. She steadied herself with one hand on the dining room table while pulling a seat out with the other. She sat down heavily.

I want Patricio? I missed them, sure, but . . . no, girl, be honest with yourself, at least. You missed him; Patricio. It was that name that set your heart to beating fast.

Why? Why should I? He hardly ever even talks to me outside of my job. "Translate this, please, Lourdes." "Is my car ready, Lourdes?" "Lourdes, have you seen the report from Professor Ruiz?" He cares more for his men than he does for me. At least he'll spend time with them when he isn't working.

Lourdes looked into the next room where, over the fireplace mantle hung Linda Hennessey's portrait. *How can I compete with that? I'm pretty enough, I guess . . . no gross defects. Not a lot of equipment but it isn't bad, what I do have. But she's dead, so she's a saint. Sometimes I hate that picture so much!*

The woman stood again, a trifle unsteadily, and walked into the living room. She looked up at Linda's portrait and asked aloud, "Do you want him to be alone? I could make him happy; I know I could. But he sits and stares and pines and, when he thinks no one is looking, he cries for you. Would you mind so much . . . ?"

The portrait didn't answer. Lourdes turned on her heel and walked up the stairs to Carrera's room, near her own. She stood there quietly, at the foot of his bed, merely sniffing. It smelled *right* to her, whatever trace of him was left in the bedding and furniture. She went to the clothes hamper, opened it and pulled out a T-shirt left from his last, very brief, visit home. *Have to speak to Lucinda about cleaning out the hampers more regularly,* she thought.

Scrunching the T-shirt in her hands she pressed it to her face and inhaled through her nose and deeply. *Oh, yes, this smells* just *right. Why are men so stupid that they can't tell a proper match the way women can?*

Presidential Palace, *Ciudad* Balboa, 13/6/460 AC

"*Tio* Guillermo, you were badly mistaken."

"Mistaken, Manuel? How?"

"They are going to get this legion finished, and *properly*. And there's precisely *nothing* I can do about it. I haven't ever seen anything like this level of . . . oh, efficiency. Certainly not since I left River Watch."

"I assumed you would do your duty and sabotage them, Manuel. Obviously you have failed," the president sneered. "You were born a failure. You remain one, a disgrace to a proud name. I wish the gringos had killed you twelve years ago. Your existence is an embarrassment."

Rocaberti cringed under his uncle's tongue-lashing. "Uncle, whatever I am, I can't do this. Parilla? You know him. He isn't so bad. But that gringo of his? Uncle, he frightens me. And Jimenez, you remember him? Jimenez wants me *dead*. He blames *me* that he lost the fight at the Estado Mayor; blames me for losing most of his men. I see it in his eyes. Can't you please, *please* get me out of this?"

"No. Get back to where you belong and *report,* at least, if you are too much the coward to do anything else. Go and at least *pretend* you're someone with balls!"

Casa Linda, 15/6/460 AC

Carrera, Parilla, McNamara, Johnson, Kennison, and
Sitnikov sipped cool drinks on the rear deck of the
house, overlooking the Gulf of Balboa. The atmosphere was informal but there was business to attend
to. The legion was almost finished with the second
phase of their training, what would be called ACT—or
Advanced Combat Training—for infantry and tankers
in the Federated States Army.

Setting down his drink, Carrera began, "Aleksandr,
how do you rate our men?"

Sitnikov had been asking himself the same question
for weeks. He made his answer honestly.

"On a purely technical level your men have done
well, especially with the heavy vehicles. My instructors
say that they have learned to drive, shoot, and maintain
better and faster than a typical group of Volgan recruits
would have. This is unsurprising, to a degree, since both
the Civil Force and the new Legion have been able to
be very selective in the recruits accepted. However,
you have weaknesses in higher-level maintenance.
Your NCO's seem as good, or probably, since they are
regulars, better than average Volgans. However . . ."

"However?" Carrera prodded.

"However," Sitnikov continued, "I cannot say as
much for all of your officers. You have some very
good ones, to be sure. Tribune Jimenez, in particular,
would be a credit to anyone's army. There are others.
Would you like to see what my instructors have to
say about the legion's leadership?"

At Carrera's nod Sitnikov turned over a list of the

Legio del Cid's commissioned leadership, tactfully without including any of Carrera's hand-picked old friends. Comments were written beside each man's name. Most were in blue, and terse. Carrera quickly gathered that these the Volgans considered good enough. Others, the best, were in black. Jimenez's name appeared in this way. About twenty names were in red. The Volgans viewed these very unfavorably. Carrera noted that Manuel Rocaberti was on that list before he passed the sheets to Parilla without comment.

Parilla noted it too. "We can't dump Tribune Rocaberti, Patricio. Too well connected, he and his family. He's the president's nephew, after all. And the president *must* have his spy in our ranks. At least with Manuel, we know *who* the spy is."

"Ummm," Carrera answered doubtfully. "Sitnikov, this about matches my own assessment. Which is why I called you here today. We have a shortage of effective, combat capable officers. I would like to make up some of that shortage from you. Also some of the maintenance deficiency. What do you say?"

Sitnikov sat silent for a long minute. When he answered, it was a deliberate, measured response. "Some of my men, maybe even more than half, would probably like to stay. Many have found girlfriends. Two, to my certain knowledge, are planning on getting married. I do not know how my government would react to that, however. If they say no, the idea of being stateless does not appeal."

Carrera looked to Parilla. Parilla gave a nonverbal assent, a shallow nod.

"What if you men could become citizens of Balboa, Aleksandr, with jobs and ranks in the LdC roughly commensurate with—okay, maybe a *bit* below—their current ranks in the Volgan Army? Would that sway them, do you think?"

"Some of them have wives, children. They would not leave them behind . . . well . . . most of them wouldn't."

"Do you think the current regime would let the men's families emigrate?" Carrera asked.

Sitnikov couldn't know for sure, but thought it likely. He reminded Carrera that not all of the Volgans were, themselves, first class military material. He had been forced to take some marginal characters, men whose only real qualification was linguistic, to meet the numerical requirements of the training mission.

"Yes, I know," answered Carrera. "I wasn't planning on keeping all of you. Moreover, while I can offer you pay and rank, I must insist that Balboans and my own people fill all combatant command positions. Most of your men will be on staff or in support. Some may be serving in positions either below their grade or below their ability."

Sitnikov laughed. "That, Legate, is no problem. It would help, though, if you could hold out a promise of equal opportunity to command once we've been citizens for a few years."

"I can do that," Carrera agreed readily. "Now find out who will stay and who will go at the end of the training period. Get me a list as soon as you can . . . say, by the end of the week. I expect you to weed out the trash yourself. Give it directly to me as the sergeant major and Tribune Kennison are going over to al Jahara to look things over."

At that moment Carrera spied his slender secretary through a door. *Jesus, what a nice rear end.* He called,

"Lourdes, have you finished making the flight arrangements for Carl and the sergeant major?"

She bridled for a moment. *"Have you got the reservations, Lourdes? Where's that personnel file, Lourdes? Why don't you shrink your tits and ass so there's absolutely no possibility I ever notice you are a woman, Lourdes?"*

That wasn't fair and she knew it. *How would I feel, how would I act, if the person I'd loved most in the world had been murdered? If my children had been murdered? It will take him some time . . . I suppose.*

She answered, calmly enough, *"Si,* Patricio. I have the tickets, visas and the press passes. And I've gotten yours to go to Hamilton, FD, the day after. I will brief them when you are done here." Her voice held not more than a trifle of anger or sarcasm, and the anger may have been directed at herself. If Carrera noticed, he didn't let on.

Carrera didn't wake up screaming as often anymore, nor did he scream as loudly as he once had. Usually. There were exceptions.

There was a low fire burning in the great stone fireplace in the living room. The troops insisted on calling it the "Dayroom" to Lourdes' immense confusion. This was an English word she had never learned and found distinctly odd, since it was almost never used except at night. The fire was unnecessary, as far as warmth went, but the men seemed to find it comforting in ways she only distantly understood. There was, in any case, never a need to designate anyone to cut firewood or build a fire. It just happened whenever any substantial group of them were in the *casa.*

Sitting across the coffee table from McNamara and Kennison, Lourdes said, "Sergeant Major, Carl, you are accredited to the *Estrella de Balboa*, our major newspaper. In theory you are going over there to cover preparations for the war. What you will actually do, I do not know and I know you can't or won't tell me. Your accreditation has been passed through the attaché at the FS embassy and is approved by the FSC's War Department."

McNamara smiled broadly and blindingly and was about to thank her when an ear-splitting shriek echoed through the *casa*. Lourdes looked terribly distressed. Kennison hung his head. The sergeant major muttered something about, "Poor bastard."

"What's wrong? What makes him do that?" Lourdes asked.

"Nightmares," McNamara answered. "I've been next to him twice when it's happened. I think . . . no, I am sure, he is seeing his family die over and over again."

"But he didn't see . . ." Lourdes began before stopping herself. "Oh, I see. That makes it worse, doesn't it?"

McNamara nodded, sadly. *Hmmm. I wonder what might make it better.* He looked once, intently, into Lourdes' huge brown eyes, measuring her. Then he looked upstairs in the direction of Carrera's quarters and back again at the girl.

She looked back, eyes narrowing inquisitively. *Do you really think that would help?*

The sergeant major's unspoken answer was, *How could it hurt?*

Flustered and not a little embarrassed, Lourdes

went to the bar and poured herself a stiff drink. This was very rare for her. She then left the "Dayroom" and went to her own room. Undressing and lying down atop the covers with her head propped on pillows, she sipped at her drink and asked herself, *How could it hurt?*

She lay that way for half an hour, thinking, sipping, wondering, sipping . . . perhaps even daydreaming. Then she arose, pulled a robe around her, and walked to Carrera's room.

She didn't knock. She just put her hand on the doorknob and, after a moment's nervous hesitation, turned it and pushed the door open. Enough moonlight entered through the windows to the room that she could make out Carrera lying on his side, his body shaking.

Walking as quietly as possible she moved to stand beside the wide bed. Then she took off her robe, letting it cascade to the floor around her feet. Her undergarments followed quickly. Again she hesitated, but only very briefly, before pulling the bed clothes down and climbing in behind Carrera, sliding between the sheets to mould her body to his back. She slid one arm around the still-shuddering form and whispered, "There . . . there . . . it'll be all right. Sleep . . ."

She felt his body spin inside the grasp of her arm. Suddenly her lips and face were being covered with kisses. Hands reached out, stroking . . . grasping . . . squeezing. Fingers probed, not always gently. She felt herself growing wet and warm. Soon—too soon, perhaps—she found herself on her back with her legs spread and Carrera hovering over. She smelled whiskey strong on his breath.

"Patricio . . . slowly . . . please," she gasped, "I've never . . . ooowww!"

She bit her lip to keep from crying out any louder. And then the strangeness of having someone inside her, thrusting, moving, took over. This was following by a spreading warmth, a sort of glow that seemed to begin between her legs and spread to every distant part of her body. She found herself thrusting back. Hard.

"Lie . . . on . . . me," she grunted. "I want . . . to . . . feel the weight . . . of your . . . body . . . on me."

She felt the strange thing inside her begin to pulse and throb. It grew as the thrusting increased in depth and force. Carrera whispered, "Oh, Linda . . . I . . . love . . . you."

Lourdes stopped pushing back and began to cry even as Carrera's body, spent, slumped onto hers. The snoring that soon followed suggested he had never really been awake.

INTERLUDE

2 October, 2067, UNSS *Kofi Annan*, along-side Colonization Ship *Cheng Ho*

A careful count of the bodies aboard ship revealed that twenty-nine people were missing, all of them either Atheist, Christian, Buddhist or Hindu. They, and the missing shuttle, must have gone below as neither radar nor lidar showed the slightest trace of the shuttle in the solar system. There was no distress signal from the shuttle. The technical manual said that the batteries should have lasted for decades. If the ship had not crashed, someone had deliberately turned the signal off.

The *Annan*'s shuttles began looking. They were few and the planet was not small. It wasn't made any easier by the fact that the survivors had landed the shuttle in a forest glade.

The continent was in the southern hemisphere of the planet. It stretched nearly ten thousand miles, east to west. On the eastern end, several geographic projections made it look something like a bull, lying on its back, with an erection. The crew named this portion of the continent "Taurus" because of that resemblance.

To the west, the continent was mostly flat, open grasslands with occasional forests and marshes, and some impressive mountain ranges near the equator. The grasslands disappeared to the east, giving way to thick virgin woods with some open areas.

Moving west to east on a sweep, *Annan's* Shuttle Number Three caught a glimpse of a flash that was unlikely to have been natural. It moved closer to investigate, finally coming to a landing a few hundred meters from the crash site.

Major Ridilla happened to be aboard that shuttle and was the first to set his feet on the ground. He wore an environmental suit, but without armor, and carried a modern rifle. Neither, as it turned out, was needed. The people, and they were fewer than the twenty-nine missing names even with the babies and young children, came out wearing badly tanned skins, thin to the point of emaciation, and ever so grateful to be rescued.

"We thought Earth had forgotten about us," their leader said. She might once have been pretty, with her high cheekbones and off-white skin with just the hint of Vedic smokiness lying below the surface. But she was a woman aged far beyond her years. "We thought we'd die here." She looked skyward. "Then again, we thought we'd die up there. I'm Marjorie Billings-Rajamana," she said, putting out her hand.

She had a very nice, upper class British accent. *Well, of course if anyone's going to survive and keep people alive that person would have a British accent,* Ridilla thought. *I mean . . . tradition and all.*

"What happened?" he asked, taking the hand and shaking it. "What happened on the *Cheng Ho*?"

"That's a long story," the woman answered. "And you'd better give me something to drink, something *strong* to drink, if you want to hear it."

Assuming that the presence of people meant the absence of disease, Ridilla removed the helmet of his enviro-suit. "I'm sorry, I don't have anything like that with me. There's some on the ship. You *do* want to go home, don't you?"

In answer, the woman laughed. Years fell away from her face, as if she had, perhaps, not laughed in all those years. She asked, "Who do I have to blow? If I never see this miserable place again it will still be too soon."

CHAPTER FOURTEEN

Grace was in all her steps, heaven in her eye,
In every gesture dignity and love.

> —Milton, *Paradise Lost*

Casa Linda, 15/7/460 AC

Carrera's first words on awakening were, "My, that was a nice..."

He was never quite sure afterwards which it was that first informed him that he had not been dreaming. Was it the mattress slumped slightly with a another human being? The scent? Some half-remembered details that were just too real to have been a dream? Or perhaps it was that all his dreams for months had been nightmares while the preceding night had definitely *not* been a nightmare.

How it would turn out, however...

"Lourdes?" he asked, uncertainly.

She sniffled, "Yes?"

Oh, shit. What the hell did I do? He asked her.

"Last night," she answered, "while you were making love to me, you didn't even call out *my* name. It was like I gave myself to you and it meant nothing." She began to cry in seriousness now.

He reached to her shoulder and pulled, rolling her over to face him. She resisted, initially, pulling her shoulder away. He was not, however, taking no for an answer. He gathered her in his arms and whispered, "It wasn't that. I was—I'm sorry to say—asleep. I don't sleep well, usually, but when I do I could sleep through a barrage. I have. Anyway, I'm really sorry. And I'll make it up to you, as best I can."

Lourdes said nothing. How someone was supposed to make up to her the ruination of what should have been the most special—or perhaps the second most special—event of her life was beyond her. She was angry, she was bitter. Above all, she was hurt.

Carrera continued on, despite her stony silence. "Frankly, Lourdes, I'm glad you came to me last night. Loneliness was killing me and you are . . . well . . . simply wonderful. Thank you."

Carrera backed off slightly to push her back onto her back. Then he proceeded to kiss her tears away and show her—without any mistakes with names, this time—that he meant what he said.

And perhaps, she thought, anger lessening, *perhaps the hurt will go away if I let it.*

Casa Linda, 27/6/460 AC

Carrera, Sitnikov, and half a dozen other Volgan officers sat in the conference room in the basement of the house. These half dozen Volgans had indicated that, while they could not, in good faith to their duties to the motherland, give up their Volgan citizenship, they were willing to stay on in Balboa under contract if they were wanted. They also represented another several dozen Volgans in the same straits. Another one hundred and twenty-one of the Volgan trainers had elected to take Legionary rank and eventual Balboan citizenship—and getting the legislative assembly to approve *that* had cost another series of bribes—and to accompany the *Legio del Cid* to al Jahara and Sumer—or *wherever*, for that matter. Legionaries take their orders and march with them. But if these men, and those they represented, remained citizens of the Volgan Republic, they could not accompany the Legion to a war to which their country was not a party.

Carrera began, "Gentlemen, first of all let me say that I appreciate and respect your decision to remain true to the country of your birth. There is no shame in that. Your absence will be felt when the legion leaves for the desert." Carrera passed around glasses, scotch, and ice as he spoke.

"Nonetheless, you may, if you wish, still remain here in Balboa to work on a few special projects that I have in mind. If you decide to stay, your pay will be commensurate with the LdC pay for the ranks you now hold. I can arrange some longevity increases as you spend more time here, but you will be, for all practical purposes, frozen in your current ranks for the immediately foreseeable future. Can you accept this?"

Carrera looked at the Volgans' faces for a reaction. Seeing no negative indicators from them, he continued. "The second condition is that you must still take an oath to the LdC to give loyal and diligent service. This includes not divulging any of the nature of the work you will do to anyone, *ever*. *This* includes divulging to the Volgan Republic. Can you accept that?"

Still the Volgans gave no indication of objection. Indeed, since their whole way of life prior to this had involved the most stringent security procedures, they did not even consider any other possibility. As to whether they would honor those oaths . . .

Carrera thought, *As if they could be trusted not to spill their guts once they go home. Still, my cautioning them may help make them feel they're part of the team and fully trusted. People are odd that way.*

Continuing, Carrera said, "Very well then. Colonel Sitnikov has decided to accept our offer of citizenship and equivalent rank. He will be in charge of you in my absence. I thank you for your decision to stay and help us. Dismissed."

When the rest of the Volgans had departed, Carrera explained to Sitnikov what it was he wanted done while the legion was gone. He had learned to trust this particular Volgan, implicitly, over the last half year.

"Aleksandr, there are a number of projects I want your people to work on over the next year or two. Probably two years."

Carrera stood up, walked to the railing of the porch, turned and leaned against it. He continued. "The first project involves the *Isla Real*. That's the big island in the Bay of Balboa. I want you, personally, to work out how to turn it into a major Initial Entry Training establishment capable of turning out up to thirty thousand trained privates a year, as well as the needed number of specialists, officers and noncoms to lead an army of about three hundred and fifty to three hundred and eighty thousand. I'll send someone over with the table of organization, equipment, and manning to guide you in your planning."

"I've already seen it in rough terms," Sitnikov said. "One of your people showed me. You really think you can turn this place into a nation-in-arms?"

"Maybe not," Carrera answered. "And maybe I won't need to. But it is certain that unless I plan for it, I won't be able to."

Sitnikov's head rocked from side to side, considering. *It's true enough, I suppose.*

"Don't, repeat *don't*, try to build anything along those lines," Carrera continued. "I will want you to build, as the money becomes available, a less ambitious facility capable of turning out seventy-five hundred to eight thousand trained privates a year, with other specialty and leadership schools as required.

"Remember, though, all you can do is plan for now. Even to buy the island, or to get the government to condemn it through eminent domain, would cost about half a billion FSD, maybe more. I don't expect to have that kind of money until and unless I can work out a deal with the Feds to hire the legion.

"In any case, let me make this clear: the planning for the building of the smaller training facility is to be open, once we own the island. The plan for expanding it to the larger capacity is to be very close hold. Even more close hold, I want you to plan for turning the island into a genuine fortress, one capable of enduring air attack and defeating amphibious attack by *any* possible enemy."

Sitnikov brushed a hand through thinning hair. *Any enemy?* he wondered. *Even the FSC? The Taurans? I wouldn't enjoy taking on the FSC, were it my fortress to command. But killing Sachsen and Gauls? Zhong? Be still, my heart.*

Sitnikov asked, "You think the others might report back even though they gave their words they will not?"

Carrera lowered his chin slightly, his eyes boring into Sitnikov as if the latter were a very dull schoolboy.

"Yes," Sitnikov admitted. "Well . . . I suppose so."

Carrera nodded and continued, "The next project is to plan to set up a major unit training center at Fort Cameron, something capable of training and testing units up to regimental size. We're going to cut you orders and get you a visa to visit the Federated States. I will also get the local FS attaché to get you permission to visit their combat training centers in the states of Arcadia and Sequoia. I'll give you more guidance on this later. For now, just go and see how the FS Army does it. And be skeptical."

Carrera paused while Sitnikov wrote this down. He began to walk from one side of the porch to the other.

"Lastly, I want—and in some ways this will be the most delicate work of all—I want a plan for organizing six junior military academies in six locations I will give you later. I will get you a professor from the University of Balboa to help with the academic requirements. The purpose of these schools will be to provide the preliminary training for recruits to the legions—yes I said, 'legions'—as and when we can expand. I also want—and this is critical—for these schools to be able to defend themselves at need and attack within fifty kilometers or so of their positions. They must be able to exit the academies and move to attack positions without being detected.

"Aleksandr . . . whatever I said to those who decided against citizenship . . . I want you to arrange things so *no one* can put together a picture of what we're doing from the bits and pieces those men will work on. Not if the KVD and OSI each had a thousand years to question every one of those men."

"That will not be easy, sir. I will have to do everything but the most mundane things myself."

"So? Lourdes will be remaining here. She can be of great assistance to you. She's a very impressive woman, actually. Now, what are your questions?"

As if on cue, Lourdes—smiling rather happily now—stuck her head out the folding glass door to the rear porch and announced, "Patricio, I've got Senator Rodman on the phone as you requested."

"Excuse me for a moment, would you, Aleksandr?" Carrera asked as he stood to go to his office.

"Patrick, dear boy, how can I help you today?" Harriet Rodman asked brightly.

Carrera went right to it. "I need an appointment, two hours or so, with Ron Campos, SecWar."

"*That* asshole? Whatever for? And why come to me?"

"I came to you because you can do it and because you are an honest politician." They both knew what Carrera meant by that. *Once bought you stay bought. And I'm keeping up the mortgage my uncle and grandfather placed on you and your antecedents.*

He continued, "As for why him; I need his help with something. Actually, Harriet, come to think of it I really should bring you into it. You, after all, are concerned with loss of Federated States citizens' and soldiers' lives. You are pretty tight with a defense drachma. Yes . . . tell you what; I'll come up a day early and brief you. At dinner, say? Perhaps at the Army and Navy Club."

"No," Rodman answered. "Too public for both our purposes. Dinner at my place, okay? Use the back door. If we're conspiring, Patrick, let's *conspire.*"

Hamilton, FD, 32/6/460 AC

"You've been doing *what?*" Rodman asked incredulously.

"Not 'been doing,' Harriet. Done. I have a large brigade, *el Legio del Cid,* a nongovernmental organization set up under the sponsorship of the government of the Republic of Balboa, organized, equipped and, *almost,* trained to fight."

"You aren't serious," she insisted. "You think these people can actually fight? Come on."

Carrera resisted, almost successfully, the outrage that he naturally felt at anyone casting even the slightest aspersion on a unit *he*—practically speaking— commanded.

Harriet knew she had overstepped her bounds when Carrera's fingers began drumming the table rhythmically. *His uncle used to do that when he was really annoyed,* she thought.

"For your information, Senator," Carrera said in an icy voice, "The legion is fully equipped. It is not equipped up to FS standards but it is still very well equipped. The core of the leadership cadres have experience of combat; many of them have much experience of combat. Moreover the bulk of the legion's leaders have been brought up to speed for modern, combined arms warfare. The younger ones have as well. The troops . . ." and the iciness left his voice as he began to describe his men.

"Ah . . . they're just *great*. The minimum IQ is 110. There is no army in the world that can boast that. The average is above 115 . . . closer to 120. In a place like Balboa, with fifty percent unemployment among young men, we could pick and choose, you see. There were about a hundred and eighty thousand unemployed young men. We only needed four thousand for now. They have been through courses of individual qualification as thorough and as rough as any in the world. They are almost frighteningly fit and healthy. They have been trained, the troops and leadership both, by some of the most combat experienced and capable trainers in the world. All they need is an extensive period of unit training, more for the commanders and staff than for the men. And that period is beginning even as we speak.

"So yes, Senator, they'll be able to fight . . . by the end of the year. They can be deployed in al Jahara before the campaign begins."

Rodman shrugged. "All right. Suppose I buy that this legion of yours can or at least will be able to fight? What do you want with Campos?"

"I want him to hire us."

The War Department gave Carrera the willies. He had always hated the place, from his first guided tour as an officer cadet to the last time he had set foot in it to tender his resignation. Everything about the comlex irked him, from the bloated staffs to the arrogant civilians to the military retirees who had sold their souls to defense contractors and made the place dangerous to walk with the slime trails they left behind them.

He loathed the décor. He loathed the special corridors set aside to pander to allies, most of whom had transformed themselves into albatrosses. He loathed the coffee shops and the pizza stands, the fast food malls and the shopping mall.

It was to him *everything* a military ought not be; an oversized, overstuffed monument to corporate bureaucracy.

"Secretary Campos will see you now, Mr. Hennessey."

As Pat stood to walk into the *sanctum sanctorum,* the holy of holies, he thought, *Hennessey . . . Carrera . . . shitbird and motherfucker. I have so many names now.*

Campos was polite, at least. He stood, walked around his desk and offered his hand in welcome to the man he thought of as Patrick Hennessey, and more importantly thought of as the heir to the Chatham, Hennessey, and Schmied empire.

Hennessey took it while, at the same time, taking the measure of Campos. *Tall man. Old but not worn. Good bearing and good health. I wish he didn't have the face of a technocrat.*

Campos began the chat. "Mr. Hennessey, how can I help you? Senator Rodman thought it imperative that we speak and, since she is on the Defense Appropriation Committee, I thought it wise to listen."

"Mr. Secretary, it's more a question of how we can help each other," Hennessey replied, in what had to be the oldest intro to a confidence game ever played. Campos took it as such but, in his line of work, expected no less.

"Please call me Ron."

"Pat, then . . . Ron. Look, I *know* that sounded like bullshit. But it's the truth. I have something *you* need. You have something *I* need."

"And those would be?" Campos enquired, innocently.

"I have an ally for you. I have an infantry brigade to assist you. I have people who will bleed and die so that fewer kids from the Federated States need to. I have people who will do so for less, much less, than it would cost you to have your own do it.

"But I need money, a *lot* of money, though less money than you would need for you own forces."

"Oh, really." Campos sounded, at best, skeptical.

"Yes, really. Shall I tell you?"

Campos consulted the watch on his wrist. *Oh, what the hell? I cleared my slate for two hours at that twat, Harriet's, insistence. I can at least hear the man out.*

"All right," he said. "You have my undivided attention for the next thirty minutes. If you can engage my genuine interest in that time you can have more."

"Fair enough," Hennessey answered. Then he began to explain what he had on offer, and a portion of why he had it. Thirty minutes stretched to an hour, to an hour and a half, to two hours, to . . . "Mildred, clear my calendar for this afternoon. I'll be busy until this evening."

That led to, "And how much is this going to cost me?"

Hennessey inhaled deeply, then sighed. "As I said, a *lot*. But less than it might.

"We believe, my people and I, that the cost for you

to use one brigade in full up combat for one month is approximately twelve billion drachma. To have that brigade in action over a longer term requires you to maintain a full division. That costs an additional four hundred million per month, base. That, you'll agree, is chickenfeed compared to the cost for actual combat."

"Whenever someone talks about that kind of money," Campos corrected, "it's *never* chickenfeed."

"All right," Hennessey conceded, smiling. "It's *not* chickenfeed. That also means that it wouldn't be chickenfeed if you could save that much, doesn't it."

Quick bastard, isn't he? Campos mused.

"Further," Carrera said, "I will deploy my legion to al Jahara in time for the upcoming campaign. I will participate in that campaign. I will undertake any mission you or your commander in the field should care to assign us that does not involve going up against masses of heavy armor or which requires that we operate more than one hundred miles from a logistics base. We're not equipped for that and frankly you don't need us for that; you need us for clearing fortifications and built-up areas. I will do so for sixty percent of the cost to you, per month, of using FS troops. That is to say, it will cost you seven point two billion FSD per month of active operations. Neither my staff nor, might I add, *yours* expects active operations to last past six weeks. Later on, if there needs to be a pacification and stabilization phase, we can also be hired. I estimate the cost to you of that to be on the order of six billion, per year, for our one brigade . . . or legion, as we call it. Since that saves you billions, you'll agree that you will not be saving 'chickenfeed,' yes?"

Campos sighed. The leathery face grew a tad weary.

"And there you had me going for a while. We can't afford that. I'd have to hide it and frankly I couldn't hide that much."

"You can't afford not to . . . Ron. And you can hide enough of it."

Campos pointed out, "We've already been helping you, you know. Harriet saw to that. Can't you come down on the price a little?"

Hennessey smiled, thinking, *We've already established what you are, young lady. Now we are merely negotiating your price.*

The next morning Campos sent for an officer stationed there in the War Department who knew Patrick Hennessey from long years' service together.

"Is this guy Hennessey on the level, Virg?"

The officer addressed, one Colonel Virgil Rivers, shrugged, sighed, looked up and finally answered, "Pat Hennessey? Well, Mr. Secretary, the first thing you have to understand about Pat is . . . well . . . he's insane. I don't mean a little odd; I mean clinically insane. Great guy, actually, but nuttier than a fruitcake."

"You mean this was all bullshit from a lunatic, this 'legion' he claims to have?"

Rivers laughed, white teeth shining in a café au lait face. "Oh, no, Mr. Secretary. If he says something is so, bet your last drachma that it *is* so. He's not crazy *that* way. He sees reality perfectly well and is annoyingly honest and irritatingly precise to boot. But he interprets it differently. It means something different than it does to the rest of us." Rivers' face grew contemplative for a moment. "That; or the rest of us are just idiots. I've sometimes wondered about that."

Campos, who was quite certain that *he* was the most intelligent man who ever lived, bridled a bit at the thought that anyone could see *him* as an idiot. "So how is he insane?" he asked.

"He's uncontrollable," Rivers answered without hesitation. "By that I mean there is nothing, *nothing*, you can do to him to deter him from something he decides is right and proper to do. Worse, his version of right and wrong come straight out of ancient history. I've never been entirely sure if it's a case of the civilized man holding the barbarian in check or if the barbarian puts the civilized man out as a cover and controls even that from behind the scenes. Of course, it could be a case of symbiosis, too.

"I have also heard him say to his own commander, and this is exactly what he said, 'You fat-fucking-pig-eyed toad, you incarnate insult to the military profession, you can't make *me* do anything. You just don't have the balls for it.' I treasured that, actually. And Pat pegged the piece of shit pretty well, too." Rivers *tsked*. "It was a shame about the relief for cause."

"Insubordinate then, is he?"

Rivers shook his head, more or less ruefully. "Oh, Mr. Secretary, you have no idea. Pat Hennessey hasn't the tiniest inkling of a clue about subordination. Mind you, he'll take any mission you give him and perform it superbly, even artistically. Any mission. But he will never let anyone else have a say in *how* he goes about performing it. He'll tell you to your face that it's none of your business. And he doesn't care what your rank is.

"By the way, if I can ask, Mr. Secretary, just what is the deal he's offering?"

"A large brigade, roughly equivalent to four Army or two and a half Marine battalions, for five point three billion drachma a month for a mid-intensity campaign and five point five to six billion a year for counterinsurgency. For that price we have to provide all medical support to include long-term care and medical evacuation, to the same standards we provide our own. We also must provide a suitable log base at no greater distance from the front than his own transportation assets can support, about one hundred miles. And we can deduct the cost of air and artillery support *he* asks for—munitions only, not wear and tear—from the base figure. Fucker bargains hard."

Rivers whistled but not for the expected reason. "That *is* a bargain, you know, sir. I've been intimately involved with the figures and it could represent a savings of about seven and a half to eight billion for either the active campaign or for a year of pacification if we need that, or both, not even counting the number of our own killed and wounded we'd save."

"Yeah, Virg, I know. But how do I hide that much money?"

Rivers, who had a sneaky creative streak, answered, "Generally speaking, funnel some of it through his government in the form of foreign aid. Some can be purely black. And some can be paid up front . . . say, on a cost-plus basis."

"Yeah . . . maybe. Tell me, Virg, if you were in command of the operation and this Hennessey person came to you, knowing him as you do, and making this offer, would you take it?"

"Sir, I gave you the bad side up front. It isn't all bad. For one thing, within certain limits, he's much the most intelligent human being I've ever met, excepting only my wife and I confess I may be prejudiced there. Pat's very loyal to anyone who deserves loyalty. Loyalty . . ." Rivers began to laugh.

"What's so funny, Virgil?"

"Well . . . he *is* very loyal. Just because he's an insubordinate son of a bitch doesn't mean he's disloyal. There was one occasion, where that same commander tried to get at Pat by busting one of his NCOs from staff sergeant to sergeant. The man . . . his name was Morse or something like that . . . anyway, he came out on the promotion list for platoon sergeant a couple of days later. Pat sat on the paperwork to bust him until that commander left command. He then talked the next guy into suspending the bust. Was that illegal? Probably. But it was right.

"And he really can do amazing—if I hadn't seen them I would say impossible—things with regard to training troops. I've got stories I could tell you . . . ah, never mind, too complex. He is tactically and operationally . . . well . . . 'deft' is not a strong enough term.

"So, yes, Mr. Secretary. If it were at all possible, I'd take him up on it."

"What do you suppose his motivation is, Rivers? Megalomania? A desire to show up the army that cast him out?"

Rivers cocked his head back in surprise. "Didn't he tell you, sir? It's much simpler than that. The bastards killed his wife and kids."

✧   ✧   ✧

The phone rang at Hennessey's Federal District hotel, an upscale but small establishment just off of Embassy Row. He answered.

"Hennessey, this is Ron Campos. This is the deal; take it or pound sand. I'm going to cover your operational and training expenses on a cost plus basis, cost plus ten percent, for the next six months. That amount will be deducted from your final bill IF we decide your group can do the job. I am sending down an officer who doesn't know you and whom you don't know—that's right, boyo, not one of your fans; Virgil Rivers warned me about that—to judge whether your legion is worth hiring. If he decides you are, you have a contract at the figures and with the provisos we discussed. If he nixes you, tough shit."

Carrera's respect for Campos went up a notch. "Done, Mr. Secretary."

INTERLUDE

A year's worth of decent feeding had returned Marjorie Billings-Rajamana to her normal state, exotic beauty. She was a natural.

The studio, however, was something of a sham, a living room-looking arrangement on one side, which the cameras faced, and a maze of snaking cables and dividers on the other. The interviewer was at least as much of a sham, his only real talent being the ability to project an air of interest and intelligence onto a face that, while *pretty*, sat in front of a fundamentally dead mind.

"It actually started on Earth," Marjorie began in explanation, her upper class British accent lending considerable dignity to her words. "We didn't know it at the time, but it started here, during the training program."

"What started here?" the interviewer asked. Well, that wasn't a mind-straining question, after all.

"A love affair," Marjorie sighed. "A *teenaged* love affair."

"Love destroyed the *Cheng Ho?*"

God, where did they get this idiot? Coming here was a mistake. Oh, well . . . stiff upper lip and all.

"Love started the chain of events that led to the troubles on the ship, yes. Then it continued to work its way to destroy it." Marjorie answered. "One of our colonists, Dr. Akbar al Damer, had a very lovely daughter, you see. Another, Dr. Immanuel Schweiz, had a handsome son. Without anyone here on Earth knowing it, those two fell in love. Touching, is it not?"

"Surely, yes," the talking head agreed, "but I hardly think—"

"On Earth, al Damer had to endure it," Marjorie plowed on. "In space, once his daughter, Besma, came up pregnant, he could not. He killed the boy and his daughter, too. Oh, there was no proof he did it. Otherwise, the captain would have spaced him. But al Damer did it, even so. Even if he had not it wouldn't have mattered. Everyone *believed* he had.

"But that was only the first incident. We'd made a great effort to integrate the passengers. That began to unravel when the first Buddhist girl married the first Buddhist guy. She moved in with his parents. Then they had a baby and there was no room. Actually, there was hardly room even to make a baby in our quarters but love will find a way." Marjorie smiled and thought, *Especially in low gravity.*

"So a Hindu family, very sweetly, offered to vacate their nearby quarters if others could be found for them. The captain had a storage chamber cleaned out, not too far from another Hindu family. And everyone lived happily ever after.

"Not. Suddenly, without anyone ever thinking about

it, we had two ethnic or religious centers of gravity. Marriages continued, and people kept shifting around. Within a year and a half there were Moslem sections, Mormon sections, Buddhist and Hindu sections, Catholic sections, Protestant sections . . . often separated by open spaces, sections of quarters left empty during the shifting. One real problem was that Moslem girls, given the chance, often preferred non-Moslem boys and would leave their sections to find husbands and, often enough, lovers among the non-Moslems.

"There was surprisingly little conflict at first, considering what came later," she said. "And then Dr. al Damer was found stuffed into the recycling bin. The dead boy's father probably did it. Within hours the Moslem section was off limits to anyone but themselves, and parties of Moslem 'youths'"—one could hear the quotations as she said it—"were rampaging and the girls were being dragged back.

"And then we had the Great Cartoon, Pig and Cow War . . ."

CHAPTER FIFTEEN

The soldiers like training provided it is carried out sensibly.

—Alexander Suvarov

Casa Linda, 7/7/460 AC

Carrera coolly regarded the Federated States Army officer standing in front of his desk, wearing the battle dress of the FSA. The officer was so incredibly average looking as to nearly defy description: average height, average build, average hair loss for a man of about forty. He wore his glasses averagely and his uniform bore an average number of the merit badges the FSA had always seemed addicted to.

"Virgil Rivers sends his best, Legate," the officer, John Ridenhour, said.

That brought a smile to Carrera's face. "How is old Virg?"

"He's fine," Ridenhour answered. "He's been selected for his first star, you know. He said to remind you,

'Who needs nukes?' If you don't mind my asking, and it seemed a damned odd thing to say, what the hell does that mean?"

"You had to be there," Carrera answered.

"He also said to tell you that I am the 'Imperial Spy,' and that you should take very good care of me." It was Ridenhour's turn to smile.

"You look the part," Carrera answered. "John, I'd set you up in a penthouse or mansion, with hot and cold running bimbos, a fast convertible and a big fishing boat with a perpetually full beer cooler if that would get me the recommendation I need from you to get my legion to the war," Carrera admitted. "On the other hand, that would be a pretty serious insult so I am *not* offering those things. Even so, do you have a place to stay?"

"The Julio Caesare," Ridenhour answered.

Carrera considered. "That's a good choice. If you're not married check out the Disco Stelaris down by the casino. If you *are* married then take my advice and *don't* check out the disco. How about a—"

From the next room Lourdes piped in, "Sergeant major has already assigned Mitchell to drive for Coronel Ridenhour, Patricio."

God, she's such a treasure.

"Okay," Carrera said. "That settles that. Mitchell has pretty decent Spanish, too, now. And he'll be armed so you needn't worry overmuch about personal security."

"I'm sure he'll be fine," Ridenhour agreed. "Besides, my Spanish is actually fairly good."

"All right then. Basically you can go anywhere, look at anything, and talk to anybody. No restrictions. Mitchell will have copies of the master training schedule and map overlay with him at all times. You need a helicopter lift somewhere, let him know in advance. I don't really recommend using our helicopters, though, because the pilots are damned near brand new and really won't be ready until just before we deploy, if we do."

"Ground trans should be fine," Ridenhour answered. "If I really need a chopper my budget can cover hiring a civilian one. I'll pass it through your man Mitchell to clear it with you if I have to do that."

"That's fair," Carrera agreed. "All I can tell you is have fun and that I think you'll be pleasantly surprised."

Guarasi "Desert" Training Area, Republic of Balboa, 7/10/460 AC

Money was less of a problem now; Campos' offer—while less than generous—had helped a *lot*. Moreover, the interest payments on the loan Carrera had personally made to the legion were being rolled into the operating cost, multiplied by the cost-plus factor, and charged to the Federated States. Thus, Carrera still retained control of the thing, notionally and nominally under Parilla, and would for the foreseeable future. While he had that control, he trained the men.

One major problem was that they were heading to the northern Sumerian desert: dusty, almost treeless, waterless away from the River Durannu, and open outside the cities. Balboa, on the other hand, was about two thirds jungle, much of that being mountainous, and most of the rest either city or valuable farm and ranch land. He could hardly use good farmland for maneuvers or, at least, not for serious ones.

Fort Cameron was about used up. It had never been large enough to train anything as large as the LdC for any purpose higher than initial training for individuals. The Imperial Range Complex, too, was overstrained as were the local training areas attached to the old Federated States military installations, most of which the legion had no access to anyway.

There *was* a useful open training area at the *Lago Sombrero*, about fifty miles down the coastal highway east of *Ciudad* Balboa. This was an old Federated States military base built to defend Balboa from attack during the Great Global War. In time, it had been returned to the Republic. Architecturally it wasn't much, a dozen barracks suitable for housing perhaps one thousand officers, centurions and men, and a large ammunition storage facility. More important was the airstrip that sat astride the main highway that paralleled the northern coast and connected Balboa with Atzlan and the Federated States to the south and east. Most important were the fifteen square kilometers of training land. Even this wasn't really enough though. Neither did it match well enough the damned desert the legion was going to fight in, *Inshallah*.

There was also a patch of ground, the Guarasi "Desert," just a bit inland from the northern coast and rather past *Lago Sombrero*. It was . . . sort of . . . kind of . . . almost . . . a desert. At least it looked something like a desert, having roughly 19,000 dusty acres of various kinds of cactus (and the odd breadfruit tree and tranzitree) amidst a barren landscape of erosion, loss of topsoil, overgrazing and general environmental devastation. It still received forty inches of rain a year so the desert analogy could sometimes seem very strained.

Carrera was—discreetly—looking into buying it permanently for the legion for a desert training area. For the nonce he was able to lease it for a low price from the government of the Republic, which owned it and had turned it into the kind of national park virtually no one ever wanted to visit except for the occasional environmentally conscious gringo or Tauran who went there to reconfirm his view that human beings just sucked and the planet would be better off without them.

On the Guarasi's eighty-one square kilometers Carrera had set Abogado's Foreign Military Training Group to running desert combat training courses for century and cohort sized units. The land had been modified to the extent of constructing several fortified areas for the troops to train on the attack. The type of fortifications differed. There were "pita" types, round raised-berm forts with trenches dug into the berms and firing positions and ramps for armored vehicles inside. There were also the more classic trench systems that the Sumerians were known to use, heavily bunkered and fronted by broad belts of barbed wire and simulated minefields. In addition, Carrera had bought about half the used tires in Colombia Central (and apparently every used tire in Balboa) and had them stacked, wired together, and filled with dirt to create buildings suitable for live fire training in city fighting. Only some of the fortifications, and all the tire houses, were sighted in places where live ammunition could be used to train. They were all, however,

sighted to present a fairly coherent picture of a broad
fortified zone suitable as an objective for a brigade—or
legion—level attack provided, at least, that no tank or
Ocelot main gun ammunition was used.

Ah, well, thought Carrera, watching a century-level
(roughly eighty men including the forward observer
team and the medic) attack on a "pita." The attack
was at night, without artillery or mortar illumination
and only about twenty-five percent of the maximum
illumination possible from one of Terra Nova's three
moons.

It was not quite as dark as three feet up a well-
digger's ass.

From his vantage point, and looking through a
large thermal imager mounted on a tripod, Carrera
observed as three machine-gun teams one hundred
meters apart slithered into position in a muddy canal
that crossed in front of the "pita." To the right side
of the machine guns, in the same muddy ditch, a
two-man rocket grenade launcher—RGL—team set
up, bowed down under a double or perhaps triple
load of ammunition.

Unseen, Carrera smiled. *I know it must have been
a bitch lowcrawling the better part of a kilometer with
that on their backs. Good boys. Tough boys.* He felt
a sudden warm glow of affection for *his* legion.

He saw one man, hunched under a backpack radio,
walk bent over extremely low from one team to another,
stopping briefly at each. Three other men followed
that one. He knew that was the sniper team by profile
of the long-barreled Draco rifles they carried. Those
four disappeared into the ditch. Behind the ditch,
stretched out in wedges about fifty meters deep and

as many across, Carrera could make out, just barely, three groups of perhaps seventeen to nineteen men, waiting silently.

Jamey Soult handed Carrera a set of headphones linked to a radio tuned to the frequency of the attacking century. He whispered, "Be only a few minutes, sir. The centurion with that century just reported to the commander that the support is in position. Now, I think, they're just waiting for an 'up' from the mortar section."

Which should long since have been *up,* Carrera fumed as he slipped the headphones over his ears. *Calm . . . calm,* he ordered himself. *People make mistakes. That's why they're out here; to learn.*

To help them learn, five of the FMTG's evaluator-trainers—not "safeties," Carrera despised the idea of special safety NCOs or officers in training for combat—stood more or less among or behind the groups along with another man that Carrera thought might be the FSA officer, Ridenhour. It was hard to tell in the fuzzy green image provided by the thermal sight.

It wasn't too much longer before he heard one long *pop* coming from two kilometers or so behind him. This repeated several times; the two mortars of the century's light mortar section beginning a preparation to drive the notional enemy into their bunkers.

With only a few seconds' delay from when he first heard the crump of the mortars, the machine guns and RGLs opened up across a front of about two hundred meters. The overall effect of the machine guns' tracers was strangely beautiful and quite surreal.

What sounded like three of the four-shot, tube-fed, pump action 43mm grenade launchers carried by an infantry century joined in with a *foofoofoomp-whawhawham*. Smallish explosions began blossoming along the front and top of the berm. A few overshot to explode inside.

Instead of one round in five, the machine guns were firing pure tracer, the glowing rounds making actinic lines through the air. This would help keep the assault teams, just now beginning to rise to their feet, from walking inadvertently into machine gun fire.

The first mortar shells fell inside the pita, their high explosive outlining the top edge of the berm in sudden harsh light as they detonated.

Behind the ditch the assault teams finished forming. Carrera thought he heard, dimly and distantly over the pounding of mortar shells and the nearer staccato bursts of machine gun fire, a young voice shouting, *"Legionarios, a pie . . . al asalto . . . adelante!"*

To add to the night's misery, Cruz and the rest of the century wore super-heavy, Federated States surplus, armored vests. These were not the obsolete ballistic nylon that might stop shrapnel but would not stop a bullet. Neither were they the roughly twenty-five pound aramid fiber vests with ceramic inserts. No, no; that would have been too easy. These vests were surplus from the time of the old Cochin war and had been intended for helicopter door gunners who were never expected to walk any farther than from the helicopter pad to the NCO club for a beer. They were ceramic, over an inch thick, weighed fifty-four pounds and would stop anything less than a heavy machine gun's bullet.

One would have thought the protection afforded by the vests would have been a comfort to Cruz. After all, there were only a couple of hundred of them, apparently, and it should have been reassuring to be given them to wear.

Not a chance. True, there were only a couple of hundred of them in the entire legion. Thus, they were only used for live fire problems, such as this one, where the chance of death or serious wounds for *somebody* was very high. Despite the fatigue of lugging himself, his weapons and equipment, two sections of live bangalore torpedo plus a blank, and the bloody-damned fifty-four pound vest, belly to the dirt, across nearly a kilometer of open space fast enough to make muscles scream in protest, Cruz trembled.

This is so *going to suck mastodon cock. Cara, I want to come* home*!*

Cruz, like the others, had learned very quickly that words in the military did not always mean what one thought they ought to mean. "Good training," for example, clearly meant, "Gonna suck." "Really good training," indicated, "Oh, shit, is this gonna suck." "Superb training," suggested something like, "This is gonna suck so hard every whore in Balboa will be unemployed for a week."

Cruz was an acting team leader for the exercise and had the responsibility for breaching the wire ahead. The section leader, Sergeant del Valle (who had gradually become a surprisingly friendly and even gentle sort once basic training was done with), had hinted that there was a good chance, unless of course Cruz screwed everything up badly, that the position might be made permanent. Since this would be a roughly twenty percent pay raise, and since he'd decided he really *did* want to marry Cara and the extra money would be useful, it was just possible that the legionary was as concerned about his performance as he was about being shot.

Well, I'd like to tell myself that anyway. Fact is, though, I am scared to death. Fucking demo. And I thought hand grenades were bad. Jesus! And a fat lot of good this vest will do me if a the bangalore goes off early. No shrapnel or bullets in me, maybe, but also no arms, legs or head. Probably no dick, either, for that matter.

The two sections of live bangalore—basically connectable pipes filled with a cyclonite-trinitrotoluene mix and weighing nineteen pounds each—lay clutched in Cruz's arms along with the one blank section. The blank was there so that if one *did* set off a mine or booby trap in the course of pushing the torpedo through the obstacle the explosion would not be carried back through the rest to prematurely detonate the torpedo and, infinitely worse, one's mortal and all too easily disintegrated body.

Two men had been hurt, one slightly and one badly, and another killed on this range about a week earlier. Cruz considered that and again shivered. Rumor was that the gringos running the training area, the FMTG, had started to add more artificial controls to keep such a thing from happening again when THE Gringo had shown up and nixed the idea.

What Carrera had, in fact, said was, "There's nothing wrong with the exercise as set up. It was a reasonable problem for the stage of training of the troops concerned, the control was generally adequate. It was a realistic simulation of what the legion will soon face. Some men were hurt because *they* fucked up, not because the exercise was. Men get hurt in training;

it's the cost of doing business. And besides, Abogado, what the fuck do you expect them to learn if someone's doing their jobs for them? You know better. I *know* you know better."

What had happened was this: the previous week a three man breach team from Third Century, 4th Cohort had assembled their bangalore and pushed it through the wire. They had then sprinted back towards the relative cover of a small depression in the ground in which the rest of the section waited. Unfortunately, because the range had been used several times before, there were sections of barbed wire embedded in the ground and sticking up above it. One of the men of the breach team had caught his foot on the wire and fallen face down. Then, with the fuse to the bangalore burning fast, the other two had gone back to free their comrade from the wire. They were still trying when the fuse reached the blasting cap and the assembly detonated, sending dozens of pieces of serrated barbed wire through their bodies.

One of the would-be rescuers was killed outright with twenty-two pieces of barbed wire in him. The other would be in hospital for quite some time. The one who had had his foot caught got away with little more damage than a few light scratches and one piece of wire embedded in his ham.

Carrera had driven to the 4th Cohort that afternoon, linked up with Jimenez, and presented the almost unhurt soldier with a wound badge in front of his peers.

"There is no moral difference between a wound received in training and a wound received in action," he had told the assembled troops.

He had then gone to the hospital in *Ciudad* Balboa

and waited for the badly wounded legionary to come out of surgery and recover consciousness. To this man he also presented a wound badge, plus the lowest step of the six awards for valor—a *Cruz de Coraje*, in Steel—for the attempt at saving his comrade. More quietly, Carrera had whispered in the soldier's ear, "You should have simply got him and yourselves low, with your helmets facing the explosion. Don't fuck it up again. Now get well and come back to us."

He had not gone immediately to see the family of the dead man, leaving that for a Survivors' Assistance NCO from Christian's II shop. Instead, he had gone to the funeral and presented the same awards he had to the wounded man to the dead legionary's family.

The civilian life insurance company that covered the men of the LdC had shortly thereafter done a few calculations, this being the thirty-seventh man killed in training so far for whom they had had to pay 100,000 FSD, and cancelled the group life insurance policy.

Which was how the *Legio del Cid* became a self-insurer.

Cara . . . Mom . . . . I hope you don't end up collecting my insurance, thought Cruz, as mortar and machine gun fire began to strike the pita ahead. He heard the century commander, a signifer, shout, *"Legionarios, a pie . . . al asalto . . . adelante!"* Legionaires, on your feet . . . into the assault . . . forward!

Rifles slung across their backs, Cruz and his breach team stood up. As he stood, finally able to *do* something, he felt fear melt away. He slung the three sections of bangalore across his right shoulder. Then, machine-gun tracers marking the path to either side and the steady flash of exploding mortar rounds outlining the objective, he confidently called, "Follow me."

Cruz and his men began to trot forward, followed by the century commander, his radio-telephone operator, and the forward observer team. When Cruz spotted the wire obstacle he was to breach—nasty looking thing!—he shouted to his team, "Down. Cover." Then he raced forward and flung himself onto the ground on his side of the wire. He felt some scraps of that wire, previously torn apart, dig into his legs as he did so.

Cruz took the blank bangalore section in both hands and began to feed it forward through the tangle. The blank piece had a rounded cap to it, which helped it slither between the strands. When he reached the last foot of that blank section he stopped and grabbed one of the two live sections, feeling first to make sure that he was *not* about to feed in the section that had been primed. Having made sure of that, he attached the unprimed live section to the blank and forced it through. Then he shouted, "Number two, on me."

Another soldier, Private Sanchez, wielding two more of the explosive pipes, trotted up and flopped beside Cruz. They attached one section, then the other, continuing to feed them forward as they did so. About half-way down the third live section of pipe Cruz told Sanchez, "Scram," before calling out, "Number three, on me." Sanchez disappeared into the night, his place being taken by another troop.

With the fourth and then the fifth live sections attached, the bangalore was too heavy, at about one hundred pounds, for one man to push forward easily. Cruz and the other legionary strained the assembly forward until they reached the end, whereupon Cruz attached his own final live section, the one that had been primed with cap, fuse and pull-igniter.

Again, Cruz ordered, "Scram." The other legionary took off, low and running.

First whispering a very short and eloquent prayer, more or less "Oh, God," Cruz screamed out, "Fire in the hole! Fire in the hole! Fire in the hole!" He then pulled on the igniter. He spent a second making sure the fuse, which had been cut to twelve seconds, had caught properly before turning himself to sprint to relative safety. As he sprinted he counted aloud, "Nine . . . eight . . . seven . . . six . . ."

Then, in the dim light of the moon, Bellona, his eye caught sight of the second man in the breach team, the one after Sanchez, on one knee apparently struggling to free himself from another grasping piece of the goddamned wire.

"Five . . . four . . . three . . ."

There was no time to free the entangled legionary. Without much thinking about it Cruz simply changed direction slightly and dove at him.

"Two . . . one . . ." *Khawhoomf!*

The explosion seemed to pick the two off of the ground where they sprawled, shake them like rats caught in a terrier's mouth, then slam them down again. Hard. Very damned hard. The shattered wire whined dangerously overhead or, in the case of pieces thrown high by the blast, lost velocity and pattered harmlessly down.

The century commander blew a whistle. At least Cruz thought it must be the whistle. It was hard to tell at first; his ears were ringing. *Ah, yep*, he thought dully, *must have been the whistle for the assault because everyone is running past me.*

Everyone is running past me?

"Bravo team, Second Squad! Assemble on me!"

Ridenhour had thought those two kids were goners when he saw the one caught fast and the other dive for him. He saw them only briefly as he took what little cover was available and tried to make himself very small. But no, once the danger from bits of jagged, flying metal had passed he saw the two sitting up, looking rather dazed and confused. He jogged over as three others likewise moved to join the pair, one of whom—the kid who'd been chosen to lead the team to execute the breach, Ridenhour assumed—began shouting in Spanish. By the time Ridenhour reached the little group they were already following the trail elements of the assault party through the wire, across the open area, and up the steep slope of the pita's berm.

This is just so fucking unsafe. *Don't they even care if they kill somebody?*

Apparently, they did not. At the point of the assault on the berm's outer edge Ridenhour found a young signifer, the century commander, directing his sections left and right to begin clearing the trenches that zigzagged along the top. He noticed the mortars were still firing, but at the far side of the pita, while the machine guns had switched from the open center to the left and right edges.

Ridenhour heard someone shout, in Spanish, "Back-blast area clear!" It took him half a second to translate and remember what that implied. This gave him about one quarter of a second to throw himself to one side as an RGL gunner let fly down into what must have been a hard target in the center of the pita. Another shout, another buffeting by the backblast, and the RGL team arose to a low hunch and moved on.

There was firing, a *lot* of firing, from the attacking sections' assault rifles and LMGs as they cleared the trench from the center to the left and right. The firing was supplemented by blasts; simulators, small demo charges, or live grenades, Ridenhour didn't know which. He crawled up the side of the berm to lay beside the century commander and peer, like the latter, over the lip of the berm in order to see the action.

Wow.

The interior of the place was lit up like Christmas by flames. One section moved in either direction around the perimeter, shooting and blasting as they cleared each bay of what looked to be an octagonal trace trench. They raced on at a speed Ridenhour thought downright foolhardy. *What the hell do they do if they run into each other? Well, at least they've lifted the mortar fire off the objective.*

The signifer commanding apparently had thought of that problem. He got on his radio and ordered one section to halt in position and guard. Then he told the other section to clear almost to the halted one.

"All right," said the signifer to the action section. "Now back up fifty meters . . . fast." He gave them half a minute to finish that move before ordering the second section to clear forward fifty meters. One way or another, the entire thing was gone over at least once.

The centurion for the century arrived and reported. "Signifer, I have all three machine-gun teams, the other RGL team, the breach team, and the scout-snipers.

Where do you want them." The century commander began bellowing orders.

Ridenhour shook his head and slithered down the berm. He had seen enough for one night.

Cruz's ears were still ringing. Moreover, he was pretty sure he had taken at least one piece of serrated barbed wire across the butt. *But . . . you know . . .* and then he started to laugh, lightly at first. Sanchez and the other man looked at Cruz, questioningly. Then they, too, started to laugh, sheepishly at first but with a growing mirth.

Sanchez was the first to put feelings into words. "Goddamn, Cruz, that was *fun*. Jesus, I love this shit."

Ridenhour and Mitchell joined Carrera and Soult shortly after sunrise. Soult was taking down the tripod with the thermal imager and stowing them in a trailer towed behind his vehicle.

Mitchell spoke first. "Sir, that was just too fucking cool."

"It wasn't bad," Carrera agreed. "Didn't lose anybody, at least."

"Not there, sir, no," Soult said. "But while you were sleeping I got the word—sorry, I should have told you before but it slipped my mind—that we lost another one, plus four wounded, on the Cohort Deliberate Attack Course at Ranges Eight and Ten at the Imperial Range complex."

"Hmmm, that would make . . . ummm . . . thirty-eight, so far. What happened?" Carrera asked. He didn't seem overly concerned.

"Half a dozen mortar rounds fell short," Soult

answered simply. Carrera shrugged. "Appears to have been an ammunition problem rather than a fire direction error. Harrington already directed that that lot be pulled out of training stocks and examined."

Carrera shrugged. You had to expect ammunition quality control problems when you bought cheap.

"You're taking this awfully calmly," Ridenhour observed. "Don't you think you're maybe pushing these units a little hard?"

"No," Carrera answered, then elaborated, "Look, John, when somebody says, "There's never an excuse for getting someone killed in training," what they really mean is, "I don't care if someone gets killed in combat later because they're not well trained enough, because that won't affect *my* career, now." It's just a damned immoral way of looking at things. And I won't permit it in the legion."

"But how the hell do you explain to a young kid's parents that he got killed for something that wasn't even battle?"

"How do I explain to a *bunch* of young kids' parents that they got killed in a battle we lost because their units weren't well trained enough?" Carrera countered.

"Are you going to have a unit left when you're done training them?"

Carrera hesitated briefly, pulling up some mental data. "I planned on one percent deaths—call it forty-nine or fifty men—in basic training and advanced individual training. We actually lost about half that. I assumed we'd lose another dozen in the *Cazador*, you would say 'Ranger,' School I had FMTG run early on for the selection process for Officer Candidate School and Centurion Candidate School. We lost seven. The unit training I anticipated would cost us another fifty and we are at eight dead so far. We probably will lose another thirty but we recruited enough to make up for those losses plus another couple of hundred more for the badly wounded."

"But what about the men's morale?" Ridenhour continued to object.

Carrera yawned. "They don't know any better. We act like it's normal and routine and so they tend not to question it. It's just not an issue. You can ask if you want, but do me a favor and don't act like the bleeding heart press when you do, less still like some hypocrite congresscritter with never a day in uniform. And *please* don't try to convince the troops that there is something wrong with training that sometimes kills.

"Remember, too, that you're trying to compare apples and oranges. The Federated States has a military tradition and a tradition of victory. There are any number of the right attitudes your young men take in more or less with mother's milk. These boys don't get the same conditioning. They *need* extreme training measures to make up for what they never got as children."

"Maybe," Ridenhour admitted reluctantly.

"Also, John, for your purpose in being here ask yourself, after what you saw last night, if you think my cohorts and centuries will be able to fight. That's really all you have to decide upon."

Soult interrupted. "Sir, it's the 11th. I think you had an appointment in Cochea."

Carrera sighed, sadly. "I didn't forget, Jamey. Thanks, though."

Cochea, 11/7/460 AC

Soult didn't even *think* about driving anywhere near the grave marker. He could pay his respects on foot. Instead he pulled up next to Carrera's in-law's house and, while his boss went inside to see the family, unloaded Carrera's gear and two liters of scotch and carried the lot by hand to the grave marker. There he erected a small shelter, a poncho hooch, and draped a mosquito net three quarters around it with enough slack to make a complete bar. Then he laid out a sleeping roll inside the shelter, erected a folding chair outside of it, and placed both liters of scotch and a metal drinking vessel next to it. He took half a dozen antimosquito torches and stuck them into the ground in a circle around the little encampment. Then he retired to the house where, since he and Carrera had been expected, Linda's family had set aside a room for him.

"Tomorrow morning, Boss?" he'd asked.

"Yes, Jamie, though probably mid-morning."

Then Carrera walked to Linda's grave, sat in the folding chair, and began to explain how things were going to the shades of his family. He drank as he talked, drank deeply and quickly.

The screaming and sobbing didn't begin until nearly midnight.

UEPF *Spirit of Peace*, 15 August, 2514

"Admiral," said Khan, the wife, over the intercom, "you asked me to keep track of that new force growing in the Republic of Balboa. My husband sent down a high altitude skimmer to look things over yesterday at the third watch. We've just finished looking over the recording and we think you ought to look at it. Actually, we have two we think you need to look at."

"What's the specific subject matter?" Robinson asked.

"The one we think you should look at first is of the Federated States Army conducting combat training. Once you have seen that, you should look at this new force and see how they do the same. My husband and I find it very worrisome."

Robinson sighed. "Very well, send them."

"Sending now, High Admiral."

Robinson turned to face the large Kurosawa. A small light below it, an original part of the *Peace*, blinked urgently.

"You have a message, High Admiral," the computer announced.

"Show me."

Immediately, the large screen began to show a top down view of what looked to be about one hundred soldiers from down below in the process of conducting some kind of attack. There was no sound—high altitude skimmers weren't even equipped for sound—but the visual was quite clear and distinct.

Robinson watched with boredom as men got up, moved, flopped to the ground, and used their weapons. All in all, it was rather unexciting, even dull. He yawned.

The images froze and the computer announced, "Ready to show second recording, High Admiral."

"Go ahead." Robinson yawned again.

Instantly, the previous, placid scene was replaced by one of smoke and fire. Other soldiers, differently uniformed, got up, ran, and used their own weapons, just as in the first recording. That much they shared.

In other particulars, however, they couldn't have been more different. Instead of being placid, this recording fairly exuded aggression and violence. Shells exploded, dangerously close to troops. Robinson could see that.

The thing that really caught his attention, though, was when a small group was apparently scythed down by a too-close shell. Dead or wounded, Robinson couldn't tell. But he could see, in full detail, that those unhit didn't even stop training.

My Annan, these people care nothing for their own lives.

"Computer, connect me to Khan."

"Have you seen, High Admiral?" she said, as soon as she came on.

"Are they always like that?"

"Pretty much, sir. You may also recall that I mentioned the possibility that this group would be even less constrained by the rules we have thrown around armed forces down below than the FS is?"

"I recall, Khan."

"Well, we've acquired another bit of intelligence. The second in command of that force, possibly the effective first in command, had his family in the Terra Novan Trade Organization headquarters on the day of the attack. They were killed."

Robinson closed his eyes and said, "Uh, oh."

INTERLUDE

From *Baen's Encyclopedia of New and Old Earth*, Edition of 442 AC

The following entries are not to appear in the Old Earth edition of the Encyclopedia

Terra Nova, Geography and Settlement of:

The major land mass of Terra Nova, Taurania, lies on its east-west axis approximately midway between the magnetic southern pole of the planet and the equator. The split between the Taurus end of Taurania, in the east, and Urania, in the west occurs arbitrarily along the Volkosk mountains and culturally and ethnically somewhat to the west of that.

Taurus, so called because it resembles an upside down male bovine with an erection, was the award of the old European Union on Old Earth. There being no equivalent supranational organization for Asia at that time, Urania was parceled out amongst various sub-supranational entities, roughly in accordance with their population, wealth, terrestrial patrimony, clout,

437

and willingness and ability to bribe members of the old United Nations Interplanetary Settlement and Boundary Committee, or UNISBC.

To the west of Urania and the east of Taurus, and lying approximately equidistant between the two, lie the Columbias, or—for Spanish speaking areas—the Colombias. These are two continents, joined by a narrow isthmus (of Balboa, q.v.), that run north to south-southeast. The larger of these, called Southern Columbia, was awarded to the old North American Free Trade Area which further subdivided the bulk of the continent almost exactly according to the wishes of the former United States of America. The two Canadas, Mexico and the Central American petty states fell into line fairly readily. Cuba was denied any colony on the new world, which denial it took with very good grace as it was believed that the entire country would depopulate itself if its people were given the chance to escape. (The government of His Revolutionary Highness, Alejandro I, son of Raul Castro, is believed to have been one of only two governments on Earth, the other being that of North Korea, that had to bribe UNISBC *not* to make any grant of land on the new world. This is unconfirmed and investigations into the matter were squelched by the then UN Secretary General, Kojo Annan.)

The other eastern continent, called Northern Colombia, was awarded to the former Mercosur, the Latin American version of NAFTA. Mercosur attempted to form a unitary colony. This, however, broke apart in a series of wars, the results of which plague Northern Colombia to this day.

Uhuru, which lies to the north of Taurania, was given

to the Organization of African States. This organization attempted a colonization project much the same as Mercosur, but with even more hideous results. (See Republic of Northern Uhuru, History of, for example. See the Mutara-Kegeli Genocide, for example.)

The Arab League parcel was not made the award of any given state. Rather, the area settled by the Arabs was unitary and later broke up or developed, depending, into something like nation states. A peculiarity of the Arab League Mandate is that a portion of it was given by the Arab League to Israel. Much was made of it, on Earth and at the time, as showing a spirit of conciliation and peacemaking. This was not the case, however. All the Arab League wanted was for some place of settlement to attract out as many Jews from Israel as possible. Arab colonists were not consulted in the matter.

For various reasons having to do with Old Earth politics, Australia was given no award on the new world though New Zealand was. The population of Australia, such as wished to settle elsewhere, tended to gravitate either to Anglia, New Wellington, the Federated States, the Republic of Northern Uhuru, or—as a distant last choice—Secordia in South Columbia.

A final subcontinental sized island, dubbed Atlantis, lies in the Mar Furioso, midway between the Columbias and Taurania. This is the enclave of United Earth . . .

Chronology, History of, Part VII:

Time on Terra Nova, on the other hand, is measured since Anno Condita, "the year of the founding." This would not be 2037, the year in which the robotic exploratory vessel, *Cristobal Colon*, actually found the rift and the planet. Rather, AC is the year in which the first, sadly failed, colonization attempt was made from Earth, in the Old Earth year, 2060.

Establishment of a local calendar spelt a considerable problem for those early settlers who followed after the *Cheng Ho disaster* (qv). The Terra Novan year corresponded very closely to the Terran year, there being 31,556,926 seconds to an Old Earth year and 31,209,799 seconds in each orbit of the new world about its sun.

For the Salafi settlers this presented even more of a problem, one made worse by the fact that, rather than the one moon of Earth by which the Islamic calendar ran, Terra Nova had three, none of which quite ran to any schedule that suited the traditional Islamic calendar. The Islamics settled this more or less mathematically, by adding a fourteenth month, to commemorate the "Second Hejira," or Pilgrimage, adding days to some months, and creating a complex set of calculations to keep this calendar in synchronization.

One advantage to the new Islamic calendar was that now, at least, it matched the actual year for the world on which it was practiced.

From all parties—Secular, Islamic, Christian, Buddhist, etc—there was strong pressure to maintain the twenty-four hour day, of which Terra Nova had three hundred and fifty-five, and the sixty minute hour. This was done by increasing the length of the Terra Novan second to 1.017533901 Earth seconds. Ten months (basically the original months of the Roman

Republic) of five weeks each were established, with an intercalary period of five or, rarely, six days between 35 December and 1 Martius.

It has worked about as well as any calendar system ever has, and perhaps a bit better than most.

CHAPTER SIXTEEN

War is too important to be left to generals.
—Georges Clemenceau

War is too important to be left to the politicians.
—Colonel Jack Ripper (in *Dr. Strangelove*)

Hamilton, FD, 6/1/461 AC

It would be wrong to say that Campos was personally planning the invasion of Sumer. After all, that was not the secretary of war's job. Instead, SecWar was responsible for administration, for expenditures, for procurement and the like.

On the other hand, when the secretary of war is convinced that he is quite the cleverest man ever to live, that most of his subordinates—indeed most of the human race—are idiots, in short when the secretary of war is something of an arrogant blockhead, one can expect him to take a hand, and perhaps an unduly heavy hand at that, in overseeing the detailed planning.

It was all water off a duck's back to Virgil Rivers. He'd been in the Army for better than two decades, been raised in the army, for that matter. Arrogant overbearing assholes were all in a day's work, provided they were at least reasonably competent.

That much one had to give Campos. He was at least reasonably competent.

Competence, however, was not infallibility. This was a problem for Campos. He aspired to not much more than competence but, since he equated himself with competence and competence with infallibility, he had rather a difficult time of it when things went wrong.

"What the hell do you mean, Virgil?" Campos fumed. "The Kemalis won't let the Fifth Division unload at their ports and won't permit them to cross the country? We *need* that division, plus the 731st Airborne Brigade, to hit Sumer from the south. Howellson from State *assured* me that the Kemalis would knuckle under."

Rivers, who had not been privy to any such conversation and knew the secretary of state, Howellson, extremely well, rather doubted that. But Campos tended to hear what he wanted to hear. Rivers also had good cause to know the Kemalis, immigrants from Turkey on Old Earth, were altogether too proud to knuckle under to anyone. Moreover, they had domestic political problems with being used as a base to attack another Islamic state, even though their own was only nominally Islamic and largely secular. Indeed, the settlers to Kemali had come largely to escape the increasing fundamentalism of their native Turkey.

"Mr. Secretary, no how, no way, are the Kemalis going to let us bring the Fifth Division through."

"Can General Thomas shift a force down to the southern part of the country?" The secretary asked.

"He says no, that everything he has he needs for the major attack from the north." Since the northern attack was already being done on a shoestring, largely as a result of Campos' unceasing nagging to reduce costs, Rivers thought that Thomas had a good argument for not being stripped of forces. Whether Campos would accept that or not . . .

"Can we fly in something to the area of Sumer we control from the Oil War?"

"Yezidistan? There are airfields there that can take heavy lift, yes. Unfortunately, Mr. Secretary, most of the heavy lift we have we need for the major operation in the north. Even more unfortunately, with Fifth Division's armor loaded on ships and essentially untouchable for anything from weeks to about a month and a half, we would have to fly a unit, along with all its supplies, in from the Federated States. That would take a lot more lift than we can spare, tens of thousands of tons."

"Allies?" Campos asked, hopefully.

"Besides the Yezidis, none," Rivers answered. "The Anglians and the other small packets from our allies are either needed for the major attack or are too small to be of any effect. And the Yezidis just aren't up to it even though they've been supplemented by our own Special Warfare people."

The Yezidis were a caste-based Kurdish group that had left the area of Mosul, Iraq, en masse early in the 22nd century. They practiced what appeared to be a pre-Islamic—pre-Zoroastrian, as a matter of fact—religion with elements of Islam grafted onto it. They had never been accepted by the majority Moslem population who thought them "devil worshippers" and among whom they had lived—usually not amicably—for centuries. The Moslems, mainstream as well as Salafi had *often* fought with the Yezidi, much to the disadvantage of the latter.

With the opening up of mass emigration to the new world the Yezidi had jumped at the chance to be on their own. They had a reputation as fine warriors. Reputation notwithstanding, they had been continuously stomped into the dirt by their neighbors and had seen their original colony parceled up among the Kemalis, Sumeris, Alawis and Farsis in the area. Even the Volgans had, at one time, had a piece of them. Rivers, who had worked with them in the past, thought they were posturing swine but, since the secretary had great expectations from the Yezidi, he kept his own counsel. He couldn't keep a look of contempt off of his face, however, and Campos saw it.

"What? You don't think the Yezidi will come through for us?"

Rivers sighed. Time for some honesty, after all, it seemed.

"Mr. Secretary, everything you need to know about the Yezidi is explained by their conduct during and after the Oil War. We told them if they arose in rebellion, in other words if they *helped* us by drawing off some of the Sumeri troops, we would help them. They rebelled all right, but they waited until after we had stomped the crap out of the Sumeri army on our own. They only rebelled when it seemed perfectly safe to rise up in the vacuum we created, and after we didn't need their help any more. Then they whined when even the shot-and-bombed-to-shit rump of the Sumeri *Haris al Watini* was able to crush their chicken-shit asses. They will do nothing for themselves or for us. Trust me on this. Politically they're unreliable and militarily they're worthless."

Campos started to object but . . . *he's been there. He should know.*

Eager to divert the subject before he said something truly career damaging, Rivers asked, "What about the Balboans? Could we use them down in Yezidistan?"

"One medium-light brigade to do the job of a heavy division, Rivers? I don't think so. Besides, that colonel we sent down, Ridenhour, has very mixed reports on them."

Rivers, who had read the same reports, looked nonplussed. "I don't understand, sir. Ridenhour was very clear that he thought they'd put up a good fight."

"But what about their losses to friendly fire in training, Virgil? According to Ridenhour they've killed nearly one and a half percent of their own people just in training and just in the last year?"

"Well . . . yeah," Rivers replied. "Losses are not something that would deter Pat Hennessey from going ahead. He might eat his own guts over it later, but he would never let that stop him. And . . . frankly, so what? It isn't like those are our people being killed."

"But that's precisely the point, Virgil. If we let a maniac like that loose near *our* people there's no telling how many . . . oh."

"Right, Mr. Secretary. In the mountains of southern Sumer—Yezidistan, if you prefer—there are not going to *be* any of our people, not until the 731st Airborne makes its drop. And if I know Hennessey, and I do, he'll just wave at the 731st as they drop and continue the march to wherever he can find a fight."

"Balboans, huh? Well . . . can Thomas get by without them?"

"Honestly, he doesn't want them. He knows Hennessey from way back and, as he so delicately put it, "If I never see the son of a bitch again, it'll still be too soon." They, ummm, really don't like each other."

"Does *anybody* like Hennessey? Oh, never mind. All right, Virgil. Work out the details and brief me. And by the way, how are we coming in modifying the plan to take advantage of the awesome shocking power inherent in our technological superiority?"

Rivers, who knew that the *only* difference had been to take the basic plan and a word processing program and add in the phrase "awesome shocking power" in one hundred and twenty-seven places, answered, "Just fine, Mr. Secretary. It's a much better plan now." *Yessir, yessir, three bags full.*

Casa Linda, 10/1/461 AC

"Son of a bitch!" Carrera cursed as he read through the dispatch sent this morning from the FS embassy in *Ciudad* Balboa. He looked rather pleased when he first began to read since the missive contained agreement that his legion would be hired at the agreed price by the FS for the coming campaign. As he had read further though . . .

"What is it, Patricio? What's wrong?" Lourdes asked.

"That motherfu . . . it's Campos. He'll hire us on but not for the mission we originally agreed to. Instead of going to the north with our equipment going by sea and then basing out of al Jahara, we have to go south—by air, mind you, which is much more expensive—and establish ourselves in Yezidistan. Then we have to fight through to where an FS airborne brigade is going to jump in, and continue operations with them until we link up with coalition forces somewhere north of Babel."

He kept reading before admitting, "Oh. Well, it isn't that bad. We get the airborne brigade's artillery and service support battalions flown in and attached to us in advance in Yezidistan. And he's offering to allow us to cost-plus the extra money we'll have to spend to get the Volgans to fly us in over what it would have cost for us to go by sea."

"So you will actually make more money than you planned?"

"Ummm . . . maybe. No telling what we'll face or what we'll lose. And I've been in those mountains before. They practically defend themselves, at least as long as they're not being defended by Yezidis. Yezidis are a net minus to combat power.

"It's going to be tough fighting, though. They're also moving up the date by a week and I am not sure we can have the cold weather gear we'll need on hand by then. Iffy. Lourdes, would you assemble the staff please? Key members only."

She was about to go, then remembered the phrase "tough fighting." That worried her. So, instead of going to use the telephone to spread the word, she locked the door to Carrera's office and went back to stand beside his chair. Then, somewhat to his surprise, she rotated the chair to face her. She dropped to her knees and began to undo his belt.

"This won't take long," she said, "I'm getting better at it. And I want to take every chance there is to remind you to come home to me when the fighting is done . . . and not to let yourself get killed."

Near Caridad's home, *Las Mesas*, Balboa, 12/1/461 AC

Ricardo Cruz leaned against a tree in a secluded spot by the creek that fed Cara's family's farm. He and the girl were asymmetrically undressed, her with her top off and him lacking trousers. She knelt on the trousers so as to leave no tell-tale dirt scuffs as her head bobbed rhythmically back and forth, lips locked in a tight, and, since it was her first occasion, rather odd feeling "O."

Cruz had returned home on leave, prior to deploying over to Sumer with the legion. Before returning home, he stopped off at a small jewelry shop on Avenida Central in *Ciudad* Balboa and purchased a ring. It hadn't been anything amazing, as far as engagement rings went. Still, when he had shown it to Cara and asked her to be his wife she had seemed to think it a marvel equal to the Anglian crown jewels. Naturally, as a well bred and brought up young man, he had asked Cara's parents' permission to marry her, after she had indicated no reluctance on her part. They, weighing his prospects, seeing that he had already been accelerated in rank past most of his peers, and liking him in general, had agreed and discreetly suggested the new couple take a walk somewhere they could plan the future. Well, Cara's parents had been young once, too.

Planning for the future, when you're that young and that in love, means little more than finding a secluded spot and racing to undress.

Ricardo had originally wanted to make love. Cara had not exactly refused, but had made what she thought was a reasonable counteroffer, a little something the girls in her high school sometimes gossiped over and sometimes bragged upon. He'd agreed, she'd tried and found that, while it was an acquired . . . errr . . . taste, it was a taste fairly easily acquired. The other taste was not so easily acquired but she'd managed. Twice. This was number three and . . . well . . . why not?

Besides, she thought, *if those groans and moans are truthful I own him now. Can this little thing really feel as good as all that. Hmmm,*

She looked up, smiled shyly and whispered, "Ricardo, I love you. So . . . if you want to make love . . ."

He'd started to lift her up, if only so he could lay her down again on the mossy bank. And then he froze in internal confusion.

I am going to war and I may not be coming back. Too, he remembered something his section leader had told the men once: *"Some day we all must die. Whether our lives will have meant anything depends on how we have lived them. Have we done well by those who cared for us, those for whom we were responsible? Have we done our duty? Who, among the innocent have we harmed? Who have we helped? How is the world better for our having lived? I think God will want to know. I think He'll ask."*

And then *what if she gets pregnant and I get killed? That would be a hard thing to inflict on her and the child both, insurance and survivor's benefits notwithstanding.*

Cruz whispered back. "I love you, too, *queridisima*. But I am going to war soon. We don't know yet what will happen. I hope I'll come back. But I don't *know* that I will. We'll wait then. Maybe when I return we can continue that conversation. For now . . ."

Understanding, Cara smiled again, bent her head, and continued her bobbing.

Herrera International Airport, *Ciudad Balboa, 15/1/461 AC*

The blue and white painted Air Balboa BG-47 bobbed up and down along the taxiway as it approached the terminal. On one side of its designated gate awaited a similar aircraft, on the other a chartered Volgan LI-68 was already boarding.

Some distance away, at the cargo terminal, teams of men, some civilians and others in the uniform of the *Legio del Cid*, loaded wide-bodied cargo aircraft—a mix of FS military, FS civilian, Balboan civilian and more Volgan military under charter—with the wheeled vehicles of the legion. Since some of those aircraft bays stood seventy feet above the tarmac, requiring that the wheels be hoisted that distance into the air on self-mobile elevators, the loading was sometimes rather precarious.

The Balboan airport was capable of receiving mid-size airships, of course. But the debarkation airport in Yezldistan was not. This ruled out using LTA craft to move any of the brigade, despite the potential cost savings.

Parilla and Carrera stood off to one side, in a pair

together and separate from the confusion around them. Carrera was used to the apparent confusion of a major deployment. Parilla was not and looked plainly concerned over it.

"Relax, Raul. This is so normal that it is the very essence of routine for something like this."

Parilla, despite this, did not seem to relax.

Carrera watched as a centurion stopped one three-ton truck before it nearly went over the side of an elevating loader. The centurion walked briskly to the driver's door of the truck, opened it, hauled the driver out with both fists and then held him in the air seven stories above the ground while shaking him and cursing. The centurion didn't drop the driver, however, but put his feet back on the ramp, pushed him back into the cab, forced him to slide over. Then the centurion climbed in himself to show how the damned thing was supposed to be done.

Parilla winced at seeing this. To Carrera it was . . . well, in small details, at least, he thought the centurions ought to have a certain latitude.

"Are we going to make it, Patricio?" Parilla asked. Carrera had never shut him out—even consulted with him frequently—but neither man had any doubt as to who was really in charge. Nonetheless, Carrera always treated Parilla as his unquestioned superior in public and a good friend in private. Politeness cost nothing, after all.

"I think so, Raul. We were lucky to have the freighters stopped before the Volgans actually began putting our armor aboard. They're going to fly the stuff into Yezidistan directly from the airport near the factory, all sixteen tanks and forty-four Ocelots, plus eight extras for floats, two tanks and six Ocelots. The other twenty-two still come here by ship, for training, of course. I'm still worried as hell about the cold weather gear, though. Those mountain passes are fucking freezing this time of year."

Parilla gave an involuntary shiver. "How badly off are we?"

Without inflection, Carrera answered, "So far we've been able to find mid-weight sleeping bags for every man, Anglian surplus, and about ten thousand heavy wool blankets for when we find out that a mid-weight sleeping bag just won't do sometimes. The Misrani tents we have will be good for summer or winter since they've got a good heavy liner to them, though with that desert pink color they'll stand out like sore thumbs whether it snows or not. The south of the country isn't desert, after all. Stoves are allegedly en route. We'll see."

"God I hate the cold." Parilla shivered in anticipation, despite Balboa's oppressive heat.

"So do I," Carrera agreed. "In any case, balaclavas have been ordered, good wool ones from Helvetia, but the order won't be filled for about ten days—ten cold fucking days, I expect—after the tail end of the legion arrives. Same deal and same source on the polypropylene-lined leather gloves. We have found some really neat polypro mittens that allow the troops to peel back the part covering the fingers for fine detailed work, but in a cold wind they'll be pretty worthless, too. Harrington's looking for leather shells to cover the mittens. Nobody had winter boots available for immediate delivery in the quantity we need and the boots we were offered were almost no better than the jungle boots the men already have. That scares me. I foresee a lot of trench foot in our future unless Harrington can come through on the boots. I told him I didn't care if the styles match, just so long as they are good, serviceable, winter boots. Maybe that will help. Then again, part of our problem is that most of the troops have shorter, wider feet than those found in all the places that make winter boots.

"On the plus side, we *have* gotten twenty-thousand sets of polypro underwear. It's already in Yezidistan and being issued, first thing, as the troops debark from the aircraft. Most of it will be too big but better too big than too small. I've had a local company take five thousand white bed sheets and convert them to camouflaged pullover smocks. Better than nothing."

"We're going be cold for a while then," Parilla commented.

"Very."

"Wish we'd had time to acclimatize the men to cold weather," Parilla said.

Was there a touch of rebuke in his voice? Carrera thought so but whether it was directed at him or not was an open question.

Parilla's aide de camp came up to the pair. "Sir," he said to the nominal senior, "the aircraft chief stewardess tells me they are ready to board you now."

"You're sure we should fly separately?" Parilla asked of Carrera.

"Absolutely," Carrera answered. "In the first place, God never intended for man to fly. Worse, He has an odd sense of humor. If one of those things comes down with both of us on it, the legion will be fucked. Go on, *Duce*. I'll be on the flight right behind you."

✦   ✦   ✦

A *bombero* band stood at attention on the tarmac playing a martial tune, one heavy on the brass and drums. The legion's main band, the pipes and drums, were already long departed and guarding the headquarters in Yezidistan.

From the movable stairway nestled against the Air Balboa jet, Parilla made a good show of turning, smiling for the cameras, and waving at the crowd of families and well-wishers bidding farewell to yet more of their soldiers. Behind him the line of mostly hung-over men waiting to board bunched briefly at the halt.

Unseen in the crowd, Lourdes waved back with her right hand. She hadn't seen Patricio since he had left the terminal lobby a few minutes after Parilla.

While Lourdes waved with her right, her left was busy catching tears in a handkerchief. Raul Parilla's elderly wife put an arm around Lourdes' narrow waist.

"I have never done this either," the older woman confided. "I am frightened for them."

Lourdes began to cry more loudly. "I am frightened for *me*."

"I know, dear. I know."

Standing not far away, a younger woman, affianced to legion Private First Class Ricardo Cruz started to bawl as soon as she saw Lourdes' tears. Seeing Cara, Parilla's wife made a motion for her to join them. Then, standing there in the lobby, the three women hugged each other and had a good, long cry.

Hewlêr International Airport, Yezidistan, 16/1/461 AC

Under the glare of the portable lights, the last of a dozen rented semi-tractors carrying Misrani Army tents pulled away from the unloading area on their way to the legion's bivouac site near Mangesh, Yezidistan. This was about thirty miles to the north and perhaps five miles from the dividing line between Sumeri controlled Yezidistan and the Yezidi safe area that had been guaranteed by the Federated States eleven years before, following the Oil War.

Despite the bitter cold the unloading crews sweated with the strain. Their breath made little horizontal evergreens of frost in the air. Nearby, Kuralski and his Yezidi counterpart, Captain Mesud, stood to one side while waiting for the Volgan LI-68s that would be flying in, among other things, a load of rather poorly made but at least warm cold-weather boots that had been stolen from Volgan army stores years before and offered to Harrington once the need was made known. Along with the boots were coming some tons of ammunition, a portion of a huge store that had been offered by the newly reunited Sachsen Reich from what had once been held by then nominally independent North Sachsen. This, too, would go to join the growing stockpile of supplies and equipment building in the middle of Yezidistan. Packaged field rations from Anglia, Gaul, the Federated States, and other places arrived at intervals as well. No rations would be coming from Zion as Kuralski had been warned about Army of Zion rations, canned goat with the hair still on it, and kosher to ensure near tastelessness. Besides, the one tasty, for certain values of "tasty," item of food in Zioni rations, *Shoug*, was a mix of ground peppers ranging from "Holy Shit Peppers" to "Joan of Arc Peppers," with a very small admixture of "Satan Triumphant Peppers." That way layeth logisticide.

Thirty miles away, at Mangesh, Sergeant Major McNamara had his hands full setting up the five hundred and forty odd tents the brigade would be moving into. Morse and Bowman were a great help, here, but—thank God!—his real salvation was that enough of these non-Yezidi, Christian Chaldeans spoke English to get his will across. Ah, well, at least he didn't have Harrington's worries. That poor bastard was torn in a hundred directions; trying to set up an Ammunition Supply Point, arrange feeding, receive the equipment that arrived in a steady stream from Hewlêr International, and, in general, prepare for the arrival of the remaining troops.

Still, between himself, Kennison, Kuralski, Johnson, and Captain Mesud—*fine officer*, thought McNamara, *rare among these wogs*—he had to admit that things were getting done. They had a tent city laid out and about half the tents raised. The ASP was also laid out and, at least to the extent ammunition had arrived, dug in. Johnson was going insane trying desperately to set up local training facilities.

In a way, that was McNamara's biggest distraction, not that he minded. Carrera—McNamara still had to force himself not to think of his boss as Hennessey—was very goddamned particular, and a little unpredictable unless you thought at his level, about how his training was set up. Johnson did better than most and Mac enjoyed filling in the small details.

Mangesh was not strange to Carrera; he'd been there before. That was part of the reason he had chosen it for his staging area. Still, the place looked rather worn down, even more so than when he had left.

After a seemingly interminable flight, followed by a long drive from Hewlêr International, Carrera and Parilla finally arrived at the legion's staging base in the Yezidistan Mountains. Kennison, McNamara, and the rest of the advanced party were on hand to greet them.

A smiling Kennison was the first to speak. "*Duce*, Pat, welcome to outer Hell . . . or maybe, since it's so frigging cold, Niflheim."

Carrera smiled back and spread his arms wide. "It's almost good to be here, Carl. Why don't you and the sergeant major show the *Duce* and myself around?"

Kennison signaled for a driver to bring up his vehicle. "Right. We planned a little show and tell after the sightseeing tour."

Siegel, standing nearby, piped in, in Italian, "*Un' espetaculo de cani e cavellini.*" A dog and pony show. At Kennison's dirty look Siegel made himself scarce.

"Good, but make it brief, will you? I'm about ready to hit the sack now."

The four—Parilla, Carrera, Kennison, and McNamara, climbed back into the vehicle. Kennison gave the driver directions to take them around the camp. As the vehicle drove around the perimeter, Kennison pointed out the main features.

It soon became obvious to Carrera that the camp

consisted of six sub-camps, a large central one and five more at a distance of about two and a half kilometers from the center.

Kennison explained, pointing at the layout, "We've put the Mechanized, Artillery, Combat Support, Service Support and Headquarters in the center. The four line cohorts and most of the Cazadors are out on the perimeter. Air is back at the airport, along with a century of Cazadors. Security of the perimeter is the responsibility of the Cazadors and the infantry. Each has about one fifth of the total area; grunts a bit more; Cazadors a bit less."

"Have you had any infiltrators?" asked Carrera.

Kennison shrugged indifferently. "Not exactly. Truth? It doesn't matter. The Yezidi did most of the work. I'd be really surprised if at least one of them, anyway, isn't reporting to Saleh, in Babel."

Carrera shrugged, as well. *Nothing much to be done about that.* Besides, except for local artillery, the only weapons the Sumeris had that could range to the camps were some crudely modified Volgan missiles. Even the unmodified versions were so inaccurate they had been known to miss entire countries before. The dictator, Saleh, would be more likely to hit the base around Mangesh if he hired a bunch of witch doctors from Uhuru and had them try to entice meteors down from space.

And even then, Carrera thought it more than likely that the UE Peace Fleet would interfere.

While the two men spoke, the vehicle continued on its way until it reached the center of the main camp. Kennison pointed out to Carrera the double-wide mobile home, air-conditioned, heated and with running water that he had set up for Carrera and Parilla's living quarters.

"Harrington sent it, along with another one to serve as the Operations, Intel and Logistics Center."

"Oh, he did, did he?" Carrera objected, glaring at the second doublewide. "There'll be no goddamned Headquarters Regency Hotel. Move it and turn it over to the medical century.

"As for the other one, the *Duce* can have that to himself. Get me a tent set up nearby, will you, Mac?"

The sergeant major didn't object. He just turned to Kennison and made a rubbing motion with his thumb across his fingers. Kennison, equally wordlessly, took out his wallet and paid McNamara a fifty drachma note. McNamara had been sure that Carrera wouldn't take quarters much more comfortable than what the troops had.

Folding the note and stuffing it in his pocket with a grin, McNamara asked, "Do you mind bunking wit' me, sir? We're kind of cramped for tent space."

Pretending not to notice the wager, Carrera simply answered that a shared tent would be fine.

While Parilla and Carrera were being shown the base, out in one of the outlying camps, Mendoza, his friend Stefano del Rio, and the tank commander, Sergeant Perez, worked over their newly issued White Eagle, though they called it a Jaguar II, tank, breaking down and checking the auxiliary weapons, checking fluid levels, and inventorying tools.

"Sergeant Perez?"

Perez looked over to where a kneeling Mendoza

was unpacking a heavy machine gun from its crate. "Yeah, what is it, Jorge?"

Mendoza stood erect. In his right hand was a piece of paper. In his left was a labeled bottle full of clear liquid. He held them out for his sergeant's inspection.

A curious del Rio hopped down from the turret to join them.

Perez took the paper and read aloud:

> Boys:
> We want you to know that this tank is good tank, the best. No effort was spared. We didn't tolerate no shoddy work. She should see you well through coming fight.
> Bottle? Well, all of us here have idea of what you going to go through soon. We thought it help. Is all.
>
> > Vaya con Dios,
> > Josef Raikin
> > Stefan Malayev
> > And the crew of
> > Overseer Team 21

"That was pretty thoughtful of them, wasn't it, Sergeant?"

Perez just nodded. *Damn, that* was *thoughtful*, he thought. He said, "Mendoza, pad it with something and lock it up with the tools. We may need it come a rainy day."

Royal Jahari Land Forces Building, al Jahara, 19/1/461 AC

The Coalition commander didn't need to worry about rain. He would barely have needed to be concerned about the near detonation of a nuclear weapon.

Underground and very safe, deep in the bowels of the Royal Jahari Land Forces Building, Carrera and Parilla waited patiently for their meeting with the commanding general of the FSC-led Coalition. Concealing his distaste at a headquarters buried so far underground, Carrera muttered something about "Fredendall" and "Kasarine Pass."

Parilla looked at him questioningly. "Never mind, Raul," he answered. "Old Earth history . . . which just goes to show that some things are eternal."

A well meaning FS Army brigadier general sat down beside the two. "Are you all ready for your meeting with the Bulldozer?" he asked.

Parilla, having limited English, looked to Carrera. Carrera shrugged and didn't bother to translate except to mutter in Spanish about people who created their own nicknames or had their public relations departments do it for them.

"Is that the name his PR folks came up with for him now?" he asked the brigadier.

The brigadier gave Carrera a quizzical look. "It's what he's always been called."

Carrera snorted, shook his head, and put on a shallow smile. "No, that's not true. When he was a mere division commander he was known to most of his division as 'Fat Normy.'"

The brigadier's face looked as if Carrera had suddenly shown signs of a career destroying disease. He hastily left. Carrera smiled wickedly, then translated for Parilla.

"Did you know General Thomas back when you were in the FS Army?" Parilla asked.

"Know him? Not well. We had one of those cases of instantaneous dislike, really, and a few unpleasant run-ins after that." Carrera suddenly laughed. "You want to hear my best story about Fat Norman?"

"Tell me."

Carrera, still smiling wickedly, said, "It was silly, really. There was this captain in the battalion I was the operations officer for that had a little run in with Norman. The division was having its annual organization day. 'Conquest Day,' they called it. Some military intelligence wimp who was running one of the competitions fucked up his station. The puke put the man from our battalion in fourth place for that particular competition when the troop had actually placed second. This friend of mine tried to get the puke to fix it but he was nowhere to be found. So my friend tried to fix it himself. Unfortunately, he'd been pretty badly hurt in a training accident the week before and was moving a little slow. Maybe, too, he was thinking a little slow from the pain medications.

"First he put the troops in the right order, the one they themselves agreed was correct. Then my friend went over to the reviewing stand on the division parade field and tried to get Normy's attention so he could fix the awards list Normy had been given. My friend got Normy's attention, all right, but the general wouldn't listen and proceeded to chew him out in front of the division. By then the awards ceremony had started."

Carrera leaned back and shook his head slightly. "Then about a dozen colonels and lieutenant colonels surrounded this poor captain, asking what the problem was. My pal was explaining it to them when Normy came to the mistake the guy had been trying to fix. When Normy turned around it was like the parting of the Red Sea for Moses. Those colonels backed away like the man had the plague. The captain came to attention and Norman began to chew again.

"Even the captain thought it was hilarious. Consider. First the guy was chewed out for trying to fix a mistake someone else had made. Then he was chewed out for not fixing it fast enough."

Parilla laughed. "And did you really call him 'Fat Normy'? he asked.

"I don't know if the whole division did. But the officers of the brigade I was in? Oh, yeah. Don't get the wrong idea. Other than that he's an asshole, he's a perfectly acceptable commander. Not brilliant, perhaps, but far from stupid. Of course, if this war takes a hero, we could be in trouble."

The conversation ended when the secretary looked up and announced, "The general will see you now." Carrera picked up a bag containing a laptop as he and Parilla rose to enter the Coalition *Sanctum Sanctorum*.

While both men saluted, only Carrera reported verbally. "*Dux* Parilla and Legate Carrera report to the CinC, sir."

The general rose from behind his desk and returned the salute. Then, hiding the sneer he felt for Carrera, he walked around the desk to firmly grip Parilla's hand. Carrera translated the English words of welcome.

Only after that did Thomas return to his seat, turn his attention to Carrera and say, "I didn't want you here and I am ever so pleased that you'll be on the other side of Sumer."

"You couldn't be half as pleased as I am,". Carrera answered, smiling. "That said, you are still stuck with me in this theater, you still need the legion *Dux* Parilla and I have brought, and so, in the interests of our common mission, why don't you just fuck off and stop being an asshole, Norman?"

Thomas' eyes flew wide with fury. "Nobody talks to me that way! Nobody!"

"It's about time somebody did," Carrera answered calmly. "Now, do you want to listen or do you want Parilla and me to pack up, go back to our base in Yezidistan, and call Campos and tell him that you've gratuitously insulted us, that we just can't work with you and that we're going home?"

"You wouldn't . . ." Thomas began before remembering that there was nothing the man he had known as Patrick Hennessey wouldn't dare to do. Since that approach wasn't going to work, the general consoled himself with finishing, "What the fuck do I need another brigade of military police for, anyway?"

That Carrera did translate for Parilla. They both began to laugh.

"What's so goddamned funny?" Thomas demanded.

"Is that what Campos told you?" Carrera asked through his laughter. "That we're *MPs?* That's the funniest thing I've heard in years."

"Not the secretary of war, no," Thomas answered,

slowly. "One of my staff officers looked up Balboa, saw that it had only twelve companies of military police, and deduced, since you *are* from Balboa, that that's what you brought."

Muttering, "MPs . . . fucking *MPs*," Carrera took the laptop computer from its bag, fiddled with it a bit, and placed it on Thomas's desk, turning the screen so that all three could see it. Then he took a remote control and pressed a button.

A picture of a White Eagle, AKA Jaguar II, tank appeared on the screen.

"That, Norman, is what we call a 'Heavy Armored Community Relations Vehicle.' It lacks a siren, mind you, but there's nothing like a high velocity 125mm long rod penetrator to get the attention of a speeding driver."

Click. Another picture appeared, this time of an Ocelot.

"This is, of course, a Light Armored Community Relations Vehicle mounting a 100mm crowd control cannon." Click to show a Volgan 122mm artillery piece. "That is a 122mm Auxiliary Riot Control Agent Dispersal Projector." Click. "The 160mm High Angle Leaflet Distribution System." Click. An aircraft appeared, propeller driven but mounting a fearsome array of machine guns and rockets. "That is our Turbo-Finch Low Altitude Riot Control Aircraft . . ."

Click, click, click, click, click.

"You aren't MPs?"

"No, we're *not* MPs," Carrera answered. "What we are is a large combined arms brigade with a core of leadership some of which was converted to military police but were infantry before that and which we converted back to infantry or to some other combat arm. That cadre has been expanded with young men of such a high quality that your own Rangers would weep with envy. In the last year that brigade has spent more time training, and under more realistic situations, than any unit in your army *except*, maybe, for the Rangers. We have used more live ammunition in that year than your entire 39th Parachute Infantry Division uses in three years."

"You can really force a pass through the Yezidi mountains?" Thomas asked.

Carrera translated that for Parilla, who snapped his fingers and answered, in heavily accented English, "Piece o' cake."

Thomas nodded, looked contemplative for a few moments, then hit his intercom and said, "Cancel the plans to fly a brigade of the 11th Division up to Yezidistan."

Turning to Parilla, Thomas asked, "Will you need a Liaison Officer?"

Parilla shook his head, no, while Carrera answered, "We have one we're happy with who's been with us for some time. He'll do."

On their way out Parilla looked mildly thoughtful. "Patricio, I'm curious. Everyone in the headquarters that I saw had a pair of those tan colored boots just like Thomas did. But I haven't seen a line trooper with a pair yet. What's going on there?"

Carrera smiled. "Raul, you have just observed the trickle down theory' of supporting combat troops. I will just about guarantee you that every rear echelon motherfucker will have a pair of those boots before a single pair finds its way to a private in an infantry squad."

Parilla looked confused. "But how can that be? The rear support types don't need them. The infantry do."

Carrera laughed bitterly. "How can it *be*? How can it *not* be? It starts with Normy himself. He gets these high-speed boots and "tests" them personally. Or, more likely, just wears them because he's the big cheese and he can. Who knows?

"Then the next senior guy below Normy will get a pair. After all, he's got to show that he's a pretty big cheese, too. So far it isn't a big problem. But then the boots get to the other REMF generals, colonels, and majors. You might think that Normy, or his deputy, could put a stop to that with an order. They could, too, if it wasn't that they lost the moral authority to do so by wearing the boots themselves first. It would be embarrassing to tell the REMFs they can't have them . . . and generals spend most of their time surrounded by REMFs.

"So by now, we've got all the more junior officers and senior non-coms in the rear wearing the goddamned boots. Well . . . how can they tell their REMF troops that the troops can't have the boots? They can't. They gave up their moral authority to do so by grabbing a pair for themselves first. So, because Normy grabbed a pair for himself and let his subordinates grab a pair too, every REMF will have to have a pair of those boots before a single set trickles down to the line. Disgusting, isn't it?"

A light seemed to flash in Parilla's brain. "Patricio . . . is that why you didn't want to use the doublewide?"

"It's a part of it, Raul. You can use yours and nothing's lost as long as I establish that there will be no palace building below you."

"I see. Maybe I should give up the palace, too."

"You could have refused it initially. Now?" Carrera shook his head emphatically. "No. It would look too much like you're following me . . . which is not the impression we want to give the troops."

"But I want to do the right thing. I *must* do the right thing," Parilla insisted.

"I should have explained how this shit really works initially, when I first saw that rolling whorehouse Harrington scrounged. My fault I didn't, not yours. Let me see." He thought intently for a short while, then said, "Raul, in about two days, at the command and staff meeting, the medical unit is going to ask about having another air-conditioned and heated facility for some of the inevitable casualties. You will ask Harrington about it. He will say that none are available and none will be for the immediate future. You will then order the sergeant major to cart off your mobile home and get you a tent. I will then tell the medicos that the very first time I see or hear of that building being used for ANY purpose but care of the wounded and ill, I will have the guilty parties staked out naked in the cold overnight."

Laughing lightly, Carrera said, "You know, I'm not sure it won't work out better this way than if you'd turned down the trailer in the first place."

Mangesh Base, Yezidistan, 20/1/461 AC

Colonel John Ridenhour approached the bunker guarding the gate with some care. When he had walked to within fifty meters of it, but no closer, a voice rang out, loud enough to be heard, but no louder, "Halt! Who goes there? Friend or foe?"

"Friend," Ridenhour answered in Spanish.

"Advance, friend, to be recognized." Ridenhour again walked forward before being halted again. He met the sentry's whispered challenge with an equally soft-spoken password.

A young Balboan sentry emerged from the bunker and brought his rifle to *present arms*. Ridenhour returned the salute.

When the sentry had moved his rifle back to a more ready position, he asked, "Sir, what the hell were you doing out there?"

"Just looking over the perimeter from the enemy's point of view."

Satisfied, the young sentry asked, in halting and accented but understandable English, "How does it look?"

"Good, son, very good. By the way, what's your name?"

"Cruz, sir. Private First Class Ricardo Cruz."

"Where are you from in Balboa?"

"*Las Mesas* Province," Cruz answered proudly.

"You're a long way from home."

Cruz smiled, white teeth shining slightly amidst the dark night. He thought longingly of Caridad. "Sir, a mile would be too far to be away from home. But if I have to be away, here's not much worse than anywhere else. Except for the damned cold, of course."

Research Building, University of Ninewa

Sada shivered as he watched the trucks loaded. There was a bitterly cold south wind blowing across the city. The scientists, soldiers and workers, like Sada, suffered in the biting breeze. Unlike him, most were allowed by their positions to find shelter wherever there was a lee.

Shaking his head sadly, Sada noted that there were only enough trucks to move half the load, all of that being money and bearer bonds. Was Saleh, the dictator of the country, incapable of coming up with enough vehicles at one time to make away with the contents of the building's basement?

If we cannot even come up with trucks, what chance have we? Sada fumed.

"We'll be back," the colonel commanding the column assured Sada.

"You'll be back *if* you aren't blasted to shit on the way," Sada corrected.

EXCURSUS

From: *Reconquista*, Copyright © Xavier
Jimenez IV, 601 AC, Carrera-Balboa Press,
Ciudad Balboa

By 155 AC Makkah al Jedidah had only one stream,
and that shallow and sluggish. The other had gone to
hide below ground. The city still had trees, about as
many as it had at the founding. Most of those trees,
however, were no longer growing but had been cut
for roof beams.

Farther out was sand with a few water holes and
oases. Caravans trekked the sand; woe betide anything
that grew near the caravan trails. The camels and
especially the goats would eat anything found green
right down to the roots.

There was little wood by this time, little to burn for
fuel. Instead, the people gathered up the droppings of
their animals and dried and burned those. Thus, even
that little bit of fertilizer never nourished the soil.

As one went farther away from the original center
of settlement one would find more greenery. Yet the
pattern was clear. The settlement of Salafi Man was

spreading fast; the existence of natural flora and fauna disappearing at the same rate or faster. The Salafis fled the desert. But they brought the desert with them, created it, wherever they went.

The nomads' flocks' hooves pounded the soil, compacting it and pulverizing it. This rendered the soil fine enough to be carried off by water and wind. And the trees that might have protected the soil, holding it in place, gathering it from the wind, shading it so that surface water did not evaporate so quickly . . . these were gone or going. Evaporation, too, brought salt to the surface, killing what plants remained and rendering the soil useless for growing.

Other colonies on the periphery of the Salafis felt the nomads' desperation. Often starving, themselves, the Salafis raided for food. They raided to spread their way of life, their purer faith. They also raided for slaves, especially women slaves. Thus, added to the now forced emigration from Old Earth, the slave women brought new Salafis into the world in continuingly large numbers.

Most of the southern shore of Uhuru, along the Tauranian Lakes, had fallen to them, as had northwestern Taurus and substantial parts of Urania and, once the Salafis took to sea, some islands of the *Mar Furioso*. This meant more slaves, more women, and more Salafis. And, except where even *they* could not overcome nature, it also meant more desert.

The other peoples of the new world began, not to strike back, but to defend what was theirs. After what they had endured from the Salafi, mercy was not a concept in common currency.

In Ardeal, five thousand Salafi raiders were impaled

at a pass following the defeat of their raiding party. At Turonensis, in Gaul, an amphibious Salafi invasion was defeated by disciplined musketry and its survivors hanged to a man, several thousand Christian slaves being liberated in the process. When a Salafi army pushed north, past the desertified coast of Southern Uhuru, seeking new lands to turn barren, it was met by the *Bulala Amalungu-* and *Bayede Nkhosi-*crying, *Shosholoza-* and *Nomathemba-*chanting, *Amazing Grace-* and *Onward Christian Soldiers-*singing, massed, Christian-Animist impis of the great King Senzangakona III of the Nguni.

Salafi hit and run tactics, on horseback, had proven no match for the Nguni numbers and their urge to close and kill at breakneck pace afoot. The Salafis and their mounts were butchered, despite their extensive use of firearms. It was said among the Nguni that the glittering sheen of their spearheads had been lit by a miraculous glow from the large gilded cross they carried as their king's standard. It was said among the few Salafi survivors, thereafter, that it was almost impossible for a man on horseback to outpace a racing Nguni impi in the long run . . . and that with the Nguni it was *always* a long run. Only the desert, creation and ultimate defense of the Salafi, had kept the impis from continuing on to exterminate the threat to their south.

Nor was the resistance limited to non-Moslems. The Salafi were a threat to *everyone*. Near Babel, in Sumer, disciplined, musket-wielding Sunni and Shia farmers on foot held the mounted Salafis at bay while their own, limited, cavalry swept in behind to trap them. Something not dissimilar happened when the Salafis faced the civilized, Moslem and Christian, Misrani along the banks of the Interu in Southwest Uhuru.

In time, the Salafi immigration from Old Earth ceased. The semi-starvation that had driven their expansion on Terra Nova began to reduce their population as, morally ingenious literalists that they were, they avoided the proscription against burying infant girls alive by first either smashing their heads with rocks or leaving them exposed for the desert animals.

And so the Salafi movement began to recede, for a time. It would come again, in the guise of an ideology. As it left, it left behind little but wasteland and corpses, and small detachments of outcast adherents. When it returned, it would be over a carpet of waste and bodies, stepping along the footholds it had left behind like a man crossing a stream on stones.

As the Salafis fell back to their desert fastness, they left little but waste and destruction—physical, moral and intellectual—behind them. Their adherents left behind in the lost lands were outcast and despised. Indeed, they were often killed out of hand, *especially* in Moslem lands. Heeding the Koran's stricture on how to deal with those who brought disorder to the world, only shortage of wood saved many Salafis from crucifixion. And those lost hands and feet on opposite sides.

Thus Salafism languished for more than two centuries while the new world progressed around them. In fact, while Uhuru, Urania and other continents were carved up by Taurana, Zhong, Yamatana and Columbians, the Salafis of the Yithrab were left in peace. This was neither altruism nor respect but a simple reflection of the fact they had nothing anyone wanted.

✧　　✧　　✧

The resurgence of radical Salafism can be dated to the discovery of substantial energy deposits, in the form of fossil fuels, in the Yithrab Peninsula and its environs, beginning in the year 348 AC. Having access to Earth's history prior to the end of emigration, the peoples of Terra Nova were never in ignorance of the value of the stuff. Civil war within the Salafi reach erupted within a few years of the discovery, the al Rashid clan eventually emerging, triumphant.

Oil revenues were initially more or less trivial to the buyers, though significant to the then-poor Salafis. Especially during the Great Global War, when all civilized constraints of behavior were thrown off, the Salafis were altogether too frightened of conquest to exert the power implicit in control of so vast a reserve of energy.

With time, however, growing awareness of the value of their resource, coupled with the post-GGW nuclear standoff between the Federated States, the Volgan Empire and the UEPF, placed the al Rashid in a position to take control of their own oil and their own destinies. Others, not merely on the periphery but around the globe, followed suit. Fossil fuel prices rose precipitously. In point of fact, they did not stop their continuous rise until the fall of the Volgan Empire freed the Federated States to credibly threaten the use of military force should prices get out of hand.

Oil brought unprecedented wealth. Money received from it went into the creation of welfare states, impressively armed if indifferently effective military and naval forces, and provided obscenely lavish lifestyles for the ruling clans. No small amount, too, went to the spread of Salafism.

Among the Misrani at the edge of Southern Uhuru, to Kashmir, to Sukarno, madrassas sprang up like mushrooms. Providing free room and board, as well as a free—if highly constrained—education, the madrassas were highly popular among the disenfranchised lower classes of the Moslem portions of Terra Nova.

And *that* was the problem. *Most* of the population of Moslem states on Terra Nova were disenfranchised and frighteningly poor. Moreover, while the first two hundred and fifty years of settlement had seen them prosper approximately as well as colonization efforts by non-Moslems, after approximately the middle of the third Terra Novan century this was no longer true. Increasingly, they had fallen behind. Increasingly they were seen to be militarily inept. Increasingly, the pride of a very proud set of people was pricked. Increasingly, they heard the message of the Salafis to return to the older, purer ways . . . to fight back with fire and sword.

PART III

CHAPTER SEVENTEEN

Behold, the fool saith, "Put not all thine eggs in the one basket"—which is but a manner of saying, "Scatter your money and your attention"; but the wise man saith, "Put all your eggs in the one basket and—watch that basket!"

—Mark Twain

Multichucha Ridge, north of Mangesh, Sumer, 21/1/461 AC

The land was compartmentalized by east-west running ridges that arose, one after another, and dominated the valleys between. A highway, a mix of gravel, dirt, potholes, and—in rare spots—asphalt, wound through the valleys and narrow gaps that appeared occasionally between sections of ridge. The highway eventually led to Ninewa and, beyond that, Babel.

Joint patrols, Yezidi and Sumeri, walked the demarcation line between the Federated States-guaranteed Yezidi Safe Zone and that portion of the Republic of

Sumer still under Sumeri control. This demarcation line, in the vicinity of the town of Mangesh, was a river. The patrols chatted amiably enough across the river despite the certainty on the part of all concerned that the area would see fighting in no more than a Terra Novan month.

In a marginally heated four wheel drive vehicle followed by a truck holding a squad of Cazadors with an engineer team to operate a mine detector, Parilla and Carrera rolled north.

"So there really is a Multichucha Ridge," Parilla observed with wonder in his voice.

"Oh, yes," Carrera, sitting in the back, agreed. There, stretching out east to west before them were five sets of enormous, naturally occurring, grass, bush, sand, rock and gravel simulacra of female genitalia.

"The one farthest east doesn't look all that realistic," Parilla continued. "But the two to the west are frighteningly real."

"Don't know about you two, sirs, but it sure makes me homesick," commented the driver.

There was a Chaldean, a native of Mangesh, in the back of the four wheel drive, next to Carrera. Fahad had grown up in the shadow of the ridge. His people had their own phrase for the terrain feature but that, too, translated as "Multi-pussy Ridge."

"Fahad," Carrera questioned in English, "are you absolutely *certain* you know a way to the top of that ridge where we can observe the Sumeri positions and that getting to which won't run us into a minefield?"

The Chaldean considered. He spoke Arabic, English, and Yezidi, along with his native tongue.. It was in English that he answered. Why not? He had done his first term of military service in the Sumeri Army teaching English at the Sumeri War College outside of Babel.

"Yes," Fahad said. "No problem. The snow makes it tougher but the path I know is broad. We should be fine."

Carrera translated for Parilla's benefit but to the latter's considerable doubt and plain discomfiture.

"I don't even like the *idea* of land mines," Parilla muttered.

"No one does," Carrera agreed. "Not until you have a horde of screaming motherfuckers coming to kill you and all that stands between their bayonets and you is a belt of land mines."

At Fahad's point of a finger the vehicles pulled over to allow the leaders, plus the Cazadors and the engineers, to dismount. Fahad led the way upward, stopping occasionally to check his memory of the path against what he believed to be certain terrain features somewhat hidden under snow. He must have guessed right; there were no loud explosions on the way up.

Just below the summit Parilla and Carrera stopped to allow the Cazadors to scout forward. At the squad leader's signal that all was clear they, too, crouched low and advanced. A dozen meters or so before the actual summit of the ridge, they went to their bellies and crawled through the hard-packed, icy snow to the top.

The sun was setting to the west. There would be no telltale flashes from the glass of the binoculars they used to scout out the opposite ridge, Hill 1647, which was to be the legion's initial objective.

"Fuck," Carrera said.

"Chingada," Parilla agreed.

From where they lay the pair saw the highway as it ran between two fortresses. Each of the fortresses was just under a kilometer across and, according to photo recon, about two thirds that deep. They were entrenched, bunkered and wired in. Moreover, according to the Yezidi, there were deep minefields in between the belts of wire. To add to the problem, a twenty-meter-wide river, low and slow moving but very cold, crossed the valley near to the base of the Sumeri held ridgelines.

"Too steep to get armor up," Parilla observed. "Even if they could get across the river."

"Maybe the lighter vehicles could make it. Maybe." Carrera countered. "If they could follow the most advantageous paths. If they could go slow. If they were not being shot at. If the best paths were clear of mines which, by all reports, they most definitely are not."

"An infantry attack?" Parilla queried. "Maybe at night."

Carrera didn't answer immediately. Looking back through his binoculars again at the thick rows of barbed wire, Carrera saw them as they might be if he ordered an assault to clear the hill, thick with the bodies, and parts of bodies, of his troops. Half a dozen possible plans flashed through his head. Each was quickly discarded before he settled on something that might be workable if short of brilliant.

"They'll get butchered by machine guns and the artillery that—I have no doubt—is on call to support the defense. And attacking at night, whatever the advantages, is confusing as hell. Too confusing to subject troops to it for their first action."

"Then how?" the *Dux* asked.

"What we have is a training issue," Carrera responded, cryptically. "That; an engineering problem and a logistics problem. Now, where are we going to get a shitpot of concrete mix and another six hundred tons of artillery and mortar ammunition on short notice?" he mused.

All the drive back to Mangesh Base Carrera pondered, mused, considered and scribbled in a notebook.

Valley between Multichucha Ridge and Hill 1647, 24/1/461 AC

They were called, after the German, *Stollen*, and they were the least offensive-seeming things imaginable. Long, narrow, and deep—rather like the Sachsen Christmas cake—the *Stollen* were nothing but shelters, passive, harmless, inoffensive shelters. Who can object, after all, to a Sachsen Christmas cake?

The river at the base of Hill 1647 marked the demarcation line. Accordingly, the *Stollen* went up two to three hundred meters south of the river, within—if barely—the Yezidi Safe Zone.

"What are they for?" all three leaders of the local Yezidi political, which were also tribal, parties asked. Since Carrera was certain that at least one of the Yezidis reported directly to Babel, he told the truth. Sort of.

"The Sumeris are likely to pound the shit out of us once the FSC begins the war. There is no place we can do our job, which is to protect you, where we will not also be in artillery range. The mountains are too rocky to dig into very well in the time we have. So I am building shelters for my men down in the valley where we can continue to protect you despite the shelling I anticipate."

This was, of course, not the complete truth. Still, reasonably satisfied at the answer, the Yezidis offered their followers as a labor force. They did not do so, naturally, without extracting a contract from the legion for pay for the labor provided. The mere fact that someone was doing you a favor was not in itself a sufficient reason not to insist on being paid for helping them do you that favor.

"I *loathe* the Yezidis," Carrera said to his chief engineer, Sam Cheatham, and Fahad when he had called them together in the valley to explain what he wanted done.

"*You* loathe them?" Fahad had answered. "Let me tell you about the Yezidis—"

"No time, Fahad," Carrera said, holding one hand up, palm out, "and I've heard all about it before."

"I wish I could put you up about sixteen of the things." Cheatham sighed, referring to the *Stollen*. "But I just don't have the material or the skilled manpower. I've only got my seventy-odd engineers, plus whatever I can use from the line cohorts' engineer sections. But they, frankly, are sappers, not builders. And the Yezidi are not going to be worth much besides scut work."

"How many can you put up that will be strong enough to take a direct hit from an eight-inch gun?" Carrera asked. "And remember, we have to be able to shelter about twelve hundred men in them for a few days."

"In the time I have," Cheatham answered, "with the material I have and with the workers I have, I can put up four, each about thirty feet by one hundred, and with a thick enough overhead cover to take a couple of eight-inch hits. By the way, sir, what makes you think the Sumeris even *have* eight inch guns?"

"Nothing," Carrera shook his head in negation. "But they *might* have them."

"Okay," Cheatham said agreeably. "Four *Stollen* coming up. This weather is going to be a problem, you know. Concrete—at least the kind I have been able to scrounge locally—doesn't set worth a shit in this kind of cold. How about if I blast a shitload of rock out of the last ridge and use that to reinforce?"

"That's fine, Sam. Do it however you think best. But get me my Christmas cakes cooked."

"What if they try to shell my engineers while they're working?" Cheatham asked, not unreasonably.

"I don't think they will, Sam, mainly because they don't have much in their strategic inventory except some sympathy from whoever hates the FSC. They'll want the coalition to fire the first shot. Even so, until H Hour-3, or at least until you're done building, you've got priority of fires—direct control if you think you need it—over all the legion's artillery plus the 105mm battalion from the 731st Airborne."

"Hmmm. Shells would arrive here before counterbattery could have any effect. So, if you don't mind, I'll start by digging some slit trenches for my people *before* we start work on the *Stollen*."

"That's fine," Carrera had answered. "Don't dawdle

over it, though. And remember I also need some special shelters built for the artillery."

For Cheatham's slit trenches he used two entrenching machines that had been purchased from the Volgans. These were of the smaller variety, having an arm of sorts that they dragged behind them and which more or less horizontally spun a series of steel buckets to cut a neat trench about seventy-five centimeters wide and a meter and a half deep. The frozen state of the ground made this a slower than normal operation but within a day the entrenching machines had scraped out sixteen reasonably sized slit trenches.

The Sumeris had paid no mind at all, so far as Cheatham could see, to the operation of the entrenching machines.

While the trench cutters were in operation, gangs of Yezidi with picks and shovels began excavating the outlines of the *Stollen* to a depth of about a meter. The Sumeris paid no attention to them, either.

When the engineers began blasting off slabs of rock from the far slope of Multichucha Ridge, the Sumeris had manned their trenches and bunkers. Still, when no attack materialized, they went back to their normal routine of shivering, freezing and, if the Yezidi were to be believed, buggering each other. In this belief Fahad and the Chaldeans seemed to concur.

They were still, so far as Cheatham could tell, buggering each other when the frameworks for the Stollen began to go up.

Perhaps they had run out of lubrication—that, or they'd discovered that weapons oil was a poor substitute—when the layer of concrete was poured.

They seemed fascinated by that, sitting atop the lips of their trenches, chatting amiably among each other, and generally having a good time watching the legion and the Yezidis work in the cold.

Supplies of a less toxic lubricant must have come through, though, because they disappeared again when the Yezidi gangs began piling dirt atop the concrete. Still, so Cheatham and the Yezidis surmised, those supplies must have been limited. They were back again to watch as the dirt was covered with large chunks and slabs of rock.

Sam Cheatham didn't bother to camouflage the *Stollen*. Anybody who thought that a six to seven meter high loaf of rock, dirt and concrete sticking up out of a flat plain in plain view of the enemy was going to be hidden by a few odd bits of grass was either smoking something or, as was perhaps the case, too busy being buggered to worry about. Besides, snow would be along any day now and it would do a better job of camouflage than anything that could be done artificially.

Hill 1647, Command Post, 2/2/461 AC

Mukkaddam, or Lieutenant Colonel, Ali al Tikriti had a problem. No, that wasn't quite right. What he had was approximately seven hundred and one problems. The seven hundred, give or take a few, were his men, whom he despised as a lot of illiterate, lazy, good for nothing peasants. The one, and that was the worst of the lot, was the dictator—Saleh, his fourth cousin, twice removed—sitting in what was likely to prove a very temporary safety in one of his palaces near Babel.

In fact, of all the people Ali had to deal with, the only one who was not a problem was the thirteen-year-old boy currently kneeling between Ali's legs with his penis in his mouth. And that was at best a temporary distraction from all Ali's other problems, problems which were altogether too likely to prove extremely and unfortunately permanent.

Ali would rather have had one of his two wives kneeling between his legs. They, however, weren't there, while the young boy was.

For an all too short period of time, the thirteen year old was able to distract Ali from his many concerns. After tousling the boy's hair and tipping him generously, Ali buttoned his trousers, refastened his belt, and left his rather luxuriously appointed, and very deep, personal bunker to walk the front trench of the rightmost of the two fortresses atop the ridge.

Ali owed his position not to military skill and competence but to family connections. Oh, yes, he'd been to all the schools—and some of them were quite decent—that his army offered. But when one is that tightly connected to the ruling clan, and able to afford substantial bribes to one's teachers, it was not strictly speaking necessary to learn one blessed thing to graduate with honors. In fairness, it had to be said that Ali had learned somewhat more than most would have in his position. At the very least, he had learned something of military engineering. Thus, his trenches were narrow and deep, his bunkers had substantial overhead cover, and his obstacles were well sighted. More than that one could hardly expect.

Ali's men cowered as he walked the line. Occasionally, and not always for any obvious reason, he would lash out with his riding crop to slash a soldier across the face or neck. His cousin ruled the country by fear; could Ali do any less? Besides, the shit-footed clumsy peasants he had to work with understood nothing but fear and the lash. Moreover, terrorizing his men helped allay the worry that the sight of those four large bunkers being built in plain view instilled in Ali. He didn't understand them, didn't understand their purpose. Why put so much construction effort into something so ridiculously obvious and so completely passive? Queries to the local Yezidi had given answers that were not been entirely satisfactory. And queries to Problem Number One, his cousin, had been brushed aside.

Approaching *Stollen* #1, 7/2/461 AC

There was a slight jingling as the unit marched, the sound of loads shifting and metal touching on metal.

Cruz brushed snow—he'd never in his life so much as *seen* snow before coming to Sumer—off of his face and shoulders as he walked towards the pass east of Multichucha Ridge. Ahead of him and behind, and on both sides of the highway, walked the rest of the four infantry centuries, minus their mortars, of 1st Cohort, plus the scout and engineer sections and the forward command post team. No vehicles were used; those were left behind. Everything, to include food and water, went in on the soldier's backs.

It was a terrible, man-killing load. Besides his rifle,

ammunition and auxiliary ammunition, Cruz carried food for five days, water for three, and a portion of the century's common equipment. In all, Cruz's load was better than one hundred and fifty pounds, and he was not the most heavily laden of the legionaries.

Nearing the pass, Cruz noticed that he could not see the genitalia that gave the ridge its nickname.

Thank God for the snow, he thought, *freezing or not. If I can't see the pussies then the Sumeris won't see me. Besides, I'm already homesick enough.*

Unseen by Cruz—or by anyone not within a few paces of the cohort commander, Tribune I Gutierrez—a noncom from Cheatham's Engineer Century met the 1st at the pass. The engineer cautioned Gutierrez, "Slow down and keep them quiet until you are in the *Stollen.*" Gutierrez dropped his pace to a crawl to reduce the sounds coming from the company, sounds that might alert the Sumeris that the *Stollen* were being occupied.

Dammit, the tribune thought, fuming at the low key jingling coming from behind him. *It isn't as if we didn't do our damndest to make sure everything was quiet and secured before we set out.* They had done what was possible. But some sound was unavoidable and in this cold air could well carry despite the muffling effect of the snow.

The engineer then led them down the road before cutting right across the open field to the shelter's narrow entrance. "File in silently," the engineer advised. A couple more engineers, these with homemade rakes, smoothed the snow behind the passing centuries.

Inside, the place smelled damp and musty, Cruz thought. It was a small surprise in construction so new.

Buckets stacked in one corner suggested that it was soon going to have a very different, and much worse, odor.

There were signs on the walls, lit only by chemical lights, or "chemlights." Other chemlights traced out boundaries on the *Stollen* floor. One of the signs said, in the sickly green glow, "1st Century." Cruz led his team to that corner and set down his rucksack. His three men placed theirs beside his and, like him, began unrolling bedding, air mattresses, sleeping bags, and blankets. As Cruz and his boys were blowing up the air mattresses someone struck a match and applied the flame to a lantern. Immediately, the greenish gloom of the place dissipated, the more so as more lanterns were lit. In the new and brighter illumination, Cruz saw two charcoal stoves, one of which the supply sergeant was in the process of lighting. The charcoal wouldn't give off any noticeable smoke, he knew, but wondered if the heat distortion might not tell too much to someone watching and paying attention. He asked the supply sergeant about that.

"The exhaust doesn't go up," the sergeant explained. "It goes to an underground pipe. That leads to a couple of dozen smaller pipes that eventually emerge above ground. All those are perforated to dissipate the smoke and heat. Clever, ain't it?"

Mangesh, 9/2/461 AC

There were caves south of the town. These were originally natural but had been further excavated and in a few cases connected by the Yezidi during their long and generally fruitless fight with the Babel regime. To these caves the legion directed the people of Mangesh, Yezidi and Chaldean both, to go for shelter from the Sumeri artillery that would, almost inevitably, devastate the town on general principle. The two double-wides were likewise moved up to shelter close in to the mountains, under cliff faces. Howitzer and mortar fire could have reached them there, were they in range. At this distance, though, only high velocity artillery had a chance of reaching and that traveled at too low an angle to search the reverse slope of the hill.

The legion's table of organization included one smallish century of mixed civil affairs and psychological operations troops. The PSYOP legionaries printed the leaflets and ran the loudspeakers that directed the townsfolk to the caves while the CA types actually physically led them, organized them, and coordinated for transport to move their food and water, their old and sick, and the bare minimum of life support.

"This is not the first time we have had to do this," said Father Hanna, the local Chaldean priest, when the CA/PO Century commander mentioned how smoothly the move was going. The townspeople looked nervous, of course, but there was no great amount of wailing from the women, or complaining from the men. Even the children were pretty well behaved and that was something the signifer *never* expected.

"No, we have had to run to the caves many times, not just once," Hanna continued. The priest was old and gray but plainly robust as he and the signifer led the people to the south. He was also multilingual, speaking—besides Chaldean—Arabic, English, Latin, French and Spanish.

When asked about that he had only answered, "Oh, I served my time at New Vatican Hill when I was a younger man."

One of the caves had been set aside as a field hospital. Father Hanna had taken some pains to find women to assist there. This was much appreciated by Carrera, who said so.

He'd also said, when out of the priest's hearing, "That son of a bitch Campos was supposed to give me medical support equal to that the FSC troops will have in al Jahara. What do I get for my men? I get an understrength medical company from the 731st Airborne and a long drive over epically shitty roads to the FSAF base in Kemal; that, or a sometimes-possible-maybe-perhaps available medevac flight from the old Sumeri airbase at Siyilopi. Motherfucker!"

"Arrest the motherfuckers as spies," Carrera commanded McNamara when told that a group of media types from the Global News Network had arrived in now-abandoned Mangesh. When told of a humanitarian medical group nosing around he had said, with equal vehemence, "Arrest them. Take them to the caves and inform them they will care for our wounded as well as any civilians. Make it clear I am *firing squad serious* about that."

"Patricio," Jimenez cautioned, "do you really think it's wise to alienate the press?"

"Errr . . . maybe not, Xavier," Carrera relented. "Though frankly I doubt it matters. The press is the enemy, as much as the Sumeris or perhaps more so. But . . . all right. We won't arrest them as spies.

"Instead . . . Sergeant Major, take the pressies and

medicos into *protective custody*, confiscate their equipment and cell phones, and confine them to the field hospital cave where they'll help care for our wounded. Don't trust the bastards; strip search them. If any of them are women see if the good father can come up with some Chaldean women to do the strip search. And if they try to escape, shoot them as spies."

Hewlêr International Airport, Yezidistan, 11/2/461 AC

The legion's air component, minus the remotely piloted vehicles that were forward based at Mangesh, was lined up at the airfield. This consisted of eight Turbo-Finch attack aircraft, twelve medium and four heavy lift Volgan helicopters, six Boiohaemum-built Cricket light reconnaissance planes plus four more slightly modified for medical evacuation, two ex-Volgan Nabakov NA-21 medium lift cargo planes and six lighter NA-23s upgraded to B300 standard.

Opposite the legion's air *ala*, by the cargo terminal, two Volgan LI-68s were still unloading artillery and mortar ammunition. Inside the terminal, near the Volgans and opposite their own aircraft, a century of Cazadors from the 6th Cohort waited for orders to board. Final orders were not expected for some time. The Cazadors would drop from two of the NA-23s.

The B300 was a much improved version of the original NA-23, having longer range, more lift capacity and much improved avionics. Dubbed "Dodos," apparently because they just looked a little awkward, the NA-23s were an early post-Great Global War-vintage design, with twin turbo-prop engines. The newest was over thirty years old. They were, however, fairly simple and robust aircraft and most were still flying even four to five Terra Novan decades later.

To get to the B300 upgrade, the original Dodos were completely disassembled and everything from struts to skin microchecked for excess stress and wear. Then, the fuselage was reassembled, with an additional meter being added between the cockpit and the main cargo compartment. Completely new wings were attached, and to the wings, in lieu of the old turbo-props, new Whitefield-Prance WPT9A-76R turbo-prop engines were added, driving five-bladed propellers. Lengthened troop seats were installed, along with new avionics, and a generally improved cockpit layout.

Before being deployed, two of the NA-23s had taken a short detour to Zion where a frame was built up around the aircraft and thin composite Carbon Fiber-Shiff Base Salt tiles added for decreased radar visibility. In addition, the original tail section was replaced with one of V-form. It was these that would drop the Cazadors.

The B300 was, for all practical purposes, a new plane superior in every way, to include operating cost, to the original Dodo. It was the reduced operating cost, as much as the increased capability, that had decided Carrera in favor of the conversion, despite a "fly away" price tag of nearly three million drachma per aircraft and five million for the two that had been stealthified. The legion could indeed, probably would have to—rely upon the Dodos for critical resupply.

One of the Cazadors due to be inserted via the stealthy Dodos, Sergeant Emmanuel Robles, paced nervously up and down that portion of the terminal set aside for the Cazadors. From time to time he took from his wallet a picture of his wife and three children waiting back home in Balboa. He also spent a good deal of time praying.

It just doesn't feel right.

Mangesh, 12/2/461 AC

Carrera frantically paced the small headquarters set up in an old Sumeri police fort on the outskirts of the town.

"I don't see how the hell you can be so calm, Raul," he said.

Parilla, sitting calmly behind a field desk with his feet up and his hands clasped behind his head answered, "Why should I worry when you are worrying enough for both of us and three more men besides?"

Carrera stopped his pacing, opened his mouth as if to retort, and then began to laugh. "Okay, you win. I'll calm down."

"Care for a drink?" Parilla asked. "The good father presented me with a bottle of the local brandy. It's actually pretty good."

The look on Carrera's face as much as said, "Gimme." Parilla poured several ounces of the brandy into a metal cup and handed it over.

"You know what's bothering me, Raul?"

"No."

"It's the coalition headquarters down in al Jahara. D-Day is supposed to be the day after tomorrow. Ordinarily, I'd expect hourly intelligence updates to have begun by now. But there hasn't been a word or, at least, not a word to us."

"Do you think they've forgotten about us way down here?" Parilla asked.

"Maybe they forgot," Carrera answered, "and then maybe they're deliberately ignoring us. I've got a call in to a friend."

"So what are we going to do if they don't answer?"

"Send in the Cazador long-range recon teams anyway, tonight around midnight. They'll need that much time to get to their positions behind the Sumeri lines."

"And if D-Day is moved up? Or delayed? How do we get them out?" Parilla asked.

"I swear to God I'll start the war on my own if it's delayed. And if it's moved up without them telling us, I just might shoot that son of a bitch down in al Jahara."

Hewlêr International Airport, Yezidistan, nearly midnight, 12/2/461 AC

Robles still didn't like it. But there were the two stealth-modified Dodos, waiting with engines idling not one hundred meters from the terminal. There, lined up by the terminal door were the chutes for each man who would jump tonight. Standing by that door was the century commander and there, in his hand, were the orders to go.

The men were singing as they lined up to chute up. Ordinarily, Robles enjoyed the singing before a jump. Now it just irritated him, especially when the song came to the lines:

Thundering motors leave each man alone.
He thinks one more time of his loved ones
   back home.
Then come, mis compadres, to spring on
   command
To jump and to die for our people and
   land . . .

Chingada. *Bunch of morbid bastards. Why the fuck did I ever sign up for this?*

And then they were at the aircraft, the crew chiefs and their assistants helping the pack-mule-laden, barely mobile men to climb the ladders and shuffle up the ramps and then walking the lines to make sure everyone was buckled in.

The engines began to thunder in truth now as the Dodos rolled down the runway. The airfield was high where the air would normally be thin. Even so, in the dead of winter the air was cold and dense enough for lift. Robles felt the plane lurch upward, leaving the runway behind. There was a winding, grinding sound followed by a pair of *thumps* as the landing gear raised and stowed away. Then the planes veered eastward towards an area where reconnaissance showed little in the way of Sumeri troops to observe—or Sumeri air defense to engage—the aircraft as they passed.

En los aviones! Los aviones!
Nunca volveremos compadres . . .

Fuckers!

Royal Jahari Land Forces Headquarters, al Jahara, 12/2/461 AC

They'd found out, so they believed, where the dictator of Sumer was hiding. Thomas had delayed going after him immediately, pending legal review by his judge advocate general. This had taken long hours as the lawyers had argued back and forth about the propriety and legality of assassination, the strategic implications, the public relations aspects. What did lawyers have to do with strategy and PR? In the Federated States Army there was *nothing* that lawyers were not intimately involved with.

Too, Thomas had not wanted to appear indecisive or at the mercy of his JAG section. So he had kept mum, pending their review and approval. This had never actually come, as the JAG section itself was evenly split on the issue. Thomas had therefore bucked the decision up to Campos who had thrown a fit that the dictator wasn't already dead. "Awful shock" readily became "Awe shucks."

It was then that Thomas moved up D-Day by twenty-four hours. This gave just enough time for his own troops in al Jahara to move to their assault positions and for his aircraft to send stealthy birds with two thousand pound GLS guided bombs winging their way towards the implicated palace.

Unfortunately, it also gave time for the dictator to change palaces as was his habit.

As unfortunately, or even more so, it did not give Parilla and Carrera time to call back the two Nabakov-23 Dodos carrying seventy-six airborne Cazadors before the planes went low behind a series of mountains and the Cazadors had jumped.

INTERLUDE

14 May, 2070, Brussels, Belgium

Money was always tight in the EU and among its member states. The only place to find it was to raise taxes (and, with the various levels of government already confiscating over sixty percent of GDP, those were already onerous and rather unpopular) or to reduce military expenditures (and at less than one percent of GDP those were already anemic and *still* rather unpopular). Only if the construction of ships could be made in the guise of social welfare legislation would there be easy acquiescence.

The United States helped quite a bit, if not with money then with free technology transfers. This was actually critical as, in this year-of-something-other-than-Our-Lord, 2070, Europe was a technological backwater. Even with the money found, or looted, the expertise simply didn't exist anymore. So many of the highly talented had left for other climes, most notably and infuriatingly for the United States, that the Old World had fallen far behind.

Between the shunting of social welfare funds to

starship construction and the technology transfers from the U.S., the EU did manage to put together a half a dozen ships. These were duly turned over to the United Nations in theory, though in practice they remained for the time being under absolute EU control.

And then the screws began to tighten. With a means of getting rid of their undesirables in hand without at the same time strengthening the Unites States, EU bureaucrats and their police minions began identifying those who most needed to go, and those they least wanted to go to the United States. No one was forced out initially; that would have been inhumane. Instead, a letter would arrive in the mail stating that "pursuant to new austerity measures X and such, you and your family will no longer be receiving any support from the government and would you please consider subsidized emigration to the new world?"

Riots ensued, of course, especially in Muslim majority or near majority states like France, the Netherlands, Belgium and Spain. This did nothing to keep the transfer payments to the indigent flowing. After all, what did hard-working, tax-paying Poland or Sweden care what happened to France or Belgium? If anything, the resulting destruction of infrastructure within the Muslim majority areas speeded up the rate at which Moslems proved willing to leave. (As an exception, Sweden did offer to make some tax transfers, but only on condition that *their* Muslims be among the first to go.)

Young Europeans were an issue. They were valuable. How else was the social welfare state to be maintained without their tax receipts? On the other hand, how were they to be kept when the more politically and economically free states on Earth—the U.S., UK,

Brazil, India, Australia and South Africa—acted as talent and willingness-to-work magnets?

The answer to that was border and emigration control. Much as had the Soviet Union decades before and much as in Cuba, still, attempting to emigrate, except as permitted by the bureaucracy of the EU, became an antisocial crime with severe penalties, both formal and informal. The reduction of the Muslim populations, coupled with the gradual deIslamicization of Europe, helped there.

CHAPTER EIGHTEEN

From our enemies we can defend ourselves but God
save us from our friends.

—Lenin

UEPF *Spirit of Peace*,
Earth Date 2 December, 2513

High Admiral Robinson had never really anticipated
the headaches that came now with increasing frequency
and never seemed entirely to go away. He wondered,
sometimes, if they were guilt driven. Certainly the
images of the people jumping to their deaths stuck
with him in much the same way as the headaches.

*And while Mustafa's people did the necessary recon-
naissance and flew the airships, I was the one who did
the structural analysis that said the buildings would
fall once the fire weakened their steel supports. I just
never imagined that I would actually see people die.
It was harder than I would have thought even if I
had considered it.*

That was one headache: guilt. He had others.

I'd thought that once the FSC invaded Pashtia they'd end up in an endless, sticky quagmire, the same way the Volgans did twenty-two local years ago. Whoever would have suspected that they'd topple the place in under a month? Whoever would have thought that they'd do it so cheaply. I'd wanted a war that would tie them up and use up their wealth so they couldn't use it to get rid of us and later attack Earth. I'd wanted a failure that would undermine their nation-state system and leave useful idiots like Wiglan in charge. Instead, this affair has seen people like Unni marginalized and the nation-state, or at least the FSC, more powerful than ever.

Did I make a mistake, helping Mustafa? Did I make an irreparable mistake?

Robinson thought about that one for a bit. Finally, he came to the conclusion, *No. It wasn't a mistake. Mustafa would have gone ahead anyway. And the result would have been the same. All I could have done was warn the FSC of what was coming and that I could never do.*

Never.

The high admiral stood and began to pace the close confines of his office, still lost in his thoughts.

I simply overestimated the ability of Mustafa's people and his allies to confront the FSC. That, and I apparently badly underestimated the ability of the FSC to impose its will through force. They're even more dangerous than I had thought they were. So, no, it wasn't a mistake to start down this road. It had to be done. What was a mistake was to think I could start down it without going all the way. The FSC must be involved in a wider war, one that disenchants its allies, dries up its treasure, kills its soldiers and demoralizes its people.

Now what do I have to do to make that *happen?*

Robinson ceased his pacing and resumed his chair.

"Computer, view screen on. Show me a map of Terra Nova, one annotated with population density, industrialization and resources."

The Kurosawa came to life. Not for the first time, Robinson wondered if the difference in the quality of the picture was the result of wear and tear on the ancient, Earth-produced, screens or if—awful thought—the Terra Novans had actually exceeded Earth's technology in this one field.

It really is an excellent picture, though, he thought. *Pity that the map tells me little.*

"Computer, add major historical events for the last sixty years."

Still nothing; too crowded.

"Computer, reduce detail to show major conflicts."

"Ah, there it is," Robinson said aloud. "Before I arrived to assume command. The Petro War."

"Computer, get me all pertinent data on the FSC-Republic of Sumer War of local year 447 plus developments in that region since then."

Atlantis Base, Earth Year 7 December, 2513

The high admiral met the Tauran Union's commissioner for culture in a little used but meticulously maintained garden not far from the island base's single major river. The garden itself was kept up by the same crew of proles brought in from Earth as servants to the families of the Class Ones, Twos and Threes that made up the bulk of the fleet's crew and the base personnel. Wiglan never saw the proles, of course. It was part of their job to be as little seen, as little noticed, as possible.

"So good of you to come, Unni, and on such short notice."

"Always a pleasure," answered Wiglan sincerely. Then, seeing the worried look on Robinson's face, she announced, "There is something troubling you."

"Yes. Yes there is, my dear. Silly of me to think I could hide it from *you*."

Silly of me to think I had to make an effort to look worried.

"Well, what is it then, Martin?"

"The war, of course. Terrible thing. All those poor civilians caught up in the FSC's imperialist games."

Never mind that previously they were caught up in bloodthirsty and fanatical Salafi and Fascist games.

"Oh, I *know*," Unni fumed. "By what right does the FSC think it can impose its will on others. Only the World League and United Earth have that kind of moral authority."

"Exactly, Love. I knew you would understánd." *Nothing.* "Tell me, is the TU going to go through with providing forces for this venture?"

"I've argued against it, Martin. All of us right thinking people have. But the TU still hasn't quite extirpated national sovereignty even in Taurus. And some of the new member states especially, the ones that think the FSC was somehow responsible for liberating them from the Volgans, are going to go along. Even Gaul and Sachsen are planning on sending some troops, though we hope to limit their rules of engagement so that they are ineffective. And," she finished with a disgusted sigh, "the Anglian lackeys of the FSC will give their full support, almost as if they were a state of the Federals themselves."

I don't suppose it would ever occur to you, Unni, that Anglia's permitting the FSC to set its foreign policy, to the extent it does, is not in principle different from any state of the TU allowing the TU to set foreign policy? You cannot logically, in principle, complain about a state giving a portion of its sovereignty to another entity and then insist that it should give it to you instead.

But then, logic is not your strong suit, is it?

"What's done is done, Unni. No sense crying over it or wishing to undo it. What concerns me more is the FSC's next step."

"You really think they won't be content with knocking out Pashtia, Martin?" The commissioner looked rather horrified.

"I am certain they won't," Robinson answered. "When you have a rogue state running free there is no limit to the damage it can do."

Wiglan agreed, her head nodding slowly, sadly and silently. "And they simply refuse to take us as their equal, either," she added.

"Unni, I am not sure that the FSC considers even the UE to be quite their equal."

And there's another repetitive thought to give me indigestion; three hundred highly militarized million of the FSC lording it over half a billion sheep on Earth and the fifty million in Class Three or higher reduced to penury or worse.

While Unni knew it was likely true that the FSC held even the UE in contempt, she was sickened to hear a major figure from the mighty UE admit to it openly. She gave a gasp of horror, her hand flying to her mouth of its own accord.

"That's . . . that's *terrible*. How can they . . ."

"They can because they have us stymied, Commissioner. We can't do anything to them because they would do the same or worse right back to us. I'd be willing to sacrifice my fleet and, of course, myself in the cause of peace but when I consider the environmental damage . . ." He meant, of course, "nuclear winter." *It's amazing how the local progressives can accept the concepts of humanocentric planetary warming and nuclear winter at the same time.*

They should see that, even if true, the one is the cure for the other. Oh, well, not my job to educate them.

"Oh, my brave and selfless High Admiral, I know you would," Wiglan nearly swooned.

Robinson made a minor show of looking very brave and very selfless.

"This is especially bad," Robinson continued, "in that I am certain that the FSC intends once again to attack Sumer. I do *so* hope, Unni, that you and right thinking people like you will be able to keep the Tauran Union's hands clean in this filthy business."

"Many will participate no matter what the TU says," Wiglan muttered. *And I feel so* terrible *about it, too.*

"Then, Unni, you must do whatever it takes, not just you but your colleagues as well, to ensure that such participation is minimal and that whatever there may be along those lines turns out to be more albatross than ally."

High Admiral's Conference Room,
UEPF *Spirit of Freedom*,
Earth Date 5 January, 2514

"All told, Admiral Robinson, the FSC can muster nearly twenty-four divisions' worth of troops. That's counting their militia organizations, which are considerably better trained, organized and led than the usual militia down below, their Regular Army and the Federated States Marine Corps."

Robinson regarded his strategic intelligence officer, a Class Two named Henkin, bleakly. All of Earth could not muster half of that, and those would be underequipped and badly trained. His own few battalions' worth of security troops hardly counted on that scale.

Seeing the admiral's bleak look, the strategic intelligence analyst hastened to add, "But not all of those are useable, few can be logistically supported in the theater of war you believe the Federated States is contemplating, and almost forty percent are part time militia, not particularly suitable for either a short and intense war or a long drawn-out, low-intensity one."

"That hardly matters, Henkin," answered the fleet's tactical intelligence officer, Commander Spiro, as he tapped a pen on the table. "The Sumeris are rotten, even more rotten—and far less well equipped—than they were the last time. Four divisions of FSC troops—five, tops—plus maybe one from Anglia, would be more than enough to knock them over. I think they could do it with three, myself."

"I don't disagree about needing only three or four

divisions for a successful invasion," Henkin admitted. "We could quibble over the number but why bother? It is afterwards that they'll need more troops, not just to wreck and defeat a fairly worthless army but to control a fairly numerous people. And *there* is where they'll have problems. Those roughly twenty-four divisions you mentioned are the equivalent of fifteen regular and nine militia. The fifteen regular can be counted on to sustain at most five divisions fighting. The militia's nine might give one division's worth, or perhaps one and a half, on continuous deployment. That's a total of *six* to six and a half useable divisions. Of those, one will continue to be needed in Pashtia. And Spiro, Admiral . . . five will not be enough."

"So you think, then, that the FSC will *not* invade, Henkin?" Robinson asked.

Henkin's face was set and sure. "They have the same data I do, Admiral. Perhaps they have better data. I don't see how they would unless they somehow felt they absolutely had to. Yes, I say this even though a lodgment in Sumer gives them access to major oil fields in every direction. The risk is simply too great."

"I wonder what would make them feel they absolutely *had* to," wondered the Admiral, idly.

Atlantis Base, Earth Date 17 May, 2514

"It's the only way I can see, Unni, to prevent this war. The FSC must be convinced that the Republic of Sumer has nuclear, chemical and biological weapons. Otherwise, the Federals are certain to invade."

"But do they have those weapons, Martin?"

"My people think they might," Robinson answered, truthfully. Indeed, the Republic of Sumer might also have time travel and the fountain of youth, though both seemed about as unlikely. There was no reason to burden the commissioner with doubts, however, or none that the high admiral could see.

"They might," he repeated, "and the dangers of letting that particular genie out of the bottle are too great not to do everything in our power to prevent even what 'might' happen."

"I see that," Wiglan agreed, though she really didn't. "But what can *I* do? I'm just the commissioner for culture; I'm not in one of the military or intelligence branches of the TU."

"You know many people who are in those branches though, don't you, Unni? You have access to them, and through them to national intelligence services."

"Yes," she agreed. "I know them . . . at least slightly, I do. You understand that we in the . . . softer services have as little to do with the military and intelligence as possible."

"Yes, Unni," Robinson answered, "and that is, normally, proper. But in this one case—"

"I'll do it," she burst out. "For you and peace and the eventual creation of true global governance, I'll do it."

EXCURSUS

From *Baen's Encyclopedia of New and Old Earth*, Old Earth Edition of 2497 (442 AC)

Freedom of Speech: This entry has been declared unfit for human knowledge by the United Earth Council for the Suppression of Hate Speech.

Freedom of Religion: This entry had been declared unfit for human knowledge by the United Earth Plenary Committee for the Advancement of Human Knowledge. See, instead, the entries on Marxism, Islam, Environmentalism, Druidism, Pan-Gaeaism . . .

Nation: This entry has been ordered expunged by decree of the International Criminal Court and legislatively confirmed by the General Assembly of United Earth. Further, this word has been declared obsolete and ordered removed and expunged from all public references, dictionaries, encyclopediae, textbooks, literary works, monuments, buildings, archeological sites, public records . . .

Weapons: This entry had been restricted to members of the UE Peace Force and holders of informational clearances above the Deputy Assistant Directorial level.

Liberty, Human concepts of: This entry has been ordered expunged as redundant. See instead the entries on Freedom from Want and Freedom from Fear.

Electricity Production: This entry has been ordered restricted to members of the United Earth Organization, Class Three and above.

Artificial Intelligence and Computers: The entry has been ordered restricted to members of the United Earth Organization, Class Three and above.

Ownership and property, concepts of: This entry has been declared obsolete and ordered expunged. See instead the entry on "Socialism and Justice."

Sovereignty: The entry has been ordered expunged by the High Commission for Semantics and Decency.

Taxation: This entry has become obsolete with the passage of the Act for the Creation of a Rational Economy, also known as the Collectivization Act of 2257.

Great Global War (Also known as "the Long Night"), History of:

An eleven year (399-410 AC) world conflict on the planet of Terra Nova that began with the use of extensive formations of horse cavalry and ended with significant usage of nuclear weapons.

By the year 399 AC, Terra Novan military technology, along with broader industrialization, corresponded roughly to that of Old Earth in the years 1920-1929. With industrialization came considerable social turmoil, along with hardship as older, more established states found themselves in mercantile competition with newer, more aggressive powers.

There was no one spark that can definitively be said to have begun the GGW. Fighting among the powers of that world, especially those of the continent of Taurus, had been endemic since at least the beginning of the 3rd century, AC. While naval conflict had spread across the planet by roughly the middle of that century, in the 4th century, ground combat moved from the continent of Taurus, itself, out to the colonies, spheres of influence, and trading blocks that had been established across the world by the Taurans, the Yamato, the Zhong Guo and the Federated States of Columbia. Thus, when the Gallic Republic declared war on Sachsen in 399, it was merely the last step in a series of smaller conflicts and battles that had been waged between these two from approximately 250 AC onwards.

What made the war such a bloodbath—indeed total deaths from all causes approached the two hundred million mark before the war closed—were the systems of alliances, some of them secret and a few mutu... exclusive and contradictory, which the major Tauran powers had bound themselves to in the preceding fifty years. Hence, in initiating its abortive invasion of Sachsen in 399, the Gallic Republic also immediately found itself at war with the Kingdom of Anglia. This relieved pressure on the Sachsens, but at the cost of the Gauls invoking their treaty with the Volgan Empire, which set in motion a Volgan invasion of Sachsen and its ally, Karinthia. Yamato, at that time an ally of the Volgans, likewise launched an attack in conjunction with Gaul upon the Sachsen and Anglian enclaves along the Zhong coast.

This early, strategically and tactically mobile, phase ended within two months as a combination of defensive technology—ranging from shovels and barbed wire at one end to artillery and machine guns on the other—combined with limitations in offensive technology, such as communications and transportation, and *severe* limits in logistics, bogged virtually every major combatant down in what would eventually become very extensive systems of field fortifications. Of course, as the fortifications became more extensive, the logistic requirements of breaking them grew still further. Moreover, those requirements grew much faster, initially, than did the means of meeting them. This phase lasted approximately two years.

The next phase, also lasting two years, found the Gauls defeated and occupied by a combination of Anglian naval blockade and amphibious invasion with Sachsen ground attack. This left Sachsen to turn its land power against the Volgans while the Kingdom of Anglia moved at sea against Yamato.

Both the Volgans and the Imperial Yamato Fleet proved much tougher customers than had been expected. The first Anglian Fleet met, and was essentially destroyed by, the IYN in the Battle of the Shujimo Straits in 403. The Sachsens, on the other hand, while initially successful against Volga, soon found that the sheer strategic depth of that empire was more than their slender logistic arrangements could well deal with. Worse, as a Sachsen general of the day observed, "What matter that we kill three or four Volgans for one of ours when there are five Volgans for every one of ours?" By 405 the Sachsens were stymied and Volga on the counterattack.

It was at this time that Tsar Vladimir Ilyich III dusted off an old and discredited political and economic philosophy from Earth and imposed it on his people in the interests of furthering the war effort. Peasants, previously freed by the tsar's grandfather, found themselves once again bound to the land as de facto serfs. Industrial workers likewise were organized and a vast array of repressive measures, backed up by an extensive secret police apparatus, were imposed.

The destruction of the Anglian power at Shujimo Straits had the side effect of radically transforming the balance of naval power in the *Mar Furioso*. Moreover, with both the Gallic and Anglian fleets out of business the Federated States was able to gather its not inconsiderable fleet in from the two oceans into which it had previously been split and concentrate it to face Yamato. This was eased by the possession, on the part of the FSC, of the Balboa Transitway, which linked the two oceans and allowed rapid redeployment. Potential threat led to tensions; tensions led to war between Yamato and the Federated States.

In this Yamato was initially frightfully successful, dealing as harshly with the FSN as they had earlier with the Anglians. Where Yamato miscalculated, however, was in confusing another island state, Anglia, which could not readily replace its fleet, with a continent-spanning empire like the FSC, which could. By 406 the Federated States was on the attack as much as were the Volgans.

The final phase of the war saw Sachsen, Anglian and Federated States troops holding a line against the Volgans across central Sachsen while the FSN approached the home islands of the Empire of Yamato. Two nuclear weapons, newly developed, were used against Yamato in an attempt to compel its surrender. The United Earth Peace Fleet likewise bombed—using rather larger, albeit much cleaner, nuclear weapons— two cities in the Federated States, San Fernando and Botulph, and threatened further bombings if nuclear weapons were again used.

Fearing nuclear destruction, the Federated States instead imposed a complete naval blockade against Yamato, while continuing mass bombing with conventional high explosives and incendiaries. It is estimated that thirty million civilians either were killed by the bombing, or starved to death, or died to disease or weather as a result of starvation-induced weakness, before that empire agreed to unconditional surrender.

Following the surrender of the Empire of Yamato, a peace treaty was negotiated between the Volgan Empire and the allied states of Sachsen, Anglia and the FSC. This peace treaty left in place the military lines existing as of 410 AC.

PART IV

CHAPTER NINETEEN

Artillery conquers and infantry occupies.

—J.F.C. Fuller

Drop Zone Hotel, southern Sumer, 0111 hours, 13/2/461 AC

Three times the green light had come on and three times a stick of seven to nine men had stood up, hooked up, and shuffled out the door of the stealthy Dodo. With each lightening of the plane Sergeant Robles had felt a corresponding sinking of his spirits.

As the others had jumped, Robles' squad had slid their posteriors down the folding troop seats lining both sides of the plane to get nearer the single, left side door. The Dodo had a ramp that could have been used but lowering it tended to destroy the stealthy characteristics added by Zion.

Robles and his Cazadors held their static lines carefully in their right hands as they slid. They hadn't bothered with reserve chutes. The jump was going to be at three hundred and fifty feet above ground level. By the time a trooper realized his main had failed and pulled the ripcord for the reserve he would already have joined molecules in a sort of disassociated way with the snow, dirt, grass and rocks below.

At the rear of the cargo compartment the crew chief ordered, "Stand up!" No one heard a thing, of course, over the roar of the engines. It didn't matter; the chief made a hand and arm motion that the men could see well enough and that got them to their feet.

"Hook up!" They didn't hear that either but saw the chief making the *hook up* motion with his right hand. They followed along.

"Stand in the door," the chief mouthed before using his hands to show the first jumper exactly where he wanted him. The men shuffled forward. Robles, in the lead, let go his static line and stood, left foot forward, with hands grasping either side of the door that was left open to the air.

Robles almost lost his footing as the plane lurched upward to crest a ridgeline and then dove downward several hundred feet.

The red light at the rear turned green. The crew chief slapped Robles' butt. The sergeant used his bent legs to propel him up and out. Once outside and past the plane's slipstream he fell and fell. There was a minor shock as the static line deployed the chute followed by a major one as the chute filled with air. In the dim and diffuse moonlight that filtered through the cloud cover overhead Robles saw other chutes deploying.

Then he saw tracers rising from the ground to try to meet the aircraft.

"Chingada," he whispered to himself. *Something tipped them off that we were coming.*

Command Post, Mangesh, 0121 hours, 13/2/461 AC

"Dodos A and B both report that their teams are inserted, sirs. Dodo B says it took fire on its last drop and that we must assume the team is compromised."

"What can we do, Patricio?" Parilla asked.

"Not a goddamned thing! Son of a bitch, Thomas."

"Do we have radio contact with the last team?" Carrera demanded of Soult, hovering over the bank of radios in the command post.

"Nothing, sir."

"What would you do if we did have radio contact?" Parilla enquired.

"Give them some artillery," Carrera answered. "Send in four of the Crickets to try to extract them. Air support. Whatever it took."

"Can we move up the attack?"

"No. Rather, we could, and then lose half the effect of the artillery—which depends on *timing*—and lose fifty more men, or five hundred, assaulting up the ridge."

"Chingada. So they're really on their own. Shit."

Hill 1647, 0337 hours, 13/2/461 AC

Robles cursed his luck, cursed the Sumeris, and cursed Parilla and Carrera, too. His ribs hurt; he thought some of them were broken. The rope tied around his neck burned where the Sumeris had pulled to lead him and his men from the spot where his team had been ambushed, pinned and forced to surrender. A truck had driven the five remaining—two had been killed to Robles' certain knowledge and another man was missing and likely dead—to the top of the fortress on Hill 1647.

Then the beatings began. First just a beating, no questions. Then more beatings, interspersed with what sounded like questions. Robles' tongue poked at the places where the Sumeris had knocked some of his teeth out. Shock and endorphins kept the pain to a barely tolerable level.

Mukkaddam Ali al Tikriti cursed as well as he punched the current object of his attention for perhaps the fortieth time. He had no Spanish; neither did any of his men. All he could manage was a little English and none of his prisoners seemed to have any or were willing to admit it if they did. Still, useless effort or not, it felt good to strike at some of the men who were part of the attack to overthrow his clan and the country they ruled.

Fiends!

The Sumeri lieutenant colonel also cursed his lack of information. He knew that the attack, by air at least, had already begun in the south. Here, though, the enemy were generally quiet, even more so than usual. He knew from the Yezidi that they had earlier moved tanks to within a couple of kilometers of Hill 1647. Was it a show of force? A demonstration? Preparations for an attack? Ali didn't know. And he had to know. The brigade commander, who was also his uncle, had told him that higher headquarters had promised reinforcements and artillery support but

only if the Balboan troops attacked or he had positive
information that they would attack.

Ali reached down to pull Robles up by his hair.
"You tell!" he screamed at the young Balboan. In
answer, Robles spit a bloody wad onto the Sumeri's
uniform.

The enraged Sumeri pushed Robles back into the
grasp of a guard. "Kill the bastard. Slowly."

The guard pushed a stick into the loop of rope
around Robles' neck. Then he began to twist the
stick, tightening the rope. As his air was cut off by
the tightening, strangling cord Robles thrashed and
twisted. His struggles were in vain. Tongue bloated
and protruding, eyes bugging from his head, fingernails
broken and bleeding where he had scratched at the
earth and rocks in his last moments, Robles died.

Ali pulled another Balboan to the fire step and
pointed to the south. "Tell me," he screamed again.
Since this soldier had no more Arabic or English than
had Robles . . .

Command Post, Mangesh,
0427 hours, 13/2/461 AC

CLICK.

As the time of action neared Carrera grew cold
and calm. Parilla, on the other hand, and despite the
Chaldean brandy, only grew more nervous. Now *he*
paced from one side of the small basement room in
the Mangesh police fort to another.

Carrera looked up at him from the table he sat
behind. "Relax, Raul, it won't be too long now."

"How can you be so damn complacent, Patricio? This is a complex operation. A million and one things could go wrong."

Carrera stubbed out a cigarette. "You are confusing detailed planning with a complex problem, Raul. Really, the problem is very simple. We pound them silly with artillery and mortars, teaching them to stay under cover and moving up and breaching their obstacles while their heads are still down. Then we assault like ten thousand screaming maniacs across the top. The Cazador teams and RPVs spot for and call in artillery to seal off the fortresses on their far sides while the rifle cohorts do a detailed clearing of the hilltops. By the time they can put in a serious counterattack, if they ever can, we are dug in and ready to beat them bloody. It's really quite simple. Relax."

Parilla just shook his head and resumed his pacing, sipping occasionally at a cup filled with brandy.

"I want to go first, with the lead elements," Parilla announced.

"We've been over this before, Raul. Your place is here. *I* am going with the lead forces."

"No, Patricio. I am either in command or I am not. Oh, yes, yes, I *know* that practical command is yours. And I've been fine with that. Really, I have. You know what you are doing and I am a comparative amateur. But for this, *precisely* because you know what you are doing and the real doing of the thing will be here, you should stay here, or in the forward command post.

"On the other hand, I am able enough to do one thing. And that is to set the example by leading from in front. So no, my sometimes subordinate, this time *I* make the rule and my ruling is that I go first."

Parilla's face looked very determined. Carrera measured it and . . .

"You're sixty years old, Raul. *Can* you lead from in front?"

"I'm as fit as I ever was," Parilla insisted, then smiled wickedly. "And if you don't believe me just call home and ask my wife. Yes, friend, I am fit enough for this."

"Oh, all right then, you old fool," Carrera agreed with seeming bad grace. He lightened and smiled after a moment's reflection. "And I understand the need. You can lead. I'll stay with the forward CP at *Stollen* Number Three."

"And on that happy note . . . Jamey, bring around the vehicle. We're moving forward."

Stollen Number Two, 0458 hours, 13/2/461 AC

It was almost time for the artillery to let fly when Parilla and Carrera reached the line of *Stollen*. They separated, Parilla going to the first and second *Stollen* while Carrera went to give a few words of encouragement to the men sheltering in the third and fourth.

Parilla could smell the excitement, overlaid with fear, in the close confines of the *Stollen*. He could smell it even over the buckets filled with shit and piss that the men had used to relieve themselves for days on end, only venturing out to empty them when the sun was down and clouds covered the moons and the stars.

Parilla exuded confidence, as well he should have since he had—reluctantly—spent most of his adult life as a politician, albeit a uniformed one. He walked around the Stollen easily enough as the men had cleared spaces when they'd stowed their personal gear away for the coming assault.

The men stood in ranks around the edges of the concrete floor. Their faces were painted in whites and blacks, proper camouflage for snowy ground. They wore their white overgarments that had been made from bed sheets back in Balboa. The Helvetian helmets, painted white, gave them a satanic look. The rifles, machine guns and rocket and grenade launchers they gripped in their hands were clean and freshly oiled. The oil, too, lent an aroma to the closed confines of the *Stollen*.

The Sapper section for the 2nd Cohort carried a mix of equipment. There were three flamethrowers, several satchel charges, and a small plastic sled which contained a rocket-propelled mine clearing line charge, or MCLC. Many of the riflemen, too, carried engineering implements: grappling hooks on ropes, sections of bangalore, and still more satchel charges.

Parilla walked among the men, clapping a shoulder here, giving a kind word there, reaching out to pat a cheek or grasp and shake an earlobe when he recognized someone from the old days. Mostly, though, he just looked the men in the faces, his own face smiling with confidence as if to say, "We can do this."

After a few minutes, Parilla turned to go. The door to the *Stollen* opened letting in the crashing thunder of the artillery and mortars. He was about to leave but then suddenly turned back to the men.

"CAN WE DO THIS?" Parilla bellowed.

"Fuckin' A, we can, sir!"

"Goddamn right.".

With that shout ringing in his ears, Parilla emerged back into the darkness of the night. Overhead he heard the mixed drone of the legion's remotely piloted aircraft, fixed wing and small helicopters both, beating their way forward to the objective.

Forward Command Post, *Stollen* Number Three, 0503 hours, 13/2/461 AC

A small portion of the shelter had been marked off and partitioned with empty ammunition boxes to create a distinct command post.

Carrera glanced at his watch. "Almost showtime, boys and girls." He stood up from his field table and walked over to the Ic, the MI, desk in one corner of the bunker. "Report."

Fernandez stood up. "Sir, we have seven deep recon teams in position. The eighth is missing. I have had the *ala* redirect a Cricket to cover that sector and to look for sign of our men. Four RPVs and four remotely piloted helicopters are moving to the far side of the objective. We observe no noticeable change in posture on the objective. Some Sumeri artillery and mortars have been identified."

Carrera looked over at the Fire Support desk. The FSO volunteered, "From the Ic I have two batteries of guns, believed to be 122mm, and one of large caliber mortars. I have assigned one section each of multiple rocket launchers to the guns and the enemy heavy mortars. Countdown to time on target has begun. Communications are excellent. The Target Acquisition and Counterbattery Century is standing by."

Carrera paced to the Ia, or Operations, desk. Kennison just raised a thumb and smiled. Carrera gave the thumbs up signal as well. He studied the map for a few minutes then, nodding and placing his helmet on his head, and walked across the bunker to the exit.

As Carrera closed behind him the double tarp that kept light from escaping from the *Stollen*, he heard the FSO beginning the final ninety seconds countdown. To his left as he walked along the trench to his observation position he saw a bright flash light up the horizon. He stopped to watch as a few, and then dozens, of flashes joined the first. He didn't try to count them. He knew there would be nearly sixteen hundred shells and rockets sent toward Hill 1647 in the first minute of the bombardment. But still he stayed to watch as the muzzle blasts of ninety-seven guns, mortars, and rocket launchers lit the landscape like so many strobe lights. It was strangely beautiful.

In the Great Global War, at its beginning, I'd have needed three times the guns for the same effect. Shells have improved. Propellants burn cooler now so guns can fire more, faster. Gotta love the modern age.

Though I wonder how much more improvement is possible. The FSC and Taurans are, allegedly, working on liquid propellant guns; railguns, too, for that matter. Will I be able to afford them when they come out? Will I be able to not *afford them, when they come out?*

Hill 1647, 0505 hours, 13/2/461 AC

The feet of the last Balboan legionary drummed futilely against the floor of the trench as the Sumeri guard made a final twist to the rope around the dying man's neck. By the diffuse light of the moons overhead Ali watched the spectacle with enjoyment. He hadn't learned anything, but oh, how satisfying to see your enemies die like cockroaches. Better even than making a Yezidi husband watch while twenty of your men raped his wife and daughters.

After the last few feeble kicks of the legionary's feet, Ali turned his attention to something off to the southeast. There were flashes lighting up the overcast sky all across his field of view. *Fuck, guns, lots of them.* The sound hadn't reached him yet but he knew what was on the way. "Incoming!" he shouted and began to run to his own bunker. He was surprised that he made it before the first rounds hit. Then he realized that the very first rounds were passing over head.

Shit, they're going after the mortars and artillery first. This isn't just a punishment bombardment.

In his well-appointed personal bunker Ali picked up a field telephone to relay this insight to his uncle, the brigade commander, when the top of the hill was swept by fire. Even so far below, a wave of concussion slammed Ali against the wall of the dugout. When he realized, semi-stunned though he was, just how close that shell had been, and how *big*, he began to shake.

Forward trench outside Stollen Number Three, 0511 hours, 13/2/461 AC

Soult joined Carrera in the slit trench, taking shelter under the overhead cover Cheatham's engineers had thrown up. Together they watched the fireworks display. Four illumination shells hung almost motionless over the hilltop. A new one would burst into light seconds before the previous one burnt out.

"Why the illumination, Boss? To ruin their night vision?"

Carrera pulled his head back from the viewport he had been looking through. "Hmm? Oh. Partly that, but mostly to make them feel observed and helpless." He went back to the spectacle.

This was Soult's first real action. He felt the compulsion to talk; many new initiates to battle did. Carrera didn't mind. Indeed, he liked explaining. One never knew when a subordinate would have to make a decision on his own. The more they understood, the more likely that decision would be the right one.

"Do you think the artillery will kill them all, Boss?"

Carrera didn't turn away from his view when he answered. "The way they're dug in? Very few, actually. That's not the point."

"Huh? Then what's the point, sir?"

Carrera thought for a while before answering. He began his answer with a question. "Have you ever almost been killed, Jamey?"

Jamey smiled. "In Balboa? The way they drive? Of course."

"Were you driving an automatic or a stick?"

"A stick," Soult answered.

"Hmm. How long before you could drive away?"

Soult took a moment before answering. "Well, you know how it is. I was driving on a mountain road in the eastern part of the country. There were actually cliffs on *both* sides. I made a turn and there was a bus coming towards me and another car passing the bus. Narrow road, too. I slowed down just in time for the car to miss me, but I ended up going fifty plus miles an hour backwards. I'd have gone off the cliff altogether except that there were three skinny palms growing close together where I went off the edge of the road. They just barely stopped me. My leg was shaking so badly at first that I couldn't use the clutch. That lasted maybe a half an hour. Then, for about two hours, I giggled like a girl at escaping."

A tremendous explosion two hundred meters away rocked the two men. It was followed by a storm of shells impacting all around the entrenchment. Carrera and Soult ducked down low. After the storm lifted Carrera picked up the radio dedicated to fire support and listened momentarily. "That was theirs. The counterbattery people are already on it," he announced.

Soult laughed. "Just like a car wreck. I'm shaking now. I see your point, Boss."

"I'm not sure you do, Jamey. You were in one— almost—car wreck. *That* was just light shellstorm. What the people on top of that hill will be going through is the equivalent of a near fatal car wreck every minute or two for the next several hours. They'll be a very long time in laughing about it."

"So you mean to break their morale?"

"Some will break, I suppose. But you know, Jamey, in battle fear and fatigue are almost indistinguishable and *are* mutually interchangeable. Those men up there are going to be so repeatedly petrified that by the time they see the first of our boys they'll be too tired and too shaken with fear to so much as shoot straight.

"And besides that," Carrera finished, "I'm *training* them."

Hill 1647, 0608 hours, 13/2/461 AC

Twice the guns had lifted and twice Ali al Tikriti had ordered his battalion back into their trenches. Twice the guns had resumed fire with as much fury as before.

During the first lull in fire the Sumeri troops had moved briskly enough under the lashing tongues of their officers. The hill had come under heavy machine-gun fire but, moving below ground level, no men were hit as they took up their positions. Then, instead of the expected ground attack, after five minutes of steady machine gunning, the artillery had reopened. A number of men were hit before reaching the safety of the dugouts. The Sumeris carried their wounded back with them.

Caught in the forward trench, Ali hadn't made it to his own bunker, but took shelter in one of the common ones.

A full thirty minutes further bombardment followed. Some of Ali's troops began a trembling that became uncontrollable whenever a shell landed close enough to rock the bunker. During the next break in fire the Sumeris hadn't moved quite so readily to the trenches. Many staggered as if drunk.

Ali and his officers and noncoms had to physically push some of them out of the bunkers.

When again the shells came in and the men had to run for shelter they did not bring their wounded back with them. Ali did see two men stop to pick up a bleeding man. They seemed to lack the strength to lift him and so he was left behind. The Sumeri lieutenant colonel was too busy running to a shelter himself to order them back. The wounded soldier lay where he fell, crying to his comrades not to leave him.

On the third lull, Ali's men wouldn't, couldn't, follow his order to man the trenches. Helpless and hopeless he sat with his back to the wall and waited for the shell that would kill them all. A shot rang out inside the bunker. Ali summoned the strength to turn his head. In the far corner of the bunker, by the light leaking in from the enemy's illumination shells, he saw a Sumeri sergeant with his rifle in his mouth. The back of his head was missing.

Forward trench outside *Stollen* Number Three, 0611 hours, 13/2/461 AC

"Call for you, sir," Soult said. "The Ia wants to move up the time for the assault. He says the RPVs showed no movement on the objective during the last lull."

Carrera considered. "Tell him no."

Soult looked questioningly.

"Like I said, I'm *training* them, Jamey. I want to teach the Sumeris a lesson, and establish a precedent. I don't want a massacre. If they are not pounded senseless the Sumeris will fight back; individually they're a tough and brave people. If they fight back to any effect, then the troops will kill damned near everything on the hill when they go in. That's the part they never teach in the law of land warfare courses: prisoners are almost never taken in a fiercely contested assault. On the other hand, if they don't resist, if they're too badly knocked around to resist, the boys will take prisoners."

"How bad is it up there, really?" Soult asked.

By way of indirect answer Carrera replied, "One or two percent of them will blow their own brains out rather than endure another minute of it. I'd call that bad enough."

"You figured this out on your own, Boss?"

"No . . . an artilleryman on Old Earth did . . . name of Bruechmueller."

Multichucha Ridge, 0700 hours, 13/2/461 AC

A three-man forward observer team equipped with a laser range finder *cum* target designator looked over the smoke-shrouded ridgeline to the north. The shells had stopped falling while the gun crews took some rest and allowed the barrels to cool. The mortars, light, medium and heavy, had extra barrels for the bombardment. These the crews changed, dropping the hot ones in the snow to cool down. This was also a longer than normal delay to ensure that the Sumeri leadership on the ridge would be able to beat and drive their men back to their bunkers. To aid the enemy in that, there were some armored vehicles, tanks and Ocelots both, moving into position on the valley floor.

"Poor bastards," said the sergeant in charge of the team, watching the Sumeris listlessly move back to position.

The sergeant was old line; the private new. They had somewhat different attitudes. The sergeant was more cop than killer; the soldier more—*much* more—killer than cop.

"Fuck 'em, Sarge," answered the private, looking through the eyepiece of the designator.

"You got target?" asked the sergeant.

"Easy. Let me know when to illuminate."

The sergeant took the radio microphone from the third, and junior, member of the team. "Zulu Five Whiskey Six Seven this is Zulu Five Whiskey Two Three, over."

The call was answered instantly. "Two Three this is Six Seven, go."

"Fire for effect, High Explosive Delay with Daredevil fuse. Target Alpha Oscar Zero Two One."

Again the radio crackled. "Roger. HEDD. Alpha Oscar Zero Two One. Stand by to illuminate . . . time of flight is thirty-nine, I repeat thirty-nine, seconds . . . shot, over."

The sergeant consulted his watch, counting off the time. When he reached thirty-three seconds he said, "Flash!" The private squeezed a trigger to send a narrow laser beam right at the bunker nearest the highway, continuing to hold the trigger down and the laser on the target until . . .

Hill 1647, 0701 hours, 13/2/461 AC

It was Robles who saved Ali's life.

The *mukkaddam* had been moving low along the trench when one of the heavy machine gun bunkers behind him simply disintegrated, tossing sandbags, wood, machinery, bodies and parts of bodies high into the air.

The blast had knocked Ali down, sending him rolling

end over end before slamming him into one wall of the octagonal trace trench.

Groggy and panicked, he'd risen and begun running as fast as he could through the zigzags his men had carved into the earth and rocks of the hill. He'd been heading, without really thinking about it, for the next bunker. There'd been a blinding flash of some kind of unseen light that stunned him further and left spots floating before his eyes. Thus he hadn't seen the Balboan bodies stretched out strangled and lifeless on the trench floor. He'd tripped over one and gone sprawling face-first down to the floor. At that precise moment another shell had struck the bunker, penetrating before exploding. The resultant demolition had ripped the bunker apart, sending—among other things—a large and jagged piece of construction steel whirring through the spot Ali had occupied just before he fell.

Now even more stunned, Ali looked up and into the rictus-smiling face of Sergeant Emmanuel Robles, late of the *Legio del Cid.* The sergeant's open eyes seemed to be staring at Ali with deepest disapproval.

Stumbling and screaming, Ali turned around once again. Halfway back to the first destroyed bunker he came to a communication trench. He recognized it as one he could use to return to his own bunker. He took the turn.

After becoming lost only once on the way, and this was understandable as the bombardment had changed the geography of the fortress more than a little, Ali found the door to his personal shelter. He opened the thick, hinged door and entered, leaving the door open behind him in his haste and his terror.

A whining, wailing sound came from under Ali's bunk. He looked to see his thirteen-year-old recreation boy cowering under the bed in absolute fright. The commander ignored the boy for the moment, rummaging around instead for a bottle of State-distilled whiskey. Finding it, he grasped the whiskey in one hand, then reached under the bed to pull the boy out by the hair with the other. He slapped the boy several times across the face, hard, to put an end to his sniveling.

Ali had lost control. Wanting something, anything, to make the terror go away, Ali broke open the whiskey bottle and took a long pull, followed by another. That helped but not quite enough. He needed to hurt something, to dominate something, since he and his command were being so thoroughly dominated by their attackers.

He put one hand on the boy's shoulder to force him down. Instead of dropping though, the wide-eyed child just shook his head, pleading. Ali was having none of that. He backhanded the boy across the bunker then followed him, reaching down to pull him up to his knees. Then he dragged the boy, still on his knees, across the bunker to his chair. Ali sat down and took another pull of his bottle before setting it down. Then he opened his belt to let his penis spring out at a forty-five degree angle. He pointed to show his boy what he wanted done but the boy just shook his head again in panicked refusal. Again, this time holding him by the hair so he wouldn't escape, Ali slapped the boy half senseless and forced his head down.

Bunker Meem Thalata (M3), Hill 1647, 0708 hours, 13/2/461 AC

Sergeant Mohammad Sabah's mother didn't raise any fools. He'd felt the destruction of bunker M1 and even managed to catch sight of the debris falling to earth. Then he'd actually *seen* M2 disintegrate. That was enough. Shooting like that did not just happen. Someone was using guided shells and systematically destroying the forward bunkers.

Sabah made the not unreasonable connection between remaining on M3 and his own untimely demise. Since remaining on the hill—period—was also likely to be life threatening and trying to get off the hill by going north would only get him shot, or worse, by his own side, he opted to head *toward* the enemy rather than away. There was a little depression a few hundred meters forward that he knew of.

"Follow me," he said to men, taking his machine gun, one corporal, and three privates. "We'll hide forward."

Maybe we can surrender, Sabah thought. *After all, we haven't done the enemy any harm, personally.*

Led by Sabah, the five Sumeris slipped over the trench and began working their way down the steep slope of the hill.

Stollen Number One, 0735 hours, 13/2/461 AC

A piper standing outside the *Stollen* played "*Boinas Azules Cruzan la Frontera*" (Blue Bonnets over the

Border) as an Ocelot bearing a long, narrow footbridge passed by. Cruz and his fire team emerged from the shelter. Some of the men who knew the new words began to sing along with the pipes:

> Many an eagle's wings
> Fly where the shellfire sings.
> Follow your crest that is famous in story.
> Stand and make ready then,
> Sons of the jungle glen.
> Fight for your legion, your God and
>   their glory.
> March, March, Principe Eugenio . . .

Perhaps they found it calming. Cruz didn't sing; he didn't feel the need to. Instead he watched. The bridge, he saw, was actually up in the air at about a forty-five degree angle, held in that position by ropes that ran to the rear of the vehicle. The bridge seemed to Cruz to be about one hundred feet long.

"Come on, shake it out!" shouted Cruz to his fire team. With his hands, he directed them to form a shallow wedge based on himself as the point man.

Right, he thought. *Maybe it doesn't make sense to take up a wide formation before we hit the footbridge, but it will make it easier to get the boys back into formation once we cross.*

Ahead the Ocelot stopped a scant two meters from the river bank. The track commander emerged from his hatch and crawled onto the rear deck. He looked across the river to make sure he had judged his spot well, then took out and swung a machete to cut the rope. The bridge hesitated briefly before plunging down to span the river. It bounced twice before finally settling. Then the sergeant dismounted to cut the footbridge loose from his vehicle's bow.

Off to the right another Ocelot approached the river bank, this one also bearing a footbridge on its prow.

The signifer for the century blew into his whistle, signaling the attack. Then he double-timed to the bridge and, without hesitation, began to cross. A shell came in, exploding on the near bank. The signifer was apparently unhurt as he increased his speed to get across the bridge.

"Come on, you assholes," Cruz shouted above the din. "The future's on the top of that hill. Follow me!"

As Cruz and his men began to cross, he chanced to look up at the hill ahead. It was—section by section— disappearing as the mortars switched from pounding it with explosives to dropping white phosphorus shells along a line on the slope to blind any of the Sumeris in the forward trace who might be still able and willing to fight.

Forward trench outside *Stollen* Number Three, 0736 hours, 13/2/461 AC

Carrera followed the progress of the men through his binoculars. He looked for Parilla, but in vain. The light was still too dim to make out individuals.

Still, up the slopes the flash of rifle and machine gun fire, punctuated by major blasts as the infantry and engineers chewed their way through the wire and mines, told the tale well enough.

The artillery and mortars suddenly switched targets, the 120mm mortars laying smoke just below the crest of both fortresses, while the artillery took to pounding targets farther back. The lighter, 60mm, mortars ceased fire as their crews packed up to begin the backbreaking trek to the slope to join their centuries once the hilltops were secured.

Now, Carrera thought, *if everyone is still following the plan* . . .

Ah, there they were, eight Turbo-Finch Avenger close air support aircraft and three Cricket recon birds winging in out of the rising sun. The Avengers formed circle a couple of kilometers to the east, taking turns to dive in and lace the fortresses with rocket and machine gun fire. Once, but only once, a light antiaircraft missile lurched up to attack the planes. All eight Avengers circling at the time had sensed the incoming missile and automatically spat out flares and chaff. The missile overcorrected and ended up ultimately crashing to the ground harmlessly.

And where are my Cazadors?

He needn't have worried. The four remaining centuries of Cazadors, borne on ten of the twelve medium lift helicopters, passed through above the highway by Multichucha Ridge and continued along it. As the choppers passed low between the fortresses atop Hill 1647 and its companion, door gunners blasted away more or less indiscriminately with machine guns. Once past, the choppers continued on. The Cazadors had a blocking position to take up farther to the north.

Slope of Hill 1647, 0745 hours, 13/2/461 AC

"Hah!" Parilla exulted as he forced his body up the hill, "Not bad for a man of almost sixty." *Even so, I wish to hell the slope ahead weren't too steep for tanks and tracks.*

Parilla was followed by a small guard from the Headquarters cohort, plus two radio-telephone operators. They were the poor slugs who had to hump the heavy radios up the hill so that Parilla could stay in communication with Carrera and the command post to the rear, as well as the infantry cohorts to the front.

The call, "Fire in the hole!" came frequently now as infantry and engineers dropped small charges to explode surface laid mines, or used bangalores to clear paths through buried belts of them. Some of the sappers dragged heavy sleds holding rocket-propelled mine clearing line charges. These, intended in most armies to replace bangalore torpedoes, had one major problem. Bangalores could be adjusted and assembled to suit the depth of the obstacle. The MCLC was one size fits all. Thus, while it took six bangalore sections of about one hundred and twenty pounds to clear two five-meter deep obstacle belts set sixty meters apart, a single MCLC, at about the same weight, could clear the first obstacle but would fall short of the second.

Fortunately for MCLC fanciers everywhere—most certainly to include engineer century commander Sam Cheatham—there was at least one broad belt of mines very near the base of the ridge. As the sappers and grunts blasted their way forward as fast as they could set a charge and duck, the more specialized engineers dragged their sleds forward, Cheatham cheering them on, ducking the flying rocks and metal as required. Their feet slipped on packed snow, and they cursed the entire way.

Parilla had to admire the engineers for their damned determination and grit. He stopped and took one arthritic knee—*Oh, that frigging* hurts—to watch as they reached the edge of the broad minefield with a MCLC.

Operation of the MCLC was simple It involved little more than removing a watertight plastic cover from the plastic sled, rotating a rocket assembly to point generally frontally, hooking up an electric connection and then running to cover. Once behind cover, the engineers merely hooked up a small generator, and *wheee*. At that point, electricity applied, the rocket took off downrange with a great deal of smoke and flame, dragging the line charge behind it. The line charge, roughly inch-thick demolition cord, set itself off after it had reached apogee and fallen to the ground. About a dozen antipersonnel mines went boom, in sympathy, when the shock wave reached them.

And then the grunts were on their feet, screaming like a thousand banshees, charging through the gap with blood in their eyes and bayonets fixed.

Main Supply Route Zeus, north of Hill 1647, Sumer, 0759 hours, 13/2/461 AC

Nineteen miles north of the twin hills, fifty odd vehicles of a Sumeri artillery battalion struggled in the dark along a winding road that led to the south. The trucks pulled behind them eighteen 122mm guns, generally

similar to those used by the legion. It was no surprise
that the guns were similar, both types had been built
by the Volgans and sold for hard, desperately needed,
cash. The guns represented the only artillery reserve
available to Ali al Tikriti's uncle, the Sumeri brigade
and regional commander.

If the guns could reach a position in range of the
hill before it was lost, there was a chance of breaking up any assault before it could reach the summit
and dig in. In time, even the shell-shocked Sumeri
defenders would recover. They'd recover, in fact, a
lot faster than their enemy could replace the shells
expended so far on the bombardment.

A few thousand feet above the battalion, unheard
over the roar of the trucks' diesel engines, a lone
Cricket observation aircraft circled in the clouds, dropping down from time to time to observe the winding
mountain road below.

The observer in the Cricket said to the pilot, "Oh,
God, I think I'm going to come just looking at this."

The pilot banked the aircraft over, took one look,
and whistled. "Oh, baby, oh, baby, oh, baby, oh."

The observer was still laughing when he used
the radio to call, "Zulu Lima X-ray Four Six this is
Tango Mike Uniform One Two. Fire for effect . . .
baby . . . over."

The radio crackled back. "Fire for effect . . . what's
this "baby" shit? Over."

"Four Six; One Two. I've got fifty, maybe sixty trucks
with a battalion of guns plodding up the highway
vicinity Target Alpha Oscar Four Five."

"Oh, baby."

❖   ❖   ❖

Far to the south, halfway from the hills to Hewlêr International Airport, the six heavy rocket launchers of the legion received the call for fire from the Cricket, Uniform One Two. Each of the launchers was capable of firing twelve 300mm rockets, bearing warheads of two hundred and thirty-five kilograms, to a range of seventy kilometers. At that range, the predictable error was under two hundred meters. Since the beaten zone of a full ripple launch was on the order of three quarters of a kilometer, square, per launcher, the dispersion was tactically insignificant.

Within four minutes from the Cricket's call, when the trucks dragging the artillery had moved perhaps five hundred meters, the area was deluged with something over fifty-one hundred two-kilogram bombs.

Two minutes after the last of the rockets had scattered its bomblets, the Cricket flew low and made a pass over the column to asses the damage. Not one of the broken, bleeding, burned or simply stunned men below even bothered to shoot at the plane.

"Oh, baby . . ."

Hill 1647, 0801 hours, 13/2/461 AC

All my life I just wanted to be a simple soldier, Parilla thought to himself as he struggled to force his armored torso up the slope while listening to the radio he held closely to his ear. *Hard to do in Balboa. Hard to do any place in the undeveloped world. All my life I was forced into politics, starting with the coup after the riots in '21 and continuing right up through when that bastard, Piña, tricked me into resigning from the force in '41. Nothing but goddamned politics. And now—finally—and thanks to you, Patricio, you gringo maniac, I get to be what I always wanted to be. Late is better than never.*

Yes, I don't have much to do. We planned and rehearsed the shit out of this. We trained back in Balboa for just this sort of thing. So I listen on the radio and provide a little moral support when I can. So what? At least I am here, a man among men, doing a man's job for once in my life.

Parilla looked up and to the right, where a legionary was carrying the gold eagle of the legion, the eagle shining bright atop its spiral carved staff. He felt a sudden warm glow. *My eagle, too. My legion, too.*

Mohammad Sabah saw the group of enemy soldiers struggling up the hill. He watched carefully, from behind a snow covered bush. *Do their faces look like they're in the mood for mayhem? Or might they be willing to . . .*

Sabah felt as much as saw the machine gunner push the muzzle through the bush that concealed them. He started to shout, "*Kif*," stop, but before he could even get the syllable out the gunner had fired.

Parilla felt the shock before he even heard the muzzle report. One bullet bounced off of one of the glassy metal plates on his chest. Two more, however, plowed into his torso, pushing aside the silk fibers of the armor and smashing meat and bone below. He went down, limp but still marginally conscious.

"It's all right," he whispered. "Better this than never knowing and always wondering what it was like . . ."

✧   ✧   ✧

"Allah curse you for a fool!" Sabah shouted at the machine gunner as his group came almost immediately under heavy sustained fire. He had no choice but to fight now. Maybe if he could hold the enemy off for a bit they might calm down and be inclined to mercy. Maybe.

The leader of Parilla's small guard force stared in momentary disbelief when he saw his *Dux* go down. Recovering, he gave the command: "Enemy in draw. Assault fire! Assault!" Leading the way, screaming, firing short bursts as they ran, the Balboans closed on the Sumeris.

The Sumeri sergeant was the first to fall. Under the legionaries' leaden hail the other members of the group were forced down into the depression in the slope. As the Balboans approached, the Sumeris threw down their arms and raised their hands in surrender. But, after seeing their commander shot, the men were not interested in taking prisoners. Muzzles spoke and bayonets flashed red under the snow-reflected light.

Several hundred meters to the west, and about one hundred and fifty forward, the recon section of Cruz's cohort, the First Infantry, reached the "lift fires" line. The cohort commander called that in via radio. Mortars ceased fire on that section of the hill altogether. The recon section took their bayonets from their rifles and the scabbards from their belts, attached the two together to form wire cutters, and began gnawing their way through the last wire before the enemy trenches and bunkers began. Other groups, straight infantry and the cohort sapper section, did so as well as they reached the last obstacle on the hill.

Hill 1647, Ali's bunker, 0811 hours, 13/2/461 AC

Ali al Tikriti, worn out as he was, still noticed the change in fires. The boy had crawled under Ali's bed for shelter again and lay there whimpering.

"Shut up, you little worm," Ali commanded. He reached for the field telephone on his desk and picked it up. Listening for a few moments to the empty sound, he turned a crank to ring the other phones on the system. No one answered.

Without the enemy artillery coming in, and even as exhausted by fear as he was, Ali felt confident enough to leave his bunker. He forced himself to his feet and left via the dog-leg that led to the communication trench. There was rifle fire to the south, and close.

Ali found his battalion's senior sergeant, along with about fifty soldiers, cowering in a bunker. He began trying to herd the troops out and into the trenches. The men stood up, staggering and swaying as their twitching hands fumbled with their rifles and machine guns. They did not, however, take so much as a single step to move forward. When Ali ordered the senior sergeant present to get the men moving, the noncom just stared at him without comprehension, not so much shell-shocked as shell-induced-fear-exhausted. The *mukkaddam* used both arms to physically turn the older NCO around and push him through the bunker entrance. Then he pushed the rest of the men, one by one, after him. Ali, himself, took up the rear.

The sergeant stumbled down the trench without really seeing it. He almost, but not quite, sensed a series of shadows leaping over it, above him. One or two of the shadows dropped something in the trench at the sergeant's feet. Grenades.

With the explosions ahead the Sumeri troops scampered back to their bunker. Ali ran back to his own.

There was little firing and most of that seemed to be friendly to the signifer in charge of Second Century, Second Cohort. Indeed, the war pipes scattered across the face of the hill were louder than the firing. Even so, there was no sense in taking chances. The officer gave the signal to begin the clearing of the trenches. The century got down and began a wholly unnecessary fire at the top of the trench ahead of them. In the center of the century the signifer and half of one section crawled up to within a few meters of the trench. A half dozen grenades made sure there were no living Sumeris waiting for them. Then they slithered on their bellies over the lip and down. The signifer landed across the inert legs of Sergeant Robles.

It took the officer a few moment to realize that he had landed on a body. A brief moment of horror followed as he noticed the small modified Balboan flag—red, white and blue with a gold-embroidered eagle—sewn to the corpse's sleeve. "Shit, we killed them."

"No, sir," answered a corporal. He fingered the rope twisted around and cutting into Robles' neck. "The fuckers murdered them."

The signifer took stock of the scene. There were five bodies, it seemed, all partially covered with dirt thrown up by the shelling. He and the corporal brushed away at the dirt until they could see that each man showed obvious signs of having been garroted.

The other men of the century, waiting at the ready, grew impatient when his signifer didn't signal the rest of the century forward. Then the man's head popped over the side of the trench, signaling the rest to come into the trench as rehearsed. When the first man in dropped down to the trench floor, the signifer stopped him.

"See that, Sergeant?"

The sergeant looked for a moment in the dim light, before exclaiming, "Jesus!"

"That's right. It's our lost recon team. The cock-sucking Sumeris strangled them. So pass the word to your men. No prisoners."

Forward Trench, *Stollen* Number Three, 0816 hours, 13/2/461 AC

Carrera did three things when he heard that Parilla had been hit. First, he radioed to make sure one of the Crickets configured for medical evacuation, or "Dustoff," was en route. Second, he called for an Ocelot to pick him up and take him up the hill as far as it could go. Lastly, he cursed up a storm that his friend and comrade had been hit.

He needn't have worried about the dustoff. The legion's medical century already had a conveyor belt operation ongoing, whereby the Crickets landed near the bridge over the river. From that point, they were physically turned around into the wind and flew the most severe of the casualties directly to the Aid

Station. From there the hurt men could be triaged and evacuated further south to the 731st Airborne's more completely equipped facilities. Less badly hit men were evacuated by ground; the bridge was safe for transit now. There had been relatively few casualties, in any case, so the evacuation capabilities being exercised were more than actually needed.

The Ocelot arrived and picked up Carrera, Soult and one radio. It then sped past the dustoff point, to the bridge, crossed that and cut sharply to parallel the base of Hill 1647. Then began a tortuous climb, zigging and zagging up the uneven slope through the breaches in wire and mines. About a third of the way up Carrera spotted four men carrying a stretcher. A fifth, wearing a medical armband and holding a transparent plastic bag overhead, walked beside. Carrera directed the track commander for the Ocelot over.

It was Parilla, alive but barely conscious. Carrera jumped down from the track and ran to stand beside his friend and nominal commander.

Carrera took one look and shouted, "Jamey, call the CP. I want a dustoff bird *there*"—he pointed at a spot a few hundred meters down the slope—"now. If I don't get it, people will die . . . and I don't mean just the wounded."

The medic spoke up, "I shot him up with morphiate, Legate. We've stopped the bleeding, but he lost a lot of blood before we could." The medic's glance went significantly to the plastic bag and down the tube that led from it to a vein in Parilla's neck. "One lung's collapsed but I sealed it off . . . the entrance wound I mean. I think he'll make it but we have to get him to a surgeon quick."

"Five minutes, Boss," Soult shouted over the rumble of the idling Ocelot's engine.

Parilla stirred. "Sorry . . . I got . . . hit . . . Patricio."

"Never mind that, Raul. A good commander leads from in front. You're good, friend."

"Thanks . . . *compadre*. You need to . . . get up top, now . . . I think."

"You take good care of him, Doc. We need him back on his feet, soonest."

Then, patting Parilla's shoulder very gently, Carrera climbed aboard the track and directed it upward. As the track reached the top of the trail it slowed down to allow the passengers to jump off. Carrera looked up after landing and saw a Balboan machine gunner blasting away at an improvised white flag sticking out of a bunker. A flame-thrower team moved to a vantage point facing the bunker. A tongue of flame licked out, pouring fire into the entrance. Inside, men screamed like small children, burning alive.

Furious, Carrera stormed over to where a Balboan signifer crouched. "What the hell is the meaning of this?"

The junior said nothing, but pointed down into the trench behind him. Carrera and Soult gazed down at the bodies of Robles and his men.

Carrera remembered something Sitnikov had once spoken of, back in Balboa. *Pashtia started like that,* the Volgan had said. *We didn't go in there trying to kill everything that lived. Hell, we went in as libera-tors. But one day two young troops from my battalion came up missing after a patrol. We found them, days later, about a kilometer from our base camp. Their hands were bound, eyes gouged out. They'd been castrated and had their throats cut. Not knowing the guilty parties, higher headquarters wouldn't permit retaliation. Can't say I blame them. But the troops retaliated on their own, anyway. I can't blame them, either. Then the Pashtun hit back, raiding a hospital and slaughtering the wounded. Soon enough, atrocity became established policy on both sides.*

Carrera pondered for all of five seconds before telling Soult, "Give me the radio." Then he made a call to the entire command net.

"This is Legate Carrera. *Duce* Parilla has been wounded but is expected to live. I am in command. On Hill 1647 we have found that the enemy has murdered five of our men. I am, therefore, and in accordance with the laws of war, ordering that no prisoners will be taken on Hill 1647. All are to be killed in a legitimate reprisal.

"Let me be clear about this. The normal rules of war remain in effect everywhere *but* Hill 1647. Enemy who clearly indicate they wish to surrender elsewhere will be taken prisoner and will be well treated. This reprisal *only* affects the enemy on Hill 1647. All parties, acknowledge."

Ali al Tikriti's Bunker, Hill 1647, 0849 hours, 13/2/461 AC

Ali clearly heard the screams leaking in from men hiding all around him. He heard some of them begging for their lives as they were shot down on the spot. He looked around frantically for something white to wave. Finding nothing, he stripped off his uniform trousers and removed his underpants. He hardly noticed that the white briefs were stained where he had shat himself. He took the briefs and tied them to his riding crop. Then he dragged the boy, still hiding under the bed, out and forced the crop into his hands.

"Wave this," Ali said, as he pushed the poor child out of the bunker. The boy flew back, bloody and ruined, when an enemy machine gun opened up on him. Aghast, Ali retreated back into his bunker, whimpering.

A small dark object flew in. Ali ducked behind his field desk, which he frantically turned over for cover from the expected blast. The explosion, when it came, burst both the Sumeri's eardrums.

Maybe they'll think everyone in here is dead now. Maybe . . .

Ali's thoughts were cut short as a stream of liquid fire bounced off one wall by the bunker's dog-legged entrance. The fire splashed into the well-appointed room. Before it managed to burn up all the oxygen and suffocate him, Ali felt the flaming stuff touch upon and begin to eat away at his skin.

From outside the bunker, the engineer manning the flamethrower heard a satisfying scream. Grimly smiling, the engineer said, "Teach you how to treat prisoners, motherfuckers."

INTERLUDE

16 Rabi I, 1497 Anno Hejirae, Nairiyah, Saudi Arabia (15 March 2074)

Times were hard for the Faithful. For a while, for many years, it had seemed they would take Europe by default. And yet the perfidious Euros had found their balls in the end, returned to their roots, and ghettoized or deported the Muslims among them. America had been more generous, in its way. It welcomed Muslims, in considerable numbers. Yet it did so in the sure knowledge that its way of life was so seductive that few, if any, among them would remain true Muslims.

In their home, yes, even in Saudi Arabia, things were no better. The Saud Clan, fickle and faithless, had turned from their Salafist roots and concerned themselves ever more with sequestering the diminishing oil wealth of the country for their own benefit. A large and ruthless secret police organization barely sufficed to keep a lid on things. Mosques were purged; holy men disappeared without a trace. All was black.

❖   ❖   ❖

The vision came to Abdul ibn Faisal as a dream, yet it was a true dream. He knew it was. No dream had ever seemed so real and when the voice of the Almighty had called in it . . .

"Servant of the Beautiful One, Servant of the Beneficent, Servant of the Most Compassionate . . ." and on through all the ninety-nine names of Allah. These, though, Abdul knew for himself. Indeed, he could have recited the ninety-nine names in his sleep. For all those ninety-nine, it could still have been just a dream.

But when the mighty voice had thundered out the one-hundredth name? *Then* Abdul had known that this was not just any dream, but a sending from the Most High.

The world around the dreaming Abdul was little beyond light and his own prostrate, quivering form. The great voice of Allah seemed to come from everywhere.

"The believers fear going to this new world, this Donya al Jedidah," rumbled the great voice. "They ask, "Where shall we turn in prayers when al Makkah is not even on the same world? How shall we make the hajj, even once in a lifetime, when the vacuum between the worlds prevents it?" Go you forth unto the believers, Abdul ibn Faisal. Tell them that they are to take a single rock from the Kaaba, in al Makkah. This rock you shall know when you see it for I shall mark it for your eyes alone. And it shall be one of those set by Abraham, stone upon stone, as a shelter for Hagar and her son, Ishmael, the Father of the Arab People.

"This stone shall be set in silver after it is taken. And you shall take it with you to *al Donya al Jedidah* where you shall build a new Kaaba. The believers, such as I shall have given the Grace to know they are chosen, shall follow you, some in one ship and others in others. There you shall settle, as Salafiyah, you and those who follow."

"I am the Maker of Universes. Obey me."

Trembling still, Abdul awakened from his dream to find himself on his bed, on all fours, and with his head down low. His second wife lay sleeping beside him; so he saw when he looked up.

It seemed to him that the light by which he saw his wife ebbed very slowly.

CHAPTER TWENTY

By steeping himself in military history an officer will be able to guard himself against excessive humanitarian notions. It will teach him that certain severities are indispensable in war, that the only true humanity lies in the ruthless application of them.

—Kriegsbrauch im Landkriege, 1902 Edition

Hill 1647, Topographical Crest,
0909 hours, 13/2/461 AC

It was too cold by far for meat to rot. Even so, the air was thick with the stench of phosphorus, napalm, explosives, blood and shit from ruptured intestines. Smoke floated thickly on the breeze. To the north, the steady *whop-whop-whop* told of the helicopters returning from dropping off the bulk of the Cazador Cohort. Behind, the muted roar of scores of tanks and other armored vehicles droned.

There were bodies *everywhere*, enough so that Carrera wanted to puke. He couldn't, of course, not in front of the troops. That would come later. And with it would come, so he strongly suspected, a new set of nightmares to steal his sleep. *So be it; so be it. What is necessary is necessary. But if I couldn't compartmentalize, I think I'd go mad.*

"The problem with a massacre . . ." *Reprisal,* Carrera reminded himself, *REPRISAL.* "The problem with a reprisal is that it can take just as much out of the men as a battle."

"Sir?" Soult queried.

"Look around, Jamey," and Carrera's hand swept over the hill to encompass hundred of listless, weary legionaries, many of them with horrified looks on their faces. "These guys aren't happy about what they've done here, many of them. They'll be useless for at least a day."

"Then why'd you order it, Boss? I'm not bitching; I'm just curious."

"Two reasons," Carrera answered. "One is that the boys were pissed and were going to do it anyway, no matter what anyone said. If that had happened, discipline would have been shot permanently. Instead, by giving them the *order* to do it, discipline is maintained. Thus, on some other occasion where maybe the enemy doesn't deserve this kind of butchery, we'll be able to hold the men in check because they *know* that if a reprisal had been warranted we would have ordered one."

"You said two reasons, Boss."

"Yeah," Carrera answered. "The other reason is that the law requires it. I'll explain later. In the meantime, give me the radio."

Soult handed the mike over. Carrera made a call

to the commander of his mechanized cohort. Brown answered, "Sancho Panzer speaking."

Carrera pulled the mike away and looked at it quizzically for a moment. When he returned it to his ear and mouth, he said, "Sancho, my armor!"

"Where you want it, Boss?"

"The pass between the two fortresses. Legate Jimenez will be taking you, plus Third and Fourth Cohorts, plus the artillery and half the engineers forward. You lead. I'll join you later. Xavier, did you copy that?"

"Roger, Patricio," Jimenez answered. "Set up a defense or keep pushing?"

"Relieve the Cazadors, then hold in place. I want to see about bringing up the rest. That, and one other thing."

"I'll need more trucks," Jimenez observed.

"You can have the helicopters for one lift. Trucks we are scrounging up."

"Fair enough. Meet you there. Er . . . what about my prisoners?"

"Base of the hill. The MP century is coming up to take charge of them."

"Wilco, then, Patricio."

Good old Xavier. On him I can rely.

Carrera handed the microphone back to Soult. "Jamey, get ahold of every one of our units on this hill. Tell them I'll speak to them on this side of the bridge in . . . oh . . . two hours. And tell the sergeant major to bring any of the pressies he's rounded up there at the same time. And I'll need the priest. Oh, and send the PSYOP chief and Fahad the Chaldean up to me. We need to make a little announcement."

✧　　　✧　　　✧

It was actually closer to two and a half hours before everyone and everything needed were assembled.

Carrera walked out and stood on a little knoll between the bridge and the base of Hill 1647. The officers, centurions and legionaries stood at attention until he called, "At ease. Break ranks. Cluster around." He held up his arms straight to his sides, to show that he wanted the men grouped to where he could speak directly to them all at once. All told, there were nearly seven hundred uniformed men.

Behind the uniforms, still under armed guard but otherwise unrestrained, were approximately thirty-four members of the press, about seven of them bearing video camcorders. As soon as the legionaries were seated one of the pressies raised a hand and opened his mouth as if to speak.

"Shut up," Carrera said, pointing directly at the man. "You have no rights here. You have no say here. You ask no questions here until you are allowed to. Shut up and learn."

Turning his gaze slightly left and then right to take in all the clustered media types, Carrera continued, "Let there be no bullshit among us. You are my enemy and I am yours. Whatever I say you will lie about. Whatever you, in your *incarnate* ignorance, hear you will not understand and will misreport. If by some strange twist of fate one of you does understand it you will certainly misreport it even more. That is one reason why I have my own camera crew here." Carrera's finger pointed to a small uniformed group with their own video cameras from the PSYOP crew.

"I intend to speak to the men in Spanish," he told the journalists. "If you can speak Spanish, you can follow along. If you cannot, fuck you, I am not going to bother to translate though a translation of the gist of it will be provided sometime later."

Switching to Spanish, Carrera continued, addressing his men. "This is a tale of two hills and one law. The hills you see behind me. One of them you just conquered. The other was taken by the Third and Fourth Cohorts in an action every bit as gallant as your own.

"On your hill you found evidence of a crime committed by the enemy upon our comrades. On the other hill, there was no such evidence. The result is plain to see." Again Carrera pointed, this time at the several hundred Sumeris sitting—either dejectedly or with relief as the mood took them—under guard by the MP century. "There are many prisoners from the unoffending hill; none from the hill and unit responsible for the murder of our men.

"Some of you are looking very dejected. Whether that is because you lost friends in the assault—and let me assure you here and now that our casualties were very light, certainly in comparison to the magnitude of the task—or because you feel dirty at shooting men who were trying to surrender, or because you are worried about some future criminal action against you, FORGET IT! Your friends are in good hands, you no more committed a crime than an executioner does when he sets the rope around the neck of the condemned. *I* gave the order to shoot those men." *Never mind that you would have done it, anyway, if I hadn't. That isn't important right now. Besides. It's my doing that you're here, my doing the way you've been trained. So if there is fault or blame, they are mine.*

"I know you have all had instruction in the law

of war. I directed that that instruction take place. I monitored it. Let me tell you now that that instruction was incomplete. Almost in the nature of things, for it to be complete would have taken weeks, and we did not have extra weeks. So, like every other worthwhile soldier on the planet, you were trained in a truncated version of the law of war, enough to keep you out of trouble. There was more."

Carrera rather hoped that the men wouldn't begin to nod off once it became apparent he intended to teach a class. He needn't have worried; the men were desperate enough for absolution and benediction that he had their full and complete attention.

"You learned that there are two bodies of law with regard to the law of war, the statutory law—treaties and such—and the customary law. There is a third which one might call 'the common law' of war. The common law of war is that which, like other bodies of common law around the world, was developed by practical men for practical problems. It was *not* developed by ignorant shits trying to score points with the equally ignorant *'international community of the very, very sensitive.'* The third body of the law of war holds, for example, that men who refuse to surrender and keep on fighting after you have closed to close combat range are to be killed.

"This sounds harsh, I know. Indeed it sounds illegal since surrender is held in many circles to be an absolute right. It is neither. In the first place, every man who ever went into a close assault with a fixed bayonet has an absolutely pat insanity defense. Thus, you cannot deter him from killing because you cannot, as a practical matter, legally punish him. Some would say that it is unwise to kill an enemy who fights too long, lest he fight to the death and drive up your own casualties. I, and the common law of war, the practical law of war, answer that without exacting a price for continued resistance, you invite the enemy to drive up your casualties by fighting *almost* to the death."

Carrera's face changed to contemplative, even musing, for a moment. "That's just an example, by the way. Yet as a fine general on Old Earth, George S. Patton, once observed, the enemy loses his right to surrender if he hasn't done so by the time you close to three hundred meters. Again, by the common law of war and as a practical matter, it just works that way and it is never punished. And, frankly, an enemy who indicates a willingness to fight beyond the point that wisdom should tell him to stop if he wants to live has already indicated he does not want to live all that much and is simply too dangerous and unpredictable to take a chance on."

The face grew hard and cold again. "That's not what we're talking about though, taking the enemy's life because of a potential immediate or fairly short term threat to your own. Those Sumeris up there really *did* want to surrender. Why did I tell you not to let them?"

Carrera looked around, slowly and deliberately, trying to catch as many eyes as he could in a single glance. "As you probably know, there is, over on the continent of Taurus, a fairly new court, the Cosmopolitan Criminal Court, or CCC. This court purports to have universal jurisdiction over certain crimes, much as any nation's courts have jurisdiction over piracy at sea. Without going into the merits of this 'universal jurisdiction' here, let me ask you what the CCC could have done to you, or to the Sumeris, that was one whit worse than what was done here today? The answer, as I am sure you are all aware, is *precisely nothing*. Courts are for civilized circumstances where people can be deterred by punishment. There is nothing any court can do to anyone, and even what it could do it cannot do very quickly, that even begins to approach what we do to each other in war, routinely. The CCC, or any similar court, is toothless as far as furthering its *stated* purpose. It might be effective, mind you, at its *true* purpose which is undermining national sovereignty and the ability of the civilized world to defend itself from barbarism. That, however, is the subject for another day.

"What is important for this day is that the law of war—customary, statutory, or common—cannot be enforced by any court, ever. Because we live in an anarchic system of sovereign states, and because the stakes in war are so high, the only thing that can enforce the law of war is the law of war itself. To do this it has one recourse: reprisal. Reprisal, which I am sure you are familiar with because Tribune Puente-Pequeño, your law of war instructor, told you about it—I've heard him, is a war crime, or conduct that would ordinarily be a war crime, but which becomes legal and legitimate in order to counter or deter an enemy from violating the law of war. It is all we have, all the world has, to make the law of war work.

"Thus, I ordered you to repulse for the murder of our men. Thus," and here Carrera stopped for a moment and pointed skyward where three Turbo-Finch Avengers were winging it northward, "I have ordered leaflets prepared, in Arabic, to be dropped ahead of our forces, to let the enemy know what we have done and to explain to him the laws which he must follow in the future if he wishes to avoid a repetition. Thus," and his finger pointed at the pressies, still standing in clueless (which Carrera was certain was their natural state) shock (at being treated with open contempt), "I had those . . . people brought here so that they, too, can spread the word. Let everyone know that if you commit a crime against the *Legio del Cid* then punishment will be immediate and frightful.

"It may seem unfair to some of you, even horrifying, that we took no account of the innocence or guilt of particular individuals on that hill. The law of war *assumes* that there is collective responsibility. We know this for two reasons. One is that, in order to be considered a legitimate combatant, and to be entitled to all the protections due a prisoner of war, one must meet four criteria: carrying arms openly, being identifiable as a combatant, being under a chain of command—and in an organization—responsible for your actions, *and* being in an organization that itself follows the law of war."

Carrera was fudging a bit there. The law did not require "being in an organization," exactly. It required that one operate in accordance with the law of war. Since individuals did not conduct operations, however, and organizations *did*, his was a logical and reasonable interpretation.

"Thus, if your organization does not follow the laws of war, even if you do, you become an illegal combatant and lose your protected status as a prisoner of war, if captured.

"The other way we know that the law of war assumes

collective responsibility is in the doctrine of reprisal itself. Say, for example, that the enemy is violating the law of war by using a hospital as an ammunition storage point. We can bomb the shit out of the hospital, or even another hospital, butchering the wounded. We can do this even though the wounded committed no crime. They may *still* be held accountable, in practice, for the actions of their side.

"Let me conclude, then, by commenting on the nature of the particular form of reprisal we took, to wit: denial of quarter and refusal to take prisoners. These were crimes. Once again, *every* reprisal is a crime. They become nonculpable, *legal*, when engaged in to enforce the laws of war. This is what we did, nothing more. We did what was *necessary* to support the law of war. We are *guiltless.*"

Carrera turned to the Chaldean priest. "Father Hanna, if you would give the men a general benediction and absolution . . ."

Hamilton, FD, 0612 hours, 15/2/461 AC

"I did warn you, Mr. Secretary, that Patrick could be hard to control."

Newspapers littered the desk, each with a screaming headline of "War Crime." The secretary of war's elbows rested on the papers, heavily. Campos adjusted the hands he had cupped around his face just enough to glare at Virgil Rivers with one eye. He did *not* like being reminded.

"Be that as it may, Virgil," Campos answered, "who would have expected this shitstorm?"

Well, Rivers thought, *frankly, I did. I'd have been surprised, as a matter of fact, if Hennessey hadn't done something, at least, to create one. It's one of his two or three natural talents.* Wisely, Rivers kept the thought to himself.

Instead he offered, "I've had the JAG here look over the statement Hennessey issued. They say that it's legally true, if unpleasant, except for one small detail."

"And that would be?" Campos asked, still glaring with one eye.

"There are actually seven requirements to making a legitimate reprisal. Hennessey snuck in an eighth. His statement said that a proper reprisal must be 'not merely proportional but also sufficient to deter future violations of the law of war.' The JAG says that is not part of the law, though it is logically and therefore legally defensible."

"But he's just a fucking . . . what was that rank he used? Legate? What's that mean? Colonel? Lieutenant Colonel? *Lieutenant?*"

"Umm . . . no, Mr. Secretary. There is, in the fine print of the contract between us, a little section that says that *Legio del Cid* ranks will be treated as, and have the power and authorities of, their traditional titles. The actual meaning of "legate" is not lieutenant or lieutenant colonel, but lieutenant *general.* Therefore, even by our rules, he has all the authority he needs."

"Sneaky bastard," Campos said, without heat.

"Yes, sir. He *is* a sneaky bastard." *Oh, to hell with it.* "I warned you."

"So what do we do?"

Rivers took a moment before answering. He walked to the window and looked out at the broad, slow-moving river that separated the War Department headquarters from the rest of the Federal District and simply stared at it for some minutes, thinking.

When Rivers turned around, he asked, "Does it make any difference, sir? I mean, really? What has Patrick done except bring into the open something that would have been just as true, even if hidden, if he had not? The press *are* the enemy. The 'international community' is the enemy. The cosmopolitan lawyers and bureaucrats are the enemy. They have been since colonization here and, back on Old Earth, for a lot longer.

"A horde of angels could come down from Heaven and make sworn depositions that everything Patrick said was true and that he acted completely correctly. That news would be buried on page one hundred and fifty-five of the *First Landing Times*. And meanwhile every paper and television station in the world, every cosmopolitan progressive, every humanitarian activist who manages to do pretty well by doing good, would still be screaming 'War Crime.'

"And if he hadn't ordered a reprisal? They would just find something else. There *is* no satisfying them because the only thing that *would* satisfy them would be if we lose the war completely."

Ar-Ramalia, Sumer, 15/2/461 AC

"Jesus, it must suck to lose," Cruz muttered as the convoy bearing him and the 1st Cohort moved into the town. The streets were full of garbage. Bodies, mostly uniformed but many not, littered them as well. Green colored leaflets—Cruz recognized them as some of those the legate had had dropped ahead of the legion—blew in the dry desert wind. A Sumeri tank burned to one side of the broad highway, its commander hanging lifeless half out of his hatch. Flames arose around the body, cooking it and lending the smell of overdone pork to the air. Cruz's nose scrunched in distaste.

The convoy stopped with the mass screaming of brakes. The first centurion of the cohort began walking the line, slapping vehicles with his palm and ordering, "All right, boys and girls, everyone off. And buckle up your goddamned armor, Sanchez."

Cruz reached over and slapped the side of Sanchez's helmet, moderately hard, before standing himself, tossing his rucksack over the side, and shuffling to the back of the truck. He jumped off, landing easily on both feet, then walked around to retrieve the ruck. When he returned, the signifer was assembling the century.

"This afternoon," the signifer announced, then consulted his watch, "in about four hours, we're going to relieve 3rd Cohort and continue clearing the town. Orders at . . ." again he looked at his watch, ". . . call it noon. Centurion?"

"Sir!"

"I'm going forward with the tribune to coordinate the passage of lines with 3rd Cohort. We own those buildings over there." The signifer pointed out the ones he meant, a series of two-story, cinder block structures with stores below and apartments above. "Take charge of the century; security, weapons maintenance, food and rest, in that order."

"Sir. Century; atten . . . shun. On my command, fall out and into those buildings the signifer indicated. Section leaders, priority of work is local security, weapons, food, rest. Report to me when you're up on the first. Be prepared to brief me on your rest plan. Fall out."

A PSYOP loudspeaker was blaring out something in Arabic as the small party from 1st Cohort arrived at the 3rd Cohort Command Post.

"What the hell is that?" the tribune asked of the 3rd Cohort's Operations Officer.

"We've had some trouble," that officer answered. "Twice we've had Sumeris come forward appearing to want to surrender and then open up when they got close enough that even *their* shitty standards of marksmanship were adequate. Another time, one came close enough to detonate himself. We lost three dead and half a dozen wounded. The loudspeaker's telling them that they're all responsible for the actions of each of them, that from now on, and because of their own treachery, if they want to surrender they have to strip buck naked and approach with their hands in the air and absolutely nothing in them."

The tribune snorted. "Any takers under those conditions?"

"Some. A few. On the other hand, we haven't lost any more of our own since we started shooting anyone approaching who *wasn't* stripped down."

"What about the women? We making them strip, too?"

"We're telling the civilians to run the other way, away from us, if possible. For those who insist on coming this way, the women have to get down to just their panties. We have *some* sense of decency, after all?"

"Okay," the tribune agreed. "Now, show me where you want our advanced parties to link up with you?"

Waiting for the order to go in, Cruz's heart thundered in his chest.

In the same room, the assistant section leader's tubular feed grenade launcher went *foomp-kaclick-foomp-kaclick . . . foomp-kaclick-foomp*. Two 43mm grenades sailed through each of the windows to the building opposite the one the section, which included Ricardo Cruz, had assembled in for their attack across the narrow street. The explosions blew out the windows' remains, and were followed by a horrible, keening cry in Arabic.

"Smoke!" ordered the section leader. Two green canisters popped as their spoons were released. The canisters landed in the middle of the alley, well to either side of the buildings concerned. The section leader waited a few seconds, to allow the smoke from the canisters to build up. Then he ordered, "Covering fire! First Team, go."

Cruz's team, Number Two, and the other one, Number Three, began blasting from their side. First Team raced through the back door and across the alley, flattening themselves against the wall when they reached it. More grenades sailed in through the windows, while the fire team leader and another man from First Team broke down the door. The Arabic cries ceased with the explosion of the hand grenades.

The section leader shouted, "Second Team, with me."

Cruz's group stopped firing and followed the sergeant across the street and into the other building. When they had disappeared, the assistant section leader led the last team, plus the weapons team, across.

"Cruz," said Sergeant del Valle, "take your men and clear upstairs. Be careful, son."

The interior of the building was dark, despite the recent destruction of the windows. Cruz took a moment to partially accustom his eyes to the dim light. When he could see the staircase that led upstairs clearly he ordered, "Follow me," and took a bent-legged crouch.

"Sanchez, left side."

Sanchez mimicked Cruz's posture. Behind them the last two men in the team, Privates Rivera and Escobedo, stood mostly erect, rifle and light machine gun pointing over the heads of Cruz and Sanchez.

"Advance."

An ununiformed Sumeri appeared above them with a grenade in his hand. Before Cruz could say anything the light machine gunner opened up, stitching the enemy and spilling his blood and intestines across the far upstairs wall. The Sumeri dropped the grenade, which exploded, further smearing the irregular.

"Up." One step at a time, and almost in step, Cruz and Sanchez ascended. When they could see over the top step they turned in opposite directions, firing down short hallways that led to rooms with closed doors. The bullets pockmarked the doors, sending wooden splinters in every direction.

"Sanchez, guard left. The rest with me." Cruz and the other two reached the landing and sprinted the few short steps to the door on that side. Rather than waiting Cruz threw himself against it, knocking it off its hinges and over into the room. The door didn't land flat, but rather came to rest unevenly and part way atop another Sumeri irregular who had probably been standing behind it when Cruz had opened fire. The Sumeri appeared not to be breathing though blood ran out from under the fallen door.

Noticing the body, Cruz had the somewhat inane thought, drummed into him in Basic, *Concealment is not cover.*

The thought was interrupted by the entrance, firing, of the last two men in Cruz's fire team. A closet door swung slowly open to allow a Sumeri body to tumble to the floor.

"Room's clear, Cruz," one of the men reported.

"Rivera, with me. Escobedo, stay here. Guard."

Leaving the light machine gun behind, Cruz and Rivera hastened back to where a prone Sanchez lay with his rifle still trained on the door opposite.

Before the three men could storm the next room they heard firing coming from behind them. Escobedo screamed. When they turned around, they saw the Sumeri who had been under the broken-down door turning an assault rifle in their direction. Rivera was a trifle faster than the Sumeri, who went down bonelessly from several close range hits. Cruz rushed back to find Escobedo hit but breathing, shot through the back.

"Motherfuckers," Cruz muttered. He went back to Sanchez and Rivera, stopping to call down the stairs, "Sergeant, I've got a wounded man up here; Escobedo. And the fuckers are *not* playing by the rules."

"Keep up the assault, Cruz," the sergeant returned. "I'll send up a medic for your man."

Instead of rushing to force down the next door, Cruz fired another long burst through it. Then he and Rivera advanced to take position on opposite sides. Sanchez got on his feet, advanced, and slammed his foot against the portal, which burst open. Cruz and Rivera then sprayed the room with fire.

Entering, Cruz saw three Sumeris, all apparently hit, one with his back against the wall. Without a word Cruz turned his rifle on the first and fired a burst. This was known as "double tapping," or making sure. He shot the second and, as he was turning to the third saw the Sumeri's eyes open wide as he reached for a rifle. Cruz shot him, too, and whispered, "Got to learn to play by the rules. Fuckers."

Looking at the bodies, Cruz felt his anger cool. Turning away from the carnage, he thought, *Cara, queridisima, I wish I could come home to you now.*

INTERLUDE

17 Safar, 1502 AH, Medina, Saudi Arabia
(22 December, 2078)

The sun was fading away to the west as the muezzin, his voice amplified by speakers mounted on the minaret walls, called the faithful to prayer. Some other place, perhaps, and the royal family might just have ignored the call if business pressed. Not here. Here the force of Allah and of the words conveyed by the Prophet were strong. Here, the king and his brother stopped their discussions, abased themselves, and prayed.

"He wants a stone, just one stone," said Bandar to his brother, the king, once prayers were over. He continued, "One stone out of sixteen hundred and fourteen outside, and who knows how many inside, and it isn't even the *Hajar ul Aswad*, the Black Stone."

"But the Kaaba is sacred, like the Word of Allah, never-changing and eternal."

"Nonsense, Brother," Bandar insisted. "The Word is eternal but the Kaaba has been rebuilt anywhere from five to a dozen times; no one's really quite sure. The most recent rebuild was eighty-five years ago, in

580

1417. It has had major components replaced, has had its shape changed from a rectangle to a square to a rectangle to a square and back to a rectangle again. It has had new stones added and old ones thrown away. And all Abdul ibn Faisal wants is *one* lousy stone to take with him to *al Donya al Jedidah*."

"We'd have to take down at least one wall to get at the stone he wants," the king objected.

"And we've taken down walls before," Bandar countered, "that same five to one dozen times I mentioned. What's one more time? We can begin right after this Hajj and have the thing rebuilt before the next, possibly even before Ramadan."

The king looked closely at his brother. "And what would be the point, after all? What good comes of it?"

Bandar took a deep breath before continuing. When he did, he said, "Brother, we have problems. The oil is going fast. Europe is plunging into blackness and all our investments there are crumbling away. Our population is growing beyond our ability to care for and beyond the capability of the secret police to control.

"We had hoped that by becoming a major food grower we could break our dependence on western imports. For a while, even, we were the fourth largest exporter of wheat in the world. We export none of that now, and again have to import wheat.

"And the Salafi are growing out of hand. We had thought the Americans would have curtailed their influence once they defeated al Qaeda. It didn't last.

"We have to advance—yes, like the West—and we cannot when every forward step we take is blocked by the Salafi."

The king's hand reached up to stroke his beard. "So you think if we give up the stone, this one of sixteen hundred and fourteen, then some sizable number of the Salafi will simply pack up and leave? Remember the disaster on the first colonization ship."

Bandar nodded. "They were mixed. We shall hire, perhaps even build or, more likely, have built, a ship or ships to take the Salafi away. Will they go? Yes, and quite possibly a large number of them. And if we can get rid of a sizable number initially, we can change this country enough to make it uncomfortable for the rest so that *they* leave too. Oh, Brother, I am *telling* you; this Donya al Jedidah is the answer to our prayers."

The king chewed on his lower lip and then reached up one hand to stroke his beard, contemplatively. "You know, there's another potential advantage here, Brother. What if we used our influence to set aside an area for the Zionists on the New World. Surely some would go; they've got to be as tired of the constant fighting as the Palestinians are, if not more so. They've got to be tired of the taxes, the constant military duty. If we can entice away some numbers of Jews, the burdens on those who remain will grow greater still. That might well make even more leave. And each who leaves makes it more likely, just as with our own fanatics, that more will leave. Get enough to go and the Zionist entity falls."

"You're dumping our problems here on the people we send out," Bandar objected.

The king shrugged eloquently. "So?"

Bandar considered. He rocked his head back and forth for a few moments. Finally, he shrugged to match his brother. "Indeed. 'So?'"

CHAPTER TWENTY-ONE

Military necessity admits of all direct destruction of life or limb of armed enemies, and of other persons whose destruction is incidentally unavoidable in the armed contests of the war; it allows of the capturing of every armed enemy, and every enemy of importance to the hostile government, or of peculiar danger to the captor; it allows of all destruction of property, and obstruction of the ways and channels of traffic, travel, or communication, and of all withholding of sustenance or means of life from the enemy; of the appropriation of whatever an enemy's country affords necessary for the subsistence and safety of the Army, and of such deception as does not involve the breaking of good faith either positively pledged, regarding agreements entered into during the war, or supposed by the modern law of war to exist. Men who take up arms against one another in public war do not cease on this account to be moral beings, responsible to one another and to God.

—The Lieber Code, Section 15

Ninewa, Sumer, 22/2/461 AC

The sand tore at *Amid* Adnan Sada's face. He didn't mind, not in the slightest.

Keeps their damned planes and attack helicopters away, at least, and so, Allah, for this I thank You.

Sada, an *Amid*, or brigadier general, in the Army of the Republic of Sumer, wore desert battle dress with insignia of his unit, rank and branch sewn on. A khaki colored cloth was tied over his mouth and nostrils; breathing was nearly impossible otherwise.

But, Allah, Sada amended, *I would really have appreciated it if you had brought the wind and the dust earlier so I could have brought in enough to feed my men.*

"And that's the problem, *Amid*," Sada's supply officer had said. "I have the ammunition, building materials, fuel and all that. But food? I have ten days' supply, or maybe fifteen on short rations. No more."

The supply officer, Major—or *Raiid*—Faush, was one of the good ones, Sada thought. *Another man might have sold the lot, or stored it to sell to the FSC when their forces arrived. Faush I can trust. Faush I can count on. And he isn't even a clan member. How often does that happen?*

In fact, in Sada's brigade it happened more often than not. He had his ways.

Sada's cell phone rang, sounding loudly even over the roar of the howling wind. He answered it, saw that it was a text message, and began to laugh.

"General?" questioned Faush.

Instead of answering, Sada just passed the phone over. Faush read.

"How *did* they get our personal cell phone numbers?" he asked, after reading. "I mean, there ought to be *something* private in life; *something* sacred."

The text message on the phone was an invitation to surrender from the FSC's Office of Strategic Intelligence.

"I don't know, Faush," Sada answered, still laughing. "Hell, it will probably work for nine out of ten of our top commanders."

"No matter, *Amid*; it won't work here." Faush sounded more confident than perhaps he felt. Not that Sada would surrender easily. *That* was never going to happen, Faush was certain. Why, in the Sumer-Farsia war of sixteen years before Sada, then a captain commanding the rump of a cut-off and undersupplied infantry battalion against uncountable and fanatical Farsian human wave assaults, had refused to surrender for weeks. He'd held the Farsians off, too, until relief got to him. There was not a man who survived that ordeal but didn't worship the ground the *amid* walked on, at least when they thought Allah might not be looking. Faush was one of those survivors, as were most of the key leaders of Sada's current command.

Achmed Qabaash, Sada's operations officer, observed, enthusiastically, "We'd better fight like hell. Everyone says the enemy coming from the south doesn't take prisoners." Qabaash liked a good fight. He was odd that way.

"I wonder if that's true," Sada said. "I know they've make no secret of not taking prisoners if the men concerned are with a unit that violated the western laws of war. But there was a division's worth of men in towns to the south of us. I doubt they killed them all."

Highway One, eighty-seven miles south of Ninewa

Dusty, tired, hungry and miserable Sumeri POWs trekked under armed guard southward, directly into the wind.

Soult, his face like his chief's handkerchiefed against the biting wind and sand, looked at the prisoners with a degree of contempt. He couldn't really understand surrendering, even on the promise of good treatment. Better to die like a soldier.

"Are they all cowards, Boss?" he asked Carrera. "We offer to take prisoners and they surrender. We kill everything moving and they still *try* to surrender. I just don't understand it. Seems chicken to me."

Carrera, sitting on the canvas seat next to Soult took a moment before answering, simply, "They're no more cowardly as a people than anyone else. Cowards don't fly airships into buildings. Cowards don't load themselves with explosives and try to get close enough to do us some harm before detonating themselves. No, Jamey, they're not cowards. But they have some problems. It's the problems that account for most of the violations of the laws of war they engage in."

Seeing from his eyes, the only uncovered part of his face, that Soult didn't really understand, Carrera continued. "The sociologists call them "amoral familists." What that means is that they are raised in such a way that they cannot really conceive of legitimate loyalty to someone who isn't a blood relation. For that matter, when it is a question of loyalty to two blood relations the one with the closer relationship is the one who gets the loyalty. Religion counts to them, too, and a lot, but that makes very different demands on them. Nation? Means nothing to most . . . or less than nothing, often enough. The family is where their important loyalties lie, the family is what will protect them from a hostile world, the family is their law and their guide."

"Yeah . . . but so?" Soult plainly didn't understand.

"It means they're completely alone, Jamey, completely alone in the most terrifying place man can exist, the modern battlefield. They can't trust their squad mates, they can't trust their officers, unless those are also blood relations. For any given soldier in a Sumeri—or Yithrabi, Jahari or Misrani—unit under serious duress the only questions are, 'Can I run or surrender before the rest do? Am I going to be stuck here, alone, to face the enemy while the rest run?' It's a self-fulfilling prophecy, true. But the way a prophecy becomes self-fulfilling is by being destined to be fulfilled." Carrera sounded sad.

"You actually like them, don't you, Boss?"

"Jamey . . ." Carrera hesitated, "I used to like them a lot. It's . . . harder now.

"Sometimes they can break out of that self-fulfilling prophecy, by the way," Carrera added, perhaps only to change the direction in which the conversation had turned. "Some of their tribally based units aren't bad, though they've got problems when the tribal chain of command and the military one don't mesh. They've also got problems in that the tribe, while it might fight well, has a very finite tolerance for casualties.

"The other way, and it has happened occasionally, is when some outsider is in command who refuses to have any truck with tribes. If he can assemble a group that has no tribal majority, preferably if he can assemble one where each member has no tribal link with any other, sometimes he can make a good unit. Sometimes. It's harder than hell to do."

Ninewa, Sumer, 22/2/461 AC

Sada walked from building to building, inspecting the positions his men were preparing as they made ready to defend the town. It was a relief to go inside, if only to escape from the dust. Some of his boys were digging up the streets to excavate trenches to connect the buildings. That would, Sada was sure, come in handy.

The lieutenant in charge of the platoon was new. Sada searched his memory. *Lieutenant Rashad is from the Bani Malik tribe. His platoon sergeant is one of my old boys, from the Farsian War, an al Hameed. Squad leaders are . . .*

"Sergeant Major?" Sada questioned.

"Sir," began the sergeant major, "no two members of the same tribe in this platoon." Sada's brigade sergeant major, and McNamara would have approved, had grown very good at reading his boss' mind over the preceding decades.

The units of Sada's brigade were organized in one of two ways. About a third of them were strictly set up along tribal lines, the only caveat to that structure being that the leadership of the unit and the leadership of the tribe *within* the unit had to match. The *amid* had run off more than one sergeant, senior in the tribe's hierarchy, who had thought to ignore his captain, who was junior.

The other two thirds, roughly, Sada and his right-hand man, the sergeant major, went out of their way to ensure had *no* tribal identity. It seemed to Sada that one of the problems—and he understood them even better than Carrera did—was that extra-tribal loyalty couldn't *grow* wherever there was a focus for tribal loyalty, but could, potentially, where there was none. The toughest part had been the officers, whom one could ordinarily have expected to loot their units if the men in those units had no blood ties.

Give the dictator this much, thought Sada. *He kept his own tribe out of my brigade, excepting only a couple of spies, and didn't mind how many men from other tribes I had shot for corruption.*

Sada had shot a few of them personally. He still smiled sometimes at the memory of Faush's predecessor, caught with his hand in the till. Sada had simply drawn his pistol and shot the man at point-blank range. That was how Faush had inherited the job.

Pity what the blood did to the books though, Sada thought regretfully.

The lieutenant of the platoon misinterpreted the look on his *amid's* face. "Sir, the men are working as hard as they can . . ."

"Show me your hands," Sada ordered.

Still uncomprehending, the lieutenant held up clean hands with unbroken nails.

Sada smiled indulgently. He leaned over to whisper in the young officer's ear. "You're new, my son. So I'll forgive you . . . this once. But officers in my brigade *work*. Officers in my brigade *lead*. *You* will work if you want to continue to *lead*. Or would you prefer to go to the penal platoon, minus your rank, now?"

Eighty miles south of Ninewa

The sun was setting on a desolate scene, made all the more so by the dust that covered everything in swirling, choking eddies. Red leaflets, prepared by the Psychological Operations Century and dropped by Cricket recon plane ahead of the legion as it advanced, also blew in the breeze. The leaflets proclaimed the list of Sumeri violations of the laws of war, to date, and the legion's bloody-handed response to them.

The press was . . . stymied. When no one responded to their charges, except to admit them and insist the reprisals were lawful, they found they had no recourse. There was no blood in the water, no struggling body filled with fear of the righteous wrath of the media. The sharks couldn't go into a feeding frenzy.

On the other hand, admitted Carrera to himself, as he exited his vehicle, *while the press is defanged, if the Sumeris had a half-functioning chain of command at army level and a couple of battalions of working armor, I'd be fucked.*

Logistically, the legion was a mess. Carrera had one cohort detached from the line to guard prisoners. There were so many of these that his one century of military police camp guards, even supplemented by the field police century, the walking wounded and as many service troops as could be spared, simply *couldn't* guard them all. In point of fact it was more important that he was feeding his prisoners than that he was guarding them.

For food, they'd stick around. Guards? Eh? They could be ducked in a thick enough sandstorm.

The rest of the legion was strung out over forty miles of bad road. The trucks were overtasked, especially given the sandstorm. The helicopters were grounded. Roughly half the armor was stuck, broken down or about to break down and waiting along the side of the road for recovery or repair. And the artillery? It was more disorganized and strung out than any other cohort in the legion.

Thank God I listened to Harrington and Lanza and paid for the B-300 Dodos. Otherwise we'd have no means of reliable resupply. As is, the Dodos can drop us enough, just enough with what the trucks can bring through, to keep us going.

About the only good thing one could say was that, between the Yezidi taking over security in the towns the legion cleared and the fact that Carrera was taking and holding prisoners rather than letting them go to become a threat to his communications, at least the trucks were getting through. When they didn't break down . . . or get lost . . . or crash into something invisible at ten feet for all the dust in the air.

There was a small school house just outside this small, insignificant Sumeri town. Kennison had grabbed it for the legion's command post. All three of the operational staff teams, Operations itself, Logistics and Intelligence, were set up there. The doors were off as were the windows, though actually it was a matter of some conjecture whether the place had ever had doors and windows. In any case, blankets were hung over whatever openings there were. It cut the dust down, but could not entirely eliminate it.

Carrera pushed aside a blanket and entered. Behind him, in the road fronting the school, a column of infantry struggled forward against the biting sand. The men were too tired to even curse. He thought this a bad sign.

Inside, Triste and Fahad the Chaldean were engaged in a low volume but still heated discussion. A Sumeri officer, a captain, Carrera saw on closer inspection, sat in obvious incomprehension on a folding metal chair off to one side.

Looking up, Triste saw Carrera observing himself and Fahad. "Boss, we gots problems," the intelligence officer announced.

Carrera made a give forth motion with one hand.

"The captain here," and Triste indicated the seated Sumeri, "has been most cooperative. He's a supply and transportation type and before we captured him had passed directly through Ninewa. He says the commander there is a Sumeri brigadier named Sada."

"I know this man," Fahad interjected. "I know him well. As Tribune Triste says, 'We gots problems.'"

"Where do you know him from, Fahad?" Carrera asked.

"I was his instructor in English at the War College outside Babel. That's one way. But I also know him from elsewhere, when I was medic on the Farsian front twenty years ago. He was my commander."

"Fahad says this guy is *really* good, Boss, tough and brave and smart. Says the men love him."

"Oh, yes," the Chaldean interjected. "Best officer in whole fucking Sumeri army. Should be in command of whole army, too, but . . . wrong tribe." Fahad shrugged.

"Does he play by the rules, Fahad?"

"Rules, *sayidi*?"

"Laws of war? Treatment of prisoners? Maintaining status of lawful combatancy?"

"Oh. Yes, Legate. Sada is straight up. Tricks, yes. Dirty tricks? No."

Carrera pondered that for a few minutes, standing in the dusty room in silence. When he had thought it through, he ordered, "Get me the PSYOP people. And Fahad, sit down and prepare to translate. Kennison, have we got a Cricket pilot crazy enough to fly in this shit?"

Ninewa, 23/2/461 AC

The sun was far from up when Faush knocked on Sada's room door.

"What is it?" Sada demanded as he sat up and began pulling his boots on.

Faush hesitated, not because he feared his commander's wrath at being awakened but because he himself was very confused.

"Is that you, Faush?" Sada thought he had recognized the knock.

"Yes, *Amid*," Faush answered through the slightly cracked door. "There is something you need to see. Leaflets from the enemy. The streets are full of them."

"Come in then." Sada struck a match to light a kerosene lantern on a table next to his narrow bed.

Faush handed his commander a green piece of paper. On the paper was printing in Arabic script. Sada read:

To the defenders of Ninewa:

It has come to my attention, from a reliable source, that despite the near continuous pattern of violations of the laws of war which have come to characterize the Sumeri defense over the last ten days, it is a distinct possibility that these violations will not be repeated in your town or by your unit. Thus, although I have previously given orders that no prisoners will be accepted unless they strip completely naked to demonstrate that they have no hidden weapons or explosives, and that—because of treachery on the part of men pretending to be wounded to gain an advantage—all remotely suspicious bodies, apparently dead or plainly living, were to be shot again for security's sake, I am *temporarily* rescinding these orders in your case.

Those orders will remain rescinded for so long as, and not one moment longer than, the defenders of Ninewa themselves continue to obey the laws of war. It is up to you to police your own. If some of your men pretend to be wounded to gain a treacherous advantage, all of your wounded will suffer. If some abuse the flag of truce, the flag of truce will no longer be honored. If some use the symbols of the Red Crescent Organization treacherously, those symbols will not be respected further. If surrendering men attack, surrenders will not thereafter be accepted. If any of my men who fall into your hands are mistreated, yours will be butchered in return.

If you fight from hospitals and mosques they will be obliterated. If you fight from behind women and children, we will take extra casualties to capture you alive so that you can be hanged in front of those same civilians whose sanctuary you will have violated.

The choice is yours.

You are reputed to be good soldiers. I hope, personally, that you and your commanders choose well.

Signed,
Patricio Carrera
Legate, Legio del Cid
Acting Commander

"What do you think of it, *Amid?*" Faush asked.

Sada didn't answer immediately. This was a strange development, unique in his personal experience. An enemy lecturing you on the law of war? *Bizarre. On the other hand, he's got a point. The conduct of the irregulars . . . and even the regulars, has been a disgrace to this army. Perhaps here, maybe, we can redeem ourselves and our country's reputation. It will take some thought . . .*

"I think I need to talk to my senior officers and noncoms," Sada finally answered. "Assemble them at daybreak, here. And have a few dozen of these leaflets, enough to pass out, collected."

Interesting, thought Sada, *that my enemy is giving us this chance.*

Surrounded by a dozen men he trusted, Sada's sergeant major listened attentively as the instructor explained to fifty of the *Fedayeen as-Sumer*, the civilian irregulars ordered raised and armed by the dictator, the finer points of convincing the enemy you were harmless in order to get close enough to them to detonate an explosive belt. The design of the belt, in particular, he thought clever.

When the instructor had finished the sergeant major stood up and asked, enthusiastically, "Are you all prepared to give your lives like this?"

"*Aywa! Aywa!*" the fedayeen answered, with an enthusiasm to match the sergeant major's own. *Yes! Yes!*

"Good," the sergeant major said calmly. Then he said to his men, "Arrest them and put them in the penal platoon. All except for their instructor. Take that one outside and shoot him."

"Ah," said Faush. "Very clever indeed." The object of the major's admiration was an ambulance bearing the Red Crescent symbol which had had its sides reinforced with plate steel to serve as a clandestine armored personnel carrier. Two others in the hospital bay had been likewise converted, while a fourth and fifth had been made into suicide truck bombs.

"Don't you agree, Sergeant Achmed, Private Omar, that this is a clever set up?"

"Oh, yes, Major," the two submachine gun bearing enlisted assistants to the logistics officer agreed. "Very clever. Absolutely clever!"

"Yes. Now please shoot the men responsible."

The major was out the door and on his way to his next inspection before the submachine guns stopped chattering.

✧   ✧   ✧

The damnable thing is, thought Sada, *I can't help but use the hospital. It's the tallest building in town and the only one that will give the miserable air defense guns half a chance of covering the troops.*

He stood in the walled yard of a mosque, looking up at the hospital building that dominated the skyline even through the dust that still swirled in the air. A company of Sada's soldiers were engaged in removing a substantial armory of everything from small arms to explosives from the mosque's interior. It was neither a small mosque nor a small armory.

While most of the company were busied with demilitarizing the mosque, one squad was engaged in removing the bodies of the mullah, two *fedayeen*, and one operative from the national secret police. Another squad had marched off the rest of the *fedayeen* to the penal platoon, which had grown to be a very large company.

Sada looked around, thinking hard. *This compound would do for a hospital,* he thought. *Big enough. Covered. And there's a generator inside, which is more than the hospital can say. Still, using a* hospital *for an air defense site . . .*

Then he considered the other reason, the secret reason, the really, really *big* secret reason he had to play by the rules. His gaze wandered in the direction of the local university—*Damned secret police had better get here and take those packages off my hands*—and then back to the hospital.

Well, I am the local governor, *after all. I have the authority to close or move a hospital. Outside of a mosque a place doesn't become sacred merely for what*

*it once was or could have been or even what it might
be. Then again, what do I get out of it? One aircraft,
maybe two. Then they flatten the building anyway.*

Sada sighed. *Still, one or two are better than nothing. And I* have *to try.*

"Faush?" Sada asked, "How long to totally move
the hospital from there to here?"

"*Amid . . .* I'm not sure," the logistician answered.
"It could be done in a couple of days, I suppose.
It might be less time if you let me use the penal
platoon as slaves."

"Do it," Sada ordered. "But when you do it remove
every trace that suggests the building is a hospital. And
paint big target symbols on the sides. Yes . . . big ones."

Command Post, *Legio del Cid*, 25/2/461 AC

"Pat," Triste began, "it's the funniest thing. We got a
message over the radio, from the enemy commander. It
was in the clear. He wanted us to know that the hospital
has been closed and may be considered a legitimate
target. He spoke really excellent English, too."

Fahad's chest swelled ever so slightly; the Chaldeans hadn't been given to excessive pride in a very
long time. Even so, you could hear the pride in the
man's voice when he said, "Well, Legate, I *did* teach
him, after all."

"The other thing is, Boss, we've taken fire from
the hospital. They took out an RPV. Before the RPV
went down, it got some good shots of the other side
of the town. The civilians are moving out and being
escorted by uniformed soldiers."

INTERLUDE

5 Duh'l-Qa'dah, 1507 AH, Makkah
al Jedidah, Al Donya al Jedidah
(19 January, 2084 AD)

If he had ever doubted that his bedroom vision was
a true one, those doubts were dispelled when Abdul
ibn Faisel took his first look out the window of the
transport and, peering through the clouds, saw the new
homeland below him. It was watered; it was green.
Wonder of wonders, there were *trees*, not merely
around oases, but in forests large and small scattered
across the landscape.

Animals grazed, Abdul saw, as the shuttle descended
lower to fly over the landscape. Great herds of them
wandered, heads down in the verdant grass or muzzles
submerged in the flowing water of the land's many
rivers and streams. Abdul did not even try to count
them; he knew that all was as Allah had foretold in
his vision.

Some of the elephants seemed impossibly large
and incredible hairy.

The view of the new land disappeared behind

flying grass and dust as the shuttle came to a hover by the spot Abdul had selected—rather, that he had *known* as soon as he had seen it on a map—for the first settlement. The engines squealed and the landing struts *thrummed* as the ship settled down to a jarring landing. There was another hydraulic sound as the two ramps, one on the side for passengers and one in the rear for cargo, lowered themselves to the ground.

Accompanied by his dozen closest followers, Abdul and his Salafis stood and moved, rifles in hand, to the relatively open area by the landing ramp. The rifles were of the older style, muzzle loading and flintlock fired. They were *Salafis*, by Allah, and dedicated to doing things in the old way. Admittedly, even the muzzle loaders post-dated the true Salafis, those generations of the Prophet's time and the two that followed. Nonetheless, the muzzle loaders *pre*-dated the influx of contaminating western ideas and, so, Abdul had judged them, in the absence of guidance to the contrary from above, as being fit to carry to the New World.

Four of his followers, specially selected for their piety and their physical strength, carried the *Stone,* the single oblong rock he had been instructed and allowed to take from the Kaaba in Mecca. From this stone, the spiritual link to the original Holy City would be maintained. Toward this stone, and the new Kaaba that would be built, the faithful would pray and their prayers be carried across Allah's infinite space.

With deep piety, the party moved down the ramp, Abdul leading the four selected to carry the *Stone* and the other eight flanking the porters as an honor guard. Abdul led the group to a spot far enough away that the litter-carried stone would not be sullied by the blast when the shuttle took off to bring in the next load. He told the four porters to guard it and then made a motion for the other eight to follow him. These he led to the shuttle's cargo ramp. Already the first of the camels, horses, sheep and goats were being offloaded by others among his followers. The armed men were not needed for that.

In all things Abdul and his followers intended to follow the ways of those who had known, or followed closely in the footsteps of, the Prophet. What was permitted by Allah must never be forbidden. What was forbidden must never be permitted. All things must be as they were.

What the guards were needed for was the other large portion of the cargo. These walked on two feet. They had been purchased from several sources. Some came from among those who had made the Hajj to Makkah. These sometimes found then that they lacked the money to return to their homelands and sold either themselves or their children. Some came from various places on Earth where certain otherwise illegal transactions were permitted, notably northern Africa, Pakistan's Northwest Frontier Province, and the Balkans. It was this cargo that would actually do the work of cutting the stone and building the new Kaaba. It was this cargo that would warm the bedrolls of the Salafis at night.

These were those "possessed by the right hand" of Abdul and his followers. These were the slaves.

CHAPTER TWENTY-TWO

The power of an air force is terrific when there is nothing to oppose it.

—Winston Churchill

Outskirts of Ninewa, Sumer, 28/2/461 AC

The sandstorm had lifted two days prior. With that lifting winter ended and a terrible, oppressive heat descended onto the playing field. With the lifting, also, planes and helicopters were able to fly in parts and men from the main depot at the airport and the smaller one at Mangesh. Convoys wandering lost in the desert or hunkered down were scouted for from the air, found and directed. Tanks were recovered and sent forward. It had even proven possible for Christian, the legion's "II," or personnel officer, to ferry in two just-graduated classes of replacements, about four hundred privates, to make up for losses suffered to date, plus a bit.

Jorge Mendoza, Stefano del Rio and the tank

commander, Sergeant Perez, pulled up in their Jaguar II to a dun-colored building fronting a small square. They were pleased to have made it this far. To this point in time, there had been little action for the tankers of the legion. In fact, only two tanks of sixteen could claim kills on enemy armor, and less than half could even claim to have fired a shot in anger at other targets.

The crew was also a little surprised. Good workmanship the Jaguar might have, and good design as well. But it had been designed for the continent of Taurus, not the desert. Half a dozen times since the sandstorm had begun the air filter had clogged with a mass of grit, choking the engine to a whining, sputtering death. The Ocelots had fared little better. Eventually Brown, the commander of the mechanized cohort, had simply said, "To hell with it," and radioed in to legion headquarters that he and his command were simply frozen. "Better we stop now," Brown had explained to Carrera, "before we ruin every engine in the command, than keep going another few miles and never move again until you fly us in a few dozen new power packs."

Since they had stopped before the dust had done their engines to death, once the sandstorm had cleared the mechanized cohort had made good progress, reaching Ninewa in less than a day and taking up positions overlooking the bridge that spanned the broad, slow-moving, and brown-silty river behind it. The bridge stood in plain view about three thousand meters away.

Perez climbed out of the tank and stood atop the turret. From there he could see the bridge easily enough, plus the tall white building his map labeled as a hospital that looked over the entire town, dominating it.

"It's got to come down," he said to himself.

Perez heard a series of *foomps*, so close together as to seem to be one, single, long explosion. He waited for a few seconds, half in analysis and a quarter in surprise. Then he shouted, "Incoming!"

Del Rio and Mendoza said, together, "What the fu . . . ?" before dropping down into the tank and buttoning the hatches behind them. Perez dived through his own hatch face first, twisting around inside the tank to get one arm onto the turret handle. This he pulled shut with a clang as the first mortar rounds began impacting nearby.

The tank shuddered under the barrage. Inside all three of its crew prayed fervently that no Sumeri shell would find the lightly armored top of the vehicle. Even a smaller shell would be dangerous if it exploded there. A 120mm, as they assumed the enemy shells were, would burst the top like an overripe grape.

The barrage ended as suddenly as it began. Giving the order, "Wait inside until I tell you it's safe," Perez popped the hatch and risked a careful look around.

"Damn," he said aloud, though without keying the tank's intercom.

His tank had survived, but not unscathed. Where once the thing had carried two whiplike radio antennae, all that remained of these were roughly sheared off nubs. It was worse farther away.

The infantry that had dismounted from their Ocelots once these had halted and had been caught in the open and flat footed. Their bodies—the bloody, torn remnants of their bodies, rather—lay stretched out, torn or eviscerated, across the square. Perez didn't try to count them but there had to be at least ten or a dozen men killed.

The wounded, and there were more of these, were worse. They screamed for pain, for "Mama," for lost legs, arms and eyes. Already medicos were busied trying to staunch the flow of blood, to keep intestines from falling out, to field-set broken bones.

A single Ocelot apparently *had* taken a direct hit on top. It burned on the opposite side of the square from Perez and his tank. Someone inside of it screamed. *No one* tried to perform first aid on its unfortunate occupants, though Perez did see a lone soldier cross himself before firing a single round into the track. The screaming stopped.

South of Ninewa, Altitude 14,000 feet, Dodo Number Seven, 28/2/461 AC

One of the nice things about modern technology—for some definitions of "nice"—was that it didn't take an ultramodern bomber or jet fighter to drop even a very large bomb accurately. Any old thing that would get off the ground with a sufficient payload would do, provided it could fly above the ceiling for light air defense or that there was no real air defense deployed.

The Dodo, as rebuilt, met these minimal requirements. It could carry, handily, six bombs of two thousand pounds each. Moreover, after a blistering tongue lashing by Carrera, the commander of the *ala* had seen to it that four of his Dodos had wooden frameworks installed internally to allow them each to carry five such bombs, with a sixth on a dispenser rack. The cursing ground crews had worked through the night, cutting, lashing and bolting together the wood scrounged up by Harrington for the purpose. Then they'd worked half the morning using the three-thousand-pound crane integral to each aircraft to load the bombs.

The bombs, themselves, came courtesy of the FS Air Force, an easy and profitable trade in which Harrington had passed over a dozen cases of eighteen-year-old scotch and received in return two dozen bombs. (It was actually more complex than this, since Harrington also had to bring in an ordnance officer from the FSAF, that officer's commander, and a couple of others to see the deal go through and the planes effectively fitted to carry and use the weapons. For simplicity's sake, though, it is accurate enough to say that one case equaled two bombs with guidance packages.)

In prior times, no plane like the Dodo could hope to place a bomb on target with anything approaching accuracy unless the planes were substantially modified. In this case, though, the bombs had been modified. Each of the two-thousand-pounders had had its normal fusing taken out and replaced with a sophisticated guidance package. The guidance package operated off of the Global Locating System the United Earth Peace Fleet had, reluctantly, permitted the FSC to loft into space. Once released, the bombs became self-actuating, if not self-aware. They would guide themselves onto target with a CEP, or Circular Error Probable, of mere meters.

(Of course, the bombs needed to be programmed and the *ala*'s ordnance folks had not the first clue as to how to do that. Moreover, they had to be kept charged until released and this required some rewiring of the Dodos. Thus, as part of the deal two ordnance men from the FSAF had had to accompany the load to teach the Balboans how to do it. As mentioned, the deal was complicated. It became more complicated when Harrington went back, some days later, for several score five-hundred-pound bombs with similar fusing and guidance packages.)

"Evacuate the hospital," the *amid* ordered abruptly.

"Sir?" asked Qabaash, the operations officer, in confusion.

"Just a feeling," Sada admitted. "But get the men out. Leave the guns. Now *go!*"

There is very little one can do with a computer that one cannot also do, albeit more slowly and with more difficulty, with a pen and paper, map and compass. The rate of fall of the bombs had been calculated and from that the release point was decided. This had been compared with the bomb's ability to guide itself and an oval shaped area was drawn on the pilot's map, now strapped to his thigh.

Back in the cargo bay, the crew, supplemented by a couple of cooks and a medic, strained to get the bomb moving down the rollered ramp that ran along the plane's center line. It was tricky and required timing.

"Five . . . four . . . three . . . two . . . release." The pilot, Miguel Lanza, pulled back on his yoke to point the nose of the plane upward slightly. This made the roll easier.

The five men of the crew, all clustered behind, heaved and pushed. The bomb began to roll to the door, picking up speed as it went down the heavy wooden ramp. The bomb disappeared from view as the plane, lightened by a ton, lurched upward. Lanza, stomach sinking as the plane arose, immediately applied throttle to get this Dodo out of the way of the next one—number two of four on the mission—coming in to the release point.

"Okay, boys," shouted the sweating, panting crew chief, leaning with one arm on the wooden frame. "Let's go back and slide the next one into position.

Amid Sada sat on a folding chair on the flat roof over his bunker, sipping a tepid fruit juice. His eyes were fixed on the hospital, standing tall and white except for black bull's-eyes painted on each side. He heard, distantly, the drone of aircraft.

Suddenly the interior of the darkened hospital lit up, showing a montage of broken glass and torn-out cinder blocks cascading from every window.

"I will never again doubt one of your hunches, sir," Qabaash admitted.

"Wait for it, my friend," Sada chided, wagging a finger. "The building still stands. It won't for long."

Seconds passed. Once again the former hospital building flashed with internal fire. This time, one corner began to sag. In half a minute another bomb, this one not so accurate as the first two, struck it on the side, almost exactly on one of the painted bull's-eyes. An entire section of masonry peeled away to fall crashing to the street below.

Qabaash looked awed. "It was likely a fluke, my friend," Sada announced.

It was nearly two full minutes before yet another

bomb hit the building, again internally. That one managed to start a fire, though the next put it out while crumbling one wing completely.

"How many, do you think, *Amid*?"

"Why, as many as it takes, Qabaash," Sada answered calmly. "And if what they have tonight isn't enough, they'll be back tomorrow. The enemy has plenty of time, and apparently no shortage of munitions."

Command Post, *Legio del Cid*, outskirts of Ninewa, 29/2/461 AC

"Truth is, Carl," Carrera admitted to Kennison, "that I'd have spared the building if I could. I couldn't. The other side probably had no choice but to use it, and made the right choice of at least not hiding behind it. But because they used it, it had to go."

"Seems like a bloody awful waste to me, Pat." For some reason Kennison seemed more troubled by the destruction of the former hospital than by anything that had gone before. Or perhaps it was a cumulative thing, with the hospital being the final straw. In either case, he had tendered his resignation to Carrera that morning, just before sunrise.

Carrera's face was a stiff mask as he folded the written resignation carefully and placed it in one pocket of his battledress, rebuttoning the pocket when he was done. "In any case, Carl, no, I won't let you go. You signed on for two years and for two years you will stay, in irons if necessary. You were under no illusions about what I intended and you've known me long enough and well enough to know how I think and how I operate. None of this should be a surprise to you."

Kennison looked utterly miserable, haggard and drawn. "That's not the surprise, Pat. Everything you say is true. The surprise is how *I* feel about it. *That*, I never had a clue to. I don't even disagree, in principle, about the things you've done. It just bothers me in ways I can't deal with. Pat . . . I haven't slept in a week and it isn't just because of the cluster fuck the sandstorm caused."

Carrera turned away for a moment, thinking hard. *I don't have a decent replacement here for him. Kuralski could do it, but he's out of country. Jimenez could, too, but I can't afford to pull him out of Fourth Cohort. I need Harrington where he is. Triste? No. Great intel guy but not an operator. Parilla could run a staff well enough provided someone else gave him the overall plan. But he's still bedridden.*

Fuck. I'll have to try to do it myself. That, and try to get Kennison back on track.

"Sergeant Major!" Carrera called.

"Sir."

"Tribune Kennison has not slept in a week. He is currently unfit for his duties. Place him under arrest. Go to my vehicle and ask Soult for a bottle—no better make it two bottles—of scotch. Take the tribune back to the last town we passed and get him drunk as a skunk. Then put him to bed. Place a guard on him with instructions to fill him with more booze when he awakens. Have the legion's chief surgeon check on him from time to time."

Kennison looked at Carrera skeptically. *Fine, we'll play it this way for now. But I don't think that's the problem.*

Sada's Command Post, Ninewa, 32/2/461 AC

The bombing had become more or less continuous, with one Dodo overhead at all times ready to drop a self-guiding bomb—mostly lighter, five-hundred-pounders—any and every time a group of Sada's men showed themselves. The bombs seemed to come down every five or ten minutes even without a visible target.

This is becoming a problem, Sada thought to himself. Another bomb fell somewhere in the town, not so far away that it didn't shake the commander even down in his bunker. *At night we have these things, during the day it's the smaller, single engine dive bombers; those, or helicopters configured to carry rockets and machine guns. Both times, day or night, we have their RPVs patrolling for targets for the aircraft, the artillery, and the heavy mortars.*

If it's becoming hard on my morale it must be worse for the men.

Right, then. Best get out of this frigging hole and go see them.

Command Post, *Legio del Cid*, 32/2/461 AC

"That's him!" Fahad shouted in the CP. "That's Sada." An RPV pilot began calling off the grid coordinates of the spot where the enemy commander had been seen.

Carrera, who was spending a lot more time at headquarters than he liked since he had sent Kennison away to sleep and rest, hurried to look at the monitor that carried an image from a circling RPV.

"Are you sure, Fahad?"

"I'm sure. No one walks quite like he does. That's him."

Already the fire direction center was on the radio, giving precise coordinates to one of the Dodos circling overhead.

"Belay that!" Carrera shouted. All chatter in the CP stopped as every face turned to their chief with looks that said plainly, "Are you out of your fucking mind?"

Carrera swept a glare back at his headquarters troops. "Yes, I am probably out of my fucking mind. But I want him alive. He's worth more to us, over there, enforcing the rules than he would be dead and some other asshole breaking them."

He did not give his real reason. *I have a use for this man, in the future, if he lives.*

Assembly Area *Principe* Eugenio, just east of Ninewa

Cruz ducked into the trench as the black flower blossomed just a hundred meters away, sending steel shards zinging through the air like homicidal bees.

"They're getting better," Sanchez said. "You've got to admit it; they *are* getting better."

Cruz knew that shells were in short supply for the legion. Allegedly, they'd been given number one priority for both trucks and aircraft coming down the highway from Mangesh Base. The problem was, so the tribune had explained, that "number one priority doesn't mean the *only* priority." Food had to be brought, and that was bulky. Nor had the water purification point been moved right up to the river that fed the city yet. The legion needed a *lot* of water, too, about forty thousand gallons a day. Other items of ammunition, notably high explosives, grenades and small arms, were also needed and took up shipping space. The rockets for the big multiple rocket launchers wouldn't fit the legion's trucks except for the trucks that accompanied the launchers, and they were already carrying what they could.

Making things worse, the gringo commander of the 731st Airborne was pissed at Carrera—no, Cruz didn't know the full story—and had pulled out his own heavy transport.

So shells were being hoarded, for now at least, and the Sumeri mortars—they didn't seem to have any artillery available, but they had a shitpot full of mortars—were having a field day.

One of the century's snipers fired a single round from his Draco. He must have missed; he cursed the thing roundly as soon as he looked through his scope. He fired again.

The flyboys claimed to have gotten some. So far as Cruz could see it hadn't made a lot of difference. The Sumeri mortars barked whenever someone from the legion had the temerity to show himself.

Still, shells *were* coming down the pike. Stockpiles *were* being built.

"Won't be long now," Cruz muttered.

"Incoming!" Sanchez shouted.

About four kilometers behind the trench in which Cruz sheltered, Mendoza, del Rio and Sergeant Perez sat in the shade of a tarp stretched out from one side of the tank to block out the setting sun. Even with the tarp it was hotter than the hinges on the gates of Hell. The air shimmered. Mendoza knew it would be even worse inside the tank. Many virtues the Jaguar had. Air conditioning was, sadly, not among them.

About seven hundred meters away a century of heavy, 160mm, mortars barked together. The blast was enough to make the tank pitch slightly. The mortars, like the tank, were out of Sumeri range.

"Bastards could warn us when they're about to do that," del Rio complained, sticking a finger in his ear and rotating it slightly to emphasize the point.

Perez shrugged, indifferent. Mendoza seemed hardly to notice.

"Something bothering you, Jorge?" Perez asked.

Jorge shook his head *no,* but then added, "I was thinking about a girl back home, Sergeant."

"Girlfriend?"

"No . . . no. Just a girl I used to see at church. Beautiful girl, perfection in miniature. I don't even know her name, never had the courage to ask. But I remember her, wearing a yellow print dress and a white sun hat."

Both Perez and del Rio turned to look.

"Never had the courage to ask her name?" del Rio asked. "What? Am I sharing my tank with a pussy? What are you going to do when we roll into town?"

"I'm not afraid of that, Stefano, but girls can be *scary.*"

Perez laughed. "Yes, Jorge, girls *can* be scary. But I'll tell you what; we get out of this, I am going to march you to that church and when the girl shows up again march you over to her and introduce you."

"Jeez, Sarge, *would* you?"

❖   ❖   ❖

"I said they were fucking getting better. I didn't want them to get this fucking good," Sanchez cursed as he fired his rifle at a Sumeri raiding party that had sprung seemingly out of nowhere.

Rivera's light machine gun chattered, sending streams of mixed ball and tracer out toward the enemy. Cruz simply moved his rifle sights from one shadow to another, firing as the sights lined up. He didn't think he was hitting anybody but one had to *try*.

From Cruz's right another, heavier, machine gun began to trace lines across the ground. As if the machine gun were a spur to action, one of the Sumeris shouted, "*Allahu akbar*," God is great. Firing from the hip the whole crew began charging at Cruz's position. The machine gun killed a number of them but, without wire to slow the Sumeris down, they were quickly out of its arc of fire and descending on the century's forward trench.

"Shit, there must be a hundred of them," Sanchez said between shots and bursts.

Cruz set his rifle down and reached for the clackers—detonating devices—that led to a couple of directional antipersonnel mines out to the front. An earlier generation, on a different planet, might have called the mines "claymores." Cruz squeezed both clackers and was rewarded with a double blast. Perhaps as many as twenty of the attackers went down, some silently, some moaning, still others screaming. The rest plunged on.

"Fix bayonets! Fix bayonets! Fix bay—" screamed Sergeant del Valle. He never finished as an unlucky bullet hit him from the side and, breaking through the softer armor there, passed through his chest. He fell without another sound.

Cruz fumbled nervously for his own bayonet, fixed to his side by his web belt and its carrier. Then he unsnapped the leather strap that held the blade in place, withdrew it, and fixed it onto the end of his rifle. He didn't have time to see to Sanchez and Rivera before the Sumeris were upon them.

A bearded face approached, shouting something unintelligible. Above the face a rifle, also with fixed bayonet, was held in both hands. It was intimidating looking, but bad technique. Cruz went under the upraised rifle and plunged his own bayonet deep into the Sumeri's gut. The Sumeri's eyes went wide as his mouth formed an "O" of surprise. His knees crumpled and, as he went to them, his body pulled Cruz's lodged rifle down with it. Cruz struggled to free the blade.

Shit! What is it about me that keeps causing sharp pointy things to get stuck in people?

"*Allahu akbar,*" sounded from another of the enemy, too close in space and time for Cruz to risk trying to free his rifle. He dropped it and faced the Sumeri, left arm and leg bent and forward, showing as little of his own body to the enemy as possible.

The Sumeri lunged. Cruz batted the rifle slightly to one side, just enough to get inside its reach. His right fist lanced upward, catching the Sumeri on the jaw. The blow wasn't enough to knock his opponent out, but it did manage to stun him. Cruz took advantage of that to land another two blows onto the enemy's solar plexus. The Sumeri dropped the rifle and went down, gasping. Cruz took the rifle away from the Sumeri, grasped it in both his own hands and smashed the butt down onto the Sumeri's head, twice.

"Cruz!" screamed Rivera from where he lay, flat on the ground.

The team leader looked up and saw two of the enemy standing over his light machine gunner. Before he could fire both had driven their bayonets down. One, it was later determined, glanced off the glassy metal plate of Rivera's armor. The other sank into his throat.

Shrieking something incomprehensible even to himself, Cruz charged, firing his captured weapon from his hip. At this range, even that way he couldn't miss. Nor did the Sumeris have body armor. They went down. Then the magazine of the captured rifle went dry. Cruz reloaded from his own magazine pouches—for both sides carried, after all, the same model rifle—and fired again, one burst each, into the two enemy soldiers.

When he turned Cruz saw two things. One was that, on the left, the rest of the century was charging to his aid. The other was Sanchez, snarling and cursing and holding off three of them on his own, his bayonet flicking back and forth to threaten each in turn.

Without help, and soon, it would be a losing game.

Cruz charged. One of the Sumeris broke and ran back from whence he had come. Still others, from different parts of the battlefield, were fleeing as well. One of the two still facing Sanchez turned instead to face Cruz.

The two Sumeris saw the rapidly approaching rest of the century. First one, then the other, dropped their weapons and raised their hands. Sanchez was about to kill his man, even so, when Cruz ordered, "No."

❖   ❖   ❖

"Three dead, sir," Cruz told Carrera the next morning on the same spot as the previous night's action. Bodies still littered the ground. "No wounded, ours or theirs. It was . . . you know . . . too close for that. Too close to take chances."

"I understand. Who was killed here?" Carrera asked.

"Sergeant del Valle, he was my section leader," Cruz answered, "plus my own light machine gunner, Rivera, and Private Aguinaldo from Second Fire Team."

The signifer added, "One of the other sections lost a man as well, Legate."

"Prisoners?" Carrera asked.

"Cruz and Sanchez took two, Legate," answered the century signifer. "I've already had them escorted to the command post. There weren't any others. Not that we've found so far, anyway."

As if to give the lie to the signifer, one of the medics forward of the trench and examining the bodies felled by the directional mines and the machine gun fire shouted, "Hey, we need a field ambulance. I've got two live ones here."

The signifer shrugged. It had been a long night and the morning was young. No surprise they found some men wounded who hadn't been in the close fight.

Carrera looked around again, counting the Sumeri bodies in and around the trench. He noted the clackers lying inside it and the swath of bodies stretched out in two triangles in front of it. He nodded at the signifer who, by prearrangement ordered, "Corporal Cruz, PFC Sanchez, Attention." The signifer, the centurion, and the few legionaries standing nearby also went to attention.

"Orders will come along later," Carrera explained, as he reached into the chest pocket of his battle dress. "We'll make it formal then, too. For now, though, I see no reason to wait. Gentlemen, I am awarding you the *Cruz de Coraje en Acero*. This is the first step in the six steps of honor the legion has instituted to recognize and reward bravery. You two are only the fourth and fifth such awards we have made since coming here though I rather doubt you will be the last." Carrera hung a medal, a simple cross on a ribbon, around the neck of Cruz. He then did the same to Sanchez.

"This medal is, as I said, only the first step. You will wear it today, as this is the day I awarded it to you. You will also wear it on the day we make it formal, read official orders over you—bless you, so to speak—and present them in front of the legion. On other days you will not wear it, until you earn the next step, the Cross of Valor in Bronze." Carrera smiled slightly. "If you like how they feel on this day and that future day, you will just have to be mindlessly brave one more time."

Clapping both men on the shoulders and shaking their hands, Carrera turned and walked away.

Cruz didn't think too much of the award. Still, he thought, *I'm a* corporal? *Really? Damn.*

Sada's Command Bunker, 33/2/461 AC

"What was the butcher's bill, Qabaash?"

"*Amid,* we sent out ninety-seven men, nearly a full company. Only forty-three returned."

"A bitter price," Sada said. "Bitter but necessary." Sada looked at Qabaash. "You don't understand why it was necessary, do you?"

Qabaash raised his chin and shook his head. Being mostly out of the action was hard on him and very depressing. "No, *Amid*, I don't. I wish I did."

Patiently, Sada explained, "What's it worth paying to make sure the enemy doesn't sleep well at night, Qabaash? What price should we pay to make sure that he spends more of his effort watching out for a surprise attack than preparing to attack us here? You're a fine fighter, Major. You have to learn to be a thinker as well."

Command Post, *Legio del Cid*, 35/2/461 AC

"Well, it's not like I didn't *try* to accommodate them," Carrera said, watching the mass of aircraft overhead and on the other side of the river. The aircraft, a mix of C-31 and C-41 medium and heavy lift, were disgorging the better part of the 731st Airborne Brigade, Federated States Army. The air was thick with parachutes.

"You robbed t'em, t'ey t'ink," answered McNamara. "T'ree times t'ey planned a drop, t'ree times we overran and passed by t'e drop zone before t'ey could execute. An', Boss, you know as well as I do t'at planning a drop takes *time* and effort. So, yeah, t'ey're pissed at you. T'at's why t'ey stopped letting their forward support battalion help us, to slow us down so t'ey *could* make a jump . . . a 'combat' jump."

"Interesting application of decision cycle theory,

anyway, Sergeant Major. First time I've heard or read of an occasion where a military organization is outmaneuvered by its *friends* because its friends just decide faster and move faster than the organization is capable of."

McNamara shrugged. Fancy theories were fine, to him, provided they didn't interfere with the actual fighting.

"Anyway, we've got a problem or, rather, several. I've got a tacit agreement with the Sumeris on the rules for this fight. The 731st is not a part of that agreement. I know their commander, and he's a dickhead. Jeff Lamprey, ever heard of him?"

McNamara scratched a cheek, idly. "Name only," he answered.

"Stuffed-shirt, stick up his ass, prig," Carrera said, disdainfully. "Tall, handsome, manly . . . who happens to be a stuffed-shirt, stick up his ass prig. Not too manly, though, some say. I've been told, by people in a position to know, that when he was a captain commanding a company his wife—beautiful girl, too, they say—used to fuck his lieutenants. I don't think he ever quite recovered from that. That's one of the reasons I'm inclined to believe the story. He's the kind of guy who insists on saluting in the field and that troops should shave daily even when drinking water is short.

"Now, technically," Carrera continued, "by the contract Campos signed with us, I outrank him. I know him though and he won't listen to that. Frankly, Sergeant Major, we loathe each other at a really deep, sincere and personal level. So we are faced with the prospect of two forces trying to take the same town

at the same time, with essentially no chance that the
two forces will or even *can* cooperate. Hmmm . . . what
to do, what to do?"

Carrera paused, obviously thinking hard. McNamara
stayed quiet for the moment, worrying about what his
boss was thinking. Then Carrera nodded to himself,
turned around, and entered the CP.

"Fire support, have we got an armed Dodo overhead?"

"Yes, sir. Two of them, actually."

"Good. Drop the bridge on the other side of town.
Immediately."

McNamara, listening, thought, *Got to hand it to
him. He cuts right to the heart of the problem and
finds a solution. It might not be an* elegant *solution. It
might even piss off everyone in the entire world. But
he does come up with a solution, every time. Jesus, I
see no fucking end of trouble out of this one.*

Lamprey and a picked group of paratroopers hit,
rolled and recovered. In an instant they had doffed
their chutes, prepared their weapons, and were racing
on foot to seize the one bridge over the river that
led into the town.

The commander of the 731st Airborne saw a dark
streak above the bridge. Even without knowing he
was still pretty sure what it meant.

"Everybody, DOWN!" he shouted, while still seven
or eight hundred meters away from his objective.

KABOOM!

Lamprey looked up to see several concrete sections
of the bridge flying up in what looked like an attempt
to achieve low orbit.

"Come on, follow me," Lamprey shouted, getting to his feet and resuming his race. He had gained perhaps another hundred meters when the bridge erupted again. Again Lamprey threw himself to the ground.

KABOOM!

"That son of a bitch, undisciplined, insubordinate *bastard*," he muttered when he reached the bridge only to discover it really didn't exist anymore.

Sada's Command Post

"But, *why*? I don't understand, I really *don't* understand, *why* they dropped the bridge, *Amid*."

So far his enemy's actions had made a certain sense to Sada. He had to confess, though that this . . .

"Makes no sense to me either, Qabaash. So it must be a trick. Move Fourth Battalion from reserve to facing the river."

"That's going to leave us stretched facing the other enemy," Qabaash objected.

"I know. But I am guessing that they dropped the bridge precisely to lull us into thinking that no attack would be coming across the river. Thus, there almost certainly *will* be an attack from across the river."

Dodo Number Two, above Ninewa, 1/3/461 AC

The load this time was five-hundred-pounders, twenty-four of them. Each of the other five birds in the mission carried a similar load, except for Number Four, which carried five two-thousand-pounders. Four was flying somewhere off to the left. Its bombs were programmed for several hardened targets, which did *not* include Sada's command bunker, within the town.

The navigator—who was doing double duty as the bombardier, to the extent the guided bombs even required a bombardier—announced, "Release in . . . five . . . four . . . three . . ."

Command Post, *Legio del Cid*

"—two . . . one," intoned Triste from where he stood between the bank of radios and the operational maps. There was a delay of about half a minute between his announcement of "one" and the first rumblings of huge aerial bombs exploding in the city.

"It takes a while for the bombs to hit ground," he explained, a little sheepishly, when Carrera turned an uplifted eyebrow towards him.

Carrera shrugged—a few seconds one way or the other didn't really matter under the circumstances—and returned his attention to the operational maps.

One of these, the largest scale one, Ridenhour was updating with the latest information from Thomas's headquarters, still ensconced in al Jahara. The Federated States had made rapid progress, despite the false start at the beginning of the campaign. Even now its armored columns closed on the capital of the Republic of Sumer, Babel. Whether they would lunge right into the town or wait to allow slower moving infantry to catch up and do the detailed clearing was a matter of some debate within the legion's own headquarters.

Ridenhour, himself, didn't know. He was reasonably sure that Thomas was still undecided. True, the Sumeri Army had mostly folded up whenever FSA troops had gotten close. But there had been exceptions, a few times and places where they'd fought like demons. This was usually the doing of some local commander. Let one or two of that sort be inside the capital with a good sized body of troops under his command and a bold lunge with armor into the town could turn into a disaster.

There's not a lot of difference it makes to us, Carrera thought, with a mental shrug. *And it's not like I can affect it one way or the other.*

He turned his attention away from the map that showed events he could do nothing about and towards the local map that detailed the actions of his own force. There, things appeared to be going pretty smoothly. Third and Fourth Cohorts were holding position. First, Second, Fifth and Sixth were either in or moving to their jump off positions south of the town.

And, he thought, *since there isn't a whole hell of a lot I can do here, I may as well go forward and at least see the action and be seen.*

"Mitch, Soult; grab your radios. We're going up to see First Cohort move in."

Assembly Area *Principe Eugenio*

Corporal Cruz, PFC Sanchez, and the two new men just arrived a few days prior, Robles—younger brother to the Cazador sergeant strangled on Hill 1647—and Correa, got as low and as forward into shelter as the shallow trench permitted.

"Any time now," Cruz said, after consulting his watch. "Any time n—."

To the east, the sky lit up as one aerially delivered bomb after another slammed in, disintegrating buildings and the men those buildings contained. Cruz and the other three, even at this distance, were buffeted and shaken by the bombardment. Bits of hot metal, some of them substantial, flew overhead or careened into the friendly side of the scraped-out trench.

The bombardment went on and on, averaging one major explosion every twelve to fifteen seconds. Cruz lost track of the time. Even before it was finished, every mortar and gun of the legion opened up, lighting up both the open desert skyline and the interior of Ninewa.

Anticipating that the regular bombardment would stay fairly regular, Cruz waited until one of the really big blasts had gone off, waited a few prudent seconds for the metal shards to either pass over or come to rest, and stuck his head up for a risky look.

"It's all smoke and fire," he shouted to his men. "I can't see everything on the edge of town for the smoke, but what I can see has been better than half obliterated." As he watched he saw a substantial building fall to the ground, pouring off bricks as it came down.

He ducked again and just in time as another aerial bomb went off.

Between the distinct sounds of the bombing, Cruz made out the sound of engines, a lot of them, swinging in from the left until they were directly behind him. Then the engines began to grow louder as they moved toward the town, coming closer.

The mechanized cohort had feinted first to the west of the town, then—leaving behind one century to maintain the deception—the rest had turned around and swung wide to three-quarters circle Ninewa again and take up a position to the east. There, behind the First Cohort, they lined up, the remaining three mechanized centuries on line, tanks leading, followed by the Ocelots carrying the infantry.

Perez stood in the hatch of his tank, scanning ahead with his eyes while del Rio, below in the turret, scanned through the tank's thermal imager. Jorge Mendoza just drove, his eyes and crown only just sticking up out of the cramped driver's compartment.

Mendoza felt his heart begin to pound when he heard the century signifer call over the radio, "Roll."

Perez acknowledged the order and echoed it, adding in the directions, "Jorge, aim for those chemlights ahead and stop when we reach them." Mendoza put the tank into gear and began rolling forward, picking up speed quickly as he went. The tank lurched into a shallow trench and then, as Mendoza applied the gas, pulled out of it. It stopped on the other side, rocking back and forth for a moment.

Perez looked around until his eyes rested on a small group of infantry, just rising out of the scraping. "Come on, come on; climb aboard. We haven't got all day." Doubting the infantry could hear him, Perez used his arms to signal that it was time.

Cruz saw the tanker frantically waving for him and his men to climb aboard. He'd never trained on this, but it seemed straightforward enough: climb on, hang on for dear life and hope that the damned thing doesn't fire the main gun until you can climb the hell off.

"Mount up, boys," he ordered over the diesel's roar. "Sanchez, take the tail."

Cruz climbed aboard first, arms grasping for purchase and legs scrambling and slipping on road wheels and treads. He eyed the reactive armor, uncertainly. Rather, he was absolutely *certain* he didn't want to be anywhere near the damned rolling target if it took a hit and one of the explosive bricks went off.

Then again, if it takes a hit does it really matter? *Probably not; probably not even a little. Just be adding insult to—mortal—injury.*

Once safely mounted, Cruz reached down an arm to help the next man, Robles, climb up. With Sanchez pushing and Robles pulling they soon had Correa up. Correa and Robles helped Sanchez while Cruz tried to speak to the tank commander.

"I'm Perez," the sergeant shouted over the engine's roar. "We're going to close to within two hundred meters of the edge of town, firing the machine guns like maniacs. Then you grunts get off, along with the rest of your people and clear the edge. After that, we'll lead and you support."

"Why just the machine guns?" Cruz asked.

"Son, you *don't* want to be on this tank if we fire the main gun," Perez answered. "It . . . hurts."

"I understand, Sergeant Perez," Cruz shouted back. "Just give me the high sign when it's time to get off."

Perez replaced his combat vehicle crewman's helmet and said something, presumably to the driver. Cruz barely had his men positioned when the tank took off again with a shudder and a lurch.

✧   ✧   ✧

Mendoza was probably the loneliest man in or on the tank. Perez had del Rio for close company. Even the grunts on back could see each other. All he had was his lonely, isolated compartment . . . that, and the intruding memory of a beautiful light brown girl in a white hat and yellow print dress singing "Ave Maria," in a church choir.

Brutally, he pushed aside the thought of the unknown, nameless girl to concentrate on his driving. He had a set of Volgan-manufactured night vision goggles on. These were plugged into the tank for juice. They were infrared, the oldest technology, but had the advantage of being able to pick out any mines that the tank's infrared light might illuminate. Jorge saw none but maneuvered around a few suspicious spots anyway, his abrupt movements throwing Perez and del Rio around the turret and certainly pissing off the grunts hanging on over the engine compartment.

Mendoza actually smiled slightly, a sort of schadenfreude, when he thought about the grunts trying desperately to hold on despite his maneuvers. He felt a little ashamed. *It isn't* that *funny,* he told himself. *Well . . . maybe it is.*

He heard in his headphones, "Tank, halt. Gunner, coax, eleven o'clock, antitank gunner in building."

The coaxial machine gun began to chatter as Cruz felt the sergeant in the hatch tap his shoulder. "Off now, and get low," the sergeant shouted, then turned to use his own pintle-mounted heavy machine gun to fire forward.

Obediently, Cruz pushed Correa off the tank, then

turned to give the boot to Sanchez and Robles. Cruz then dove off himself and rolled to a stop next to Correa.

No sooner had he done so than the tank's main gun spoke, the muzzle blast assaulting Cruz's ears painfully and causing his internal organs to ripple. Downrange a building flashed, then exploded, as a high explosive round with delay set on the fuse burst through its wall and detonated inside. Men and parts of men flew out with the walls. The tank rolled forward, its machine guns still spitting at the buildings opposite.

Even though stunned by the muzzle blast, Cruz stood up to a crouch, Correa doing likewise beside him. He looked to the left and saw Sanchez and Robles doing the same. Cruz pointed at the tank's rear panel and pulled Correa along to get them both behind it. Sanchez and Robles joined them there a split second later.

Advancing with the tank, Cruz leaned out and fired a burst at nothing in particular. He hoped the tracers would remind the commander of the tank that he had infantry following. The only thing more frightening to a foot soldier than a friendly tank lurching about without control is an enemy tank lurching about with malicious intent. And the difference in fear factor is not large.

Other tanks, to the left and the right, fired machine guns and high explosive shells into the town. To these suppressive fires were added those of the Ocelots and the supporting infantry. There was some return fire, but the wall of lead put out by the attackers made it, at best, unaimed.

At the very edge of the town, taking cover behind still smoking buildings, the tanks stopped. Like the other infantry, Cruz and his boys surged into the town, to root out the defenders with rifle, bayonet and grenade.

INTERLUDE

13 May, 2092, Karolinska University Hospital, Stockholm, Sweden, European Union

Her breathing was labored now. No matter, it wouldn't be long and Margot Tebaf already had had a life with much to be proud of in it.

It has worked out, she thought. *It has worked out as we hoped it would.*

The pattern of outworld emigration, demographic flux, and expansion of political control by the United Nations, other supranationals, nongovernmental organizations and their supporters had been intimately linked.

The toughest part had been maintaining a working population sufficient to meet needs while getting rid of only enough useless mouths that the progressives of the European Union could maintain power. Once that power had solidified, though, it had become possible to so undercut the semblance of democracy that the votes of the elderly and indigent, the culturally unassimilated and inassimilable had become superfluous.

Old people don't riot when their pensions are cut

631

or eliminated and their children, if any, refuse to take them in, Margot thought. *They just die.*

Without off world emigration to dump the Moslems, their departures spurred by almost total elimination of welfare and the unavailability of work, it wouldn't have worked either.

Yet their colony on the New World was also a great draw. May they have luck with it.

Better and more satisfying, the cut-off of European immigration forced the United States to accept larger and larger numbers of immigrants as inassimilable as the Moslems were here. Now? Better than half their population owes and feels no loyalty to America, and votes for what it does feel loyalty to. And as we have expanded our power around the world, we have been able to force the United States to accept more and more of our way of doing things. They're still an economic powerhouse, but they can't impose their will anymore.

Even better than that, though, has been the effect of off-world emigration on the Americans. For each one that left has made the place less comfortable for those that remained. And each drop in the comfort level has made more leave. They still think of themselves as a real country. But they're dying. They predicted demographic death for us, but we will be at their funeral.

It was a cheery, if not perfectly accurate, thought for Margot. Thus, when the evening nurse came to check on her, her corpse was smiling broadly.

CHAPTER
TWENTY-THREE

Animals flee this hell; the hardest stones cannot bear
it for long; only men endure.

—Leutnant Weiner,
24th Panzer Division,
Stalingrad, 1942

Ninewa, Revolution Square, 6/3/461 AC

Cruz turned and began to throw up at the base of
the half-crushed wall behind which he had his team
sheltered. It was bad enough seeing the things done
to men in the town. But when a donkey staggered
by, dragging its entrails on the ground until its rear
legs twisted in them and it fell, bleating piteously?
That was just too much.

Sanchez apparently couldn't stand it either. He took
the Draco he was carrying, sighted it, and put the
poor animal out of its misery. Sanchez beat Robles,
carrying the light machine gun vice Rivera, by only
a fraction of a second.

"How long we been here?" Robles asked.

"*Here,* here, *or in the town,* here? Five days in the town. Here by the square maybe twenty minutes," Sanchez answered. "This time. Last time we got here we lasted a whole hour before they kicked us out again."

"Anyone know how Correa's doing?" Cruz asked through a dry, dusty and overtaxed throat.

"He . . . died, Cruz," Sanchez answered, sadly. "Yesterday. The medics told me last night."

"Damn," Cruz said, too tired to show any emotion. "Kid was only eighteen."

"Hey, Corp," said Robles. "I'll be sure to let you know when being eighteen saves you from anything. Besides, what are you? Nineteen?"

"Yeah . . . almost nineteen," Cruz answered.

As Sanchez had said, the square had changed hands numerous times. The statue of Saleh, the Sumeri dictator, that stood in the center of it was pockmarked and missing an arm. Bodies, both from the legion and from the Sumeri Army, littered it. The bodies, like those of Cruz and his two remaining men, were covered with a mix of dust, minute particles of pulverized adobe, concrete and stone, sweat, explosive residue and—in the case of those lying in the square—blood. There were many times more Sumeri bodies than Balboan, largely a function of the body armor worn by the legionaries; that, and their superior training in marksmanship.

"Heads up," Cruz ordered. "White flag, two o'clock."

"Surrender?" asked Sanchez.

"No . . . don't think so. The Sumeri looks like he still has fight in him. To me it looks like a request for truce to let medical and burial parties in."

Robles lifted his light machine gun as if to fire.

Cruz saw this, understood the anger and bitterness that might lead a young man to violate the flag of truce and said, "Knock it off, Robles. We got even for your brother one hundred times over." The private, reluctantly, lowered the weapon's muzzle.

The signifer for the century, a broad but filthy bandage covering half his face and one eye, walked out into the square, a white—well, it had started as white—flag tied onto a pole he held up and ahead. He and the Sumeri met midway, almost at the colossal statue. They nodded at each other in a way that was, if not quite friendly, at least respectful.

The Sumeri made a sweeping gesture which took in the square and all the bodies, living and dead, within it. Then he made something like the sign of the cross, but on one arm, pointing for emphasis at the bandage over the signifer's face.

The signifer nodded agreement, then pointed to his watch. He held up the fingers of one hand, twice. *Ten minutes?*

The Sumeri shook his head regretfully, once again sweeping around the square with one arm. *Too many bodies . . . and our people are stretched.*

Agreeing, the signifer held up all the fingers of the same hand, and repeated the gesture four times. At this the Sumeri seemed happy . . . or as happy as one could be under the circumstances. He then flashed his five finger sign once again and made as if putting a pistol in his holster. *Start the truce, officially, in five minutes.* The signifer agreed.

The Sumeri then made a sign as if drawing his pistol and firing it three times into the air. *That will be the signal to resume.*

At this the signifer nodded, as well. Then both shook hands and walked back.

Five minutes later, parties of legionaries and Sumeris warily entered the square, no weapons in evidence. They searched impartially for the wounded, of which there were a few. These the Balboans took away, irrespective of uniform. They could care for the wounded much better than could the Sumeris' poor medical staff. Moreover, while there was some advantage to making the Sumeris take their own wounded, to make them eat up the little food remaining, Carrera had ordered that starvation was not, in this case, to be used as a weapon.

The dead were taken away by their respective sides, the Sumeri dead to a mosque that had been turned into a morgue not far away, the Balboans to another ad hoc morgue that had been set up in the gymnasium of a captured high school. All the dead were treated with the greatest respect by both sides.

Both sides moved as briskly as exhausted men could be expected to. It was not quite briskly enough. Nearing the end of the truce the original Sumeri officer—lacking decent body armor, generally, they had many more dead to carry away—asked for another ten minutes, which was granted.

Then, exactly thirty-eight minutes and twelve seconds after the first white flag was shown, the bagpipes picked up, three well-spaced shots were fired into the air, and the slaughter resumed.

The only way tanks could lead in city fighting was if there was no real fighting to be done, in other words, if the enemy was either nonexistent or worthless. With a brave and *competent* enemy, and Sada's boys had shown themselves to be that, it was generally suicide for armor to lead. In that case, and in this, infantry led while armor followed and supported at a distance, suppressing with machine guns or clearing the way with the main gun. They'd proven particularly useful in clearing streets of the mines and booby traps the Sumeris had laid down lavishly.

The really bad part was that the streets made it impossible to use the armor in mass. Instead, one tank or sometimes two would be attached to one infantry century. Sometimes they'd have an Ocelot or two in support and sometimes not. In either case, though, when the rifle, sniper and machine-gun fire came in the crews had to button up and hope the infantry could keep the enemy's antitank teams away while the tank dealt with the threat that it sometimes couldn't really see very well.

In the close confines of the town of Ninewa, and despite having quite good night vision equipment, Perez, del Rio and Mendoza just couldn't see very well, generally. Not having slept much in days didn't help, either.

Still worse, they had no really good communications with the infantry century they were supposed to support. Their blasted antennae had been replaced; that wasn't the problem. Nor was it negligence on the part of the infantry. The grunts had simply lost so many leaders that a sergeant was leading the entire group with the senior section leader a mere corporal, and only one of those. The century had basically *lost* its ability to coordinate with their supporting tank.

Even worse than that, this century was not the original one. The tanks were in such short supply, never more than sixteen to begin and four had been lost completely, that they had to shunt around from unit to unit.

Neither Perez, nor del Rio, nor Mendoza could remember when they'd slept last. Mendoza thought he might have eaten something the day prior but couldn't be sure. The stewed camel over rice was not something the cohort mess section was really used to preparing, but they'd been reduced to that for the last three days. He might have skipped it yesterday; hard to remember. Too sleepy, too—

"Jorge, back up! Back up! Back up! Gunner, HE, RGL, two o'clock. Jorge, goddammit, back UP!"

Still half asleep Mendoza automatically shifted gears and backed the tank fifty meters. Before he had gone that distance, though, a rocket-launched grenade lanced out from the half-shattered wreck of an adobe building. It missed the tank, barely, and exploded against a wall behind Jorge and to his left. The tank's automatic defense system hadn't fired because all the blocks on the front had been used up and there hadn't been any spares to replace them. Maybe tomorrow . . .

Del Rio was apparently not half asleep since the main gun roared even before Jorge applied the brakes. That woke him up fully and in time to watch the adobe building to his right front disintegrate to dust.

Ninewa, Command Post, *Legio del Cid*, 6/3/461 AC

A Cricket's engine sputtered outside where it had come to a hasty landing just a few seconds ahead of a heavy machine gun's tracers. A short, dark, and stout man, chest still swathed in bandages, climbed painfully down from its high door.

Parilla had to be helped into the building. The first thing he heard upon entering was Patricio Carrera, cursing a storm into a radio. "Listen carefully, you miserable son of a bitch. I said I want . . ."

Parilla sat heavily and wearily in a folding chair inside. Outside the Cricket that had brought him had its tail picked up by four legionaries and turned to face away from the wind. Once loaded, it would taxi again and face into the wind for takeoff. Another pair of men, wearing white armbands with red crosses, loaded a stretcher in through the rear of the aircraft, then helped another legionary with his chest and shoulder heavily bandaged to climb into the front passenger seat. Loaded, the Cricket took off again in a cloud of propeller-raised dust. Behind the Cricket a NA-23 Dodo with "Lolita" painted on the nose waited patiently while more wounded either boarded or, if stretcher cases, were loaded.

Carrera took one look and asked, "Raul, what the fuck are you doing here? You're still hurt."

Parilla sighed and answered, "I couldn't stand it anymore, lying there while they brought in more and more wounded kids, most of them worse off than I was. So, one of the advantages of being *Dux*," and he emphasized the title as if to say, *which means people do what I tell them to, generally*, "is that when I say, 'I want to be flown to the front,' someone is going to bust ass to get me flown to the front."

Carrera smiled. "I missed you, you old bastard. Things are not going all that well and we sure needed you here."

"That's why I came, Patricio."

"Are you up to running things from here?" Carrera asked.

"Yes . . . with help," Parilla admitted.

"Okay then. Let me show you how things stand." Carrera walked to the map and began to trace with his finger. "We've got about two-thirds of the town, plus this airport," Carrera's head inclined in the direction of the Nabakov-23. "The Sumeris are still hanging on to the local university, backed up here against the river, and this corner." The finger showed the northeast area of the town, marked as being still in Sumeri hands. "This group didn't go into the school, by the way, to try to gain shelter by hiding in an off-limits target. They knew we wouldn't feel terribly restricted by that and sent a parliamentaire to assure us we could engage them there. They're only in it because it's all they have left."

"Fighting strength is down" Carrera continued, "dangerously down. We've got nothing but MPs and walking wounded guarding prisoners and we've cannibalized the rear echelon for riflemen. Even so, average century rifle strength is only about three-quarters, more in some, less in others. That's even *with* the four hundred replacements fresh out of training that Christian rushed us from Balboa."

Parilla raised a finger. "I can shed a little light and hope on the replacement situation. Another one hundred and fifty . . . ummm . . . fifty-four are due in day after tomorrow. And another one hundred and eighty or so in ten days."

"That might help; the next contingent, I mean. If we haven't finished taking this place before ten days are up, I'll resign."

Parilla inhaled deeply and, with obvious reluctance and distaste, said, "And that's another problem. The papers back home are howling for your head over these reprisals. Some of the politicos are, too. You haven't been up on international news here, have you?"

"No, why?"

"The Taurans are talking about putting out a warrant for your arrest from the Cosmopolitan Criminal Court."

"Fuck 'em," Carrera answered, with no noticeable degree of concern.

"Okay, just thought you might like to know. Anyway, I can handle things here." Parilla looked over the manning charts hanging on one wall. "Legate, you need to get forward to *lead* this legion."

Carrera looked at the same charts, even as Parilla did. "Can you get by without a couple of the staff?" he asked.

"Who did you have in mind taking?"

"Rocaberti, Daugher, Bowman. Plus Mitchell and Soult. I had to shift Johnson to 3rd Cohort to replace its commander."

"Where's Carl Kennison?" Parilla asked.

"Here, *Duce*," Kennison answered unexpectedly from the door.

Carrera raised a single eyebrow, which Kennison answered by saying, "I'll be fine for now, Pat. We can talk later, after the battle's over."

Carrera nodded. "Fine. I'll be on my way then." He glanced around to make sure all five men he'd said he wanted to take were present. "You people I mentioned; on me in ten minutes, ready to rock."

❖   ❖   ❖

Manuel Rocaberti had done his level best to be as useful at headquarters as possible, hoping thereby to escape being sent anywhere but. He wasn't lazy, after all; he just wasn't too terribly brave. He'd learned that over a decade ago when, in the face of an FSC attack on Balboa he had run, deserting his men and his command. He'd have been shot, he knew, if his side had actually won. Fortunately, for him, they had not and in the chaos after the fall of Piña, the ex-dictator, no one had thought to prosecute him. Rather, no one in a position to had ever thought to. He was reasonably sure that Jimenez, among others, would have been glad to see him dead.

Thus it was with a mix of relief and trepidation that Rocaberti found himself suddenly placed in command over an understrength infantry century with a single tank attached. The relief came from the fact that no one in the century or the cohort over it had any obvious reason personally to want Rocaberti dead. The trepidation came from the fact that the century was facing a large number of Sumeris who *did* want him dead, albeit only in an impersonal way. That was small comfort.

Even so, Rocaberti was an experienced officer, an experienced commander, and well above the rank normally associated with the command of a single century. There was some good he could do. He began well enough, reorganizing the century and letting one badly overtasked sergeant become his assistant, rather than having the entire weight bearing down on the poor sergeant's own young shoulders. Then he'd seen to the supply situation, ensuring especially that more ammunition was ordered. Lastly, after talking amiably with some of the men, he'd set upon the cooks. There would be something better than boiled camel over rice this evening.

So many of Sada's officers were down that he was reduced to, if not quite leading charges himself, at least guiding the assault parties forward and giving them their final instructions. With another Sumeri commander, this sort of thing would have been expected and, as expected, such assaults would have petered out quickly once out of that stay-behind commander's gaze.

Sada, by contrast, spent so much time at the front, and so much time exposed to enemy fire, that his men understood that if he stayed behind it wasn't in regard for his own safety, but in regard to the mission. They knew they weren't being sacrificed by a coward. That his reputation for this kind of conduct went back almost twenty years didn't hurt matters.

The hardest thing for Sada to learn, this campaign, had been the effectiveness of modern night vision. In the Farsi War there had been little and what little there had been had been almost all on his side. In the Oil War of a dozen years before, while the enemy coalition had had a massive advantage, it hadn't affected him or his men much as they were in another part of the theater, killing Yezidis. They'd been bombed silly more than once, true, but night vision hadn't had a lot to do with it.

Here though, the disparity was both gross and *everywhere*. The enemy had sights that would see through dust, through smoke, through *walls*. He'd lost a lot of men figuring that out. Now his men didn't try to restrict their movements to the night that the enemy owned. Instead, day or night they moved underground wherever possible, in tunnels—often no more than crawlspaces—that stretched from building to building and under roads and parks. Even where tunnels had not been possible, trenches were, and these helped shield Sada's men at least from the ground mounted thermal and light amplifying sights, if not from those loitering above, in the air.

It was a hard-learned lesson: *If the enemy owns the night, fight, where possible, in the day.*

So, ratlike, Sada and his soldiers moved in small groups, through trenches and tunnels, between buildings and under and across roads and parks before emerging, several hundred of them, in a series of apartment buildings still held by his side. The worst part was crawling through a trench that led across a children's park. Sada had fretted over that badly, finally ordering enough troops into five buildings that dominated the park so that any aerial recon could be driven off or shot down. At the end of the park, the trench went underground again, before turning left to enter several apartment building basements.

In the apartment buildings' basements—named by Sada "Assault Position Ramadan"—too tired to be nervous over the possibility of aerial bombs or heavy mortar shells, Sada and his men slept the night, awaiting morning and their attack.

And I must *attack, at least often enough to keep the enemy from feeling secure enough to methodically peel us away like the shell from an egg,* Sada thought, as he drifted off to fitful sleep.

4th Cohort Command Post (Forward), 7/3/461 AC

The Forward CP was wherever Jimenez happened to be, with a couple of radiomen, a forward observer team with another radio, and a few more soldiers detailed as security.

It was just after midnight. Jimenez and his small party hunkered down behind some furniture hastily thrown up and then reinforced by sandbags, the whole mess being on the ground floor of a government building facing a broad and dusty open area. This had some children's amusements to suggest it had once been dedicated as a park.

One would have to look twice, though, to see that now. The children's amusements were smashed, littered here and there with bodies, and the otherwise smooth and level fields of dust were pockmarked with shell craters. Further detracting from the image of playground were the long trench dug into the field and the barbed wire that was strung from end to end.

Jimenez had reason to know the place was mined, too. Even if he might have forgotten, the grim light cast by the flickering flames of one of his Ocelots— immobilized by a mine and colanderized by rocket launched grenades—would have reminded him.

At least we got the chingada *crew out.*

Five apartment buildings, the center one of seven ntories, flanked by two of six, with those flanked by two of five stories, dominated the open field. They were exactly the kind of unattractive and tasteless government housing projects one might have expected from any government involved in public housing; blank, featureless, concrete "machines for mass living" with all the humanity carefully excised.

Their ugliness was even worse now—even more real—for it was from these that fire had poured down on Jimenez's men as they'd tried to cross without adequate armored support. It was from these that the RGLs had smashed one of the few armored vehicles Jimenez had available to him.

Carrera had called, just after the last attack, asking if Jimenez couldn't *somehow* force the field and get a toehold on the buildings opposite.

"Patricio, there is no way I can get across on foot. We tried. We paid, too. If you've got a bright idea, let me know because I am fresh out."

"Wait, out." The radio had gone silent then for half a minute. When Carrera had come back he'd said, "Yes, I've got an idea. It'll be dangerous, though, and it will take some time to set up, to coordinate between the artillery, the flyboys and the Cazadors. Say . . . between four and eight hours. Hang tight. I'll get back with you."

The artillery wasn't a problem. Neither was getting half a dozen helicopters configured for a mixed infantry-gunship load. The problem was the Cazador Cohort.

"They're spent, Jamie," Carrera said, looking around at a collection of not so much dispirited as simply bone-weary men. "For at least a day, more likely two days, they're just out of it. Sending them back in, in this state, would be murder."

Soult had nothing to say to add to that. Instead, he simply asked, "What are you going to do about it?"

"Something I'd really rather not," Carrera admitted. "Call the CP and have Colonel Ridenhour meet us here."

Tactical Operations Center, 731st Airborne Brigade, northwest of Ninewa

Colonel Jeff Lamprey was frantic, frustrated and infuriated, his face beginning to match his flaming red hair. He paced the close confines of his tented command post, set up just out of range of 120mm mortars, lashing out at all who crossed his path. His headquarters troops tried to avoid him, as best they could.

There was a low *thrum* from overhead. This, Lamprey hadn't heard before, at least on his side of the river. He left the tactical operations center, or TOC—a fancy name for a command post, stepping outside in time to see a crude and primitive looking aircraft on high, grasshopper leglike landing struts set down lightly less than one hundred meters away. The door to the plane had painted on it an armored knight with curved wings attached to his back armor and rising overhead.

Lamprey, who had had a week to study the organization across the river recognized it as one of the *Legio del Cid's* light recon and command birds. He snarled.

The door to the plane swung open to allow a man in FSA-style desert camouflage to climb down. It was too far to see the man's rank clearly, but Lamprey, who had an instinct for general officers—indeed his entire life's ambition was to join that exclusive club—was reasonably certain that the just-arrived officer was not one. Perhaps he was a colonel like Lamprey himself, perhaps some lesser being.

Suppressing his rage and putting on an utterly false smile, Lamprey walked halfway to the Cricket to meet his visitor. He saw that the man was, like himself, a colonel and, upon closer inspection of the embroidered tape over his right breast pocket, that his name was Ridenhour.

Ridenhour didn't waste time on trivialities. "You want into the fight?" he asked.

"Damn straight. And if that son of a bitch on the other side—"

"Which other side?" Ridenhour asked with a wintery smile. "I have direct access to *Dux* Parilla and Legate Carrera. But if you want to talk to the enemy commander, *Amid* Sada, you're on your own . . . though you could probably funnel a message through the legion." Ridenhour smiled, "The relationship is quite close and rather cordial, considering."

"You know damned well who I mean, Ridenhour." Lamprey's frustration and anger threatened to leak out.

"Ah. Well, Carrera is willing to negotiate."

"Negotiate, hell, that motherf—"

"Ah, ah, ah," Ridenhour wagged a finger. "Temper, temper. Carrera had sound reasons for keeping you out, initially, just as he has sound reasons for letting you in now . . . in a limited fashion."

"In a *limited* . . . arrrghgh!"

"That's right. He is willing to let your brigade take some buildings. It's an important set of targets. They'll be plenty of medals and commendations to go around. *If* you're a) interested and b) willing to fall under his—rather, *Dux* Parilla's—command."

"Details?" Lamprey asked, forcing his temper down.

Ridenhour nodded; this was easier than he'd thought it would be. He pulled a map out of his left leg cargo pocket and began to speak, while pointing. "In about four hours there will be six helicopters, Volgan-built IM-71s, landing four kilometers south of your positions. At the moment they land there will be an aerial attack on the objective I mentioned. That will be followed by a mortar bombardment on and around the objective. When the helicopters land here, and this is assuming you agree, of course, you will board the first echelon of one battalion—call it one reinforced company of one hundred and forty-four men, maximum—or one reinforced platoon of each of three companies of one battalion; your call. The helicopters will make a total of three sorties each, so the most you are getting over there is a single battalion, plus maybe a little reinforcement."

Ridenhour looked up to see if Lamprey was still with him. Seeing that he was, he continued. "The helicopters will follow this route. They will halt, briefly, at a range of five hundred meters and blast the living shit out of the targets, which are five apartment buildings of five to seven stories, each. Then they'll move in by pairs. As pairs, they will fly in your men and drop them on top of the buildings. Your job is to clear them to ground level, then pass through a . . . well . . . call it a 'battalion' from the legion. The cohort concerned—their commander is Xavier Jimenez, good man—will fall under your command until they pass through, just as you will fall under legion command as soon as you board."

Lamprey's eyes lit up slightly. Ridenhour was morally certain that what he was thinking about was a comment on his next Officer Evaluation Report Support Form to the effect of, *Commanded a foreign battalion during combat operations in Sumer in 461*, just above the comment that said, *Cooperated fully with allied forces during combat operations in severe city fighting in Sumer in 461*.

"If—and it's a big *if*, I know—you do this and it works out," Ridenhour continued, "Carrera will use his assets to ferry over your entire brigade and subdivide the city into two sectors for operational purposes. You will still be under legion command, however. Do you accept?"

Before Lamprey could answer, Ridenhour laughed. "If you don't, he will take the city on his own, damn the cost, and you will look like the Grand Old Duke of York, except that the air transport that got you here so that you could sit around jerking off is much more expensive than the shoe leather the duke wore out marching his men up a hill and down again."

"I could simply ignore the bastard and cross on my own," Lamprey insisted. "I've got my people back in the rear working on getting me rubber boats even now."

Ridenhour sighed deeply. How to explain to one arrogant world-class asshole that there was a much bigger, and infinitely more ruthless, asshole nearby.

"Have you ever stopped to consider that dropped bridge, Jeff?" Ridenhour asked. "Do you really think it was just a mistake? I've gotten to know the man and he doesn't make or permit that kind of mistake. Now what do you suppose he might be willing to do if you try to force a river crossing against his wishes? What do you think it will do to your career if there's a massive friendly fire incident here between you and the legion and you end up losing over half the total of men killed in this campaign? You did want to see stars someday, didn't you?"

Forward Command Post, 4th Cohort

Xavier Jimenez heard the IM-71s *whop-whopping* behind him as they moved from the captured airfield to cross the river to where the gringo Airborne troops waited. Truth be told, Jimenez had doubted the FS Army commander on the other side of the river would roll for it. It had been an awfully dirty trick, he thought, Patricio dropping the sole useable bridge right under the paratroopers' noses.

The helicopters' sound rose, then began to drop again. Almost immediately, four Turbo-Finches appeared overhead. Singly they began to dive on the apartment buildings, firing machine guns and rockets down to clear the rooftops of any enemy who might be waiting there. Jimenez didn't know how effective the attack would be, though he did see one enemy soldier running along a roof be driven over the side by a blast to fall, screaming and arms flailing, to the ground.

That attack went on for several minutes while the helicopters got farther away. Just as Jimenez lost track of them completely, the aerial attack stopped, the birds winging it out of the area on full throttle.

Even as the last Turbo-Finch emptied its rocket pods, there came a massive roar from the legion's heavy mortars, in firing position somewhere to Jimenez's rear. He'd seen and heard so much mortar fire of late that he didn't even bother to try to count the seconds until impact. Instead, at about the right time, he ordered his command party to, "Duck!"

The mortar rounds that came in were almost all airbursts, set off by variable time fuses as they neared the vertical walls of the apartment building or the ground below. Their shards sometimes landed near Jimenez and his men. More often, the shards crashed against the apartment buildings' walls or entered the rooms through open or smashed doors and windows. The firing stayed steady, at about thirty heavy rounds a minute, for several minutes.

Sometime after the heavy mortars had begun firing, Jimenez heard the sound of the helicopters coming from behind and growing. They held up and hovered at a holding position several hundred meters behind Jimenez. That was his signal.

"Patricio, this is Xavier. Cut the heavies."

"Roger, out."

The muzzle blasts from behind stopped, though the shells continued detonating for half a minute. The last four shells were smoke. These exploded and sent burning bits of phosphorus down to the ground trailing tails of white smoke. Jimenez counted them off, carefully, before ordering, "Fourth Cohort! Support the assault by fire!"

Rifle and machine gun fire erupted from Jimenez's side of the children's park.

Assault Position Ramadan

Sada was most pleased to wake up and discover he was not dead, as he had half-expected to become when he'd closed his eyes to sleep the night before. Around him, his men were also awakening, shaken rather than shouted at by their sergeants and lieutenants. The sun was just beginning to seep through the basement assembly area's few slits and crevices.

"Qabaash, check the troops to the right," Sada ordered. "I'll go left."

The two then split up, walking where possible and crawling where not, to inspect the soldiers Sada was about to send into an attack that was, on its face, hopeless. They returned after several minutes, meeting with the commander of the battalion about to assault.

"Let me go with them, *Amid*," Qabaash begged. The major just *quivered* with excitement at the pending assault.

"No," Sada answered, firmly. "You have other things to do." He turned to face the new battalion commander. "You know your orders?"

"Yes, *Amid*," the captain commanding the assault battalion answered. "They're simple: attack, do damage, break through and go hunting through the rear for the support areas. Then become such a pain in the ass in the enemy's rear that he has to stop his attack to the northeast." The battalion commander—he was the sixth officer to hold the post in as many days—looked like a man who has resigned himself to death, as indeed he had.

"Allah's blessing upon you then," Sada said, placing one encouraging hand on the *naquib*'s shoulder. He looked at a firing slit, and then at his watch. Judging the time about right, Sada said, "*Allahu akbar,* my friend. Attack."

Ordering "Fixed bayonets" and taking up the cry, "*Allahu akbar!*" the battalion commander led his men out of their sheltering cellar and into the light.

"*Allahu akbar!*" came from three hundred throats as the storming party, pleasantly surprised not to be shot to bits as they emerged from the basements, charged across the street in full battle fury.

As they stormed, six blocks away a barrage was unleashed on another Sumeri position.

Command Post, Rocaberti's Century

Timely provisioning was something Rocaberti had always prided himself on, even back in the old days of the Balboan Defense Corps. He also saw much benefit in an orderly dispensing of rations. His acting centurion, still the sergeant who had previously led the century, had had other ideas. The sergeant had demanded to maintain fifty percent security rather than lining up three sections out of four to make chow go more smoothly and efficiently. The sergeant had demanded and Rocaberti had overruled him. All the sergeant could do now was get the men through the line and back to the front as quickly as possible. This he tried to do. He was still trying, when the heavy mortars to the rear had opened up on some apartment buildings well off to the right front. The men had shuddered, as nervous and tired men will, when the first shell bursts had gone off.

"Ignore it," the sergeant insisted. "Get your goddamned food and get back to the line."

The last time Manuel Rocaberti had heard massed artillery so close it had been at the commencement of the invasion of his country by the FSC. It had set him to trembling then. It did no less now.

Then, though, it had not been the artillery that frightened him so much as the prospect of a ground attack. *That* had convinced him to desert his command and run for it. So, when over the shock waves of the big guns he heard, louder and much closer, the massed cry of *"Allahu akbar,"* and looked up to see a mass of armed Sumeris boiling up seemingly from the earth, Rocaberti did three things: he dropped his jaw, he dropped his breakfast and he dropped the pretense of courage.

While his sergeant shouted, "Action front," and tried to push, pull and prod the legionaries into some semblance of a position they might hope to defend, Manuel Rocaberti, son of the Federated States Military Academy at River Watch, Class of 438, former major in the Republic of Balboa's Defense Corps, tribune in the *Legio del Cid,* bolted.

Daugher straight-armed the bolting, panic-stricken legionary, dropping him flat on his back. Carrera and his party had headed toward the sound of firing as soon as they'd heard it. When it had grown into a cacophony they'd broken into a run to get there. They'd slowed when they saw the soldier fleeing without his rifle.

Carrera bent down and, grabbing the soldier with one arm, backhanded him across the face with the hand of the other. "What the fuck is going on, trooper?"

The kid just shook his head back and forth saying, "I don't know, I don't know, I don't know—"

"Mitchell, this soldier is under arrest. Follow. The rest of you, either side of the street. Let's go see."

Carefully, the headquarters party advanced, Carrera just behind Bowman on one side, Daugher taking point on the other. Mitchell, taking up the rear, prodded the arrested soldier forward at muzzle point. They saw no more fleeing troops. On the other hand, they did see small groups of Sumeris advancing across an intersection without any obvious opposition.

Carrera took the radio microphone from Soult. He called Parilla first, to tell him what he thought had happened and to warn the *Dux* to be prepared to defend the CP and the airfield. Parilla was already shouting instructions before he released the microphone on his end.

Confident that at least the Command Post wouldn't be taken unawares, Carrera next called the Cazador Cohort.

"Tribune," he'd said, "I don't care if your men are tired. I don't care if they're dragging their guts behind them. Meet me at . . ." he stopped to look at his map . . . "Meet me at Checkpoint Alpha Seventeen. Now . . . yes, your whole fucking cohort."

"What now, Boss?" Bowman asked, eagerness and excitement in his voice.

"Now? Now we go seal off that intersection and try to buy some time."

Daugher and Bowman said, together, "Yeehaw!"

Carrera's only responses were a smile, the word, "Lunatics," and the order, "Let's go."

Jimenez had to admire the elegance of the thing. While his men fired up the lower stories of the apartment buildings across the park, the choppers pulled pitch and lifted up above Jimenez's own positions. They advanced above the park blazing away, lacing the fronts of the enemy-held buildings with fire. As they crossed from overhead to his high front, Xavier saw that even the crew chiefs were leaning out the side doors and windows to add their machine guns to the din.

With no significant return fire coming, the center two IM-71s arose, then swooped down, one falling in behind the other, to the center—and tallest—of the apartment buildings. The first disgorged its troops there, then moved forward to give room to the helicopter following.

When it did, the far side of the building—the side where there was no suppressive fire and which had not been touched by the mortar barrage—erupted with machine guns and RGLs. The helicopter tried to get away, but its own downdraft corrected at least one grenade in flight, straightening it out by the wind on the fins and causing it to surge upwards. This struck it on the tail, wrecking the tail rotor and causing the helicopter to tilt half over to one side and go into an uncontrolled spin. Spinning still, it spiraled to the ground behind the apartments and crashed in smoke and flames. Pinned tight by centrifugal force, none of the crew escaped.

Jimenez didn't see the crash. He caught a single

glimpse of the spinning tail boom and then heard the fiery explosion. "Shit," he said quietly, nausea gripping at his stomach.

Lamprey and his RTOs landed even as the previous bird was beginning its death spiral. The pilot of the IM-71 that disgorged this second group saw what had happened to his predecessor and had *no* intention of following. Fortunately, he didn't have to. The first bird had taken the dangerous route out to clear the rooftop as quickly as possible for the second. Since only two were scheduled to carry troops to the tallest of the buildings, the second chopper didn't have to get out of anyone's way and could take the time to lift and do a fairly leisurely turn.

Once it had cleared the rooftop, the third and fourth helicopters eased in to the lower buildings flanking the center one. Before they touched down, forty of the forty-eight paratroopers of the 731st that had already landed had burst through the rooftop and were clearing out the Sumeris hiding below in vicious, no quarter, room-to-room and hall-to-hall fighting.

Lamprey, staying on the roof, led from the rear.

Rocaberti stopped running only after having sprinted half a mile and zigzagged several times to make sure he was out of the line of fire. It was a not unimpressive performance from a man in his early forties. Gagging with exhaustion, he leaned against a wall to catch his breath. Behind him, he heard enough firing to suggest that his entire command had not been exterminated.

This was a problem.

When Rocaberti heard the roar of a big gun—a

tank, he thought—he knew he had a really big problem. If the century somehow held out there would be witnesses, dozens of them, against him at his future court-martial. He considered the way Carrera had treated enemies who had broken the rules. What would he do to nominal friends who had? Thinking of ropes and short drops, the tribune automatically felt around his neck.

Not that Rocaberti considered Carrera a friend; the legate had always been a bit distant. In fact, the sinking feeling in the deserter's stomach might not have been quite so deep if Carrera had been a friend.

"What difference does it make though?" he wondered aloud. "Jimenez is his best friend and Carrera would even have *him* shot if he'd run as I did. Fuck; fuck; fuck! Why did I ever let my uncle force me back into uniform?"

Though it did not answer the question, another blast from a tank's muzzle half a mile behind him did punctuate it.

Mendoza had to admit, the food *was* a bit better this morning than it had been. He sat in his driver's compartment, surrounded by the dials and controls of his tank, eating breakfast, fried sausage and some yellow-greenish stuff that probably had egg in its ancestry somewhere. Del Rio had gone and fetched it for all three men; the infantry century they supported still hadn't quite figured out what to do with them.

Between bites Mendoza watched the legion's attack aircraft swoop in on some targets blocked by the buildings to either side. Between those attacks, his mind wandered to a pretty girl in a yellow dress . . .

The cry of *"Allahu akbar"* echoed down the street. Mendoza heard Sergeant Perez shout, "Oh, shit!" He looked up from his food and saw a part of the Sumeri wave washing down the street. Without orders, Mendoza pushed the starter button to bring the tank's engine to life. With only the slightest hesitation he tossed the food up and out of the driver's compartment, then pulled on his combat vehicle crewman's helmet in time to hear Perez ordering, " . . . HE, Infantry."

The tank rocked as del Rio fired a round point blank into the oncoming Sumeris. The shell exploded a bit farther than would have been ideal but the Sumeris went down anyway, killed or wounded or merely stunned by the explosion behind them.

Perez shouted into the microphone, "Jorge, back up! Back up, dammit!" Mendoza threw the tank into reverse and stepped on the gas. These actions were automatic; he didn't need to see. Instead, he looked up and saw parties of the enemy racing along the roofs on both side of the street. Several of them carried rocket grenade launchers.

Distracted by the threat above, Mendoza lost track of the direction his tank was going. Instead of moving directly back, it lurched at a slight angle to the lay of the street. Thus, just after passing an intersection, the left rear struck the wall of a building, smashing it and lurching up on the mound of adobe fragments it created. The tank bellied up and stuck on the mound.

Perez was firing the heavy, pintle-mounted machine gun in front of the commander's hatch, the steady hammering feeling like blows to the driver. Maybe Perez saw the attackers above; maybe he didn't. The firing stopped, in any case, when the tank crashed into the wall and came to a sudden halt. Mendoza, stunned but not out, keyed the microphone on his CVC and tried to warn Perez. "Sergeant Per—"

Whatever warning he was about to give was cut off when an RGL round, fired from above, struck the top of the tank, over the engine compartment. Jorge didn't see the hit, but he felt the sudden overpressure all around him as if it were a set of massive clubs, applied equally and simultaneously to every square inch of his body.

He didn't feel the second round impact on the roof of the turret. Nor did he feel it when a round of the ammunition, caught halfway between the armored carousel below the turret and the breechblock of the gun, went off.

Having seen off the spoiling attack, Sada, Qabaash and a few of their men retraced their steps back toward the command post. It was daylight now and, even though he knew in principle that he was at least as likely to be seen crossing the trench across the park at night as in the day, it still took all the courage Sada could muster to take that first crouched-over step out into the sunlit trench.

The shelling had stopped, which seemed to Sada a good thing as the shards from the airbursts might well have found them out even below ground level in the uncovered ditch. On the other hand, the helicopters above *seemed* as threatening.

"But they're not looking down here at all," Sada said to himself. "Hmmm. If I *had* an RGL would it be worth the shot? No matter, since I don't."

Halfway across the park Sada and his party turned left and followed a narrower, zigzagging section of the trench that led to the apartment building's basements. Nobody saw them, all the enemies' eyes still fixed on the buildings looming above.

Private Muqtada Fawash saw one RGL round strike the tank's rear grill, setting it alight. The blast knocked forward the man in the tank's commander's hatch who had been stoutly serving his machine gun until the moment the blast hit. Muqtada didn't know if that blast had killed him. He was certain that the second round impacting had been fatal though; it was so close to the enemy tanker's body that it should have cut his torso nearly in two.

As impressive as that was, it was as nothing to the blast that came a fraction of a second later when, so the private assumed, the second RGL set off some—almost certainly not all—of the tank's internally stowed ammunition.

Right before Fawash's eyes two bodies were blown completely out of the tank. The first—the tank commander's—flew almost straight up and in two pieces, a geyser of flame following it. The second was expelled from the driver's compartment. The force must have been something awful, for it had caused the driver's legs to be nicked off when they struck the inside ring of the hatch.

Fawash winced in sympathy.

Muqtada was a bit of an oddity in the Sumeri Army, though not all that uncommon in Sada's brigade. He whispered a prayer as his hand reached up to caress a small golden cross hung about his neck. Then, he hurried to where the second body had fallen to see what he could do to help a fellow Christian.

There wasn't much, Muqtada saw, once he got a good look at Jorge Mendoza's body. *Still, what I can; I must.* He cleared Jorge's airway and made sure he could breathe. Then he took the cord from the CVC helmet and tied it around one leg to stop the gush of blood. The victim's belt did for the other. *Best I can do.* He made a quick sign of the cross over Jorge just as his sergeant barked, "Fawash, get your *Nazrani* ass in gear."

"Yes, Sergeant."

Fawash hurried, like a good soldier, following his sergeant. In accordance with the prearranged order, this small group of a dozen men was to fan out left and find some position that could be defended and which would block or delay the enemy advance into the area just reconquered.

Daugher and Bowman trembled with an almost sexual excitement. This was going to be so much *fun*. Carrera, Soult and Mitchell were calmer. *Let what is coming, come.*

The Sumeris came on fast, a dozen of them, right up the street. It wasn't bad tactics, Carrera thought, just a desperate mission that required throwing the book away. They were plainly looking more to accomplishing their mission than to safety.

Amateurs initiate an ambush by doing something silly like shouting, "Fire!" Professionals begin one by simply opening fire with their most powerful weapon. In this case, that was a light machine gun carried by that human fireplug, Mitchell, who still kept the fleeing trooper from earlier beside him. Carrera waited until the Sumeris were well into the kill zone before slapping

Mitchell's back. From behind the flattened automobile tire where the two had taken cover Mitchell depressed the trigger and stitched an entire rotary drum magazine, seventy-five rounds, into the Sumeris, spraying bullets out as if from a water hose. Men twisted and fell, spilling blood across the street. Before the drum was empty the barrel was smoking.

On the other side of the street from Carrera, Daugher and Bowman joined in gleefully but taking more care to target individuals. Bowman counted off, "One . . . two . . . three . . ." He was counting bodies, not bursts.

By the time the last Sumeri was down, a uniformed tribune dropped beside Carrera and Mitchell. "Legate, it's Tribune Valdez, 6th motherfucking Cazador Cohort. What are my *chingada* orders?"

Carrera answered, simply, "Contain and destroy that outbreak ahead."

The tribune arose, made a half a salute and then turned to urge his men forward.

"C'mon, you scrofulous pieces of runny shit!" Valdez cried. "There's enemy up ahead and you can *kill* their buggered asses. Now *move*, fuckheads!"

As he was moving forward, still cursing a storm, Valdez happened to look down at the Sumeri bodies in the street and was struck by the glint of a small golden cross, strung around the neck of one of them.

INTERLUDE

12 April, 2092, Rift Transition Point

The technology had improved considerably. Ships were larger, lighter and stronger. They could carry more. Moreover, deep sleep techniques had improved to the point that the colonization ships could be stuffed almost to the rafters with people who, thus suspended, needed neither food nor air. Only the crews remained awake during the voyages, and even they slept for as much as two thirds of the time. The crews had shrunk considerably as the ships had grown more reliable and automation had further improved.

The colonists' livestock, too, could be sent in greater numbers and variety. There was even room for seeding the new world with the animals, especially the endangered animals, of the old. (Though some of Old Earth's endangered animals were themselves dangers to Terra Nova's.) Moreover, cows could make cows, rice plants could be set in moist earth to make more rice seed, horses made more horses. Little machinery was shipped, and that mostly of the simplest types.

Books came digitalized. Medicines and some medical equipment were sometimes sent.

There were ninety-seven ships, either built, laid, or planned. They were, in comparison to earlier vessels, huge, capable of hauling as many as fifty thousand passengers in deep sleep. Their light sails . . . well, "enormous" hardly did them justice. The ships took months to load and unload.

To fill those ships voluntarily, however, required an end point at which the passengers would feel comfortable. The Agreement of 2087 divided up the new world into sections roughly comparable to the areas held by the nations and supranationals of Earth, which sections were then often further subdivided. In the division, some got a bit more than they'd had; some got a bit less. Switzerland's colony, Helvetia, had a bit less mountain and a bit more pasture. Japan's Yamato was an island chain of three large islands and numerous small ones, and was somewhat larger in land area—though just as mountainous and almost as resource poor—as the home islands. Canada got a largely frozen wasteland. It also was next to the colony for the United States. As Canadians saw it, this made sense. They knew their Americans and knew that no American-founded colony would stint their war department. Thus, how else could their settlers ultimately get the best defense in the world and have to pay nearly nothing for it.

Mexico, too, wanted a land border with the gringo colony. From the point of view of the upper classes that had ruled Mexico to their own benefit for so very long, how else could they hope to export the masses of the jobless and hungry their preferred system was sure to create unless there were to be a labor hungry and prosperous land nearby? They were reasonably certain the Americans, wherever they went, would create such a land.

Not everyone was a volunteer, of course. The nations of Earth sometimes used their allotted ships to send off their criminals en masse. Unsurprisingly, their criminals often did very well in the new land. Others used it as a population control measure. China's people often took the space route to fecundity, since the one-child policy, except for party leaders and the rich, was being strictly enforced again. India's poor were given the choice of departure or continuing to sleep on the pavement and starve. They went in droves and died in droves.

Weapons were permitted to the new settlers by most Earth governments, if the settlers could afford them. Wisely, most elected to bring a level of technology, roughly that of late seventeenth- to early eighteenth-century Earth, which could be sustained. Some Earth companies, for example, made not-so-small fortunes building flintlock rifles for the emigrant trade. Flint could be found; percussion caps required industrial manufacture.

This load, leaving the solar system and transiting the rift on the 12th of April, 2092, consisted of colonists from the Republics of Panama, Costa Rica, Colombia, Nicaragua, El Salvador and Honduras, all in the vessel *Amerigo Vespucci*, Captain Ngobe Mzilikazi, UNSN, Commanding. The *Vespucci* departed without incident, accelerated to the requisite speed for transition, reached the rift, and disappeared from Earth's view.

CHAPTER TWENTY-FOUR

The courage of your enemy honors you.
—Arab saying

Ninewa, 9/3/461 AC

It took two days to contain and clear out the remnants of the spoiling attack Sada had launched. When it was finally done, the legion was pleased to discover that about half the century that had been under assault had managed to hold out in a stout adobe building and beat off all attacks. Even the wounded who had not made it to the building were found, as often as not, neatly laid out and, to the extent practical, cared for, in nearby structures. The sergeant in charge, though wounded, was still ready to fight when the first relieving troops reached him.

He didn't have a bad word to say about the Sumeris, but he had more than a few for Manuel Rocaberti. After hearing the sergeant out, Carrera had returned to the command post and had a long conversation with Parilla.

❖   ❖   ❖

Parilla and Carrera were still talking as Manuel Rocaberti entered the legion's command post. A private, looking very frightened, stood to one side under a guard supervised by McNamara. The *Dux* and legate immediately stopped whatever the conversation had been and turned to face the tribune. The private was the same one who been stopped and arrested for desertion under fire.

"Manuel," Parilla began, "The legate and I were just discussing what to do with this man. Carrera wants him shot before the legion. I think maybe we should be kinder, under the circumstances. You're still officially his commander. What do you think?"

Rocaberti had been surprised that he had not been arrested when he'd shown up to report the destruction of his century. He assumed, then, that they must have all been killed but for this private. It was either that, or the position of his uncle, that was acting to save him. Perhaps it was both. Still, that also made the private the only possible witness against him.

"Shoot him," Rocaberti answered. "Court-martial him and shoot him. Discipline ought to be maintained."

Though it jarred his half-healed wound, raising a wince, Parilla's fist lashed out of its own accord, catching Rocaberti on the jaw and knocking him to the floor. He was surprisingly fast for someone nearly in his sixties.

"*That* was your last chance, Manuel," Parilla said. "Sergeant Major McNamara, arrest this man. He is charged with desertion under fire. And release the private back to his unit."

University Quarter, Ninewa, 10/3/461 AC

The sun was up enough to cast long shadows across the streets and parks of the town.

Carrera sighed, a bit wistfully, looking from his high perch down onto the grounds of the university below. *Be a shame to destroy it; it's the only bit of decent architecture I've seen since coming here.*

The University of Sumer at Ninewa was smoothly white and surrounded on three sides by a three-meter high wall that, but for the bullet marks, would have been equally smooth and equally white. The river bank made up the fourth side. A green strip of park, fed from the waters of the river, framed the university. Two-lane, one-way boulevards ran to either side of the park.

Because it was older than most of the smashed city behind him, Carrera knew that the University predated the current dictator of the country and so hadn't suffered his megalomaniac urge towards heroic monumentalism or outsized construction. It was low-lying, for the most part, and tasteful in the way that traditional Arabic architecture almost always was, all high windows and graceful arches, with geometric decoration on the walls where those walls were not smooth.

There were three gates into the compound, one in the center facing to the southwest and two more flanking that one to the northwest and southeast at a distance of about four hundred meters. Another broad boulevard led from the town directly to the main gate.

"Patricio, I think you're insane," commented Parilla,

standing next to Carrera and looking out over the same scene. "Let someone else go. Send *me*."

Behind the two, Soult added in, "Goddamn straight."

"Besides," Parilla continued, "you don't know you can trust this man."

Not turning his head to address his friends, Carrera insisted, "He's fought like a soldier so far. No tricks . . . well, no *dirty* tricks. He's been a tricksy enough bastard in every permissible way though; that I'll give you."

Clasping his hands behind his back, Carrera began to pace. "Raul, we can't send you," he said. "Your English is, at best, so so. Fahad doesn't speak Spanish. I'm the only one with the right combination of languages and rank. And I don't think it's right to insult this man by sending anyone lesser."

"We could just blast them out, you know," Parilla objected.

"Yes," Carrera agreed slowly. "But then how would we get any future use of them? And I think we're going to need them in the future. I think we've got the best group of Arabs on Terra Nova, right here."

The party went silent then as two assault teams composed of mixed armor and infantry moved into firing position and spent five minutes or so each blasting two large gaps in the university walls. A *"practicable breach,"* Carrera had called it.

"Order the troops to cease fire except in self-defense," he commanded. "Get the air *ala* circling overhead."

"*Amid,* there's a white flag showing near the main gate," Qabaash informed Sada. "Just three men, one holding the flag, another with a small loudspeaker, and the last standing there with his arms folded. You suppose they want to surrender? The loudspeaker asked for you, personally."

Sada looked around at some of the remnants of his filthy, ragged command and answered, "Somehow I doubt they intend to surrender to us."

"Are you going to meet them, *Amid*? If so, I need to have the barriers at the gate cleared away."

"Can't hurt to talk, I suppose," Sada answered. *Every minute we gain . . . gains us . . .* nothing. "Have someone shout to them that I'll be along in thirty minutes. And, yes, open the gate."

It had begun hot enough, standing there in the open and waiting for the Sumeris to respond. As the sun arose, it grew hotter still, despite the wide swath of pockmarked greenery on which they stood. Sweat poured off the faces of Carrera, Soult and Fahad. Their uniforms, and Fahad's civilian clothing, grew soaked with it even though the dry, dusty air sucked it away almost as fast as it formed.

"There he is," Fahad said. "Magnificent, isn't he?"

Carrera agreed, though he said nothing. The man approaching under flag of truce was caked with sweat and dust, but tall, well built, and walked like a man of fierce courage still.

Carrera's party stood in place while the Sumeri approached. Sada stopped only once, gaping at Fahad from just recognition distance. Fahad made a small bow, *Yes, my general, it is me.*

"How may I be of service?" Sada asked in polite, Anglian accented English. He looked at Carrera's eyes and thought, *Creepy, like the Blue Jinn.* Glancing at Fahad again, he added, to Carrera, "I gather you know who I am."

Taking the hint, Carrera offered his hand, which Sada took, and introduced himself, adding, "Your men have fought well, as have you."

"Thank you, *Liwa* Patricio." In the Arab way, Sada used rank and first name. "And, might I add, they're ready to keep on doing so."

Carrera bit his lower lip, doubtfully. "For a while," he conceded. "But the rest of your army, elsewhere, has folded. These are the only men who've made a good stand. It would be a shame to rob your country of them now, don't you think?"

Overhead, six NA-23s and a like number of Turbo-Finches circled in two separate groups. Reinforcing these, ten helicopters, ostentatiously bearing rocket and machine gun pods, hovered. Carrera didn't have to point them out; their noise reached the ground with a low, steady *thrum.*

"The other thing is . . . you can surrender to me or you can surrender to the Federated States Army which, now that it has nothing better to do, is sending a division this way to reinforce us. You'll get better treatment from me. So will your men."

Seeing that Sada was still full of fight—*Fahad was right about this one. A wonderful enemy. Even in defeat he's got pluck*—Carrera put in a sweetener. "I've got medical teams standing by, just behind the line, to go in and see to your wounded." His eyes swept around the grassy strip. "We can medevac them from right here."

"I have a lot of wounded," Sada answered, wavering slightly.

"I know. And not much food and not much ammunition. And no medicine. Friend, this is the best thing you can do for your men, hurt or unhurt. For reasons I'll explain later, it's also the best thing you can do for your country and your people."

Sada's shoulders, previously proudly squared off, sank just a little. "Terms?" he asked.

"The usual," Carrera answered, "except that I'll want officers to take their sidearms even into captivity to maintain order."

"We don't have enough nine millimeter ammunition left to maintain order."

"No problem; we'll give you enough." *That* was an almost unprecedented offer of grace.

Sada nodded, then let his face hang downward.

"And I'll want your men to march out under arms, like honorable soldiers, colors flying and band playing."

"I don't have a band," Sada objected.

"That doesn't matter. *I* do."

Sada looked . . . well, he looked ripped up inside. "This is hard. *Hard.* I've never surrendered my command. In three wars I've never given up."

"I understand," Carrera commiserated. "It's the hardest thing one can do. But is your pride worth getting the only part of your army that consistently fought well destroyed? Your country is going to need these men. Is your pride more important than that?"

Sada inhaled deeply. When he gave up that breath his shoulders slumped even more than they had been. "When? How do you want it done?"

The sun was high overhead and the PSYOP cameras were rolling when Sada reappeared at the gate. From above, confirmed by both observation teams and the still circling aircraft, the remnants of his command were formed up behind him. Medical teams from the legion were already inside the compound, triaging the wounded and treating them where practical. Fahad and Soult had accompanied the medics and doctors to translate. The three-way translation was slow and awkward, but ultimately effective enough.

Precisely at noon Carrera reappeared in the green strip fronting the gate. This time he was accompanied not by a mere two men. Instead, he had the dozen each pipers and drummers of the legion, their Secordian-born pipe major, plus an honor guard of one century from the 1st Cohort. The pipes and drums stood to Carrera's right, the honor guard to the left. Well behind him, on the far side of the boulevard, Parilla and the legionary staff stood on a makeshift platform raised above the rear decks of two tanks. The one gold and eleven silver eagles of the ground and air elements of the legion were drawn up, held aloft by their bearers, in front of the stand.

Sada appeared within the gate. Behind him were his staff and his brigade colors, a splash of green against the white background.

Carrera looked right and nodded at the pipe major who raised his baton and lowered it. Immediately the drums began a marching beat. Four beats later the pipes joined in with *"The Muckin' o' Geordie's Byre."*

Qabaash looked terribly forlorn and depressed, slumping behind Sada. He turned his head and gave the order to "Mark time, march." The men began to march in step, lifting their feet in time to the beat. This was followed by, "Forward . . . march." Sada, the staff, the brigade colors, and the first group of soldiers stepped off.

Four abreast the Sumeris flowed out of the gate. Weary as they no doubt were, still the pipes and the drums gave them a bit of energy they'd perhaps not known they'd had. They came forward, dirty and ragged but in good dress and step, until Sada reached a point six meters in front of Carrera. There Qabaash gave the order, "Brigade . . . halt." The pipes and drums ceased.

Sada and Carrera exchanged salutes. Then Sada walked forward, unbuckling the sword—a great prize and artifact of his clan—to present to Carrera. Carrera held up his hand in refusal, saying, "I am not the commander." He turned and pointed to Parilla, standing on the platform, and said, "Your sword and your colors go to him. Have your command follow me and then peel off in line along the grass."

With that, Carrera executed a letter-perfect about face and once again nodded to the pipe major. The drums and the tune picked up as the honor guard marched forward to insert itself between Sada's colors and the bulk of his brigade. Following Carrera, the Sumeris advanced into the boulevard to just before Parilla's reviewing stand. Behind Sada the remaining units peeled off right and left to form a line of columns. They were few and took up comparatively little of the space.

At the reviewing stand Carrera saluted Parilla, reporting, "Al Sada Brigade, present and accounted for and ready to surrender after a gallant defense." The pipes and drums automatically cut out.

Parilla returned the salute and answered, "Continue with the ceremony."

Carrera turned and nodded at Sada. Sada, in turn, gave the orders in Arabic for his colors to follow him. They marched in time, pipes silent and drums only beating a slow march. There Sada once again unbuckled his sword belt and gave it to Parilla, who took it and passed it to Sergeant Major McNamara. Parilla then, followed by McNamara, walked gingerly down some rickety steps that led to the flat below the stand.

Sada turned and took the brigade colors from their bearer. *Oh, this hurts.* He turned once again, in place, and offered these to Parilla who took them as well. Parilla held them in his hand, momentarily, savoring the ultimate battlefield commander's high, the capture of the enemy's soul. Then, smiling, he gave them back to Sada.

"I don't understand," the Sumeri said, in English.

McNamara translated to Parilla who answered, through him, "You've earned t'e right to keep t'em."

Sada felt unmanly tears begin to form. He bit his upper lip and, nodding gratefully, returned the colors to their bearer. He saw Qabaash the Fierce suddenly lose his dejected demeanor and stand tall. By the time Sada turned again, Parilla had retrieved his sword from McNamara and was offering that back as well.

The tears began to course then in truth. Sada hung his head in embarrassment. Parilla just smiled broadly and slapped the Sumeri's shoulder, saying something in Spanish that Sada had no clue to.

McNamara handed a small hinged box to Parilla, who took from it a medal on a ribbon. This Parilla hung about Sada's neck while his head was bowed.

"*What?*" the surprised Sumeri asked.

❖   ❖   ❖

"*Can you identify forty or fifty men—officers, noncoms or enlisted, makes no difference, except I'd prefer some of each—who just did a really good, really courageous job here?*" Carrera had asked. "*I mean soldiers that everyone in your brigade would recognize as being number one fighters, first-class men?*"

"*Forty or fifty? I could probably give you four or five hundred.*" Sada had answered with pride, standing there on the green strip as the two worked out the final details of surrender.

"*No . . . let's not be too ostentatious. Forty or fifty will do, for now.*"

"Follow t'e commander," McNamara said to Sada, as Parilla walked to the group of fifty Sumeris who had followed just behind the colors and were centered in middle of the remnants of the brigade. Sada did so, with the sergeant major following. Another legionary followed the sergeant major, bearing a scrounged metal tray on which were laid out fifty Steel Crosses.

"What the hell is he doing?" Sada asked of the sergeant major.

"T'ere is no bar in our regulations," McNamara answered, "to decorating for bravery an enemy who has fought well. As a matter of fact, if you read t'em t'e right way, it is required, at least where possible."

"No shit?" Sada asked.

"No shit . . . sir."

Well, this was certainly something different. With a very odd mix of feelings, Sada followed Parilla as he walked down the five ranks of ten and hung a medal around the necks of each of the Sumeris Sada had identified as particularly worthy. At each man

Parilla shook hands and said a few words, technically incomprehensible but in practice quite clear. "Good man . . . brave soldier . . . it was an honor to fight you . . . wear it with pride."

With the presentation of the last award, Parilla again shook Sada's hand. Again they exchanged salutes. Sada walked back to his position in front of his staff while Parilla went back to the reviewing stand.

Carrera gave the order to Sada, "Have your soldiers ground arms."

Unit by unit, starting from the right of the line as they faced, the remnants of the Sumeri units grounded their rifles and machine guns on the grass strip, the men bending at the waist to carefully lay the weapons down before recovering to attention.

When the last unit had disarmed, Carrera ordered, "Have your brigade follow me." With another head nod, the pipes and drums picked back up again. The Sumeris began to march, first marking time in place and then, as the way cleared, wheeling left or right and moving forward behind the colors following their commander who, in turn, followed Carrera.

The honor guard from 1st Cohort stepped out to stand beneath the reviewing stand, between the eagles and the boulevard. When Carrera reached the stand he turned his eyes to the right and saluted the *Dux* and the Eagles. The sergeant major ordered, "Present . . . arms."

Carrera dropped the salute and continued on.

Taking the hint, Sada gave the command, "Eyes . . . right," and rendered "Present Arms" with his clan's sword. The colors of his brigade dropped to a forty-five degree angle until he ordered, "Ready . . . front." The silver eagles likewise lowered but to a lesser degree.

As the group of Sumeris Parilla had just decorated reached the stand they, too, executed an eyes right. Parilla saluted and dropped it. Then Parilla began to applaud. The staff on the stand joined him, holding the applause until the Sumeri honorees had passed.

That night, Sada met with Parilla and Carrera in a large and tacky office in one of the local municipal buildings that had been mostly spared in the fighting. The cheap but ostentatiously gilded furniture glinted in the now dim and then flaring kerosene lamps.

Fahad was in attendance in case translation should be needed.

"Your men? Settled in? Fed? Watered?" Parilla asked in his marginal English.

"Yes, sir," Sada answered. He was still in mild shock at the decent, even gallant, treatment he and his men had been accorded. Indeed, back in the wire-ringed temporary camp in which he and his troops were housed under first class Misrani tents his staff was still scratching their collective head.

"I have to apologize for the food," Parilla said, through Carrera. "Frankly, we're not eating all that well, either. We're supposed to have a somewhat improved supply situation in a few days."

"That's fine," Sada said. "After a week of boiled camel and rice, and not much of that, the men are happy just to be full."

"Drink?" Carrera offered, indicating a mostly full bottle and some mostly clean glasses.

"Please. We Sumeris are not, generally speaking, Salafi fanatics, you know."

Fahad poured for the four. There was no ice so it was scotch, neat.

They sipped, in silence and contemplatively, for a few minutes before Carrera began to speak.

"The FSC-led coalition has ordered your entire army to disband, the fucking idiots," he said heatedly. "Allegedly they'll provide a month's severance pay, at least to the officers."

Sada laughed, low and deprecatingly. "I can't even begin to tell you what a bad idea that is. You're going to suddenly *un*employ several hundred thousand young men, all trained to arms, and—my brigade excepted—with every reason to hate your guts. Oh, my. Saleh, wherever he's hiding, must just be coming in his pants over *that* one."

"Not us," Carrera corrected, "the FSC. Seems some civilian, never-heard-a-shot-fired-in-anger-idiot there, decided for the military that troops who had run away and surrendered were just not worth keeping around. Mind you, the money was all allocated to keep them under arms and employ them. But, no, this dipshit civilian with never a day in uniform thinks he knows better."

Sada shrugged. "Well," he admitted, "they're mostly *not* worth keeping around for the good they can do the FSC. At least not any immediate good. They're worth keeping around for the *harm* they might do if left to their own devices."

"We agree," Carrera said. "That's why we don't want to let your brigade go."

Seeing Sada bridle at the thought of his men spending some uncountable amount of time locked up behind wire, Carrera hastened to add, "Wait. I don't mean we want to keep them as prisoners past the time we must. I mean *we* want to hire them. And you."

Well . . . that was different. "So that's what all that pageantry was about."

"Partly," Carrera admitted. "But only partly. You and your men deserved it, too. What we have in mind, what we need, is three things. We want to hire about one hundred and fifty of your men as auxiliaries. They'll go to school to learn Spanish for about four months. Then they'll be assigned right down to century level to act as guides and interpreters for our units."

"That's . . . do-able," Sada agreed. One hundred and fifty men was only a fraction of the men he had who would need employment.

"The second thing we want is for you to reform a regular brigade of three or four infantry battalions. Call it two to three thousand men. You and they will fall under command of the legion and, frankly, be used."

"I don't have that many men," Sada objected, "not unhurt anyway."

"We expect you to recruit. We expect you to recruit very carefully because this brigade *must* be really first rate."

"Assuming you're paying, I suppose I can recruit. But I'll have to be very careful *who* I recruit."

"We know," Carrera agreed. "We expect you to take your time about it. It's going to be a few months before the insurgency we expect to come about can really kick off. You have to be ready by then."

"The insurgency is in place," Sada answered. "It's

been in place. And with the FSC letting all those soldiers go, it's going to grow fast."

"Yes, but not *here*, not in our area."

"Maybe not," Sada said, noncommittally. "But it will spill over even so."

"That's the third thing we need. After you subtract for the translator-guides and the cadre for your new brigade, we want . . . watchers."

"In the towns?" Sada asked. "To spy and report?"

"And assassinate," Carrera added. "And to terrorize, if and when that becomes necessary. But the whole thing has to fall under your command. For any number of reasons, but mostly financial, we can't do some of the necessary dirty work. Some of that dirty work involves . . . well . . . let's say it involves information control."

Sada held out his glass to Fahad, who automatically refilled it. "*Shokran, ya* Fahad," he said, while using the moment to think.

"You realize, then, that no one can rule this place except through fear. I always despised the dictator except for one thing; he was able to hold us together. No one else could have. Carrot and stick is all well and good, but the donkey has to be able to see the stick."

"We understand that," Carrera answered.

"Pay?" Sada asked, more curious about whether it would be enough to keep his men and their families fed than out of any sense of greed.

Carrera handed over a sheet with pay scales. "It's about half what we pay our own, and about thirty or thirty-five percent more than the pay rates under the dictator. Plus there are some bonuses and extra pay for translators and the watchers. And we can work out special event bonuses for some utterly necessary but distasteful actions."

Sada put the sheet down. It was enough not to need to quibble over. More importantly, "How many of my wounded are expected to recover?"

"About six hundred," Carrera answered. "Maybe a few more."

"So . . . two thousand men to be your translators, form a secret police network, and cadre for a brigade. It's . . . possible, but only just possible."

"Best start now then," Parilla said, after Carrera had translated. "Pay starts as soon as you begin."

Sada was leaving, under escort, when Fernandez stopped him in the corridor. He introduced himself and explained, "I'm the military intelligence section. Rather, I'm the dirty part of it. I know what Carrera and Parilla asked you for. I need something, too."

"Yes?"

"You won't have any of what I need in your brigade," Fernandez began to explain. "But, given your former position, you'll have connections to what I need."

"And that would be, Tribune?"

"Interrogators," Fernandez answered simply. "And I have my own budget. I'll pay better than normal rates for what I have in mind."

Ninewa, 12/3/461 AC

It was hard, if not quite as hard as the decision to surrender his command had been. *What do I do?*

Sada asked himself. *What do I do about the special . . .*
packages. I don't have a use for the weapons. I don't
even want my country to have the filthy things. The
funds? I can see better uses for them than they're
likely to receive if Saleh's people get control of them.
And what about if they get control of the weapons?
Allah, that's a horrible thought.

But to turn them over to the enemies who just con-
quered us? Is it treason? Is it treason when the govern-
ment that I swore an oath to has ceased to exist?

On the other hand, the Balboans have hired me.
Wouldn't it be treason to my new bosses to fail to
give them the weapons? God, I don't know.

After two days of thinking about it, Sada asked to
see Carrera and Parilla again. Standing orders were
that he was to be given every possible leeway and
privilege. The MPs guarding the camp accordingly
escorted him to headquarters, which had been moved
to the fairly undamaged university. The gate guard
had apprised Carrera that Sada was coming.

"There is a reason I was here," Sada announced
without fanfare.

"Well, of course . . ."

"No. Another reason. Your men wouldn't have found
it, not yet. Can you assemble a guard, a very reliable
guard, quickly? They'll need flashlights."

That took a bit, perhaps an hour. When the guard was
assembled Sada told Carrera, "Follow me, please."

He led the party to a building in an isolated part
of the university compound, almost at the surrounding
wall. There, he continued on down into the basement
by way of a wide staircase. At the base of the stairs
Sada opened what looked to be a gray metal circuit

breaker box. He flicked a few switches and a hidden door opened up in the wall, moving out of the way with an irritating screech.

Sada took a flashlight from one of the legionaries and led the way through the door.

"None of my men knew about this," he explained, waving the light from side to side of a long, broad corridor. "Just me and a few *mukharbarat* I had shot before the battle."

Sada and Carrera walked to one of the open doors that fronted the corridor. There, the Sumeri turned the flashlight into a room and played it about. "That's money," he said. "I don't know how much but I'm guessing it's at least several hundred million, maybe a billion. Maybe more. Mostly it's Tauran Union currency, with some FS drachma and Anglian pounds. Come on, there's more."

"More money?" asked Carrera incredulously. "It's already more than we can easily funnel into rebuilding the country."

"No, not money . . . other things."

"Those two lead to chemical agents and the makings for more," Sada said, as they reemerged into the corridor. He flicked the light from one of two further doors to the other. "I wouldn't open those, not until you have men equipped to deal with a possible leak." He flashed another door and said, "That one's bio. Smallpox and anthrax. Scares the shit out of me and if you can figure out a way to destroy it without opening the doors I'll be very grateful."

Sada's light came to rest on a final door. "This is the important thing I wanted to show you," he finished, as he turned himself and the light toward a door marked with radiation symbols. He had to open another box and flick several more switches to make that door open.

Inside, Carrera saw twenty-one plastic cases, each about the size of a footlocker. Some, but not all, of those were likewise marked with radiation symbols.

"Jesus Christ!" he uttered. "Are these . . . ?"

"Yes. And it's more like Shaitan," Sada corrected. "There are seven of them here. I *think* that was all there were. They're in sets of three cases to a weapon: nuclear material, conventional explosive, and control device. Only three have been reconditioned to work. The others could be, but there was no time. They were supposed to go to another place, I don't know where—for safekeeping and possible future use. You must take control of them."

"I must, indeed," Carrera agreed.

Ninewa, 15/3/461 AC

Drums beat and bagpipes skirled as the legion marched onto the field from a hidden position behind the sand dunes. Carrera, Parilla, most of the cohort commanders and a party of about sixty Sumeris stood on a reviewing stand that had been bulldozed up out of the sand.

Sada asked, "Where the hell did you get those pipers, anyway, Patricio? I wouldn't have picked Balboa for a place where bagpipes would be popular."

Carrera chuckled. "It's a funny story actually. The Balboans love the horrid things to the extent they know about them. But you're right. They're not that well known in the country. We got these by a sort of roundabout route. A lot of our people emigrated to Secordia during Piña's time in power. Even before that, too, as a matter of fact. Often they eventually return. One of our women, living down there for a few years, married a Secordian who was a reservist in their army.

"She got homesick, so she and her husband left Secordia and came to Balboa. The husband took over her father's ranch. When the call was sounded to come here the husband couldn't resist joining up. He brought his pipes with him to training.

"I heard him playing out on the parade field at Fort Cameron one night—that's where we did our initial training—and went to ask about it. He said he learned in the Secordian Army. So I asked him if he could teach a few others to play. He thought he could. We ordered a few dozen chanters, some instructional materials, and the dozen pipes you see.

"In point of fact they really can't play them. Except for the Secordian, they just know about twenty or so tunes by rote."

"I'd like to get some pipes and instruction for my brigade, when we form it," Sada said.

"Consider it done."

By the time Carrera finished his explanations the legion had formed on line with cohorts in blocks. An extra, smaller formation of about one hundred men stood off to one side. Kennison, as the Commander of Troops, reported to Parilla. Salutes were exchanged. Parilla then walked to a microphone and began to speak in Spanish. Sada had no idea what was being said. When Parilla was finished he backed away from the microphone. An announcer began to read a long list of names and places.

In English, Carrera explained to Sada what was going on. "After the invasion of Balboa, fourteen years ago, no one ever thought to reward those Balboan soldiers who had done a good job. We're taking this opportunity to correct that as well as to reward some who, like your own men, fought exceptionally well here. The announcer is reading the list of those killed in action, and their home towns. On the assumption that a man who has died for his country and cause has given and done all he can, each of the fallen is being awarded the *Cruz de Coraje in Acero*, the Cross of Courage in Steel. A few of those who we know for a fact fought exceptionally well are being given the next step up, the CC in Bronze, as well. You can, if you wish, put in all your dead for CCAs."

After the announcer finished reading the list of posthumous awards Parilla stepped down from the reviewing stand, his feet raising little bursts of dust on the sand ramp. He was followed by a signifer carrying a cloth-covered board on which lay rows of medals with ribbons.

The first man to be awarded was Jimenez. After Jimenez had received his award, Parilla quietly told him to move out. He trotted off happily to where another important duty awaited.

Parilla, once the presentation of awards was finished, returned to the microphone.

"Soldiers!" he began, "I join you in the pride you must feel today at seeing so many of your brave comrades rewarded for their courage and service to the country and the legion. Honoring them honors us all. Unfortunately, we have one among us who fell so far short of the standards expected of a soldier of the legion that his continued existence among us would be a shame upon us all."

Parilla then ordered the men of the brigade to stand at ease.

At that command a truck pulled out from behind a row of tents to a place a hundred meters or so to the left of the reviewing stand. A detail of men threw a framework from the back of the truck, then dismounted to set it up. When it was upright, it appeared to be a heavy pole supported by an even heavier X frame underneath it. The detail then pulled a coffin out of the truck and placed it beside the pole. The truck then left, with the detail of men.

As soon as the truck was gone, the band struck up a dirge. From a place off to the left of the legion ten Balboans began to march, Jimenez leading the party. Behind Jimenez three men marched tightly together. All were in battle uniform with helmets. The middle man was bound hand and foot with only enough slack in the rope around his ankles to take half steps. Behind the three marched another six men, these carrying scoped Draco rifles at port arms.

Jimenez reached a position about fifty meters in front of the reviewing stand and stopped while the rest marched to stand behind him. When they were in position he ordered, "Right face," and reported to Parilla that the firing party was ready. Parilla gave the order, "Proceed."

The announcer began to read off the charges and sentence against Rocaberti while the firing squad marched to a position forty meters in front of the framework. Jimenez and the two guards on Rocaberti dragged him to stand a few feet in front of the framework's upright pole.

Jimenez first removed Rocaberti's Helvetian helmet and tossed it to the sand. Then he loosened the condemned man's web belt and cut away his load-carrying equipment. It, too, was thrown to the ground. Next Jimenez tore off Rocaberti's insignia of rank. The shirt was ripped open, buttons falling scattered to the sand. Lastly, Jimenez deftly cut away the" Leg. del Cid" tape over Rocaberti's left pocket.

As the last insignia to be removed from Rocaberti's uniform fluttered away, the two guards half carried him to the pole. They quickly bound him to it at the chest, waist, and thighs. One of the guards put his head to Rocaberti's chest, then taped a bull's-eye to the bare skin. The guards stepped back.

Jimenez looked toward the announcer who switched the public address system to enable it to pick up from a microphone attached to the framework. From that time on the entire legion was able to listen to Rocaberti's last few minutes. He sobbed.

Jimenez then advanced to stand directly in front of the prisoner. He took a black bag from one pocket. Before placing it on, however, he reached up to slap Rocaberti, once, hard, across the face. Then the bag brought Rocaberti into the night from which there would be, for him, no dawn.

"Pass in review."

No dirge this time; the band picked up a martial tune. Down the line of cohorts the command echoed. First Cohort, Eagle held high in front, wheeled to make its pass by the reviewing stand. The commander of the

Principe Eugenio gave the order, "Eyes . . . right!" in time for the men to see the shattered body hanging from the ropes that held it to the pole. The men on the reviewing stand saluted the Eagle as it passed.

By the time the last cohort made its wheel, the band doing a fair job with "Hielen Laddie," Jimenez had rejoined the party on the reviewing stand. The band changed tune to "Blue Bonnets over the Border" as that last cohort reached the pole and corpse.

"That was very well done, Xavier," Carrera said, later. "My compliments to yourself and the detail. I've already given orders to break out a bottle of 'medicinal' rum for them."

Jimenez shrugged and answered, "Well, I won't turn it down. But, honestly, we don't need it. Every man on the detail was an eager volunteer. We were glad to shoot the miserable son of a bitch."

Then Jimenez told Carrera, "We rehearsed it, you know."

"I assumed so," Carrera said.

"No, Patricio. You don't understand. We rehearsed it with Rocaberti himself. Eleven times in all. Every step from marching him out, to commanding the squad to fire, to my giving him the 'Coup de Grace' with my pistol to the back of his head, to throwing his carcass into the coffin. Every little step we rehearsed. We even buried him once."

Carrera snorted, saying, "You are a vengeful man, Xavier. I like that. You'll go far."

Ninewa, 22/3/461 AC

Carrera was staying. Parilla, Jimenez and about half the staff were going back to Balboa, along with a few hundred of the initial cadre and all the badly wounded. Their job, once returned, was to form a second echelon of cohorts to replace the echelon already in country. It was going to be a long war and, ultimately, there needed to be two or, preferably, three more cohorts, some of them mere cadres in school, for each cohort deployed. Eventually, it was intended that the *Legio del Cid* would rise to division strength, about thirteen and a half thousand men, with another thirty-five to thirty-seven thousand in Balboa forming and training units to replace the ones already there as those units grew understrength and weary.

That was going to take years, not less than four and probably more like six. The plan was to send back up to half the deployed legion, as quickly as replacements arrived. These would go to leadership schools run by Abogado's FMTG. The replacement funnel would then be aimed at the new units, which would fill and come over as cohorts to replace the old ones.

The old cohorts, once back in country, would increase in size by a factor of just over three. These would again be deployed as they were filled and trained. Then the second echelon would go back and do the same. When the first echelon of cohorts returned to Balboa they would split and fill.

Eventually, Carrera hoped to have one division at roughly full strength deployed and fighting for a year, one at slightly over full strength and training as a group to deploy, one still building to just over full strength and averaging about seventy percent strength during that year, and one reduced to a cadre of about forty percent, those being mostly in school or supporting school and training for a year. This would give one year of school, one year of building up and doing low level training, one of higher level and more difficult training, and one fighting.

In actuality, it was going to be a lot more complex than that as not every type of cohort was suitable for replacement at the cohort level. The Combat Support and Artillery cohorts, for example, had to replace by centuries, later to be maniples of roughly one hundred and twenty to two hundred men, while the Headquarters and Service Support cohorts, and the Aviation *ala*, were best served by individual replacement.

"This is *so* going to suck for Tom Christian," Carrera had observed, more than once.

The plane coming in, a Volgan-built Nabakov-21 flown by the air *ala*, stopped at the end of the runway, turned under its own power, and began to taxi to the terminal for the Ninewa Airport. The engines, shrieking in protest, suddenly reversed themselves as the plane neared, throwing up a mass of dust.

The Nabakov dropped its tail ramp once it had come to a complete halt. First off was Dan Kuralski who was followed by—

"Lourdes, what are you doing here?" Carrera asked, trying to keep the anger he felt out of his voice. This was not really all that difficult as, *Jesus, she looks good, even after twenty hours in the air.* It was made even easier by the fact that she had launched herself at him with a happy squeal as soon as she'd reached lunging range. Some of the troops waiting nearby to go home made a number of ad hoc and mildly obscene sounds. Carrera glared at them but that only seemed to encourage the bastards.

Hard to be angry with a woman in this position.

"You can blame that on both of us, Patricio," Parilla said, trying to hide a smile and failing miserably. "My wife told me how much Lourdes missed you. I suggested she come along on this flight since you are not planning on going home for at least another year. I asked Tom Christian if there was any bar to it under the regulations. Since there wasn't . . ."

"Besides, Patricio," Lourdes pointed out, reasonably enough, "you've lost weight and you stink to the heavens. Obviously no one has been taking proper care of you."

"Proper care of" can have so many meanings, Carrera thought, not without a bit of eager anticipation.

"So be it," Carrera said, defeated. "As long as you're here, you can come with me to see off the badly hurt troops we're evacuating back to the Federated States and Balboa for recuperation. Maybe they'll give you some idea of what a really bad idea it was for you to come here, my stink and my weight loss notwithstanding."

That was an education Lourdes might just as soon have forgone. The troops missing eyes, arms and legs were chipper enough, remarkably so, under the circumstances. She just wanted to *cry*.

One case in particular was bothersome. That boy, and he couldn't have been over eighteen, was missing both legs and had been blinded to boot. *Handsome boy, though*, Lourdes thought. *What a shame.* She immediately cursed herself, inside, for thinking that it would have been any better if the kid had been ugly.

"Hello, Private Mendoza," Carrera said, after he looked at the medical charts to find the name. Mendoza didn't answer, but just nodded to show he had heard.

On the other hand, when Lourdes introduced herself he sat upright and, politely answered, "Hello. Who are you?"

"I'm Legate Carrera's . . . secretary, Lourdes Nuñez. I wanted to see the brave boys of the legion before you were shipped home."

Mendoza's face grew downcast. "I don't have a home. I'll never really have a home, not like this."

"I don't understand," Lourdes said, "of course you have a home. You came from somewhere."

Mendoza sighed. "We have a farm. My mom is too old to work it and I am the last boy left. Do you think we'll be able to keep it? No. When's the last time you saw a blind farmer? And a home means a wife, eventually. What girl would marry me now?"

Carrera said, "You can keep the land or sell it, Mendoza. You're a member of the legion until you die and your pay stays until that day, too. It's enough to live on. As for a wife . . ."

"You are selling our countrywomen short if you think that little things like legs will stop one of them from wanting to marry you," Lourdes supplied. "And even if you can't see out of your eyes *I* can still use them to see inside *you*. Any woman could. You'll have a wife, trust me. As a matter of fact . . ." Lourdes went silent.

"In any case," Carrera continued, "you'll have legs

again. About a million drachma worth of legs. It's going to take you some time to learn to use them once you get home, though. And it's going to be hard."

"That's something, I suppose," Mendoza answered.

"Where are you from, Jorge?" Lourdes asked.

"*Las Mesas*," he answered. "Why?"

"Really! I have family there," Lourdes said, without quite answering.

EXCURSUS

From: *Legio del Cid: to Build an Army* (reprinted here with permission of the Army War College, Army of the Federated States of Columbia, Slaughter Ravine, Plains FSC)

Despite the impressive combat record amassed by the legion, both during the initial invasion of Sumer and later during the counterinsurgency operation there, and still later, in Pashtia and other theaters, the legion became a magnet for criticism. Much of this came from elements within the Federated States. Some of these objected to the cost, though these raised no practical alternative except for sending even costlier Federated States forces, which forces did not even exist at the time to send. Still others insisted on greater reliance on allied troops, with those allies presumably paying their own way. This foundered on the clearly stated objections of those very allies who, to quote the Chancellor of Sachsen, would come, "Not now, not ever, no how, no way."

Moreover, the performance and staying power of most of the coalition troops left something to be desired. Castilla, for example, deserted in less than a year, taking with it the not inconsiderable number of Colombian states that had sent small formations to the war. Etruria and other Tauran forces likewise drew down as things appeared to bog in what the media insisted was a quagmire. Some allies from along the rim of the *Mar Furioso* sent substantial numbers, and paid for them, but always over strenuous domestic objections and usually at substantial domestic political cost. Moreover, these troops were almost invariably limited in their portfolio to peacekeeping in sectors where there was no great insurgency. They were useful in such places, but only that.

The only really reliable troops proved to be those of Anglia, the Federated States themselves and the quasi-mercenary Balboans.

It was precisely that quasi-mercenary nature to which much of the world objected. Indeed, since approximately half of Terra Nova had signed on to Additional Protocols One and Two to Old Earth's Geneva Convention Four, which barred the use of mercenary troops, the presence of these Balboans was used as an excuse *not* to send troops. The mercenaries, it was said, tainted the entire enterprise and made it illegal. Curiously, no one claimed that Anglia's and Gaul's use of mercenaries was illegal.

Then again, from the World League to the Tauran Union to every humanitarian activist non-governmental organization on the planet, plus the United Earth Peace Fleet circling overhead, one and all insisted that the war itself had been illegal. Thus, it seems unlikely that any troops would have been forthcoming even had the Balboans been sent packing.

This was the view of the Federated States' Department of War, in any case, and that view prevailed. The Balboans continued to be used and paid for.

In that use, the legion, later legions, became noteworthy not only for impressive combat performance, but also for a ruthless application of the Laws of War.

They were notable, as well, for a more general ruthlessness. This was especially to be seen in their treatment of anyone and everyone associated with the cosmopolitan progressive movement. Humanitarian activists attempting to operate in any zone of responsibility (ZOR) over which the Balboans held sway found that security and logistic support would not be provided. Moreover, any who didn't take that hint were often set upon and killed by parties unknown. Curiously, those who were approved and guarded by uniformed Balboan troops were *never* given any trouble by the guerillas who were said to infest the land.

The key to being accepted by the Balboans was simple. A humanitarian organization wishing to operate in their area had to meet a simple test. If they were "neutral" or anti (and neutral, in this context, generally meant "anti"), they were not welcome. If they had no substantial assets and expertise to lend to the effort, they were likewise not welcome. If, on the other hand, the groups were willing to help and had the ability, they were welcomed with open arms. A certain number of groups who came willing to provide nothing more than labor were accepted, as well.

If harsh treatment was the lot of many of the humanitarians, this was even more true of the press. With these, not only were unfriendly members not authorized, any found within the Balboans' ZOR were likely to be arrested, tried, found guilty of spying or subversion, and sentenced to death. After the Balboans shot a news team of four from the Arabic news channel, *al Iskandaria*, newspapers and television networks generally had to pay a substantial, even crippling, fine to retrieve any of their people who had been found, unauthorized, in the BZOR. Others, who toed the line and did not slant their reporting, were made welcome and, generally speaking, treated rather well. Indeed, the Balboans went out of their way to welcome those who engaged in truly *constructive* criticism.

The Balboans proved not to be above conducting "sting" operations to humiliate and discredit the cosmopolitans. Some of these were very elaborate and, it is clear in retrospect, had been planned well in advance. . . .

PART V

CHAPTER
TWENTY-FIVE

"The enemy gets a vote."
　　　　—Common wisdom, understood
　　　　by all decent armies, and
　　　　completely lost on the press.

Ninewa, 24/3/461 AC

People were beginning to return to the town now, indeed to return to all the villages of the roughly forty thousand square kilometers of the Balboan Zone of Responsibility or BZOR. The people numbered anywhere from a million to two million; no one really knew and aerial surveys were of little help.

The populace of Ninewa returned to what was mostly a ruin. There were no functioning utilities, no governmental administration, no schools, no jobs. Whatever local money the people had was worthless except perhaps as toilet paper. Then again, since the Sumeris did not, by and large, *use* toilet paper it didn't really have even this small value.

On the plus side, there was food—plenty of it, as a matter of fact—in the granaries and silos of the former government. These were under guard by the legion, which had taken control by right of conquest. There was water no worse than what they had been used to drinking. As this same water might well have been responsible for the deaths of tens of thousands in the years leading up to the invasion, this was small recommendation.

There was also plenty of work to be done. With work, with money, with food for the money to buy, there was some hope. Electricity was nice, but it could wait. Clean water was more important, but it could wait, too, albeit at cost in lives. For now, what the people needed were jobs, money, and food to buy with the money.

And therein lay a problem, for although plenty of the food had been captured, enough to last until the next harvest came in, following right on the heels of the invading armies had come the cosmopolitan progressives.

The progressives came in one of four or, rather, five categories. Some had assets or skills and were willing and eager to help the Sumeri people by helping the invaders. Others had assets and skills, money at least, but were totally unwilling to cooperate with the invading armies even though that was the only way to help the Sumeri people. Some had neither assets nor skills and only enough money to ensure that their representatives in Sumer could live rather well while by being gadflies. Some came with nothing but a willingness to work and were willing to live pretty poorly while they did so. And then, for the fifth group, there was the press, which was unwilling to do anything useful and, indeed, was most eager to see the entire enterprise fail, preferably miserably.

The cosmopolitans, most of them, did not want the food sold. They did not want the people forced to work to earn the money to buy it. Food was a "human right" and it was morally wrong to withhold it.

Carrera said, "Fuck off." The cosmopolitans lived to be appreciated, that and for their perks, and rough language was not something they were used to. This cavalier treatment sent many of them packing but, in both Carrera's opinion and Sada's, too many of them stayed.

The legion called a meeting of the Kosmos, sending patrols out throughout its ZOR to so advise them. About half showed up. These were given their marching orders and rules of engagement. They were also promised that security would be provided by the legion as long as they followed the legion's program.

The rest? Those without the obvious security of uniformed legionaries? Sada's watchers came to the fore here, showing up in the middle of the night to threaten, to beat, in a few cases to kill. The only limit on their conduct was, "no rapes." This rule was not always followed and Sada had to have a few of his men, with regret, hanged in public squares.

Some more of the Kosmos packed up, true, but even more came to Carrera's next meeting.

The press waxed lyrical about "the growing lawlessness and terror in Sumer."

That, Carrera admitted, was a problem but not one admitting of an easy solution. That he had hired Sada's brigade, and even expanded it, helped. Still, that was only about three thousand young men employed. There were anywhere from a third to three-quarters of a million men without jobs, though many of these were farmers and could be said to be constantly employed. For the nonfarmers, he could decorate every non-functioning lamppost in the BZOR with hanged bodies and *still* men would rob to feed their families. And who could blame them?

Again, Sada's watchers provided a partial solution. Sent out to all the larger towns and in all the neighborhoods of the city of Ninewa, they reported on the crime status in their areas, naming names. Carrera's helicopters would then fly in, surrounding the town concerned with Sada's troops. Hangings, sometimes mass hangings, quickly followed. That was the province of the mullahs Sada had found, the chief mullah charging a price of one gold drachma per death sentence.

The press added, "Travesty of Justice" and "Death Squads" to their existing repertoire of "growing lawlessness and terror."

"In the long run, though," Sada told Carrera, "however necessary they seem now, the hangings might do us more harm than good on their own."

"Why's that?" Carrera asked, puzzled.

The two men sat conversing in one of the university buildings, the entire complex still being under occupation by the legion. Fortunately, the furniture had not been looted precisely because of that occupation. The rest of the town had been somewhat looted, what little there was to take, by the returning people. It was only "somewhat" because of a dozen or so street lynchings that had taken place supervised by the men of Sada's brigade.

"We're not individuals the way you people are," Sada explained. "Everyone we hang is a member of a family and a tribe. It doesn't really matter if the bastards we string up are guilty because right and wrong here do not mean objective right and wrong, they mean, "What is good for my tribe is right; what is bad for my tribe is wrong." Executing young men who could bring in money and eventually father families is therefore inherently wrong."

"How many have your boys hanged so far?" Carrera asked.

"Eighty-seven," Sada answered, instantly. "As of yesterday. Fortunately, they're mostly from two of the smaller tribes. Also, fortunately, they were mostly here in Ninewa where tribal affections are slightly looser."

"How did the dictator maintain control if killing a tribe member makes enemies of the entire tribe?" Carrera asked, even more puzzled than he had been before.

"Well . . . see," Sada explained. "He changed the equation. Resistance meant something between tribal culling and tribal extermination and not a man or woman in the country but believed he meant it. Therefore *that* became the ultimate wrong, risking the complete death of the tribe."

"I can't exterminate entire tribes," Carrera said. *Jesus, I've got* some *decency left.* "You have a solution?"

"Work? We have to provide work for the young men. We might also slip some money, under the table, to the leaders of the tribes we've affected."

Carrera answered, "No . . . I won't reward people

for failure to control their young men. I'm willing to
provide work, though."

"It'll help," Sada answered with a shrug. *And I
can take care of bribing the tribal leaders, even if
Patricio will not.*

"Let's look at the map," Carrera suggested.

The map, marked up with grease pencils, showed
the borders of the BZOR, which was a near square
of about two hundred kilometers on a side. Ninewa
was approximately in the center of the eastern side
along the River Buranun.

"We need to build a base here," Carrera pointed
to a spot just northeast of Ninewa. "I'll also need one
more smaller base for each infantry cohort, though
those will need to be big enough to house three times
that many, eventually, and assuming the war goes the
way I expect it to. Can your people handle that kind
of construction?"

Sada snorted. "Back on Old Earth my people were
building magnificent palaces and cities when yours
were still painting themselves blue." He did some
quick calculations in his head. *Let's see. An average
cohort base will need to house about fifteen hundred
men when it grows. At sixty square meters per man
that would be ninety thousand. A square of three
hundred meters on a side . . .*

"How are you planning on building your bases?"
Sada asked.

"Basically square. Ditch. Earthen wall," Carrera
answered. "Maybe adobe housing. Small airstrip inside
for the Crickets. A full-length strip, maybe twelve-
hundred meters, at the main base."

"Okay . . . that would be about one square kilometer

you'll need to rent or lease—trust me, Patricio, you'll want to lease it rather than just take it—for each cohort base. A fair price, depending on the quality of the land, would be somewhere in the range of twenty to fifty thousand FSD per year for each."

"That's *all*?"

"Yes, somewhere in there. Probably on the low end provided you make it clear that the housing will stay when you leave. Then, for the walls . . . ummm . . . call it two or three thousand men employed with shovels for a month, for each base. Housing would be . . . honestly I don't know anything about housing."

"I know someone who does," Carrera answered. "Get me Tribunes Cheatham and Clean," he shouted out the office door.

"Two to three thousand each would work for the outlying bases," Carrera said. "Here in Ninewa it would have to be quite a bit larger."

"Yes," Sada agreed. "Including my brigade it would have about four times the area and twice the perimeter. Call it four to six thousand men for a month."

"That would make a big dent in the unemployment situation here in Ninewa," Carrera said. Unenthusiastically, he added, "But only for a month or so. Speaking of your men and families, has yours arrived here safely?"

"Yes, just this morning. I've taken over a couple of rooms here in the compound for them."

"We'll need to secure the families of your men as well, you know," Carrera observed.

"Just so. But the university hasn't enough space. For now, the families are safer where they are. When we build the base, we can make room for them as well and move them there."

Cheatham knocked on the door, accompanied by the Anglian, Clean. "You called us, sir?"

"Yeah . . . how much would we need in housing, presumably adobe housing, for the troops?"

"Adobe?" Clean asked, visibly interested. "As it so happens, I've always had a great interest in adobe construction. Did you know that it can be as strong as concrete and, if labor is cheap, also much, much cheaper? It's a wonderful building material for the very rich and the very poor."

It took Clean and Cheatham some days to work out the plans and the requirements. Still more time was spent in negotiations with local leaders for the leasing of land. After that it took more time for PSYOP and word of mouth advertising to assemble work crews. Within a month or so, however, about fifteen thousand of the otherwise unemployed Sumeris had found work in base construction. This was less of a drop in the bucket than it seemed as each Sumeri with money to spend created jobs for the otherwise jobless.

It helped, but not enough.

Zabol, Pashtia

Fadeel al Nizal was a man with a problem.

Actually, I have more problems than I can count. Starting with this one.

"This one" meant Mustafa ibn Mohamed ibn Salah, min Sa'ana. And Mustafa was not a happy camper, nor even a happy troglodyte.

"You shame me for being a member of the same

race," Mustafa stormed. "I gave you money, hundreds of thousand of FS drachma, and what do you show for it? Nothing!" he raged. "I've given you access to our data base to recruit your own group and what have those you have recruited done to resist the infidel? Lain around buggering each other for all that anyone can see!"

Abdul Aziz ibn Kalb, standing well off to one side, flinched even though he was not the target of the tongue lashing.

"Sheik Mustafa," Fadeel began, "I admit, we were taken by surprise by the speed of the infidel conquest. But then," and Fadeel looked around at the walls of the cave as if to say, *Aren't* you *a little surprised to find that your impregnable Pashtia, the Pashtia that did to death the might of the Volgan Empire, is reduced to this little hole in the ground?*

"Don't try me, little man," Mustafa glared. "If we are here it is due to the will of Allah. *He* is the great strategist. Ours is but to fight in His cause."

"Indeed," Fadeel agreed. "And all will turn out well, even in Sumer. But we do have problems there."

"Like what?" Mustafa demanded.

"Number One is a turncoat Sumeri general named Sada. For reasons I dearly pray the Almighty will reveal to me someday, this man fought the infidel gloriously . . . and then surrendered and joined him. Worse, this Sada, the dog, took his brigade over with him."

"He is in the infidel's pay," Mustafa said, with a glare of hate. "His family must pay."

"Easier said than done, Great Prince. The turncoat's family is already beyond our reach. Those of his men will be . . . harder to identify and find. We are working on this."

"Ah, so you actually *have* done something."

"We have done what we could. I have just over one hundred future martyrs operating in Sumer. About twenty of them are in the area of the traitor, Sada. It would be more except that about half, or a bit more, of what I sent simply disappeared. I suspect he has a network of informers. And I can't eliminate the informers without knowing who they are. I can't find out who they are without getting more of my people in place. And I can't get my people in place, as long as the area crawls with informers. Only in the city of Ninewa, mostly because it is of a size that makes it impossible to identify strangers, have I been successful in infiltrating. That; and that there been a major displacement of people and disruption of society wherever there was serious fighting."

"And you have a plan for the use of what you do have?" Mustafa asked, growing visibly calmer.

"I do. Noting that everything is in the hands of the Beneficent, the Merciful, still I am prepared to begin attacks against these crusaders very soon."

"With what?"

"I have too few men to conduct a proper suicide campaign at this time," Fadeel admitted. "But I can do kidnappings, I can plant bombs, I can do some assassinations. Watch and see. There are munitions scattered unsecured all over Sumer. My people are buying these up. Very soon the invader will feel our sting."

Ninewa, 1/4/461 AC

Tariq Mohsem was one of the town's few Christians. A bit shorter than most of the Sumeri norm, and also a bit stouter as befit a normally prosperous shopkeeper, he was also one of the first merchants to reopen for business. Tariq's shop, one of Ninewa's largest before the invasion, was a general store that sold food along with some dry goods, household appliances, tools, and such.

He'd returned to find the shop looted and heavily damaged. He had some funds, not the worthless Sumeri pounds but hard currency from the FS and TU. It had been his escape money. Instead of using it to escape with his family, however, he'd decided to stay and rebuild. Factoring large in that decision had been the very forthright way the occupying forces—or liberating, for those who insisted on more aesthetic terms—had shown early on that they were intent on maintaining order. Perhaps the clearest indicator of this was the young man Tariq had found dead in the shop, though visible from the street, hanging by the neck from a cross beam—*Who would have thought a neck could stretch that far?*—and with a sign on his chest proclaiming, "Looter."

"If the invading forces provide safety and order," Tariq had told his wife, "why not stay? This is home, after all."

So, instead of using the money to flee, Tariq had hired a couple of carpenters to put his shop back in order. The rest he had used to buy food from the invaders. He had to admit, they'd charged a fair price.

"Thank God," he'd also said to his wife, "that they are, too. If we were further north, in the Anglian or FSC sector, they'd be giving the food away and no one would shop from us."

Things were going well enough, so far, too. He'd bought the food at about forty percent of what the invaders told him he could sell it for. *And don't the bastards stop by from time to time to make sure I'm not gouging, too? Of course, that doesn't stop me from taking some of the grain and trading it for other foodstuffs, which I can mark up rather more than that.*

With the profits, and given that he was one of the first stores to reopen, Tariq not only hired two assistants, he also took on an armed guard for the evenings when he closed shop.

Of course, not everyone had a job yet. The six thousand or so men employed by the legion, locally, were only a fraction of those needing work. On the other hand, those six thousand with money created a certain amount of work on their own, as did the men of Sada's brigade and even the damned foreigners. In any case, Tariq was finding business picking up almost to preinvasion levels. As to whether it would drop off again, as more competition reentered the market; who could say? Tariq hadn't gotten where he was by inability to compete or to work hard. Indeed, in a freer market he expected to do rather better.

No one noticed when the tall, slender man with the oddly and unevenly shaped eyes pulled the beat up, dented and dirty white van to the front of the store. Even the lack of a license plate excited no interest;

many, perhaps even most, of the automobiles operating in the town were unlicensed. Perhaps they had once had licenses; who knew?

The slender fellow had a friendly face, although anyone who saw him probably thought it seemed a bit distant. He fiddled with something in the van, something below door level. No matter, everyone in the country was still in a state of shock, even those for whom the shock was not unpleasant. Nor was there anything particularly suspicious in the driver's reaching below the dash.

Opening the van's door and stepping out, the driver simply walked into the store. No one thought it odd that he consulted his watch and left after approximately four minutes. And no one walking by the storefront connected the man departing with the parked van.

Standard military time fuse burns at a rate of forty seconds per foot. The fuse had been cut to a length of fifteen feet. Thus, between the time he reached below the dash, and subtracting a few seconds to enter Tariq's store and five minutes inside, the slender man had just over four minutes to walk away at a fairly leisurely pace. He was almost three hundred meters away when . . .

"What the fuck was the point?" Carrera asked Sada.

"I'm not sure," the Sumeri answered. "Does it have to have a point?"

The two men, surrounded by legionaries with a few of Sada's men as well, stood in front of what had once been a store. The street was mostly still there, barring only a four foot deep crater, but the front of the store itself was gone. Indeed, much of the back was gone as well. Bodies and parts of bodies remained. Some of those parts were very small.

"Do we know how many people?"

Sada asked one of his men before answering, "At least fifty-seven. That many are more or less intact. As to the parts . . ."—he spread his arms, shrugging—". . . hard to say."

Carrera's eyes focused on one very small part. It was a leg, small, slightly olive in tone, with a shoe on the foot. A baby girl's leg, he thought. *A baby girl . . . like my Milagro. So fucking what if she was a Moslem, she was still just a baby girl. Bastards!*

Sada looked at the legate, looked away quickly, and offered, "It is no shame to cry, my friend. The shame would be in doing nothing about this atrocity."

Wiping a hand across his face, which did little more than streak the dust that had gathered there, Carrera forced the sorrowful tone away and asked, bitterly, "What can we do? It's in the nature of these things that they leave little evidence."

Sada laughed grimly. "Remember what I said about us being the sort of people who become exceedingly resentful about losing family members? Well . . . I think we have here the recruiting brochures"—his hand swept the scene, taking in the bodies and parts of bodies—"to acquire some numbers of people who will do anything to get even for what's just been done to *their* family. Watch and see if I'm not right."

He bellowed something to one of his officers supervising the soldiers at the bombing site. The officer came over and Sada spoke to him briefly. Then he turned back to Carrera and said, "I've just ordered

Lieutenant Faroush to round up as many relatives as
he can find and bring them to the university. I don't
suppose your people are up to teaching a course in
counter-terror? No? Well, we'll think of something.
After all, it isn't as if we Sumeris have never had
experience in crushing dissidents."

Village of Qadir Karam, Ninewa Province, 10/4/461 AC

Sada's adjutant had narrowed the number of applicants
down to thirty-six.

Since this was *Sada's* adjutant, the officer didn't do
the normal thing for Sumer and select based on who
could offer the highest bribe. Instead, he screened
out those too old, or too young, those who didn't look
strong enough and those with wives and children still
living. Not that the others were turned away completely.
Instead, they were redirected to neighborhood militias.
Some joined; some did not.

After that, the adjutant selected for intelligence and
desire for revenge. This required personal interviews,
literacy being far from universal in Sumer and vin-
dictiveness something that could never be objectively
tested for. This process took time but narrowed the
number of suitable candidates considerably.

Those few dozen were gathered now in a plain and
somewhat run-down adobe mosque in this plain and
ramshackle Sumeri town. Indeed, the only brightness
to the assembly came from the flickering lamps along
the walls and the shining, hating, vengeful eyes of the
men assembled. Along with the few dozen was another,

smaller group of specialists Sada had recruited from the dictator, Saleh's, secret police.

"So," Sada began, in addressing them, "you have agreed to give up your old lives, to become instruments of justice and vengeance? Excellent. Let me tell you what you are going to do. In a few minutes I am going to turn you over to one of my officers and a couple of special people he has selected to teach you how to become the instruments you wish to be. Before that happens, I am going to take your oaths, in the name of Allah, that you will obey every order you are given without question. You will be trained, over the next few months, in how to kill. More than that, you'll be trained in how to kill in the most terrifying manner. After that, you will return to your homes. In time, orders will come. You will gather in small groups to prepare and then you will hunt down and kill—or otherwise punish—those whom you are told to, wherever they may be and *who or what*ever they may be.

"Let me explain something to you, two things, actually. One is that once you have taken the oath, you may not release yourself from it. Your families are hostages, wherever *they* may be, for your continued obedience. The second is in the nature of what you are to do.

"You see, there are three kinds of terrorism. The first is what you have suffered, random acts of senseless violence. This kind almost *never* works," Sada sneered. "Witness the Federated States of Columbia. When their people were randomly killed, they merely went to war to exact vengeance and destroy the terrorists. Two regimes, here and in Pashtia, which formerly were great supporters of terrorism around the world, have fallen. More than that, as boys in school you all read—at least those of you who had the chance to attend school did—of the great terror bombings of the Great Global War. That was all random terror; it targeted nobody in particular. Note that no one ever knuckled under to them until nuclear weapons were used. So much for random terror.

"The other kind of terror is specific. With this kind, punishment is inflicted on particular persons, either on themselves or on those whom they love. To be the target of specific terror is a fearsome and terrible thing. Specific terror works. If it didn't, would the dictator have lasted a week?"

The eyes of the men assembled seemed to glow. *Yes, yes*, they thought. *This is what we want: specific terror.*

"The third kind of terror is genocidal. With this an entire people and even civilization is threatened with destruction. Thus, it includes specific terror because, if all are killed, then all whom you love are killed as well. Anyone who does not believe that this kind of terror works is a fool. Genocidal terror was all that kept the Federated States and the Volgan Empire from destroying each other and, incidentally, probably us as well. Genocidal terror is probably all that keeps the United Earth Peace Fleet and the Federated States from using nuclear weapons on each other now.

"So there are your three types. The kind that was used on you and brought you here and the other two, which are the kinds you will use to retaliate. Are there any questions?"

Seeing there were none, Sada said, "Very well. Stand and raise your right hands . . ."

University Compound, Ninewa, 12/4/461 AC

Ricardo Cruz was just leaving the gymnastics building where he had showered when it happened.

The first warning was a flash in the distance, behind some houses in the town. Next came the muffled sound of a small explosion. Then came the first blast, much nearer. Only after that could anyone make out the freight train rattle of incoming mortar rounds.

Cruz screamed, "INCOMING!" as he threw himself into partial shelter at the angle where steps met building wall.

The rounds came in at even intervals, a dozen of them, about two seconds apart. Whoever was on the other end apparently knew what he or they were doing. They landed with about thirty meters between shells, moving in a slightly arcing line from near the broad front steps to the main office of the campus and across an open field. Between the even spacing and the even timing it was the obvious work of a well-trained mortar crew, using the traversing wheel on the bipod to quickly and expertly lay the rounds. Before the last round had landed someone caught on the field was screaming out in pain.

"I knew this shit was too good to last," Cruz muttered as he picked himself up from his temporary shelter and then ran to offer aid, toward the still incoming blasts.

I swear I will kick my own ass if I ever go to the showers without my body armor again.

The mortar attack was over almost as soon as it began. Automatically, the legionary Command Post's duty officer ordered a reaction century of mechanized troops and a mixed flight by a Turbo-Finch and a Cricket.

The Cricket was airborne in minutes, the Finch following almost immediately thereafter. The mechanized troops were bursting through the university gate to race into the town scant moments later.

Mistake. Big mistake. Big, bad, *fucking* mistake.

Khalid al Marri kept in the shadows atop the half wrecked apartment building. It was the same building that had been taken by the now departed FSA 731st Airborne Brigade. People lived in it, still, but not in anything like what had been its pre-war capacity. That was a shame, because al Marri's mission was to get the crusader dogs to overreact, to kill some number of the civilians now living inside. Ah, well; between his own surface to air missile and the other one located a kilometer away and overlooking the same area, one was sure to take down a crusader aircraft and cause a reaction.

From his vantage point, al Marri saw the flashes of the mortar firing and the impact of the shells inside the university compound. *Not much time now.*

Despite his prediction, al Marri was still somewhat surprised at how quickly the enemy got aircraft into the air. *Just like the dogs, to have airplanes standing by to kill the people,* he thought, his heart overflowing with hatred for the infidel invader.

To the outsider, privileged to look into al Marri's mind, that would have seemed incongruous. There he stood, ready to do his best to bring violence and destruction down onto the innocents of the apartment building beneath him, and hating those he intended to provoke into that violence because of their willingness to engage in it.

There was no real contradiction, though. To al Marri, and he shared this much, at least, with much, perhaps even most, of the cosmopolitan progressive community, things were neither good nor bad in themselves, but only in relation to the end being sought. To some extent, they shared that viewpoint with Carrera, at least as he had come to be, the major difference being only the end in view.

In any case, one of the infidel airplanes was coming his way. Still keeping to the shadows, al Marri picked up the tube he had carried to the top of the apartment building and placed it on his shoulder, fitting his eye to the sight. He aimed the sight and tube at the noise he heard coming from the craft's engine. Then he flicked a switch and was rewarded with a low hum as the seeker head went active and coolant circulated to drop its temperature so it could make out the heat of the airplane's engine.

The engine stood out in fuzzy view in the sight's eyepiece. Al Marri squeezed the first trigger and was rewarded with a beep which told that the sight saw the target. Elevating the tube until the target was near the bottom of his field of view, he then squeezed the second trigger. The sealed back of the tube blew off as the missile went airborne, al Marri feeling a slight push from his front as the missile's exhaust pushed him backwards.

Though he was too busy to note it, the other missile, launched from a kilometer away, likewise took off within a couple of seconds of his own.

✧　　✧　　✧

Tribune Miguel Lanza of the legion's air *ala* wasn't really a scout pilot, despite the Cricket he strapped himself into. Instead, he'd flown transports most of his adult life; "hauling the trash," as he liked to say, especially when the trash consisted of human beings who could hear him say it. Nobody minded; Lanza had been a fixture in the old *Guardia Nacional*, then in the Defense Corps, the Civic Force and now, finally, in the legion.

At nearly fifty, Lanza was a bit long in the tooth for the Turbo-Finches. Those birds went through gyrations that pulled the blood from the brain and made an old man faint. Even so, he had checked out on them. One never knew, after all, when a pilot would be needed. Likewise, he'd gotten himself qualified on the NA-21s and -23s—which were similar to his normal bird—and the Crickets. The helicopters were still beyond him but he intended to fix that if he ever got a chance to get back to Balboa.

Lanza loved to fly. Moreover, he believed in leading from in front. For a pilot, leading from in front meant flying, even flying the dangerous missions. That was why, despite command responsibilities as the senior officer of the *ala*, he'd been standing by on alert when the word had come of the mortar attack. First to the Cricket despite his years, Lanza had told the younger pilot just behind him in the sprint to, "Fuck off, sonny. This one's mine. You can observe."

An amazing aircraft, the Cricket; one hundred feet of take-off run and the thing had gone up like an eleva-tor, pulling Lanza's stomach down to his butt despite the low speed. Lanza's observer was already fiddling with the radio before the thing was off the ground, getting the latest intel update from the command post.

There wasn't much intel; *that* was, after all, why the command post had ordered the Cricket launched in the first place. Aviation was mostly about reconnaissance and always had been.

The command post did have a presumed firing position for the mortar or mortars—no one knew for certain if there had been more than one—that had fired at the university. This Lanza set his heading towards. It led over a set of five modern and ugly looking apartment buildings.

Once airborne, Lanza pulled one of the two sets of night vision goggles the Cricket carried over his head and onto his eyes. The observer did the same. Lanza looked back and over his left shoulder, catching sight of the Turbo-Finch that followed at a discreet distance. Confident of support, Lanza turned his eyes back to the flight path. Then, with both pilot and observer looking forward, both sets of goggles suddenly flashed brightly and went blank.

"Shit!" Lanza shouted as he pushed the Cricket's nose down with one hand, tearing off the goggles with the other. "Shitshitshitshitshit!"

The missile wasn't what one could call "bright." As a matter of fact, where the FSC had poured money into "brilliant" munitions, the Volgans—and they had made the thing some years prior—concentrated instead on "competent" ones. *Competent* was another way of saying, "good enough for the purpose, especially if used in mass."

It saw the target, a glowing greenish blur, and sped towards it. The target attempted to duck by dropping and the missile duly corrected itself, following the target down. The missile's dim but "competent" mind went something like, "Oh, boy, I'm going to hit . . . Oh, boy, I'm going to hit . . . Oh, boy, I'm going to hit," as it got closer. Still, the target went erratic. "Oh, boy, I'm going to hit," changed to, "Oh, shit, I missed."

The missile promptly blew itself up, scattering numerous small rods of hot metal through the air, some of which connected with Lanza's Cricket.

Lanza felt the plane shudder, first from the blast and then, slightly and unevenly, from the metal rods scattered by the warhead. The observer felt rather more, and let it be known with a piercing scream, as one of the rods passed through the upper portion of the cockpit's Plexiglas rear canopy, through his seat, through his harness and into his back. He slumped forward.

The important thing is not to panic, Lanza reminded himself as he played with the controls to assure himself that his plane would still respond to command and fly. His heart was pounding, and it showed in his voice, as he called the CP and said, "This is Lanza . . . We've got *SAMs*! *Shitpots* of 'em. My Cricket is hit and my observer wounded . . . I think they got the Finch that was following me . . . I'm heading back and I suggest that no more planes be launched for now, not until we can reduce the SAM threat."

Al Marri felt a great joy overflowing. True, and it was a shame, his own missile had failed to bring down its target. Yet he had seen the other crusader aircraft go up in a fiery ball of light. His partner in this enterprise had clearly scored against the enemy. Of course, the towering apartment building was still standing. Perhaps that would change. For now, al Marri decided to follow orders and leave. There would be other days. Besides, the enemy armored column that had left the university a few minutes prior was just now reaching the part of the town from which the mortar attack had come. The next few minutes would be interesting.

The mechanized century had taken some pretty fierce losses in the fight for the town. These hadn't been made good yet. Instead of having four tanks, five Ocelots, and fifty-eight men, the century had three, four and forty-six. Worse, maybe, the leadership was low. Both the century's key men, the signifer and centurion, had been killed, with command devolving onto a sergeant.

Not that Sergeant Paredes was a bad sergeant, not at all. The kid had actually been tapped for centurion track before the legion had even left Balboa. He was slated to be replaced by a newly graduated signifer, due in on the next transport. You really couldn't bitch; the whole legion was straining for leadership, what with the losses in the invasion and the scramble to form replacement units back home.

The problem was that the sergeant hadn't really been trained for the job he had. Smart? Check. Good attitude? Check. Aggressive? Check. Brave? Double check. Wise?

Kaboom!

❖   ❖   ❖

Three of al Marri's comrades in Fadeel's organization were waiting for the armored column as it approached. There were only so many roads into the area, a small open spot surrounded by buildings. Along each of the major ones a very large explosive device had been improvised from an automobile or, in one case, van. These were primed to be set off remotely, by radio. The radio control devices and solenoids were, after all, cheap and readily available for purchase from any good hobby store in the TU or FS.

True to form, the arrogant invaders took the easiest, quickest and broadest route to the mortar site. One of the men standing by with a handheld remote control device watched as the lead vehicle in the column passed the van he had parked earlier. The first three vehicles were tanks, followed by the four that carried infantry. The bomber had thought that getting an expensive tank would be the greater prize but his team leader, who was also Fadeel's brother-in-law, had assured him that killing more men was better in the long run.

Thus he waited as the clumsy tanks passed. When the first infantry carrier reached a spot next to the van he pushed the button.

Kaboom!

The explosion physically threw the Ocelot's front around by ninety degrees, knocking Paredes' helmet off. He was slammed to one side, splitting the skin over his scalp and breaking one arm with a sickening *crunch*. The driver, who had had his head stuck up out of the hatch, was knocked unconscious. From what Paredes could see, only half of the track commander made it into the track. Where his upper torso had gone? Who could say?

With blood seeping into his eyes and his arm shrieking in protest Paredes crawled to the back of the track and twisted the door latch open. The door still didn't move—perhaps the hull was slightly deformed—until the sergeant kicked it open. When he emerged, weaponless, helmetless and using one arm to try to keep the other in place, the building walls to either side were lit by fire, despite the smoke.

In shock, Paredes looked to one side and saw a tipped over Ocelot, with flames pouring out of it. *No survivors,* he thought, grimly.

His assistant, a corporal, ran up asking, "What the fuck, Paredes? I mean, what the fucking *fuck*?"

"Bomb," the sergeant answered, simply and a bit distantly. He was swaying on his feet as he continued, "I'm . . . a little hurt. Stop the tanks and get them back here. Set up a perimeter. Report to higher. And take over because . . ."

The sergeant pitched face first onto the asphalt.

University of Ninewa, legionary Command Post, 17/4/461 AC

Sada was there, representing and in command of his Sumeri Brigade. So were all the cohort commanders as well as the primary staff and McNamara.

"Let's be honest," Carrera was saying. "We got over-confident and we got sloppy. Some of that's understandable; post invasion let down and all. We had the boys on an adrenaline high for weeks. When the adrenaline went, they just went on a natural downer. It was to be expected and we *should have expected it. . . . I* should have expected it.

"That's in the past. We can only affect the future. For the future I have some other news, most of it good. There have been attacks all through the country over the last several days. For the most part, we got off lightly. The Anglians and the FS troops were hit a lot harder. I think we can thank *Amid* Sada's watchers for the fact we weren't hit as badly. They've identified and helped round up about half of the insurgents, so we think, who infiltrated our ZOR . . ."

Carrera waited for a few moments for a translator to pass what he had said on to Sada who answered, "They did, Pat, and thank you. But they're only part of it. If there had been no work here, then the attacks would have been a lot worse."

"I know," Carrera agreed. "In any case, there is some good news. The FSC's War Department is finally waking up to the fact that we have an insurgency here and it's not going to go away on its own. We've been offered a long-term contract to keep a legion here and to expand that legion to roughly divisional strength. The details don't matter much except that the rate of reimbursement we get is going to be based on our strength in country. Even so, we're not going to hurry that expansion. For one thing, the Area of Responsibility we get assigned, the size of it, goes up as our strength does. For another, if we break ourselves in trying to get big faster than our school system and recruiting standards would currently permit, we'll soon find ourselves unemployed." *And I'll find myself without the means of finding and destroying those who murdered my wife and children.*

"It isn't just the insurgents, Patricio," Fernandez said. "We've got to go after those who feed them, those who support them, those who supply them and those who'll spread their propaganda, too. Everybody."

INTERLUDE

5 January, 2095, Terra Nova

The unloading proceeded in accordance with a schedule designed to get one national or ascriptive group completely off the transport before another was unfrozen. The Panamanians came first, roughly ten thousand of them, as their colony, named Balboa, was the westernmost of the six colonies the *Amerigo Vespucci* had come to settle. Even among the Panamanians, there was a split as *Chocoes* Indians were to be dropped before the European- and Mestizo-descended people. The *Vespucci* would merely accelerate slightly in its orbit to assume the best position for unloading each of the others.

Ngobe Mzilikaze, Captain of the *Vespucci*, thought this was needless and excessive care. True, there had been problems with the colonies from Europe, from farther south in Latin America, and from Africa. And what happened with the colonists from the Balkans, the one time they had been awakened without regard to ethnicity, ought not even be talked about. But the Central Americans, despite having had a few wars amongst themselves over the centuries, had no real or deeply engrained hatred of each other. They much preferred civil to foreign war. Nonetheless, since the *Cheng Ho* disaster, standard procedure was to unload ascriptive, national, religious and ethnic groups as separately as humanly possible.

Ngobe hoped the settlement went smoothly. He carried important dispatches for the UN enclave on the island they called Atlantis, dispatches he was bound to deliver personally. Yet he could not, consistent with his duty, abandon his post aboard the *Vespucci* until all of his cargo was unloaded.

Belisario Carrera had never even believed it was possible to be so cold. Shivering worse than a leaf in hurricane, worse even than a high living leader of a Kosmo charity faced with an audit, he sat up in his deep freeze cubicle like a corpse arising at a funeral.

That was not the only *Finnegan's Wake* aspect to the resurrection, either. As soon as he sat up a white-coated technician handed him a plastic cup containing several ounces of nearly pure ethanol mixed with what passed for orange juice.

"Drink this," the technician ordered. "Primitive, I know, but we've found it's the best thing to get the blood moving and to warm you up."

The tech didn't mention that, after many dozens of voyages now, it had also been found to calm colonists who sometimes tended to panic when they realized they were suddenly, from their point of view suddenly, an uncrossable distance from a home and family they would never see again in this life.

Gratefully, too cold even to enquire as to the

young wife who had accompanied him, Belisario took the proffered ethanol and drank quickly and deeply. He barely choked on the liquid as it burned its way down his throat and began to light small fires in his veins and arteries.

Beginning to warm now, and finally able to think more or less clearly, Belisario asked about his wife, still lying frozen in the next compartment.

The tech checked the meters on the compartment and answered, "She's fine. Would you like to be here when she awakens? It sometimes helps."

5 January, 2101, UNOG (UN Offices, Geneva)

High Admiral Kotek Annan looked out over a skyline gone dark. It was far too much to say that Earth had become "a world lit only by fire"—though fire all too often lit it—but there had been a steady drop in all the activities that might have brought light. At least here in Europe there had, though Europe had started off on so high a plain it still exceeded most of the world. China was doing well enough, as were India, Brazil, and a few other places. The United States, along with those portions of what had once been known as western Canada and which now made up six of America's sixty-three states, was still a powerhouse though there were indicators that that was changing. The U.S. still tried to act as if the UN didn't exist, too.

"The secretary general will see you now, High Admiral," a flunky announced.

Nodding slightly, Annan turned from the window and the darkness it showed and walked briskly into the well-appointed, even *luxuriously* appointed, offices of the secretary general, Edouard Simoua.

"Kotek, my fine boy," said Simoua, rising and taking the younger man's arm warmly. "So good to see you. And how is your most excellent great-great-grandfather?"

"He is well, Your Excellency, in rigorous good health. I saw him in Kumasi just a few days ago. He told me to pass along his thanks, both for my appointment and for the antiaging treatments you ordered for him."

"Well," began Simoua, "it is sad but we are just in the infancy of antiagathic therapy. If your esteemed ancestor can hang on, even greater things may be possible. Besides, we people of the right views have to watch out for each other, do we not? And no one else is going to if we don't, eh?"

"Indeed, Your Excellency," Annan readily agreed. How could he not? His family—and he, personally— benefited immensely from the "I'll scratch your back; you scratch mine" philosophy of nearly all of those elites who worked for the great supra- and transnational organs of the Earth.

"Please, sit, my boy. Can I have anything brought to you? Coffee? Tea? Something stronger, perhaps?"

Annan shook his head as he sat in the proffered chair. "No, thank you, Your Excellency."

"As you wish," said Simoua, taking a chair himself opposite Annan, "I wanted to discuss your new command, the *Amistad*, and the others that will follow."

"Ah, yes," Annan agreed. "I have been up to see my new ship. It's a wonder."

"Indeed. It is the finest that America could build."
Simoua laughed. "We took it in lieu of a UN dues payment that they would never have given us anyway."

"A wonderful ship it is, Excellency, but I confess I am a bit confused about my mission."

"Govern the island on the new world that is our enclave. Atlantis, they call it. Observe . . . for now," answered the secretary general. "Spread our influence. Organize the fleet we will send you. It's going to be thirty-three ships, eventually, you know."

CHAPTER
TWENTY-SIX

In the Cain-and-Abel conflicts of the 21st century, ruthlessness trumps technology.

—Ralph Peters

Hospital *Ancon*, *Cerro Gorgia*, *Ciudad Balboa*, 15/7/461 AC

Mango trees and chirping birds surrounded the long, five-story hospital atop *Cerro Gorgia*, or Gorgia Hill. They stood, and smelled, in pleasant contract to the unadorned brick walls, antiseptic odor, and continuous business bustle of the "body shop."

The hospital had once had a different name. This was when it had been the major medical facility for the FSC forces in Balboa. It was not so major now; not every ward had been reopened. At the very least, though, it was fully staffed and equipped for Jorge Mendoza's needs. Now that they were not so pressed for medical care, and the question had become merely one of money, Campos and the War Department had

737

come through on their promise of equivalent care, restoration and prosthesis for the legion's wounded. In some cases, this meant anything up to millions of drachma for the very latest.

His new "legs" were a marvel. Flexible, strong and computer controlled; they'd cost half a million drachma each from the Sachsen company that made them. Jorge would rather have his old ones back. Marvelous these new legs may have been, but they couldn't feel. Worse, he was still not really able to use them naturally and spent most of his time not in bed in a wheelchair.

He took the loss of the legs well enough, if not precisely cheerily; he was that kind of young man. But his eyes . . .

"Jorge, there is nothing wrong with your eyes that I can find," the doctor had said. "Here, let me show you." The doctor flicked a finger at Jorge's eye. The eye blinked.

"Did you feel that?"

"Feel what?" Jorge asked.

"The blink. I just poked my finger at your eye and you blinked. Your eye blinked because it saw my finger. But your brain won't let vision through."

"I saw nothing," Mendoza insisted. "I just blinked because . . . well . . . people blink."

The doctor poked at the eye again and, again, it dutifully blinked. "Twice in a row is not coincidence, Jorge," the medico said.

The orderly at the desk just melted when the tiny . . . well, tiny, yes, that . . . but perfectly symmetrical, *charmingly* symmetrical, *vision* of a young girl fluttered her eyelashes and asked if she could *please* visit Private Jorge Mendoza. She'd said her name was "Marqueli Cordoba."

"Jorge, a Miss Cordoba to see you."

Private Mendoza turned his wheelchair toward the voice, bumping his bed as he did so. Blind, with both legs off below the knee, his reconstructive surgery had only been able to heal the more visible scars. Mendoza's green hospital robe hung down below the point at which his legs ended. The young soldier looked his age, about eighteen years old.

Cousin Lourdes didn't tell me he was so gorgeous, Marqueli thought, no eyes for the legs but only for the face.

It was characteristic of Balboan society that the government didn't do much. Nor had the legion had time and opportunity to set up a large and complex bureaucracy to deal with personal problems. Instead, the extended family took care of things. Thus, naturally, when Lourdes had seen a problem to be dealt with she hadn't thought of anything too very formal as a solution. Instead she'd called a family member, in this case Marqueli, and said, "There's a really nice soldier who was hurt in Sumer. Could you go make sure he's all right?" Lourdes being family, Marqueli had, also naturally, agreed.

As a system it wasn't much. Where it worked it tended to work well. Where it didn't it failed completely. Looking over Jorge Mendoza, Marqueli decided instantly that here, at least, it was going to work.

"Private Mendoza, I'm Marqueli Cordoba. My cousin, Lourdes, suggested I look you up. It's wonderful to meet a hero who's fought in the war."

Mendoza scratched behind his ear. He caught the slightest whiff of perfume. He sensed someone small and somehow soft sitting in the chair next to his bed. "I don't know if I fought. It's more like they fought me."

"It's fine," Marqueli answered. "You're fine." She turned and asked a nurse on the ward, "How is his recovery going?"

"Jorge is doing very well. He has some minor reconstruction still to go. Then we have to get him used to his new legs. That's going to take longer. And then, of course, there's physical therapy, and—"

"But he *will* be getting mostly better, then," the girl announced, in a voice like a love song. "I'm sorry it's taken me so long to get here, Jorge. Do you mind if I call you 'Jorge'? I was in school. And it took me a while to find out where you were since you started out in the hospital near Hamilton."

She has a nice voice, thought Mendoza. "No, Miss Cordoba, I don't mind."

"Wonderful!" she bubbled and the sweet sound cheered up the entire ward. She reached out to touch a hand. "And, please, I'm Marqueli."

"Marqueli," he said, uncertainly, ". . . yes, I was in Warren Branch Hospital in the FSC for a while. They did a lot of the work on me there. Hmmm . . . Lourdes," he puzzled. "I don't know any . . . Ohhh, the Legate's . . . wife."

"They're not married," Marqueli laughed, bouncing lightly on her chair. "Wicked, naughty Lourdes. Bad, bad, *bad* Lourdes. I hope they will be sometime but my cousin told me she was willing to wait."

"She seemed like a nice woman," Mendoza observed neutrally.

"She's wonderful," Marqueli enthused. "Smart and clever and tall and . . . well, she's just *slinky*. And those eyes! I'd like to be just like her except that she's almost a foot taller than I am and I don't think I'm going to grow."

Mendoza made an estimate of Marqueli's height based on where the voice seemed to be coming from. True, she was sitting in a chair but, even so, just under five feet was his best guess.

God, though, she smells and sounds wonderful. Height? Well, I'm a shorty myself. Otherwise I'd never have ended up in one of those cramped Volgan tanks. Moreover, I am especially short now, he thought. *Shorter by a couple of feet . . . and two legs.*

Camp Balboa, Ninewa, 20/7/461 AC

Whatever she lacked in height, Irene Temujin of Amnesty, Interplanetary (a subsidiary of the Marquisate of Amnesty, Earth) made up for in determination. She barged furiously past the guards on the headquarters gate to force her way in and directly to Carrera's office. How she got onto the compound, how she got into the *freaking* BZOR, had to wait. She was here and, Carrera supposed, she had to be dealt with.

Just shooting the bitch is right out, I suppose, since she hasn't technically violated any rules. I might have the fucking guards shot, though; that or make them wish that I had.

"Legate Carrera, I am—"

"I know who you are, Ms. Temujin." Carrera interrupted, sliding onto his desk the report he had been reading. "I read the papers when I can. What I don't know is why you are here."

"I'm here to investigate credible reports that you and your . . . *mercenaries,*" Temujin spat out the word, "are torturing prisoners in your camp."

Carrera's face assumed a highly amused look. "Mercenaries is *such* a loaded term. Inaccurate, too, since, under Additional Protocol One we are no such thing. My men make about the same pay as in the Civil Force of Balboa, you see, and there's nothing in the rules to suggest one is a mercenary unless one meets *every* condition. As for torturing people here . . . no . . . no, I'm afraid we're not. Sorry, but your reports are ill-founded."

Temujin sneered, "Then you wouldn't mind if I looked around?"

"Considering your affection for and affiliation with the enemy," Carrera answered, calmly, "I would. But, if you are willing to be confused a bit, so that I know you are not pacing off corrections for the mortar attacks we seem to receive about twice a week, then yes, I'll let you . . . look around. To your heart's content, as a matter of fact. I'll even escort you myself."

Fernandez burst into Carrera's office. "Patricio, I just hea—"

"Ms. Temujin, may I introduce Tribune Omar Fernandez, my intelligence officer? Tribune, this is Ms. Irene Temujin of Amnesty, Interplanetary. I've just told her she could look around the camp . . . 'to her heart's content.' Ms. Temujin seems to think we are torturing people here. And," Carrera sighed deeply, "she doesn't seem to want to take my word for it that we are not."

His face assuming a very somber expression, Fernandez answered, "That is most sad, Legate."

"I'm going to escort her myself. Ms. Temujin, did you bring a camera team with you? Ah, you did not. Fernandez, would you call the PSYOP people to provide a camcorder and operator for Ms. Temujin?"

"I'll see to it, sir," Fernandez answered, as he hurried out of the office.

"Ms. Temujin? Some coffee while we wait for the camcorder team?"

The camp was still under construction. Indeed, it would remain under construction for years if things worked out as Carrera planned. While some things were complete, work continued in part to provide better living arrangements for his troops but equally to provide continued work and—at least as important—job training for the Sumeris who worked there. The legion had become the largest single employer in the province, and that wasn't even counting the several hundred Sumeri whores—widows, many of them, with no other recourse—who had been given a small quadrant of the main and each outlying camp.

Well . . . they're going to work at what they do, anyway, had been Carrera's thought. *It only makes sense to protect and regularize them. Keep down the incidence of clap among the troops, too.*

The perimeter was roughly rectangular, but only roughly. A thick berm of earth zigzagged to provide lines along which any attacking enemy would have to bunch up for easy harvesting by the machine guns at the angles and corners. The berm had been formed from a deep ditch excavated out of the soil. It stopped

at the river edge, where one corner of the camp
continued on the other side. The water purification
equipment, four Secordian-built reverse osmosis water
purifiers, or ROWPUs, were dug in at the friendly
side of the river by that corner. A few small motor
launches stood bobbing in the murky water, tied to
a short pier. Another, longer pier was being built as
it was intended, eventually, to bring in parts of the
classis to patrol the river.

Topping the berm were dozens of towers, each standing about fifteen meters high. They were effectively
indistinguishable. No one not a long-time denizen of
the camp could hope to find their way about by reference to the towers.

On each side there was a complex gate. Like the
walls, these were formed of earth. Moveable barbed
wire barriers helped to control vehicular access and
block off any dismounted enemy that might try to
force one of the gates.

From the gates four dirt and gravel roads ran
inward to a central parade field fronting the headquarters building. On either side of the roads, and all
around the parade field, mixed crews of legionaries
and locals worked at putting up adobe buildings. Not
every legionary was in adobe, however. Many tents,
pink Misrani-manufactured ones, still stood. These
were beginning to grow a little ragged.

For the purposes and under the circumstances,
adobe was a nearly ideal material. Once the legion
had received its long-term contract from the FSC's
War Department, it had let a further contract to a
machinery company in Hindu-speaking Bharat for a
fairly large number of earth-block forming machines.

Some of these were automated; still others used muscle power. The blocks, a uniform ten inches by fourteen inches by three and a half, were emplaced by hand without mortar, indentations on each side and at the edges serving to hold them together.

Irene Temujin thought them interesting.

"The block houses are reasonably cool, once we add a double roof," Carrera explained. "Moreover, they're also fairly bullet and shrapnel proof. At the current rate of progress, we should have the camp completed, at least for the number of troops on hand, within a month or so. It's taken longer than we thought it would. For after that, we've formed a building company from the Sumeri workers here who will take possession of the machines and build housing for the locals . . . for profit."

Despite her initial fascination with the machines, the word "profit" drew a sneer from Irene.

"Ahhh," Carrera said, understanding instantly. He smiled broadly. "You're one of those Kosmos who used to be a Marxist, aren't you? Tell you what: I'm putting Sumeris to building decent housing for money. In all the other ZORs every bleeding heart organization in the world is trying to put up housing for free. Let's make a bet . . . any sum you care to name and put in escrow," Carrera smiled wickedly, "*any* sum, that in six months I'll have a larger portion of the population housed, more decently, than anywhere else in Sumer outside of the capital at Babel."

Temujin merely scowled.

"Up to you," Carrera said, grinning. "But if you decide to take me up on it just let me know. I'll be happy to take your money."

Two uniformed men trotted up, one of them bearing a camcorder. They stopped and the senior saluted, reporting, "Sir, Corporal Santiago and Private Velez, PSYOP, reporting as ordered."

Carrera returned the salute, saying, "Gentlemen, this is Irene Temujin of Amnesty, Interplanetary. She wishes to tour the camp, which request I have approved. You are going to film whatever it is she wants filmed. You will then, when the tour is done, turn the film over to her *without altering it in the slightest*. Understood?"

"Yessir. Only it's a disc, sir, not film."

"Whatever. Ms. Temujin, will a disc do? Good. As I said earlier, you *are* the enemy and I can't have you pacing off correction for insurgent mortars. I'm going to blindfold you now, spin you like a top, and drive you someplace where you will not recognize exactly where you are. Then I'm going to spin you like a top, again. After that, and from there, you can remove the blindfold and go wherever you would like."

"I am *neutral*," Temujin insisted.

"Yes. As I said, you're the enemy. Now, do we blindfold you or do I have you tossed out of the camp? Your choice."

Gritting her teeth, Irene answered, "Blindfold me then."

"Corporal," Carrera ordered.

One of the escorts from Fernandez's section took a black blindfold from his pocket and placed it over the woman's eyes. Then he spun her around several times, in both directions. At Carrera's summons a four wheel drive vehicle pulled up, into which the woman was helped. The vehicle sped off, doing several otherwise unnecessary turns, before stopping at one wall.

Temujin was helped out of the vehicle, spun more, and her blindfold removed.

"From here, go where you like," Carrera said. "We're just along for the ride."

After almost two hours of aimless wandering during which Temujin saw nothing, Carrera's attention was caught by Siegel, standing at a camp street corner. Siegel gave the thumbs up.

"Ms. Temujin, you really want to see our POW compound, don't you?" Carrera asked. His finger pointed down one street. "It's just down that way, about a quarter of a mile."

"You mean now that you've had to chance to hide the evidence," she growled.

"We've hidden absolutely nothing," Carrera assured her.

Gathering her soiled dignity about her—representatives of major cosmopolitan progressive organizations like Amnesty were used to more *respect*!—she walked in the direction indicated.

Irene Temujin first heard the screams when she reached a point about one hundred meters from the separately walled compound. She began to hurry. The guards at the gate attempted to bar her way until Carrera signaled that it was all right for her to enter. Once past that inside gate, the screaming grew oppressively loud.

A row of five gallows, wire nooses hanging empty, stood just inside the gate. They were low structures, each with a stool underneath, obviously intended to let their victims strangle rather than to mercifully break their necks. Temujin almost retched at seeing them.

Worse was the stink. As soon as Temujin entered the adobe building nearest the gate her nostrils were assailed with the mixed smell of feces, piss, blood, and burnt pork. Once again, a guard made as if to bar her way until Carrera signaled that she was to be allowed in.

Once inside, she saw four men, their arms bound behind them, hanging by those arms from meat hooks attached to the wooden beams of the ceiling. The men's heads hung low, the very picture of abject misery, while their toes barely touched the floor.

"Would you like to record their faces?" Carrera asked genially. When she didn't answer immediately he walked up to the nearest of the hanging men and, grabbing him by the hair, lifted his face for the camera.

Temujin was so shocked she didn't even wonder at Carrera's arrogance in showing her all this horror. *Doesn't realize I'm from* Amnesty? *Or that I have* pull *around the globe?*

"Be sure to get this, gentlemen," he told the camera team. "Ms. Temujin will want it all recorded." He did the same with each of the others.

"Irene, would you like to see the rest?"

Normally tawny face gone white with horror, the woman gulped and answered, "Yes."

In the next cell, a small room showed a half naked man bound to a metal chair. Wires led from a field telephone to the floor where they were lost in a mass of wires. Wires also were attached directly to the prisoner's genitals. A Sumeri, in the uniform of Sada's brigade, asked questions of the bound prisoner. When answers were not forthcoming, another Sumeri sitting at the table began to turn the crank on the field phone. The bound prisoner screamed and writhed piteously. There was a puddle of urine on the floor. A smell of overripe shit escaped the cell's small window.

The next cell showed a man on a wooden table. Another interrogator asked questions while an assistant played a blowtorch over the far side of the prisoner's leg, farthest away from the door. The screaming was absolutely hideous and nauseating. There was an overwhelming smell of burnt pork.

Temujin turned and began to storm out. Before she made it she bent over suddenly, adding the smell of her own vomit to the sickening stench that pervaded the facility.

Babel, Hotel Ishtar, 21/7/461 AC

Carrera had provided an escort for Irene all the way to Babel. "It would never do," he explained, "for you to be killed in my ZOR." *At least once we've accepted you in and assumed a sort of tacit responsibility.* The escort had consisted of two light wheel vehicles and a heavier truck with a tarp pulled over it. Fernandez had volunteered to serve as escort officer.

Once back at her hotel, Temujin had wasted no time in calling for a press conference. At that, she had made her statement and shown her video of the horrors being perpetrated near Ninewa. She called, forcefully and sincerely, for, "This illegal occupation to end."

At about that time, Fernandez walked into the back of the large press room containing hundreds of reporters. He had a fairly large armed escort with him. Temujin, closing her prepared statement, wondered for a moment if they were here to arrest her. She pointed and started to say, "There's one of the torturers—" when she recognized the face of one of the armed men standing by Fernandez's side.

Oh, shit, she thought. *The bastards.*

She didn't need to say it. As one the assembled media types turned around and saw for themselves.

The man to whom Irene had pointed had appeared on the film she had just shown. He appeared on the film not as one of the guards or interrogators, but as one of the "victims," the very first one hanging with his arms behind him, as a matter of fact. (For, unnoticed by Irene, another rope had run from the bound hands to encircle his waist under his clothing.) Despite the current highly amused smile, the face was completely recognizable. So were the faces of every other man in Fernandez's escort, every man who had ridden to Babel in the back of a tarp-covered truck, every man who had been seen under "torture."

Yet here he was, here they were, free and armed. That meant . . .

The reporters turned their questioning faces back toward Temujin who sat there, dumbly.

"If she'd seen nothing," Fernandez shouted over the hubbub, "she'd still have reported the same thing. It's her *business* to find torture in the world. It's so much her business that she didn't even think to question the show we put on for her. I've got to ask you people, how stupid are *you* that you would assume accurate reporting from a woman as gullible as *that*?

"Now, if any of you would like to talk to the 'victims,' they're at your disposal."

Camp Balboa, Ninewa, 22/7/461 AC

"Patricio, that was just *mean!*" Lourdes chided as they watched the television in the three-bedroom adobe bungalow the troops had put up for them. The party, Carrera and Lourdes plus Sada and his wife, sat on the floor on cushions. Ruqaya, Sada's wife, had shown Lourdes how to make a first class *kibsa*, which sat mostly eaten (with fingers) on a tray in the middle.

Carrera couldn't answer at first; he was laughing too hard.

"He was perfectly correct to do this, Miss Lourdes," Sada insisted. "Prestige drives these people, that and their perks. Humiliation is what they fear the most. That woman is personally crushed, probably forever. Her entire organization is humiliated. Patricio has pulled the incisors of a major enemy."

"It was really Fernandez's idea," Carrera submitted humbly, though it was a hard statement to get out through his laughter. "Frankly, I couldn't believe that she'd be stupid enough to fall for it, that *anyone* would be stupid enough to fall for it. The tricky part was collecting the special effects, the blood and shit and such, to make it seem real. Fortunately, one of the mess halls had some pork we could burn up with a blowtorch. And the 'victims' and 'interrogators' had already been rehearsed."

"Those were important, Legate Patricio, but she saw what she expected to see," Sada explained. "She made *herself* fall for it."

"It was still *mean*," Lourdes insisted.

"But it was *clever*," Sada's wife, Ruqaya, answered, sipping at her tea.

Hospital *Cerro Ancon*, 23/7/461 AC

If I were truly *clever,* thought the doctor, *I'd have thought of this myself. It's just amazing what a young girl looking on or helping can do to move progress along.* The doctor smiled indulgently as young Private Mendoza *walked*—with difficulty, true, but he walked—with one arm over the shoulder of the lovely young girl who came to see him every day. Her arm was about his waist.

"This is so hard, 'Queli," the boy said, "and I'm too heavy for you."

"Nonsense, Jorge. Did you forget I'm a farm girl, not some soft, city-bred wilting flower?"

Mendoza had wondered what she looked like. At some level he knew it could not matter to him so long as he couldn't see. On the other hand, looks or not she was *shaped* right. That, he could tell from the press of her tiny body against him and the times they walked with only his arm around her waist for support. *God, is she shaped right!*

The pair reached as far as they could in the physical therapy and prosthetics area. Marqueli guided Jorge in a half-stumbling turn and they began the return promenade.

"I heard Legate Carrera and *Duce* Parilla have decreed a *beca*"—an educational scholarship—"for all seriously wounded or decorated veterans," Marqueli said.

"Something to think on," Mendoza agreed. "But I've only got a high school education. And then there's the farm to think about."

"Well, as to the farm," the girl answered, "you really don't need to worry about it. Your mother told me over the phone that she's found someone to work it for her."

"I know . . . but that land's been in our family for over four hundred years. It doesn't feel right having someone else work it."

Marqueli understood that call of the land. Her family, too, had been ranching the same patch for as long as Mendoza's. Indeed, she'd checked the local histories and birth records and discovered that they'd both had ancestors who'd ridden with the semilegendary Belisario Carrera in his war against Earth. The *reason* she'd checked, though, had been to find out degree of consanguinity. They were, it seemed, roughly seventh cousins . . . though it was more complicated than that as there was more than one link. The reason she'd checked *that* . . . well . . . that was for later.

In the interim, there was the torture of Jorge learning to walk to see to.

SS *Hildegard Mises*, Yithrabi Coast, 23/7/461 AC

Relatively few people were actually tortured on the ship. For most, a tour of what was available was generally sufficient. While Jorge and Marqueli worked out his new legs, and Irene Temujin wallowed alone in the abject misery of worldwide embarrassment, other people arrived at a ship registered to Balboa and currently coasting off of Yithrab. The ship was unremarkable, a freighter with nothing much to distinguish it on the outside except for what appeared to be a helicopter platform. An IM-71 helicopter sat on the pad, but only for so long as it took to disgorge five tightly bound men and a woman.

They were prisoners. They'd had all the due process anyone might expect, however, and been found guilty of numerous war crimes to include failure to meet the requirements for legal combatancy. They were *illegal* combatants, in other words.

Identified as outsiders by the men of his brigade that Sada had spread out as "watchers," four of the men had been grabbed from a safe house set up by Sumer's dictator in the days before the invasion for just such a purpose. The other two were the homeowner and his wife. All six had been captured in a raid by the Cazador Cohort, aided by some Sumeri guides from Sada's brigade.

The prisoners had been taken, in secret, to another safe house, this one controlled by Sada's men. There all six had been court-martialed, separately, *in camera* and sentenced to hang. A mullah—Carrera had asked Sada for, "An honest mullah, one who will stay bought."—and two of his associates had approved the penalty as fitting under Islamic law. Fernandez had given the mullah six gold drachmae as a reward, to be divided as the mullah, Hassim, thought fit.

The executions had been duly announced, along with the notice that the bodies had been cremated and the ashes scattered against the Day of Judgment when Allah could rejoin their atoms or not, as he saw fit. Instead of having been executed, however, the six were taken at night in a sealed vehicle to the airfield inside the camp and loaded aboard the helicopter. This had then flown them, also in secret, to the ship, the helicopter skimming the waves and even venturing into Farsian airspace to confuse radar.

Gagged with duct tape, none had been given a chance to talk with each other since their capture.

On the ship they were separated and carried individually to separate containers that had been soundproofed. There they were chained to the walls while the program for each was worked out by the Sumeri interrogators on Fernandez's Black Budget.

Looking over the files on each, the chief interrogator, Warrant Officer Achmed al Mahamda, tapped his fingers on first one picture, then another. *These are either brothers or close cousins,* Mahamda thought. *What one knows the other will know as well.* He placed the files together on his desk and wrote on a slip of paper, "Interrogation Course M."

This meant that the cousins, or brothers, would be used as a check on each other. If their stories failed to match in any particular, pain would be first threatened and, if that failed, applied until they did match.

It's funny, thought Mahamda, *well, funny for certain values of funny, that for all that relatives and comrades try to concoct a story beforehand, they can never get all the details right. They might agree on, "We were just minding our own business going to the goat auction," but they never think of "What's Khalid's mother's maiden name?" They never remember to work out and commit to memory a purely spurious route or set of connections and events. Even if they did, they wouldn't remember to update it daily and couldn't commit it to memory even if they tried. And once we get them screaming and talking, once they*

*lose confidence in each other and the story, there's no
stopping point and they'll spill everything.*

The others were more problematic. At this stage, the
insurgency wasn't really well developed enough—even
the bi-weekly mortaring of Camp Balboa had grown
somewhat listless—for there to have been much intelligence to gather. Sada's watchers watched, of course,
even so.

The first course of the treatment, for each of the
prisoners, was to give them a guided tour of the
ship. This was usually enough to loosen even very
fixed tongues.

Muhammad al Kahlayleh was the first of the new-
comers to be given the tour. His interrogator introduced himself genially. "I'm Warrant Officer Achmed
al Mahamda, and you are going to tell me everything
I want to know."

Al Kahlayleh told Mahamda, a very genial seeming and somewhat overweight former member of the
dictator's *Mukhabarat*, or secret police, "I'll tell you
nothing."

Al Mahamda just kept the genial smile and answered,
very confidently, "Yes, you will. Trust me on this. I've
been at this business a long time. It's just a job to me
but it's a job I do very well."

With al Kahlayleh's hands cuffed to a chain about
his waist, and accompanied by two stout escorts, al
Mahamda led the prisoner to the first chamber. This
contained a dental chair, with all the usual appur-
tenances and some extra features for holding the
"patient" firmly in place.

"We usually begin here, my friend," al Mahamda
began. "The teeth are not strictly necessary for life,

can be repaired almost indefinitely, and are extremely painful to have drilled without anesthesia."

A smiling Sumeri in a white coat bobbed his head, also genially, agreeing, "Oh, yes, it is truly awful what we can do here, more or less indefinitely." Al Kahlayleh's tawny face blanched, as much at the present geniality as at the future prospect.

"Of course, there are other methods," al Mahamda continued, still smiling. "This way, please."

The next chamber held another chair, not unlike the dental chair in the first, but without any of the instruments.

"This is worse," the warrant officer said. "Here, we do more or less permanent damage. The chair is to hold you still for it."

"Permanent damage?" the prisoner asked.

"Oh, yes. Here fingernails are removed. Gonads are crushed. Also we can attach an electrode to your penis and stick one up your ass." Al Mahamda shook his head. "If you think a dental drill is painful, well . . ." Mahamda shuddered delicately. "Come on, only fair to show you the rest."

The next chamber held a similar chair. Along one wall was a bench on which were neatly laid out a series of obscure instruments.

"This one is particularly fascinating," al Mahamda said, picking up a complex metal assembly with places for neck, knees and wrists, plus a rack and pinion method for closing the entire apparatus. "It's called the 'Scavenger'—I haven't a clue why—and it does everything the old rack used to do, but in a fraction of the space. It will break your bones, deform your spine, dislocate your joints. It's pretty awful, but very little effort for us which, as you may imagine, we appreciate."

The prisoner gulped.

"And then there's this," the warrant continued, holding up what looked like an outsized wooden shoe with handles and screws. "We put this on one of your feet and simply crush that foot a millimeter at a time. You know," he said, with a trace of wonder in his voice, "as I said, I've been at this business a long time and I've never seen anyone resist this for long. I think it must be the idea that they'll be crippled for life that gets to them. What do you think?"

"I think I'll tell you whatever you want to know," answered al Kahlayleh, shivering. "Just keep that shit away from me."

So much for "I'll tell you nothing," thought al Mahamda.

"You sure you wouldn't like just one little demonstration?" al Mahamda asked. "Just so you know we're sincere."

"No, no," the would-be insurgent answered. "That won't be necessary. No, not at all necessary. I'll cooperate."

"You're *sure* you wouldn't like a demonstration?" al Mahamda asked again, pleasantly. "Just as a show of our good faith."

"Please, no," the prisoner whimpered.

"Very well, then." Al Mahamda put the boot down, as if reluctantly. "You do realize, don't you, that if we catch you in a lie, now or later, you will get the treatment before I deign to talk to you again."

"I *said* I'll talk," al Kahlayleh shouted. "Just get me out of here."

"Very well. In light of your cooperative attitude, I think we can dispense with the rest of the tour. Come with me."

The four men began walking toward the bow of the ship when they passed an area marked, in Arabic, "Surgical Ward."

"Is that for if someone has a heart attack while being questioned?" the prisoner asked.

"Oh, no," the interrogator answered. "Well, that, too. But mostly this is for the really hard cases. See, we give them sex change operations before we strangle them so that they go to Allah as women."

Kahlayleh's eyes rolled up in his head as he moaned and crumpled to the deck.

Mahamda couldn't help but laugh. "You know, boys, it's amazing how often we get that reaction. That infidel, Fernandez, was a pure genius for thinking of this trick."

Not that it was actually a trick, of course.

First Landing, Hudson, 33/7/461 AC

Matthias Esterhazy, representing the firm of Chatham, Hennessey, and Schmied had no trouble securing an appointment with Irene Temujin. Indeed, since it seemed as if the entire world had turned their backs on her, unwilling to be contaminated by her apparent gullibility, she was positively eager to see anyone who might contribute to the organization and so help her expiate her shame. She had been thinking of resigning her post and going to work for the World League, where even idiocy could be, and generally was, rewarded. But before she took that cut in pay and prestige, perhaps Esterhazy would offer her the means to regain her lost status.

Esterhazy ignored the woman's voluble gratitude. He wasn't here to dispense money, but rather to show the power and influence money could buy. Taking his seat he opened an expensive looking leather briefcase and took from it a folder, which he opened. He slid a picture onto Temujin's desk.

"A photo of my son at school? I don't understand."

Matthias didn't answer. Instead, he slid another across, this one of her family in Kashmir, which was her home. This was followed by another of her daughter in finishing school in Helvetia. The last was of her husband, taken apparently as he left his place of employment with the World League in First Landing.

"Let me be blunt," Esterhazy said, Sachsen accent coming through strongly. "You are now shown to ze verld, fittingly or not, as an hysteric und a fool. Very little you say is likely to be believed by anyvun who matters. Ever. Again."

Irene began to blanch.

"Zus, ze rest of vat I haff to say, you could repeat to no good effect. Zat is, if you were shtupid enough to repeat it. If, even zo, you do repeat it, everyone you care for in zis verld vill disappear." His hand pointed toward the photos now littering Irene's desk. "Moreover, if you do not call your organization's dogs away from the *Legio del Cid*, eferyvun you care about in life vill disappear. Let me add to zat, zat zey are all being vatched and ze disappearance of any vun of zem vill cause all ze rest to disappear. Phones, too, are being monitored as is zeir mail.

"My principal in zis matter is someone you don't want to fuck viz, Ms. Temujin. He has no scruples, not anymore. If you get in his vay you vill be crushed. Going after him or his organization, or trying to, is even more silly zan it vould have been for you to go after ze olt Volgan Empire in zeir days of power. Ze Volgans, at least, vere slightly sensitive to public opinion vile my principle is not in ze least."

Esterhazy further explained, "Ze problem, you see, Ms. Temujin, is zat you and zose like you are aesthetically razer zan morally focused. You object to what you can see razer zan to vat is true. Zus, you can see what you like to zink of as torture because the civilized East *lets* you see it. You cannot see ze harm that ze torture seeks to prevent und zo you ignore it. Frankly, since it does not fit your verld view, you ignore ze harm even ven you can see it. In ze old days, you made a show of being "neutral" with regard to the Volgan Empire. Never mind zat, morally speaking, ze Volgan Empire vas as evil a political construct as man has efer known and should have been ze focus of *all* of your efforts. Ze Volgans did not let you *see* ze evil zey did and so, zey vere not truly evil to you. Ze democratic world did let you *see* zeir much lesser degree of evil and so zey were ultimate evil to you.

"You are like ze drunk who lost ze keys to his vehicle on vun side of ze road, but insists on looking for zem on ze ozer where zere is more light.

"Zat will be all, zank you, madam."

Without another word Esterhazy stood, took the photos, returned them to his briefcase, and left.

INTERLUDE

Earth Date 27 March, 2102,
Island of Atlantis, UNENT
(United Nations Enclave, New Terra)

"Ungovernable, untaxable, unsupervisable, and uncivil, High Admiral," the outgoing governor, a short and slight, sandy-haired bureaucrat named Lubbing informed Annan. "Our staff here is too small to really supervise or govern. Nor is the population density high enough for them to pay enough in tax to justify a larger staff. The land mass is extensive and the people just move around as they see fit. It's hopeless, at least until their population grows."

It was a feature of UN policy with regard to the new world that, while countries and groups on Earth were awarded settlement rights, most of those countries didn't really care about, or have the clout to interfere with, the UN's attempt at governing those colonies. Most especially did the UN's heavy hand fall, as it did on Earth, upon the poor and weak.

"Govern through the Terra Novans?" Kotek asked.

"They won't cooperate. The people who came here

wanted to escape taxation and supervision. That, or they're just dirt-scrabble subsistence farmers forced to leave. And those have nothing to give."

Annan shrugged his shoulders eloquently. "It doesn't matter. The point of this exercise is to get them off Earth, both the useless and inefficient and the extremely efficient but unenlightened and ungovernable. I had just hoped to make this trip worth the time away from Earth. As a practical matter, when my tour here is done I'm allowed to return with as much as I can carry."

"I know," the bureaucrat agreed. " And *that*, High Admiral, you *can* do. There are some nice things available here, including some things you can't find on Earth at any price."

"Like what?"

The outgoing governor's eyes lit up. He already had a rather large haul that would accompany him back to Earth at UN expense. "Gold, jewels, rare woods, other precious metals can be obtained quite cheaply. I am taking back two dozen *Smilodon* rugs and several score bales of other furs. Mastodon tusks sell well back home, too, especially since the great herds here are already disappearing. You *did* bring trading materials with you from home, yes?"

"Yes," Annan confirmed. "Mostly medical and electronic. Some primitive firearms."

"I made that mistake too," admitted Lubbing. "Forget the flintlocks; they're making their own now. If you had something modern perhaps . . ."

"No. That particular ban I thought it wise to keep. Tell me, what are the chances of picking up slaves for concubinage at a fair price?" Annan asked. "Female slaves, of course. Oh, yes, I know I couldn't keep them in Europe; appearances and all. But in Kumasi? No problem."

"Very small," Ludding said. "Oh, there are some, particularly among the Salafis of Yithrab. But the prices are high and the quality comparatively low. And don't try raiding. The locals will fight. In any event, you can get better deals in the Balkans, Africa, or the Arabian Peninsula back home. If you are willing to pay well, then you could find a girl or two among the Salafis, something you could make do with, at least, here. But I really don't see the point. The entire female staff of the mission here on Atlantis—to say nothing of the fleet as it grows—would, I am sure, be happy to be at your disposal."

CHAPTER TWENTY-SEVEN

Ancient gods used to "kill us for their sport," but modern Olympians are content to regulate and preach at us.

—John O'Sullivan, *Gulliver's Travails*

UEPF *Spirit of Peace*,
Earth Date 20 August, 2515

"Oh, Hammerskjold," Robinson laughed in the privacy of his quarters, "That's just *priceless*."

Robinson sat on an overstuffed brown chair he'd had purchased from below and brought up. The matching sofa held Captain Wallenstein, who leaned on one arm of the piece, her breasts poking through a thin negligee and her long legs folded under her.

"She was almost one of ours," the captain pointed out, with residual anger in her voice, "hand picked by our own Amnesty to do our work below among the savages."

"Oh, I know," Robinson agreed, sobering. "And

surely we can't just let this pass. But on the other hand, what *can* we do about it?"

"Not much," Wallenstein admitted. "She's asked for asylum for herself and her family. It seems that, not content with just publicly humiliating her, the locals have made threats which, based on their record to date, they'd carry out in a heartbeat."

"Have you spoken with the woman?" Robinson asked.

"Not personally," Wallenstein answered. "I sent one of my people to see her though. She has some very . . . quaint notions of life on Atlantis, aboard ship and on Earth. Her idea of her place in the big scheme of things is even farther off base."

Robinson made a tent of his fingers, tapping them together under his nose. "Is she attractive? Could we get enough for her as a slave on Earth to justify the expense of shipping her and hers back?"

"Not a chance; she's not much to look at. There are some prole positions on Atlantis, cooks and maids and gardeners and such. Shall we send her and her family there?"

"Whatever you think best," Robinson answered, now grown very serious. "Just so long as she has no chance of ever escaping. Wouldn't do for her to tell the local progressives just where progress is going to lead them now, would it?"

Wallenstein laughed in agreement before changing the subject. "Speaking of progress, how is the war down below going?"

"Mixed bag," Robinson said, putting out his hand and wiggling his fingers. "The invasion by the FSC and the coalition went a little better for them than

I had hoped. On the other hand, they haven't found any of the weapons that provided some of the excuse for the invasion. I've passed the word to our people below who deal with the press to play that up and play down any of the other reasons for the invasion. It's been hard, though, to get the anarchist bastards to pay much attention what with all the atrocities they've fixated on that are taking place in the Balboan sector."

"Well . . . won't that hurt the FSC?"

"Yes and no," Robinson said, further explaining, "there are two ways to look at it. In the first place, the Balboans are doing a much better job of controlling the insurgency than the FSC or the Anglians are. If the press would play that up they might have more of an impact on undermining support for the war effort in the FSC simply by making them appear inefficient. But, on the other hand, by playing up the Balboans' war crimes, the press is helping build an unbreachable wall to further participation by the states of the Tauran Union. It's a hard call and I don't know which way to nudge it," the high admiral admitted.

"What *is* the deal with the Balboans anyway?" Wallenstein asked. "I looked them up. They've got no really modern military tradition though they were a serious pain in the ass to us four centuries ago. Tied to trade as they are, you would think they'd be more globally minded, more like the Taurans. Yet they've got a larger percentage of their population over there fighting than anyone else, about three times larger."

"I wondered about that, too," Robinson admitted. "Computer?"

"Working, High Admiral," a speaker answered.

"Bring up the file on Patrick Hennessey."

The Kurosawa view screen, previously taken up with a soothing show of geometric patterns, changed almost instantly to show a somewhat grainy picture of Carrera.

"He caused it," Robinson explained. "You can look his file over later at your leisure."

Unconsciously, Wallenstein ran her tongue over her lips. "Can't we control him, then?"

"I'm not sure how," the high admiral admitted, shaking his head with frustration. "He's got no family to threaten, or none that he cares enough about anyway. He appears to have no civilized moral constraints; he's a pure barbarian, in other words. Nor is he hurting for money. Actually, he appears to have more money than he really knows what to do with."

"A direct attack?" Wallenstein suggested.

Robinson exhaled, forcefully. "I wish, but no. He's an important enough ally of the Federated States that they might consider taking him out to be an act of war by us on them. And *that* we can't afford."

"I suppose not," Wallenstein conceded. "They're touchy swine. How about having one of the Novan states take him out for us?"

"It's highly questionable whether they even could," Robinson laughed. "Outside of a very few of them the rest are unlikely to be able to field a force of a competence or size capable of getting through his security. On the other hand, that does give me an idea . . . but it will take some time to set that up.

"In any case, the insurgency is going reasonably well," the high admiral continued. "They're terribly short of money, though. So Mustafa told me last month on Atlantis." Yes, he'd had to bring Wallenstein in even on that.

"Is there any way to funnel them funds?" Wallenstein asked.

"Probably, but the FSC has gotten almost incredibly good at ferreting out their accounts. Anything we did would have to be *very* discreet."

"Or not," the captain answered, cryptically. "I think I know a way."

Ciudad Balboa, 26/8/461 AC

Jorge Mendoza handed a roll of bills to the girl who sat next to him in the taxi. She counted out the fare, rounded it up for a tip, and paid the driver. The driver attempted to return the money but a look from Marqueli and a vigorous shake of her head told him that Jorge would be insulted if the driver refused his fare. The driver nodded his understanding and took the money with a sincere "*Muchas gracias, señor.*" Then Marqueli gave the change to Mendoza and opened the door on her side of the taxi.

Mendoza slid across the seat towards the open door. His metal and carbon fiber legs caught briefly on the transmission hump in the middle of the taxi floor. He unhooked the flexible metal feet at the end of the tubes that ran up to join the remnants of his own legs, then swung them out onto the street. Marqueli took his arm to help him stand. Passersby stopped momentarily to look over the smartly uniformed soldier being led by a tiny girl. An off-duty policeman saluted Mendoza's wound badge and the ribbon—all he was allowed to wear—of his "*CC en Acero*" and continued on his way. Marqueli nodded to the policeman in recognition of the salute. As the taxi pulled away, Mendoza took a moment to secure his balance. Then he followed Marqueli to the door of the restaurant, lifting his artificial legs especially high to avoid the rise of the sidewalk.

This was Mendoza's first time in public since being equipped with his prosthetics. Understandably he was nervous about it. But, at his doctor's prompting, Marqueli had taken him out. Some of the other troops of his ward had gone over his dress uniform with a fine tooth comb. Everyone there was just pleased as punch to see one of their own with a beautiful girl.

"'Queli, I feel like people are staring at me."

"It's only your imagination, Jorge. However, they *are* staring at me; I'm *sooo* pretty." She laughed at herself. The sound was like the bubbling of a newly discovered jungle stream, infinitely joyful and refreshing. "Now relax. I won't let you fall. Okay, you can start lifting your legs now. There is a staircase in front of us. Here, put your hand on the rail, right here." With one hand on the rail, the other held by the girl, Mendoza was just able to make his way up the stairs without making it look too difficult.

At the top of the steps, Marqueli opened the door and held it for Mendoza to enter the restaurant. A waiter appeared to escort the two to their table. The table was next to the long windows that looked out over the Bahia de Balboa and towards the *Isla Real*.

"The view is so lovely here," said Marqueli. Then she realized that Jorge couldn't see any of it. "Oh, I'm sorry, Jorge. I forgot." She reached over to hold his hand lightly. The touch surged through Mendoza like an electric jolt.

He said, "That's all right. Tell me what you see and I'll try to imagine it."

"If you like. We are sitting in a restaurant, at a table with a white table cloth. To your right is a clean window. Below the window children are playing on a slanted rock wall that runs from street level down to the water. The water doesn't look too clean this close, I'm afraid.

"But just a ways out there are boats. Let me see . . . I count . . . ah, seventeen of them. All waiting to go through the Transitway or to leave. There are a few small boats moving among the ships. And I see crewmen working on the ships too."

Mendoza wrinkled his brow in concentration, willing his mind to see what his eyes no longer would. "I think I can hear the children playing. And maybe the engines of the small boats."

Marqueli smiled and gripped Mendoza's hand tighter. "There is a boat you *can't* hear. A big sailing ship with . . . three, no four masts. It's painted white and has none of its sails set. There is no one on that ship that I can see. It just rocks there, with the waves. It's a beautiful ship."

"I can almost see that."

The waiter came and placed menus down for the couple. Marqueli just took them and asked "Why don't you let me order for both of us, Jorge?" The soldier agreed without comment. Marqueli looked over the menu, decided lobster was impossible, and settled on something that didn't require sight to eat neatly.

While they waited for their meals to be prepared,

Marqueli continued to chatter on, describing the bay to Mendoza. "Far away, on the other side of the bay, Jorge, there is a row of white buildings. I can't make out much but there seems to be movement around the buildings."

"That's probably the police cavalry squadron. I remember that they keep a base there."

"Yes, you must be right. I don't remember that the legion has one there, anyway. But the base really looks lovely from here." Marqueli was silent for a while, looking out over the tranquil scene.

Mendoza too was quiet. *If things had been different, if I hadn't been hurt, I might have been able to find a girl like this someday. But if I hadn't been hurt, it would not have been this girl. And, when she is with me, it feels like it must be this girl, not some other. But it can't ever be this one. I wouldn't saddle her with a cripple.*

Marqueli looked over at the boy. *Can he tell when I stare at him, I wonder? If she were still alive, my mother would say I was crazy, if she thought I was beginning to fall in love with a cripple. Am I falling in love? I don't know, I've never been in love before. But it hurts, inside, when we're not together. And Jorge isn't crippled in any way that matters. We could have children. He could be a good husband and father. And he needs me. I like being needed . . . by him. But he's not going to ask me. I'd better tell him myself.*

The waiter brought out two steaming trays and set them on the table. Marqueli assisted Jorge by cutting his meat first and then switching plates.

"You said you were a soldier's daughter, 'Queli?" he asked, while she cut.

"Yes." She sighed, sadly. "My father was killed by the gringos when I was very little. I don't remember much but broad shoulders and a big smile for me. A couple of years ago my mother died, too. I don't think she ever got over losing him."

"How did you . . . ?"

"Oh, we went to live with my uncle and my mother worked to support us until she died. If Legate Carrera had not begun supporting those of us who lost family in the invasion I don't know what I'd have done."

"He's a gringo, you know," Mendoza said. "He was even in on the invasion. It may have been him, or his men, who killed your father . . . or my brother."

"I know . . . but . . . if he did, he's gone a long way to make up for it."

"That's true," Mendoza admitted. "And he's done all right by me." *Better than all right.*

"In more ways than one, Jorge," she amended.

Now the only question is tell him or trap him. Marqueli turned to her dinner with a grin unseen by Mendoza.

Babel, Sumer, 28/8/461 AC

Her given name meant "assistant." It was fitting.

Senta Westplatz waited impatiently at the corner of two busy streets. Though Sachsen-born, Senta was a Muslim. Like virtually all of those around her, Westplatz wore the hijab. Since it was important that she also be recognizable, her outer covering was olive on the outside, with enough of a sky blue lining showing to mark her as distinctive. Between that, her light eyes and her Sachsen features, she hoped the freedom fighter coming to claim her would have no problem.

Though Sachsen-born, Senta had lived long in Sumer. She had friends there, many of them. Many of those friends were involved, deeply involved, in the resistance. It was a case of like attracting like.

She'd done odd work for the resistance from time to time, her cover as an aid worker giving her free access throughout most of the country, though the BZOR remained problematic. The mercenaries seemed to neither have, nor permit, any illusions about the humanitarian Kosmos.

Senta was a committed pacifist. Though willing to help, she had drawn the line at transporting weapons or explosives, instead acting as a courier, transporting fighters under cover of her humanitarian organization, providing medical supplies and occasionally spying. Then, too, some of the FSA's civil-military affairs personnel were more civil than military and gave away more information than they should have.

When some of her Sumeri friends suggested to Senta that she might help the resistance by voluntarily becoming a hostage for ransom, she'd jumped at the chance. She could think of no better way to help the cause.

Simply taking her off the street would have been easy, especially given her intention of helping in her own kidnapping. On the other hand, such a kidnapping might be inherently suspicious. To allay that suspicion, Westplatz had reported to the occupation authorities that she had received nonspecific threats. That way, her side and her country—nominally, *very* nominally, allied to the FSC—could also blame the

FSC for failing to provide security for her when she was taken.

The automobile, when it pulled up, proved to be a nondescript dirty white four door sedan made in Yamato. There were three men inside. Each pulled his keffiyah, the traditional checked Arab headdress, across his face and tucked it into the opposite side as the car slowed to a stop.

Once the car stopped, two of the men emerged waving pistols. They simply grabbed Senta as she stood there and bundled her into the car.

Potsdam, Sachsen, 31/8/461 AC

The old, gray, stone building rang with the sounds of workmen engaged in restoration. It was slow work but much had been accomplished already. The key officers of the cabinet of the Sachsen Republic, for example, all had habitable offices.

"They want five million Tauros and the release of Ali Mahmoudi," the chancellor's greasy-looking assistant, Herr Hoyer, said, in the secure confines of his chief's centrally located suite of offices. Even to the chancellor, Hoyer seemed to be something of a *Schmierfink*.

"Ali Mahmoudi . . . ?" The Chancellor groped for a memory. "Oh . . . *him*."

"Yes, him. The FSC seems to know some of the details of the offer," the assistant advised. "Well . . . after forty years of occupation and keeping us from liberation by the Volgan Empire, while preserving our own fascists, it's no surprise they have their friends in

Sachsen, too. In any case, they're already pressuring us to turn Mahmoudi over to them before we can release him. Of course, we would have turned him over years ago except that two of our own people are being held hostage in Mahmoudi's old stomping ground in Bekaa. We were promised that they would be killed if we let the FS have him. This was obviously a political impossibility."

The chancellor was no friend of the Federated States, less still a supporter of the war in Sumer. Deep down he wasn't even a supporter of the war in Pashtia, though he had had to send some forces. Even there, he'd made sure their rules of engagement were such as to make them as useless as possible, all under the guise of preserving Sachsen life.

Notwithstanding any of this, however, he had his domestic opponents who were sure to take advantage of his discomfiture whichever way he rolled. And roll he would; there was no doubt about that. The only question was the direction of the roll and the degree of spin that would be needed. And there really wasn't much question about the direction, either.

Majrit, Castilla, Terra Nova, 21/9/461 AC

Of course, the Sachsen chancellor *did* release Mahmoudi. There really had never been much question about that. Whatever physical harm the terrorist might do in the future was unimportant compared to the damage that would be done to the chancellor's domestic political power in the present were Westplatz to be killed. This release of the terrorist had to be made public though every effort was made, largely unsuccessfully, not to link the two as having been the subjects of a trade.

The trade couldn't be hidden, really. What could be, and was, hidden was the amount of ransom money paid over. This was the full five million Tauros that had been demanded. Even with the obvious linkage between Westplatz and Mahmoudi, the chancellor was a believer in Abraham Lincoln's truth: you *can* fool all of the people some of the time.

Of course, thought the Chancellor, *it's much easier when all of the people desperately want to be fooled.*

The money went to a number of useful places. Some purchased influence in Sumer and elsewhere. Some went to arms inside the country and out. A fair amount went to explosives, detonators, the odd book bag and backpack, and living expenses for certain persons inhabiting various parts of the continent of Taurus.

It was amazing how far a few million Tauros could go when overhead was low, arms and explosives cheap, and with most of Salafis within Taurus already being supported by the generous doles provided by the Tauran Union's member states and some lesser amounts from Yithrabi-funded madrassas and mosques.

Some small percentage went to fund a critically important operation in Castilla.

The operation had cost less, far less, than holding a Kosmo conference at a five star hotel on the picturesque island of Melosia concerning the dreadful problem of forced assimilation of migrant widget pickers in Eastern Westfuckistan. (Or perhaps it was Western

Eastfuckistan. No matter; the point was never really to solve the problem, so much as it was to have a lovely conference by a lovely beach at someone else's expense. Why, if the problems were actually to be solved the free luxury conferences might end. That would never do.)

In any case, Fadeel's organization was able to plant fewer than a dozen bombs, kill under two hundred Castillanos, and drive that country completely out of the coalition in Sumer. Rarely in history had such a significant strategic objective been achieved at so little cost, though the Salafis would remember when it had, if anyone would. Westplatz agreed that the lives lost, while regrettable, had been well spent. Even so, she slept poorly for three entire nights over it, she felt so badly, and felt very virtuous at her own suffering thereafter.

UEPF *Spirit of Peace*, Earth Date 19 September, 2515

"I've got to confess, my dear Captain, that your plan was brilliant, *brilliant,* I say!"

"Why thank you, Martin," Wallenstein answered, preening. "It gets better, too. Our collaborators down below have rounded up dozens of people willing to be 'kidnapped.' We've got news reporters, humanitarian aid workers, international lawyers, priests and ministers. There are even two rabbis and as many homosexuals as one could imagine. I never thought that would happen. I really don't see us ever running out of people, actually. And every one taken means five or ten million transferred to the resistance in

Sumer and even in Pashtia. Of course, some of it will go to Taurus, too, and while I don't expect anyone to fold as readily as Castilla did, governments *will* fall, alliances will be weakened."

"I've been thinking a bit myself," the high admiral said. "I think the best way to handle the success the Balboans have been having is to split the effort in the media, with half comparing them to the FSC to the latter's detriment and half insisting that the FSC boot them out of the country and arrest their leaders for war crimes."

Wallenstein sipped at her drink. "Not sure I follow."

"The people down below who support us engage in a very interesting form of double think," Robinson answered. "They seem to have these little mental compartments in which they store their hatreds. The compartments let in or reject evidence, but seem never to objectively analyze it. They accept anything they hear that fits their world view or supports the ends they believe in, and reject what does not, logical consistency be damned. Thus, they're perfectly capable of believing both things as true at the same time, provided they hear them from different sources.

"It's like those homosexuals you mentioned who are willing to be kidnapped as hostages. They're going to help people who would string them up by their necks in a heartbeat. Why? It can only be mental compartmentalization amounting to insanity."

Wallenstein thought that very witty. She added to the high admiral's thought, "Well, our ancestors, the ones who took over Old Earth, didn't compartmentalize. Like us, however, they were very capable of using those who did."

"Quite," Robinson agreed. "In any case, I do intend to push their Cosmopolitan Criminal Court into having the Balboan leaders arrested, if possible, but it has to be at the right time. That time is not quite yet. I *am*, however, working on the Balboan government. Apparently the agreement under which they agreed to sponsor the forces in Sumer allowed them a total of one thousand FSD per man per month from the profits. This is about twice what an individual private in that force is paid, by the way. It's also become a substantial portion of the government's revenues, about seven percent and rising. The government, however, sees no reason anymore that they shouldn't be receiving *all* of it, which would increase their total funding several times over."

"So what stops them from simply issuing a decree and taking over?" Wallenstein asked, confused.

"Fear, I think. They've only got a few thousand under-equipped police in country. The mercenaries match that fully with their secondary formations of soldiers, damned well-armed soldiers, too, being raised under the government's nose. Still, let's let the ambassador see what he can do. No need to tell him in advance how unlikely success is."

Embassy of United Earth, *Ciudad* Balboa, 1/10/461 AC

"What you ask is, sadly, impossible," President Rocaberti insisted. "Yes, Mr. Ambassador, I would very much like to see those two bastards out of the way. I lack the power even to get at the one that's in this country. If I tried, I'd soon find myself decorating a lamppost."

The ambassador of United Earth to the Republic of Balboa was nonplussed. A small man, very dapper and precise, he found it hard to imagine a semi-private military force able to ignore a genuine government, though he understood that nonmilitary nongovernmental organizations did so with impunity all the time. That was *different* though.

"I really don't understand," the ambassador admitted.

"It's like this," the president explained. "I have about eleven thousand police, most of them civil rather than military. Of the military police there are about four thousand, a quarter of which are brand new. They lack heavy weapons and training for combat. Moreover, those most suitable for combat were let go to join this "legion" Parilla and Carrera—that's not his real name, did you know that?—set up. We've since made up the numbers, but not the . . . oh, I suppose 'quality' is the best word. Worse, there are strong ties of affection between the Civil Force and the *Legio del Cid*. My police are, frankly, unreliable to me.

"In Balboa now, there is a second legion forming. My people tell me this legion is about half strength in the units—call it twenty-five hundred soldiers—and has about as many still in training. They are led by what are now rather experienced and rather good combat commanders; so I'm told. They're frighteningly well armed, too. They'd go through my skeleton of a military police force in days . . . maybe hours. If the police didn't just go ahead and join them.

"So you see, I can neither arrest them, not even the ones in country, nor do a damned thing to force them to pay a fair share of their revenues."

The ambassador almost asked whether it might not

be possible to have the FSC, the ultimate guarantor of Balboan democracy, or what passed for it, force the change in receipts and likewise reinforce the police to make the arrests. He started, and then realized that there was no chance—zero, zip, zilch, nada—that the FSC would do a blessed thing to undermine their real allies in the conflict that currently mattered. Still, there was *something*, something just at the edge of conscious thought.

Rocaberti saw and understood the fleeting look that crossed the ambassador's face. "Yes, that's exactly right. Under the circumstances of this war, with the Balboan legion being the third, soon to be second, largest contingent, there is no chance of any support from the gringos. My best hope is to keep the legion for the most part out of the country."

The ambassador half closed one eye, cocking his head and twisting it on his neck as he struggled for that something which seemed to be eluding him. *Aha*.

"Mr. President," he asked, "what if Tauran Union troops came to secure your government?"

UEPF *Spirit of Peace*, Earth Date 13 October, 2515

"Now isn't *that* an interesting idea?" muttered Robinson as he considered the ambassador's proposal. "It would never work on its own, of course. But if there were to be another attack on Balboa, then the legion they have overseas would have to be sent home *or* other security forces would have to be brought in."

"Which security forces, Martin?" the captain asked.

"The FSC can't, they're already overstretched in the first place but in the second place, after a century of occupation and an invasion, the people there would not welcome their troops."

"After I looked over the file on this Hennessey or Carrera person, I also looked into the country he's recruiting from. I doubt their president could politically stand the uproar if he invited the FSC back."

"I know," Robinson agreed genially. "That's why the ambassador suggested that Tauran Union or other coalition troops be used."

"You would have to be careful," she cautioned. "The Yamatans are notable for being dicks when overseas. The Sachsen *Army*, whatever its government might feel, is still at heart a staunch ally of the FS. The Anglians? I'm not sure why but the Balboans seem to not much like the Anglians. What's that leave? Gauls and Castilians?"

"Yes," Robinson agreed happily. "And some few others. Precisely those who are no friends of the FSC and those who are most friendly to us and our aspirations. But there will need to be an incident to justify calling for help. And if it kills some civilians down below, it's still better than people of our classes being killed, eventually, back home."

Ciudad Balboa, 25/10/461 AC

Not every asset available to Mustafa had been used in the attacks of two years prior. He still had his command and control team which had never been used and was perfectly capable of easing the arrival of other, operational, teams.

Those teams, two of them of three men each, came in on a single large yacht that anchored at one of the country's many yacht clubs, debarking their hidden passengers at night.

Moreover, the passengers fit right in once they were ashore. It was elegant, really. There were a dozen good Salafis from Castilla who spoke Spanish and needed to get out of the country. There was a job for half that many men skilled with explosives in a country where one needed to speak Spanish. Sometimes problems had a way of solving each other.

The men had escaped from Castilla barely ahead of the police and hidden out in Bilad al Sham for some weeks. From there they'd flown via that nation's national airline service to Farsia. Once in Farsia they'd languished for a bit, their informal leader, Mohammad Ouled Nail, doing his best to keep their spirits up after the ecstatic excitement of the attacks.

While they'd languished, however, the Farsian intelligence service had been very busy, preparing identification and passports. Properly documented, the six chosen reboarded an airplane, the first of a series that ultimately saw them arrive in San Vicente, not far from Balboa. There they were met by a representative of some local import-export business known locally as M-31. This business imported money and exported illegal drugs. They imported a bit more money, some small portion of what was paid for Senta Westplatz, for seeing the six by sea to Balboa and providing them with certain useful materials and implements. Business was business, after all.

Kaboom! Kakakakakaboomoomoomoomoom!

Camp Balboa, Sumer, 26/10/461 AC

Carrera found Fernandez weeping quietly and staring at the photo of his daughter. A faxed message sat, crumpled on the desk, alongside a color newspaper page from home showing the carnage.

Beautiful girl, Carrera thought. *She must have resembled her mother. What a goddamned fucking waste.*

He placed one hand on his intel chief's shoulder, in sympathy. "I just heard, Omar. There are no words . . ."

Fernandez looked up, not trying to hide his tears. "She was all I had after her mother died. And then these . . ."

". . . bastards," Carrera supplied. "We'll get them, if we can, Omar. I wish I could promise you—"

"It's for me to promise you, Legate. We'll get them, all of them, no matter what it takes."

Of all men, Patricio Carrera probably best understood Fernandez's suffering. And one had to be impressed with the conviction behind his promise.

Aeropuerto Internacional Herrera, *Ciudad* Balboa, 3/1/462 AC

You had to be impressed. The fund-starved and despised armed forces of the various states of the Tauran Union had never managed to deploy much of anywhere without the FSC not only footing the bill but providing the taxis . . . and the lunch counters . . . and the fuel . . . and the bulk of the ammunition . . . the administration . . . the medical support, the . . . ah, but why be petty? Nonetheless, in what was lightning speed by TU standards, the first troops of the Kingdom of Castilla and the Republique de la Gaule arrived in country within a fortnight of the second series of attacks.

These had been directed away from infrastructure and towards people. This focus was not exactly unusual, for the terrorists, but it was critical here. Had they actually succeeded in destroying the Balboa Transitway, the above-sea-level canal that connected Terra Nova's two major oceans, there might not have been a reason to deploy. Moreover, killing people (and they killed many in attacks on churches, especially) was much more likely to garner sympathy.

Best of all, from the Tauros' point of view, was that no one at home could object to sending soldiers to protect Balboa. This was as plainly a nonaggressive move as one could conceive of. Even the pacifists approved.

The FSC had very mixed feelings, of course. The Transitway was theirs. They'd paid for it, built it, defended it, and even once invaded to make sure the Balboans didn't soon forget who really owned it. On the other hand, the FS really didn't have available the troops required to defend it, what with running two campaigns in Sumer and Pashtia. Even worse, with the growing insurgency in Sumer, the legion couldn't be released to defend their home turf.

There wasn't much to do but acquiesce.

Las Mesas, Balboa, 3/1/462 AC

Jorge would never surrender to being a mere cripple.

But your problem, old son, is that there is only so much you can do that's fun. Mendoza laughed at himself. *Okay, there's only so much you can do . . . period. The fun part could wait. Seriously though, I can't take her swimming outside of a pool. And I'm not comfortable in a pool. Movies are less than ideal for me and so she doesn't enjoy them as she should. The worst are the ones in English with Spanish subtitles. Long walks are out for the next few years. But this horse has advantages over walking anyway.*

Actually, thought Mendoza, *my body—what there is of it—isn't so big a problem as the fact that I am scared to death of Marqueli . . . or rather of losing her. I'd love to tell her how I feel, but what if she just ran away from me? A cripple for a friend is one thing. But for something more than a friend . . . ?*

It was Marqueli who hit upon the idea of horseback riding. She had gone to her uncle who raised horses and asked him if he could provide a couple of gentle ones. The uncle, being told of Carrera's interest in Mendoza and eager to stay on Carrera's and the legion's good side, had agreed immediately.

So Marqueli asked the doctor in charge of Jorge's recovery if a car and driver could be provided, telling him why they needed them. "Piece-o-cake," tho doctor had answered, snapping his fingers.

A few days later Mendoza and Marqueli found themselves staying in separate rooms on her uncle's ranch. Every day began with a ride. Marqueli took along a picnic lunch. As she and Jorge rode she described the scenes they passed and warned him of any undulations in the ground that would affect his horse. Sometimes they just rode in silence.

He's remarkable, thought Marqueli. *He never complains, he never whines. How many men would take such a beating from life and still be trying?*

She asked, "Jorge, what are you going to do now?"

Mendoza didn't answer immediately. When he did, his answer came slowly, as if he were still thinking. "There's the *beca* the legion is offering to badly wounded troops. It's generous, much more so than the one being offered to regularly discharged legionaires. I've been thinking along the lines of taking them up on that offer . . . going back to school, to the university."

The girl clapped her hands together, startling the horses slightly. "That's wonderful. To study *what*, do you think?"

"History, maybe. The legate and *Dux* have said they'd need teachers at the schools they're starting. It would carry a warrant-officership when I finish. I'll keep drawing my regular pay until then. Only problem is . . . how do I write a paper when I can't see the typewriter?"

"Oh, Jorge don't be silly. I'll type your papers for you, once we're married." The girl said it so matter of factly that Mendoza didn't at first realize what she had said. He answered "Well, of course you could . . . did you say married?" He reined his horse in tightly.

"Yes, silly. Do you think I spend all my available time with you because I hate you? 'Married.' Why not?"

"Pity?" Mendoza asked.

"When you start feeling sorry for yourself, maybe I'll feel sorry for you, too. In the interim, since I do plan on children, and since I plan on them being yours, and especially since my family would disown me if they were illegitimate, then 'married.' To you. Or don't you want me?" She leaned over Mendoza's horse and kissed his cheek.

Speechless for the moment, Jorge just inclined his head at an odd angle. "Married. Señora Marqueli Mendoza. Children. Oh, wow . . . I love you 'Queli."

"I know. I've known for months. Though why you never said so . . . *well!*"

"Married." He whooped and gave a nudge to his horse's midriff. The horse picked up to a trot, heading down the road.

Marqueli followed, reaching to grab Jorge's horse's leads. "You damned fool. A broken neck might be a little bit too much, don't you think?"

Marqueli, being not much past sixteen, needed her family's permission to marry. This was forthcoming once Jorge explained to her uncle that, despite his injuries, he would be able to maintain a wife and family. Following that step, the next had been to introduce Marqueli and his mother.

His mother had wept, of course, at first. She'd wept, too, when she'd first heard the news of his loss and then again when she'd seen him at the hospital. The image of her line strong son, bedridden and crippled, had been just too much. However, where before she had wept in despair, now it was with relief and even happiness. And *married*? To such a fine girl?

While the driver had taken Marqueli to her family's house, not too far away, Jorge and his mother were left alone to talk.

"Oh, she's a wonderful girl," Mama Mendoza said. "A beautiful little thing. How in the world did you ever find her?"

"She found me . . . sort of, *Madre*. It seems she's the cousin of the . . . to be honest, the mistress of Legate Carrera."

"Really? Well . . . she's not only beautiful but she has a very nice singing voice," the mother said innocently.

"*What?*"

"You're the girl?" Jorge asked, as his horse sauntered besides 'Queli's mare.

"The girl?"

"You sang in the choir, didn't you? You wore a white hat and a yellow print dress."

"Sometimes. How did you know?"

"I didn't, I had no idea until my mother mentioned it. I always stayed in the back and I used to watch you, you were so beautiful."

Marqueli's heart leapt. *He remembered.*

INTERLUDE

Earth Date 16 May, 2104 (Terra Novan year 45 AC), Continent of Southern Columbia, Balboa Colony, Isthmian Region, Terra Nova

The raiders had come before, though not to Belisario Carrera's newly founded settlement of Cochea. Still, even with word of mouth and jungle telegraph, he was not surprised when one of the village boys ran to the center of the spread out, ramshackle town to breathlessly report that a helicopter was disgorging armed men.

Taxes? Belisario wondered. *No, not that. We have nothing much to take. These are looking for something else.*

At that moment Belisario's beautiful wife—she would one day have a multi-great-granddaughter named Linda who would be her very image—emerged from their hut. He knew then what the armed men were coming for.

"What is it, husband?" she asked.

"Trouble," he answered. "Raiders. Gather up all the women and children, except for the boys over twelve.

791

Take them to the caves downstream from here to the east. Send the men and the older boys to me. Tell them to bring their guns and bows."

Trade is all well and good, Kotek thought, *but why trade for what you can take?*

The base was already well established. Command of the *Amistad* took little of his time; after all, he had "people" to do that sort of thing for him. So Kotek spent much of his time hunting. He'd already bagged half a dozen saber-tooths, well over a score of impressively tusked mammoth, and sundry other bits of wildlife useful for their pelts and feathers (the antifur fetish on Earth—as with all such fads—having long since passed into mere quaintness).

Indeed, he'd grown rather tired of the game. There really wasn't much challenge in shooting stupid animals and the rewards, while reasonable, were far off in time. What Kotek wanted was more immediate satisfaction.

Besides, while he had purchased a couple of female slaves from a reputable Yithrabi dealer, they were poor, drab and miserable things. Anything beyond bending over or kneeling down and quietly accepting was beyond them. No, Kotek wanted some females with a bit of *life* in them. And for those, he had to go hunting himself, as his ancestors in distant Ghana had hunted to feed the slave markets of Virginia, Panama, Cuba and Brazil.

Then, too, it was reputed that there was a great deal of gold found in these parts and *that* would be even more negotiable upon his return to Earth than matched pairs of mastodon or mammoth tusks.

The helicopter had landed Kotek and two squads of UN Marines, nineteen men in total, not far from a small village set in this mountain-fringed part of Balboa colony. One squad of Marines Kotek sent sweeping south of the village to set up a cordon while he and the other prepared to drive the inhabitants out of their village and into the net. The Marines were armored and armed with both lethal and nonlethal weapons, the better to take worthwhile females and young boys alive.

I might get a decent price on some of the boys, too, Kotek thought, *or at least be able to trade them to the Yithrabi for a better class of female.*

Kotek Annan stood up when he and the Marines had reached a line within two hundred meters of the village. They began firing immediately, but only over the heads of the villagers. They assumed the sound would panic the people into running into the cordon. It was a great surprise for Kotek when, instead of panicking, the people disappeared and began returning fire with their primitive rifled muskets. His accompanying Marines looked, if anything, more surprised. But the next surprise, a few minutes later, was better, as two dozen or more clouds of smoke suddenly bloomed to Kotek's right flank.

Even so, the best surprise was the .57 caliber ball that smashed into Kotek's right thigh, rending the flesh and smashing the bone. It also nicked the femoral artery but not so badly that Kotek didn't have the chance to see a hard, hate-filled face, lighter than his own but still quite dark, that came up to glare down at him. The face spoke some words in a language Kotek didn't understand.

✧   ✧   ✧

Belisario was no soldier. Still, he had three great assets, common sense, knowledge of the lay of the land, and the sure knowledge that he had to kill these raiders or see—or rather more likely not *live* to see—his wife and daughters dragged off to serve foreign masters. This much he had learned on Old Earth; the progressives who said they came to do good only came to do well.

It also didn't hurt that his enemies were clumsy, being unused to genuine field work. He heard their twin columns, even as small as they were, before he ever saw them.

"One coming from the north, one from the south. They won't attack from two directions at once; that might cause them to shoot each other. So . . . one's a driving force, the other's a net. We hunt that way, sometimes, after all. But which is the net? South, I think, on the other side of the river."

South of the town there was a river that ran east to west. It was down this Belisario had sent his wife and the other women, girls and very small boys. His wife had carried her own *escopeta*, or shotgun, as had some of the others. The town itself was a mere twenty-three huts holding perhaps one hundred and fifty people of all ages.

Belisario counted heads at the people assembled around him, their faces looking frightened but determined. *Sixty-one men and older boys with rifles, another dozen with homemade bows and arrows. All right. The raiders are . . . not many, based on little Pablo's report, but they'll be better armed.*

Dividing his men into three groups, Belisario

explained his plan quickly. No one interposed a better one. Leaving one group—about a quarter of the total—behind at the village, he sent another quarter downstream to cross the river at a ford he knew and which the raiders were unlikely to. The others he, himself, led to a tree line to the northeast.

"Keep low, dammit," he whispered. "For your lives, your wives and your children, for God's sake keep low."

The men following Belisario through the woods lay down along the edge and waited. Surely enough, ten men, nine of them armored and all of them armed, emerged into the open and began firing generally at the village. The group that had been left there went low and returned fire, generally ineffectively.

That doesn't matter, Belisario thought. *I don't want you to be effective. I want you to be* enticing.

The skirmish line advanced toward the village, their own rifles firing low now to suppress the defenders. Belisario waited . . . waited . . . waited . . . "READY . . . Fire!"

Over the sound of their own fusillades, the raiders didn't hear him. Thus, it was with considerable shock that the heavy bullets slammed into them, knocking half down immediately. Some of the villagers had climbed into trees to fire down on their enemies. Soon enough, there was not a single man left unhurt among the UN Marines.

"Reload," Belisario ordered before leading the men with him out. "Kill them all, then we'll go after the other group." Desultory firing to the south told him that the cordon, too, was being engaged.

One man, differently clothed from the Marines and

less well armored, lay on his back trying to staunch the flow of blood that poured from a shattered thigh. Belisario walked up to him, kicking the man's expensive looking rifle away from his reach. The man put one arm up, either begging for mercy or trying to fend off the machete Belisario drew from a scabbard at his waist.

"I should burn you alive," Belisario said. "I should burn you alive, you bastard, but there isn't time. Still, you won't live to gain revenge for this." He raised his machete high.

Four hundred and fourteen local years later all that remained of a very beautiful woman, one of Belisario's many multi-great grandchildren, would be interred very close to the spot where High Admiral Kotek Annan's hand and head rolled free of his body.

(And that, boys and girls, was how the office of High Admiral of the UN Space Fleet and its successor, the UEPF, was rendered nonhereditary.)

CHAPTER TWENTY-EIGHT

My troops are just poor . . . boys in rude shirts, but they're good soldiers, and they'll soon have *better* shirts.

—Charles XII, of Sweden

The new year saw some material things change while many remained the same. Desert uniforms changed to a new tiger-striped and pixilated pattern Carrera had ordered from a company in the FSC. Another pattern was created for the radically different jungles of Balboa, Carrera believing that any pattern which tried to do both would do each only half as well, if that. The *loricae*, the silk and glassy metal vests the legion used for body armor remained the same. The basic design of their Helvetian helmets didn't change, but they grew lighter as a new model, likewise manufactured from glassy metal, made its appearance.

Two new rifles were in development. Both were in 6.5mm. The nearer to perfection was a Volgan design, the Bakanova, superficially similar to the Samsonov already in use. The Bakanova inside was radically different, however, having a rammer to half feed a fresh cartridge during the extraction process and thus increase the rate of fire to eighteen hundred rounds per minute, for two rounds anyway. This made burst fire a practical and useful capability for the first time in a general issue rifle on Terra Nova. To take full advantage of the burst fire capability, the Bakanovas were to be modified to fire a Montgomery Arsenal 6.5mm Jotun cartridge. The barrels were also modified—increased by four inches—to take full advantage of the more powerful round. The Bakanovas, however, had not yet been perfected.

Even there, an improved rifle was only considered to be a stopgap. Carrera wanted something new and had formed a group under Terry Johnson to investigate possibilities. Among the possibilities being looked at were combustible casings, semicombustible casings, electronic priming with the rate of fire controlled by a computer chip in the rifle, near simultaneous feeding and extraction to bring the rate of fire up to two thousand rounds per minute, and carbon fiber wrapped thin steel barrels to reduce weight and improve cooling.

There *were* some new rifles issued, but only for the snipers. These came in three calibers, .34, .41 and a reduced charge .510 that, with a silencer attached, was extremely quiet. For these rifles, frightfully expensive in themselves but with money no longer being so much of a limiting factor, thermals sights were obtained.

Two new machine guns, a heavy in .41 and a general purpose MG in .34 were likewise under slow development.

Mortars and MRLs remained unchanged: 60mm,

120mm and 160mm mortars, and 300mm rocket launchers. Artillery was being switched from 122mm to a 155mm lightweight gun pirated by the Volgans from an Anglian design. The numbers grew, too, from the seventy-eight systems the legion had first gone to war with, inching upward to the one hundred and fifty-two it would need to field when it reached the equivalent field strength of a full division.

Helicopters and fixed wing aircraft had, so far, proven mostly satisfactory. The Turbo-Finches were retained, but modified for additional armor protection for the pilots and with a semiactive defense system against shoulder-fired surface-to-air missiles added. This came at a small cost in ordnance carried but, in the circumstances of a guerilla war against small, scattered, and for the most part poorly armed irregulars, Carrera considered it a fair trade off. The IM helicopters and NA cargo aircraft likewise had done good work and were retained. Some of the NA-23 Dodos were converted to aerial gunships firing a mix of ordnance, .50 caliber, 23mm and 40mm. Like the artillery, the numbers of aircraft increased towards the final goal of one hundred and thirty-two deployed systems, exclusive of aerial medical evacuation.

Heavy armor had proven mostly good enough during the invasion and the subsequent occupation. Contracts were let, therefore, for an additional six hundred and ninety combat systems, mixed tanks and Ocelots, exclusive of simple armored personnel carriers, to be delivered over four years. This was enough, if barely, to keep Khudenko's factory in Kirov employed. Some of his workers were invited to Balboa to set up a depot for heavy maintenance on the armor.

One of the legion's larger purchases, in every sense, was in the form of an old light aircraft carrier, once called Her Anglic Majesty's Ship *Revenge*, and more recently known as the *Amazonia*. This had been offered for a price not much above its value as scrap metal or about the cost of three Jaguar tanks. It needed work, of course, before it would be fit to fight, but its engines were good and it could already sail. It also needed a trained crew, for which purpose Abogado's FMTGRB added another subdivision. Other ships for the naval *classis* of the legion were manned and, approximately, ready sooner.

The legion was growing. It *had* to; the insurgency around it was growing even faster. Worse, it had spread.

Pashtia, which had fallen very quickly to the FSC led coalition, was already showing some signs of future problems as the *Ikhwan* reconsolidated in neighboring Kashmir and sent teams forward to contest the land. Carrera expected it to become a major theater of war again, though it would be, he thought, some years.

Within the oil states of the Yithrabi Peninsula there were terrorist strikes wherever the local government chose to accommodate the wishes of the FSC. From Mustafa's point of view the results of these strikes were a very mixed bag. In some cases, true, the government had ceased such support to the infidel. In others, disastrously, it had instead struck back at the *Ikhwan*, arresting and imprisoning holy men, sometimes even as they preached the jihad from their pulpits. Worse, the government security and intelligence forces had taken to searching out and destroying *Ikhwan* cells, seizing weapons caches and, most damnably, interfering with the flow of money to the cause.

Along the northern border of the Volgan Republic there had been some remarkably effective strikes, proof to the *Ikhwan* of the holiness of the cause. No longer could Volgan mothers pack their children off to school without fear. No longer could Volgan soldiers march with impunity, even within their own country.

Uhuru was beginning to see flare ups, some trivial but many quite bloody, between Christian and Moslem factions. Overall, the Moslems had the edge there, however. Long lines of black Christians and Christian-Animists now marched as coffled slaves towards the markets of Yithrab. Meanwhile highly civilized Taurans and progressives in the FSC wrung their hands and wept at the plight of the Uhurans. That, however, was all they did. After all, weeping and hand wringing made them feel virtuous while forceful action would have been a rebuke to their worldview.

It was actually quite easy to trace the troubles. All one had to do was run one's finger over a map of the planet. Wherever Salafis or Salafi inspired or controlled Moslems shared a border with anyone else—Christians, Christian-Animists, Buddhists, Confucians, Hindus . . . *anyone*—that border was awash in blood. Even at sea blood was beginning to flow as Salafi pirates in the Nicobar Straits and along the coast of Xamar attacked shipping for loot, ransoms, and slaves.

Santissima Trinidad, Bahia de Balboa, 3/1/102 AC

The surplus special operations and patrol boat was capable of mounting up to ten .50 caliber machine guns or some combination of those and either 30mm or 40mm grenade launchers. It could have been fitted for missiles or torpedoes as well, but in this case was not. Indeed, only four of the possible ten weapons stations were filled.

She was low and lean and predatory. Made of aramid and carbon fiber composites, the boat was eighty-four feet from stem to stern and seventeen and a half feet in beam. Capable of better than fifty knots, it was one of, if not *the*, fastest things smoking on the water.

That his crew was only half trained, the boat's skipper, Warrant Officer Pedraz, knew. *Then again, I'm only about half trained, too. How much training do you need to run down a yacht moving at fifteen knots? Not much, I think. It's an easy target to practice intercepts on. Hopefully they won't mind too much.*

The target yacht was named *The Temptation*. This seemed fitting to Pedraz, since his patrol boat had *Santissima Trinidad* painted across her stern.

It was just a routine run, a training run. They approached from astern to within one hundred meters of the *Temptation*. Pedraz had no idea that there was anything amiss with the yacht until he heard frightening cracking sounds splitting the air overhead.

"Holy shit, Chief, that fucking boat is firing at us!"

The speaker was Able Bodied Seaman Miguel Quijana, a young recruit to the legion's *classis*. At barely seventeen, Quijana had never before been shot at.

Well, dammit, neither have I, thought Pedraz as he ducked low behind the boat's superstructure, his finger pressing the klaxon for "battle stations."

When you've got the range advantage, use it, the

chief remembered one of his FMTG instructors telling him. Gunning the engine, Pedraz twisted the wheel hard left and swung his boat past the *Temptation*. The *Trinidad*'s wake caused the *Temptation* to rock, upsetting the aim of the men aboard. The chief kept a nervous watch behind him until he had determined his ship was out of small arms range.

He put his head up. Each of the .50 caliber machine guns was manned by two anxious looking crewmen. He nodded to them and turned to face the yacht. Moving at only twenty knots or so, the *Trinidad* closed the distance, aiming for an intercept point about two hundred meters ahead of the yacht.

"One hundred rounds per gun," Pedraz ordered, when he judged the position right, "FIRE!" Immediately the air was rent by hundreds of powerful muzzle blasts a minute. The recoil wasn't enough to rock the boat or upset the gunners' aim. Downrange, however, the superstructure of the yacht began to come apart under the hammering of high velocity fifty caliber slugs. Even with a half-trained crew, the fire was fierce enough that several of the gun-wielding men aboard the yacht went down, ripped apart by the heavy bullets. The others soon dropped their weapons in abject terror.

Slowly, the *Trinidad* approached, her crewmen rocking with the boat and keeping their machine guns trained on the yacht. One two-man gun crew could not see the yacht as the *Trinidad's* own cockpit blocked their line of sight. These Pedraz selected to board with him, along with the boat's cook and one of the radar crew.

"Spoon!" Pedraz shouted to the cook. "Draw five

submachine guns out of the armory. Francais," he said to his second in command, "take the con. I'm boarding."

"I've got it, Chief," Francais answered.

Thus armed, all five men of the boarding party loaded a small rubber boat with a motor. This sped, cook manning the outboard, to cross the short distance between the two boats, leaving a white wake V-ing out behind it.

Blood dripped out the runnels in the yacht's side, Pedraz noted, as the rubber boat touched the target's side. He went first, keeping the yacht's passengers covered until a second sailor, ABS Dextro Guptillo, could board. Then he tied the rubber boat to the yacht. The rest of the sailors followed.

None of the yacht's crew resisted. Most were down anyway, dead, wounded, or having shat themselves silly. After making sure the remaining few were disarmed, Pedraz ordered the *Trinidad* over. The crew conducted a thorough search of the yacht, stem to stern.

Pedraz expected drugs. There weren't any. Failing that, money? Not much. Arms? Only what had been used to shoot at his boat.

He was puzzled, really puzzled. *Why the hell did they shoot at me? Makes no sense. It was a serious overreaction to our playing games.* He asked one of the unwounded men on the yacht and got a sullen answer. That also made no sense. And then it hit him, *Castilian accent . . . bombings in Castilla . . . similar bombings here. Bingo.*

Balboa Base, Ninewa, 3/1/462 AC

Fernandez's daughter's murder remained a festering hate within him. He nursed that hate, guiding and developing it from a small planting into a full-blooming tree. He didn't let it distract him from his work.

"Where—where the *fuck*—are the explosives coming from!?" Carrera asked Fernandez as he looked over the latest casualty figures from roadside bombings in the BZOR. His anger was not at his chief of intel, but at the enemy.

Fernandez rubbed a finger over his upper lip. He answered, "The . . . ummm . . . ship reports that they're coming in from Farsia right across the border and from Bekaa by way of Bilad al Sham. They're being bought from either the Volgans—the criminal organizations there, not the government—or the Zhong. Some, too, may have been bought in other places. A fair amount was bought right here. The money appears to have come from Sachsen."

"Sachsen? That Westplatz twat?" Carrera asked.

"So I would surmise, her and some of the others."

"Evidence?"

Without a word Fernandez turned in his wooden swivel chair and, opening a cabinet, extracted a thin red file. This he handed over.

Taking the file and opening it, Carrera began to read. When he was finished, he said, "Get Sada and bring him here. I have a mission or three for some of his *special* workers."

"Wilco, Patricio. By the way, next week I need to

go visit the *Hildegard Mises*. We have some special *prisoners* I want to see to . . . personally."

Carrera thought on that and suspected it meant Fernandez was going to oversee something that a man ought not oversee, not if he wanted to keep his soul. He didn't want to see it, either. Nonetheless, he said, "I think that, this time, I should join you there."

SS *Hildegard Mises*, 9/1/462 AC

Mohammad Ouled Nail spat at Warrant Officer Mahamda as the latter set about giving the customary tour and demonstration. Mahamda looked questioningly at the short, wiry, dark man standing nearby.

"I think the tour will be unnecessary," Fernandez said. "Let's go right to interrogation."

Nail lifted his nose and clamped his mouth shut, almost theatrically. *I won't say a word to you pigs.*

Fernandez just smiled as two stout guards picked up the bomber of Castilla and Balboa and carried him, struggling, to a dental chair. They expertly strapped him in to the point he was almost completely unable to move.

Silly man, Fernandez thought. *You should have thought a bit more carefully on what it meant when you were tried, sentenced to death, reported hanged, and yet found yourself here.*

A sort of articulated cage was fitted onto Nail's head, with metal projections to fit between gums and lips and blunt-tipped screwbolts to hold the head to the frame. The guards set the helmet on Nail's head and began turning cranks on each side of the helmet.

When it was firmly affixed, a far from painless process in itself, they rotated the jaw separator down. Nail refused to open his mouth, of course. One of the guards picked up a small hammer and deftly whacked Nail between the legs. *That* opened his jaws for a scream. They then forced the device into his mouth and turned another crank, which spread the device, separating the invading bits of metal and forcing the terrorist's lips and jaws apart.

"He's ready, Doctor," one of the guards called out. In walked a white-jacketed dentist who looked over the arrangement and nodded satisfaction. The dentist put in earplugs and covered his ears with muffs. Then he picked up one of his drills and stepped on a pedal. The drill began to whine.

Nail's fear-filled eyes followed the drill bit as it inched closer to his mouth, ultimately crossing just before the bit touched enamel.

In a few moments he was screaming, pleading, begging to be permitted to talk, but over the whine of the drill no one seemed to be able to hear him.

Ar-Ramadi, Ninewa Province, 14/1/462 AC

Giulia Masera didn't have Westplatz's local connections. Still, she wanted to help the cause. Indeed, she'd been fighting for the cause all her life. For the better part of the last year she'd been fighting in the role of a journalist, uncovering the misdeeds of the FSC and its running dogs. When a Sumeri, apparently having noted her sympathies, approached her with the offer of a kidnapping to both raise funds for the resistance and discredit her own fascist government, she jumped at the chance. She'd have made the offer herself if she'd only known where to find members of the resistance.

If one had asked a Roman Catholic why he or she believed in the Bible and the teachings of the Church, the nearest to an honest answer might have been something like, "That's how I was raised." Masera was not different. She'd grown up at the knee of the hero of her life, her grandfather, who had been an antifascist partisan in her native Etruria during the Great Global War. Both her mother and father had been Marxist activists and had made the easy transition to cosmopolitan progressives.

She didn't *like* the Salafis or even the more secular terrorists she supported. But when she considered the evil she saw in the FSC, in capitalism, and in the travesty that passed for democracy, she saw something that justified even support for murderers, oppressors of women, and theocratic fascists. *Sometimes you have to choose the lesser of two evils.*

Giulia was picked up off the street without incident and taken to a residential basement somewhere in the city. The men who took her were as polite as she'd expected they would be, being allies and all.

In the basement, a small TV studio had been set up. Her co-fighters spent a few hours coaching Giulia before she made a teary-eyed plea for her government to come to her rescue by withdrawing their troops from this imperialist war and paying the just ransom demanded.

Imagine her surprise then when, taping apparently completed, her newfound comrades tossed a rope over a hook in the ceiling, tied her hands to the rope and hauled her up to her tippy toes. Imagine her greater surprise when she was stripped to the waist and, out of deference to Islamic modesty, turned around to face away from the cameras, her legs being likewise tied by the ankles to bolts in the floor to prevent her from twisting and shamelessly showing her breasts to the camera.

Neither of those surprises, however, compared to the surprise she felt when the whip first bit a bright red, oozing strip out of her back.

"Now howl like a dog, bitch," her captors instructed as one of them lay on the whip for another stroke. Still in shock from the first stroke, Giulia shook her head in shocked misunderstanding. No matter, the second lash evoked a piercing scream that was every bit as good as a howl.

When the flogging was done, another twenty-three strokes later, and Masera sobbing and hanging by her wrists from the rope, the leader and the other captors pulled balaclavas over their faces and lined up three to either side of her shuddering, bleeding body. Into the camera the leader said, "Twenty-five million Tauros," he said, "or this twat gets fed feet first into a wood chipper for the nightly news."

At that, all the captors raised their weapons above their heads, shouting, *"Allahu akbar!"*

SS *Hildegard Mises*, 16/1/462 AC

They'd let Nail talk, but only after drilling away most of the enamel on his two front upper teeth. This had been replaced with a temporary filling material. There was no sense, after all, in wasting the good stuff on a walking corpse.

Talk he did, intending to lie. Sadly for Mohammad, lies required concentration and pain destroyed it. They'd caught him in a lie, a trivial thing, really, from his own badly abused mouth.

He'd thought he'd get the drill again and shat himself at the thought of it. He'd probably have been happier if they had gone the dental route. Instead, though, they'd moved him to a different chair after stripping off his trousers. Even over the pain, he'd been deeply embarrassed when his captor had stuck something cold and hard up his ass, then put his penis in what looked like a light socket.

There were things, he discovered, that hurt worse than dental work without anesthesia.

23 Al Rasul Street, Doha, 17/1/462 AC

Although weapons were easier to obtain on the Yithrab peninsula even than slaves, the four Sumeris had brought in their own. These were silenced pistols, in 9mm. Other weapons, though it was to be hoped they would not be needed, were secured in the rental car's trunk.

The team waited near the guarded gate for the chauffeured limousine that always came at this time every day but Friday. Not that they intended to attack the limo, far from it. But the limousine carried four children, two boys and two girls, to and from their school every day. Its arrival thus signaled that all the targets were present at home.

Seeing the limousine pull through the guarded gate at the front of the mansion, the rental car's driver waited five minutes before following the same course. The gate opened and an ethnic Bengali emerged, wearing a uniform far, far too hot for the climate.

"May I be of assistance, *sayidi*?" the Bengali asked of the driver. In answer, the man sitting beside the driver shot the gate guard with his silenced pistol. One man got out to drag the Bengali's body behind some well-tended bushes. The car proceeded through the gate, and into the mansion complex.

Al Iskandaria Studios, Doha, Terra Nova, 17/1/462 AC

"I won't show this perversion," Sheik Hamad insisted to the vicious looking man seated opposite him in his plush blue and green themed office.

Hamad was a study in contrast to his visitor. The sheik was tall and lean, with the sharp features of a desert nomad accentuated by his pure white *keffiyah*. His visitor was short and a bit overweight, perhaps the scion of some peasant family.

Probably a Sumeri peasant family, the sheik thought, *based on the accent*.

"Yes, you will," the visitor answered amiably. "By the way, have you spoken to your wife today? Why don't you give her a call? They live at Twenty-three al Rasul Street, do they not? Here, use my cell phone. The number is already dialed."

SS *Hildegard Mises*, 19/1/462 AC

Nail knew they were working over his captured comrades, just as they had worked over him. He knew it because they often played his comrades' screams over the speakers in his cell when he was not, himself, under the torture.

They'd gotten pretty direct in their approach. They were being direct now.

"What is the address for the safe house you used in *Ciudad* Balboa?" Mahamda asked.

The captive spat out an address. Mahamda consulted an earpiece stuck into his right ear and shook his head, sadly. "Your answers don't match, Mohammad. You know the price of that."

"Please . . . no . . . I am telling the truth," Ouled Nail begged.

"Perhaps you are and perhaps you are not. Listen to this." Mahamda turned on a speaker so that Ouled Nail could hear the pleading screams of his comrade. Nail couldn't know it, but the transmission was on a time delay controlled by the interrogation team to ensure that no one undergoing questioning could, between screams, coach anyone else on a story.

"He's just lost a fingernail," Mahamda said calmly. "Now it's your turn." He flicked off the speaker and turned on a microphone. He nodded at an assistant.

Mahamda's assistant grabbed Ouled Nail's middle finger on his left hand firmly, then took a pair of needle-nosed pliers and jammed one end under the nail. The terrorist shrieked into the microphone then, sobbing, begged, "For the love ... of Allah ... please ... please tell them ... the truth."

It took three nails each before the addresses given matched perfectly. There were seventeen more nails to go, along with much skin, many teeth, and a virtual infinity of nerve endings. Indeed, there were more than enough nerve endings to learn everything Ouled Nail had ever known or even suspected.

Neue Ulm, Sachsen, 21/1/461 AC

Senta Westplatz was busy packing for her return trip to Sumer. An agent of the freedom fighters was supposed to give her the tickets at the airport. In the background *Fernsehen Sachsen* droned. Senta paid no attention to the television until she heard the name of a friend and comrade, Giulia Masera, mentioned. Even that really didn't catch her attention—Giulia was often in the news—until she heard the words, "kidnapped" and "torture."

She ran to the TV barely in time to catch the last four strokes of the whip that set her comrade to howling, much like a dog. Hand clenched over her mouth as she watched the spectacle, Senta was simply horrified, so much so that the knock at the door barely registered until it had been repeated several times.

Finally, Westplatz did go to the door, pulling her hijab over her hair automatically as she walked.

"Yes? How may I ... ?" she asked the delivery-man standing there, impatiently, holding a wrapped package.

The blow to her solar plexus came as a shock to

Senta. She went down like a sack of rice, loosely and almost without a sound. The deliveryman entered the apartment, closing the door carefully behind him. He hit the woman once again, hard, in the chest. She wouldn't be screaming for help any time soon. From his pocket he drew a very small digital camera with which he took a short video of Senta moving feebly and gasping for air.

Returning the camera to his pocket, he then squatted down by the shocked almost-corpse and picked it up. He looked around quickly and identified the bathroom. Then he carried Senta to it, stripping her body and placing it in the tub. Another few seconds were spent recording that scene as well. After putting on some rubber gloves, he flicked the switch to close the drain and turned the tap to let the water fill.

Taking a towel with him, the deliveryman then went to the kitchen and carefully opened the drawers until he found a sharp knife. He had one with him, of course, but it would be better in the short term if the implement came from the house. Returning to the bathroom he found that Senta, still gasping desperately, had sat up. He pushed her back and grabbed her left wrist, which he twisted toward the far wall. Senta struggled but feebly.

With the knife he made a long slash lengthwise up the radial artery. The cut went deep and blood spurted out, staining the tiled far wall and turning the water filling the tub red. The deliveryman released the arm and took another short video of the blood flowing. Then he took that hand and wrapped it around the handle of the knife, holding it firmly. With this he made a not very deep and deliberately ragged cut up the right wrist. Then he let both knife and hand go free. He watched for a minute as blood loss took away consciousness. When the water had mostly filled the tub he shut off the flow and waited for ten minutes. A quick check of the carotid confirmed the woman was quite dead. He took some more video of the corpse.

The deliveryman then retrieved the package and removed from it a change of clothing, another pair of rubber gloves, a false moustache, a digital camera and a plastic bag. He exchanged clothing, putting his old, blood-spotted clothes in the bag and the bag back in the package, which he rewrapped loosely. He put on the gloves and began to search the apartment. Since no suicide was very likely to be packing a bag for a trip, he returned the articles of clothing to what seemed logical places. In the course of his search, he found a folder at the bottom of the bag. He did not find any air or train tickets. The folder he set aside for the moment.

Continued searching of the apartment turned up nothing further, not even a computer. Walking to the door, folder and package in hand, the man stopped to listen for a few moments. Nothing. Then he opened the door, exited, and closed the door behind him.

By the time the police began to suspect that Senta had been murdered, the assassin would be long gone, leaving no personal trace. The video would be posted on the Globalnet as a warning to other Kosmos who might be inclined to help the Salafi *Ikhwan*.

SS *Hildegard Mises*, 24/1/462 AC

The walls of the cell were covered with color photographs of the victims of the bombs he'd helped set off in Balboa. He couldn't escape them; his eyelids had been sewn open. When he looked at the pictures, in his mind's eye he saw his own family laid out butchered as he was sure they would soon be.

Mohammad Ouled Nail wept as the cell door opened in front of him. Mahamda entered with that small dark man—Fernandez, he was called—who seemed to be in charge. Another man, taller and lighter skinned than Fernandez, stood there as well.

Nail's hands were bandaged but blood oozing from the fingertips had stained the white gauze red.

It wasn't just pain that made Nail weep; it was also the shame.

He'd thought he was tough and brave. He'd thought he had faith in his God. He'd been sure they could never break him. He'd been sure, too, that he could lie.

He knew, now, in his innermost being, that there was no God. He knew he couldn't keep a story straight when in agony. And he knew he couldn't take the pain.

His joints were, half of them, dislocated from the little metal framework—the "Scavenger," they'd called it—they'd placed him in and tightened. They hurt almost as much from the decompression chamber he'd endured. His face—they'd made him look in a mirror—was blotched with burst blood vessels.

The evil looking infidel, Fernandez, made his pronouncement. "Murdering bastard! Turn him into a woman, then hang him . . . her . . . *it*." Then, horror of horrors, the evil infidel had bent down and whispered, "I'm sending a team to exterminate your family in Castilla, you son of a bitch."

Topside, far from the screams, Carrera and Fernandez sat on a large pipe, staring across the dark vastness of the ocean toward the lights of the Yithrabi coast. In these confined waters the ship rocked gently, slowly. It didn't matter; Carrera was sick to his stomach anyway.

"Do you ever have nightmares, Omar?" Carrera asked of Fernandez.

The Balboan shrugged. "Everyone has nightmares, Patricio."

"Do they?" He shook his head. "Not like mine, I don't think. Not like mine.

"Did you know," Carrera continued, "that I was raised to be a civilized man? I don't advertise it but my mother and father were progressives, cosmopolitans, in fact. I sometimes wonder if that's why I was able to transfer my loyalty from the Federated States to the legion; because I wasn't raised to be loyal to the Federated States, even though for many years I was and, to some degree, still am. An interesting thought, is it not; that maybe the end result of the destruction of ties to nations is not loyalty to mankind, but loyalty to even smaller and more exclusive groups than nations? To family most of all."

Fernandez's mind was not the sort to worry about such things. He kept silent. Besides, what was wrong with having an ultimate loyalty to one's family? As far as he could see that *was* the default state of mankind.

Carrera flicked a cigarette butt over the side, then reached for a tumbler of whiskey resting on the deck by his feet. From this he drank deeply.

"Ever read any Shakespeare from Old Earth, Omar? *Henry the Fifth*, maybe?"

Fernandez shook his head in negation. "I've heard of it; that's all."

"No surprise, I suppose. It's a play; never underestimate the benefits of a classical education. There's a scene there . . . where the king insists that he is not to blame for the condition of his soldiers' souls should they be killed in battle for him."

Carrera laughed, bitterly. "Damn old Will. He answers the questions he wants to but not the one you want him to. Tell me, Omar, what do you think? If Henry's soldiers had sacked Harfleur, would he have been responsible for the sack? For the rape of the 'shrill shrieking maidens'? For the dashing of old men's heads to walls? For the 'naked infants spitted upon pikes?' Where would the blame lie then?"

"Patricio," Fernandez began, "I don't thi—"

Carrera cut him off. Nodding his head toward the hatch that led into the bowels of the ship, he asked, "And where does the blame lie here? Who is to blame for that obscenity taking place below? If it's you, does that relieve me of anything? I don't think so."

Sighing, Fernandez asked, "Do you want me to shut the program down?"

Taking another hefty slug of the whiskey, Carrera coughed and then answered, "That's the worst part: no."

Ic (Intelligence Office), Camp Balboa, Ninewa, 29/1/462 AC

Thank God Patricio didn't succumb to the weaker part of his nature, thought Fernandez while sitting at his desk in Sumer. *Bad enough he shows too light a hand with some of our adversaries. But we* must have *the information that comes out of that ship, whatever it costs.*

The desk sat deep inside the Intel Office, which was the most secure building in the camp. It was built of a double wall of pressure formed adobe bricks with the interior space filled with earth as well. The office was surrounded by another wall, this one topped with barbed wire and with a tower at each corner of the compound. Guards manned the tower, the narrow gate, and the inside of the building continuously.

There was no air conditioning; Carrera simply forbade it on the theory that troops given air conditioning would never grow acclimated to the heat, which was, while drier, even worse than Balboa's. The four exceptions to this rule were the religious facilities, the field hospital, the troop messes and the small brothel quadrant full of Sumeri whores, most of them widows or orphans.

So instead of air conditioning, Fernandez sat under an overhead fan. Paperweights—generally of steel, glass, or fired clay—held the papers on the desk in place against the breeze of the fan.

It was better to be seated. After days on the *Hildegard Mises* Fernandez found himself still swaying when he walked on dry land. He hoped it would go away soon.

It had been worth it, though. Normally Fernandez was, while willing enough, not a man who enjoyed inflicting pain. This time had, obviously, been different.

They were still on the ship, the one named Ouled Nail and the other three who had survived. They'd be hanged when they'd healed from their surgery; be hanged, incinerated and their ashes dumped out with the garbage.

Big mistake to survive, Fernandez thought. *Worse mistake to survive after killing my blood and then being captured. Bastards. Well, let's see what today brings.*

What today brought were dispatches from Sada, received from Sachsen. These included a folder taken from the not-quite-packed bag of a woman. Most of the names in the folder were of no interest. Rather, they were of no obvious interest as they had no markings against them in the folder to indicate any importance beyond the merely personal. They would, of course, be investigated anyway.

Two names were interesting. One of them was a woman, this one living in the City of Akka in Bekaa. She appeared in the folder as Westplatz's main contact with the insurgency.

"Odd," Fernandez said to himself, "very odd that a Spanish name should appear among our adversaries, yet be living in Bekaa." He decided to pass the name on to the research section.

When the name came back, a few days later, with a healthy file including pictures both before and after the plastic surgery, all Fernandez could say was, "Ohhh," before passing the file back to Sada's office.

Akka, Bekaa, 2/2/462 AC

Standing on a second floor, iron railed balcony overlooking the Tauranian Lakes, Layla Arguello shivered despite the warm night air. There was something going on that was monstrous in its implications. People, *her* people, good and trusted comrades of many years of struggle, were disappearing right and left. She was pretty sure they were disappearing *right*.

She'd been something of an icon in her youth, had Layla. Borderline pretty, with a simple, sincere face masking a devious mind, a photographer had once taken her picture with her hair covered by a man's keffiyah and a man's rifle slung over her shoulder with the muzzle projecting above her back. This photograph had rocketed around Terra Nova, propelling Layla into an unwanted, even unfortunate, stardom. Songs had been written about her in several tongues. The stardom, in turn, had made it nearly impossible for her to continue her mission, which was, by and large, the hijacking of aircraft.

Nothing deterred, Layla had undergone a series of plastic surgeries to hide her true face and make it possible for her to continue boarding aircraft in order to hijack them. The significant part of *that* was that she had endured the surgery *without* anesthesia, this being by way of a gesture of solidarity with the suffering *People* of the world

Later in life, after many hijackings and many terms in prison, Layla had married a comrade from the struggles in Colombia Latina. Later still, she'd entered politics, winning office repeatedly based largely on her revolutionary past and her potential for continuing the revolution into the future. As a politician, her new face became even better known than had been her old. Likewise well known were her residence, office, domestic arrangements and family situation.

Is it time to go undercover again? she wondered, staring at the stars winking in the waves below. *No . . . I can't. The cause needs me here, easy to find and with all my connections intact. But I think I ought to improve my security.*

Camp Balboa Base, Ninewa, Sumer, 3/2/462 AC

Sada, Fernandez and Carrera met in a conference room in the intelligence offices. The conference room was small; the idea of a large conference in the shadowy, dirty world of intelligence, counterintelligence and direct action was something of a contradiction in terms. A few flies buzzed—Fernandez had reason to believe they were the only bugs in the room—and the rotating fan whined despairingly overhead.

"There are a few people, very few," Fernandez admitted, "who *won't* break under torture. She's going to be one of them."

"She has two sons," Sada had pointed out. "She might not talk over threats to a husband, or even her father and mother, but she's an Arab, an Arab *mother*; she'll talk to save her sons."

"What do you think she's going to know to justify torturing and killing her sons?" Carrera had asked. "Remember, we do not torture anybody we have not announced that we have killed and are not planning to kill. If you tell me she's part of a plot to set off a nuke in a major city, maybe that would justify it. Maybe. Or if you tell me that you *know*, not suspect but *know*, that her sons are in on the whole thing. Can you do that?"

Sada shook his head. "No, we can't say that. Both of them are still in school. One's in college; the other in high school. They're likely to join the enemy at some point in time, yes, but for now? No, as far as we can tell they're innocent enough."

Fernandez grew heated. "If the sons will grow up to become terrorists, and they will, we should kill them now while we can. If we're willing to kill them then why not do the rest?"

"It just seems wrong." ·

"Patricio," Sada said, "you heard me when we first began working together but I don't think you listened. We Arabs are not like you people, and it isn't just a matter of religion. After religion, and not far behind . . . maybe even ahead, family is what really matters to most of us. We stopped, or at least cut down on, the hangings because it was making enemies of entire clans. The same logic applies here. At least the clans and tribes here could be bought off. But unless you are willing to kill the sons who will avenge this woman—and the right or wrong of it matters not at all—you are better off not touching her. What's the sense of killing or taking one terrorist if, in the process, you create two? On the other hand, if you're reluctant to take and use the sons to loosen their mother's tongue, at least let us kill the lot of them."

Fernandez inclined his head toward Sada. "Adnan is quite right, Patricio. Moreover, what's the difference between that and an air strike that takes out a whole family to get one terrorist? There isn't any and you know there isn't." Fernandez's voice and face grew desperate. "Patricio, for God's sake they created *you* by killing your family and leaving you alive. They have brought out the very worst in *me*. This is not different."

Carrera thought about that. He'd done some terrible things, let innocent people be killed to get at the guilty. But this was just . . . wrong somehow. He couldn't deliberately order the deaths of the two boys on the mere chance that they *might* someday become a threat.

"No. Kill the woman, fine. Leave her family alone."

"Well," Sada said, acquiescing, "if it's to be a simple assassination then there's no sense in using my own boys for it. Can we afford to hire a hit team?"

Fernandez, still shaking his head in disgust at Carrera's squeamishness, asked, "Of course we can *afford* it. A hit team from whom?"

"Possibly the Anti-Zionist People's Liberation Front; they're strong in Bekaa and never liked the fact that Arguello, a woman, garnered so many headlines. Or maybe the ZII, the Zion Intelligence Institute, could suggest someone. Maybe they'd be willing to do it themselves. Give me a week to work it out."

"You have contacts with the *ZII*?" Fernandez asked incredulously.

"Just one good one," Sada answered and then refused to say more.

Akka, Bekaa, 9/2/462 AC

As it turned out, ZII wouldn't touch it. The head of the organization, Mickey Zvi Maor, who knew Sada from school in Anglia, was firm on that. Oh, they wished the woman dead, one thousand times over dead. But they were such an obvious candidate for the hit that Maor begged off. He did suggest contacting one of the religiously affiliated parties in Bekaa, all of whom distrusted women in positions of power.

Sada sent one of his more trusted lieutenants, Major Qabaash, to Bekaa to do the negotiations.

"Qef halak, ya sheik," Qabaash began at the audience he had secured with the leader of the Monotheism Party in a suburb of Akka. The sheik lived simply enough, in a rambling adobe house with a fountained central courtyard. The fountain was not ostentation. In the fierce heat of the Bekaa desert the fountain served to cool the courtyard without the pollution of the infidel's electricity.

Serene and dignified, the sheik—his given name was Ghaleb—returned the greetings and swept his hand down, inviting Qabaash to sit near him on some cushions placed where they would receive the most benefit of the fountain's cooling effect.

Serving women, some the sheik's wives and concubines, others his daughters, brought in trays ostentatiously laden with more food than two men could hope to eat. Besides the usual lamb, there were bowls of red maize paste, flavored with native "holy shit peppers."

Holy shit peppers were at the low end of piquancy compared to some of Terra Nova's natural spices. Above them were Joan of Arc peppers, only for the very daring or masochistic. At the very high end were the plants known as "Satan Triumphant." No one had ever managed to eat these, whole, though they had found a use during the Great Global War when distilled into a potent chemical agent similar in its power and effects to phosgene oxime. Highly diluted, they could have been used for food preservation. Unfortunately, STs were so vile that the slightest underdilution would have preserved the food indefinitely as no human being could have hoped to eat it. Mixed in *minute* proportion in *shoug*, a fiery popular paste, was about as useful as "Satan Triumphant" peppers ever got.

Besides the red maize paste were pitas made from the flour of the chorley. There were half a dozen Terra Novan "olives" on the trays, as well. These had little resemblance to Old Earth olives, being roughly the size of plums and gray in color. They grew in clumps of three on a plant that looked like a stunted, anemic palm, except that unlike the palms of Old Earth this one's trunk was green while its fronds were gray. The taste was said to be similar to normal olives, though slightly more astringent.

One did not get right down to business when dealing with the sheik or, indeed, with nearly any Arab; there were the niceties to observe first. A full two hours of mostly meaningless pleasantries followed. Mostly, however, does not mean *entirely*. By the end of the two hours, from hints and suggestions, Ghaleb had learned that the heretic woman, Layla Arguello, needed to die and Qabaash had learned that the price of her death, her husband's and her sons would be fifty thousand FSD, half payable up front and half on confirmation that she was truly dead. Two of Terra Nova's three moons, Eris and Bellona, had risen by the time the two reached this point.

"It would be better," observed the sheik, getting down to business, "if her sons did not grow up to avenge her."

"I could not agree more, O Wise One," Qabaash answered. "Yet those are our limitations. The people I represent will not countenance the killing of the sons."

Ghaleb's smiled slightly as his fingers pulled at one ear. "Easterners, eh? It never ceases to amaze me how little they understand us and how completely they insist on trying to fit us into their own mold. For the woman and the sons I would charge fifty thousand. For the woman alone, the price is one hundred thousand, for I will have to recompense families when the sons grow up to exact their revenge."

"It is fair, O Sheik, and the amount in within my discretion."

To himself Qabaash mused, *If this were the FSC, they would, at a cost many times greater, drop a large and expensive guided bomb from an aircraft costing more than this country earns every year. The bomb would kill Arguello, and the FSC would congratulate itself for its discretion and humanity. The bomb would also kill fifty genuine innocents and probably miss her sons. For a mere fifty thousand I could get rid of the lot and kill no true innocents if only I were permitted. Life is strange and the Almighty's sense of humor unfathomable.*

Akka, 17/2/462 AC

Ordinarily, the sheik would have merely given a sermon in the mosque on the subject of female iniquity and mentioned Layla's name as an example. Several of his followers would have read between the lines, hunted her down to her home and killed her and her family. Word would have leaked so that the sheikh could reward his diligent followers properly, but only within the close confines of the clan, so that the police could pretend bafflement. Because of the absurd requirement that her family not be hurt, more direct and less subtle methods were required.

A team of Ghaleb's followers was thus handpicked and given its marching orders. They were experienced and bright men; they had no real difficulty finding Layla's residence and office. They did find it suspicious that she changed her routes between the two more than daily. This meant that the killing would have to take place either in or in front of either her office or her home. Given that they were, unaccountably, forbidden from killing her family it would have to be the office.

Purchasing weapons and explosives in the market in Akka was like buying dates and figs. Finding Layla's residence and office was equally easy, reconning them not much more difficult.

Unfortunately, what the hit team did not count on was the woman herself. Layla Arguello was not some untrained, innocent Kosmo journalist or humanitarian aid worker. She was, herself, a trained and *experienced* terrorist. Moreover, her long career should have told the team she was a *smart* trained terrorist. Smart and trained terrorists, in the circumstances of Akka, Bekaa, did not go about unarmed.

What should have been an easy hit turned into a somewhat lengthy firefight. With six men with rifles engaging one woman with a pistol the result would normally been foreordained. Not so with Layla.

Near her office, her car was suddenly cut off by another that swerved in front and forced her driver to crash into a parked car by the curb. The car following Layla's smashed into the rear of her own to further shock the occupants. Her driver and the guard sitting in the front seat were thrown forward—the use of seatbelts indicating a certain lack of piety among their people—and stunned.

Layla, however, was not shocked. She had the door open and was crouching outside, digging in her purse for a pistol and her trademark hand grenade, even before the men in the assaulting cars had their feet to the pavement. Her hand closed on the grenade first. This she donated to the following car. It went off on the asphalt, laying out two just emerging assassins with multiple shrapnel wounds. Red pools began to spread across the pavement.

The remaining four assassins were momentarily shocked. This gave Layla enough time to dig out her pistol, a 9mm job made in Sachsen. With the pistol in hand, she stuck her head over the trunk of her own immobilized automobile and fired at the passengers of the car that had rammed hers from behind. She hit one, she thought.

A long burst of fire from the car that had swerved

in front of hers smashed the windows of her own, sending the glass shards tinkling to the asphalt and killing the driver. None of the barely aimed bullets hit her, but spraying glass scored her forehead and face, causing blood to run into her right eye. Desperately Layla used her left hand to try to wipe the blood away and clear her eye for shooting. Even through the haze she managed to jack a couple of rounds in the direction of the first auto.

Achmed, nephew of Ghalib, was shocked by the return fire. The explosion of what he assumed was a hand grenade had been bad enough. But for the woman to have the effrontery to actually shoot back? This was too much.

Unfortunately, the return fire was also too much. Achmed, feeling ashamed, closed his eyes and kept low to the ground to escape the bullets this damned heretic woman seemed to have in great supply.

The rough pavement dug into his face. Achmed forced his eyes open and saw a woman's foot and a knee exposed under the floor of the target vehicle. He pointed his rifle in the general direction of the foot and pulled the trigger.

Layla was reloading her pistol from one of the four spare magazines she kept in her purse when she felt the blow just above her knee. Partly from the physical force of the blow and partly in automatic response to the instant and intense pain, her leg spun out from under her, causing her to drop the loaded magazine she had been struggling to insert. She fell to one side even as her hand groped the asphalt for the magazine.

Unable to stand or kneel any longer Layla forced her back to the rear wheel of her car while her hand continued to feel around, searching for the lost magazine. She found and grabbed it with a joyful cry.

Before she could reload, she stopped. Two angry looking men were standing above her, each with a rifle pointed towards her head and torso. A third sprayed her guard, still sitting in the front seat, knocking his bloodied corpse over onto the lap of the dead driver.

No chance now, Layla thought, dropping the magazine but retaining the pistol.

Layla's last acts in this life were to smile as if her own death were a triumph and to spit at her assailants.

The rifles opened fire. At this range even very bad marksmanship could not miss. Over forty bullets entered Layla's body. When they were done she lay dead against the rear tire, her head lolling to one side and the pistol still held tightly in her hand.

Camp Balboa, Sumer, 19/2/462 AC

Layla's bullet-riddled body was barely in the ground in Bekaa when the first replacement units began to arrive in Sumer. This was the Second Cohort of the now renamed 1st Tercio (*príncipio Eugenio*). Whereas the 1st Cohort had never had a strength above four hundred and sixty, the replacement was closer to a real battalion's strength of nearly seven hundred. It was still organized in six subunits though these, in deference to the increase in strength, were called now "maniples" rather than centuries and were subdivided into platoons rather than sections. The platoons were still rather small, as platoons went.

Sporting new sergeant's stripes on his collar, Cruz didn't care about that. In truth, he didn't care much about anything except that this combat tour was over and he was going *home* for a while, home to his Cara and, hopefully, home to marriage and the beginning of a family. He had a good job with the legion, work he liked and work he had proven good at. He intended to stay even though this would mean frequent separation from his loved ones.

Waiting with his gear for the trucks that would take himself and the rest of the cohort to the Ninewa airport, Cruz mused upon the meeting he and his cohort's tribune had had with Carrera and the legion's sergeant major, that crusty old bastard, McNamara.

He'd been shocked, more than a little, when Carrera had announced that he'd been selected for Cazador School and, if he passed that, further selected for the Centurion Candidate Course.

"They'll be harder than combat, Sergeant Cruz," McNamara had informed him. "I know you don't believe that now but, before you accept the appointment, just trust me on this."

He'd sat silent for a while at that, thinking hard. Finally, he'd decided, "I think I can take it, Sergeant Major . . . Legate. After all, I have good reasons to."

INTERLUDE

Earth Date 27 May, 2104 (Terra Novan year 45 AC), Atlantis Base

The shuttle came down from the *Amistad* carrying a full platoon of thirty UN Marines, all the ship had available. It screeched in to Atlantis base furiously. The Marine commander directed his troops to wait at the small terminal while he went to collect his orders from the Base's deputy, acting in High Admiral Annan's stead.

"The helicopter went off the air several days ago," the deputy advised the major commanding the Marines. "I don't know if they crashed or what."

"Where were they heading?" the major asked.

The deputy's finger played over his computer's keyboard, bringing up a somewhat undetailed map of Balboa colony. "The high admiral said he was going here. 'Hunting,' he said." Since the deputy had some idea of just what it was that Annan had intended to hunt, and since that was technically illegal, even for a high admiral, he kept his mouth shut as to what Annan's objective had been.

"I've been in contact with our office in *Ciudad*"—the Deputy laughed; to call such a miserable collection of shacks a city was absurd—"Balboa. They say the high admiral stopped there on his way."

The major could have surmised the hunt's objective but long years in UN service had conditioned him not to dig into, not to even think upon, the foibles of his superiors. He had his own life to worry about and another four years would see him retired to his Botswanan village on a very comfortable, Noblemaire-Rule-driven, pension.

Following Annan's flight path, the shuttle stopped off at the local UN supervisory office in *Ciudad* Balboa. The bureaucrats there had nothing to add. It struck the Marine major that the guards on the office seemed even more slovenly and undisciplined than was the UN norm. Still, it was close enough to that norm to excite no real interest. After refueling the shuttle from local stocks, and seeing that his men were given a decent meal and some rest, the ship took off heading east.

The shuttle was *not* equipped to scan the jungle below. Even if it had been, it might well not have noticed the several dozen armed men on horseback over whom it flew, riding hell for leather, westward, beneath the thick triple canopy.

The helicopter was easy enough to find; it had landed in the open and there it still was. When the shuttle descended to a leaf- and grass-churning landing, the major and his men debarked. They found the helicopter, along with twenty-two insect-eaten heads on stakes in a circle around it. Of the high admiral's body, or those of the eighteen Marines who had accompanied him, there was not a trace. The bodies of the three-man crew, or what was left of them after ants, *antaniae*, and buzzards had taken their share, were found right by the helicopter.

The nearby village was abandoned. No footprints told where the villagers had gone. Prints of horse hooves, some dozens of them, led off to the east but disappeared in the sodden jungle. The major was about to organize and send off search parties when he received a distress call from the UN supervisory office, now some hundreds of kilometers away.

The call for help ended almost as soon as it began. By the time the shuttle arrived back at the office it was nothing more than a corpse-draped, smoking ruin.

The shuttle landed nearby. This was a mistake.

Among the weapons found in the supervisory office's armory had been a single sample of a very special type. This was a magazine-fed, bolt action rifle in 14.5mm, with its own limited visibility scope, recoil absorption system and a muzzle brake to further reduce the otherwise shoulder-shattering recoil of the piece. For all that, it was no different in principle from any of the bolt-action rifles in use on Earth. It was this simplicity that recommended the weapon to both Belisario and the UN, though the latter used it exclusively for hunting mammoth, not men nor their machines.

Belisario lay now beside the sniper he had chosen, a *cholo* from Panama with a deserved reputation as a marksman. The *cholo*'s, or Indian's, name was Pedro.

"Pedro, can you hit the gas tank?" Belisario asked.

"No, *señor*," the *indio* answered. "I don't even know where it will be. But I can hit an engine, no problem."

"Make it the engine then, *compadre*. But *make* it the engine. We can't afford a miss."

The pair lay in a shack overlooking the UN office. More particularly, their field of fire covered the marked, concrete shuttle landing pad to one side of that office. What they would do if the shuttle landed elsewhere, Belisario didn't know. His men were scattered in small groups in other buildings. Perhaps that would be enough.

He'd told them no cooking fires, an order that had not gone over particularly well. He hoped they'd listen, but had less than absolute confidence that they would. What he could do about it he didn't know. Rather, he hoped he didn't know.

Will it come to that? Belisario wondered. *Will I someday end up having to shoot some of my own men if they won't follow orders? God . . . if there is a God . . . deliver me from this, please.*

His thoughts were interrupted by the whine of the UN shuttle circling the area before coming in for a very soft, though leaf and dust churning, landing.

Belisario was just rising and turning his head toward Pedro to give the order to fire when the *cholo* fired *sua sponte* . . . and immediately screamed and rolled from the gun, clutching a broken shoulder. So much for recoil absorption systems. The muzzle blast half-stunned Belisario, knocking him right back on his arse.

"What the—?"

On hands and knees, shaking his head, Belisario

crawled back to the low window through which Pedro had engaged the shuttle. As he neared the opening, he heard and felt the familiar blasts of his own men's muzzle loaders, combined with the rattle of machine guns. Belisario hoped at least *some* of those machine guns were among those he and his followers had captured at the UN's office armory.

The first thing Belisario saw from the window was smoke. True to his word, Pedro had struck an engine. The engine had then caught fire, a fire which spread to other parts of the shuttle. The entire machine seemed about to burst into flames.

While Belisario watched, it *did* burst into flame, the fireball catching several of the UN Marines, sending them running as shrieking human torches. The Cochean felt no satisfaction at this, but only pity and perhaps even a bit of regret. He regretted, too, that any equipment that might have been on the shuttle was now irretrievably lost.

A near miss knocked bits of wood off of the wooden window frame causing Belisario to duck. Taking a moment to steel his soul he returned to his observation point. There were no more near misses, however. Instead, with his head now rapidly clearing from the shock of Pedro's muzzle blast, Belisario saw a dozen or fourteen—it was hard to be sure under the circumstances—UN Marines, cowering at the edges of the burned area. He suspected that those, plus the ones he had seen burn, were all that had gotten out of the shuttle. Those survivors were tightly pinned by the machine gun fire coming from Belisario's looted weapons.

Between the machine gun and rifle fire, plus the

real fire from the shuttle, first one, then another, then a group of three of the Marines dropped their weapons and stood up, arms raised high. It wasn't *their* bloody fight and if the locals were willing to take prisoners they were willing to become prisoners.

Belisario was still in the first phase of a very steep upward learning curve. He'd never thought to arrange for a signal to cease fire. Fortunately, his followers were not cold-blooded killers but simple farmers and ranchers and artisans who would kill only most reluctantly. Fire ceased as the gunners and riflemen saw that the Marines were, in fact, trying to surrender. As the fire let up, and seeing those trying to surrender standing unharmed, the rest of the UN troops quickly put down their weapons and stood, as well.

Saying, "I'll send someone for you, Pedro," Belisario left the room and walked out of the shack towards the UN Marines. He was met, not too far from the burning shuttle, by one very shaken Botswanan major with his arms raised high over his head.

CHAPTER TWENTY-NINE

It is expedient for us, that one man should die for the people.

—John 11:50

Las Mesas, Balboa, 28/2/462 AC

Was there ever a sweeter sounding word? Cruz was *home*!

Admittedly, it was only for four weeks leave and, even worse, he had an allegedly nasty leadership selection course to run through, to be followed by more advanced training. But he was *home*, he was a sergeant, and at last he could marry his lovely and sweet Caridad.

Actually, there was one sweeter word . . . or rather, one sweeter phrase. Standing beside him in a white dress—well, she was still, *technically*, a virgin—surrounded by both their families and with Cruz wearing the new, black and silver dress uniform of the legion that he'd been issued at *Fuerte* Cameron, Cara had said, "I do."

Feast followed and honeymoon, altogether too brief a one, followed feast. As for the honeymoon . . . well, newlyweds are entitled to a certain amount of privacy.

Main Bus Terminal, Ciudad Balboa, 8/3/462 AC

It was just after midnight, with the lights of the city washing out the stars overhead. Under the bright streetlamps, Caridad Morales-Herrera de Cruz fought to keep control of her voice. But it was just so damned unfair. She and her Ricardo had barely had time to get to know each other again before he had had to go.

I refuse to cry. I refuse. I refuse.

She cried anyway.

Around the young couple, hundreds of other Cazador hopefuls and their nearest kin awaited the buses that would bring them to the nearest thing to Hell man's imagination could create on Terra Nova. Many a young girl and elderly mother wept. Cazador School had gained a well-deserved reputation for misery and danger in its brief existence.

Cruz stiffened and Cara began softly to cry with the sound of the first horn. Cruz pulled her close, stroking her long midnight black hair and murmuring words of comfort into her ear. Around them, unnoticed, others left behind by loved ones joined in a low floating wail.

Camp Gutierrez, Balboa

A long line of students wound from the class headquarters building down to the tiny unkempt parade field. To either side of the students CIs roamed like ravenous beasts of prey.

Standing at rigid attention, shorn of hair, rank, and the external trappings of personal dignity, Cruz listened attentively to the CIs' grandiloquent vituperation. *Might come in useful someday.*

The students had managed a couple of hours' sleep on the buses to Camp Gutierrez. No breakfast had been offered, as a matter of policy. Cruz listened to the rumbling of his deprived stomach: *Hey, asshole, don't you remember me? You know, the one you're supposed to fucking feed? Your stomach?*

As classmates ahead of him completed their inprocessing, Cruz neared the school headquarters building. Ahead was a large curved sign, yellow with black letters, held up by columns. *CAZADOR*, Cruz read. He could see concrete pyramidal blocks lining both sides of the trail past the sign. A student did pushups, hands on the ground, feet elevated on the concrete at each block.

The rain began to fall. Still, the students stood and marched forward at attention. The rain lifted and the bright Balboan sun turned the sodden uniforms to clinging, stinking, steamy prisons. Cruz passed under the *CAZADOR* sign.

"Get your feet up on that block, *Cazador*! Fifteen for the ones who preceded you," commanded an impersonal CI. Cruz mounted his feet on the block and began to perform push ups, as the others before him had. His arms pumped out the pushups smoothly.

Turning his head to one side Cruz saw an inscription on the concrete block opposite. It was from the Bible: "And his meat was locusts: Matthew 3:4." Below that were written the names of three Cazador students who had lost their lives in training. Cruz moved up to the next block as the flow of students moved onward. The inscription Cruz read now was: "And when he had fasted forty days and forty nights, he was afterward an hungered: Matthew 4:2." More names of the dead were proclaimed below that quote. "I came not to send peace, but a sword: Matthew 10:34" followed that.

Hours later, still unfed and wanting sleep, Cruz and his newly assigned *"Cazador Compadre,"* Rafael Montoya, a lanky boy from *Valle de las Lunas*, emerged from the headquarters building with all that they would be allowed to possess as Cazador students. A huge pile of sandwiches, cookies, cakes and other goodies fed the ants and birds in the field behind the headquarters.

Camp Gutierrez, 22/3/462 AC

Already Cruz's uniform was beginning to hang on him loosely. The purely technical aspects of Cazador School were behind him—map reading, the steps in troop-leading procedures, radio communications, physical fitness tests, and so on. He could do all those things perfectly well before coming here. But—and this made it special—all of it had been done on under an hour and a half's sleep per night and with a constant pain in the belly.

Almost a fifth of those who had begun the course with Cruz had already dropped out or been dropped. None had yet been killed, though two had been injured badly enough in the hand-to-hand combat pits that they had to be recycled. These did scut work in a separate compound called, none of the students knew quite why, the "Gulag."

This was the first patrol. The patrol, really a large squad, was halted in a cigar-shaped perimeter. Men looked out to all sides, fighting to keep their eyes open. The CI took a position in the center, watching Cruz more closely than Cruz knew. Mosquitoes buzzed in ears, taking their part of each student's daily donation of a pint of blood to the jungle pests. Outside the perimeter foul-mouthed *antaniae* murmured, "*mnnbt . . . mnnbt . . . mnnbt.*" No one really worried about the *antaniae*. They were too nasty to eat and, while their mouths were septic, they were a cowardly species which, for the most part, posed danger of infection only to the very young.

"Montoya. Goddammit, Montoya, wake the fuck up!" Cruz whispered as he jostled his assigned buddy.

Montoya snapped up with a start. "I wasn't sleeping, Centurion."

"Save the lies for the CI. It's me, Cruz. Pull out your poncho and put it over us."

Cruz took a red filtered flashlight and his acetated map in his hands and joined Montoya under the cover of the poncho. Unheard by either, the CI crept to within a couple of feet to listen.

"Cazador Cruz, you have failed this patrol." The CI laid his judgment out without cushioning. Cruz hung his head in shame. The CI then proceeded to explain precisely why Cruz had failed: improper contingency plan so that when the perimeter had been hit, Montoya hadn't known where to take the patrol to link up; inadequate supervision on Montoya's part after Cruz's departure leading to sleeping troops who couldn't detect the approaching enemy, failure to navigate properly so that the patrol had to stop too close to the objective leading, so the CI said, to interception by a random security sweep by the unit at the objective. Of course the security sweep hadn't been random at all, but Cruz couldn't know that.

The rain began to fall once again as Cruz made his miserable way back to his patrol.

Camp "Greasy" Gomez, 26/3/462 AC

Balboa's climate was hot and wet. Ordinarily, it wasn't possible to become cool there in the outdoors, let alone cold. Still, when deprived of food and sleep, worked too hard, and kept soaking wet for days on end, men would shiver.

Where the swamp water came midway up Cruz's chest, it was closer to neck deep on Dominguez. That was why Cruz never noticed that Dominguez was shivering until his teeth began to chatter.

"'Minguez, are you okay?"

"No, Cruz . . . cold, getting colder."

Shit. Cruz told Dominguez to wait in place—the patrol wasn't going anywhere fast—and waded forward to find the CI.

"Centurion, I think one of my men is coming down

with hypothermia." They'd been lectured on that particular danger early on in the course.

The CI waded back with Cruz, both of them sloshing through the darkened water to where Dominguez still stood. None of Terra Nova's three moons were up much so the CI broke out a blue filtered flashlight and played in over the shivering man's face. After a brief visual inspection, plus a quick feel of the all-too-cooled forehead, he decided Cruz was right.

"We've got to get him out of some of this water. It's not so deep up ahead. You two, pick him up and carry him forward." Montoya and another man named Saldañas lifted Dominguez bodily out of the water.

At the shallow spot, the CI took his knife out and stuck it perpendicularly into a tree. Then he took a blue fuel tablet out of a metalicized pouch. He laid the fuel tablet on the knife. Reaching into the student's web gear, the CI took out Dominguez's steel canteen cup and filled it with water. He lit the fuel tab, letting it begin to burn over its entire surface, before placing the cup squarely upon it. He pulled both knife and cup away from the tree, holding them together.

The CI looked around and announced, "I need a crap load of sugar."

Montoya went around the gathering students. "C'mon. Give it up, goddammit. Dominguez needs sugar." The men reached into hidden stores for sugar packets filched from the mess on those rare occasions the students were allowed to eat in the mess.

The CI gently slid the knife out from under the cup. The fuel tablet stayed, magically stuck to the cup's bottom. With its own bottom exposed to the air, it flared into a respectable flame. Soon the water was hot enough for a decent cup of coffee, heavily laden with sugar.

Montoya, standing with his hands cupped around sugar packets, looked with wonder at the CI's method of coffee preparation in a soaking wet environment. "I believe that is the neatest thing I've ever seen," he said, mostly to himself.

Lago de Ajuela, Balboa, 28/3/462 AC

Today was a test day of sorts. Its objective was to run out a portion of those students who could not overcome physical fear. All the candidates had already been in combat, of course. This proved little as, in combat, no one was really watching to *see* how they reacted to danger.

"This is more like what I signed up for when I volunteered for this stinking course," announced Montoya, looking over the various tests.

Saldañas, standing on the other side of Cruz from Montoya, looked ghastly pale. "Man, I am terrified of heights." Saldañas was a sailor with the still growing naval *classis*. In the legion even sailors and members of the air *ala* had to demonstrate combat leadership before being allowed leadership of any kind.

Another student—Dominguez, Saldañas' Cazador buddy—answered "Cheer up, friend. You're a squid. At least you can swim well."

The class tac, a retired FSA master sergeant working for the FMTG and named Olivetti called the class to attention, then "at ease."

"The purpose of today's exercise," the CI said, "is to

separate from the school those who lack an essential characteristic needed in a combat leader—physical courage."

At Olivetti's last words twin explosions erupted from the water. The students shuddered from the shock. A Balboan CI, carrying a pulleylike device with a handle attached, ran from the woods toward a steel I-beam set upright in the ground, with a small platform on top and a wire cable running at an angle down to the water. The CI howled as he ran.

Reaching the I beam, the CI rapidly clambered up its seventy-five odd feet until he reached the platform. There he hooked the pulley around the wire cable, grabbed hold of the handle and lifted his feet off the platform. He sped down the cable gathering speed. Another CI, standing on a floating platform near where cable met water, signaled when it was time for the slider to let go of the handle.

Montoya watched, wide-eyed, as the slider's feet struck the water first, causing him to spin head over heels a half dozen times before knifing headfirst below the surface.

That has got to take practice, thought Cruz admiringly.

Fifty times the son of a bitch does it right in rehearsal, thought Olivetti, *then he screws it up in practice. Idiot.*

The CI surfaced and then swam toward the shore. Olivetti announced "What you have just seen is called the 'Slide for Life.' The CI is now approaching the Log Walk/Rope Drop."

Still howling, the demonstrator ran from the shore to the Log Walk. This consisted of three on-line poles set upright into the muck below. At a height of some thirty-five feet—shrewdly calculated to be the most frightening height to be at for a human being—the poles were surmounted by a log, topped by a flat plank, with steps in the middle. The logs swayed as the CI raced upward. At the top the CI bound down the plank, not stopping or slowing even for the steps in the middle. He took a quick seat at the far end.

Olivetti continued his explanations. "Once you have successfully negotiated the Log Walk you will take a seat while awaiting your turn for the Rope Drop."

The demonstrator CI rolled to his side and began to pull himself out onto another steel cable that ran slightly upwards toward the summit of a taller pole. Set more than halfway up, a Cazador tab painted on wood hung. The CI slapped it once, screamed, "Cazador!" and eased his body smoothly off the cable until he was hanging by both hands. The CI released his right hand from the cable, executed a smart hand salute and said, "Centurion, Cazador Torres requests permission to drop."

Olivetti returned the salute and answered, "Drop, Cazador." The CI on the cable let go with his left hand, placing it over his crotch as he fell. The right hand went under the chin, fingers cupping the nose. The water splashed more than halfway to the cable when he hit.

Turning his attention back to the students, Olivetti said, conversationally "Easy as Hell, isn't it? See, we don't ask too much of you."

Oh, God, I hate heights, thought Saldañas, as he began the long climb up the I beam. Rather than look upward as he climbed, which would remind him of how far he had to go, or—worse—downward, which would tell him how far he had gone, Saldañas kept his eyes on the rusted steel of the beam, parallel to the ground. Even when his pulley, hanging off his shoulder by a strap, caught on one of the rungs, he freed it purely by touch, rather than risk seeing the ground. He closed his eyes every time a student ahead of him took off down the slide, making the beam shudder. The climb seemed endless and limitlessly terrifying.

"Get your ass up here, Cazador," shouted the CI atop the little platform. Saldañas carefully eased through the little trap door, fingers turning white from his clenching grip on whatever seemed solid. The CI saw this.

"Scared are you, son?"

Teeth clenched to keep them from chattering, he forced out a, "Yes, Centurion."

"No shame in that, son," the CI said, not unkindly. The CI took the pulley from Saldañas' shoulder and hooked it onto the cable. Then he grabbed the back of Saldañas' shirt and pulled him under the pulley. The student resisted giving up his grip on the platform.

"Open your eyes, son. The point is to see what scares you and overcome it." Saldañas obeyed and immediately lunged for the I beam.

"Cazador, there is only one way off this platform. You either get a grip on yourself and take hold of this handle or I am going to kick your shitty butt out into space, hear me?"

Half guided by the CI, Saldañas, trembling, forced himself to stand under the pulley and take a grip on the handle.

"Now when I tell you to go, I want you to lift up with your arms. When you get away from platform a ways, bend your body into an 'L' shape. Watch the man with the flag standing at the anchor dock. He'll tell you how high to lift your legs and when to let go of the pulley. Got it? Oh, yes. One other thing. If you don't keep your eyes open to see the drop signal you are going to slam into the dock at the other end of the cable at about 100 kilometers per hour. Guaranteed fatal. You will keep your eyes open?"

Saldañas could only nod, two or three times, quickly.

"Go!" Saldañas, after a moment's hesitation, lifted off and went . . . nowhere. The CI still had a grip on his shirt. "Okay. Let's try it again, this time with your eyes open. Go." Again Saldañas didn't slide but he did keep his eyes from closing.

"All right, son. That was fine. Now this time I really am going to let go. Ready? . . . Go!"

At first Saldañas felt nothing. Then he realized he also could not feel the CI's grip on the back of his shirt. By the time this registered he felt the beginnings of forward motion. He screamed, "*Jeeesuuusss!*" as he picked up speed. Chuckling and thinking, *it's funny how he called upon the only man who can save him now*, the CI called out, "Next Cazador. Get your ass up here, boy."

Dimly, Saldañas realized on his way down, *It's a good thing I'm landing in water. No one will see the piss.*

Caridad Cruz's parent's home, 31/3/462 AC

"Cara? Cara, I have a letter for you from Ricardo!"

At her mother's call Caridad ran, breathless, for the front hall. She tore the letter from her mother's hand and opened it.

"Dearest Cara,

I'm terribly sorry that I haven't written before . . . there simply hasn't been any time at all. The only reason I can write now is that this is sort of a screw off day; terrifying but not difficult. "Terrifying?" I hear you ask. Very.

We were all (except Montoya, I'll tell you about him later) scared of heights. I still am but at least I can deal . . . now. The interesting one was Saldañas. He's a sailor who's bucking for officer (did I ever tell you even the squids have to graduate Cazador School to become centurions or officers?). I can't prove it, but I'd almost swear Saldañas wet himself on one of them. But he's a gutsy one. You could see he'd rather have died than walk over some steps that were thirty-five feet in the air. The steps were in the middle of one of the obstacles. But he'd rather die than fail, too. He made it over, with help, but almost in tears. We're all really proud of him.

For the rest, my mates and I are starving, and more than two weeks behind on sleep. They feed us so little here, one scanty ration

a day, most days, that there isn't enough to
allow the body to heal even a little cut. I
have a couple I got early on that are still
running sores.

Nonetheless, I am making it so far. I
failed my first patrol, but it didn't count. I
passed the second. Tomorrow we're off to
the mountain school.

Give your parents and mine my best.

All my love,
Ricardo

Cara put the letter back in the envelope. *He didn't
even mention sex. That's not the Ricardo I know.*

Camp Bernardo O'Higgins, Hephaestus, *Valle de las Lunas*, 32/3/462 AC

O'Higgins was the mountain training center for the
expanding legion and the second phase of the Cazador
School.

In this camp Cruz's class had suffered its first fatal-
ity. In front of all four hundred odd Cazador students
still with the class, a piton securing a rope snaking up
the side of a cliff broke free. The reactions of both
climber and safety man were too slowed by fatigue
to grab a handhold; the next piton broke free as well.
A long scream tore through the air, and those nearby
heard a dull thud.

An ambulance came to claim the body. Other than
that, none of the school cadre took any special pains
over the death. In a few days a new name would be

added to the monuments that stood by the entrance to the camp and the concrete plinths in front of the school headquarters at Camp Gutierrez. A memorial service was held at the close of that day's training. No other official notice was taken. That night fifteen men resigned.

Unofficially, and unobtrusively, Olivetti made note of those who had not resigned but who seemed more upset than most. These, in ones and two, as the schedule permitted, he spoke to over the next several days. One reported to him now.

"Cazador Cruz, reporting as ordered, Centurion."

"Sit, Cazador." Olivetti made a show of looking over Cruz's school file. He closed the file. "This is counseling, Cazador Cruz. We counsel each Cazador student several times during the course of the school . . . to help you learn, to improve. That's all this is. In looking over your file, and it's a short file now, I observe that you have been a somewhat better than average Cazador. True, you failed your first patrol. Most do. Nonetheless, the evaluations of your peers in your squad speak highly of you as a leader. And the CI for your first patrol thought that mostly you were let down by your assistant, Montoya."

Cruz bristled. "Montoya's okay. He just took a little longer than most getting used to the lack of sleep."

Olivetti shrugged. Alone he was a much friendlier sort than the ravening beast he usually put on for the students. "Forget about Montoya for now. You have been acting more listless than short rations and lack of sleep alone account for. What's the problem?"

Cruz hesitated to speak for a moment. When he did finally begin to talk, it came out in a torrent. "I don't understand this place. You starve us. You won't let us sleep. You keep us in constant fear of failure. You work and march us to death. And then, when somebody dies because he's too tired to pay attention and too weak to hang on to something, you act like it's just routine business. What's the point of that? This is supposed to be a leadership school. How can we learn when it's all we can do to stay awake? What does losing twenty pounds have to do with the ability to lead men in battle? Or is this all just some initiation rite at the legion's expense?"

Olivetti answered calmly, "No, it isn't an initiation rite, not entirely. Let me try to answer your questions with other questions. Ask yourself what battle is like. I know you have two awards for valor, the *Cruz de Coraje* in Steel and Bronze. Was battle stressful? Did it put stress on your leaders? Did they need the ability to cope with stress to deal with it? Is that ability innate, learned, or a combination of both? Can we give you all the stress of battle in the form it takes in battle? What kinds of stress can we put you under without surely killing too many of you? Will you be able to cope better with one kind of stress by learning to cope with another? Is it more likely or less likely that graduates of the Cazador School will have shown more of an innate ability to cope with stress? Do men become brave by doing brave acts?"

Cruz remained as silent and sullen as he thought he could get away with. Even so, Olivetti's logic nagged at him. *Maybe he has a point. Maybe.*

"You don't have to answer. Just think about the questions for a while.

"As for Cazador Enriquez, he was on the centurion

track. He will get every benefit of the doubt and be buried as Optio Carlos Enriquez, of the 6th Mechanized Tercio, with a *Cruz de Coraje* in Gold; he already had Steel, Bronze And Silver. Very brave trooper, was Enriquez."

Olivetti grew thoughtful. "One of the things I like about how the legion does business is that you"—as part of FMTG Olivetti was not technically or legally a legionary—"don't distinguish between training and battle deaths."

He continued, "What more do you want us to do? Would Enriquez be happier, do you think, if his mates had missed valuable training? In battle would we stop a fight while it was ongoing to mourn a fallen comrade?

"You feel bad about Enriquez. So you should. You're sorry he died. So am I. And the training killed him, no doubt about it. Was Enriquez's life more valuable than the lives of the men he would someday have led? More valuable than yours and the men you will someday lead? Don't those men, and their mothers and fathers, their wives and children, deserve the best leaders we can give them?

"Your main complaint, however, seems directed at the fact that we don't seem to emphasize the . . . oh . . . skills a leader needs as much as we do the character. More questions for you to answer for yourself: Are those skills something that can be taught or only learned? Do we give you the opportunity to learn even though no one can necessarily teach them? Don't we coach you to learn them for yourself? And do we not teach them, too, in a way? When, Cazador Cruz, will you in the future forget that men need food and sleep to keep going at top performance? When, in battle, when you're a centurion leading a platoon, will you forget to take care of your troops because if you don't they won't be able to take care of you? When will you forget that fear and fatigue are interchangeable, that frightened men get weak fast? That tired men frighten easily? Enriquez died so you would learn those lessons in a way you will never forget.

"Finally, ask yourself what character a leader in battle must have. I think when you do you may discover that no one who graduates this school can be very deficient in any important aspect of it. But you'll have to find the answers to those questions yourself. Send in Saldañas, please."

Camp O'Higgins, 34/3/462 AC

Just keep putting one foot in front of the other, thought Cruz as he trudged his weary way along the side of the mountain. His legs and back ached mercilessly from the uneven path and off-center walk it required.

The patrol stopped suddenly. Cruz almost walked into the back of the man ahead of him, despite the dim glow of the two florescent strips sewn on the back of that student's hat.

Men took a knee at alternate sides of the patrol's perimeter, forming a rough cigar shape on the ground. Cruz struggled to keep his eyes open. The assistant patrol leader came forward from the rear of the little column to inquire about the halt. As he passed each man he whispered, "Take off your hats."

The students complied without argument. They'd

learned that the hat became a little house and they'd fall asleep in a heartbeat if they felt themselves at home. A sleeping Cazador was a Cazador who would be left behind by his patrol. There was no greater shame and no more likely cause for dismissal from the course.

At the point of the column Cruz heard the CI loudly berating the patrol leader, Montoya, for becoming lost. Montoya fumbled verbally, trying to make an excuse. What Montoya didn't do was insist that he *did* know where the patrol was, even though he did.

The CI gave Montoya a location on the map that seemed plausible but was incorrect. Rising to their feet again, the men took off in a new, and false, direction. They would march all night up and down the side of this one mountain, with no time for sleep or to eat even the wretched amount of food they carried.

With each step, the burning pain in their legs increased. When they realized that they were walking in circles around a single summit, getting nowhere, the frustration, and the pain, brought tears to the eyes of some. In the morning, the CI would tell the patrol leader that he hadn't been lost at all, but that his lack of self-confidence had cost everyone. Montoya, the leader, told the squad what had happened. He hung his head for days.

Unknown to the patrol, it was all planned. Cazador Instructors evaluating each patrol did the very same thing at about the same time. Each patrol, as a result, became lost and wasted the night. The number of students dropped still further.

Jungle Camp, Yaviza, Balboa, 13/4/462 AC

Now what's the holdup? Cruz cursed under his breath at the school, the CIs, the rain, the piss warm swamp water that sloshed around his waist. Wiping rain from his brow—the hat he wore was so soaked that it didn't shed water anymore—Cruz felt his feet sinking slowly into the mud below him. He shifted to a fresher spot and let the sinking process begin anew. Lightning flashed, illuminating the murky scene.

I am so hungry. So very hungry. He thought warmly for a moment of his wife, Cara. He felt a moment's chagrin as he realized that he didn't think of sex anymore, hadn't in weeks. *And a sad thing it is, too, when your pecker stops working.* The stress- and starvation-induced impotence was something of a class joke for every Cazador class. "Hung our balls on the centurion's office wall when we reported in."

As he sometimes did when there was time and nothing better to do with it, Cruz played a mental game. He had discovered, almost two months prior, that just dreaming of having enough to eat was unsatisfying. Instead, he gave himself an imaginary twenty drachma, then went on an imaginary shopping spree at the supermarket with only that twenty to spend. The limitation, imaginary and artificial as it was, gave more substance to his dreaming. It also, sometimes, caught his stomach up in the dream so that the organ stopped nagging, *Feed me, Motherfucker, feeed meee.*

He roused himself back to reality as he realized the patrol was moving on. The man to his front reached back to tap him; too many times a patrol had become separated after a halt to a seemingly interminable march. Men had learned that they could fall asleep on their feet. The students no longer took chances. Cruz likewise tapped the man behind him. "Come on, Montoya. We're moving out again," he whispered.

Montoya nodded. Speech took too much energy. The group continued their fight with the water and the muck.

Jungle Camp, 16/4/462 AC

A light rain, unusually light for Balboa, fell on the patrol. Montoya walked back to the center of the perimeter, where Cruz minded the radio. "I failed another one, Cruz."

"Shit."

Montoya collapsed in a heap next to the radio. "Not to worry, friend. They're going to keep giving me back-to-back leadership phases until I pass. I'm leader, again, for this one. I'm fucked. You all are even more fucked."

Cruz, who had already tabbed out—made the requirements to graduate the course—made sympathetic sounds. Saldañas, Ramirez, and Dominguez walked over and sat down as well. They, too, already, had made the grade.

"Heard you're on the intensive track, Montoya." That from Ramirez.

Cruz interjected, "It just isn't possible. He can't do any more." Montoya didn't argue the point.

"He can't, but *we* can. Listen." Cruz listened as Saldañas laid out his plan for how the four of them would do as much of Montoya's work for him as the CIs would permit.

Montoya looked up, hope dawning in his eyes. His eyes clouded. "I can't make it on charity."

Dominguez took his shoulder in a firm grip. "It's not charity, Montoya. When Saldañas, here, froze on the log walk, who went up and talked him across? You, friend.

"And when Dominguez fell off the side of the hill at Camp O'Higgins, rolling end over end while his own machine gun tried to beat him to death, who carried the gun and the pack for two hours until he was capable of carrying them again?"

"Me, too, Montoya," said Cruz. "When I fucked up and didn't order chow for the platoon . . . and we all had nothing at all to eat for a day. Who talked me up to keep on going. They're right. We can help you, and it isn't charity. It's just paying a debt."

Montoya bowed his head, humbled and grateful.

Ramirez, silent until now, said, tersely, "Now let's get to work."

Graduation Exercise Area, Camp Gutierrez, 5/5/462 AC

Unique among militaries, the legion, at Carrera's insistence, had a requirement that all officers and centurions be combat tested before receiving their commissions or centurion's batons. This was so even though almost everyone sent to the Cazador School, followed by OCS, CCS or WOCS, was a veteran of combat already.

"Eventually, there will be peace, however transitory it will prove," Carrera had said. "The tradition of combat testing starts now so it will be kept then."

This was the most dreaded mission in the school, although much of the danger was still more apparent than real. Nonetheless, students *were* wounded or killed by design rather than by accident.

The live fire took place on an area of rough ground. The objectives consisted of well fortified battle positions, with bunkers and trenches, protected by broad belts of barbed wire and concertina. Interspersed among the bunkers, sometimes in place of them, very heavily uparmored tank turrets with anti-spalling liners—lead shields to absorb the little splinters of steel that often flew off of the inside of armor when it was struck by fire—were set into concrete. These held the defenders of the positions.

The tanks had the main guns removed. Unlike the ones the school used elsewhere, however, the crews of some of these tanks would try to hit the students rather than merely frighten them. Ordinarily, this would mean serious casualties. To keep these within acceptable limits, the turrets' machine guns only carried one round in ten live. The rest of the belted ammunition was plastic tipped. This was still dangerous close up but the plastic rounds lost velocity rapidly due to their low density. Every burst would be aimed with evil intent, but only one round in ten would actually have a bullet in it. The machine guns were, moreover, set loosely in their cradles to allow the fire to spread to cover an area as a normal ground-mounted machine gun would. Therefore, even if the gunner was dead on target, inclined to shoot that target, and that target was a real student, and the burst happened to have a live round in it, the odds were good that the bullet would go low, high or wide.

Other turrets had both main gun and machine guns removed. These had sniper rifles locked firmly into place. The "sniper" turrets fired all live ammunition, but their job was to try to fire as close as possible to the students without actually hitting any of them. Still, mistakes happened. And, it was widely rumored, the CIs manning the sniper rifles would deliberately shoot a man if provoked by incompetence. The rumor was only occasionally true and they *never* shot to kill.

Still, the students weren't entirely helpless. The things they had learned, careful reconnaissance, thorough planning and rehearsals, control, and teamwork could, properly applied, allow them to put effective fire on the turrets. The turret crews would cease fire for fifteen seconds after taking a hit from a bullet. There were also two small, upper body shaped, targets on the front of each turret. If the students hit both of these in an area about ten inches in diameter, the tank would cease fire completely. It was possible, though very uncommon, for no turrets on an objective to have a chance to fire.

Turrets never fired deliberately at a CI. Indeed they avoided them as completely as possible.

As an added measure, the students were issued the heavy, fifty-four pound, ceramic torso armor and extra-heavy helmets. Face, arms and legs were still exposed, but the odds of a fatal hit were lessened. Statistics said that out of a typical class of about three hundred to three hundred and fifty, 8.4 men would be shot as a result of the day's training, 1.4 of them fatally.

Olivetti, wearing more complete body armor, painted white to mark him as a CI, stood in front of the class, explaining these things to the students. "Those casualty rates are only averages. Sometimes a class comes through without a scratch. Once we had seventeen men shot. Four died. If anyone wants to resign now, step to the rear and see Sergeant Major Schetrompf. He'll take your resignations." The CI didn't mention that after that particular day, the course had changed to give sixteen hours unbroken rest and five complete meals to the students before sending them to the graduation exercise. It was better they should believe the course was even more dangerous than it was.

Inside the ranks men wavered, Olivetti could see it in the way they shifted weight from side to side, looked around to see what their peers were doing.

Montoya finished their mental self debate for them. Speaking loudly, he said "You've made me shit myself more than once already, Centurion, although with the little bit you feed us there wasn't much shit. I'll be damned if all that, plus starving us and making us walking dead from lack of sleep, was for nothing. Bring on your fucking tanks, Centurion Olivetti. Besides, I need to pass one more patrol to graduate anyway." A few students laughed nervously. The moment of wavering was broken.

Olivetti nodded, seeing the men quiet down in the ranks. *That's why you're still here, Montoya. You can't lead for shit. Your squad has carried you through every leadership phase you passed. But you're a tough little bastard and you don't quit. Your legion has use for those, too.* At his signal, the three, much truncated, student companies began to shake out into tactical formations, separating and moving toward their objectives. Olivetti fell in with the center company, talking on his radio as he did so.

Overhead, real artillery, not simulators or preplaced charges, began to rumble across the sky toward small impact areas offset from the objectives. Though frightened, the men grinned. It was almost over.

Parade Field, Camp Gutierrez, 8/5/462 AC

The school commandant, Major Broughton, FS Army (retired), stood on a low reviewing stand. He looked over the ranks, 331 men of six hundred and ten who had started. Four were dead, about par for the course, most of the rest dropped with prejudice or quit. Some of those dropped were medicals. If they recovered, these would have a chance to continue the course with another class. A few others, hospitalized with wounds from the final exercise, would be graduated, and decorated, in their beds later in the day, their squads in attendance.

Broughton walked up to the microphone and began to speak. At his command the class stood at ease. He told the graduating students how tough they were, and brave; how they represented the best of their countries, and some of the best in the world. He said he expected great things of them, as they had proven themselves capable of great things.

Cruz whispered to Montoya, standing at his left, "You feel tough, bud?"

Montoya answered, likewise in a whisper, "He must be talking about some other people. I don't feel tough."

Broughton finished, calling the class to attention and ordering the school adjutant to call the roll.

The adjutant took Broughton's place at the microphone and began to read off names.

"Optio Enriquez."

The entire class answered, as rehearsed "Here!"

"Signifer Trujillo."

"Here!"

The adjutant finished the last names on his list of dead, each with the rank he would have held had he finished Cazador School and the next course for which he was scheduled. Following the last "Here!" he gave the command, "Open ranks, march!"

As the companies opened their ranks, the CIs of Camp Gutierrez trotted out, one to each rank of each platoon, each CI carrying a cloth bag draped over one shoulder. Olivetti came to attention to Cruz's right front.

"Present the tabs!"

Olivetti took one step forward, halted and faced left. He nodded, "Cazador Cruz?"

"Blood tab, Centurion." In the school's short life no Cazador had yet failed to ask for a "blood tab." It was an article of faith among the students that the first one to do so would have his name publicized across the entire legion.

Olivetti reached into the cloth bag and pulled out a full color black and gold half circle with the word "CAZADOR" spelled in bold, gold letters. A safety pin ran through the tab. Olivetti unlocked the safety pin, grabbed Cruz's sleeve near the shoulder, and drove the pin into the emaciated flesh beneath before withdrawing it, pushing it through the cloth, and hooking it back onto itself. Cruz controlled his flinch. *What's a little more pain, after all?*

"Good job, Cruz." Olivetti held out his hand.

"Thank you, Centurion. You, too." Cruz shook the hand with real feeling.

Olivetti passed on to Montoya.

Montoya smiled. "Blood tab, Centurion." He held his smile as the point pierced him.

"You're a shithead, Montoya. But you're a damn fine soldier. Congratulations."

When the last of the tabs had been awarded, Broughton returned to the reviewing stand. "Pass in review!"

Without further fanfare, the platoons faced right and began to double time past the reviewing stand. They only dropped to a walk when the last of them had passed. The students—no, full fledged Cazadors now—began to sing as they walked back to barracks.

Once he arrived back in *Las Mesas*, Cruz was very pleased to discover that his impotence was only temporary. Caridad was *very* pleased, as well.

INTERLUDE

15 June, 2104 (Terra Novan Year 45 AC), Atlantis Base

The acting commander of Atlantis base was at wits' end. High Admiral Annan was gone; reported dead. The Marines and shuttle he had borrowed were gone as well and he had to presume them to be dead or captured, likewise the Supervisory Office in Balboa colony. He had no more Marines to spare. He had no more shuttles and only three helicopters. And until a new ship came in system he had no way of getting any more, either.

It was bad enough that Anglia colony, for now, reported only to its home government back on Earth. No one ever expected anything different from the stinking Americans beginning to fill up Southern Columbia, or indeed anyone from Earth's Anglosphere except for the people settling Secordia. But the colonies from the Earth's Third World? These were *supposed* and expected to stand by the UN, to toe its line, to build one-world government here to match the one building back home. Otherwise, Terra Nova would become just another twentieth-century Earth. And that, the acting commander knew, spelled danger.

"Commander?" an aide broke in, giving the honorific despite doubt about whether the title would become permanent. "News from our office in San Jose colony. They're under attack by hundreds of men armed with modern weapons."

"Shit!"

"It gets worse, Commander. The rebels are broadcasting from the radio station at our Balboa office— what used to be our Balboa office—calling on everyone to 'throw off Earth's chains.' And we have little or nothing to stop it."

That bastard, Annan, the acting commander thought. *He could have bought all the little girls he wanted from the Yithrab, or even bought them from Earth at one of the open markets and brought them here. But* nooo, *the cheap son of a bitch had to go outside channels and avoid paying the little bit asked for. God save me from hereditary bureaucrats and their offspring. Now I get to sit, helpless, while the world we wanted to construct here falls apart around me.*

"Can we contact the leader of the . . . rebels?"

The aide thought about that for a minute. "He's probably directing the attack in San Jose colony, sir. We can probably contact him *after* he's finished storming it."

"Great," the acting commander muttered, leaning his weary head down to rest it in his hands. "Advise the office in San Jose to surrender. Tell them to *ask* him to speak with me. Maybe I can make a deal to keep this from spreading."

✧   ✧   ✧

"*Comandante*," Pedro said, "the Earthpigs want to talk to you. They want to arrange a ceasefire before this war spreads."

Belisario considered. *Should I? I could stop the carnage now, probably. But then, what prevents them from using the bases they retain to come back? What do I owe my fellow colonists languishing under the heel of the UN Birkenstock? How will my wife and our children ever sleep safely with slavers and tax gatherers hovering at the edges of our domain?*

"Tell the pig to kiss my ass, Pedro," Belisario answered. "The war goes on until we are, all of us, free."

Resolution 4999 (2127)
Adopted by the Security Council on its
16128th meeting,
On 1 June, 2127

The Security Council,

Recalling its previous resolutions, in particular resolution 4547 of 2107 and 4569 of 2108, concerning the situation off world among the colonies of Terra Nova,

Reaffirming its commitment to peace, prosperity and freedom as expressed and implied in the Charter,

Welcoming a just resolution to the ongoing conflicts on the planet of Terra Nova,

Acknowledging the difficulties inherent in administering and securing a world light years away,

Reiterating in the strongest terms its desire to accord self-determination to all mankind,

Stressing the importance of the recent peace accords between itself and various insurgent governments and movements on Terra Nova,

Welcoming the joint communiqué between its representatives on Terra Nova and the representatives of the United Front for the Liberation of New Earth,

Expressing its continuing responsibility toward the peoples of that world and its firm commitment to their continuing welfare,

Determining that the maintenance of its rule on the world of Terra Nova is beyond its abilities,

1) *Retires* its offices and security facilities to its base on the Island of Atlantis on the new world,

2) *Requests* a cease fire from all still-engaged armed or political agencies, governments, organizations and movements on the new world.

3) *Reiterates* its request for prisoner of war exchange and repatriation,

4) *Directs* the redesignation of its fleet around the new world as the United Nations Peace Fleet, to be further renamed the United Earth Peace Fleet at such time as the General Assembly may direct, and

5) *Declares* the conflict on the new world to be at an end.

CHAPTER
THIRTY

We have done with Hope and Honour,
 we are lost to Love and Truth,
We are dropping down the ladder rung by rung,
 —Kipling, "Gentlemen Rankers"

Ninewa, Sumer, 10/5/462 AC

Fadeel al Nizal's problems had multiplied. On the plus side, though, at least Mustafa was no longer one of them. If anything, the relationship had reversed itself with Fadeel becoming a major financial supporter of the rest of the movement and Mustafa being along mostly for a distant form of moral support. Not that the movement didn't have money. It had a great deal, most of it untouchable for the infidel accountants who watched for the slightest excuse to freeze suspicious accounts. Even Fadeel had lost money that way.

He'd have gladly accepted a great deal more of Mustafa's former chiding if he could have eliminated some of the other things bearing down upon him.

For a while it had seemed that the willing cooperation of the Kosmos—the cosmopolitan progressives who believed in one-world government, under
themselves—were the answer to most of his prayers.
With the money gained from the crusader governments
with the progressives' cooperation, his organization
had flown as high as the aircraft he had managed to
bring down early on in the campaign.

For a while, rather than having to listen to lectures
from Mustafa, Fadeel had found himself in a position
to repay the start-up money he'd received and even to
make a substantial gift to his principle. That gift had
been gratefully received, Mustafa having fallen upon
rather hard times. Moreover, he'd managed to knock
one crusader state, Castilla, almost completely out of
the war. He'd failed to knock Balboa out of the war.
That rankled. Worse, they were hunting down and
killing his men. And the damnable locals seemed to
be helping them do it, which was worse.

Unfortunately, the supply of Kosmo hostages had
dried up completely. There were no more Taurans
willing to volunteer, nor had there been since that
one woman, Giulia Masera, had been fed feet first
into a wood chipper and a tape of the murder
turned over to al Iskandaria News Network. Fadeel
was still puzzling over what had caused al Iskandaria to broadcast the tape. After all, they'd been
wise enough to refuse to show the death of one of
Masera's countrymen when he had defied Fadeel
just before his well-deserved execution. At the time,
Fadeel had been rather angry at the television network for refusing the tape. On reflection, though,
he had come to agree that showing a citizen of the

crusader coalition dying bravely and well would have been damaging rather than helpful.

At that, it would not have been nearly as damaging as broadcasting the death of Masera. She had been emulsified from the bottom up, her mouth opening and closing like a fish stuck out of water as she sank feet first into the wood chipper, her reddened, lumpy remains spitting out the bottom. Fadeel had rather enjoyed the show, naturally, but even he had seen it was a dangerous move for whichever comradely organization had been responsible.

That was another puzzle. Fadeel didn't know and had not been able to find out who was responsible for that execution. He'd thought at first that it must have been one of his own cells, naturally under very loose control due to the circumstances of the fight for God in Sumer. Not one of his people, however, had been willing to admit to it. Nor had any of the ransom money shown up.

I could surely have used another twenty-five million Tauros in the fight against the crusaders.

Not everything was going against him, fortunately. He'd had a few bad moments there, when the satanic Federated States had introduced automatic explosive sniffers. A number of bombs and great quantities of bomb-making material had been lost to the cause of the righteous and the just that way. Then the local mercenaries had brought in dogs to hunt for and warn of bombs.

The solution had been both beautiful and elegant in its simplicity. Fadeel had set some hundreds of young boys with small spray bottles to randomly spraying wheel wells of automobiles and trucks with water with which minute quantities of powdered explosive had been mixed. When everything smelled of bomb then nothing smelled of bomb. The dogs and the operators of the sniffing machines had been driven half insane, Fadeel and his followers had had a few good laughs, and more than a few crusaders had been enticed into the range of actual bombs.

Now the dogs were used only for tracking and the sniffing machines sat uselessly in a warehouse somewhere in Babel. Better still, the flow of explosives continued as it had before the infidels had tried their clever tricks.

Thinking about that, about the machines sitting idle and useless, set Fadeel to laughing yet again.

He sobered immediately. It wasn't enough to make up for the fact that after Masera's grisly execution the weak crusader governments had refused to give *any* ransoms. More than three dozen kidnappings and executions without so much as a drachma changing hands was enough to convince him it was a losing game.

Fadeel supposed that the charge of bad faith, after the Masera butchery, was enough to shield those governments from the domestic fallout of not paying.

When the governments had a reasonable and obvious chance to get "their" people back alive the pressure was tremendous. Now? Now nobody trusts us to deliver the goods.

Oh, yes, his people still went after the humanitarians and the journalists. The FSC even tried to stop them or rescue the peace-lovers in the other parts of the country. Here around Ninewa, for some reason, the Balboans generally didn't even make the attempt. And the other aid workers, the ones Fadeel thought might elicit a response from the mercenaries? Those were always too well guarded to even try.

Maybe they want me to kill off the ones I take. Something to think upon, anyway. Fadeel scratched his head in puzzlement. He was, at heart, a fairly simple man rather than a devious one. Grand strategy was Allah's job, not his. He was for fighting.

For that fighting he had a new recruit as well, though this particular recruit's time in the organization was destined to be short.

Ishmael Arguello, an earnest boy of seventeen, had taken the death of his mother hard. The younger of the two boys, and the handsomer if not the brighter, Ishmael had always been his mother's favorite. Moreover, Layla had been the center of Ishmael's universe. He had been cast adrift when Layla was cut down in cold blood. His father had been little help. No more so had his brother. School friends and teachers had been sympathetic, of course, and when one of the teachers had suggested continuing his mother's work Ishmael had decided that that was for him. The teacher had also, very considerately, put the boy in touch with a . . . recruiter, for lack of a better term. That was close enough.

The overhead fan turned slowly and quietly in Fadeel's basement office. He sat on a cushion on the floor, his legs crossed underneath him, feet pressed against thighs, while he continued to muse on his problems.

In some ways this enemy understands us very well, Fadeel thought, *damn him. In other ways he is almost as ignorant as the rest of this crusader alliance. He knows, for example, that disadvantaging clans by killing some of their workers causes more discontent. Why he never followed through on that understanding to the logical conclusion that killing very large numbers of clan members would destroy his enemies and serve as a salutary lesson to other clans, I just don't understand. He knows, absolutely he knows, that we are a people who take revenge. Why he can't figure out that he should eliminate people who are sure to become enemies by reason of the blood of relations . . . well, it's just impossibly foolish.*

I understand that in Taurus and the FSC, guilt and innocence are entirely individual matters because their people are individuals, individuals who can be encouraged and deterred by what happens to them, personally. But here, we are not individuals. No system of punishment can mean as much to us without a collective, blood-related, aspect.

Of course, some of the bastards do understand that. How many times have I had my men lost to the infidel because he rounded up twenty or so clansmen from clans sympathetic to the cause of Allah, tried them for crimes and threatened to hang them if information—oh, and captures, of course—was not forthcoming? More than I care to count. How many times have the clans captured, bound, and turned over my holy warriors to secure the release of their kin? I can count how many, but I'd rather not.

And now, instead of the insurgency being fed by locals as I had planned, I have more foreign born mujahadin than I do Sumeri. And the supply of foreign born will dry up, too, if the enemy ever figures out

how to target their families back home. Pray Allah,
they never shall.

Fadeel cut his musings short. He had people to
meet, notably some new volunteers to the cause.

Ishmael was given some travel funds, just enough
to see him to the next station on his journey. From
home he'd traveled by bus halfway through Bilad al
Sham, spending several nights in a safe house in the
capital while there.

The safe house had been a shock after the spacious, well furnished and maid-swept expanse of his
own home, back in Akka. Besides its being cramped
and filthy, Ishmael had found himself with the first
case of lice in his life.

If the quarters had been bad the food was . . . well,
the less said about the food the better. The *most* that
could be said for it was that it prepared a man for
leaving this life without regret. After a few days of
undercooked rice and goat with the hair still on, what
was there to fear with death?

From the safe house, Ishmael had moved on to a
school, of sorts. This was where he was to be trained.
Surprisingly, his training, along with that of another
four boys about his age, was not very military. In fact,
based on the little Ishmael knew about the subject
from his mother, it wasn't military at all. Certainly it
was nothing like the courses of instruction Layla had
told him about her having attended in her glorious
youth. He never even saw a rifle, except for the two
in the hands of the guards posted at the front gate
to the school's walled compound.

Instead, Ishmael's training was ninety-nine percent

religious, though whether the Prophet would have recognized it as such was debatable. It was geared, in the main, towards producing a young man willing to martyr himself. At that, the school was very efficient, especially when it had good material to work with.

"You came looking for martyrdom," Fadeel observed to the new recruits. "We shall help you to find it. More than that, we shall help your martyrdom to be of the greatest effect here on *al Donya al Jedidah*. To that end, each of you will make a tape. In those tapes you will explain yourselves and your commitment to the cause of Islam, Triumphant. The tapes will later be broadcast by al Iskandaria to inspire the masses and bring yet more volunteers. In the end, we cannot lose. There are over a billion of us; few of the crusaders."

Fadeel smiled benignly at the martyrs to be, the smile changing in a moment from benign to ferocious. Voice rising, he said, "By your courage, you will earn a place in Paradise and bring us victory here."

Al Kuwaylid Girls School, Ninewa, Sumer, 12/5/462 AC

Ishmael felt ridiculous. Worse than ridiculous, he felt *dirty*.

Bad enough they'd shaved his face and made it up to look more girlish. After Fadeel's people had rigged him with a suicide vest they dressed him in hijab and even added a veil! It hadn't been made any better by the profuse apologies and explanations they'd offered either.

Ishmael had grown up in liberal Akka. He didn't think girls were all that inferior a sex, or not more so than most boys anywhere on the planet would think. But for all that he didn't want to *be* one or to look like one.

They'd insisted though, harping on the theme of, "Your mother would be proud of you. More than changing clothes; she changed her entire *face*." In the end, of course, Ishmael had gone along, letting them shave him, make him up, load him with thirty pounds of explosive and shrapnel laden vest and bra, and rig him with a radio so that his handler could direct him and talk him through his part. They'd even coached him on walking like a girl, easier to seem to do in a burka than in any kind of infidel garb.

He wasn't allowed to drive himself to the vicinity of the school even though he'd had a license for almost two years.

"You don't know the area," Fadeel's people had explained. "You don't know which checkpoints are tighter than a houri's hole and which are manned by more easygoing sorts. You don't know where to park. Besides, how can your control direct you if he can't see you? You don't have the right accent if someone stops you. No, Martyr to the Cause," they'd insisted, "*we* will drive you."

Ishmael had been dropped off around the corner from the school. Doing his best to walk girlishly he'd turned that corner, walked about fifty meters forward and joined the stream of girls—some dressed in burkas or hijab and others in more modern clothing—that flowed through the gate and into the school yard.

Once inside the gate the girls who wore them had

begun immediately to remove their Islamic outer coverings. Several were quite pretty and shapely, Ishmael noticed, with big brown eyes being the norm. They spoke to each other in high musical voices he found most enchanting and . . .

"I can't do this," he said into the radio that ran from his explosive vest to an earpiece *cum* microphone. He turned to leave the school.

Sadly for Ishmael, more sadly for the girls at the school and their families, the radio had another purpose besides control. It also served as a remote detonator. With or without any words from Ishmael, the controller's instructions were to detonate it when a certain time had passed after Ishmael had walked through the gate or if it appeared he wanted to back out. That time was up. So was Ishmael's.

So was the girls'.

Balboa Camp, 12/5/462 AC

The bottoms of Carrera's and Sada's boots were stained red. That was as nothing to the red Carrera was seeing, a seething bloody red that arose to infuse his brain and cloud all his thoughts.

Fernandez was waiting for them at Carrera's and Lourdes' quarters. Lourdes was horrified, weeping. Carrera was simply outraged, though he mostly hid it behind an automatic stone mask.

"Have you seen the *al Iskandaria* broadcast, Patricio?" Fernandez asked, after Lourdes had dragged Carrera to a chair and forced a scotch over ice into his hand.

"No, why?" Carrera asked evenly.

"Our girlabomber was the son of that woman we had taken out in Akka, Layla Arguello. It was broadcast half an hour ago." Fernandez's look said more eloquently than could have any words, *And that's your fault.*

"Fuck."

"Fuck," Fernandez repeated. Neither he nor Sada bothered to remind Carrera of their advice concerning the family of the Arguello woman.

Unconsciously echoing Fadeel al Nizal's thoughts of a couple of days earlier, Sada observed, "Your Christian heritage of individual accountability has no use here, Patricio. It can never be of use in a place where the individual places so much importance on family ties. Moreover, you seem to insist that groups cannot be responsible for the actions of individuals. This is nonsense, my friend, and *worse,* it's immoral. Mothers and fathers raise their sons to be such and must be held accountable. Moreover, by your own laws of war you hold organizations accountable. When the organization is a family it is *illogical* not to hold them equally accountable."

Carrera leaned back in his chair and closed his eyes. It didn't help; he still saw a red-stained courtyard filled with the bodies and parts of bodies of young, innocent girls. *I become just like my enemy,* he thought. *Well, so be it then. After all, I'm already better than halfway there.*

"Is Fadeel responsible?" he asked.

"Clearly," Fernandez and Sada said together.

"Grab his family. Do it as soon as possible. Kill whomever we can't get at otherwise. All ages and sexes. *Punish this motherfucker!*"

"You don't really mean that, Patricio," Sada said. "We don't have to go that far."

"But you said . . ." Carrera began.

"I said you sometimes had to demonstrate a willingness to seriously hurt a tribe or family to control it. We can do that without exterminating it. Besides . . ."

"Besides?"

"You're not a complete barbarian, Patricio. Neither am I and neither is Omar, here. We still have to live with ourselves. We can be more selective."

Carrera breathed deeply, realizing what he had ordered. *Jesus, what am I becoming?*

"Thank you, my friend. Yes, please . . . be selective."

"Your boys, Adnan," Fernandez offered.

"Yes," the Sumeri agreed. "It will take a while to set up."

"Fine, so long as it gets done. I have to go to the FSC for a bit anyway."

Hamilton, FD, 21/5/462 AC

Campos was considerably warmer in his greetings than he had been the first time he and Carrera had met. He was practically effusive in shaking Carrera's hand and welcoming him back.

"Legate Hennessey, it is so good to see you once again."

"I go by Carrera now," came the dry answer. "That, or Pat."

"Fine, fine," Campos said. "I wanted to talk to you about your new and expanded area of responsibility.

That, and the way you are conducting the war in your sector."

"For that," Carrera answered, "I could have spoken to your commander in Sumer or your ambassador. I didn't need to traipse halfway across the world with my . . . secretary. And I fight the war in accordance with the law, so don't bother."

Campos decided to drop the question of war crimes. After all, technically the legion did stay within the bounds of the law, at least insofar as anyone could prove. Shrugging, he continued with the important part, "Both General Abramovitz and the Ambassador thought it would be better coming from me. They seem to feel you're maybe a little hard to control."

"I am," Carrera admitted. "I'd still have at least *listened*."

"I'm sure you would have," Campos tactfully lied. "By the way, how many men do you have in Sumer now?"

"About seventy-seven hundred. And another five thousand or so back home, not counting those still in initial training. Why?"

Campos didn't answer directly. Instead he asked, "And we're paying you how much?"

"Now? Now it's fifty-five percent of what it would cost you to field an equivalent combat force. It was just under eight billion per annum. It's now over twelve. It's *still* a bargain for you," he added.

"Didn't say it wasn't." Campos conceded easily. "It's a great bargain. *But* . . ."

"But?"

"We need to adjust your sector from what we originally agreed to."

I should have seen this coming, Carrera thought. "Show me."

Campos led him over to map spread across his desk.

"Going to cost you another one point two billion," Carrera announced when he had seen the border shift Campos wanted.

"We're already paying you the agreed rate," Campos insisted, growing heated.

"Let me point out that our current contract is not for major conventional operations," Carrera pointed out. He stuck his finger to the map, resting it on the midsized city of Pumbadeta, Sumer. "Your people lost control of that town months ago. To get it back . . . and . . ." Carrera thought for a moment before his face lit in a broad smile. "Ohhh, I see. You're having an election soon, aren't you? You need the town reduced before then, but you don't want to take any serious casualties before then, either."

Campos scowled but admitted the charge.

"Yes . . . well, our contract is for low intensity operations. This is something different. It's going to take a shitpot of ammunition, fuel, food, air movement. It's also likely to cost me a thousand men dead or wounded. For that matter, I really don't have the force yet. In another year I would . . ."

"We can't wait—"

". . . another year," Carrera finished. "Yes, I can understand that you can't wait. Even so, I don't have the forces myself."

"We can give you control of three or four battalions of ours, provided *you* do the bulk of the actual clearing," Campos conceded.

"No, you can't," Carrera contradicted. "I fight my way. The old way. The *true* law of war way. You either can't or won't."

"I don't see . . ."

Carrera clasped his hands behind his back, turned from the map, and began to pace. "Do you know how I'd take that place?" he asked. Without waiting for an answer he continued, "I'll surround it. I'll cut off the food. I'll announce what I'm doing and let leave only those I am required to allow out: the very sick, pregnant and nursing women, and such. I *will* check for actual pregnancy and actual illness. And I'll take my time about just when they'll be allowed to leave, too. After that, if any civilians try to escape I'll engage them and drive them back so that they help eat up the food. I will do my damnedest to destroy any food stocks I can identify, too. Any humanitarian effort to bring food in by ground will be stopped and the food confiscated. Any aerial attempt will be shot down; I do have that one maniple of air defense troops I've been using for checkpoints, after all."

He stopped his pacing and turned back to the map. One finger made a rotating motion over the spot of the city of Pumbadeta. "About a week or two after aerial reconnaissance informs me there isn't a dog or cat left walking the streets of the town—in other words when I am *sure* they've been eaten because the people are starving—I'll let the civilians out. The women and children, that is. No men will be allowed to leave, period. Then I'll let them starve some more. They'll attack, of course; it's a quicker death than starving. But I still won't let any out. And I will refuse to recognize any emissaries that try to surrender as lacking authority.

Individual attempts at surrender will be treated as the civilians were. After all, if I can engage civilians and use them as a weapon to eat up the food, then the law of war, despite what it seems to say about there being an absolute right to surrender, makes no sense if it requires that I let men, potentially armed men, go. Anyway, no surrender will be accepted until I am very nearly ready to assault. Then I'll go in and kill damned near everything.

"Now, Mr. Secretary, are you suggesting that FSA and FSMC troops will stand for that? That they'll be willing to shoot up women and kids to drive them back to starve? I don't think so. What's more, you don't want them to. Remember me? I'm supposed to be the heavy in this play."

"But in any case, I can't do it. Not counting the river, the place has a perimeter of nearly thirteen kilometers or about eight miles. That's too much for me alone while still clearing the place and holding the ZOR I already have, even with the Sumeris that *I*, at least, was smart enough to keep under arms."

"Well," Campos answered. He didn't even want to *think* about the disaster of letting all the Sumeri ex-soldiers go. "Maybe you can and maybe you can't. But I am allowed, by our *contract*, to adjust your boundaries in accordance with your combat strength and what we pay you for it. And remember that the penalty clauses run both ways. So, Bubba, you own Pumbadeta anyway. How you deal with it is your problem."

' Lourdes had expressed an interest in shopping and, since they had a couple of days before they had to return to Sumer and since Carrera knew the city—"I hate this fucking place!"—and she didn't, he took her on a shopping expedition.

He'd hired a car and driver from a limousine service, though he'd expressly insisted that they not be driven in a limo. "No damned tacky, nouveau riche, limousine bullshit," was the way he'd expressed it to the company. He'd also taken on three guards, fairly expensive, high-end guards, from a security company that was recommended to him by a friend in the War Department. A perusal of resumes led Carrera to call McNamara, who vouched for one bodyguard. That one vouched for the others.

Good as it's going to get, I suppose.

Lourdes had wanted to see the city as well, so the shopping trip began with a tour. For that, Carrera didn't need to hire anybody, though he took the guards along. He'd spent a few of the most miserable years of his life in Hamilton and knew where the monuments and museums were.

As they drove through the crowded streets, Lourdes looked out at the people. "The women all look so . . . desperate," she observed.

"They are," Carrera agreed. "This place not only has the greatest population, per capita, of young, unattached women in the world, most of them working for the FS government or companies that do business with the FS government, the women themselves tend to come here looking for husbands. And they're not just looking for any old husband. They want movers and shakers; rich and powerful men, preferably not too old. They have a hard time finding any and so their lives are lonely, and given the cost of living in this place and the need to dress for success the women here tend to become bitter and, yes, desperate very quickly."

The driver parked the car not very far from the War Department, in a multistory parking garage that attached to one of the major department stores.

Carrera expected Lourdes to head for "Ladies Fashions" immediately. He was surprised then, when instead she headed to "Children's."

Actually, surprised wasn't quite the word. Shocked silly? That came close.

"You're *what*?"

"About two months along, Patricio. You had so much on your mind I didn't want you to worry. Besides, I wasn't really *sure* until two weeks ago." She looked, unaccountably, shamefaced when she asked, "Do you mind?"

"Mind? Are you insane? It's . . . wonderful. But . . ."

"But?" the woman stiffened, waiting for the hammer to fall.

"What about your parents? We're not married."

Lourdes sighed. "Marriage would be . . . more proper, yes. But, in all the time you've lived among us you still haven't figured it out, have you? As long as I am your woman and you recognize the child as yours then marriage doesn't mean all that much extra. It's nice . . . it would be nice. But you don't have to marry me."

Carrera nodded. Yes, he'd known that at some level. He turned and asked a shop girl if the store had a jewelry department.

"No, sir. Sorry," had been the answer. "But there is a very nice one in the building next door."

"Let's try to do this as properly as we can, under

the circumstances," he said to Lourdes, taking her hand and leading her to an elevator. "First the proposal: will you marry me?"

Her eyes lit up happily as she answered, "Yes, of course."

"Good. Be awkward otherwise. Now let's go find a ring. *Then* we go shopping for the baby."

It was after looking at the thirty-fourth ring that it hit him. *Crap . . . two-edged sword. Now the enemy has something to use against me, if I go after their families. Note to self, security detail for Lourdes, soonest. Obstetrician, soonest. Bunker the living hell out of our quarters at Camp Balboa, soonest.*

Later, in the hotel where he'd rented a suite, Carrera mentally kicked himself for not having noticed her breasts had, in fact, swollen noticeably already. She actually looked better than she ever had. Where she'd once been rather girlishly slender, now hips and breasts had both filled out a bit, making her look more womanly. Also more desirable, if that were possible.

He looked at her nipples, lovely pert things, and said, "If I sucked those as hard as I liked, I'm afraid I'd hurt you. And your breasts have got to be tender now. If I did hurt you by playing with them too roughly, I apologize."

She just smiled as she gathered his head to her chest. She had him now and she knew it.

"Suck them as hard as you want," she said in a husky voice. "Play with them as roughly as you want. I'll tell you if it ever gets too hard or too rough. But . . . I *like* it . . . and they're there for *you*."

Ciudad Balboa, 23/5/462 AC

From Hamilton Lourdes and Carrera had flown north to Balboa. After the endless dun color of the Sumeri desert and the mud brick of both city and base, followed by the barren stone of Hamilton, the country that passed beneath the airplane windows looked almost shockingly green.

"I'd almost forgotten . . ." Lourdes whispered.

"There are reasons green is the more or less sacred color of Islam," Carrera observed. "It is very beautiful, though, isn't it? It'll be good to be home for a week."

The charter jet had landed and taxied to the military terminal on the other side of the airfield from the civilian one. Parilla, Jimenez, most of the staff and Esterhazy were there to greet Carrera and Lourdes. Carrera was unsurprised at being met by a band of pipes and drums. He was more than a little surprised that he was also met by what appeared to be a full infantry cohort, supported by tanks, and with aircraft circling overhead.

"It's the Taurans," Parilla explained, when Carrera's surprise became obvious. "Remember, there's a warrant for your arrest from the Cosmopolitan Criminal Court. The government is being openly ambivalent about it, but there's no doubt they'd like to see you and me both gone. And since the Taurans are here the civil government has started to use the police and military police to push us a bit. They've sacked some of our friends in the Civil Force and most of the rest are running scared. I can't go anywhere anymore without an armed guard. Neither can most of our higher commanders. I'll be glad when the base on the *Isla Real* is finished and we can move our enterprise there completely."

"The sale is going through then?" Carrera asked. With everything else on his mind in Sumer he hadn't really followed developments in Balboa as closely as he might have wished to.

Esterhazy answered, "Oh, yes. Ve haff already bought vell ofer half ze island, plus *Isla* San Juan and *Isla* Santa Paloma. Ve haff options on most of ze rest.

"Some of the gringos who built houses along the beaches didn't want to sell," Parilla added with a smile. "But we opened up about twelve square kilometers as an artillery and mortar impact area and, once their sleep started being interrupted nightly by exploding shells, they dropped their opposition and became, oh, ever so much more cooperative.

"For now," Parilla continued, "we have about half the casernes about half built. Sitnikov is over there supervising. In a year, or maybe a year and a half, we'll be able to move most of the enterprise to the island."

"Speaking of Sitnikov and his projects, how is the boys' school going?" Carrera asked.

"First stop on the tour that begins tomorrow," Parilla answered. "For now, we're heading to the *Casa* Linda where you and Lourdes can rest. We're having a big dinner for you two, the staff, and key commanders."

Puerto Lindo, Balboa, 24/5/462 AC

Balboa had free and compulsory education. Sort of. Between the need for parents, often poor parents, to buy school uniforms for their children, along with books, paper, writing implements . . . well, it was actually a fairly expensive proposition. That the country still had, despite this, one of the highest literacy rates on Terra Nova was testament to the value the people placed on education.

Still, it *was* an expense. So when a new school, the *Academia Militar Sergento Juan Malvegui*, had been created promising not only free uniforms, but free everything including room and board, many parents had jumped at it. The kids even received a small stipend. Not that it was open to everyone. Prospective students had to be male, of the right age, in perfect health, and pass what amounted to an IQ test. Only about one in five of the applicants had been accepted.

The academy was sited at an old stone fortress from the second century after colonization. The fortress looked out over an almost perfectly rectangular bay and had been intended to defend the bay from the Anglian and Gallic pirates that had once infested the Shimmering Sea.

A mix of Volgan, Balboan and FSC instructors and cadre manned the school. These, bright and early, were out with the boys on the fortress' broad green parade ground. The school commandant, Carrera, and Sitnikov stood atop a covered reviewing stand on one side of the parade field.

"They have academics four days a week," Sitnikov

explained, leaning over to speak into Carrera's ear. He'd flown in the night before from the *Isla Real* expressly to show off his handiwork. "Two days are devoted to more military subjects. On the last day they rest, as the Bible insists. This summer will be their first. Half of it will be spent in a military course. The other half will be vacation at home . . . if they want vacation."

The school's adjutant, a crusty old Volgan, reported to the commandant. Salutes were exchanged and the commandant ordered, "Pass in review."

There was no band. Perhaps it could come later. For now, the green- and gray-uniformed boys sang wherever they marched, something they had apparently picked up from their Volgan instructors.

As the first company of about one hundred and fifty boys wheeled and began to march past the reviewing stand, Carrera heard them sing:

> *Juventud adelante, cantando feliz*
> *Si hay sol o si llueve*
> *Juventud adelante, cantando feliz*
> *A muerte o victoria*
> *Assaltamos el mundo con pasos fuertes . . .*

Carrera looked upon the marching boys' dark faces and bright eyes with a smile. "Very good," he judged, nodding slowly. Then, turning slightly to Sitnikov, he asked, "The other five schools?"

"Next year two more will have been built. This group will be split into three, one for each of the schools. They'll be able to assume some of the leadership responsibilities themselves, which will allow us to use fewer cadre members, per capita. Teachers for civilian subjects are like beans; we'll just buy more. The following year the last three academies will be built. We'll split the student body again. After that, it's just maintenance. It's not particularly cheap, though. Each one of these kids costs about seven thousand drachma a year to keep clothed, fed and educated. When all six schools are filled with their full compliment of eighteen hundred kids it will cost almost eighty million drachma a year."

"Small change," Carrera scoffed. "Eighty million for nearly eleven thousand fanatical potential infantry? A bargain. Besides, we have the money."

But I have to take that fucking hellhole, Pumbadeta, to keep the money flowing. Bastard, Campos. Shit.

Enroute to Ninewa Airport, 27/5/462 AC

The legion AN-21 was something less than comfortable. Lourdes didn't complain, though, and Carrera hardly noticed. She slept with her head on his shoulder and he with his cheek resting against the top of her head.

Halfway through the flight, he suddenly sat erect, waking her and causing concern among the crew. He cursed himself for an idiot.

"Sorry, Lourdes," he apologized. Carrera then walked to the cockpit and asked if it was possible to make a telephone call to Hamilton, FD. Assured that it was, he gave the radioman/navigator a number to dial.

"Mr. Secretary? Carrera. I can do it. But it's still going to cost you the extra figure I quoted. And I *am* going to need those battalions you promised."

Pumbadeta, Sumer, 35/5/462 AC

The FS Marines never patrolled the streets of the city anymore, Fadeel was pleased to see. Moreover, whoever among the local police had not come over was surely cooperating anyway. Perhaps the entire family hanging by their necks from one of the bridges over the river had something to do with that.

This had not been the first family put to death in the city, of course, merely the first for whose execution Fadeel had been present. It had been a grisly, awful thing, even by Fadeel's atrophied moral standards. The father and mother had been forced to watch first as each of their five children, aged four to eleven, were hoisted up. The ropes were thick and the children light. After watching for a quarter of an hour of slow strangulation, the children's faces slowly purpling and their legs kicking frantically for purchase, Fadeel had told his men to hang onto the legs to put the kids out of their misery. Both mother and father had been too grief-stricken, horrified and shocked, thereafter, to even struggle as the ropes were placed around their own necks. They'd died more quickly and far more easily than had the children.

A small price to pay, however distasteful, to ensure the rest cooperate, was Fadeel's judgment.

And cooperation had indeed been forthcoming. Crews of conscripted civilians dug ditches and tunnels wherever they were directed to. Streets were being blocked off; mines, booby traps and improvised explosive devices were being set all across the city. More than twenty-five hundred holy warriors, too, had gathered for a climactic showdown. Best of all, the cost of stockpiling food for the coming siege—and there would. be something like a siege, Fadeel was certain of it—had been borne by various worldwide humanitarian organizations. Since more than a few of these were Islamic, supply of ammunition had also been seen to.

We'll make the infidels pay a price in blood that will open their eyes to the truth, Fadeel thought, *that they can never pacify and control Islamic lands.*

INTERLUDE

6 Jumadah I, 1529 (20 May, 2105 AD),
Makkah al Jedidah (New Mecca), Al Donya
al Jedidah (the New World)

Abdul ibn Fahad wasn't entirely comfortable with
the new calendar system. He still went by the old,
though he also—as a very holy man—kept both sets
of religious holidays and festivals. That took up quite
a bit of time. Worse, celebrating two Ramadans a
year was exhausting. Fortunately, at least occasionally
they coincided.

In twenty-one years they had coincided twice. In
twenty-one years the population of the colony had
blossomed. Not only did the women bear children in
vast numbers, but every month it seemed new ships
arrived bearing colonists from among the most faithful, the most traditional, back on Earth. The colonists,
of course, brought many slaves with them to tend
to the farming. It was well that they did so; the life
expectancy of a slave was naturally lower than that
for a freeborn man.

Sitting, as it did, at the confluence of two streams,

Makkah al Jedidah was green and lush and lovely. This was as it should be, as this was a holy place, especially marked by Allah to be a reminder of the blessing of Paradise that awaited the Faithful.

Farther out, the greenery lessened. It was hardly noticeable to the new colonists, coming as they did from the barren deserts of Old Earth. As more people arrived, more trees had to be cut for their homes. As more people arrived so, too, they brought more domestic animals with them. These ate the grass. The goats, in particular, ate the grass down to the roots. Without trees, without grass, the sand blew. Already, one of the two streams that fed the settlement was noticeably shallower than it had been.

Abdul didn't worry about that. *It is good,* he thought, *if by the Grace of Allah we return here to the desert from whence we sprang. Life has been too easy. Too much green and the faithful might forget that greenery is the gift of the Almighty. A green and holy Makkah al Jedidah should be enough to remind them of the bounty that awaits in the hereafter.*

The hereafter was more and more on Abdul's mind of late. He hadn't been precisely a young man when he'd made the *hejira* to the new world. Now he was well advanced in years. Soon, very soon, his time would come.

CHAPTER THIRTY-ONE

I will leave your flesh on the mountains, and fill the
valleys with your carcasses. I will water the land with
what flows from you, and the river beds shall be filled
with your blood. When I snuff you out I will cover
the heavens, and all the stars will darken.

—Ezekiel 32: 5-7

Northern Boundary, Ninewa Province, Sumer

It began with a gradual repositioning of troops along
the boundary. From all appearances, this was merely
an attempt to seal off infiltration into the BZOR from
the insurgent held city of Pumbadeta. There were
a fair number of firefights, mostly in the nature of
ambushes, over the following week. Some of those
were staged purely for show but some really did stop
infiltrating vehicles and small units of insurgents.

The other effect the move had was that it placed
the troops an average of fifty miles closer to the town.
It also put them within one day's very hard march.

Moreover, a fair amount of artillery was moved into range, ostensibly to support the interdiction line. Lastly, because the interdiction line was somewhat remote from any substantial place of habitation, it lessened the chances that anyone would report the sudden move away from that line, either by foot or by helicopter, in anything like a timely fashion.

Pumbadeta, Sumer, 1/7/462 AC

The stars were unseen through the cloud cover over the city as the remotely piloted vehicle made its pass. The RPV was nearly silent. Certainly, it was quiet enough that no one noticed it over the normal noise of the place.

Normally it might have been seen, of course, by any of the city's population of nearly three hundred thousand or by any of the now three thousand, approximately, of the mujahadin who had also taken up residence. The cloud over the city prevented that. The cover did not, could not, prevent the thermal imagers the RPV carried from seeing down and recording the town below. Among other things, the operator of the RPV, sitting comfortably in a cool adobe building in Balboa Base, was counting dogs and cats running free in the town.

Cloud cover overhead could not prevent the people, or the mujahadin, from seeing outward, though, as hundreds of helicopter sorties landed and took off, removing the FSMC troops who had been partially investing the city for some months. After giving the populace of the town a good look at the Marines leaving, the Marine artillery and mortars expended their white phosphorus and HC, hexacloroethane-zinc, shells to screen the pickup zones.

Thus, the mujahadin, no great shakes at patrolling in the desert anyway and very loathe to risk fighting the Marines in the open, really didn't see the men of the deployed cohorts of the 1st through 4th Infantry *Tercios* of the *Legio del Cid* as the men landed in the helicopters ostensibly coming in to pull Marines out. Nor, given the dark, did they notice that not all the helicopters inbound were of the types favored by the FMC's armed forces.

Camp Balboa, Ninewa, Sumer

In the cool adobe building, more of a bunker really, the RPV's controller watched his screen. He pulled back on his stick slightly and nudged it to the left, causing his bird to begin a slow left-banking spiral up to height. As it gained altitude, more of the city spread out below on the green-toned control monitor.

The city abutted the river at a spot where it turned south, then north, then south again to form an N. By that N, coming from the city to the west of the river and continuing on, was a highway that cut through the center of town. East were two bridges, close together. It was too far up for the RPV pilot to make out how many bodies were hanging by the neck from the spans. Previous flights had seen a variable number from four to, on one day, thirty-one. Some of those bodies had seemed very small, even to the distant pilot.

The town jutted out west of the river. It was almost

rectangular and about three kilometers, north to south, by perhaps five, east to west. A multilane highway ran northwest to southeast, west of the town. The narrower highway, Highway 1, ran through the town from a cloverleaf on the major highway to the two bridges over the river.

As the RPV inched higher, more and more of first the city and then the surrounding lands became visible. Lights marked landing/pickup zones where groups of men, their body heat gleaming on the monitor, boarded hot-engined helicopters.

The command post for the legion was lit red inside. The usual ceiling fans turned slowly and, for the most part, silently overhead. Messengers and staff officers hurried to and fro on various missions. Not all of those messengers were legion troops, either. There were plenty of Sada's Sumeris and more than a few FS Marines. Briefings were being conducted in three languages in different corners of the CP.

"I wish to hell my men and I were going in with you," the crusty FS Marine Corps colonel told Carrera.

"No, you don't," Carrera corrected. "Trust me on this; it's going to be nasty and the nastiest part isn't even going to be the fighting."

"Even so," the Marine countered, "It's going to be the best brawl since Gia Long, in the Cochin War. My boys will hate to miss it."

"Well . . . maybe we'll save you some. You just make sure that things here don't go to shit while we're gone."

"No chance of that," the Marine assured the legate. "I've got all three of my battalions, plus another two coming from the army, to hold down your ZOR. Plus, you're leaving me enough Sumeri and Balboan liaison that we won't exactly be strangers. And I'll have that one battalion of Sada's troops; they look pretty competent. We'll do fine."

I hope to fuck you do. Carrera was actually desperately worried about the situation in the BZOR. He, Sada and most of their troops were going to be gone for over a month, possibly two. A lot of unpleasantness could come to pass in even a month.

Still, they are FS Marines, good troops. Campos could have given me Tauros to cover my sector in my absence. Thank God for small blessings.

Landing/Pickup Zone Bluejay, 1400 meters north of Pumbadeta, Sumer

Carrera had had Jimenez flown in two weeks prior just for this operation. He'd been the first Balboan on the ground, arriving to coordinate with the Marines ten days prior to the shuffle.

A young tribune commanding a maniple ran from a group that had just debarked from a Marine helicopter and reported to Jimenez. "Sir, Tribune Rodriguez, Maniple B, 2nd Cohort, 3rd Tercio, Commanding. Where do you want us?"

"You brought the mines?"

"Yes, sir," Rodriguez answered. "Every man is carrying a couple and the helicopters left us six bundles with . . . well, shit, sir . . . *craploads.* Plus a fuck of a lot of wire and stakes. We can mine and wire maybe three kilometers. I counted the wire before we left.

It was six hundred rolls and maybe fifteen hundred stakes."

Jimenez nodded. "Good." His finger pointed in the dark. "See that red chemlight to the right, Tribune?"

Rodriguez looked, saw it and answered, "Yes, sir."

"Your sector starts there and then works over to the left along the berm the FS Marines left us. You'll know when to stop when your line reaches the green chemlight to the left. Occupy and then move forward to just outside effective small arms range. Then mine and wire in. Don't forget to tie in with the units to your left and right."

"Yes, sir. I won't, sir. I mean, no problem, sir."

"Good lad. Off with you now."

There had been four Marine battalions surrounding the town. This was not considered enough to take it. It would have been enough to seal it off *if* they had really been permitted to seal it off. They hadn't.

Each of the Marine battalions was flying out by one or two pickup zones. The legion and most of Sada's brigade were flying in via the same spots. The continuous landing and lifting of masses of helicopters raised a cloud of dust that spread for miles downwind.

Sneezing at the dust assailing his nose, Fadeel climbed to one of the highest spots in the city—a thin, graceful minaret that soared over the walled compound of a mosque. Try as he might, Fadeel had never been able to obtain one of the thermal imagers the FS forces seemed to use everywhere. He did have a number of Volgan-built passive vision devices—relatively cheap and simple light amplification scopes—but these were much inferior. In any case, it had proven impossible to train his men to use them or, as important, maintain them. He did have a few superior Haarlem- and FSC-made passive vision scopes, but these used odd batteries and were, for the most part, useless now.

Harder to get a hold of the batteries than it is to get explosives, Fadeel thought bitterly. He had no idea that many an FS Army and FS Marine Corps supply sergeant had had the same thought over the years.

The scope Fadeel had with him he had batteries for, enough, at least, for a few nights' work. It had once been mounted on a rifle. That mounting was broken now, had been broken, as a matter of fact, in the action in which the scope had been captured. Still, it did perfectly good service, if only for reconnaissance.

Fadeel flicked a switch. The scope came on without the noticeable and annoying hum of the Volgan versions. He raised it to his eye. A folding rubber sphincter kept the green glow of the thing from lighting up that eye as a target for a sniper until it was safely pressed to his face.

From this vantage point Fadeel could see west, southwest, and south. The lights of the helicopters that landed and took off in seemingly endless numbers drew lines in the scope. They were not bright enough to permanently harm it, however. Looking down, Fadeel saw groups of men stringing wire. Some of them seemed to be laying mines.

"What? Do the crusader Marines think I am stupid enough to attack them in the open where they have all the advantages? Not likely, that. I could order some

sniping, I suppose, but to what purpose? They're too far away to hit—and despite having a fair number of sniper rifles Fadeel knew his men were not great shots at any range—*and the return fire might be devastating. Besides, what do I care if they wire in the whole city? The humanitarians will still make sure we are fed. "It's for the children, after all."* Fadeel laughed softly and bitterly, thinking of very small bodies hanging from the bridge behind him. *"For the children."*

While Fadeel sneered, high, high above those gently swaying bodies the NA-23 nicknamed *Lolita* circled. *Lolita* carried, this sortie, five two-thousand pound bombs. Another five were carried in her sister, *Anabelle*. It was believed that the bridge that could take four of five direct strikes with two-thousand pounders hadn't been built yet and, even if it had, it had certainly not been built in Sumer.

The bombs were only a moderately heavy load, but most of the extra two and a half tons more lift still available to the planes was taken up with fuel. The aircraft could loiter for quite some time.

Ninewa-Pumbadeta Highway

Sumer's old dictator, Saleh, had expended considerable capital on modernizing the country, though "modernization" was, itself, a word open to some interpretation. One of these programs had been to give Sumer a truly modern highway system. It would have been more accurate to say that Saleh had given Sumer a post-modern highway system, in the same sense that post-modernity meant familial corruption, vice, graft, kickbacks, bribes . . . and a shoddy product.

Carrera had actually spent quite a bit of the legion's money, and hanged more than a few Sumeris who sought graft, turning that highway system into a model within the BZOR.

Despite the improvements, the armored columns stayed off the asphalt highway except at the bridges over streams and irrigation canals. There was no better way for a heavy force to strangle itself, logistically, than to drive on and thereby destroy the very roads down which ran its lifeblood of fuel, food, parts and ammunition. The columns raised great clouds of dust. With the wind blowing from the west this was little problem to the drivers of the westernmost column. For the soft-skinned, untracked vehicles, which included the military police, engineers, and artillery prime movers moving along the hard surfaced road, and for the other armored column moving in the dirt east of those, it was a misery of choking, stinging dust.

A PSYOP vehicle, a four-wheel-drive light truck, preceded the column. Loudspeakers mounted on it proclaimed that any interference with the column would mean the destruction of whatever town the interference was met in. The tone of the speaker and the words suggested very strongly that the people of such a town would not survive the experience. There was, unsurprisingly, no resistance whatsoever. The people stayed inside and closed the shutters to their hovels, each of them hoping that no hothead would take a shot at the foreign soldiers. In several cases village elders confiscated arms and held them in order to prevent any such incident.

NA-23, *Lolita*, above Pumbadeta

Jimenez's voice crackled in Miguel Lanza's headphones. "What have you got for me, *Lolita*?"

"X-ray Juliet Five Two this is *Lolita*. I'm two NA-23s out of Ninewa Air Base carrying five two-thousand pounders, each, on GLS guidance systems. Per coordination my mission is to take out the bridges."

"Do it, *Lolita*."

"Wilco, out."

The previous jury-rigged bombing system was history now. Instead of that, there was a specially built rack and drop system that could be installed for those rare occasions when a cargo aircraft was called on to do double duty as a precision bomber.

Lanza flicked the switch for the ramp, which lowered itself with a vibrating, hydraulic hum. He was lead bird, thus he didn't have to buck the turbulence of a Nabakov ahead of him. At this altitude, and despite the season, cold air rolled in as soon as the ramp began to drop. The strong smell of kerosene exhaust entered the aircraft along with the thin, cold air. To Lanza the stench of the burnt kerosene was perfume. He smiled broadly.

If there was going to be any substantial error on the bombing run, it was going to be along the axis of flight. Lanza played with his controls, hand and foot both, and brought the throttle down to reduce speed. A tone sounded in his headphones as he passed precisely through a checkpoint.

"Pilot to crew, five minutes. Stand by to roll."

"Chief to pilot, bomb crew standing by."

Lanza waited for another tone, the one that would tell him to begin the bombing run. It came quickly. He keyed his microphone again, saying, "Roll to the ramp."

He couldn't feel the bomb crew straining muscle to move the thing down the line to the ramp. He could and did feel the vibration of the bomb itself as it rattled along horizontally, then the final *kachunk* as the crew eased it into the down-angled cradle that held it locked in position on the ramp itself. *Lolita* nosed upward slightly with the rearward weight shift and Lanza adjusted the controls, his left arm pushing on the yoke while that thumb played with the trim button to keep her level. Another tone. "Releasing." For a brief moment he felt overweight as the plane ballooned slightly, then weightless as it dropped. Lanza's right hand adjusted the throttle to increase speed. No sense in hanging around, after all. Despite intel, the enemy just might have something in the way of air defense. Besides, he had to get well out of the way of *Anabelle*, coming in close behind.

Lanza turned hard left, flipping his night vision goggles down and looking towards the ground. He didn't expect to see the bomb hit the target; there was too much cloud cover for that. But just seeing the flash was satisfying all on its own. Besides, he knew that all bombs were one hundred percent accurate. They never failed to hit the ground.

"I love my job," he said aloud, as the flash of the two-thousand pounder lit up the clouds around him.

Fadeel heard the aircraft overhead, but distantly, as if they were a noise coming from another room.

He didn't hear the whistle of the bombs until after the first explosion.

"What the . . . ?" he asked aloud from his perch on the trembling minaret. *Why would the crusaders drop the bridges?*

Hastily, he descended from the minaret to where a few of his subordinates waited below. "Go to the bridges. Investigate."

Fadeel wasn't worried. *What matter if they take out the bridges,* he thought. *The worst it means is that we get no more resupply by that route. The Kosmos will find another.*

"X-ray Juliet, this is *Lolita*. Request bomb damage assessment on the bridges."

"One's down, one's still standing," Jimenez answered. "The northern bridge is the one down. Repeat on the southern."

"Wilco, X-ray Juliet. *Lolita*, out."

This time, both *Lolita* and *Anabelle* dropped. The southern bridge went down.

"*Lolita* this is X-ray Juliet. Both bridges are down. Go to your secondary targets."

"Roger, X-ray Juliet. Heading for food warehouse number one now. Note, X-ray, we've got two more birds inbound. The warehouses are priority targets for them."

"Roger," Jimenez answered. "So long as the food is destroyed, out."

The messenger stopped at the base of the minaret and gasped out, "*Sayidi,* they're going after the food stockpiles."

Fadeel's eyes went wide. What was wrong with these crusaders? Didn't they understand that the entire world would condemn them for destroying food? Didn't they *care*?

"By Allah," he whispered, a measure of truth finally dawning on him, "what will we do if the crusaders stop *caring* about their image among their undeclared enemies?"

Pumbadeta, Sumer, 2/7/462 AC

"Tighter than a houri's hole," Sada announced triumphantly, when Carrera emerged from the IM-71 helicopter that had carried him down to the landing zone west of the city where he planned to make his command post.

"It's cut off," Jimenez agreed. "So far, there's been no reaction. I mean, I expected *something* by now. A probe . . . some mortar fire . . . maybe a little sniping. But . . . nothing."

"I don't think they contemplated the possibility of being *actually* besieged," Carrera said. "If you look at it from their point of view, they had no worries. They had absolute political control of the town; their logistics were being handled by the Kosmos; and the FSC's coalition was obviously unwilling to risk the casualties."

"Big mistake on their part," Sada said. "Speaking of the Kosmos, Patricio, there's a representative of GraceCorps that wants to speak to you, a Ms. Lindemann. They've got a column of trucks loaded with food that we stopped."

"Fine. I expected that, or something like that, anyway. I'll speak with her."

Sada pointed at a long line of tractor-trailers, led by a white-painted sedan. "She's over there."

Carrera didn't consider GraceCorps to be the enemy. Did he think they were stupid? Absolutely. Misinformed? Generally. Inexact? Especially. Hopelessly optimistic? Of course. But they weren't the enemy. They did what they did, help the needy, and they did it rather better than most of their sort. They were among the few Kosmos of whom it could be said, in his opinion, that they were more interested in doing good than in doing well.

So he was polite, unusually so for him in his dealings with the Kosmos.

Smiling affably, he began, "Ms. Lindemann, how can I help you?"

She smiled as well. "You could begin, sir, by having your men let us through."

He shook his head, as if with regret. "No . . . no. I'm afraid that won't be possible. This town is besieged."

Lindemann didn't seem to understand. "What difference does that make?"

"It means we've cut off all access. If you have medicine that might be needed by the inhabitants, I can arrange an airdrop. The law of war requires that. But no food is going in and no people are coming out anytime soon."

"You can't do that!"

"Why?" Carrera's face seemed genuinely puzzled.

"Food's a *human right*," she answered. "Those people will starve."

"So?"

She opened her mouth again, as if to speak. No words came out.

Carrera reached into his pocket and pulled out a small sheaf of folded paper. This he handed over, saying, "This is the law of war as regards sieges. I intend to abide by it completely. Read it, then come back to me. Note that while the country that has sponsored us, Balboa, is a signatory to the Additional Protocols, neither my organization, nor our principles, the Federated States, are."

Lindemann was at least somewhat familiar with the laws of war. After all, her organization often came in on the tail end of human-inspired and created destruction.

"You're required to let out pregnant women, the very ill, and very young children," she said.

"Really? What a surprise," Carrera answered. Then he asked his own question. "When?"

Lindemann looked confused. "When?"

"Yes. *When* does the law of war say I must let them go? I'll save you the trouble. It doesn't."

"But the garrison may not feed them!" she countered.

"That'll be their doing, not mine," he answered.

At that time another series of explosions rocked the town. Even at this distance, several kilometers, Lindemann and Carrera were rocked by the blasts.

"What was that?" she asked.

"We're destroying the food stocks in the town," he answered, calmly. "This is a *siege*, Ms. Lindemann, not a game. This is war, not a boxing match. Now, you can take your trucks back, or you can sit here, or you can do whatever you like . . . *except* resupply that city. That you will not be permitted to do."

"What about when the people try to escape? You know they will."

"Then, Ms. Lindemann, we will do what the law of war permits. Besides, before they get out they'll have to clear mines. They're not really equipped for that. We won't let them, anyway."

"You *are* going to let them out at some point, aren't you, Patricio?" Jimenez asked.

"'Course I am, Xavier. I can't tell you when, exactly. I'll let the Kosmos beg, and chide and nag for ten days or maybe a couple of weeks. Then, I'll exact some concessions from them. I'm still thinking about what concessions I'll want. Maybe we'll make them grovel and thank us for abiding so completely by the law of war. Maybe we'll just make them feed us first. Maybe both and maybe more.

"After that, we'll drop some leaflets and let the pregnant women and the sick out. Then the Kosmos can care for them a few miles downstream."

Pumbadeta, Sumer, 9/7/462 AC

The leaflets fell from the sky—specifically, they were dropped by Crickets—before sunrise. On one side they showed pictures and diagrams of who would be allowed out and where. The pictures showed one woman with a large belly, a man on a stretcher, and a very small child. The diagram was simply the place where Highway 1 met the encircling berms and minefields.

More complex instructions were written on the back. Most of Pumbadeta's adult residents, male and even female, could read.

Fadeel was mixed about the prospect. Food was already scarce; this would reduce the number of mouths he had to feed. On the other hand, he was counting on the presence of large numbers of noncombatants, when the assault finally came, to sully the reputation of the coalition. Then he remembered:

This part of the coalition doesn't care a goat's ass for their reputation with the humanitarians. They'll kill without compunction. Better, then, to let go whoever will be allowed out, to stretch out the food that remains.

Three hundred thousand people, give or take, had been trapped when the siege fell on the city like a thunderclap. Of those, perhaps five or six thousand were truly sick. An additional ten or eleven thousand women may have been pregnant or nursing. And there were many small children.

Nothing like that number came out. Nursing women would be allowed to leave, but what if they had children over the age of six, which was Carrera's stated cut off? Would they leave those behind? For the most part, they would not. What about women with children who would be allowed out as well as children who would not be? They tended to stay behind as well. And the sick? If they were truly ill, they needed to be carried. Stretcher bearers from the legion were standing by to take their litters. Few men inside the town were willing to bear them to the demarcation berm.

In all, perhaps five thousand, or a few more, of

the citizens of the town actually left. Then the wall closed down again.

As that wall closed, Fernandez and his people, supplemented by Sada's, descended on the refugees, pumping them, without violence, for any information they might have on the defenses and the defenders. Most knew little. A few were better informed.

"Why so few sick?" Lindemann asked. When Carrera explained, she volunteered, on behalf of herself and her workers, to go in and carry the deathly ill out.

"No . . . you would just be held and become hostages," he answered, feeling a measure of grudging admiration. "They get out on their own, or with the help of those inside, or they stay there. I'm still willing to airdrop medicine, remember."

"What good is medicine without doctors to administer it?" she asked.

"Not my concern. But if you can talk Mustafa into letting Doctor Nur al-Deen—he's the enemy's overall number two, you know?—jump in by parachute, I'll be glad to let him do so. Course, I'll hang the bastard right after we take the town."

Pumbadeta, Sumer, 11/7/462 AC

The air defense maniple that loosely ringed the city was useful only for low flying aircraft. For any that flew higher Carrera had Turbo-Finches armed with machine gun pods. These, with a top speed of only about two hundred and fifty miles per hour, were extremely poor interdiction aircraft.

On the other hand, the Castilla-built Hacienda-121

was a very good light cargo aircraft, but its top speed was only two hundred and twenty-five miles an hour. Thus, when the pilot of the circling Turbo-Finch saw the Hacienda kicking bundles out the door, he had little trouble closing the distance and investigating. The Hacienda was decorated with a Red Crescent, sign of the Islamic version of the Red Cross. The serial numbers on the side of the Hacienda indicated Yithrabi registration.

Since he was weapons free, meaning he could engage any aircraft that fit his rules of engagement, and since he was expressly instructed not to permit any airdrops or aerial deliveries into the town without prior authorization, he armed his gun pods. If he worried even in the slightest about his commander's reaction to his shooting down a civilian aircraft he had only to remember that this was the third anniversary of a very important date to that commander.

It was unlikely that Carrera would mind, *today*, if he dropped a nuke.

Before shooting, though, the Finch pilot tried to warn the Hacienda off with a burst that flew parallel to the cargo plane. The plane shuddered, as if the pilot were surprised, but quickly got back on course. It was as if the Hacienda pilot simply couldn't believe that anyone would violate the rules the Kosmos had set up to protect just such activities. At that point, the Finch pilot shifted slightly to line his guns up, and opened fire with a short burst of several hundred rounds. Perhaps a third of these impacted the Hacienda, which heeled over to one side and began a rapid smoking descent to the ground.

And that was the last attempt at aerial resupply of the town by any Kosmo organization.

✧   ✧   ✧

"Don't you have any sense of humanity?" Lindemann asked, furious and in tears.

Carrera thought about that for a few seconds before answering, "As you would define it? Perhaps not. Am I supposed to? If so, why?"

Fadeel was shocked, *shocked* at seeing the Hacienda go down in flames. He'd never believed any of his enemies would have the sheer . . . the sheer . . .

They're as ruthless as I am. And much better armed. I'd better figure a way out of here for myself and my key subordinates or I'm screwed.

The sun had set several hours prior, leaving three spark-bright moons to shine onto the planet. They would set about midnight. In those hours, Fadeel had massed just over three hundred of his mujahadin and a thousand unarmed civilians in buildings on the north side of town, at a place where the ground was a bit rougher and where a man, once free of the encirclement, might have a chance to escape. He told his followers that this was a raid with the purpose of getting into the besiegers' rear area and ruining their supply arrangements. Liberally doped with hashish as many of those followers were, there had been no questions.

Ordinarily, Fadeel would have waited until perhaps three in the morning to launch his raid. That would be the time when the enemy would be at his lowest level of alert. Unfortunately, that would also not give him enough darkness before sunrise to effect his escape. The attack would be at midnight.

✧   ✧   ✧

The legion had purchased two NA-23s for the express purpose of converting them to aerial gunships. Eventually, there would be four in a deployed legion, twenty total for the entire force, but for now, two would have to do. These were just enough, with maintenance schedules, to keep one on station throughout the night, most nights. Instead of "NA," these birds bore the designation "ANA"; "A" for Attack.

Out the left-hand side of each of the planes stuck the muzzles of five tri-barrel fifty caliber machine guns. These were chain guns, driven by electric motors to very high rates of fire, eighteen hundred rounds per minute, per gun. Between the five of them, the planes could spit out nine thousand rounds in just sixty seconds. The guns were carefully aligned so that number three, in the center of the left-hand side, fired to the center of the beaten zone, number one fired high, number five low, and two and four in between. The guns were somewhat loosely mounted as a certain amount of spread was deemed desirable.

Modifying the planes had not been particularly cheap. It had seemed worthwhile, therefore, to give each a fairly sophisticated suite of sensors, especially low light television and thermal imagers. The thermals alone were an appreciable percentage of the cost of the final system.

The price had been worth it. Alerted of the assembling enemy by the ever-roaming RPVs, the one ANA-23 on station was waiting when the mujahadin and the civilians emerged from their cover.

The gunner for the plane tapped his monitor to mark one edge of the enemy formation. He then tapped the perceived center of mass, and then the other end of the group. A computer registered the taps and calculated a flight path and attitude for optimal dispersion of fire. This was fed to the pilot's console automatically. The pilot aligned his plane on the calculated path, heeled over and began his firing run.

Fadeel's men crept forward, driving the civilians before them, toward the enemy-held berm that surrounded the town. He and his select followers waited in the covering buildings for a path to be breached. *Any minute now . . .*

"*Il hamdu l'illah!*" Fadeel exclaimed when the eye-searing lines began to burn down from the heavens onto his men. "I never saw—"

He stopped speaking when the near horizon lit up with what appeared to be a moving wall of flame.

Not only had the RPV alerted the ANA-23, it had also alerted base, which had sent out two sorties of Turbo-Finches carrying incendiaries, plus rocket and machine gun pods. The Finches followed hard on the heels of gunship's tracers with the leftmost bird in the lead and the rightmost following in echelon.

The Finches opened up with rockets first. These sped downrange until their time fuses exploded them about twelve hundred meters from the insurgents. Each ship fired two pods of nineteen rockets. Each rocket further launched eleven hundred and seventy-nine, give or take, flechettes. Between the two planes, four pods, and seventy-six rockets a total of nearly ninety-thousand flechettes took flight.

As if the flechettes weren't enough, the pilots of the Finches armed their machine gun pods and fired several bursts each at whatever clusters of warm, or cooling, bodies were in their view. Then, as the planes neared the beaten area, they further armed and dropped the two incendiary canisters each carried slung under its wings on the hard points nearest the fuselage. These tumbled down, end over end, before reaching the ground and breaking open to spill their contents in long, licking tongues of flame.

After the gunship, then the flechettes, then the Finch's machine gun pods, there were relatively few insurgents or civilians in a position to notice the flame. Most of those who were screamed like girls as they burned.

"That is *illegal, Illegal, ILLEGAL!*" screamed Lindemann at Carrera.

"Nonsense," he answered, more amused by her anger than made angry himself.

"It is forbidden to use flame as a weapon!" she insisted.

"Still nonsense. What you apparently misread was the provision in the applicable convention on using incendiaries expressly to destroy cities and their civilian inhabitants. This was put in, perhaps even sensibly, to try to prevent the kind of city burning that took place during the strategic bombing campaigns of the Great Global War. It has no applicability to tactical uses."

Near tears, for the screams had carried far, even over the roaring of the flames, she said, "But you didn't have to burn them *alive.*"

Carrera shrugged. "Explosives would have damaged the minefields we laid to isolate the city. Flame does not."

He didn't add, *Besides, you haven't seen the pictures*

of the little children these bastards murdered here and elsewhere. They deserved to burn alive.

Camp Balboa, 24/7/462 AC

"Not a single one left," the RPV pilot muttered. "Not a dog or a cat nor, so far as I can tell, even a rat left wandering. They must be getting mighty hungry in there."

This was not exactly time-sensitive information. The pilot merely made a note of it on his flight journal. He'd report it to intelligence as soon as his bird was safely home.

Carrera was back at base, leaving Jimenez in charge forward at the wall of circumvallation around Pumbadeta. The Marines had actually done splendidly in his ZOR, enough so that he wondered if he was perhaps unduly prejudiced by long service with the FS Army. Doing splendidly or not, though, it was worth coming back to check from time to time.

He was standing at a map board, analyzing it for serious incidents that had occurred in the last month as compared to the previous three. There had been a couple more roadside bombings than normal, a couple of suicide bombings more than usual, as well. But firefights were down. This he attributed to most of the enemy fighters being in Pumbadeta, safely—for certain values of safe—locked up.

A private working for the command post took some cigarette ash and a cloth to clean off a small portion of one chart labeled, "Dog and Cat Report." This was divided into days. Carrera noticed that the number had been steadily dropping for a week. Now, the private marked in "0."

Not a single dog or cat to be seen from the air with thermals, he thought. *They have got to be getting very hungry, indeed. Oh, sure, there are probably a number left. But if so, it's because people are keeping them indoors, either for safety from foragers or to eat themselves.*

We'll give them a couple more days and let all *the woman and smaller children out. Better tell the MPs to shift some women to do visual inspection and physical search of the Sumeris. Maybe Sada can help there, too.*

Pumbadeta, Sumer, 27/7/462 AC

If one thing marked the throng of people leaving the town it was tears. For some, even many, these were tears of relief. For others they were tears of pain from hunger, disease, or even thirst.

The night before leaflets had been dropped advising the civilians that it was time for the women and children under twelve to leave. No men or boys over twelve would be allowed out, the leaflets said.

This time there were nearly two hundred thousand that took the exit being offered. Each of them was sure the insurgents would never have let any of them go unless the food were almost completely gone. But it was either feed the families, or let them go, or face an insurrection by the one hundred thousand *men* who were in the town and were *not* necessarily with the insurgents. Since most of those men were armed . . .

The line was thick and long and very, very slow. Each family group had to descend into one or another of the pits that had been dug by the access points. The pits had long, gradually sloping ramps. Cloth barriers divided them into two, one for boys and the other for women, babies, and girls. Armed men oversaw each, prudery be damned. On a few occasions rifle fire split the air as men were identified trying to escape under burkas. On one occasion fire was opened when it was revealed that a young woman was wearing a suicide vest under hers.

GraceCorps was there but was not in control. As the families exited the pits they were interviewed by Sada's people, then photographed. The photographs did two things. One was to provide identity cards that the people were told *must* be kept on their persons and displayed at all times. The other, less obvious reason, was that the machines used to make the photographs also scanned in the facial features, entering them into a data base that could be used by a new technique—new to Terra Nova, in any case—Face Recognition Technology. This measured certain factors that could not be easily disguised by such things as beards, distance and angle from corners of eyes to nose, for example. A face entered into an FRT database could be reliably picked out, even from a crowd, until its wearer went to a *talented* plastic surgeon.

From the ID Card/FRT stations the families went to medical clearing points. This also had two purposes. On the one hand, the legion wanted to avoid the spread of disease and even had an interest, minor to be sure, in preventing loss of innocent life. Thus inoculations were given. On the other, it was a way of getting a DNA sample from everyone in the town.

Senior women from each group were then sequestered from their families and from each other. While their families went to one of the forty small and fairly comfortable tent cities being run now by GraceCorps, the senior women had to stay behind to identify other groups and individuals and vouch that they came from the neighborhoods they said they did, the ones that were shown on their ID cards. In case of doubts, the new families were shown to much less civil camps run by Carrera's MP and Civil Affairs maniples. In case of demonstrating a pattern of not telling the truth, the senior women were themselves shown to the relatively unpleasant military-run camps.

It took four days to run the people through the various checkpoints. The last two days, it was probably fair to say that the refugees were beginning to approach starvation. On the other hand, few of them died.

There was also one smaller camp outside the walls around the city. This was full of a group of Kosmos who had come to protest the siege. It was *very* unpleasant, the diet consisting entirely of bread and water for the thirty-seven odd days of their confinement.

INTERLUDE

29/4/69 AC, Cochea, Balboa

And so it is over, they say, thought Belisario Carrera, sitting on the front porch of his small house and looking at the dormant volcano to the east. *Will it ever really be over, though?*

It had been a long war for Belisario, a man who had never thought to have found himself in a war, let alone leading the band that had struck terror into the forces of Earth from past San Jose colony to the northern half of Santander.

Twenty-five years of war, he mused tiredly. *Thank God it's ended for now, at least. I am old, too old to have gone on much longer.*

It hadn't just been a long war, it had been a hard one. The small family graveyard not far from the porch held the bodies of a dozen of Belisario's sons, sons-in-law, and grandsons, fallen in action, along with some of the women and girls killed by Earth's retaliatory random terror bombing. Sometimes there was no body, or only a part of one, beneath a marker. Yet all were remembered, all missed, all grieved for.

It was possible that no one on the New World had given as much of his blood as had Belisario in the cause of freedom.

He'd never really been a "general," he knew, no matter what his followers had called him. Indeed, his "army" had never numbered more than about five hundred, and usually much less. Their arms had been a motley collection of homemade and primitive supplemented with captures, here and there, from the UN Marines. Some of his men had *been* UN Marines who had deserted with their arms. One of his daughters-in-law—a tall, slender and beautiful Zulu girl—was one such. He thought that perhaps those desertions, and they had become increasingly common as the war dragged on, had had more to do with Earth's throwing in the towel than whatever success he and the other bands across Terra Nova had had in the field.

Idly, Belisario wondered how it might have been if he'd been a real general, not a mere horse rancher and farmer operating off instinct. Perhaps more of his sons and grandsons might have lived, he thought. *Then again,* they *had the trained generals and they lost. So perhaps it was as well I had only instincts.*

In his mind's eye, Belisario saw a montage of scenes: his horsemen slipping through the jungle flats, the burning buildings and the smoke of Earth's aircraft in the distance. In his memory he heard the high-pitched shriek of UN attack aircraft strafing his columns, the screams of the wounded and the exultant shouts of victory.

The last was best remembered, bringing to his face a smile. That face was still smiling when his wife found him, cold and stiffening, on the front porch.

CHAPTER THIRTY-TWO

Whosoever saveth the life of one, it shall be as though he had saved all mankind.

—The Koran, Sura V

Pumbadeta, Sumer, 34/7/462 AC

Fadeel had expected the assault by the crusader mercenaries to begin as soon as the last of the women and children had been evacuated. He'd expected wrong. Instead, the blockade continued, with the pitiful food stocks running lower and lower. His men were already on quarter rations. The civilian men of the city got nothing.

Which is a problem, as Fadeel unhesitatingly admitted to himself. *They're getting no food, except for whatever they may have hoarded, but they still have guns. And the second I try to take the guns, I'll have a full scale revolt on my hands. Besides, if the crusaders couldn't get the Sumeris to surrender their weapons, what chance have I?*

Hmmm. I wonder if I can't use them to my purposes before *they become dangerous to me. Hmmm.*

35/7/462 AC

It was no real problem for Fadeel's twenty-seven hundred remaining committed fighters to round up several hundred boys between the ages of thirteen and sixteen. They simply tooled through the streets on their SUVs, grabbing whomever they chanced upon that was unarmed. Moreover, given that the insurgents already had perhaps twenty *thousand* small arms in the city, together with millions of rounds of ammunition, arming the boys, once conscripted, was even easier.

Dawud ibn Haroun, aged fourteen and scrawny even in good times, searched fruitlessly through a garbage can in an alley. An orphan about whom no one had cared since he was a baby, Dawud was perhaps better placed to survive amidst the siege-induced starvation than most of the city's people. Even so . . .

Even so, it's a frightful thing, indeed, when even the garbage cans are empty.

His head was stuck in a dumpster, legs and feet trailing to the ground, when Dawud heard, "Hey, boy? You looking for something to eat?"

Overcoming his first instinct, which was to run, Dawud eased himself out of the dumpster and turned to face the voice. He saw an SUV, unevenly painted, as if with a can of spray paint, a sort of dun color, and containing three armed men. One of the men, presumably the one who had spoken, held his hand out, palm down, and jerked his fingers to the hand's heel in the Arab method of beckoning.

"Come with us," said the one who seemed to be the leader. "We'll feed you. Once anyway."

Seeing little option, Dawud climbed into the SUV, which sped off. It stopped twice more, once to summon another street urchin little different from Dawud and once simply to grab and carry off an older boy who refused to enter the auto.

Briefly, Dawud wondered if the number of boys taken corresponded to the number of fighters in the car. It was not impossible. Then again, he'd been through that, too, in his short and unpleasant life. He'd survived it once; he could again.

But no, the men hadn't taken the boys for fun and games. Moreover, true to their word, they had taken them to a large warehouse on the edge of town and fed them. Perhaps the food had been less than ideal, the meat scanty and the rice undercooked, but it had still been more than Dawud had seen in one place in weeks.

Food was followed by a lecture from a mullah, the lecture mostly concerning the iniquity of the besiegers, the duty of all Moslems to fight in the jihad, and the rewards of paradise. Dawud was no dummy and absolutely didn't like the direction in which the sermon was plainly going.

He liked it even less when the fighters had begun passing out arms and ammunition, and explaining, briefly, how to load, aim—more or less—and fire the things. The insurgents had the boys practice dry firing a few times before they led them off, by various routes, with two insurgents to each group of ten boys to ensure there would be no "desertions."

The last thing the fighters had done was explain the boys' mission. "Better for you to keep going in the attack," they'd added. "We'll support you in that. But death at the end of a rope awaits any so cowardly as to turn around from their duty."

A sound eerie to Balboan ears poured across the desert floor. It was a muezzin calling over loudspeakers.

Jimenez looked out over the dry and barren desolation that stretched from the circumvallating berm to the edge of the city. There was one almost full moon tonight, Hecate, plus partial luminescence from another, Bellona. Thus, even without using his night vision goggles, he could see easily across the open expanse.

Oh, oh, he thought as the first armed combatants stepped out into the light and began to walk forward.

"Engage now, sir?" asked the platoon centurion lying next to Jimenez on the friendly side of the berm. He had seen them too.

"No . . . no, wait until they hit the leading edge of the minefield. Any we can draw out and kill are that many fewer we'll have to fight when we finally assault the town."

The speakers on one of the near minarets crackled to life as the boys emerged from their shelters on the edge of town. A muezzin began reciting from the Koran over the speakers, his recital focused on the path of holy war.

One boy—Dawud thought it was the last one who had been taken in the vehicle that had brought him in—lay down in dirt, apparently taking cover. Dawud paused briefly, his eyes glancing over to look down at the boy. He began moving forward again almost instantly as a burst of automatic fire coming from behind impacted the slacker, causing blood to spurt from the body as it caused little geysers of dust to spurt from the ground.

From the speakers the muezzin decreed that death was to be the lot of slackers and cowards.

"This feels dirty as shit, sir," the centurion told Jimenez as the mob flowed closer.

I'm trying to remember the last clean war there was, Jimenez thought to himself. To the centurion he said, "Nothing for it but to get it over with then. But give them a couple more minutes. Until we can be sure none are going to be able to escape."

Jimenez slid down the berm's embankment and gestured for his radio telephone operator to hand over the microphone. With the radio, he called the command post to ask if there were a gunship overhead. Informed that there was not but that one would be overhead within ten minutes, he cursed and began the crawl back up to the berm's edge. His RTO followed.

"Do you have a forward observer attached?" he asked the centurion.

"Yes, sir. Shall I get him?"

"Please. Immediately."

Dawud's young heart pounded in his chest as the men following began to shout, "*Allahu akbar*, CHARRRGE!"

while firing their weapons from behind the boys and forward, over their heads. The shouting grew more distant the farther Dawud's legs carried him.

In his brief course of instruction the orphan had been taught to fire the rifle once each time his left leg hit the ground. He began to do so, keeping the rifle generally pointed to the north. Each burst took him a little by surprise. He found the sensation of recoil both unpleasant and frightening. He found the thought of being shot in the back by the men he assumed were still following to be more so.

There was an explosion ahead, somewhere to Dawud's right front. When he looked at the flash it was just in time to see three bodies flying through the air before hitting the ground. At the same time, two sets of bright shining lines were drawn across the front, one coming from the east and one from the west. Not only didn't Dawud know these were tracers, he was far too ignorant of matters military to realize that one tracer also meant another four bullets. He also didn't know enough to identify the explosion as having come from a land mine.

"This is just fucking murder," the centurion said to Jimenez over the continuous rattle of machine guns assaulting both men's ear and from both sides. He repeated, "Just fucking murder."

Jimenez ignored it, concentrating on the bodies being harvested in long lines at the edge of the minefield and where the machine guns were laid along their final protective linen.

The centurion's right. This is just murder. These poor bastards are clueless. It isn't even worth calling in some artillery or mortars on them. Why waste the shells when they just offer themselves up for butchery?

Dawud never saw the bullets that cut his legs out from under him. One minute he was running forward, the next he felt both legs struck out from underneath and found himself spinning, literally head over heels, to fall to the dirt.

It didn't hurt at first, nor even for several minutes. Then the burning began, followed by pain such as the boy had never even imagined. He began to cry and then, as the pain grew greater, infinitely great, to scream.

His screams were no more than a few notes in the hellish symphony.

The centurion's eyes glowed even in the darkness. He shrugged, "So court-martial me, sir, but I'll be damned if I'll let that shit go on. Just *listen* to them, won't you? Those were just fucking kids. Just kids! So I'm going out—we've got clear lanes through the wire and mines—and I'm bringing them back with me, as many as I can and as many as any of my men who'll volunteer to go with me can."

Jimenez sighed. He'd not have the centurion court-martialed, not when he wanted to go out himself. *Poor little bastards. They* are *just kids, too. Maybe one man might sound like that. But not every one of hundreds.*

"Wait a few minutes until I can get a smoke screen laid then, centurion. Then you can go."

Field Hospital Number Two, *Legio Del Cid*, 2/8/462 AC

When Dawud came out of surgery he was unconscious and legless. The surgeons had tried but . . . well, the damage had been too great. Keeping the legs would only have condemned the boy to a harder death from gangrene.

He remembered nothing of how he had come to be captured and treated, though after the centurion who had ventured out into no-man's-land had come by the field hospital to check on him, Dawud had been told the story by a Sumeri auxiliary nurse.

He'd miss the legs, he knew. Then again, what use were legs to a beggar boy? Perhaps it had been a fair trade. After all, at least he was eating well.

The boy bore no grudges. He didn't even know who to blame, the men who had shot him or the men who had driven him forth to be shot. In his world, bad things happened—usually to him—and it wasn't really anyone's fault. *Il hamdu l'illah.*

In any case, he had no hard feelings. The Sumeris working the field hospital had even suggested that it might be possible to go to school again on the legion's ticket. "Stranger things have happened," they'd all agreed. So, when the intelligence warrant officer had come to question Dawud, he had held nothing back. Not that he had much to tell. Yet from little bits of color are mighty works of art created. Dawud had a few such little bits to offer.

Given the ready cooperation, it was unsurprising that the boy was identified to the PSYOP maniple as a possible source for a telling interview.

Pumbadeta, Sumer, 3/8/462 AC

It was Dawud's voice carried on the dusty air from the loudspeakers of the legion to the ears of the men, and they were virtually all men, remaining inside the city.

Listening to it, Ehmed al Hanawi sat in a circle of other Pumbadetites. Like them his face was darkened with fury. Like them, too, his empty stomach rumbled. Like them his teeth ground against each other.

"So much for my boy's having volunteered for martyrdom," he cursed. "Taken without warning and forced into a meat grinder by our 'liberators.' The bastards."

The others nodded. Ehmed was the only one of the group who had lost a son in this way. But they were all fathers, and many of them still had boys trapped inside the town.

One of them men lifted up his Samsonov rifle and shook it. "I say we clean these bastards out. Who the fuck do they think they are, bringing this trouble upon us? Clean 'em out, I say."

Though almost all of the men assembled were at least functionally literate, only one among them could have been called really well educated. Mullah Thaqib had even attended school in far off Yithrab. He, too, had borne arms to the meeting. Those who insisted on calling Islam the "religion of peace" had obviously missed something important.

"It is easy to say 'Clean them out,' my friend," Thaqib answered. "But before we revolt," Thaqib said, "we must know if it is to any purpose. Will those who surround us let us live if we kill their enemies here for them?"

"Most of those surrounding us do not speak Arabic," Ehmed pointed out, "nor even English. Are there any here who can speak with them?"

Not even the mullah could speak Spanish.

"Most," he agreed. "Not all. There are some sections of the wall around us manned by Sumeri soldiers."

Ehmed answered dejectedly, "What difference, really? They let no one approach, preferring we all starve here."

"Where are the Sumeris stationed?" the mullah asked.

"One battalion—I *think* it's a battalion—is on the other side of the river."

"'Whosoever saveth the life of one . . .'" quoted Thaqib. "I will go to them."

Battle Position Sargon, 2nd Battalion, Sada's Brigade, 4/8/462 AC

If a Catholic priest had appeared alone in front of one of the portions of the front held by Balboan troops the effect would have been much the same. With a mullah, a bit wet and dripping perhaps but still recognizably a man of the cloth, the Sumeri troops likewise didn't fire.

The mullah climbed up the bank of the river and posted himself near the far end of the ruined, green-painted-steel girder bridge and leaned against it to catch his breath. He had a torch with him, and a lighter, but these were both soaked. He had to wait a time for them to dry. Fortunately, even this close to the river the air was dry enough to suck away life, let alone a bit of muddy water from the stream.

Although around four-fifths of the city the distance between buildings and circumvallating walls was nearly half a mile, here at the river the lines were close. Moreover, given a shortage of mines, the far bank was bare of them. Nor was there any wire, Sada having deemed, with Carrera's agreement, that the river itself was obstacle enough.

Thaqib didn't know that, of course. It was an act of desperate faith and belief in his God that caused him to light the torch, stand erect and walk forward.

He did have one thing going for him that he knew about. The insurgent fighters under Fadeel were an undisciplined lot. They rarely stayed awake to guard at night.

At least I don't have to worry about being shot in the back, he thought. *That's some small comfort anyway.*

"*Naquib! Naquib!* Wake up. There is a holy man who has crossed to our lines and wishes to speak with General Sada."

"Send him back," the captain commanding the company answered, firmly. "You know the rules on line crossers."

The sergeant normally wouldn't have bucked his commander. He liked the boy for one thing. For another, they were cousins. It was precisely that fact that made the sergeant stand up. "Sada will want to talk to this one, cousin. Trust me on this."

✧   ✧   ✧

When Sada arrived and had spoken to the mullah he congratulated the captain on his wisdom and made a mental mark to look the man over closely for possible promotion. Breaking rules and violating orders—let alone disturbing their commanders at frightful hours!—was not something that came easily to Sumeri officers.

Hearing the mullah out took hours. By the time it was done the sun was beginning to rise, its glorious light casting the shadows of buildings across the ground.

"Carrera will want to hear this, Thaqib," Sada advised. "But he may have you shot."

"That will be as it will be."

By noontime two things had happened. For one, the desert had returned to its normal state of open oven. For another, Carrera had decided that there might be a way to end this without destroying the town and killing all the men inside.

"Are you willing to go back? To organize a rebellion?" Carrera asked in Arabic. "I *would* spare the men, but they must *earn* it." Unsurprisingly, his Arabic had started to become quite good rather than just adequate, though it still lagged well behind Lourdes' under Ruqaya's instruction, or Sada's English for that matter. This was annoying to him, in a distant way, as he had already spoken some Arabic long before Lourdes had ever come to Sumer.

"I am willing," Thaqib answered. "As to whether I am able? The men inside will likely not let me return."

"Do you have some people who are jump qualified?" he asked Sada.

"You're shitting me, right, Patricio?" Seeing that Carrera was serious, Sada thought about it and said, "Myself. Qabaash. Oh, he'll be hot for this. Possibly half a dozen troops. But the mullah is *not* trained. How do we get him out the airplane and down on the ground?"

Carrera just smiled and turned to Thaqib. Conversationally, he asked, "How's your faith in God?"

Fifteen-hundred feet over Pumbadeta, Sumer, 6/8/462 AC

A half a day of ground school and twelve jumps were hardly enough to make Thaqib an expert parachutist. On the other hand, he took it philosophically.

I am sure to hit the ground, no matter what happens, he thought. *The ways of Allah are inscrutable but are as certain as His Grace. And best of all, after this one it will be the last time I'll ever have to do anything like this again. For this, Beneficent One, I thank You.*

They waited until the moon, Eris, which was nearly full, had set. Sada jump-mastered the operation for one bird. Qabaash had the other. They both thought the idea was insane—a definite point of appeal to Qabaash—but were willing to take the chance to prevent the otherwise inevitable bloodbath in what was, after all, one of their cities and filled with their people.

Sada looked Thaqib straight in the face, searching for signs of hesitation. Seeing none, he laughed aloud. "Mullah, when this is done, if we live, how would you like a job as a chaplain in my brigade?"

Given the warm, thin air right at the surface, the Crickets had had to strain to lift even two men with parachutes. Any idea of using the next smallest airplane available, however, the NA-23, was simply out of the question. Crickets were designed to be quiet, their single engines muffled. NA-23s could be heard from far away.

Lanza—hell, he flew everything and every chance he had, too!—looked back over his right shoulder and told Sada, in English, "Crossing the river now." Sada knew that meant less than two minutes to jump at this speed.

The engine suddenly went dead. This was by design rather than a flaw. The Cricket was perfectly capable of gliding quite some distance without engine power, once it was up among the cooler, thicker air.

Sada helped Thaqib to ease himself to the Cricket's door. As with every prior jump, the cleric stiffened once he was in position, but then forced himself to a more relaxed calm. Reciting some of his favorite hadiths helped. At the proper time, Sada pushed the mullah out the door, then quickly threw himself behind him.

Above, the Cricket sailed on until near the edge of the city, at which point Lanza reengaged the engines.

Sada, Qabaash and the young soldier accompanying them, Sergeant Ali, landed easily enough in the broad park near the center of town. Mullah Thaqib nearly screamed at his landing as he came down with one leg on a concrete pad and the other just off it. This caused the ankle that hit first to twist, dislocating it with an audible sound that was almost as bad as the pain shooting up Thaqib's leg.

"Oh . . . *God!*" Thaqib gasped when Sada reached him. One look at the odd angle of the foot was enough to tell the general that there was no chance of the man walking on his own power any time soon.

"Qabaash, you and Ali hide the chutes." He hesitated. They had not been sure, even after planning and aerial recon, just where they *could* hide the parachutes. "Mmm . . . over there. I'll meet you." Sada's finger pointed to an apparently abandoned apartment building.

While that was being done, Sada half-stripped and put on a long flowing robe and keffiyah. His weapon was indistinguishable from those carried by the insurgents so that would be no problem. Slinging the rifle across the left side of his neck, Sada helped the mullah to his good leg and assisted him to hobble, one-legged, to where Qabaash and Ali waited. They'd also donned local, civilian costume and already had their boots off and replaced with sandals.

Qabaash and Ali both looked at the mullah's ankle and the bone pressing out and said, together, "Shit."

"We'll have to splint it before we try to move him any farther. Sergeant Ali, can you find a couple of stout sticks?"

The sergeant nodded and walked farther into the building, muttering something about, "Darker than three feet up a well digger's ass at midnight . . . a *moonless* midnight."

Sada and his two men had no real difficulty moving Mullah Thaqib to his home. The streets were dark, the insurgents mostly less than alert, and their appearance nothing remarkable. Once there, they set

Thaqib down on a pallet while his wife fussed over him. Sada used the break to call the legion's command post with a single code word, repeated three times: "Badr . . . Badr . . . Badr."

Legionary Command Post, 7/8/462 AC

"They're in and safe," Jimenez announced, when the message was received. A subdued cheer rang throughout the command post.

Fahad, standing by for just this word, breathed a sigh of relief.

"You really care about Sada, don't you?" Carrera asked. "Moslem or not you still care about him?"

The Chaldean thought about that for a minute before answering. "He was . . . still is, my *commander*, sir. We've been through the . . . through the shit together. Bonds like that go past things like religion. Besides . . ."

"Yes?"

"If this country is ever going to amount to anything ever again, it will be because of Sada and the few men like him, men who stand above tribe and religion and sect. Honorable men."

"Isn't that an interesting thought," Carrera said slowly. "Sada and a few like him. I confess; I see Sumer as doing better in his hands than in those of the pack of jackals down in Babel. He *is*, as you said, an honorable man . . . and a brave one. Yes, that's a *very* interesting thought, Fahad."

"Sir?" Fahad asked, clearly not understanding.

"Never mind, friend. We will see what we will see."

Pumbadeta, Sumer, 7/8/462 AC

A man has to play the hand he's dealt. Sada didn't even try to form a working chain of command based on military experience. Instead, he selected out the couple of dozen experienced senior officers and NCOs from the old Sumeri Army (for while virtually every man in town had some military experience, trained leaders were few and far between) and assigned one or two to each group of tribal and clan leaders. The traditional chiefs would command; the former soldiers only advise.

In analyzing his assets all Sada could think was, *There are damned few of them. I've got numbers but I lack everything else. No radios, no heavy weapons, limited ammunition, no special purpose ammunition.*

More than anything, it was those last two that decided him to begin the rebellion on the side of the town by the river. If he could clear that, then his troops could throw a temporary bridge over the stream and not only add their own weight to the fight but also bring in whatever the rebellion would need.

He had another consideration though. *Even after we seize the near bank, Fadeel's men will just fall back and make us root them out of every little building and shack. Bad for the town, and bad for the townsmen's lives.*

Sada knew, from prior planning, that the legion would be making a great show of preparing to assault from every side. The intent was to draw the insurgents out from the center of town, leaving it for the townsfolk to occupy. This would make life very difficult for the insurgents, once they began to fall back.

That's not enough, though. They will *still fall back. How do I use that?*

He closed his eyes and began to think. *Okay . . . let's imagine I first grab the near bank. The insurgents will run to that to try to retake it and stop us. Let them in or keep them out? Hmmm. Let them in, I think, as many as want to go.* Then *we rise up to seize the center of town. Both of my battalions here cross the river at about the same time and begin the resupply operation for the locals. Then we push the insurgents into the center of town,* which we hold . . . *and ambush the hell out of them as they flee to new positions to the west. Now . . . where to draw the line?*

"Qabaash, do you have the centers of gravity for the clans and tribes, yet?"

In response, Qabaash left the group of elders with whom he'd been talking and from whom he'd taken the information to annotate his acetate-covered map, came over, and laid the map in front of Sada.

Sada rubbed his hand across his sprouting beard wearily. *No really good lines to seal off the area. But . . . there is this government complex in the center of town. It's tall and fairly visible from everywhere.*

The trick, he knew, would be assigning the tribes missions that directly related to the security of their own homes, that blocked the fighting from those homes. Sada read off a tribal name that Qabaash had scrawled inside a circle drawn on the acetate along with a number indicating likely fighters. "Dulaim tribe?"

"Here, *sayidi*," answered a bearded old man in a dusty robe.

Sada's finger pointed to the map near the northern edge of town. "I'll want your people to assemble here and keep anyone from fleeing westward. Let as many as want to come east, but nobody goes west. Got it?"

"Yes, *sayidi*," the old man answered after looking carefully enough at the map to make sure he could find the right spot. "When do we start? I don't own a watch."

"Noon," Sada answered. "We will begin seizing the river bank at first-light. Give these stinking, murdering foreigners plenty of time to move to contain us, and have this position blocked by high noon."

"Yes, *sayidi*. We can do this."

Sada slapped the old man on the shoulder, then turned his attention back to the group. "Muntafic tribe . . . ?"

Fadeel no longer used his minaret lookout. It was no fine sense of obligation or newfound respect for convention that kept him out. Rather, the filthy, ass-fucking crusaders made a habit of sniping at anyone found near the city's edge who looked remotely like an observer.

They were damnably good shots, too. Worse, some of the rifles they used were subsonic and silenced. One never knew where the shot might have come from that blew out a man's chest or disintegrated his head amidst a spray of brains, blood and bone.

So, instead of his usual minaret perch Fadeel found himself looking through an irregular loophole knocked in the wall of a used car dealership.

Something's definitely up, he thought, looking out over the crusaders' surrounding berm. The air past the berm was heavy with the dust thrown up by what had to be heavy vehicles, *lots* of heavy vehicles, moving into position.

A large explosion rocked Fadeel. *And they're blowing lanes in their own obstacles. We're in for it, right enough.*

Fadeel left the shelter of the used car lot headquarters and began moving toward the center of town. While he did, he stopped at a couple of spots to count the aircraft circling like vultures overhead. He stopped counting when he reached forty and then saw over thirty more helicopters winging in from the south. *Shit.*

Carrera and Jimenez choked on the dust in the air. A nearby light truck deliberately raised those clouds, dragging behind it several rolls of concertina wire stretching out in the dirt. It was one of dozens being used for the purpose. They dragged the concertina up, raising the clouds, then collapsed the wire and drove back away from the city and repeated. From the inside of the town it had to look like a massive assembly of troops and armor.

Soult handed over a radio microphone with the announcement, "Sada, Boss."

"Yeah, Adnan?"

"We're ready to start, Patricio. What's the word from overhead?"

"Not much reaction, yet," Carrera answered. The air folks reported some massing toward the bridges but as near as we can figure that's your people."

The radio keyed and Carrera heard a heavy rattle of rifle and machine gun fire before Sada said, "Well, it's time. Wish me luck, friend."

"Rack 'em up, Adnan."

✧   ✧   ✧

Qabaash laughed heartily. Normally quiet, he was one of those odd folks who only came alive when the bullets were flying and he could shoot back. He hadn't had nearly enough chance to do that, of late. Under his direction a group of townsmen assaulted a building overlooking the river. They had no grenades, except for a few dozen they'd captured when they'd taken the insurgents unawares. These had been passed out already and, for the most part, used. Now it was rifle and bayonet in every room.

"Allah forgive me but I love this shit," Qabaash murmured. He raised his own rifle to take a potshot at an insurgent running across an alleyway. Much to his irritation, he missed.

No problem, friend. We'll get you later.

The radio crackled. "Qabaash, Sada. Progress?"

"We've almost cleared the river bank, *Liwa*. There's one big building held by the enemy that's blocking our way. The engineers on the other side can't get a bridge up until we take that building. Any word on grenades?"

"Waiting on the other side, Qabaash. Will the building burn?"

Qabaash looked at it. It was an older one and likely to have something flammable to it. "Maybe."

"Good. Burn 'em out."

Qabaash looked around the street. *Hmmm . . . I wonder how many of those cars have gas in the tank.* He ran over to one and flopped to the ground. Crawling underneath, he tapped the gas tank. *Maybe half full. Hmmm.*

Running back to where a group of townsmen

waited, Qabaash ordered, "Bottles and hoses. Drain the tanks of the cars. We'll give them a taste of the hellfire that awaits."

Little bits of concrete dust burst into the air as bullets struck the walls and windows of the building. Below, at street level, a steady stream of men and boys ran across the open area to toss a bottle or two into the ground floor. The whole area stank of gasoline.

The other bottles had not been lit. Qabaash, however, had a more conventional Molotov cocktail in his hand. After seeing what had to be fifty or sixty liters of gas dumped in the building, he trotted across the street and took cover against the building wall. Reaching into a pocket he pulled out a cigarette lighter and flicked it to light the Molotov. *Build a man a fire and keep him warm for the night. Set a man on fire and keep him warm for the rest of his life.* With a smile he hurled the flaming contraption into the building and began to run back . . .

And was knocked flat on his face as the gasoline inside suddenly caught in something that was only just less than a full up fuel-air explosion. Only the many open portals of the building kept it from going up in a huge, contained, thermobaric *kaboom.* By the time he had rolled on his back and sat up, the entire ground floor poured forth flames. Before he had gotten to his feet the second and even some of the third floor windows had tongues of flame licking out.

The screaming inside the buildings went on for a very long, very satisfying, time.

✧   ✧   ✧

"Hump it, you bastards, hump it!" Qabaash shouted across the river to the struggling gangs of Sumeri engineers frantically rebuilding something that would do for a floor to the smaller of the two bridges spanning the river. Even while they built, thin squads of uniformed Sumeri soldiers, Sada's men, carefully crossed onto the near bank along creaking a foot path laid along the bridge's skeleton. These assembled as they crossed under their own leaders. A news team was mixed in with one column, having bribed one of the lesser commanders to let them in.

Even Sada's brigade couldn't change human nature.

The members of the GNN camera crew were careful to place the still burning building as a backdrop to their reporter. This seemed easy but wasn't. There were confident looking regular Sumeri troops standing below the building. Obviously they had to be left out. Worse, there were armed civilians who were not only not fighting the soldiers, but were actually welcoming them and helping them.

In the end, they'd settled on placing the camera low and the reporter on a small earthen ramp they'd thrown together. This allowed the reporter to speak about the terrible destruction—though, admittedly, other than that one building it didn't seem so terrible—without letting in the unwanted messages of welcoming townsfolk and competent Sumeri troops. Best of all, this angle showed the stinking mercenaries' aircraft overhead. The obvious implication of ruined edifice in the near background and flying combat aircraft farther off was that the legion was smashing the town like a bully child.

"Pumbadeta is dying," the reporter began . . .

✧   ✧   ✧

Fadeel didn't want to die just yet. Some of the crusaders leveled charges of cowardice against him. None of his own men did. He had work to do and could not let death inconvenience that work. They knew that and accepted it.

How to prevent it though; that was the problem. Taken by surprise by the men of the city he'd already lost one quarter of Pumbadeta. Much worse, as his men fell back onto prepared positions farther in, they'd run into ambush after ambush. The very positions they'd prepared they often found in enemy hands as they reached them.

This town is lost, Fadeel thought. *Nothing for it but to lie low, blend in, hope my fighters take some with them, and then escape to rebuild. Next time, I'll know better than to count on the Kosmos to come to my rescue. In the interim, best to hide out, I think, until the fighting passes and I can join the mob.*

GNN had a mission and a message. The farther the crew moved into the town, the less they found to back up that message. Yes, there were dead bodies damned near everywhere, but they were almost all armed. The town itself, though, had suffered little destruction so far.

"Well, we'll make do," announced the reporter. He directed his camera crew to remove weapons from several dozen bodies to make them look like innocents caught up in the fighting. It wasn't perfect but it was better than nothing.

Fadeel's first thought when he saw the camera crew was *My salvation.*

He walked directly over and introduced himself in good English as "Ahmad Habib al Fadel. Can I help you?"

Pleased to have someone who spoke English and Arabic with him the reporter hired Fadeel on the spot. He proved, over the next few hours, to have a real knack for setting up the bodies of those killed in the fighting to look incredibly innocent and pitiable.

When the day's shooting was done, the reporter asked Fadeel if he would like a lift somewhere.

"Anywhere away from this madhouse," was Fadeel's answer.

The reporter and his crew, no less Fadeel, were quite surprised and shocked to discover that, while a bribe might have gotten them in, even high powered media types were *still* not being allowed *out* of Pumbadeta.

Checkpoint X-ray, Wall of Circumvallation, 10/8/462 AC

The excuse was to pay those who had fought and to make sure the town was thoroughly swept of insurgents. Using the same checkpoints as they had previously used to filter out the women and the children, the legion likewise filtered out the townsfolk from the insurgents.

The first step had been for the tribal leaders and those military advisors Sada had selected for them to come out and take charge of their displaced, tent city "neighborhoods." Having done so, and confirmed that the women and children were alive and well, they returned to the town and began to lead their fighters, and those who had taken no part in the fighting but for whom they were still responsible, out through the checkpoints. No one left except for those who were vouched for by their tribal leaders.

The men leaving were separated into those who had fought and those who had not. Both groups were subject to paraffin tests to see if, in fact, they had fired small arms. The purpose was quite different. Among the groups identified as fighters by the tribal leaders and whose clothing showed traces of small arms propellant, one hundred drachma was paid immediately. The fact that the legion's original cadre had been police who were used to gathering evidence helped here.

Any in the other group who showed such traces raised immediate suspicions. Some were identified as "okay" by their own relatives. Others could not be identified. After a very quick trial these were shot by firing squads organized by the religious leadership of the town, a substantial bounty being paid to the tribes who brought in outsiders who could not claim and prove membership in a local tribe. Those so identified who showed traces of a foreign accent were hanged.

Among those shot was a GNN camera crew which tried to bully its way through a checkpoint. They were not shot for the bullying. Rather, they were shot for attempting to help escape one Fadeel al Nizal. They claimed innocence but, given that the man's picture was in worldwide circulation, that their news network had shown nothing but harshness and contempt toward the war and those who fought in it (barring, of course, the insurgents), and that their own video found in the camera demonstrated an attempt at what was really enemy propaganda, neither the mullahs, nor Sada, nor Carrera, were convinced. They went to the wall, in tears, and still pleading.

Fadeel was not hanged on the spot. Neither was he shot. Instead, at an interview with Carrera and Sada, he was told, "Friend, you are going to take a long, long cruise."

Even then, Fadeel was most uncooperative, despite the threat and reality of pain, until his parents, kidnapped in an operation long planned, were brought to him aboard the *Hildegard Mises*.

EPILOGUE

I

With Hecate and Bellona hurtling overhead, from just outside the cave's mouth that led down to his underground command post, Mustafa min Sa'ana, prince of the *Ikhwan* contemplated a bleak present and a bleaker future.

Why, O Merciful One, do you try me so? Why do you seem to favor the infidel? Why have you caused us to lose in Sumer? Is it my failings? Or is it that the Sumeris, themselves, are unworthy of your redemption? Or is it, perhaps, that you required us to lose there so that when we win this world, as we eventually must, we and our descendants will be in no doubt that it was You who gave us the victory, and not our own efforts?

Oh, yes, we will hang on in Sumer for a few more years, perhaps even a decade. We are a stubborn people, as You made us to be, and an optimistic one. But the tide is against us I know this, no matter what I tell my followers. And the chief of the space infidels, the pigs from Old Earth, likewise assures me that our cause there is lost. He tells me that terror met terror there, and the greatest terrorists won.

Who would have believed it; that an infidel from the greatest of infidel states should have become a greater terrorist than even the bloody handed Fadeel al Nizal?

Curse him, O Mighty One, this filthy pig, Carrera.

And where is Fadeel, anyway? He has disappeared from the world and left no trace. I think he must have been taken, though. Too many cells around the world of which only Fadeel and I and my closest associates knew have likewise gone into the ether. Too many accounts with too many millions in them have also gone. I think Fadeel must have lived and I think he must have talked.

What could make a man like Fadeel talk? Oh, he was a lion, despite our occasional differences. No ordinary interrogation would have broken Fadeel. This Carrera swine must be deep into Shaitan's clutches if he could make Fadeel betray trusts.

Unconsciously, Mustafa's teeth ground together with the sheer hate and frustration of it all. He began to pace the mouth of the cave, hands clutched tightly behind him.

Allah, we've got to win. I have been to Taurus, I have been to the Federated States. I know what they are like. I know . . . You know, how they have begun to contaminate even the faithful.

It is an abomination. Especially is it an abomination where women are concerned. Women working outside the home? Women choosing their own mates? Women free to fuck whom they will without marriage, even within marriage? Women baring their bodies in public like wantons? Women learning to read? Women voting? Women free?

Abomination, abomination, *ABOMINATION!*

You have created the one above the other, the man above the women, just as You have placed the faithful above the infidel and the dhimmi. And these infidels would seek to recreate the worlds in ways contrary to your will? Forbid it, Almighty Allah! Help us to forbid it and to bring your just rule to this world, to this universe.

You, O Allah, are the greatest plotter of all. Help us and guide us, your faithful servants.

Mustafa had a sudden and unsettling, even an awful, thought.

He asked aloud of the night air, "Is it my fault that we have lost, my God? Is it my misspent youth? The days of uselessness and the nights of drunkenness and debauchery? I regret them all, O Most High. I know they all should have been either my wives or those held under my right hand before I touched them. I humbly ask—I humbly beg—Your forgiveness. I knew not then what I know now."

Facing toward Makkah al Jedidah, Mustafa prostrated himself, bowing repeatedly and whispering his prayers and his penance. When he was finished, his mind was clearer, clear enough to think upon the future which looked so bleak.

So we have lost in Sumer. So be it. What is there to gain, then? How shall we proceed?

Further attacks on the Federated States? The last one didn't work out precisely as planned, now did it? Why was this? I had thought them much weaker than they proved to be. I had thought them as weak as the Taurans. No, then; no more attacks on the FSC until and unless I can make them truly crippling. No more threats unless the threat is so deadly even they will not face it.

But what is left then? What is left when they have won in Sumer?

There are the Xamar pirates. They owe me, many of them. Perhaps they can be persuaded to integrate their individual efforts, to join the higher holy cause. I will dispatch Abdul Aziz to that end as soon as possible. Perhaps the pirates of the Nicobar Straits, too, can be brought into the fold. Most of them are of the faithful, after all.

And then there is Pashtia. Yes . . . perhaps Pashtia can be reopened as our major effort. After all, the mujahadein and the money that would go to Sumer otherwise are still available; will still be coming. And then, too, Pashtia has few roads and railroads, no ports, not many airports. Can the infidels even supply a larger force in Pashtia? Perhaps not; the Volgans never could.

Yes, Pashtia is where we shall fight them. Pashtia is where we shall crucify the swine.

II

Carrera half lay on a supply pallet outside the field hospital at Balboa Base. His legs hung off with his feet on the ground. Both arms were outflung on the pallet, the hand on the right one holding a smoldering cigarette. Under the other arm was strapped a pistol in a shoulder holster. He looked up at the stars and the moons, speaking to Linda in his mind.

I almost murdered a city, love. I was ready to. I had

everything needed to destroy it. I'd have given the order in a few days if one bloody mullah hadn't saved me from it. What do I owe, do you suppose, to a man who kept me from getting more blood on my hands than I could ever wash off? I'm building him a new mosque, a grand one. But I don't think it's nearly enough.

Carrera didn't bother to stifle a yawn.

I'm tired, Linda, so tired. Not just of the work but of the means. My boys are great, they do whatever I want them to. But they can do it only because the sins are all on my head.

It was easy, baby, when I first began. Then it was all abstract; I didn't have to think. And I was too full of hate to feel much else.

I wish it were over. But it never will be, will it? Not in my lifetime.

He stopped thinking for a while, feeling the cool night air, seeing the twinkling stars, and conscious of the pistol strapped to his chest.

That would be the easy way, wouldn't it. And I'd like to; I really would. But I can't do that either. I owe it to you and the babies to continue the fight. And I owe it to my men not to abandon them.

I owe it to Lourdes, too, her and the new baby. And . . .

Sada materialized next to the supply pallet. "Ruqaya says it's time, Patricio."

Sitting up, Carrera tossed the cigarette. It would never do to bring fire inside a place where pure oxygen flowed. He stood and turned to follow Sada to the maternity ward. At the door, a nurse helped him into a hospital gown. Sada stayed outside as Carrera entered.

The look on Lourdes' face was one of pure excruciation. Standing in the adobe field hospital, wearing the hospital gown to cover his battle dress, Carrera took her hand. He felt every contraction and spasm right along with her. Though Sada was not allowed into the delivery room, his wife, Ruqaya, held Lourdes' other hand, stroked her damp hair and forehead and whispered words of encouragement to her.

Carrera had tried to send Lourdes back. In this one particular, though, her will had been iron.

"My mother bore four children with never a doctor in attendance," she'd said. "My grandmother had eight and all in her own bed, on her own and my grandfather's farm. Without even *electricity*. I'm no wilting flower, either. I am *your* woman. My place is with you and I WILL NOT GO!"

It was a surprising show of resistance from such a normally serene and cooperative person. He'd known he was not going to win that fight. Instead, bowing to the inevitable, he'd flown in an obstetrician from Balboa. At some level he'd felt a certain guilt about that; using his position for special consideration for his own family.

Am I becoming like the Balboans, placing family first? Am I becoming like the Islamics? Certainly Adnan and Ruqaya, Fernandez and Jimenez, and—so far as I can tell—each and every one of the troops, approved. I must think on this . . . later.

To his own question he'd had no answer or, in any event, not one that satisfied. He'd sent the doctor out, always under heavy guard, to deliver babies all over the BZOR to try to give the appearance of having brought specialist medical aid for the mission and not for his own sake or that of his new wife.

And in that, too, it seems I am becoming more like my enemies. Do I care so much about appearances? I never did before.

And that was another thing. A few days before he'd had one of his horrible nightmares. This one was different, though. Linda had been there, as usual, along with Julio, Lambie and Milagro. But so had Lourdes and the baby.

It was the picnic nightmare, again, only with the oddity that Lourdes and Linda, *both*, were his wives and seemed quite content with that situation. It was positively Islamic and even worse than usual when all six screamed and turned to rotten meat, then crumbling bones, before his eyes.

His reveries were interrupted by a loud, piercing, wailing scream from Lourdes and a painful squeeze of his hand. Her head was up off her pillow, bobbing as she gasped for air. In a few moments of hard struggle it was over. Lourdes' head returned to her pillow. She still gasped and—Carrera had no doubt—was still in agony. Compared to agony of actual delivery, though, what she felt now was probably small beans. Indeed, by comparison it was likely pure relief. He could see that on the smile that shone through her tears.

Carrera heard a slap and then one very, very affronted wail. He was distantly aware of the flash of a scalpel and of the baby being passed to Ruqaya.

"Behold, Patricio," Ruqaya said, flicking a miniature penis with an index finger "you have a son."

Before placing the child at Lourdes' breast, Ruqaya held the boy's tiny ear to her mouth and whispered, "*La illaha illa Allah; Muhammadan rasulu Allah.*" There is no God but God; Muhammad is the prophet of God.

Carrera let it be. On the other hand, *What religion should the boy be raised in? I'm a Catholic, if a bad one. Lourdes is Baptist, and a good one. But, who knows; maybe Ruqaya has a point.*

Nah.

He looked at the boy again, now nuzzled into his mother, and felt something he had not felt in a very long time. It wasn't love; he loved Lourdes and had for a lot longer than he'd been willing to admit it. If she was not Linda, she was still the finest—and based on her just concluded delivery one of the toughest and bravest—human beings on the planet.

No . . . it's not love that I feel anew. It's . . . it's . . . He struggled with the concept before realizing, *It's a sense of future, of having a continuing place in the march of Man. I lost it when Linda and the children were killed. Lourdes has just given it back to me.*

With his right palm stroking Lourdes' hair he bent over her and placed a gentle kiss on her forehead. "I love you, Lourdes," he said. "In all this world I love you and our child above all. You, and he, have given me my future back."

And for that future I will fight.

Carrera rested his head upon hers and lay that way for several minutes. At length, he became aware of a hubbub of sorts coming from outside the field hospital.

Sada stuck his head in the door. "Patricio, there are over a thousand soldiers outside, maybe two thousand, including mine, and they want to see the baby."

Looking at Lourdes, Carrera saw her smile again and head nod, weakly. "Show them, Patricio," she said.

The doctor shrugged and said, "I think it's safe

enough. There are some stairs down the hallway that lead to the roof. You can use those."

"Show them, Patricio," Ruqaya agreed.

Gingerly, for he had not held a newborn in a very long time, Carrera took the still naked child from Lourdes' breast and placed it on his own shoulder, one hand under the baby's head. The baby—they'd already agreed he would be named Hamilcar Xavier Adnan Carrera-Nuñez—took it pretty well, not crying but peering curiously at the out-of-focus, barely perceived world around him.

Lots different from my last digs, thought little Hamilcar. *Might be fun. And there's so much more room to grow here.*

Still cradling the baby, Carrera gave Lourdes another warm and gentle look. Then he left the delivery room and walked to the stairs, Sada and Ruqaya following. These they ascended. At the top of the stairs they emerged onto the roof, itself surrounded by a low adobe wall built in the Arab fashion. Stars shone down on the roof, as did Hecate and Bellona. There was a murmuring sound, as if coming from thousands of throats. The sound was gentle and quiet, though, as if, also, those making it were reluctant to disturb the new mother.

New mother or not, the murmur arose to a roar when the legionaries of *el Cid* and the *askaris* of Sada's brigade saw Carrera's head, then shoulders, and then the baby,

To the roar of the men was added a round of mass applause. *Good job, Legate. Fine work, Lourdes. Welcome to the legion, little one.*

Carrera placed one hand, then the other, under

Hamilcar's arms and gently lifted him overhead, to display to the troops. The applause and the cheering grew louder still, which seemed not to bother the baby one bit.

Behold my son, Carrera thought. *Behold: I have a future. And for that future I will fight.*

Carrera looked up at the sky once again, looked at the stars, and wondered which of them were ships of the UEPF.

On the horizon, Eris was just beginning to rise anew.

III

Robinson sat on the observation deck of *Spirit of Peace* watching as Eris rose and Hecate prepared to plunge behind the planet. In his hand he held hard copies of dispatches from the Consensus on Earth.

The future is black, he thought. *Everything is going black. I should nuke Terra Nova now, while I can.*

It wasn't just the situation in Sumer that had Robinson's mood down in the pits. The dispatches from home were at least as depressing: riots in Rome—the caliph had been torn limb from limb by a mob. Raiders from the reversions—those areas on Old Earth that the Consensus lacked the means or will to keep civilized—had struck civilization in three places; just west of the Dahlonega Glacier, along the edge of the Arabian reversion area, and at the mines in central Africa. The Consensus itself was split, with some advocating further pullbacks from the reversions and others—notably the druids and neopagans—demanding an increase in the strength of the security forces to roll back the reverted areas.

So they're compromising by ordering me to send back half my security force. How the hell am I supposed to even guard Atlantis Base with half my troops, such as they are, gone? What will be next; ordering me to send back half the fleet to nuke the reversions into submission?

Oh, Holy Annan, what am I to do?

Robinson placed his elbows on his thighs, rested his head in his hands, and tried desperately to think.

All right, my best way of guarding Atlantis Base is probably bluff. I think I can keep the locals from sensing half my force is gone by ordering the remainder to be more aggressive about their patrols and enforcing the exclusion zone to surface shipping and air transport even more rigorously than we do. That will help . . . for a while, anyway.

Robinson's thoughts were interrupted by the sound of elevator doors *whooshing* open, then closed, and soft footsteps on the deck behind him. He recognized the footsteps.

"Hello, Marguerite," he said, raising his head from his hands but staring out the large rectangular viewport rather than turning to see her.

"High Admiral," *Peace*'s captain answered, with an unseen nod. She knew what was troubling him; she'd seen the dispatches from Earth before he had and she knew that Sumer was, from the Earth's and Robinson's point of view, a failure.

She gracefully took a seat on the padded bench next to Robinson. There she remained, quietly, allowing him to continue to think undisturbed.

Robinson broke the line of silence by saying, "It's odd, isn't it? That, outside of Europe, it is the first areas of home to come under real Consensus control that were also the first to revert? That, outside of Europe, it is the areas that came in last that provide the core and the strength to our system?"

Wallenstein shrugged. She tried *not* to think about that, nor about what it implied for the system as a whole.

"What are you going to do?" she asked, changing the subject.

"Send them the troops, I suppose. Though I'm sorely tempted to recruit some mercenaries like that Carrera bastard and ship *them* to help the Consensus with its problems."

"Martin, you can't! If the locals ever saw what home was like—"

"I know that," he answered. "I wasn't serious when I said it. Send back thousands of local mercenaries who are not only willing to but actually know *how* to fight? Abomination! They'd destroy our system of governance even faster than the reverters would. And we could never control them."

Wallenstein breathed a small sigh of relief. "So you will send the troops back. How will we keep Atlantis Base secured?"

"The same way we keep the FSC from blowing us from the sky—bluff."

"And if we're discovered? If someone calls our bluff?"

"Marguerite . . . I don't know."

"The longer it takes to win down below, the more likely it is our bluff will be called," the captain observed.

Robinson sighed, himself. "That much I *do* know. I think we're going to have to help Mustafa and the TU to destroy the FSC more directly than I've been willing to. There's only so much time, after all."

Wallenstein nodded. The two went silent then, as the orbits of Bellona and Eris carried the moons to close juncture. After long minutes she stood and walked to a panel to the right of the transparent view screen. There she pressed a button. From either side doors began slowly and silently to close on the scene. She walked and stood in front of the high admiral of the fleet.

"Come, Martin. Let's go to bed. Tomorrow we can begin to plan. Pashtia, do you think?"

"Yes," he said, rising and taking her hand. "They've won too much already. In Pashtia we will break them, because we must."

To be continued.

WARNING: Read further at your own risk.

AFTERWORD

This is becoming a habit, you know, and probably
not a good one. But you had some questions, you
said? Something about Kosmos, on our world known
as "Tranzis," torture, and the prospect of becoming
what you fight.

I'll try to answer . . . and to be brief . . . something
I have signally failed to do with this book and fully
expect to fail in future volumes, of which there may
be as many as eight. Pull up a chair. Scotch? Iced
or neat? The cigars are in the humidor over there.
Try one of those Magnum Force #42s. They're just
excellent.

I had cause, recently, to do some research on the
definition of insanity. One I found, and that I *almost*
agreed with, said that "Insanity consists of doing
everything the same and expecting a different result."
I say "almost" because there is a corollary to that:
"Insanity also consists of doing everything differently
and expecting the same result."

This is perhaps the only real difference between a current day Marxist and a current day Transnational Progressive, or Tranzi. The Marxist expects a different result from doing everything important the same, as if there is any freedom that doesn't include economic freedom, as if there is _any_ path to socialism that will not be paved with bodies, as if socialism has ever managed to create anything beyond corpses, poverty and oppression . . . oh, and lots of pieces of third-rate military equipment and a new entrenched upper class backed by a ruthless secret police and outrageous propaganda, too, of course.

The Tranzi, on the other hand, expects to maintain and expand modern, enlightened, prosperous, liberal society while opening up the borders that shelter that society to unlimited numbers of the least assimilable and most reactionary, most traditional and hidebound, least economically productive cultures on the face of the Earth. This wouldn't be so bad, or so insane, did they not at the same time insist that nothing be done to even try to assimilate the immigrants from those cultures to modern, enlightened, liberal values. (Do you suppose there were pro-Vandal, pro-Hun and pro-Goth immigration public interest groups in ancient Rome? Societies usually rot from the inside out so it does seem likely.)

The Tranzi also insists on enlightening the rest of the world, but rejects any and every means that might actually _work_.

This, friend, is the other kind of insanity.

Of course, that first definition is not the only interesting quote that has an amusing corollary. For example, it has been said more than once that you should choose enemies wisely, because you are going to become just or, at least, much like them. The corollary to this is that your enemies are also going to become very like you.

In human conflict this really is and always has been everywhere apparent: Hannibal adopts Roman arms and something like the manipular legion for his forces. Sparta and Rome, landpowers to begin, face Athens and Carthage, seapowers, and both Rome and Sparta build enormous and effective fleets. German tank designers adopt Russian tank design philosophies. Russians become operationally deft. British and American troops are plagued with Indian irregular tactics and techniques during the French and Indian War and so adopt light infantry and riflemen. The Soviet Union provides free meals to school children and we begin to as well. (And then there are those, all over the world, who hate the United States and express that hatred regularly and virulently. One wonders why they never contemplate what it will be like when *we* begin to really hate *them*. They should be afraid, very afraid.)

It's partly propaganda driven but partly also driven by the act and process of learning from those who have most to teach us, by harming us, our enemies.

If I could speak now to our enemies, I would say: Do you kill innocent civilians for shock value? So will we learn to do, in time. Do you torture and murder prisoners? So will we. Are you composed of religious fanatics? Well, since humanistic secularism seems ill-suited to deal with you, don't be surprised if we turn to our churches and temples to find the strength to defeat and destroy you. Do you *randomly* kill our loved ones to send us a message? Don't be surprised, then, when we begin to target *your* families, *specifically*, to send the message that *our* loved ones are not stationery.

This seems lost on the current enemy but, then, he's insane. It's very sad. Yes, it's very sad for us, too.

In any case, *that*, friend, is some of what I've tried to illustrate in this book. Do I like torture? No. It's a nasty technique that dirties everything it touches. No sane man who engages in it is likely to ever be quite right in his head and heart again, for he will have seen man at his lowest and joined him there. No sane man ought want to engage in it. No society that uses it to any great extent is likely to feel moral again for quite some time.

This, however, is not the same thing as saying it never works, as any number of either very stupid or very dishonest people have tried to claim.

(Do I like reprising against civilians who happen to share blood and culture with specific enemies? No. I don't particularly like reprising against, in effect, wounded in hospitals that an enemy is using for ammo dumps, either. The latter, however, is clearly necessary sometimes and, when your enemy is socially organized not as formal military units but around ties of blood, the former may well be unavoidable if the enemy is to be deterred from certain kinds of conduct. Or beaten, for that matter.)

Stupid and dishonest . . . it's sometimes hard to tell the difference, isn't it? What's one to make of a politician, one who has experienced torture personally, to all appearances a decent and brave man, who can say in one breath that (I'm probably paraphrasing, here),

"People will say anything under torture," and in the next say, "Torture doesn't work"? He's either dishonestly pandering to the crowd (Am I being redundant by saying "politician" and "dishonestly pandering to the crowd"? I suppose I am.) or he's too dumb to realize that, if torture's that bad, and with a modicum of ability to spot-check for truth, the victim of torture will also tell the truth rather than risk more torture. One has to wonder about the fitness for high office of such a man. I mean, *really*? It's being neither *cleverly* dishonest nor *honestly* stupid. I'd prefer he say, "Even though torture works, we would prefer to be destroyed or enslaved than violate our principles and use it."

Of course, he'd get few votes that way. He sure as hell wouldn't get mine, though at least he'd have my respect. What *would* get my vote? Oh . . . something like, "*Whatever* it takes to preserve our civilization, our nation, our people, and our way of life, without hesitation or unnecessary restraint, and consulting no one who does not have *our* best interests at heart, *that* shall I do, always remembering that there's a price for everything."

Votes . . . what does it say about us or our preferred democratic system that so many of our people prefer the palatable lie to the unpleasant truth? Nothing good, surely. Thomas Carlyle had this much right, though: "A lie will not stand." Indeed, the Islamofascists are going to knock it down around our heads while at the same time removing any restraint of ours behind which they hide. Then again, as mentioned, they're insane.

"'Are going to?'" you ask. Oh, yes. This goes back to torture. Many people who would otherwise object to torture would permit it in the so-called "Ticking Bomb Scenario." This is, though few seem to realize it, an admission that, given a means of immediate feedback, torture works. But what is al Qaeda, what is the entire Islamic Fundamentalist movement, in an age of nukes and bugs and gas, except one big ticking bomb with an unknown time of detonation?

Is it the immediacy of the threat that makes torture valid in the ticking bomb scenario? Immediacy hardly seems an absolute moral principle. How about immediacy times potential harm; isn't that better? So if you can morally break out "Skevington's Daughter" (Look it up; I don't have a sample here to show you. Not my thing.) for five hundred pounds of TNT in a van somewhere now, can't you break it out also for a nuke in New York in ten years? For a dozen nukes scattered about the U.S. or Europe in twenty-five? For a world-scourging plague in fifty?

I think you can. If the threat is real, I think you—we—must.

As I said, it's very sad.

And then, too, let us not forget the *real* poltroons. You know the type: "We'll officially forbid torture but if you—soldier or law enforcement officer or intelligence agent—engage in it illegally with the intent of protecting me and mine and it turns out that you just might have protected us then we'll pardon you. Then we can feel clean and safe and pure and virtuous and still be properly grateful."

Despicable moral cowardice; that's what that is.

Someone (Michael Kinsley, I think) called all this, "salami slicing." He was right, of course, it often *is* salami slicing. Salami slicing is not one of the classical logical fallacies. Ever try to eat a large salami without slicing it? If it's a question of slicing the salami or starving do you prefer to die? Go ahead with my blessings. Before you expire though, could you pass over the salami, the knife and the crackers? Yes, they're there in the little refrigerator, in behind the beer.

Thanks. Care for some salami? Go on, have some. It might help keep you alive.

The following is an excerpt from:

STORM FROM THE
SHADOWS

DAVID WEBER

Available from Baen Books
March 2009
hardcover

✧ CHAPTER ONE

"TALK TO ME, JOHN!"

Rear Admiral Michelle Henke's husky contralto came sharp and crisp as the information on her repeater tactical display shifted catastrophically.

"It's still coming in from the Flag, Ma'am," Commander Oliver Manfredi, Battlecruiser Squadron Eighty-One's golden-haired chief of staff, replied for the squadron's operations officer, Lieutenant Commander John Stackpole. Manfredi was standing behind Stackpole, watching the ops section's more detailed displays, and he had considerably more attention to spare for updates at the moment than Stackpole did. "I'm not sure, but it looks—"

Manfredi broke off, and his jaw clenched. Then his nostrils flared and he squeezed Stackpole's shoulder before he turned his head to look at his admiral.

"It would appear the Peeps have taken Her Grace's lessons to heart, Ma'am," he said grimly. "They've arranged a Sidemore all their own for us."

Michelle looked at him for a moment, and her expression tightened.

"Oliver's right, Ma'am," Stackpole said, looking up from his own display as the changing light codes finally restabilized. "They've got us boxed."

"How bad is it?" she asked.

"They've sent in three separate groups," Stackpole replied. "One dead astern of us, one at polar north, and one at polar south. The Flag is designating the in-system force we already knew about as Bogey One. The task group to system north is Bogey Two; the one to system south is Bogey Three; and the one directly astern is Bogey Four. Our velocity relative to Bogey Four is just over twenty-two thousand kilometers per second, but range is less than thirty-one million klicks."

"Understood."

Michelle looked back at her own, smaller display. At the moment, it was configured to show the entire Solon System, which meant, by definition, that it was nowhere as detailed as Stackpole's. There wasn't room for that on a plot small enough to deploy from a command chair—not when it was displaying the volume of something the size of a star system, at any rate. But it was more than detailed enough to confirm what Stackpole had just told her. The Peeps had just duplicated exactly what had happened to *them* at the Battle of Sidemore, and managed to do it on a more sophisticated scale, to boot. Unless something reduced Task Force Eighty-Two's rate of acceleration, none of the three forces which had just dropped out of hyper-space to ambush it could hope to overtake it. Unfortunately, they didn't need to physically overtake the task force in order to engage it—not when current-generation Havenite multidrive missiles had a maximum powered range from rest of over sixty million kilometers.

And, of course, there was always the possibility that there was yet *another* Havenite task group waiting in hyper, prepared to drop back into normal space right in their faces as they approached the system hyper limit. . . .

No, she decided after a moment. *If they had the hulls for a fourth force, it would have already translated in, as well. They'd really have us in a rat trap if they'd been able to box us from four directions. I suppose it's possible that they* do *have another force in reserve—that they decided to double-think us and hold number four until they've had a chance to see which way we run. But that'd be a violation of the KISS principle, and this generation of Peeps doesn't go in much for that sort of thing, damn it.*

She grimaced at the thought, but it was certainly true.

Honor's been warning us all that these *Peeps aren't exactly stupid,* she reflected. *Not that any of us should've needed reminding after what they did to us in Thunderbolt! But I could wish that just this once she'd been wrong.*

Her lips twitched in a humorless smile, but she felt herself coming back on balance mentally, and her brain whirred as tactical possibilities and decision trees spilled through it. Not that the primary responsibility was hers. No, that weight rested on the shoulders of her best friend, and despite herself, Michelle was grateful that it *wasn't* hers . . . a fact which made her feel more than a little guilty.

One thing was painfully evident. Eighth Fleet's entire operational strategy for the last three and a half months had been dedicated to convincing the numerically superior navy of the Republic of Haven to redeploy, adopt a more defensive stance while the desperately off-balance Manticoran Alliance got its own feet back under it. Judging by the ambush into which the task force had sailed, that strategy was obviously succeeding. In fact, it looked like it was succeeding entirely too well.

It was so much easier when we could keep their command teams pruned back . . . or count on State Security to do it for us. Unfortunately, Saint-Just's not around anymore to shoot any admiral whose initiative might make her dangerous to the régime, is he? Her lips twitched with bitterly sardonic amusement as she recalled the relief with which Manticore's pundits, as well as the woman in the street, had greeted the news of the Committee of Public Safety's final overthrow. *Maybe we were just a little premature about that,* she thought, *since it means that this time around, we don't have anywhere near the same edge in operational experience, and it shows.* This *batch of Peeps actually knows what it's doing. Damn it.*

"Course change from the Flag, Ma'am," Lieutenant Commander Braga, her staff astrogator announced. "Two-niner-three, zero-zero-five, six-point-zero-one KPS squared."

"Understood," Michelle repeated, and nodded approvingly as the new vector projection stretched itself across her plot and she recognized Honor's intention. The task force was breaking to system south at its maximum acceleration on a course that would take it as far away from Bogey Two as possible while maintaining at least the current separation from Bogey Four. Their new course would still take them deep into the missile envelope of Bogey One, the detachment covering the planet Arthur, whose orbital infrastructure had been the task force's original target. But Bogey One consisted of only two superdreadnoughts and seven battlecruisers, supported by less than two hundred LACs, and from their emissions signatures and maneuvers, Bogey One's wallers were pre-pod designs. Compared to the six obviously modern superdreadnoughts and two LAC carriers in each of the three ambush forces, Bogey One's threat was minimal. Even if all nine of its hyper-capable combatants had heavy pod loads on tow, its older ships would lack the fire control to pose a significant threat to Task Force Eighty-Two's missile defenses. Under the circumstances, it was the same option Michelle would have chosen if she'd been in Honor's shoes.

I wonder if they've been able to ID her flagship? Michelle wondered. *It wouldn't have been all that hard, given the news coverage and her "negotiations" in Hera.*

That, too, of course, had been part of the strategy. Putting Admiral Lady Dame Honor Harrington, Duchess and Steadholder Harrington, in command of Eighth Fleet had been a carefully calculated decision on the Admiralty's part. In Michelle's opinion, Honor was obviously the best person for the command anyway, but the appointment had been made in a glare of publicity for the express purpose of letting the Republic of Haven know that "the Salamander" was the person who'd been chosen to systematically demolish its rear-area industry.

One way to make sure they honored the threat, Michelle thought wryly as the task force came to its new heading in obedience to the commands emanating from HMS *Imperator*, Honor's SD(P) flagship. *After all, she's been their personal nightmare ever since Basilisk station! But I wonder if they got a fingerprint on* Imperator *at Hera or Augusta? Probably—they knew which ship she was aboard at Hera, at least. Which probably means they know who it is they've just mousetrapped, too.*

Michelle grimaced at the thought. It was unlikely any Havenite flag officer would have required extra incentive to trash the task force if she could, especially after Eighth Fleet's unbroken string of victories. But knowing whose command they were about to hammer certainly commodores to make them any *less* eager to drive home their attack.

"Missile defense Plan Romeo, Ma'am," Stackpole said. "Formation Charlie."

"Defense only?" Michelle asked. "No orders to roll pods?"

"No, Ma'am. Not yet."

"Thank you."

Michelle frown deepened thoughtfully. Her own battlecruisers' pods were loaded with Mark 16 dual-drive missiles. That gave her far more missiles per pod, but Mark 16s were both smaller, with lighter laser heads, and shorter-legged than a ship of the wall's multidrive missiles like the Mark 23s aboard Honor's superdreadnoughts. They would have been forced to adopt an attack profile with a lengthy ballistic flight, and the biggest tactical weakness of a pod battlecruiser design was that it simply couldn't carry as many pods as a true capital ship like *Imperator*. It made sense not to waste BCS 81's limited ammunition supply at a range so extended as to guarantee a low percentage of hits, but in Honor's place, Michelle would have been sorely tempted to throw at least a few salvos of all-up MDMs from her two superdreadnoughts back into Bogey Four's face, if only to keep them honest. On the other hand . . .

Well, she's the four-star admiral, not me. And I suppose—she smiled again at the tartness of her own mental tone—*that she's demonstrated at least a* modicum *of tactical insight from time to time.*

"Missile separation!" Stackpole announced suddenly. "Multiple missile separations! Estimate eleven hundred—one-one-zero-zero—inbound. Time to attack range seven minutes!"

Each of the six Havenite superdreadnoughts in the group which had been designated Bogey Four could roll six pods simultaneously, one pattern every twelve seconds, and each pod contained ten missiles. Given the fact that Havenite fire control systems remained inferior to Manticoran ones, accuracy was going to be poor, to say the least. Which was why the admiral commanding that group had opted to stack six full patterns from each superdreadnought, programmed for staggered launch to bring all of their missiles simultaneously in on their targets. It took seventy-two seconds to deploy them, but then just over a thousand MDMs hurled themselves after Task force Eighty-Two.

Seventy-two seconds after that, a second, equally massive salvo launched. Then a third. A fourth. In the space of thirteen minutes, the Havenites fired just under twelve thousand missiles—almost a third of Bogey Four's total missile loadout—at the task force's twenty starships.

❖   ❖   ❖

As little as three or four T-years ago, any one of those avalanches of fire would have been lethally effective against so few targets, and Michelle felt her stomach muscles tightening as the tempest swept towards her. But this *wasn't* three or four T-years ago. The Royal Manticoran Navy's missile defense doctrine was in a constant state of evolution, continually revised in the face of new threats and the opportunities of new technology, and it had been vastly improved even in the six months since the Battle of Marsh. The *Katana*-class LACs deployed to cover the task force maneuvered to bring their missile launchers to bear on the incoming fire, but their counter-missiles weren't required yet. Not in an era when the Royal Navy had developed Keyhole and the Mark 31 counter-missile.

Each superdreadnought and battlecruiser deployed two Keyhole control platforms, one through each sidewall, and each of those platforms had sufficient telemetry links to control the fire of *all* of its mother ship's counter-missile launchers simultaneously. Equally important, they allowed the task force's units to roll sideways in space, interposing the impenetrable shields of their impeller wedges against the most dangerous threat axes without compromising their defensive fire control in the least. Each Keyhole also served as a highly sophisticated electronics warfare platform, liberally provided with its own close-in point defense clusters, as well. And as an added bonus, rolling ship gave the platforms sufficient "vertical" separation to see past the interference generated by the impeller wedges of subsequent counter-missile salvos, which made it possible to fire those salvos at far tighter intervals than anyone had ever been able to manage before.

The Havenites hadn't made sufficient allowance for how badly Keyhole's EW capability was going to affect their attack missiles' accuracy. Worse, they'd anticipated no more than five CM launches against each of their salvos, and since they'd anticipated facing only the limited fire control arcs of their fleeing targets' after hammerheads, they'd allowed for an average of only ten counter-missiles per ship per launch. Their fire plans had been based on the assumption that they would face somewhere around a thousand ship-launched counter-missiles, and perhaps another thousand or so Mark 31-based Vipers from the *Katanas*.

Michelle Henke had no way of knowing what the enemy's tactical assumptions might have been, but she was reasonably certain they hadn't expected to see over *seven* thousand counter-missiles from Honor's starships, alone.

"That's a lot of counter-missiles, Ma'am," Commander Manfredi remarked quietly.

The chief of staff had paused beside Michelle's command chair on his way back to his own command station, and she glanced up at him, one eyebrow quirked.

"I know we've increased our magazine space to accommodate them," he replied to the unspoken question. "Even so, we don't have enough to maintain this volume of defensive fire forever. And they're not exactly inexpensive, either."

Either we're both confident as hell, or else we're certifiable lunatics with nothing better to do than pretend *we are so we can impress each other with our steely nerve*, Michelle thought wryly.

"They may not be cheap," she said out loud, returning

her attention to her display, "but they're a hell of a lot less expensive than a new ship would be. Not to mention the cost of replacing our own personal hides."

"There is that, Ma'am," Manfredi agreed with a lopsided smile. "There is that."

"And," Michelle continued with a considerably nastier smile of her own as the leading salvo of Havenite MDMs vanished under the weight of the task force's defensive fire, "I'm willing to bet Mark 31s cost one hell of a lot less than all those *attack* missiles did, too."

The second attack salvo followed the first one into oblivion well short of the inner defensive perimeter. So did the third. And the fourth.

"They've ceased fire, Ma'am," Stackpole announced.

"I'm not surprised," Michelle murmured. Indeed, if anything surprised her, it was that the Havenites hadn't ceased fire even sooner. On the other hand, maybe she wasn't being fair to her opponents. It had taken seven minutes for the first salvo to enter engagement range, long enough for six more salvos to be launched on its heels. And the effectiveness of the task force's defenses had surpassed even BuWeaps' estimates. If it had come as as big a surprise to the bad guys as she rather expected it had, it was probably unreasonable to expect the other side to realize instantly just how hard to penetrate that defensive wall was. And the only way they had to measure its toughness was to actually hammer at it with their missiles, of course. Still, she liked to think that it wouldn't have taken a full additional six minutes for *her* to figure out she was throwing good money after bad.

On the other *other hand, there* are *those other nine salvos still on the way*, she reminded herself. *Let's not get too carried away with our own self-confidence,*

Mike! The last few waves will have had at least a little time to adjust to our EW, won't they? And it only takes one leaker in the wrong place to knock out an alpha node . . . or even some overly optimistic rear admiral's command deck.

"What do you think they're going to try next, Ma'am?" Manfredi asked as the fifth, sixth, and seventh salvos vanished equally ineffectually.

"Well, they've had a chance now to get a feel for just how tough our new doctrine really is," she replied, leaning back in her command chair, eyes still on her tactical repeater. "If it were me over there, I'd be thinking in terms of a really massive salvo. Something big enough to swamp our defenses by literally running us out of control channels for the CMs, no matter how many of them we have."

"But they couldn't possibly control something that big, either," Manfredi protested.

"We don't *think* they could control something that big," Michelle corrected almost absently, watching the eighth and ninth missile waves being wiped away. "Mind you, I think you're probably right, but we don't have any way of knowing that . . . yet. We could be wrong. And even if we aren't, how much accuracy would they really be giving up at this range, even if they completely cut the control links early and let the birds rely on just their onboard sensors? They wouldn't get very good targeting solutions without shipboard guidance to refine them, but they aren't going to get *good* solutions at this range anyway, whatever they do, and enough *bad* solutions to actually break through are likely to be just a bit more useful than perfect solutions that can't get past their targets' defenses, wouldn't you say?"

"Put that way, I suppose it does make sense," Manfredi agreed, but it was apparent to Michelle that her chief of staff's sense of professionalism was offended by the idea of relying on what was essentially unaimed fire. The notion's sheer crudity clearly said volumes about the competence (or lack thereof) of any navy which had to rely upon it, as far as he was concerned.

Michelle started to twit him for it, then paused with a mental frown. Just how much of a blind spot on Manfredi's part—or on her own, for that matter—did that kind of thinking really represent? Manticoran officers were accustomed to looking down their noses at Havenite technology and the crudity of technique its limitations enforced. But there was nothing wrong with a crude technique if it was also an *effective* one. The Republican Navy had already administered several painful demonstrations of that minor fact, and it was about time officers like Oliver Manfredi—or Michelle Henke, for that matter—stopped letting themselves be surprised each time it happened.

"I didn't say it would be pretty, Oliver." She allowed the merest hint of reprimand into her tone. "But we don't get paid for 'pretty,' do we?"

"No, Ma'am," Manfredi said just a bit more crisply.

"Well, neither do they, I feel fairly confident." She smiled, taking the possible sting out of the sentence. "And let's face it, they're still holding the short and smelly end of the hardware stick. Under the circumstances, they've made damned effective use of the capabilities they have this time around. Remember Admiral Bellefeuille? If you don't, *I* certainly do!" She shook her head wryly. "That woman is *devious*, and she certainly made the best use of everything she had. I'm afraid I don't see any reason to assume the rest of their flag officers won't go right on doing the same thing, unfortunately."

"You're right, Ma'am." Manfredi twitched a smile of his own. "I'll try to bear that in mind next time."

"'Next time,'" Michelle repeated, and chuckled. "I like the implication there, Oliver."

"*Imperator* and *Intolerant* are rolling pods, Ma'am," Stackpole reported.

"Sounds like Her Grace's come to the same conclusion you have, Ma'am," Manfredi observed. "That should be one way to keep them from stacking *too* big a salvo to throw at us!"

"Maybe," Michelle replied.

The great weakness of missile pods was their vulnerability to proximity kills once they were deployed and outside their mother ship's passive defenses, and Manfredi had a point that incoming Manticoran missiles might well be able to wreak havoc on the Havenite pods. On the other hand, they'd already had time to stack quite a few of them, and it would take Honor's missiles almost eight more minutes to reach their targets across the steadily opening range between the task force and Bogey Four. But at least they were on notice that those missiles were coming.

The Havenite commander didn't wait for the task force's fire to reach him. In fact, he fired at almost the same instant Honor's first salvo launched against *him*, and whereas Task force Eighty-Two had fired just under three hundred missiles at him, he fired the next best thing to eleven thousand in reply.

"Damn," Commander Manfredi said almost mildly

as the enemy returned more than thirty-six missiles for each one TF 82 had just fired at him, then shook his head and glanced at Michelle. "Under normal circumstances, Ma'am, it's reassuring to work for a boss who's good at reading the other side's mind. Just this once, though, I really wish you'd been wrong."

"You and I, both," Michelle replied. She studied the data sidebars for several seconds, then turned her command chair to face Stackpole.

"Is it my imagination, John, or does their fire control seem just a bit better than it ought to be?"

"I'm afraid you're not imagining things, Ma'am," Stackpole replied grimly. "It's a single salvo, all right, and it's going to come in as a single wave. But they've divided it into several 'clumps,' and the clumps appear to be under tighter control than *I* would have anticipated out of them. If I had to guess, I'd say they've spread them to clear their telemetry paths to each clump and they're using rotating control links, jumping back and forth between each group."

"They'd need a lot more bandwidth than they've shown so far," Manfredi said. It wasn't a disagreement with Stackpole, only thoughtful, and Michelle shrugged.

"Probably," she said. "But maybe not, too. We don't know enough about what they're doing to decide that."

"Without it, they're going to be running the risk of completely dropping control linkages in mid-flight," Manfredi pointed out.

"Probably," Michelle repeated. This was no time, she decided, to mention certain recent missile fire control developments Sonja Hemphill and BuWeaps were pursuing. Besides, Manfredi was right. "On the other hand," she continued, "this salvo is ten times the size of anything they've tried before, isn't it? Even if they dropped twenty-five or thirty percent of them, it would still be a hell of a lot heavier weight of fire."

"Yes, Ma'am," Manfredi agreed, and smiled crookedly. "More of those bad solutions you were talking about before."

"Exactly," Michelle said grimly as the oncoming torrent of Havenite missiles swept into the outermost counter-missile zone.

"It looks like they've decided to target us this time, too, Ma'am," Stackpole said, and she nodded.

TF 82's opening missile salvo reached its target first.

Unlike the Havenites, Duchess Harrington had opted to concentrate all of her fire on a single target, and Bogey Four's missile defenses opened fire as the Manticoran MDMs swept towards it. The Manticoran electronic warfare platforms scattered among the attack missiles carried far more effective penetration aids than anything the Republic of Haven had, but Haven's defenses had improved even more radically than Manticore's since the last war. They remained substantially inferior to the Star Kingdom's in absolute terms, but the relative improvement was still enormous, and the gap between TF 82's performance and what *they* could achieve was far narrower than it once would have been. Shannon Foraker's "layered defense" couldn't count on the same sort of accuracy and technological sophistication Manticore could produce, so it depended on sheer weight of fire, instead. And an incredible storm front of counter-missiles raced to meet the threat, fired from the starships' escorting LACs, as well as from the superdreadnoughts themselves.

There was so much wedge interference that anything resembling precise control of all that defensive fire was impossible, but with so many counter-missiles in space simultaneously, some of them simply *had* to hit something.

They did. In fact, they hit quite a few "somethings." Of the two hundred and eighty-eight MDMs *Intolerant* and *Imperator* had fired at RHNS *Conquete*, the counter-missiles killed a hundred and thirty-two, and then it was the laser clusters' turn. Each of those clusters had time for only a single shot each, given the missiles' closing speed. At sixty-two percent of light-speed, it took barely half a second from the instant they entered the laser clusters' range for the Manticoran laser heads to reach their own attack range of *Conquete*. But there were literally thousands of those clusters aboard the superdreadnoughts and their escorting *Cimeterre*-class light attack craft.

Despite everything the superior Manticoran EW could do, Shannon Foraker's defensive doctrine worked. Only eight of TF 82's missiles survived to attack their target. Two of them detonated late, wasting their power on the roof of *Conquete*'s impenetrable impeller wedge. The other six detonated between fifteen and twenty thousand kilometers off the ship's port bow, and massive bomb-pumped lasers punched brutally through her sidewall.

Alarms screamed aboard the Havenite ship as armor shattered, weapons—and the men and women who manned them—were wiped out of existence, and atmosphere streamed from *Conquete*'s lacerated flanks. But superdreadnoughts were designed to survive precisely that kind of damage, and the big ship didn't even falter.

She maintained her position in Bogey Four's defensive formation, and her counter-missile launchers were already firing against TF 82's second salvo.

"It looks like we got at least a few through, Ma'am," Stackpole reported, his eyes intent as the studied the reports coming back from the FTL Ghost Rider reconnaissance platforms.

"Good," Michelle replied. Of course, "a few" hits probably hadn't done a lot more than scratch their target's paint, but she could always hope, and some damage was a hell of a lot better than no damage at all. Unfortunately . . .

"And here comes their reply," Manfredi muttered. Which, Michelle thought, was something of an . . . understatement.

Six hundred of the Havenite MDMs had simply become lost and wandered away, demonstrating the validity of Manfredi's prediction about dropped control links. But that was less than six percent of the total . . . which demonstrated the accuracy of Michelle's counterpoint.

The task force's counter-missiles killed almost nine thousand of the missiles which *didn't* get lost, and the last-ditch fire of the task force's laser clusters and the *Katana*-class LACs killed nine hundred more.

Which left "only" three hundred and seventy-two.

Five of them attacked *Ajax*.

Captain Diego Mikhailovic rolled ship, twisting his command further over onto her side relative to the incoming fire, fighting to interpose the defensive barrier of his wedge, and the sensor reach of his Keyhole platforms gave him a marked maneuver advantage, as well as improving his fire control. He could see threats more clearly and from a greater range, which gave him more time to react to them, and most of the incoming X-ray lasers wasted themselves against the floor of his wedge. One of the attacking missiles managed to avoid that fate, however. It swept past *Ajax* and detonated less than five thousand kilometers from her port sidewall.

The battlecruiser twitched as two of the missile's lasers blasted through that sidewall. By the nature of things, battlecruiser armor was far thinner than super-dreadnoughts could carry, and Havenite laser heads were heavier than matching Manticoran weapons as a deliberate compensation for their lower base accuracy. Battle steel shattered and alarms howled. Patches of ominous crimson appeared on the damage control schematics, yet given the original size of that mighty salvo, *Ajax*'s actual damage was remarkably light.

"Two hits, Ma'am," Stackpole announced. "We've lost Graser Five and a couple of point defense clusters, and Medical reports seven wounded."

Michelle nodded. She hoped none of those seven crewmen were badly wounded. No one ever liked to take casualties, but at the same time, only seven—none of them fatal, so far at least—was an almost incredibly light loss rate.

"The rest of the squadron?" she asked sharply.

"Not a scratch, Ma'am!" Manfredi replied jubilantly from his own command station, and Michelle felt herself beginning to smile. But then—

"Multiple hits on both SDs," Stackpole reported in a much grimmer voice, and Michelle's smile died stillborn. "*Imperator*'s lost two or three grasers, but she's essentially intact."

"And *Intolerant*?" Michelle demanded harshly when the ops officer paused.

"Not good," Manfredi replied as the information scrolled across his display from the task force data net. "She must have taken two or three dozen hits . . . and at least one of them blew straight into the missile core. She's got heavy casualties, Ma'am, including Admiral Morowitz and most of his staff. And it looks like all of her pod rails are down."

"The Flag is terminating the missile engagement, Ma'am," Stackpole said quietly.

He looked up from his display to meet her eyes, and she nodded in bitter understanding. The task force's sustainable long-range firepower had just been cut in half. Not even Manticoran fire control was going to accomplish much at the next best thing to two light-minutes with salvoes the size a single SD(P) could throw, and Honor wasn't going to waste ammunition trying to do the impossible.

Which, unfortunately, leaves the question of just what we are going to do wide open, doesn't it? she thought.

Several minutes passed, and Michelle listened to the background flow of clipped, professional voices as her staff officers and their assistants continued refining their assessment of what had just happened. It wasn't getting much better, she reflected, watching the data bars shift as more detailed damage reports flowed in.

As Manfredi had already reported, her own squadron— aside from her flagship—had suffered no damage at all, but it was beginning to look as if Stackpole's initial assessment of HMS *Intolerant*'s damages had actually been optimistic.

"Admiral," Lieutenant Kaminski said suddenly. Michelle turned towards her staff communications officer, one eyebrow raised. "Duchess Harrington wants to speak to you," he said.

"Put her through," Michelle said quickly, and turned back to her own small com screen. A familiar, almond-eyed face appeared upon it almost instantly.

"Mike," Honor Alexander-Harrington began without preamble, her crisp, Sphinxian accent only a shade more pronounced than usual, "*Intolerant*'s in trouble. Her missile defenses are way below par, and we're headed into the planetary pods' envelope. I know *Ajax*'s taken a few licks of her own, but I want your squadron moved out on our flank. I need to interpose your point defense between *Intolerant* and Arthur. Are you in shape for that?"

"Of course we are." Henke nodded vigorously. Putting something as fragile as a battlecruiser between a wounded superdreadnought and a planet surrounded by missile pods wasn't something to be approached lightly. On the other hand, screening ships of the wall was one of the functions battlecruisers had been designed to fulfill, and at least, given the relative dearth of missile pods their scouts had reported in Arthur orbit, they wouldn't be looking at another missile hurricane like the one which had just roared through the task force.

"*Ajax*'s the only one who's been kissed," Michelle continued, "and our damage is all pretty much superficial. None of it'll have any effect on our missile defense."

"Good! Andrea and I will shift the LACs as well, but they've expended a lot of CMs." Honor shook her head. "I didn't think they could stack that many pods without completely saturating their own fire control. It looks like we're going to have to rethink a few things."

"That's the nature of the beast, isn't it?" Michelle responded with a shrug. "We live and learn."

"Those of us fortunate enough to survive," Honor agreed, a bit grimly. "All right, Mike. Get your people moving. Clear."

"Clear," Michelle acknowledged, then turned her chair to face Stackpole and Braga. "You heard the lady," she said. "Let's get them moving."

BCS 81 moved out on Task force Eighty-Two's flank as the Manticoran force continued accelerating steadily away from its pursuers. The final damage reports came in, and Michelle grimaced as she considered how the task force's commanding officer was undoubtedly feeling about those reports. She'd known Honor Harrington since Honor had been a tall, skinny first-form midshipwoman at Saganami Island. It wasn't Honor's fault the Havenites had managed to mousetrap her command, but that wasn't going to matter. Not to Honor Harrington. Those were her ships which had been damaged, her people who had been killed, and at this moment, Michelle Henke knew, she was feeling the hits her task force had taken as if every one of them had landed directly on her.

No, that isn't what she's feeling, Michelle told herself. *What she's doing right now is wishing that every one of them had landed on her, and she's not going to forgive herself for walking into this. Not for a long time, if I know her. But she's not going to let it affect her decisions, either.*

She shook her head. It was a pity Honor was so

much better at forgiving her subordinates for disasters she knew perfectly well weren't there fault than she was at forgiving herself. Unfortunately, it was too late to change her now.

And, truth to tell, I don't think any of us would want to go screwing around trying to change her, Michelle thought wryly.

"We'll be entering the estimated range of Arthur's pods in another thirty seconds, Ma'am," Stackpole said quietly, breaking in on her thoughts.

"Thank you." Michelle shook herself, then settled herself more solidly into her command chair.

"Stand by missile defense," she said.

The seconds trickled by, and then—

"Missile launch!" Stackpole announced. "Multiple missile launches, *multiple sources!*"

His voice sharpened with the last two words, and Michelle's head snapped around.

"Estimate seventeen thousand, Ma'am!"

"Repeat that!" Michelle snapped, certain for an instant that she must have misunderstood him somehow.

"CIC says seventeen thousand, Ma'am," Stackpole told her harshly, turning to look at her. "Time to attack range, seven minutes."

Michelle stared at him while her mind tried to grapple with the impossible numbers. The remote arrays deployed by the task force's pre-attack scout ships had detected barely four hundred pods in orbit around Arthur. That should have meant a maximum of only *four* thousand missiles, so where the hell—?

"We've got at least thirteen thousand coming in from Bogey One," Stackpole said, as if he'd just read her mind. His tone was more than a little incredulous, and her own eyes widened in shock. That was even more preposterous. Two superdreadnoughts and seven battlecruisers couldn't possibly have the fire control for that many missiles, even if they'd all been pod designs!

"How could—?" someone began.

"Those aren't *battlecruisers*," Oliver Manfredi said suddenly. "They're frigging *minelayers!*"

Michelle understood him instantly, and her mouth tightened in agreement. Just like the Royal Manticoran Navy, the Republic of Haven built its fast minelayers on battlecruiser hulls. And Manfredi was undoubtedly correct. Instead of normal loads of mines, those ships had been stuffed to the deckhead with missile pods. The whole time they'd been sitting there, watching the task force flee away from Bogey Four and directly towards *them*, they'd been rolling those pods, stacking them into the horrendous salvo which had just come screaming straight at TF 82.

"Well," she said, hearing the harshness in her own voice, "now we understand how they did it. Which still leaves us with the little problem of what we do *about* it. Execute Hotel, John!"

"Defense Plan Hotel, aye, Ma'am," Stackpole acknowledged, and orders began to stream out from HMS *Ajax* to the rest of her squadron.

Michelle watched her plot. There wasn't time for her to adjust her formation significantly, but she'd already set up for Hotel, even though it had seemed unlikely the Havenites' fire could be heavy enough to require it. Her ships' primary responsibility was to protect *Intolerant*. Looking out for themselves came fairly high on their list of priorities as well, of course, but the superdreadnought represented more combat power—and almost as much total tonnage—as her entire squadron combined. That was why Missile Defense Plan Hotel had stacked her battlecruisers vertically in space, like a mobile wall between the planet Arthur and *Intolerant*. They were perfectly placed to intercept the incoming fire . . . which, unfortunately, meant that they were completely exposed *to* that fire, as well.

"Signal from the Flag, Ma'am," Stackpole said suddenly. "Fire Plan Gamma."

"Acknowledged. Execute Fire Plan Gamma," Michelle said tersely.

"Aye, aye, Ma'am. Executing Fire Plan Gamma," Stackpole said, and Battlecruiser Squadron Eighty-One began to roll pods at last.

It wasn't going to be much of a response compared to the amount of fire coming at the task force, but Michelle felt her lips drawing back from her teeth in satisfaction anyway. The gamma sequence Honor and her tactical staff had worked out months ago was designed to coordinate the battlecruisers' shorter-legged Mark 16s with the superdreadnoughts' MDMs. It would take a Mark 16 over thirteen minutes to reach Bogey One, as compared to the *seven* minutes one of *Imperator*'s Mark 23s would require. Both missiles used fusion-powered impeller drives, but there was no physical way to squeeze three complete drives into the smaller missile's tighter dimensions, which meant it simply could not accelerate as long as its bigger brother.

So, under Fire Plan Gamma *Imperator*'s first half-dozen patterns of pod-launched Mark 23s' drive settings had been stepped down to match those of the

Agamemnons' less capable missiles. It let the task force put six salvos of almost three hundred mixed Mark 16 and Mark 23 missiles each into space before the superdreadnought began firing hundred-and-twenty-bird salvos at the Mark 23's maximum power settings.

All of which is very fine, Michelle thought grimly, watching the icons of the attack missiles go streaking away from the task force. *Unfortunately, it doesn't do much about the birds they've already launched.*

As if to punctuate her thought, *Ajax* began to quiver with the sharp vibration of outgoing waves of *counter-*missiles as her launchers went to sustained rapid fire.

The Grayson-designed *Katana*-class LACs were firing, as well, sending their own counter-missiles screaming to meet the attack, but no one in her worst nightmare had ever envisioned facing a single salvo this massive.

"It's coming through, Ma'am," Manfredi said quietly.

She looked back up from her plot, and her lips tightened as she saw him standing beside her command chair once more. Given what was headed towards them at the moment, he really ought to have been back in the shock frame and protective armored shell of his own chair. *And he damned well* knows *it, too*, she thought in familiar, sharp-edged irritation. But he'd always been a roamer, and she'd finally given up yelling at him for it. He was one of those people who *needed* to move around to keep their brains running at the maximum possible RPM. Now his voice was too low pitched for anyone else to have heard as he gazed down into her repeater plot with her, but his eyes were bleak.

"Of course it is," she replied, equally quietly. The task force simply didn't have the firepower to stop that many missiles in the time available to it.

"How the *hell* are they managing to control that many birds?" Manfredi continued, never looking away from the plot. "Look at that pattern. Those aren't blind-fired shots; they're under tight control, for now at least. So where in hell did they find that many control channels?"

"Don't have a clue," Michelle admitted, her tone almost absent as she watched the defenders' fire ripping huge holes in the cloud of incoming missiles. "I think we'd better figure it out, though. Don't you?"

"You've got that right, Ma'am," he agreed with a mirthless smile.

No one in Task force Eighty-Two—or anyone in the rest of the Royal Manticoran Navy, for that matter—had ever heard of the control system Shannon Foraker had dubbed "Moriarty" after a pre-space fictional character. If they had, and if they'd understood the reference, they probably would have agreed that it was appropriate, however.

One thing of which no one would ever be able to accuse Foraker was thinking small. Faced with the problem of controlling a big enough missile salvo to break through the steadily improving Manticoran missile defenses, she'd been forced to accept that Havenite ships of the wall, even the latest podnoughts, simply lacked the necessary fire control channels. So, she'd set out to solve the problem. Unable to match the technological capability to shoehorn the control systems she needed into something like Manticore's Keyhole, she'd simply accepted that she had to build something bigger. *Much* bigger. And while she'd been at it, she'd decided, she might as well figure out how to integrate that "something bigger" into an entire star system's defenses.

Moriarty was the answer she'd come up with. It consisted of remotely deployed platforms which existed for the sole purpose of providing telemetry relays and control channels. They were distributed throughout the entire volume of space inside Solon's hyper limit, and every one of them reported to a single control station which was about the size of a heavy cruiser . . . and contained nothing except the very best fire control computers and software the Republic of Haven could build.

She couldn't do anything about the lightspeed limitations of the control channels themselves, but she'd finally found a way to provide enough of those channels to handle truly massive salvos. In fact, although TF 82 had no way of knowing it, the wave of missiles coming at it was less than half of Moriarty's maximum capacity.

Of course, even if the task force's tactical officers had known that, they might have felt less than completely grateful, given the weight of fire which *was* coming at them.

Michelle never knew how many of the incoming missiles were destroyed short of their targets, or how many simply got lost, despite all Moriarty could do, and wandered off or acquired targets other than the ones they'd originally been assigned. It was obvious that the task force's defenses managed to stop an enormous percentage them. Unfortunately, it was even more obvious that they hadn't stopped *enough* of them.

Hundreds of them hurled themselves at the LACs— not because anyone had wanted to waste MDMs on something as small as a LAC, but because missiles which had lost their original targets as they spread beyond the reach of Moriarty's lightspeed commands had acquired them, instead. LACs, and especially Manticoran and Grayson LACs, were very difficult for missiles to hit. Which was not to say that they were *impossible* to hit, however, and over two hundred of them were blown out of space as the tornado of missiles ripped into the task force.

Most of the rest of Moriarty's missiles had been targeted on the two superdreadnoughts, and they howled in on their targets like demons. Captain Rafe Cardones maneuvered Honor's flagship as if the stupendous superdreadnought were a heavy cruiser, twisting around to interpose his wedge while jammers and decoys joined with laser clusters in a last-ditch, point-blank defense. *Imperator* shuddered and bucked as laser heads blasted through her sidewalls, but despite grievous wounds, she actually got off lightly. Not even her massive armor was impervious to such a concentrated rain of destruction, but it did its job, preserving her core hull and essential systems intact, and her human casualties were minuscule in proportion to the amount of fire scorching in upon her.

Intolerant was less fortunate.

The earlier damage to *Imperator*'s sister ship was simply too severe. She'd lost both of her Keyholes and all too many of her counter-missile launchers and laser clusters in the last attack. Her sensors had been battered, leaving holes in her own close-in coverage, and her electronic warfare systems were far below par. She was simply the biggest, most visible, most vulnerable target in the entire task force, and despite everything BCS 81 could do, droves of myopic end-of-run Havenite MDMs hurled themselves at the clearest target they could see.

The superdreadnought was trapped at the heart of a maelstrom of detonating laser heads, hurling X-ray lasers like vicious harpoons. They slammed into her again and again and again, ripping and maiming, tearing steadily deeper while the big ship shuddered and bucked in agony. And then, finally, one of those lasers found something fatal and HMS *Intolerant* and her entire company vanished into a glaring fireball of destruction.

Nor did she die alone.

HMS *Ajax* heaved indescribably as the universe went mad.

Compared to the torrent of fire streaming in on the two superdreadnoughts, only a handful of missiles attacked the battlecruisers. But that "handful" was still numbered in the hundreds, and they were much more fragile targets. Alarms screamed as deadly lasers ripped deep into far more lightly armored hulls, and the *Agamemnon*-class were podlayers. They had the hollow cores of their type, and that made them even more fragile than other, older battlecruisers little more than half their size. Michelle had always wondered if that aspect of their design was as great a vulnerability as the BC(P)'s critics had always contended.

It looked like they—and she—were about to find out.

Oliver Manfredi was hurled from his feet as *Ajax* lurched, and Michelle felt her command chair's shock frame hammering viciously at her. Urgent voices, high-pitched and distorted despite the professionalism trained bone-deep into their owners, filled the com channels with messages of devastation—announcements of casualties, of destroyed systems, which ended all too often in mid-syllable as death came for the men and women making those reports.

Even through the pounding, Michelle saw the icons of both of her second division's ships—*Priam* and *Patrocles*—disappear abruptly from her plot, and other icons disappeared or flashed critical damage codes throughout the task force's formation. The light cruisers *Fury*, *Buckler*, and *Atum* vanished in glaring flashes of destruction, and the heavy cruisers *Star Ranger* and *Blackstone* were transformed into crippled hulks, coasting onward ballistically without power or impeller wedges. And then—

"Direct hit on the command deck!" one of Stackpole's ratings announced. "No survivors, Sir! Heavy damage to Boat Bay Two, and Boat Bay One's been completely destroyed! Engineering reports—"

Michelle felt it in her own flesh as HMS *Ajax* faltered suddenly.

"We've lost the after ring, Ma'am!" Stackpole said harshly. "*All* of it."

Michelle bit the inside of her lower lip so hard she tasted blood. Solon lay in the heart of a hyper-space gravity wave. No ship could enter, navigate, or long survive in a gravity wave without both Warshawski sails . . . and without the after impeller ring's alpha nodes, *Ajax* could no longer generate an after sail.

—end excerpt—

from *Storm from the Shadows*
available in hardcover,
March 2009, from Baen Books